JOHN EDWARD HARDY

The Modern Talent

AN ANTHOLOGY OF

SHORT STORIES

HOLT RINEHART AND WINSTON

New York · Chicago · San Francisco · Toronto

Foreword

THE nineteenth century, in some quarters, was a great age of short fiction. Moreover, some of the writers of this fiction provided basic critical definitions of the short story form which have been little improved upon since. But it is obviously in the present century that the art has reached its fullest, most subtle, and varied development.

I have, therefore, no design of intellectual condescension in offering to the university audience, for which this book is primarily intended, a selection from the literature of our own era. For that matter, the world of a James Joyce or a Willa Cather is hardly less remote than Maupassant's or Hawthorne's from that of a university student in the mid-sixties. But there is, in any event, no reason for assuming that the literature of earlier periods is necessarily more worthy of serious study than that of one's own, simply because it is older. By and large, the stories in this volume will offer to the student, by virtue of their modernity, not less but more intellectual resistance.

To be sure, there is a certain advantage, for engaging the student's initial interest, in the relatively familiar "life material" of these stories. It is an advantage that the experienced instructor will not minimize. But the intellectual discipline is in discovering what the writer has done with the material. The familiarity of the subject matter does not prevent its being profoundly reflected upon, intricately shaped to an artistic purpose. I have chosen to make the collection not only modern but basically American. And one of my reasons for doing so is that the book is to be used primarily by American students, who can be expected to respond most readily to fiction written in an American idiom and about aspects of American life with which they are more or less intimately acquainted. But, again, it so happens that the American short story writers of the twentieth century are, as a national group, at once the subtlest and the toughest-minded practitioners of their art in the world, the most boldly experimental, and of the most improved sensibilities.

In every way, however, I have tried to stretch my principles of selection just as far as they would go without breaking. It is a modern collection. We should be aware of the short story as a living and changing form, and to this end I have chosen a few stories by relatively unknown writers, whose work will challenge students and instructors to an effort of interpretation free of the inevitable prejudices imposed by reputation. And yet, the contemporary is only one aspect of the modern. The character of growth in an art is always to some extent determined by the artists' consciousness of formal tradition. One has to know conventions, even to violate them effectively. A good number of the stories, therefore—those by Hemingway, Fitzgerald, Faulkner, and the like—are already modern classics. And many of the other writers are at the very least "standard" authors.

It is basically an American collection. But nine stories, four of them in translations from three different languages, are by European and British and Irish writers. I have insisted that the Americans, as a group, dominate the field of the short story, and have noted the initial advantage to the student in the familiarity of the American subject matter. But what was first an advantage can easily become a hindrance to intellectual development if we are never tempted to venture abroad. The modern American short story, despite its peculiarly interesting native characteristics, is no exception to the general rule that no part of our national literature (no part of our national life, indeed, as reflected in the literature) can be adequately studied without awareness of what we have, and have not, in common with the Europeans.

I would not emphasize the seriousness of literary studies to the exclusion of enjoyment. There is no going against the ancient principle that a work of art is meant to give pleasure. The kind of seriousness I have been talking about, the kind of discipline, is meant to enhance pleasure rather than diminish it. And one of the principal elements of pleasure is variety. Therefore, without becoming burdensomely conscious of such a design either, I have selected stories that represent a wide range of human types and situations—social, religious, and so on. There are stories about young people, old people, men, women, Negroes, Protestants, Catholics, citizens, outcasts, artists, workers, the bourgeoisie, the aristocracy, stories of the farm, of the prison, of the great world, and the demimonde, of the small town, and, of course, of New York and Paris, stories of love and of unlove, of the beautiful and the ugly, the commonplace and the grotesque, day stories, night stories, twilight stories. Within the American group, many different regions of the country are represented.

Consciously, I have neither preferred nor rejected stories of any particular technical order. There are some very simple stories in the group, some moderately difficult, and some which might be considered in one way or another obscure. But I have not arranged them in any kind of *graded* series. The stories also vary considerably in their emphasis upon one or another aspect of the art. In some, for example, the element of plot is very important, while others are all but plotless, do not in the usual sense "tell a story" at all; in some, the central emphasis is moral-psychological, in others a structure of symbolic motif may be of prime importance; in one story the action may be all but entirely external, in another it may occur exclusively within the mind of a single character. But I have not grouped the selections according to any preconceived scheme of analysis. Twenty or thirty years ago there was a real need for a fiction text that would systematically educate the instructor as well as the student in a critical methodology. I do not believe that need any longer exists. Any book that is very elaborately organized, with pretensions to revealing a wholly original theory of analysis, is likely these days only to antagonize the well-trained instructor. And the book that merely refurbishes at length the clichés—about the "elements of fiction," about conflict, point of view, irony, and what not—will bore him. The minimal freedom that ought to be left to us as teachers is the right to bore ourselves, and our students, on our own initiative, and in our own way.

There might be some advantage, for organization of a course, in having the stories grouped according to theme. But I have preferred leaving this, too, to the instructor—either to do it entirely on his own, or, if he thinks that I have done it unawares, to discover for himself the concealed principle of order.

On the other hand, in most courses in which an anthology is used the students are required to write analytical papers on the stories. I know from my own teaching experience that it is very difficult to show freshmen, especially, what is wanted when they have never read such commentaries. No amount of classroom discussion will acquaint them with the problems. And it is difficult, with a large class and limited library facilities, to enforce uniformity in collateral reading assignments. For this reason, if for no other, I have supplied six *sample* commentaries—choosing the stories with regard to the variety of critical problems they present. I have also provided a few study questions for each of the stories, which may be helpful to the student in stimulating critical interest for his own, preliminary reading, or to the instructor in organizing class discussions.

But the study questions have been placed unobtrusively at the back of the book. And neither they nor the six brief commentaries are meant in any way to impose restrictions upon the reader's approach to the stories. I should hope that they will provoke argument rather than satisfaction. No one of the little essays and no set of questions represents an attempt to exhaust the meaning of the story concerned or to provide a definitive reading.

I have, of course, my considered opinions about modern fiction, and about modern criticism of fiction. I know what I like, and I think I know why. I have not, as a teacher, ever had much respect for the kind of textbook in which the editor remains wholly anonymous. To the discerning eye, the rhetorical strategies of the commentaries—a certain recurrent terminology there and in the study questions—will reveal at least the kind of problems I consider most important, a bent of mind if not a bias. And I am not reluctant to make at the outset a few admissions.

My emphasis is on the unique structure of the individual work as a self-contained whole, generating its own principle of order.

But this emphasis by no means excludes other interests. The commentaries and study questions should amply illustrate an awareness of certain dominant, recurrent themes in modern literature—for example, the theme of the "quest for identity"—and a sense of their importance beyond the strictly literary sphere. I think it vitally important that the student be trained to consider *why* there are so many stories in modern American literature of the type called "initiation" stories. In short, to insist that the individual work has its own unique order whose principle must be discovered if we are to understand it, that each story is in a formal sense self-contained, is not the same thing as to say that literature as a whole is self-contained or self-sufficient. It is not simply that literature has much to tell us about ourselves and our culture but also that the culture has much to tell us about literature.

Likewise, the discipline of literary criticism, as I conceive it, can never be wholly autonomous. Especially and increasingly since the end of the nineteenth century the sciences of modern psychology and anthropology, for a major example, have exercised a profound influence on the techniques and themes of fiction. Dream invades the realm of waking consciousness and asserts its equal if not superior "reality." The simplest practical action has ritual significance, its ultimate motivation intelligible only by reference to a symbolic system. The child, with a vengeance, is father to the man. Past is everywhere contained in present, or present in past, or both in future, and the chronological order of plot—action flowing in rationally intelligible sequence from thought and decision—is lost. Given a fiction in which these things have occurred, it is useless to approach it with a critical method that would tag as "extraliterary" even the rudimentary terminology of the disciplines under whose influence the changes were brought about. No one wants to turn literary criticism into psychology or anthropology—or sociology, or theology, or history, or metaphysics. There is no reason, however, so long as the critic is really sure of his own purposes, why any of these sciences should not be put to work for criticism.

But I have taken the greatest care not to let the book become a covert treatise. Even the idea of attaching a glossary of critical terms was rejected on these grounds; for every definition is a treatise in little. A textbook, especially an anthology, is not a formal work of criticism. Ideally, it provides only materials for work—work that is to be done in the classroom by the students and their instructor. The basic materials are the stories themselves, and no greater dignity, surely, need be claimed for whatever I have added.

J.E.H.

Notre Dame, Indiana
February 1964

ACKNOWLEDGMENTS

I am deeply indebted to my daughters Leonore and Margot for their collaboration on the German translations, and again to Leonore, and to my wife, for assistance in the preparation of the manuscript. I would also thank my colleagues, Professors James Robinson, Robert Christin, and Seymour Gross, for valuable advice on the plan of the book, and my students David Kubal and Mother Cor Mariae Schuler for many irksome scholarly chores cheerfully done and for help on the composition of study questions. Finally, it is impossible for me adequately to express my gratitude to Richard Giannone, whose generosity, energy, and intelligence were drawn upon at every stage and in every phase of the work.   *J.E.H.*

Contents

JAMES JOYCE

An Encounter

. . . .

T WAS JOE DILLON who introduced the Wild West to us. He had a little library made up of old numbers of *The Union Jack, Pluck* and *The Halfpenny Marvel*. Every evening after school we met in his back garden and arranged Indian battles. He and his fat young brother Leo, the idler, held the loft of the stable while we tried to carry it by storm; or we fought a pitched battle on the grass. But, however well we fought, we never won siege or battle and all our bouts ended with Joe Dillon's war dance of victory. His parents went to eight-o'clock mass every morning in Gardiner Street and the peaceful odour of Mrs. Dillon was prevalent in the hall of the house. But he played too fiercely for us who were younger and more timid. He looked like some kind of an Indian when he capered round the garden, an old tea-cosy on his head, beating a tin with his fist and yelling:

"Ya! yaka, yaka, yaka!"

Everyone was incredulous when it was reported that he had a vocation for the priesthood. Nevertheless it was true.

A spirit of unruliness diffused itself among us and, under its influence, differences of culture and constitution were waived. We banded ourselves together, some boldly, some in jest and some almost in fear: and of the number of these latter, the reluctant Indians who were afraid to seem studious or lacking in robustness, I was one. The adventures related in the literature of the Wild West were

From DUBLINERS by James Joyce. Originally published by B. W. Huebsch in 1916. Reprinted by permission of The Viking Press, Inc.

remote from my nature but, at least, they opened doors of escape. I liked better some American detective stories which were traversed from time to time by unkempt fierce and beautiful girls. Though there was nothing wrong in these stories and though their intention was sometimes literary they were circulated secretly at school. One day when Father Butler was hearing the four pages of Roman History clumsy Leo Dillon was discovered with a copy of *The Halfpenny Marvel.*

"This page or this page? This page? Now, Dillon, up! 'Hardly had the day' . . . Go on! What day? 'Hardly had the day dawned' . . . Have you studied it? What have you there in your pocket?"

Everyone's heart palpitated as Leo Dillon handed up the paper and everyone assumed an innocent face. Father Butler turned over the pages, frowning.

"What is this rubbish?" he said. "*The Apache Chief!* Is this what you read instead of studying your Roman History? Let me not find any more of this wretched stuff in this college. The man who wrote it, I suppose, was some wretched fellow who writes these things for a drink. I'm surprised at boys like you, educated, reading such stuff. I could understand it if you were . . . National School boys. Now, Dillon, I advise you strongly, get at your work or . . ."

This rebuke during the sober hours of school paled much of the glory of the Wild West for me and the confused puffy face of Leo Dillon awakened one of my consciences. But when the restraining influence of the school was at a distance I began to hunger again for wild sensations, for the escape which those chronicles of disorder alone seemed to offer me. The mimic warfare of the evening became at last as wearisome to me as the routine of school in the morning because I wanted real adventures to happen to myself. But real adventures, I reflected, do not happen to people who remain at home: they must be sought abroad.

The summer holidays were near at hand when I made up my mind to break out of the weariness of school-life for one day at least. With Leo Dillon and a boy named Mahony I planned a day's miching. Each of us saved up sixpence. We were to meet at ten in the morning on the Canal Bridge. Mahony's big sister was to write an excuse for him and Leo Dillon was to tell his brother to

say he was sick. We arranged to go along the Wharf Road until
we came to the ships, then to cross in the ferryboat and walk out
to see the Pigeon House. Leo Dillon was afraid we might meet
Father Butler or someone out of the college; but Mahony asked,
very sensibly, what would Father Butler be doing out at the Pigeon
House. We were reassured: and I brought the first stage of the plot
to an end by collecting sixpence from the other two, at the same
time showing them my own sixpence. When we were making the
last arrangements on the eve we were all vaguely excited. We
shook hands, laughing, and Mahony said:

"Till to-morrow, mates!"

That night I slept badly. In the morning I was first-comer to
the bridge as I lived nearest. I hid my books in the long grass near
the ashpit at the end of the garden where nobody ever came and
hurried along the canal bank. It was a mild sunny morning in the
first week of June. I sat up on the coping of the bridge admiring
my frail canvas shoes which I had diligently pipeclayed overnight
and watching the docile horses pulling a tramload of business
people up the hill. All the branches of the tall trees which lined the
mall were gay with little light green leaves and the sunlight slanted
through them on to the water. The granite stone of the bridge was
beginning to be warm and I began to pat it with my hands in time
to an air in my head. I was very happy.

When I had been sitting there for five or ten minutes I saw
Mahony's grey suit approaching. He came up the hill, smiling, and
clambered up beside me on the bridge. While we were waiting he
brought out the catapult which bulged from his inner pocket and
explained some improvements which he had made in it. I asked
him why he had brought it and he told me he had brought it to
have some gas with the birds. Mahony used slang freely, and
spoke of Father Butler as Old Bunser. We waited on for a quarter of
an hour more but still there was no sign of Leo Dillon. Mahony,
at last, jumped down and said:

"Come along. I knew Fatty'd funk it."

"And his sixpence . . . ?" I said.

"That's forfeit," said Mahony. "And so much the better for us—
a bob and a tanner instead of a bob."

We walked along the North Strand Road till we came to the

Vitriol Works and then turned to the right along the Wharf Road. Mahony began to play the Indian as soon as we were out of public sight. He chased a crowd of ragged girls, brandishing his unloaded catapult and, when two ragged boys began, out of chivalry, to fling stones at us, he proposed that we should charge them. I objected that the boys were too small, and so we walked on, the ragged troop screaming after us: "*Swaddlers! Swaddlers!*" thinking that we were Protestants because Mahony, who was dark-complexioned, wore the silver badge of a cricket club in his cap. When we came to the Smoothing Iron we arranged a siege; but it was a failure because you must have at least three. We revenged ourselves on Leo Dillon by saying what a funk he was and guessing how many he would get at three o'clock from Mr. Ryan.

We came then near the river. We spent a long time walking about the noisy streets flanked by high stone walls, watching the working of cranes and engines and often being shouted at for our immobility by the drivers of groaning carts. It was noon when we reached the quays and, as all the labourers seemed to be eating their lunches, we bought two big currant buns and sat down to eat them on some metal piping beside the river. We pleased ourselves with the spectacle of Dublin's commerce—the barges signalled from far away by their curls of woolly smoke, the brown fishing fleet beyond Ringsend, the big white sailing-vessel which was being discharged on the opposite quay. Mahony said it would be right skit to run away to sea on one of those big ships and even I, looking at the high masts, saw, or imagined, the geography which had been scantily dosed to me at school gradually taking substance under my eyes. School and home seemed to recede from us and their influences upon us seemed to wane.

We crossed the Liffey in the ferryboat, paying our toll to be transported in the company of two labourers and a little Jew with a bag. We were serious to the point of solemnity, but once during the short voyage our eyes met and we laughed. When we landed we watched the discharging of the graceful three-master which we had observed from the other quay. Some bystanders said that she was a Norwegian vessel. I went to the stern and tried to decipher the legend upon it but, failing to do so, I came back and examined the foreign sailors to see had any of them green eyes for I had some confused notion. . . . The sailors' eyes were blue and grey and even black. The only sailor whose eyes could have been called green was a tall man who amused the crowd on the quay by calling out cheerfully every time the planks fell:

"All right! All right!"

When we were tired of this sight we wandered slowly into Ringsend. The day had grown sultry, and in the windows of the grocers' shops musty biscuits lay bleaching. We bought some biscuits and chocolate which we ate sedulously as we wandered through the squalid streets where the families of the fishermen live. We could find no dairy and so we went into a huckster's shop and bought a bottle of raspberry lemonade each. Refreshed by this, Mahony chased a cat down a lane, but the cat escaped into a wide field. We both felt rather tired and when we reached the field we made at once for a sloping bank over the ridge of which we could see the Dodder.

It was too late and we were too tired to carry out our project of visiting the Pigeon House. We had to be home before four o'clock lest our adventure should be discovered. Mahony looked regretfully at his catapult and I had to suggest going home by train before he regained any cheerfulness. The sun went in behind some clouds and left us to our jaded thoughts and the crumbs of our provisions.

There was nobody but ourselves in the field. When we had lain on the bank for some time without speaking I saw a man approaching from the far end of the field. I watched him lazily as I chewed one of those green stems on which girls tell fortunes. He came along by the bank slowly. He walked with one hand upon his hip and in the other hand he held a stick with which he tapped the turf lightly. He was shabbily dressed in a suit of greenish-black and wore what we used to call a jerry hat with a high crown. He seemed to be fairly old for his moustache was ashen-grey. When he passed at our feet he glanced up at us quickly and then continued his way. We followed him with our eyes and saw that when he had gone on for perhaps fifty paces he turned about and began to retrace his steps. He walked towards us very slowly, always tapping the ground with his stick, so slowly that I thought he was looking for something in the grass.

He stopped when he came level with us and bade us good-day.

We answered him and he sat down beside us on the slope slowly and with great care. He began to talk of the weather, saying that it would be a very hot summer and adding that the seasons had changed greatly since he was a boy—a long time ago. He said that the happiest time of one's life was undoubtedly one's schoolboy days and that he would give anything to be young again. While he expressed these sentiments which bored us a little we kept silent. Then he began to talk of school and of books. He asked us whether we had read the poetry of Thomas Moore or the works of Sir Walter Scott and Lord Lytton. I pretended that I had read every book he mentioned so that in the end he said:

"Ah, I can see you are a bookworm like myself. Now," he added, pointing to Mahony who was regarding us with open eyes, "he is different; he goes in for games."

He said he had all Sir Walter Scott's works and all Lord Lytton's works at home and never tired of reading them. "Of course," he said, "there were some of Lord Lytton's works which boys couldn't read." Mahony asked why couldn't boys read them—a question which agitated and pained me because I was afraid the man would think I was as stupid as Mahony. The man, however, only smiled. I saw that he had great gaps in his mouth between his yellow teeth. Then he asked us which of us had the most sweethearts. Mahony mentioned lightly that he had three totties. The man asked me how many I had. I answered that I had none. He did not believe me and said he was sure I must have one. I was silent.

"Tell us," said Mahony pertly to the man, "how many have you yourself?"

The man smiled as before and said that when he was our age he had lots of sweethearts.

"Every boy," he said, "has a little sweetheart."

His attitude on this point struck me as strangely liberal in a man of his age. In my heart I thought that what he said about boys and sweethearts was reasonable. But I disliked the words in his mouth and I wondered why he shivered once or twice as if he feared something or felt a sudden chill. As he proceeded I noticed that his accent was good. He began to speak to us about girls, saying what nice soft hair they had and how soft their hands were and how all girls were not so good as they seemed to be if one only knew. There was nothing he liked, he said, so much as looking at a nice young girl, at her nice white hands and her beautiful soft hair. He gave me the impression that he was repeating something which he had learned by heart or that, magnetised by some words of his own speech, his mind was slowly circling round and round in the same orbit. At times he spoke as if he were simply alluding to some fact that everybody knew, and at other times he lowered his voice and spoke mysteriously as if he were telling us something secret which he did not wish others to overhear. He repeated his phrases over and over again, varying them and surrounding them with his monotonous voice. I continued to gaze towards the foot of the slope, listening to him.

After a long while his monologue paused. He stood up slowly, saying that he had to leave us for a minute or so, a few minutes, and, without changing the direction of my gaze, I saw him walking slowly away from us towards the near end of the field. We remained silent when he had gone. After a silence of a few minutes I heard Mahony exclaim:

"I say! Look what he's doing!"

As I neither answered nor raised my eyes Mahony exclaimed again:

"I say . . . He's a queer old josser!"

"In case he asks us for our names," I said, "let you be Murphy and I'll be Smith."

We said nothing further to each other. I was still considering whether I would go away or not when the man came back and sat down beside us again. Hardly had he sat down when Mahony, catching sight of the cat which had escaped him, sprang up and pursued her across the field. The man and I watched the chase. The cat escaped once more and Mahony began to throw stones at the wall she had escaladed. Desisting from this, he began to wander about the far end of the field, aimlessly.

After an interval the man spoke to me. He said that my friend was a very rough boy and asked did he get whipped often at school. I was going to reply indignantly that we were not National School boys to be whipped, as he called it; but I remained silent. He began to speak on the subject of chastising boys. His mind, as if magnetised again by his speech, seemed to circle slowly round and round its new centre. He said that when boys were that kind they ought to be whipped and well whipped. When a boy was rough and unruly there was nothing would do him any good but a good sound whipping. A slap on the hand or a box on the ear was no good: what he wanted was to get a nice warm whipping. I was surprised at this sentiment and involuntarily glanced up at his face. As I did so I met the gaze of a pair of bottle-green eyes peering at me from under a twitching forehead. I turned my eyes away again.

The man continued his monologue. He seemed to have forgotten his recent liberalism. He said that if ever he found a boy talking to girls or having a girl for a sweetheart he would whip him and whip him; and that would teach him not to be talking to girls. And if a boy had a girl for a sweetheart and told lies about it then he would give him such a whipping as no boy ever got in this world. He said that there was nothing in this world he would like so well as that. He described to me how he would whip such a boy as if he were unfolding some elaborate mystery. He would love that, he said, better than anything in this world; and his voice, as he led me monotonously through the mystery, grew almost affectionate and seemed to plead with me that I should understand him.

I waited till his monologue paused again. Then I stood up abruptly. Lest I should betray my agitation I delayed a few moments pretending to fix my shoe properly and then, saying that I was obliged to go, I bade him good-day. I went up the slope calmly but my heart was beating quickly with fear that he would seize me by the ankles. When I reached the top of the slope I turned round and, without looking at him, called loudly across the field:

"Murphy!"

My voice had an accent of forced bravery in it and I was ashamed of my paltry stratagem. I had to call the name again before Mahony saw me and hallooed in answer. How my heart beat as he came running across the field to me! He ran as if to bring me aid. And I was penitent; for in my heart I had always despised him a little.

HENRY JAMES

The Two Faces

I

HE SERVANT, WHO, in spite of his sealed, stamped look, appeared to have his reasons, stood there for instruction, in a manner not quite usual, after announcing the name. Mrs. Grantham, however, took it up—"Lord Gwyther?"—with a quick surprise that for an instant justified him even to the small scintilla in the glance she gave her companion, which might have had exactly the sense of the butler's hesitation. This companion, a shortish, fairish, youngish man, clean-shaven and keen-eyed, had, with a promptitude that would have struck an observer—which the butler indeed was— sprang to his feet and moved to the chimney-piece, though his hostess herself, meanwhile, managed not otherwise to stir. "Well?" she said, as for the visitor to advance; which she immediately followed with a sharper "He's not there?"

"Shall I show him up, ma'am?"

"But of course!" The point of his doubt made her at last rise for impatience, and Bates, before leaving the room, might still have caught the achieved irony of her appeal to the gentleman into whose communion with her he had broken. "Why in the world not——? What a way——!" she exclaimed, as Sutton felt beside his cheek the passage of her eyes to the glass behind him.

"He wasn't sure you'd see anyone."

"I don't see 'anyone,' but I see individuals."

"That's just it; and sometimes you don't see them."

"Do you mean ever because of *you?*" she asked as she touched into place a tendril of hair. "That's just his impertinence, as to which I shall speak to him."

"Don't," said Shirley Sutton. "Never notice anything."

"That's nice advice from you," she laughed, "who notice every-thing!"

"Ah, but I speak of nothing."

She looked at him a moment. "You're still more impertinent than Bates. You'll please not budge," she went on.

"Really? I must sit him out?" he continued as, after a minute, she had not again spoken—only glancing about, while she changed her place, partly for another look at the glass and partly to see if she could improve her seat. What she felt was rather more than, clever and charming though she was, she could hide. "If you're wondering how you seem, I can tell you. Awfully cool and easy."

She gave him another stare. She was beautiful and conscious. "And if you're wondering how *you* seem——"

"Oh, I'm not!" he laughed from before the fire; "I always perfectly know."

"How you seem," she retorted, "is as if you didn't!"

Once more for a little he watched her. "You're looking lovely for him—extraordinarily lovely, within the marked limits of your range. But that's enough. Don't be clever."

"Then who *will* be?"

"There you are!" he sighed with amusement.

"Do you know him?" she asked as, through the door left open by Bates, they heard steps on the landing.

Sutton had to think an instant, and produced a "No" just as Lord Gwyther was again announced, which gave an unexpectedness to the greeting offered him a moment later by this personage—a young man, stout and smooth and fresh, but not at all shy, who, after the happiest rapid passage with Mrs. Grantham, put out a hand with a frank, pleasant "How d'ye do?"

"Mr. Shirley Sutton," Mrs. Grantham explained.

"Oh yes," said her second visitor, quite as if he knew; which, as he couldn't have known, had for her first the interest of confirm-ing a perception that his lordship would be—no, not at all, in general, embarrassed, only was now exceptionally and especially agitated. As it is, for that matter, with Sutton's total impression that we are particularly and almost exclusively concerned, it may be further mentioned that he was not less clear as to the really handsome way in which the young man kept himself together and little by little—though with all proper aid indeed—finally found his feet. All sorts of things, for the twenty minutes, occurred to Sutton, though one of them was certainly not that it would, after all, be better he should go. One of them was that their hostess was doing it in perfection—simply, easily, kindly, yet with something the least bit queer in her wonderful eyes; another was that if he had been recognised without the least ground it was through a tension of nerves on the part of his fellow-guest that produced inconsequent motions; still another was that, even had departure been indicated, he would positively have felt dissuasion in the rare promise of the scene. This was in especial after Lord Gwyther not only had announced that he was now married, but had mentioned that he wished to bring his wife to Mrs. Grantham for the benefit so certain to be derived. It was the passage immediately produced by that speech that provoked in Sutton the intensity, as it were, of his arrest. He already knew of the marriage as well as Mrs. Grantham herself, and as well also as he knew of some other things; and this gave him, doubtless, the better measure of what took place before him and the keener consciousness of the quick look that, at a marked moment— though it was not absolutely meant for him any more than for his companion—Mrs. Grantham let him catch.

She smiled, but it had a gravity. "I think, you know, you ought to have told me before."

"Do you mean when I first got engaged? Well, it all took place so far away, and we really told, at home, so few people."

Oh, there might have been reasons; but it had not been quite right. "You were married at Stuttgart? That wasn't too far for *my* interest, at least, to reach."

"Awfully kind of you—and of course one knew you *would* be kind. But it wasn't at Stuttgart; it was over there, but quite in the country. We should have managed it in England but that her mother naturally wished to be present, yet was not in health to come. So it was really, you see, a sort of little hole-and-corner German affair."

This didn't in the least check Mrs. Grantham's claim, but it started a slight anxiety. "Will she be—a, then, German?"

Sutton knew her to know perfectly what Lady Gwyther would

"be," but he had by this time, while their friend explained, his independent interest. "Oh dear, no! My father-in-law has never parted with the proud birthright of a Briton. But his wife, you see, holds an estate in Würtemberg from *her* mother, Countess Kremnitz, on which, with the awful condition of his English property, you know, they've found it for years a tremendous saving to live. So that though Valda was luckily born at home she has practically spent her life over there."

"Oh, I see." Then, after a slight pause, "Is Valda her pretty name?" Mrs. Grantham asked.

"Well," said the young man, only wishing, in his candour, it was clear, to be drawn out—"well, she has, in the manner of her mother's people, about thirteen; but that's the one we generally use."

Mrs. Grantham hesitated but an instant. "Then may *I* generally use it?"

"It would be too charming of you; and nothing would give her —as, I assure you, nothing would give *me*, greater pleasure." Lord Gwyther quite glowed with the thought.

"Then I think that instead of coming alone you might have brought her to see me."

"It's exactly what," he instantly replied, "I came to ask your leave to do." He explained that for the moment Lady Gwyther was not in town, having as soon as she arrived gone down to Torquay to put in a few days with one of her aunts, also her godmother, to whom she was an object of great interest. She had seen no one yet, and no one—not that *that* mattered—had seen her; she knew nothing whatever of London and was awfully frightened at facing it and at what—however little—might be expected of her. "She wants some one," he said, "some one who knows the whole thing, don't you see? and who's thoroughly kind and clever, as you would be, if I may say so, to take her by the hand." It was at this point and on these words that the eyes of Lord Gwyther's two auditors inevitably and wonderfully met. But there was nothing in the way he kept it up to show that he caught the encounter. "She wants, if I may tell you so, for the great labyrinth, a real friend; and asking myself what I could do to make things ready for her, and who would be absolutely the best woman in London——"

"You thought, naturally, of *me*?" Mrs. Grantham had listened with no sign but the faint flash just noted; now, however, she gave him the full light of her expressive face—which immediately brought Shirley Sutton, looking at his watch, once more to his feet.

"She *is* the best woman in London!" He addressed himself with a laugh to the other visitor, but offered his hand in farewell to their hostess.

"You're going?"

"I must," he said without scruple.

"Then we do meet at dinner?"

"I hope so." On which, to take leave, he returned with interest to Lord Gwyther the friendly clutch he had a short time before received.

II

They did meet at dinner, and if they were not, as it happened, side by side, they made that up afterwards in the happiest angle of a drawing-room that offered both shine and shadow and that was positively much appreciated, in the circle in which they moved, for the favourable "corners" created by its shrewd mistress. Her face, charged with something produced in it by Lord Gwyther's visit, had been with him so constantly for the previous hours that, when she instantly challenged him on his "treatment" of her in the afternoon, he was on the point of naming it as his reason for not having remained with her. Something new had quickly come into her beauty; he couldn't as yet have said what, nor whether on the whole to its advantage or its loss. Till he could make up his mind about that, at any rate, he would say nothing; so that, with sufficient presence of mind, he found a better excuse. If in short he had in defiance of her particular request left her alone with Lord Gwyther, it was simply because the situation had suddenly turned so exciting that he had fairly feared the contagion of it—the temptation of its making him, most improperly, put in his word.

They could now talk of these things at their ease. Other couples, ensconced and scattered, enjoyed the same privilege, and Sutton had more and more the profit, such as it was, of feeling that his interest in Mrs. Grantham had become—what was the luxury of so

high a social code—an acknowledged and protected relation. He
knew his London well enough to know that he was on the way to
be regarded as her main source of consolation for the trick that,
several months before, Lord Gwyther had publicly played her.
Many persons had not held that, by the high social code in question,
his lordship could have "reserved the right" to turn up in that way,
from one day to another, engaged. For himself London took, with its
short cuts and its cheap psychology, an immense deal for granted.
To his own sense he was never—could in the nature of things never
be—any man's "successor." Just what had constituted the predeces-
sorship of other men was apparently that they had been able to
make up their mind. He, worse luck, was at the mercy of her face,
and more than ever at the mercy of it now, which meant, moreover,
not that it made a slave of him, but that it made, disconcertingly,
a sceptic. It was the absolute perfection of the handsome; but
things had a way of coming into it. "I felt," he said, "that you were
there together at a point at which you had a right to the ease that
the absence of a listener would give. I reflected that when you made
me promise to stay you hadn't guessed——"

"That he could possibly have come to me on such an extraordinary errand? No, of course, I hadn't guessed. Who *would?* But
didn't you see how little I was upset by it?"

Sutton demurred. Then with a smile, "I think *he* saw how little."

"You yourself didn't, then?"

He again held back, but not, after all, to answer. "He was
wonderful, wasn't he?"

"I think he was," she replied after a moment. To which she
added: "Why did he pretend that way he knew you?"

"He didn't pretend. He felt on the spot as if we were friends."
Sutton had found this afterwards, and found truth in it. "It was an
effusion of cheer and hope. He was so glad to see me there, and to
find you happy."

"Happy?"

"Happy. Aren't you?"

"Because of *you?*"

"Well—according to the impression he received as he came in."

"That was sudden then," she asked, "and unexpected?"

Her companion thought. "Prepared in some degree, but confirmed by the sight of us, there together, so awfully jolly and sociable over your fire."

Mrs. Grantham turned this round. "If he knew I was 'happy' then—which, by the way, is none of his business, nor of yours either —why in the world did he come?"

"Well, for good manners, and for his idea," said Sutton.

She took it in, appearing to have no hardness of rancour that could bar discussion. "Do you mean by his idea his proposal that I should grandmother his wife? And, if you do, is the proposal your reason for calling him wonderful?"

Sutton laughed. "Pray, what's yours?" As this was a question, however, that she took her time to answer or not to answer—only appearing interested for a moment in a combination that had formed itself on the other side of the room—he presently went on. "What's *his?*—that would seem to be the point. His, I mean, for having decided on the extraordinary step of throwing his little wife, bound hands and feet, into your arms. Intelligent as you are, and with these three or four hours to have thought it over, I yet don't see how that can fail still to mystify you."

She continued to watch their opposite neighbours. " 'Little,' you call her. Is she so very small?"

"Tiny, tiny—she *must* be; as different as possible in every way —of necessity—from you. They always *are* the opposite pole, you know," said Shirley Sutton.

She glanced at him now. "You strike me as of an impudence——!"

"No, no. I only like to make it out with you."

She looked away again and, after a little, went on. "I'm sure she's charming, and only hope one isn't to gather that he's already tired of her."

"Not a bit! He's tremendously in love, and he'll remain so."

"So much the better. And if it's a question," said Mrs. Grantham, "of one's doing what one can for her, he has only, as I told him when you had gone, to give me the chance."

"Good! So he *is* to commit her to you?"

"You use extraordinary expressions, but it's settled that he brings her."

"And you'll really and truly help her?"

"Really and truly?" said Mrs. Grantham, with her eyes again upon him. "Why not? For what do you take me?"

"Ah, isn't that just what I still have the discomfort, every day I live, of asking myself?"

She had made, as she spoke, a movement to rise, which, as if she was tired of his tone, his last words appeared to determine. But, also getting up, he held her, when they were on their feet, long enough to hear the rest of what he had to say. "If you do help her, you know, you'll show him that you've understood."

"Understood what?"

"Why, his idea—the deep, acute train of reasoning that has led him to take, as one may say, the bull by the horns; to reflect that as you might, as you probably *would,* in any case, get at her, he plays the wise game, as well as the bold one, by assuming your generosity and placing himself publicly under an obligation to you."

Mrs. Grantham showed not only that she had listened, but that she had for an instant considered. "What is it you elegantly describe as my getting 'at' her?"

"He takes his risk, but puts you, you see, on your honour."

She thought a moment more. "What profundities indeed then over the simplest of matters! And if your idea is," she went on, "that if I do help her I shall show him I've understood them, so it will be that if I don't——"

"You'll show him"—Sutton took her up—"that you haven't? Precisely. But in spite of not wanting to appear to have understood *too* much——"

"I may still be depended on to do what I can? Quite certainly. You'll see what I may still be depended on to do." And she moved away.

III

It was not, doubtless, that there had been anything in their rather sharp separation at that moment to sustain or prolong the interruption; yet it definitely befell that, circumstances aiding, they practically failed to meet again before the great party at Burbeck. This occasion was to gather in some thirty persons from a certain Friday to the following Monday, and it was on the Friday that

Sutton went down. He had known in advance that Mrs. Grantham was to be there, and this perhaps, during the interval of hindrance, had helped him a little to be patient. He had before him the certitude of a real full cup—two days brimming over with the sight of her. He found, however, on his arrival that she was not yet in the field, and presently learned that her place would be in a small contingent that was to join the party on the morrow. This knowledge he extracted from Miss Banker, who was always the first to present herself at any gathering that was to enjoy her, and whom, moreover—partly on that very account—the wary not less than the speculative were apt to hold themselves well-advised to engage with at as early as possible a stage of the business. She was stout, red, rich, mature, universal—a massive, much-fingered volume, alphabetical, wonderful, indexed, that opened of itself at the right place. She opened for Sutton instinctively at G——, which happened to be remarkably convenient. "What she's really waiting over for is to bring down Lady Gwyther."

"Ah, the Gwythers are coming?"

"Yes; caught, through Mrs. Grantham, just in time. *She'll* be the feature—everyone wants to see her."

Speculation and wariness met and combined at this moment in Shirley Sutton. "Do you mean—a—Mrs. Grantham?"

"Dear no! Poor little Lady Gwyther, who, but just arrived in England, appears now literally for the first time in her life in any society whatever, and whom (don't you know the extraordinary story? you ought to—*you!*) she, of all people, has so wonderfully taken up. It will be quite—here—as if she were 'presenting' her."

Sutton, of course, took in more things than even appeared. "I never know what I ought to know; I only know, inveterately, what I oughtn't. So what *is* the extraordinary story?"

"You really haven't heard——?"

"Really," he replied without winking.

"It happened, indeed, but the other day," said Miss Banker, "yet everyone is already wondering. Gwyther has thrown his wife on her mercy—but I won't believe you if you pretend to me you don't know why he shouldn't."

Sutton asked himself then what he *could* pretend. "Do you mean because she's merciless?"

She hesitated. "If you don't know, perhaps I oughtn't to tell you."

He liked Miss Banker, and found just the right tone to plead. "*Do* tell me."

"Well," she sighed, "it will be your own fault——! They had been such friends that there could have been but one name for the crudity of his original *procédé*. When I was a girl we used to call it throwing over. They call it in French to *lâcher*. But I refer not so much to the act itself as to the manner of it, though you may say indeed, of course, that there is in such cases, after all, only one manner. Least said, soonest mended."

Sutton seemed to wonder. "Oh, he said too much?"

"He said nothing. That was it."

Sutton kept it up. "But was *what?*"

"Why, what she must, like any woman in her shoes, have felt to be his perfidy. He simply went and *did* it—took to himself this child, that is, without the preliminary of a scandal or a rupture—before she could turn round."

"I follow you. But it would appear from what you say that she *has* turned round now."

"Well," Miss Banker laughed, "we shall see for ourselves how far. It will be what everyone will try to see."

"Oh, then we've work cut out!" And Sutton certainly felt that he himself had—an impression that lost nothing from a further talk with Miss Banker in the course of a short stroll in the grounds with her the next day. He spoke as one who had now considered many things.

"Did I understand from you yesterday that Lady Gwyther's a 'child'?"

"Nobody knows. It's prodigious the way she has managed."

"The way Lady Gwyther has——?"

"No; the way May Grantham has kept her till this hour in her pocket."

He was quick at his watch. "Do you mean by 'this hour' that they're due now?"

"Not till tea. All the others arrive together in time for that." Miss Banker had clearly, since the previous day, filled in gaps and become, as it were, revised and enlarged. "She'll have kept a cat from seeing her, so as to produce her entirely herself."

"Well," Sutton mused, "that will have been a very noble sort of return——"

"For Gwyther's behaviour? Very. Yet I feel creepy."

"Creepy?"

"Because so much depends for the girl—in the way of the right start or the wrong start—on the signs and omens of this first appearance. It's a great house and a great occasion, and we're assembled here, it strikes me, very much as the Roman mob at the circus used to be to see the next Christian maiden brought out to the tigers."

"Oh, if she *is* a Christian maiden——!" Sutton murmured. But he stopped at what his imagination called up.

It perhaps fed that faculty a little that Miss Banker had the effect of making out that Mrs. Grantham might individually be, in any case, something of a Roman matron. "She has kept her in the dark so that we may only take her from her hand. She will have formed her for us."

"In so few days?"

"Well, she will have prepared her—decked her for the sacrifice with ribbons and flowers."

"Ah, if you only mean that she will have taken her to her dressmaker——!" And it came to Sutton, at once as a new light and as a check, almost, to anxiety, that this was all poor Gwyther, mistrustful probably of a taste formed by Stuttgart, might have desired of their friend.

There were usually at Burbeck many things taking place at once; so that wherever else, on such occasions, tea might be served, it went forward with matchless pomp, weather permitting, on a shaded stretch of one of the terraces and in presence of one of the prospects. Shirley Sutton, moving, as the afternoon waned, more restlessly about and mingling in dispersed groups only to find they had nothing to keep him quiet, came upon it as he turned a corner of the house—saw it seated there in all its state. It might be said that at Burbeck it was, like everything else, made the most of. It constituted immediately, with multiplied tables and glittering plate, with rugs and cushions and ices and fruit and wonderful porcelain

and beautiful women, a scene of splendour, almost an incident of
grand opera. One of the beautiful women might quite have been
expected to rise with a gold cup and a celebrated song.

One of them did rise, as it happened, while Sutton drew near,
and he found himself a moment later seeing nothing and nobody
but Mrs. Grantham. They met on the terrace, just away from the
others, and the movement in which he had the effect of arresting
her might have been that of withdrawal. He quickly saw, however,
that if she had been about to pass into the house it was only on
some errand—to get something or to call someone—that would
immediately have restored her to the public. It somehow struck him
on the spot—and more than ever yet, though the impression was not
wholly new to him—that she felt herself a figure for the forefront
of the stage and indeed would have been recognised by anyone at
a glance as the *prima donna assoluta*. She caused, in fact, during
the few minutes he stood talking to her, an extraordinary series of
waves to roll extraordinarily fast over his sense, not the least mark
of the matter being that the appearance with which it ended was
again the one with which it had begun. "The face—the face," as
he kept dumbly repeating; that was at last, as at first, all he could
clearly see. She had a perfection resplendent, but what in the world
had it done, this perfection, to her beauty? It was her beauty,
doubtless, that looked out at him, but it was into something else
that, as their eyes met, he strangely found himself looking.

It was as if something had happened in consequence of which
she had changed, and there was that in this swift perception that
made him glance eagerly about for Lady Gwyther. But as he took
in the recruited group—identities of the hour added to those of the
previous twenty-four—he saw, among his recognitions, one of which
was the husband of the person missing, that Lady Gwyther was not
there. Nothing in the whole business was more singular than his
consciousness that, as he came back to his interlocutress after the
nods and smiles and handwaves he had launched, she knew what
had been his thought. She knew for whom he had looked without
success; but why should this knowledge visibly have hardened and
sharpened her, and precisely at a moment when she was unprece-
dentedly magnificent? The indefinable apprehension that had somewhat sunk after his second talk with Miss Banker and then had

perversely risen again—this nameless anxiety now produced on him, with a sudden sharper pinch, the effect of a great suspense. The action of that, in turn, was to show him that he had not yet fully known how much he had at stake on a final view. It was revealed to him for the first time that he "really cared" whether Mrs. Grantham were a safe nature. It was too ridiculous by what a thread it hung, but something was certainly in the air that would definitely tell him.

What was in the air descended the next moment to earth. He turned round as he caught the expression with which her eyes attached themselves to something that approached. A little person, very young and very much dressed, had come out of the house, and the expression in Mrs. Grantham's eyes was that of the artist confronted with her work and interested, even to impatience, in the judgment of others. The little person drew nearer, and though Sutton's companion, without looking at him now, gave it a name and met it, he had jumped for himself at certitude. He saw many things—too many, and they appeared to be feathers, frills, excrescences of silk and lace—massed together and conflicting, and after a moment also saw struggling out of them a small face that struck him as either scared or sick. Then, with his eyes again returning to Mrs. Grantham, he saw another.

He had no more talk with Miss Banker till late that evening— an evening during which he had felt himself too noticeably silent; but something had passed between this pair, across dinner-table and drawing-room, without speech, and when they at last found words it was in the needed ease of a quiet end of the long, lighted gallery, where she opened again at the very paragraph.

"You were right—that *was* it. She did the only thing that, at such short notice, she *could* do. She took her to her dressmaker."

Sutton, with his back to the reach of the gallery, had, as if to banish a vision, buried his eyes for a minute in his hands. "And oh, the face—the face!"

"Which?" Miss Banker asked.

"Whichever one looks at."

"But May Grantham's glorious. She has turned herself out——"

"With a splendour of taste and a sense of effect, eh? Yes." Sutton showed he saw far.

"She *has* the sense of effect. The sense of effect as exhibited in Lady Gwyther's clothes——!" was something Miss Banker failed of words to express. "Everybody's overwhelmed. Here, you know, that sort of thing's grave. The poor creature's lost."

"Lost?"

"Since on the first impression, as we said, so much depends. The first impression's made—oh, made! I defy her now ever to unmake it. Her husband, who's proud, won't like her the better for it. And I don't see," Miss Banker went on, "that her prettiness *was* enough —a mere little feverish, frightened freshness; what *did* he see in her? —to be so blasted. It has been done with an atrocity of art——"

"That supposes the dressmaker then also a devil?"

"Oh, your London women and their dressmakers!" Miss Banker laughed.

"But the face—the face!" Sutton woefully repeated.

"May's?"

"The little girl's. It's exquisite."

"Exquisite?"

"For unimaginable pathos."

"Oh!" Miss Banker dropped.

"She has at last begun to see." Sutton showed again how far *he* saw. "It glimmers upon her innocence, she makes it dimly out— what has been done with her. She's even worse this evening—the way, my eye, she looked at dinner!—than when she came. Yes"— he was confident—"it has dawned (how couldn't it, out of all of you?) and she knows."

"She ought to have known before!" Miss Banker intelligently sighed.

"No; she wouldn't in that case have been so beautiful."

"Beautiful?" cried Miss Banker; "overloaded like a monkey in a show!"

"The face, yes; which goes to the heart. It's that that makes it," said Shirley Sutton. "And it's that"—he thought it out—"that makes the other."

"I see. Conscious?"

"Horrible!"

"You take it hard," said Miss Banker.

Lord Gwyther, just before she spoke, had come in sight and now was near them. Sutton on this, appearing to wish to avoid him,

reached, before answering his companion's observation, a door that opened close at hand. "So hard," he replied from that point, "that I shall be off to-morrow morning."

"And not see the rest?" she called after him.

But he had already gone, and Lord Gwyther, arriving, amiably took up her question. "The rest of what?"

Miss Banker looked him well in the eyes. "Of Mrs. Grantham's clothes."

ERNEST HEMINGWAY

The Battler

NICK STOOD UP. He was all right. He looked up the track at the lights of the caboose going out of sight around the curve. There was water on both sides of the track, then tamarack swamp.

He felt of his knee. The pants were torn and the skin was barked. His hands were scraped and there were sand and cinders driven up under his nails. He went over to the edge of the track down the little slope to the water and washed his hands. He washed them carefully in the cold water, getting the dirt out from the nails. He squatted down and bathed his knee.

That lousy crut of a brakeman. He would get him some day. He would know him again. That was a fine way to act.

"Come here, kid," he said. "I got something for you."

He had fallen for it. What a lousy kid thing to have done. They would never suck him in that way again.

"Come here, kid, I got something for you." Then *wham* and he lit on his hands and knees beside the track.

Nick rubbed his eye. There was a big bump coming up. He would have a black eye, all right. It ached already. That son of a crutting brakeman.

He touched the bump over his eye with his fingers. Oh, well, it was only a black eye. That was all he had gotten out of it. Cheap at the price. He wished he could see it. Could not see it looking into the water, though. It was dark and he was a long way off from anywhere. He wiped his hands on his trousers and stood up, then climbed the embankment to the rails.

He started up the track. It was well ballasted and made easy walking, sand and gravel packed between the ties, solid walking. The smooth roadbed like a causeway went on ahead through the swamp. Nick walked along. He must get to somewhere.

Nick had swung on to the freight train when it slowed down for the yards outside of Walton Junction. The train, with Nick on it, had passed through Kalkaska as it started to get dark. Now he must be nearly to Mancelona. Three or four miles of swamp. He stepped along the track, walking so he kept on the ballast between the ties, the swamp ghostly in the rising mist. His eye ached and he was hungry. He kept on hiking, putting the miles of track back of him. The swamp was all the same on both sides of the track.

Ahead there was a bridge. Nick crossed it, his boots ringing hollow on the iron. Down below the water showed black between the slits of ties. Nick kicked a loose spike and it dropped into the water. Beyond the bridge were hills. It was high and dark on both sides of the track. Up the track Nick saw a fire.

He came up the track toward the fire carefully. It was off to one side of the track, below the railway embankment. He had only seen the light from it. The track came out through a cut and where the fire was burning the country opened out and fell away into woods. Nick dropped carefully down the embankment and cut into the woods to come up to the fire through the trees. It was a beech-wood forest and the fallen beechnut burrs were under his shoes as he walked between the trees. The fire was bright now, just at the

edge of the trees. There was a man sitting by it. Nick waited behind the tree and watched. The man looked to be alone. He was sitting there with his head in his hands looking at the fire. Nick stepped out and walked into the firelight.

The man sat there looking into the fire. When Nick stopped quite close to him he did not move.

"Hello!" Nick said.

The man looked up.

"Where did you get the shiner?" he said.

"A brakeman busted me."

"Off the through freight?"

"Yes."

"I saw the bastard," the man said. "He went through here 'bout an hour and a half ago. He was walking along the top of the cars slapping his arms and singing."

"The bastard!"

"It must have made him feel good to bust you," the man said seriously.

"I'll bust him."

"Get him with a rock sometime when he's going through," the man advised.

"I'll get him."

"You're a tough one, aren't you?"

"No," Nick answered.

"All you kids are tough."

"You got to be tough," Nick said.

"That's what I said."

The man looked at Nick and smiled. In the firelight Nick saw that his face was misshapen. His nose was sunken, his eyes were slits, he had queer-shaped lips. Nick did not perceive all this at once, he only saw the man's face was queerly formed and mutilated. It was like putty in color. Dead looking in the firelight.

"Don't you like my pan?" the man asked.

Nick was embarrassed.

"Sure," he said.

"Look here!" the man took off his cap.

He had only one ear. It was thickened and tight against the side of his head. Where the other ear should have been there was a stump.

"Ever see one like that?"

"No," said Nick. It made him a little sick.

"I could take it," the man said. "Don't you think I could take it, kid?"

"You bet!"

"They all bust their hands on me," the little man said. "They couldn't hurt me."

He looked at Nick. "Sit down," he said. "Want to eat?"

"Don't bother," Nick said. "I'm going on to the town."

"Listen!" the man said. "Call me Ad."

"Sure!"

"Listen," the little man said. "I'm not quite right."

"What's the matter?"

"I'm crazy."

He put on his cap. Nick felt like laughing.

"You're all right," he said.

"No, I'm not. I'm crazy. Listen, you ever been crazy?"

"No," Nick said. "How does it get you?"

"I don't know," Ad said. "When you got it you don't know about it. You know me, don't you?"

"No."

"I'm Ad Francis."

"Honest to God?"

"Don't you believe it?"

"Yes."

Nick knew it must be true.

"You know how I beat them?"

"No," Nick said.

"My heart's slow. It only beats forty a minute. Feel it." Nick hesitated.

"Come on," the man took hold of his hand. "Take hold of my wrist. Put your fingers there."

The little man's wrist was thick and the muscles bulged above the bone. Nick felt the slow pumping under his fingers.

"Got a watch?"

"No."

"Neither have I," Ad said. "It ain't any good if you haven't got a watch."

Nick dropped his wrist.

"Listen," Ad Francis said. "Take ahold again. You count and I'll count up to sixty."

Feeling the slow hard throb under his fingers Nick started to count. He heard the little man counting slowly, one, two, three, four, five, and on—aloud.

"Sixty," Ad finished. "That's a minute. What did you make it?"

"Forty," Nick said.

"That's right," Ad said happily. "She never speeds up."

A man dropped down the railroad embankment and came across the clearing to the fire.

"Hello, Bugs!" Ad said.

"Hello!" Bugs answered. It was a negro's voice. Nick knew from the way he walked that he was a negro. He stood with his back to them, bending over the fire. He straightened up.

"This is my pal Bugs," Ad said. "He's crazy, too."

"Glad to meet you," Bugs said. "Where you say you're from?"

"Chicago," Nick said.

"That's a fine town," the negro said. "I didn't catch your name."

"Adams. Nick Adams."

"He says he's never been crazy, Bugs," Ad said.

"He's got a lot coming to him," the negro said. He was unwrapping a package by the fire.

"When are we going to eat, Bugs?" the prizefighter asked.

"Right away."

"Are you hungry, Nick?"

"Hungry as hell."

"Hear that, Bugs?"

"I hear most of what goes on."

"That ain't what I asked you."

"Yes. I heard what the gentleman said."

Into a skillet he was laying slices of ham. As the skillet grew hot the grease sputtered and Bugs, crouching on long nigger legs over the fire, turned the ham and broke eggs into the skillet, tipping it from side to side to baste the eggs with the hot fat.

"Will you cut some bread out of that bag, Mister Adams?"
Bugs turned from the fire.

"Sure."

Nick reached in the bag and brought out a loaf of bread. He
cut six slices. Ad watched him and leaned forward.

"Let me take your knife, Nick," he said.

"No, you don't," the negro said. "Hang onto your knife, Mister
Adams."

The prizefighter sat back.

"Will you bring me the bread, Mister Adams?" Bugs asked.
Nick brought it over.

"Do you like to dip your bread in the ham fat?" the negro
asked.

"You bet!"

"Perhaps we'd better wait until later. It's better at the finish
of the meal. Here."

The negro picked up a slice of ham and laid it on one of the
pieces of bread, then slid an egg on top of it.

"Just close that sandwich, will you, please, and give it to Mister
Francis."

Ad took the sandwich and started eating.

"Watch out how that egg runs," the negro warned. "This is for
you, Mister Adams. The remainder for myself."

Nick bit into the sandwich. The negro was sitting opposite
him beside Ad. The hot fried ham and eggs tasted wonderful.

"Mister Adams is right hungry," the negro said. The little man
whom Nick knew by name as a former champion fighter was silent.
He had said nothing since the negro had spoken about the knife.

"May I offer you a slice of bread dipped right in the hot ham
fat?" Bugs said.

"Thanks a lot."

The little white man looked at Nick.

"Will you have some, Mister Adolph Francis?" Bugs offered
from the skillet.

Ad did not answer. He was looking at Nick.

"Mister Francis?" came the nigger's soft voice.

Ad did not answer. He was looking at Nick.

"I spoke to you, Mister Francis," the nigger said softly.

Ad kept on looking at Nick. He had his cap down over his eyes. Nick felt nervous.

"How the hell do you get that way?" came out from under the cap sharply at Nick.

"Who the hell do you think you are? You're a snotty bastard. You come in here where nobody asks you and eat a man's food and when he asks to borrow a knife you get snotty."

He glared at Nick, his face was white and his eyes almost out of sight under the cap.

"You're a hot sketch. Who the hell asked you to butt in here?"

"Nobody."

"You're damn right nobody did. Nobody asked you to stay either. You come in here and act snotty about my face and smoke my cigars and drink my liquor and then talk snotty. Where the hell do you think you get off?"

Nick said nothing. Ad stood up.

"I'll tell you, you yellow-livered Chicago bastard. You're going to get your can knocked off. Do you get that?"

Nick stepped back. The little man came toward him slowly, stepping flat-footed forward, his left foot stepping forward, his right dragging up to it.

"Hit me," he moved his head. "Try and hit me."

"I don't want to hit you."

"You won't get out of it that way. You're going to take a beating, see? Come on and lead at me."

"Cut it out," Nick said.

"All right, then, you bastard."

The little man looked down at Nick's feet. As he looked down the negro, who had followed behind him as he moved away from the fire, set himself and tapped him across the base of the skull. He fell forward and Bugs dropped the cloth-wrapped blackjack on the grass. The little man lay there, his face in the grass. The negro picked him up, his head hanging, and carried him to the fire. His face looked bad, the eyes open. Bugs laid him down gently.

"Will you bring me the water in the bucket, Mister Adams," he said. "I'm afraid I hit him just a little hard."

The negro splashed water with his hands on the man's face and pulled his ears gently. The eyes closed.

Bugs stood up.

"He's all right," he said. "There's nothing to worry about. I'm sorry, Mister Adams."

"It's all right." Nick was looking down at the little man. He saw the blackjack on the grass and picked it up. It had a flexible handle and was limber in his hand. It was made of worn black leather with a handkerchief wrapped around the heavy end.

"That's a whalebone handle," the negro smiled. "They don't make them any more. I didn't know how well you could take care of yourself and, anyway, I didn't want you to hurt him or mark him up no more than he is."

The negro smiled again.

"You hurt him yourself."

"I know how to do it. He won't remember nothing of it. I have to do it to change him when he gets that way."

Nick was still looking down at the little man, lying, his eyes closed in the firelight. Bugs put some wood on the fire.

"Don't you worry about him none, Mister Adams. I seen him like this plenty of times before."

"What made him crazy?" Nick asked.

"Oh, a lot of things," the negro answered from the fire. "Would you like a cup of this coffee, Mister Adams?"

He handed Nick the cup and smoothed the coat he had placed under the unconscious man's head.

"He took too many beatings, for one thing," the negro sipped the coffee. "But that just made him sort of simple. Then his sister was his manager and they was always being written up in the papers all about brothers and sisters and how she loved her brother and how he loved his sister, and then they got married in New York and that made a lot of unpleasantness."

"I remember about it."

"Sure. Of course they wasn't brother and sister no more than a rabbit, but there was a lot of people didn't like it either way and they commenced to have disagreements, and one day she just went off and never come back."

He drank the coffee and wiped his lips with the pink palm of his hand.

"He just went crazy. Will you have some more coffee, Mister Adams?"

"Thanks."

"I seen her a couple of times," the negro went on. "She was an awful good-looking woman. Looked enough like him to be twins. He wouldn't be bad-looking without his face all busted."

He stopped. The story seemed to be over.

"Where did you meet him?" asked Nick.

"I met him in jail," the negro said. "He was busting people all the time after she went away and they put him in jail. I was in for cuttin' a man."

He smiled, and went on soft-voiced:

"Right away I liked him and when I got out I looked him up. He likes to think I'm crazy and I don't mind. I like to be with him and I like seeing the country and I don't have to commit no larceny to do it. I like living like a gentleman."

"What do you all do?" Nick asked.

"Oh, nothing. Just move around. He's got money."

"He must have made a lot of money."

"Sure. He spent all his money, though. Or they took it away from him. She sends him money."

He poked up the fire.

"She's a mighty fine woman," he said. "She looks enough like him to be his own twin."

The negro looked over at the little man, lying breathing heavily. His blond hair was down over his forehead. His mutilated face looked childish in repose.

"I can wake him up any time now, Mister Adams. If you don't mind I wish you'd sort of pull out. I don't like to not be hospitable, but it might disturb him back again to see you. I hate to have to thump him and it's the only thing to do when he gets started. I have to sort of keep him away from people. You don't mind, do you, Mister Adams? No, don't thank me, Mister Adams. I'd have warned you about him but he seemed to have taken such a liking to you and I thought things were going to be all right. You'll hit a town about two miles up the track. Mancelona they call it. Good-bye. I wish we could ask you to stay the night but it's just out of the question. Would you like to take some of that ham and some bread

with you? No? You better take a sandwich," all this in a low, smooth,
polite nigger voice.

"Good. Well, good-bye, Mister Adams. Good-bye and good
luck!"

Nick walked away from the fire across the clearing to the railway tracks. Out of the range of the fire he listened. The low soft
voice of the negro was talking. Nick could not hear the words.
Then he heard the little man say, "I got an awful headache, Bugs."

"You'll feel better, Mister Francis," the negro's voice soothed.
"Just you drink a cup of this hot coffee."

Nick climbed the embankment and started up the track. He
found he had a ham sandwich in his hand and put it in his pocket.
Looking back from the mounting grade before the track curved
into the hills he could see the firelight in the clearing.

ERNEST HEMINGWAY'S *"The Battler"*

In "The Battler," we have an excellent example of
Hemingway's famous "athletic" prose. It is no accident that much of his
fiction concerns the doings of sportsmen—big-game hunters, fishermen,
bullfighters, jockeys, and, in an extended sense of the term "sportsmen,"
soldiers. The preoccupation with sport, with the conflict conducted
according to a hard-and-fast *code* of behavior, is essentially related to
his stylistic practice.

In this instance, of course, as indeed in many of his stories, there
are certain ironies to be taken into account. The professional athlete
here, Ad Francis, is not really the central figure of the narrative. It is
Nick Adams in whose reactions we are principally interested, whose
consciousness gives the happenings their significance. And Francis is,
at least at first glance, an entirely pathetic figure—old, crazy, deformed
by beatings, a tramp, living only on the recollections of his former glory
as a champion boxer. But we can set these considerations aside for the
moment.

The general point still holds, that the prose style directly "imitates"
the code-sense of the sportsman. It is a bare, stripped-down, deliberately

From COMMENTARIES ON FIVE MODERN AMERICAN SHORT STORIES, by
John Edward Hardy, Verlag Moritz Diesterweg. Frankfurt/Main. Copyright
1962 by Moritz Diesterweg.

simple style. The code, the set of rules, of any sport is established and maintained by the deliberate exclusion of certain, natural human impulses generated in the situation of conflict. The object of the game is not simply to win (by punching one's opponent in the nose, or whatever) but to win *according to the rules*. The keeping of the rules, indeed, is the "game."

This situation furnishes not only the model for Hemingway's moral sense, but the exact analogy for his style. He is, stylistically, no more a true naturalist than he is a traditional rhetorician. His short, simple sentences; his habit of repeating himself, with the same object described, or simply referred to, over and over again in the same words; his narration of events in a straight line of succession, one incident leading only to the next, without "flashbacks" or other complications of the time sense—all this may, at first glance, look merely childish and "innocent," uninstructed. But it is not; it is the most stringent and deliberate economy, severely calculated, highly artful. The rigorous discipline that excludes from his work, on the one hand, almost all the devices of traditional rhetoric (complexities of sentence structure and prose rhythm, overt use of metaphor and other tropes, etc.) is identical with the artificiality of style, its *unnaturalness*.

We may take as a good example of this in "The Battler" the account of Nick's walk along the railroad track after the brakeman has knocked him off the train. The action of the brakeman, notice, is taken by Nick entirely "philosophically." Nick determines the extent of his injury, washes his hands, allows himself a moment's—but only a moment's—anger against the brakeman, and a determination to revenge, and then starts walking ahead up the track. The emotions are all but entirely "ritual," we may say. To be hit, and to hit back when one gets the chance, is all merely "a part of the game." There is no elaboration of feelings—the brakeman is, repeatedly, a "lousy crut," a "crutting son of a brakeman"—and nothing really personal in it; Nick's anger is as much against himself, for having been "sucked in," as against the brakeman, and is expressed in a partial repetition of the same terms—his own behavior, in falling for the man's trick, has been equally "lousy." ("What a lousy kid thing to have done.") He has, in short, simply forgotten the "rules" for a moment. Now, having been reminded of them, having learned his lesson, he does not waste time with superfluous emotion, but walks away determined only to "get to somewhere," and to keep firmly to "the track."

Just *where* he will get to is of no great importance. What is important is simply to keep going, without misgivings, without looking aside or backward—to move ahead, by the shortest route possible, to wherever it is. And the track (observe how many times Hemingway repeats the word) is the exact objective symbol—so exact, indeed, so simple and perfect that we are likely not to notice it—of this uncompromising state of mind. It was "well ballasted, and made easy walking . . . solid walking"; it "went on ahead." Where it goes on ahead, Hemingway tells us, is "through the swamp." And we might like to hear more about that swamp. It looks interesting; it is "ghostly," with the mist rising from it. Could we not be entertained with some weird sounds, perhaps; a moment's terror on Nick's part, stopping and looking apprehensively about him, his hair rising? Some small, human weakness or uncertainty of purpose anyway, at one point or another? But no; he (Nick or Hemingway) stays on the track; and the swamp, not very interesting after all, "*all the same* on both sides of the track," is behind us before we know it. It is not, perhaps, that it would be unmanly of Nick to show fear, or other errant emotions. In fact, Hemingway gives us enough—with the one word "ghostly" in description of the swamp, and then again with the image of the loose spike falling between the ties into the "black water" under the bridge—to permit us to assume that Nick does feel afraid, and lonely, and lost. Not unmanly, but it would be unsporting, undisciplined, to be distracted by these things. The "game" demands that we put them aside.

The track, product of man's work and instrument of his purpose, cutting straight and uncompromising through the countryside, is also the symbol of the specifically *human* situation, as Hemingway sees it. Nonhuman, external Nature, represented by the varying landscape— the swamp, and then, after the river, the hills, and beyond them the lowland woods—is neither hostile nor friendly to man, but essentially indifferent. It is all, whether rising or falling, dry land or swamp, "all the same" from the human viewpoint, from "the track." The variations of scene are minimally interesting as something to be observed, but are insignificant as to human purpose.

Nick leaves the track, entertains any thoughts besides his single-minded determination to keep going, only when he sees the light of the fire—that is, the sign of a human presence. It is ironic, of course, that what he discovers is *hardly* human; the battered, little man with his sickeningly mutilated, "dead looking" face, his sinister, half-appealing, half-threatening manner, his abnormally slow pulse-beat that Nick consents gingerly to feel; something only half alive. But Hemingway typically prefers to deal with human beings in what we might call "marginal" situations of this kind. Cast out, ruined, with no or few companions, maimed, living in the woods. He prefers it to the purpose, finally, just of emphasizing the more strongly that it *is* human; that the closer we get to the margin between the human and the inhuman, the bestial, the more important the little difference becomes, the more surely does it make "all the difference."

Ad Francis is almost over the line. Nick has quickly recognized and accepted his fellow-humanity, the feeling-of-the-pulse being the symbolic act of recognition. But the little man's returning insanity, after the Negro has arrived, threatens to cancel this out—and, but for Bugs' interference, would do so.

We have not the space to enquire very far into the psychology of the Negro's attitude. But the Negro is, of course, the most commonly recognized type of the pariah in American society; and Hemingway's basic intent in assigning the "nigger" to the part of sole companion to Francis, himself an outcast, ought to be obvious enough. It is only, we feel, a Negro who could have not merely compassion enough to devote himself to the care of such a man, but also a certain pride in the office. With all apparent, naïve sincerity, he tells Nick that he considers himself "living like a gentleman" in his relationship with the old boxer!

And yet, I think, the final irony is that this is not just the "nigger's" view. Bugs, in the end, is Hemingway's spokesman. We are meant finally to see old Ad Francis, after the Negro has explained him to Nick, as not merely human but the best of humanity—as a hero, indeed—and therefore to accept Bugs' office of attendance upon him as a truly noble one, the true life of the "gentleman."

It should be observed that Francis' *insanity*, when he threatens to fight Nick, is precisely identifiable with his hallucinatory return to the days of his fame. (He imagines himself to be somewhere again in an apartment, or hotel room, seeing Nick as one of his hypocritical, false admirers, a freeloader, smoking his cigars and drinking his liquor.) The implication is, then, that he is by contrast *sane*—most normal, most genuinely human and admirable—when he recognizes and accepts his present, real condition as an outcast.

Not that there is anything wrong with being a prizefighter. The memory of what gave him his fame, his skill and toughness, his ability to "take it," is what makes him interesting. But Hemingway does suggest that there is something wrong with *success*, in itself. To be successful, the "champion," is inevitably to make oneself subject to the capricious will of the audience, the fans—those nameless "they" whom Bugs speaks of—who can destroy a man's reputation as quickly as they have built it up. The only thing really worth having is the skill and the endurance itself, the knowledge of the game, and the ability to recognize an opponent worthy of one's prowess—the sportsman's sense not to use it in an unequal contest. And all of this, essentially, Ad Francis still has in his periods of sanity, and is more likely to keep in his present situation than when he was in his public glory.

Hence, to go back to the opening situation of the story, Nick Adams has never actually "left the track" with his brief visit to Ad and Bugs' campfire. What he has learned there is only an amplification of the lesson he took from his encounter with the brakeman, that a man's gallantry, true self-esteem, is measured precisely and only by his capacity for living according to his code—whatever the code may be.

We may properly question whether Hemingway's view is an entirely adequate one. *Is* life a game? And, if not, can we consider that a major art which mirrors it as such? But, whatever its ultimate limits, it is an art the integrity and clarity of which cannot be questioned.   *J.E.H.*

D . H . L A W R E N C E

The Christening

HE MISTRESS OF THE British School stepped down from her school gate, and instead of turning to the left as usual, she turned to the right. Two women who were hastening home to scramble their husbands' dinners together—it was five minutes to four—stopped to look at her. They stood gazing after her for a moment; then they glanced at each other with a woman's little grimace.

To be sure, the retreating figure was ridiculous: small and thin, with a black straw hat, and a rusty cashmere dress hanging full all

From THE PRUSSIAN OFFICER in THE COMPLETE SHORT STORIES OF D. H. LAWRENCE, Vol. I (Compass Edition). All rights reserved. Reprinted by permission of The Viking Press, Inc.

round the skirt. For so small and frail and rusty a creature to sail with slow, deliberate stride was also absurd. Hilda Rowbotham was less than thirty, so it was not years that set the measure of her pace; she had heart disease. Keeping her face, that was small with sickness, but not uncomely, firmly lifted and fronting ahead, the young woman sailed on past the market-place, like a black swan of mournful disreputable plumage.

She turned into Berryman's, the bakers. The shop displayed bread and cakes, sacks of flour and oatmeal, flitches of bacon, hams, lard and sausages. The combination of scents was not unpleasing. Hilda Rowbotham stood for some minutes nervously tapping and pushing a large knife that lay on the counter, and looking at the tall, glittering brass scales. At last a morose man with sandy whiskers came down the step from the house-place.

"What is it?" he asked, not apologising for his delay.

"Will you give me sixpennyworth of assorted cakes and pastries —and put in some macaroons, please?" she asked, in remarkably rapid and nervous speech. Her lips fluttered like two leaves in a wind, and her words crowded and rushed like a flock of sheep at a gate.

"We've got no macaroons," said the man churlishly.

He had evidently caught that word. He stood waiting.

"Then I can't have any, Mr. Berryman. Now I do feel disappointed. I like those macaroons, you know, and it's not often I treat myself. One gets so tired of trying to spoil oneself, don't you think? It's less profitable even than trying to spoil somebody else." She laughed a quick little nervous laugh, putting her hand to her face.

"Then what'll you have?" asked the man, without the ghost of an answering smile. He evidently had not followed, so he looked more glum than ever.

"Oh, anything you've got," replied the schoolmistress, flushing slightly. The man moved slowly about, dropping the cakes from various dishes one by one into a paper bag.

"How's that sister o' yours getting on?" he asked, as if he were talking to the flour-scoop.

"Whom do you mean?" snapped the schoolmistress.

"The youngest," answered the stooping, pale-faced man, with a note of sarcasm.

"Emma! Oh, she's very well, thank you!" The schoolmistress

was very red, but she spoke with sharp, ironical defiance. The man grunted. Then he handed her the bag, and watched her out of the shop without bidding her "Good afternoon."

She had the whole length of the main street to traverse, a half-mile of slow-stepping torture, with shame flushing over her neck. But she carried her white bag with an appearance of steadfast unconcern. When she turned into the field she seemed to droop a little. The wide valley opened out from her, with the far woods withdrawing into twilight, and away in the centre the great pit steaming its white smoke and chuffing as the men were being turned up. A full rose-coloured moon, like a flamingo flying low under the far, dusky east, drew out of the mist. It was beautiful, and it made her irritable sadness soften, diffuse.

Across the field, and she was at home. It was a new, substantial cottage, built with unstinted hand, such a house as an old miner could build himself out of his savings. In the rather small kitchen a woman of dark, saturnine complexion sat nursing a baby in a long white gown; a young woman of heavy, brutal cast stood at the table, cutting bread and butter. She had a downcast, humble mien that sat unnaturally on her, and was strangely irritating. She did not look round when her sister entered. Hilda put down the bag of cakes and left the room, not having spoken to Emma, nor to the baby, nor to Mrs. Carlin, who had come in to help for the afternoon.

Almost immediately the father entered from the yard with a dust-pan full of coals. He was a large man, but he was going to pieces. As he passed through, he gripped the door with his free hand to steady himself, but turning, he lurched and swayed. He began putting the coals on the fire, piece by piece. One lump fell from his hands and smashed on the white hearth. Emma Rowbotham looked round, and began in a rough, loud voice of anger: "Look at you!" Then she consciously moderated her tones. "I'll sweep it up in a minute—don't you bother; you'll only be going head-first into the fire."

Her father bent down nevertheless to clear up the mess he had made, saying, articulating his words loosely and slavering in his speech:

"The lousy bit of a thing, it slipped between my fingers like a fish."

As he spoke he went tilting towards the fire. The dark-browed woman cried out; he put his hand on the hot stove to save himself; Emma swung round and dragged him off.

"Didn't I tell you!" she cried roughly. "Now, have you burnt yourself?"

She held tight hold of the big man, and pushed him into his chair.

"What's the matter?" cried a sharp voice from the other room. The speaker appeared, a hard well-favoured woman of twenty-eight. "Emma, don't speak like that to father." Then, in a tone not so cold, but just as sharp: "Now, father, what have you been doing?"

Emma withdrew to her table sullenly.

"It's nöwt," said the old man, vainly protesting. "It's nöwt at a'. Get on wi' what you're doin'."

"I'm afraid 'e's burnt 'is 'and," said the black-browed woman, speaking of him with a kind of hard pity, as if he were a cumbersome child. Bertha took the old man's hand and looked at it, making a quick tut-tutting noise of impatience.

"Emma, get that zinc ointment—and some white rag," she commanded sharply. The younger sister put down her loaf with the knife in it, and went. To a sensitive observer, this obedience was more intolerable than the most hateful discord. The dark woman bent over the baby and made silent, gentle movements of motherliness to it. The little one smiled and moved on her lap. It continued to move and twist.

"I believe this child's hungry," she said. "How long is it since he had anything?"

"Just afore dinner," said Emma dully.

"Good gracious!" exclaimed Bertha. "You needn't starve the child now you've got it. Once every two hours it ought to be fed, as I've told you; and now it's three. Take him, poor little mite—I'll cut the bread." She bent and looked at the bonny baby. She could not help herself: she smiled, and pressed its cheek with her finger, and nodded to it, making little noises. Then she turned and took the loaf from her sister. The woman rose and gave the child to its mother. Emma bent over the little sucking mite. She hated it when she looked at it, and saw it as a symbol, but when she felt it, her love was like fire in her blood.

"I should think 'e canna be comin'," said the father uneasily, looking up at the clock.

"Nonsense, father—the clock's fast! It's but half-past four! Don't fidget!" Bertha continued to cut the bread and butter.

"Open a tin of pears," she said to the woman, in a much milder tone. Then she went into the next room. As soon as she was gone, the old man said again: "I should ha'e thought he'd 'a' been 'ere by now, if he means comin'."

Emma, engrossed, did not answer. The father had ceased to consider her, since she had become humbled.

" 'E'll come—'e'll come!" assured the stranger.

A few minutes later Bertha hurried into the kitchen, taking off her apron. The dog barked furiously. She opened the door, commanded the dog to silence, and said: "He will be quiet now, Mr. Kendal."

"Thank you," said a sonorous voice, and there was the sound of a bicycle being propped against a wall. A clergyman entered, a big-boned, thin, ugly man of nervous manner. He went straight to the father.

"Ah—how are you—" he asked musically, peering down on the great frame of the miner, ruined by locomotor ataxy.

His voice was full of gentleness, but he seemed as if he could not see distinctly, could not get things clear.

"Have you hurt your hand?" he said comfortingly, seeing the white rag.

"It wor nöwt but a pestered bit o' coal as dropped, an' I put my hand on th' hub. I thought tha worna commin'."

The familiar "tha", and the reproach, were unconscious retaliation on the old man's part. The minister smiled, half wistfully, half indulgently. He was full of vague tenderness. Then he turned to the young mother, who flushed sullenly because her dishonoured breast was uncovered.

"How are *you?*" he asked, very softly and gently, as if she were ill and he were mindful of her.

"I'm all right," she replied, awkwardly taking his hand without rising, hiding her face and the anger that rose in her.

"Yes—yes"—he peered down at the baby, which sucked with

distended mouth upon the firm breast. "Yes, yes." He seemed lost in a dim musing.

Coming to, he shook hands unseeingly with the woman.

Presently they all went into the next room, the minister hesitating to help his crippled old deacon.

"I can go by myself, thank yer," testily replied the father.

Soon all were seated. Everybody was separated in feeling and isolated at table. High tea was spread in the middle kitchen, a large, ugly room kept for special occasions.

Hilda appeared last, and the clumsy, raw-boned clergyman rose to meet her. He was afraid of this family, the well-to-do old collier, and the brutal, self-willed children. But Hilda was queen among them. She was the clever one, and had been to college. She felt responsible for the keeping up of a high standard of conduct in all the members of the family. There *was* a difference between the Rowbothams and the common collier folk. Woodbine Cottage was a superior house to most—and was built in pride by the old man. She, Hilda, was a college-trained schoolmistress; she meant to keep up the prestige of her house in spite of blows.

She had put on a dress of green voile for this special occasion. But she was very thin; her neck protruded painfully. The clergyman, however, greeted her almost with reverence, and, with some assumption of dignity, she sat down before the tray. At the far end of the table sat the broken, massive frame of her father. Next to him was the youngest daughter, nursing the restless boy. The minister sat between Hilda and Bertha, hulking his bony frame uncomfortably.

There was a great spread on the table of tinned fruits and tinned salmon, ham and cakes. Miss Rowbotham kept a keen eye on everything: she felt the importance of the occasion. The young mother who had given rise to all this solemnity ate in sulky discomfort, snatching sullen little smiles at her child, smiles which came, in spite of her, when she felt its little limbs stirring vigorously on her lap. Bertha, sharp and abrupt, was chiefly concerned with the baby. She scorned her sister, and treated her like dirt. But the infant was a streak of light to her. Miss Rowbotham concerned herself with the function and the conversation. Her hands fluttered; she talked in little volleys, exceedingly nervous. Towards the end

of the meal, there came a pause. The old man wiped his mouth
with his red handkerchief, then, his blue eyes going fixed and
staring, he began to speak, in a loose, slobbering fashion, charging
his words at the clergyman.

"Well, mester—we'n axed you to come here ter christen this
childt, an' you'n come, an' I'm sure we're very thankful. I can't see
lettin' the poor blessed childt miss baptizing, an' they aren't for goin'
to church wi't——" He seemed to lapse into a muse. "So," he resumed, "we'n axed you to come here to do the job. I'm not sayin'
as it's not 'ard on us, it is. I'm breakin' up, an' mother's gone. I
don't like leavin' a girl o' mine in a situation like 'ers is, but what the
Lord's done, He's done, an' it's no matter murmuring. . . . There's
one thing to be thankful for, an' we *are* thankful for it: they never
need know the want of bread."

Miss Rowbotham, the lady of the family, sat very stiff and
pained during this discourse. She was sensitive to so many things
that she was bewildered. She felt her young sister's shame, then a
kind of swift protecting love for the baby, a feeling that included
the mother; she was at a loss before her father's religious sentiment,
and she felt and resented bitterly the mark upon the family, against
which the common folk could lift their fingers. Still she winced
from the sound of her father's words. It was a painful ordeal.

"It is hard for you," began the clergyman in his soft, lingering,
unworldly voice. "It is hard for you to-day, but the Lord gives
comfort in His time. A man child is born unto us, therefore let us
rejoice and be glad. If sin has entered in among us, let us purify
our hearts before the Lord. . . ."

He went on with his discourse. The young mother lifted the
whimpering infant, till its face was hid in her loose hair. She was
hurt, and a little glowering anger shone in her face. But nevertheless
her fingers clasped the body of the child beautifully. She was
stupefied with anger against this emotion let loose on her account.

Miss Bertha rose and went to the little kitchen, returning with
water in a china bowl. She placed it there among the tea-things.

"Well, we're all ready," said the old man, and the clergyman
began to read the service. Miss Bertha was godmother, the two
men godfathers. The old man sat with bent head. The scene became
impressive. At last Miss Bertha took the child and put it in the

arms of the clergyman. He, big and ugly, shone with a kind of unreal love. He had never mixed with life, and women were all unliving, Bibical things to him. When he asked for the name, the old man lifted his head fiercely. "Joseph William, after me," he said, almost out of breath.

"Joseph William, I baptize thee . . ." resounded the strange, full, chanting voice of the clergyman. The baby was quite still.

"Let us pray!" It came with relief to them all. They knelt before their chairs, all but the young mother, who bent and hid herself over her baby. The clergyman began his hesitating, struggling prayer.

Just then heavy footsteps were heard coming up the path, ceasing at the window. The young mother, glancing up, saw her brother, black in his pit dirt, grinning in through the panes. His red mouth curved in a sneer; his fair hair shone above his blackened skin. He caught the eye of his sister and grinned. Then his black face disappeared. He had gone on into the kitchen. The girl with the child sat still and anger filled her heart. She herself hated now the praying clergyman and the whole emotional business; she hated her brother bitterly. In anger and bondage she sat and listened.

Suddenly her father began to pray. His familiar, loud, rambling voice made her shut herself up and become even insentient. Folks said his mind was weakening. She believed it to be true, and kept herself always disconnected from him.

"We ask Thee, Lord," the old man cried, "to look after this childt. Fatherless he is. But what does the earthly father matter before Thee? The childt is Thine, he is Thy childt. Lord, what father has a man but Thee? Lord, when a man says he is a father, he is wrong from the first word. For Thou art the Father, Lord. Lord, take away from us the conceit that our children are ours. Lord, Thou art Father of this childt as is fatherless here. O God, Thou bring him up. For I have stood between Thee and my children; I've had *my* way with them, Lord; I've stood between Thee and my children; I've cut 'em off from Thee because they were mine. And they've grown twisted, because of me. Who is their father, Lord, but Thee? But I put myself in the way, they've been plants under a stone, because of me. Lord, if it hadn't been for me, they might ha' been trees in the sunshine. Let me own it, Lord,

I've done 'em mischief. It would ha' been better if they'd never known no father. No man is a father, Lord: only Thou art. They can never grow beyond Thee, but I hampered them. Lift 'em up again, and undo what I've done to my children. And let this young childt be like a willow tree beside the waters, with no father but Thee, O God. Aye, an' I wish it had been so with my children, that they'd had no father but Thee. For I've been like a stone upon them, and they rise up and curse me in their wickedness. But let me go, an' lift Thou them up, Lord . . ."

The minister, unaware of the feelings of a father, knelt in trouble, hearing without understanding the special language of fatherhood. Miss Rowbotham alone felt and understood a little. Her heart began to flutter; she was in pain. The two younger daughters kneeled unhearing, stiffened and impervious. Bertha was thinking of the baby; and the young mother thought of the father of her child, whom she hated. There was a clatter outside in the scullery. There the youngest son made as much noise as he could, pouring out the water for his wash, muttering in deep anger:

"Blortin', slaverin' old fool!"

And while the praying of his father continued, his heart was burning with rage. On the table was a paper bag. He picked it up and read: "John Berryman—Bread, Pastries, etc." Then he grinned with a grimace. The father of the baby was baker's man at Berryman's. The prayer went on in the middle kitchen. Laurie Rowbotham gathered together the mouth of the bag, inflated it, and burst it with his fist. There was a loud report. He grinned to himself. But he writhed at the same time with shame and fear of his father.

The father broke off from his prayer; the party shuffled to their feet. The young mother went into the scullery.

"What art doin', fool?" she said.

The collier youth tipped the baby under the chin, singing:

> *"Pat-a-cake, pat-a-cake, baker's man,*
> *Bake me a cake as fast as you can. . . ."*

The mother snatched the child away. "Shut thy mouth," she said, the colour coming into her cheek.

"Prick it and stick it and mark it with P,
And put it i' th' oven for baby an' me. . . . ."

He grinned, showing a grimy, and jeering and unpleasant red mouth and white teeth.

"I s'll gi'e thee a dab ower th' mouth," said the mother of the baby grimly. He began to sing again, and she struck out at him.

"Now what's to do?" said the father, staggering in.

The youth began to sing again. His sister stood sullen and furious.

"Why does *that* upset you?" asked the eldest Miss Rowbotham, sharply, of Emma the mother. "Good gracious, it hasn't improved your temper."

Miss Bertha came in, and took the bonny baby.

The father sat big and unheeding in his chair, his eyes vacant, his physique wrecked. He let them do as they would, he fell to pieces. And yet some power, involuntary, like a curse, remained in him. The very ruin of him was like a lodestone that held them in its control. The wreck of him still dominated the house, in his dissolution even he compelled their being. They had never lived; his life, his will had always been upon them and contained them. They were only half-individuals.

The day after the christening he staggered in at the doorway declaring, in a loud voice, with joy in life still: "The daisies light up the earth, they clap their hands in multitudes, in praise of the morning." And his daughters shrank, sullen.

SHERWOOD ANDERSON

I Want To Know Why

E GOT UP AT four in the morning, that first day in the east. On the evening before we had climbed off a freight train at the edge of town, and with the true instinct of Kentucky boys had found our way across town and to the race track and the stables at once. Then we knew we were all right. Hanley Turner right away found a nigger we knew. It was Bildad Johnson who in the winter works at Ed Becker's livery barn in our home town, Beckersville. Bildad is a good cook as almost all our niggers are and of course he, like everyone in our part of Kentucky who is anyone at all, likes the horses. In the spring Bildad begins to scratch around. A nigger from our country can flatter and wheedle anyone into letting him do most anything he wants. Bildad wheedles the stable men and the trainers from the horse farms in our country around Lexington. The trainers come into town in the evening to stand around and talk and maybe get into a poker game. Bildad gets in with them. He is always doing little favors and telling about things to eat, chicken browned in a pan, and how is the best way to cook sweet potatoes and corn bread. It makes your mouth water to hear him. When the racing season comes on and the horses go to the races and there is all the talk on the streets in the evenings about the new colts, and everyone says when they are going over to Lexington or to the spring meeting at Churchill Downs or to

Latonia, and the horsemen that have been down to New Orleans
or maybe at the winter meeting at Havana in Cuba come home to
spend a week before they start out again, at such a time when
everything talked about in Beckersville is just horses and nothing
else and the outfits start out and horse racing is in every breath of
air you breathe, Bildad shows up with a job as cook for some outfit.
Often when I think about it, his always going all season to the
races and working in the livery barn in the winter where horses are
and where men like to come and talk about horses, I wish I was a
nigger. It's a foolish thing to say, but that's the way I am about
being around horses, just crazy. I can't help it.

Well, I must tell you about what we did and let you in on what
I'm talking about. Four of us boys from Beckersville, all whites and
sons of men who live in Beckersville regular, made up our minds
we were going to the races, not just to Lexington or Louisville, I
don't mean, but to the big eastern track we were always hearing
our Beckersville men talk about, to Saratoga. We were all pretty
young then. I was just turned fifteen and I was the oldest of the
four. It was my scheme. I admit that and I talked the others into
trying it. There was Hanley Turner and Henry Rieback and Tom
Tumberton and myself. I had thirty-seven dollars I had earned
during the winter working nights and Saturdays in Enoch Myer's
grocery. Henry Rieback had eleven dollars and the others, Hanley
and Tom, had only a dollar or two each. We fixed it all up and
laid low until the Kentucky spring meetings were over and some
of our men, the sportiest ones, the ones we envied the most, had
cut out—then we cut out, too.

I won't tell you the trouble we had beating our way on freights
and all. We went through Cleveland and Buffalo and other cities
and saw Niagara Falls. We bought things there, souvenirs and
spoons and cards and shells with pictures of the falls on them for
our sisters and mothers, but thought we had better not send any
of the things home. We didn't want to put the folks on our trail
and maybe be nabbed.

We got into Saratoga as I said at night and went to the track.
Bildad fed us up. He showed us a place to sleep in hay over a
shed and promised to keep still. Niggers are all right about things
like that. They won't squeal on you. Often a white man you might

meet, when you had run away from home like that, might appear
to be all right and give you a quarter or a half dollar or something,
and then go right and give you away. White men will do that, but
not a nigger. You can trust them. They are squarer with kids. I
don't know why.

At the Saratoga meeting that year there were a lot of men from
home. Dave Williams and Arthur Mulford and Jerry Myers and
others. Then there was a lot from Louisville and Lexington Henry
Rieback knew but I didn't. They were professional gamblers and
Henry Rieback's father is one too. He is what is called a sheet
writer and goes away most of the year to tracks. In the winter
when he is home in Beckersville he don't stay there much but goes
away to cities and deals faro. He is a nice man and generous, is
always sending Henry presents, a bicycle and a gold watch and a
boy scout suit of clothes and things like that.

My own father is a lawyer. He's all right, but don't make much
money and can't buy me things and anyway I'm getting so old
now I don't expect it. He never said nothing to me against Henry,
but Hanley Turner and Tom Tumberton's fathers did. They said
to their boys that money so come by is no good and they didn't
want their boys brought up to hear gamblers' talk and be thinking
about such things and maybe embrace them.

That's all right and I guess the men know what they are talking
about, but I don't see what it's got to do with Henry or with
horses either. That's what I'm writing this story about. I'm puzzled.
I'm getting to be a man and want to think straight and be O.K.,
and there's something I saw at the race meeting at the eastern
track I can't figure out.

I can't help it, I'm crazy about thoroughbred horses. I've always been that way. When I was ten years old and saw I was growing to be big and couldn't be a rider I was so sorry I nearly died.
Harry Hellinfinger in Beckersville, whose father is Postmaster, is
grown up and too lazy to work, but he likes to stand around in
the street and get up jokes on boys like sending them to a hardware
store for a gimlet to bore square holes and other jokes like that. He
played one on me. He told me that if I would eat half a cigar I
would be stunted and not grow any more and maybe could be a
rider. I did it. When father wasn't looking I took a cigar out of his

pocket and gagged it down some way. It made me awful sick and the doctor had to be sent for, and then it did no good. I kept right on growing. It was a joke. When I told what I had done and why most fathers would have whipped me but mine didn't.

Well, I didn't get stunted and didn't die. It serves Harry Hellinfinger right. Then I made up my mind I would like to be a stable boy, but had to give that up too. Mostly niggers do that work and I knew father wouldn't let me go into it. No use to ask him.

If you've never been crazy about thoroughbreds it's because you've never been around where they are much and don't know any better. They're beautiful. There isn't anything so lovely and clean and full of spunk and honest and everything as some race horses. On the big horse farms that are all around our town Beckersville there are tracks and the horses run in the early morning. More than a thousand times I've got out of bed before daylight and walked two or three miles to the tracks. Mother wouldn't of let me go but father always says, "Let him alone." So I got some bread out of the bread box and some butter and jam, gobbled it and lit out.

At the tracks you sit on the fence with men, whites and niggers, and they chew tobacco and talk, and then the colts are brought out. It's early and the grass is covered with shiny dew and in another field a man is plowing and they are frying things in a shed where the track niggers sleep, and you know how a nigger can giggle and laugh and say things that make you laugh. A white man can't do it and some niggers can't but a track nigger can every time.

And so the colts are brought out and some are just galloped by stable boys, but almost every morning on a big track owned by a rich man who lives maybe in New York, there are always, nearly every morning, a few colts and some of the old race horses and geldings and mares that are cut loose.

It brings a lump up into my throat when a horse runs. I don't mean all horses but some. I can pick them nearly every time. It's in my blood like in the blood of race-track niggers and trainers. Even when they just go slop-jogging along with a little nigger on their backs I can tell a winner. If my throat hurts and it's hard for me to swallow, that's him. He'll run like Sam Hill when you let him out. If he don't win every time it'll be a wonder and because

they've got him in a pocket behind another or he was pulled or got
off bad at the post or something. If I wanted to be a gambler like
Henry Rieback's father I could get rich. I know I could and Henry
says so too. All I would have to do is wait 'til that hurt comes when
I see a horse and then bet every cent. That's what I would do if
I wanted to be a gambler, but I don't.

When you're at the tracks in the morning—not the race-tracks
but the training tracks around Beckersville—you don't see a horse,
the kind I've been talking about, very often, but it's nice anyway.
Any thoroughbred, that is sired right and out of a good mare and
trained by a man that knows how, can run. If he couldn't what
would he be there for and not pulling a plow?

Well, out of the stables they come and the boys are on their
backs and it's lovely to be there. You hunch down on top of the
fence and itch inside you. Over in the sheds the niggers giggle and
sing. Bacon is being fried and coffee made. Everything smells
lovely. Nothing smells better than coffee and manure and horses
and niggers and bacon frying and pipes being smoked out of doors
on a morning like that. It just gets you, that's what it does.

But about Saratoga. We was there six days and not a soul from
home seen us and everything came off just as we wanted it to, fine
weather and horses and races and all. We beat our way home and
Bildad gave us a basket with fried chicken and bread and other
eatables in it, and I had eighteen dollars when we got back to
Beckersville. Mother jawed and cried but Pop didn't say much.
I told everything we done except one thing. I did and saw that
alone. That's what I'm writing about. It got me upset. I think about
it at night. Here it is.

At Saratoga we laid up nights in the hay in the shed Bildad had
showed us and ate with the niggers early and at night when the
race people had all gone away. The men from home stayed mostly
in the grandstand and betting field, and didn't come out around the
places where the horses are kept except to the paddocks just before
a race when the horses are saddled. At Saratoga they don't have
paddocks under an open shed as at Lexington and Churchill Downs
and other tracks down in our country, but saddle the horses right
out in an open place under trees on a lawn as smooth and nice as
Banker Bohon's front yard here in Beckersville. It's lovely. The

horses are sweaty and nervous and shine and the men come out and smoke cigars and look at them and the trainers are there and the owners, and your heart thumps so you can hardly breathe.

Then the bugle blows for post and the boys that ride come running out with their silk clothes on and you run to get a place by the fence with the niggers.

I always am wanting to be a trainer or owner, and at the risk of being seen and caught and sent home I went to the paddocks before every race. The other boys didn't but I did.

We got to Saratoga on a Friday and on Wednesday the next week the big Mullford Handicap was to be run. Middlestride was in it and Sunstreak. The weather was fine and the track fast. I couldn't sleep the night before.

What had happened was that both these horses are the kind it makes my throat hurt to see. Middlestride is long and looks awkward and is a gelding. He belongs to Joe Thompson, a little owner from home who only has a half dozen horses. The Mullford Handicap is for a mile and Middlestride can't untrack fast. He goes away slow and is always way back at the half, then he begins to run and if the race is a mile and a quarter he'll just eat up everything and get there.

Sunstreak is different. He is a stallion and nervous and belongs on the biggest farm we've got in our country, the Van Riddle place that belongs to Mr. Van Riddle of New York. Sunstreak is like a girl you think about sometimes but never see. He is hard all over and lovely too. When you look at his head you want to kiss him. He is trained by Jerry Tillford who knows me and has been good to me lots of times, lets me walk into a horse's stall to look at him close and other things. There isn't anything as sweet as that horse. He stands at the post quiet and not letting on, but he is just burning up inside. Then when the barrier goes up he is off like his name, Sunstreak. It makes you ache to see him. It hurts you. He just lays down and runs like a bird dog. There can't anything I ever see run like him except Middlestride when he gets untracked and stretches himself.

Gee. I ached to see that race and those two horses run, ached and dreaded it too. I didn't want to see either of our horses beaten.

We had never sent a pair like that to the races before. Old men in Beckersville said so and the niggers said so. It was a fact.

Before the race I went over to the paddocks to see. I looked a last look at Middlestride, who isn't such a much standing in a paddock that way, then I went to see Sunstreak.

It was his day. I knew when I see him. I forgot all about being seen myself and walked right up. All the men from Beckersville were there and no one noticed me except Jerry Tillford. He saw me and something happened. I'll tell you about that.

I was standing looking at that horse and aching. In some way, I can't tell how, I knew just how Sunstreak felt inside. He was quiet and letting the niggers rub his legs and Mr. Van Riddle himself put the saddle on, but he was just a raging torrent inside. He was like the water in the river at Niagara Falls just before it goes plunk down. That horse wasn't thinking about running. He don't have to think about that. He was just thinking about holding himself back 'til the time for the running came. I knew that. I could just in a way see right inside him. He was going to do some awful running and I knew it. He wasn't bragging or letting on much or prancing or making a fuss, but just waiting. I knew it and Jerry Tillford his trainer knew. I looked up and then that man and I looked into each other's eyes. Something happened to me. I guess I loved the man as much as I did the horse because he knew what I knew. Seemed to me there wasn't anything in the world but that man and the horse and me. I cried and Jerry Tillford had a shine in his eyes. Then I came away to the fence to wait for the race. The horse was better than me, more steadier, and now I know better than Jerry. He was the quietest and he had to do the running.

Sunstreak ran first of course and he busted the world's record for a mile. I've seen that if I never see anything more. Everything came out just as I expected. Middlestride got left at the post and was way back and closed up to be second, just as I knew he would. He'll get a world's record too some day. They can't skin the Beckersville country on horses.

I watched the race calm because I knew what would happen. I was sure. Hanley Turner and Henry Rieback and Tom Tumberton were all more excited than me.

A funny thing had happened to me. I was thinking about Jerry

Tillford the trainer and how happy he was all through the race. I liked him that afternoon even more than I ever liked my own father. I almost forgot the horses thinking that way about him. It was because of what I had seen in his eyes as he stood in the paddocks beside Sunstreak before the race started. I knew he had been watching and working with Sunstreak since the horse was a baby colt, had taught him to run and be patient and when to let himself out and not to quit, never. I knew that for him it was like a mother seeing her child do something brave or wonderful. It was the first time I ever felt for a man like that.

After the race that night I cut out from Tom and Hanley and Henry. I wanted to be by myself and I wanted to be near Jerry Tillford if I could work it. Here is what happened.

The track in Saratoga is near the edge of town. It is all polished up and trees around, the evergreen kind, and grass and everything painted and nice. If you go past the track you get to a hard road made of asphalt for automobiles, and if you go along this for a few miles there is a road turns off to a little rummy looking farm house set in a yard.

That night after the race I went along that road because I had seen Jerry and some other men go that way in an automobile. I didn't expect to find them. I walked for a ways and then sat down by a fence to think. It was the direction they went in. I wanted to be as near Jerry as I could. I felt close to him. Pretty soon I went up the side road—I don't know why—and came to the rummy farm house. I was just lonesome to see Jerry, like wanting to see your father at night when you were a young kid. Just then an automobile came along and turned in. Jerry was in it and Henry Rieback's father, and Arthur Bedford from home, and Dave Williams and two other men I didn't know. They got out of the car and went into the house, all but Henry Rieback's father who quarreled with them and said he wouldn't go. It was only about nine o'clock, but they were all drunk and the rummy looking farm house was a place for bad women to stay in. That's what it was. I crept up along a fence and looked through a window and saw.

It's what gives me the fantods. I can't make it out. The women in the house were all ugly mean-looking women, not nice to look at or be near. They were homely too, except one who was tall and looked a little like the gelding Middlestride, but not clean like him, but with a hard ugly mouth. She had red hair. I saw everything plain. I got up by an old rose bush by an open window and looked. The women had on loose dresses and sat around in chairs. The men came in and some sat on the women's laps. The place smelled rotten and there was rotten talk, the kind a kid hears around a livery stable in a town like Beckersville in the winter but don't ever expect to hear talked when there are women around. It was rotten. A nigger wouldn't go into such a place.

I looked at Jerry Tillford. I've told you how I had been feeling about him on account of his knowing what was going on inside of Sunstreak in the minute before he went to the post for the race in which he made a world's record.

Jerry bragged in that bad woman house as I know Sunstreak wouldn't never have bragged. He said that he made that horse, that it was him that won the race and made the record. He lied and bragged like a fool. I never heard such silly talk.

And then, what do you suppose he did! He looked at the woman in there, the one that was lean and hard-mouthed and looked a little like the gelding Middlestride, but not clean like him, and his eyes began to shine just as they did when he looked at me and at Sunstreak in the paddocks at the track in the afternoon. I stood there by the window—gee!—but I wished I hadn't gone away from the tracks, but had stayed with the boys and the niggers and the horses. The tall rotten looking woman was between us just as Sunstreak was in the paddocks in the afternoon.

Then, all of a sudden, I began to hate that man. I wanted to scream and rush in the room and kill him. I never had such a feeling before. I was so mad clean through that I cried and my fists were doubled up so my finger nails cut my hands.

And Jerry's eyes kept shining and he waved back and forth, and then he went and kissed that woman and I crept away and went back to the tracks and to bed and didn't sleep hardly any, and then next day I got the other kids to start home with me and never told them anything I seen.

I been thinking about it ever since. I can't make it out. Spring has come again and I'm nearly sixteen and go to the tracks mornings same as always, and I see Sunstreak and Middlestride and a new colt named Strident I'll bet will lay them all out, but no one thinks so but me and two or three niggers.

But things are different. At the tracks the air don't taste as good or smell as good. It's because a man like Jerry Tillford, who knows what he does, could see a horse like Sunstreak run, and kiss a woman like that the same day. I can't make it out. Darn him, what did he want to do like that for? I keep thinking about it and it spoils looking at horses and smelling things and hearing niggers laugh and everything. Sometimes I'm so mad about it I want to fight someone. It gives me the fantods. What did he do it for? I want to know why.

FRANZ KAFKA

In the Penal Colony

Newly translated by John Edward Hardy and Margot Hardy Minczeski

T IS A REMARKABLE piece of machinery," said the officer to the explorer, as he gave the apparatus a familiar and admiring glance. It seemed that the explorer had only accepted out of politeness the commandant's invitation to be present at the execution of a soldier who had been convicted of disobedience and insubordination. Interest in this execution was not very great in the

Reprinted by permission of Schocken Books Inc. from ERZAEHLUNGEN by Franz Kafka. Copyright 1935 by Schocken Verlag, Berlin, Copyright 1946 by Schocken Books, Inc., New York.

This translation copyright © 1964 by Holt, Rinehart and Winston, Inc

penal colony either, it would appear. At least, outside of the officer
and the explorer, there was no one present in the deep sandy little
valley surrounded on all sides by naked crags, except the condemned man, a stupid, wide-mouthed creature with bewildered
hair and face, and the soldier who held the heavy chain to which
were attached several smaller chains that bound his wrists and
ankles and also his neck. These chains, too, were connected to each
other by separate links. Actually, the prisoner looked so like a dog
that one got the impression he could readily have been allowed to
run freely among the hills until the beginning of the execution, at
which time a mere whistle would bring him back.

The explorer showed little interest in the machine and paced
back and forth behind the prisoner with obvious indifference while
the officer busied himself with final preparations, first crawling
around underneath the machine, which was built on a foundation
that went deep into the ground, and then climbing a ladder in order
to inspect the upper section. This was work which apparently could
have been left to a mechanic, but the officer performed it with great
zeal, either because he was especially fond of the apparatus or
because for some reason the work could be entrusted to no one
else. "Everything is ready now," he called finally and climbed down
from the ladder. He was perspiring all over and breathing heavily,
mouth wide open—he had stuffed two dainty women's handkerchiefs down into his collar. "These uniforms are really too heavy
for the tropics," the explorer commented, instead of asking some
question about the apparatus, as the officer had expected. "They
are, at that," answered the officer, and began washing his oil- and
grease-stained hands in a nearby pan of water, "but they are part
of home to us, and we wouldn't want to forget our home—but now,
look at this machine," he went on, drying his hands on a towel and
indicating the machine at the same time. "Until now some manual
work was still necessary, but now it functions entirely by itself."
The explorer nodded and followed the officer. The latter, anxious
to insure himself against all eventualities, then said, "Naturally
there are disturbances from time to time. I do hope nothing will
interrupt today, but we must always be prepared to cope with anything that should come up. The machine should run for twelve

hours without stopping. But if by chance something should fail to operate, it would only be a very small matter, easily corrected."

"Don't you want to sit down?" he asked finally, pulling a cane chair out of a pile of them and offering it to the explorer, who could not refuse. He now sat at the edge of a pit into which he glanced for only a moment. It was not very deep. On one side of the pit the loosened dirt had been packed together to form a wall, on the other side stood the machine. "I don't know," began the officer, "whether or not the commandant has already explained to you how this machine operates." The explorer gestured vaguely, but the officer needed no further encouragement to begin the explanation himself. "This machine," he said, supporting himself with a hand on a connecting-rod, "is the invention of our former commandant. I assisted him in the preliminary experiments and had a part in all the work up until its completion. The credit for the invention, however, must go to him alone. You have heard of the former commandant? No? Well, I am not exaggerating when I say that the design for the entire penal colony is his work. We, his friends, knew even at the time of his death that the pattern for the colony was so well thought out that his successor, had he a thousand new ideas, would find no reason to alter the old plan for many years to come. Our prediction came true; the new commandant must face this fact. It is unfortunate that you were not acquainted with the old commandant.—But, I digress, and his machine stands before us. It consists, as you can see, of three sections. Over a period of years certain popular expressions have come into use to indicate each part. The lower one is called the Bed. The upper is known as the Designer and this middle, moving part is called the Harrow. "The Harrow?" asked the explorer. He really hadn't been paying much attention—the sun shone so strongly in the shadowless valley; it was difficult to collect one's thoughts. The officer seemed all the more amazing in his tight-fitting, full-dress uniform, which was amply braided and weighted down with epaulettes; he pursued his subject with such zeal, and even went about tightening a screw here and there as he spoke. The soldier seemed to be in a mood similar to the explorer's. He had wound the prisoner's chains around both wrists, propped himself with one hand on his rifle, let his head loll forward, and was completely oblivious to everything. This wasn't

surprising to the explorer, because the officer spoke French, and it
was obvious that neither the soldier nor the prisoner understood a
word of that language. It was therefore the more remarkable to
observe that the prisoner did attempt to follow the officer's explanations. With a kind of lethargic obstinacy he kept glancing in whatever direction the officer indicated with his gestures; and now, as
the explorer's question interrupted, he too turned to look at him.

"Yes, the Harrow," replied the officer. "The name fits. The
needles are set in like the teeth of a harrow and the whole thing
operates somewhat in the manner of one, although only in one
place, and much more artistically, of course. You will see what I
mean in a moment. The prisoner lies here on the Bed.—I'll describe
the apparatus first of all and then set the machine in motion.
You'll be able to follow the process much better that way. Besides,
one of the cogwheels in the Designer is badly worn; it creaks a lot
when the machine is working—you can hardly hear yourself speak.
Spare parts are rather hard to come by here. Well, anyway, here is
the Bed, as I said. It is completely covered with a layer of cotton
wool; you will see the reason for this soon. The condemned man is
laid face down on the cotton wool, quite naked, of course; there
are straps here for the hands, for the feet and for the neck, to hold
him still. At the head of the Bed here, where the man, as I said,
first lays his face, is a little gag made of felt, which can easily be
adjusted to go straight into the mouth. This is to stop him from
screaming and biting his tongue. Naturally, the man is forced to
take hold of the gag, because otherwise his neck would be broken
by the strap. "Is that cotton wool?", asked the explorer as he bent
forward. "Yes, of course," said the officer smiling, "feel it for yourself." He grasped the explorer's hand and guided it over the Bed.
"It is a specially prepared cotton wool; that's why it looks so strange
—I will explain its purpose later." The explorer already was beginning to take a certain interest in the machine; shielding his eyes
from the sun with one hand, he gazed up at the towering structure.
It was a huge thing. The Bed and the Designer were of the same
size and resembled two dark wooden chests. The Designer hung
about two meters over the Bed, and both were held at the four
corners by brass rods which almost flashed out rays in the sunlight.
Between the chests the Harrow swayed on a narrow band of steel.

The officer had hardly noticed the explorer's former indifference, but he was instantly aware of his dawning interest; he therefore stopped his explanations for a moment in order to allow the explorer time for undisturbed observation. The condemned man did likewise; not being able to use his hands, he stared up into the air without shading his eyes.

"So the man lies down," said the explorer, leaning back in his chair and crossing his legs.

"Yes," said the officer as he pushed his cap back a little and passed one hand over his heated face, "now follow what I say. The Bed as well as the Designer has its own electric battery; the Bed needs one for itself, the Designer for the Harrow. As soon as the man is bound fast, the Bed is set into motion. It quivers in tiny, very rapid vibrations from side to side and also up and down at the same time. You must have seen similar machines in hospitals, only with our Bed all the movements are precisely controlled; that is, they must correspond quite exactly with those of the Harrow. And the Harrow is the actual executor of the sentence."

"Of what does the sentence consist?" asked the explorer. "You don't know that either?" said the officer, astounded, and bit his lip. "Forgive me if my explanations are incoherent; I do hope you will excuse me. The commandant used to be in the habit of giving these explanations; the new commandant, however, shirks this duty; but that such an important visitor—." The explorer sought to deprecate such honor with both hands, but the officer would not be swayed—"that such an important visitor should not even be informed as to the sort of sentence we use is something new indeed, which—"; he had been on the point of using strong language but checked himself and said then: "I was not informed of this, it is not my fault. Anyway, I am certainly the most competent one to explain how our sentences run, for I have here"—and he indicated his breast pocket—"the relevant drawings made by the former commandant."

"The commandant's own drawings?" asked the explorer: "Was he everything all in one, then? Was he soldier, judge, mechanic, chemist, and draftsman?"

"That he was," said the officer nodding, with a glassy, faraway look. Then he looked critically at his hands; they didn't seem quite

clean enough for handling the drawings, so he went over to the
water basin and washed them again. Then he pulled out a small
leather wallet and said, "Our sentence doesn't sound very harsh.
Whatever rule it is that the prisoner has broken is written on his
body with the Harrow. This man, for instance"—the officer indicated the prisoner—"will have written on his body: RESPECT
YOUR SUPERIORS."

The explorer looked for a moment at the man; when the officer
pointed at him, he put his head down and listened in a huge effort
to understand what was being said. But the movements of his big
lips, as he pressed them tightly together, made it obvious that he
was unable to understand a word. There were various things which
the explorer wanted to ask about, but at the sight of this man, he
asked only, "Does he know his sentence?" "No," said the officer,
eager to proceed with the explanation, but the explorer stopped
him: "He doesn't know his own sentence?" "No," said the officer
again; he paused a second as if he expected the explorer to elaborate
on his question, and then went on: "there would be no use in telling
him. He'll learn it on his body." The explorer hadn't wanted to
continue, but he felt the prisoner's gaze upon him as if to ask
whether he approved of what he'd just been told. Therefore, although a moment before he had leaned back, the explorer bent
forward again and persisted: "But he at least knows that he has
been sentenced?" "Not that either," said the officer, and smiled at
the explorer as if awaiting some further unusual comments. "No,"
repeated the explorer, wiping his forehead, "then the man also
doesn't know yet whether his defense was effective?" "He had no
chance to defend himself," said the officer and looked to one side,
as if he were speaking to himself, in order to spare the explorer the
embarrassment of having self-evident matters explained. "But he
must have had a chance to defend himself," said the explorer, and
rose from his seat.

The officer, realizing that he was in danger of having his explanation of the machine held up for a long time, walked over to
the explorer and took his arm. With one hand he indicated the
prisoner—who now stood bolt upright since he had so obviously
become the center of attention, causing the soldier to give the chain
a little jerk—and said: "This is how things are here. I have been

appointed judge in the penal colony, in spite of my youth. Also, any matter concerning punishment was my business as well as the former commandant's, and then, too, I am best acquainted with the workings of the apparatus. The main principle to which I adhere is this: Guilt is not to be doubted. Other courts cannot use this principle, because they depend on the opinions of several people and also have higher courts to contend with. But that is not the case here, or at least it wasn't as far as our former commandant was concerned. The new man has been overly inclined to interfere with my running of the court, but so far I have been able to discourage this for the most part, and I shall continue to do so.—You wanted me to explain this particular case. It is as simple as any of them. A captain reported this morning that this man, who acted as his orderly and sleeps before his door, was asleep on duty. It is his duty, that is, to stand up whenever the clock strikes the hour and to salute before the captain's door. It is certainly not a very difficult task, yet surely an essential one, because he must be alert both as a sentry and as a servant. Last night the captain wanted to see whether or not the orderly was performing his duty. At the stroke of two he opened the door and found him curled up asleep. He took his riding whip and lashed him across the face. But instead of getting up and begging forgiveness, the man grabbed his master around the legs, shook him violently and cried out: 'Throw the whip away or I'll eat you up.'—Those are the details of the matter. An hour ago the captain came to me, I wrote down his report, and attached the sentence directly to it. Then I had the man put in chains. That was all very simple. If I had first had the man appear before me and questioned him, nothing but utter confusion would have come of it. He would have lied; if it had been possible for me to disprove these lies, he would have replaced them with others, and so on. But now I have him and won't let him go.—Does that explain everything? But the time is getting away from us; the execution is due to begin, and I'm not yet finished with my explanation of the machine." He indicated that the explorer should resume his seat, walked over to the machine again, and began: "As you see here, the Harrow corresponds to the shape of the human body; here is the Harrow for the upper portion of the body, here are the Harrows for the legs. There is only this small spike for the head. Is that clear?" He bent amiably toward the explorer, ready to go into greater detail.

The explorer looked at the Harrow and wrinkled his forehead. The explanation of the judicial system had not satisfied him. He always had to remind himself that one was concerned here with a penal colony, that special laws were necessary, and that military discipline must be strictly adhered to. But even so he placed some hope in the new commandant, who was attempting, however slowly, to introduce new procedures which the officer's rather limited mind found impossible to grasp. In this train of thought the explorer asked: "Will the commandant attend the execution?" "It's not certain," said the officer, set off balance by the pointed question, his amiable expression changing suddenly: "It is for precisely that reason that we must hurry. As it is, I'll have to cut my explanation short, much to my regret. But then tomorrow I could go over the more complicated details when the apparatus has been cleaned up again—that is the machine's only drawback, that it gets so dreadfully messy. But now, the most important things.—As soon as the man lies down on the Bed and it begins to quiver, the Harrow is lowered onto the body. It regulates itself in such a way that the needles barely come into contact with the skin; as soon as contact is made the steel ribbon stiffens into a rigid band. This begins the actual performance. Anyone not versed in the details of the process would see no difference between one punishment and another. The Harrow seems always to operate in the same way. Quivering, it inserts its needles into the skin, which also is set into motion by the Bed. Further to facilitate observation of the actual execution of the sentence, the Harrow was constructed of glass. There were a few technical difficulties in attaching the needles, but this was accomplished after many attempts. We spared no effort. And now everyone can look through the glass as the inscription appears on the body. Would you like to come over here and take a closer look at the needles?"

The explorer slowly pulled himself up, walked over and bent down over the Harrow. "You see," said the officer, "two kinds of needles arranged in a multiple pattern. Every long one is paired with a short one. The long one does the actual writing and the short one sprays water to wash away the blood and keep the inscription clear. The bloody water is then conducted into small runnels here and finally goes into this main runnel which enters a waste pipe leading to the pit." The officer traced with his finger the path which the blood and water took. In order to make the picture as clear as possible, he spread both hands out at the mouth of the wastepipe as if to catch the outflow and at this point the explorer drew back his head and, groping behind him with one hand, attempted to return to his seat. Then he noticed, to his horror, that the prisoner had likewise accepted the officer's invitation to take a closer look at the Harrow, and had followed him. He had jerked the sleeping soldier a little forward on the chain and was now bent over the glass. He sought with uncertain eyes to see what the two gentlemen had just observed, but because he had missed the explanation, comprehension was impossible. He peered about here and there, his gaze always returning to the glass. The explorer wanted to pull him back, since what he was doing was most probably an offense of some sort. But the officer held onto the explorer with one hand, took a clod of dirt from the wall with the other hand and threw it at the soldier. The latter shot up, eyes wide open, and seeing what the prisoner had dared, dropped his weapon, dug his heels into the ground and jerked the condemned man back, so that he suddenly toppled over. He then stood looking down at him as he struggled and rattled his chains. "Get him on his feet!" yelled the officer, for he was aware that the explorer's attention was too much on the prisoner. Indeed, the explorer leaned right over the Harrow completely unconcerned with it, and wanting only to see what was going on with the prisoner. "Be careful with him," yelled the officer again. He ran around the machine, grabbed hold of the prisoner under the shoulders and, with the soldier's help, pulled him to his feet, which kept sliding out from under him.

"Now I understand it all," said the explorer as the officer returned. "All except the most important thing," the latter replied, as he took hold of the explorer's arm and pointed up: "In the Designer there are the cogwheels which regulate the movement of the Harrow; these cogs are set according to whatever inscription the sentence demands. I still use the inscriptions initiated by our former commandant. Here they are"—he pulled some sheets out of the leather wallet—"but I'm sorry that I cannot allow you to handle them; they are the most prized things I have. Sit down—I'll show them to you from here and you'll be able to observe everything quite well." He produced the first sheet. The explorer would have liked to say something knowledgeable, but he saw only a labyrinth of multiple lines which crossed and recrossed the page, covering it so thickly that there were hardly any blank spaces visible. "Read it," said the officer. "I can't," said the explorer. "But it is quite clear," exclaimed the officer. "It's very artistic," said the explorer, wishing to evade the issue, "but I can't make it out." "Yes," replied the officer, laughing as he put away the wallet, "it is hardly child's play. One must study it for some time. But after a while you too would certainly recognize it. Naturally, the script must not be too simple; it's not supposed to cause death at once—only, on the average, within twelve hours' time; the turning point is reckoned to be at the sixth hour. Therefore, there must be numerous flourishes around the actual script; the essential inscription forms only a narrow band about the body; the rest of the body is used for the embellishments. Can you now see the real extent of the Harrow's work and the possibilities of the entire apparatus?—Just look!" He ran up the ladder, turned a wheel, and called down: "Look out— step aside!" and the whole thing was set into motion. If the wheel hadn't creaked, it would have been fantastic. The officer shook his fist at it as if this disturbance had astonished him, then shrugged apologetically in the explorer's direction, clambered down, and proceeded to inspect the lower part of the apparatus. Something which no one save the officer could have noticed was still out of order; he climbed up once more, groped around with both hands inside the Designer and then, instead of using the ladder, came sliding down one of the rods as fast as possible. In order to make himself understood above the racket, he now yelled into the explorer's ear at the top of his lungs: "Can you see how it works? The Harrow is starting to write; as soon as the first layer of writing on the man's back is complete, the pad of cotton wool begins to turn, rolling the body over onto its side in order to provide more space for writing. In the meantime, the part which has already been torn open by the needles is laid directly on the cotton wool, which is specially treated to stop the bleeding and so to prepare for the ever-deepening inscription. The teeth here at the edge of the Harrow tear away the padding from the wounds as the body turns, throw it into the pit, and so provide the Harrow with further work. In this way, and for a full twelve hours, it goes on writing deeper and deeper. For the first six hours the prisoner stays about the same, suffering only pain. After two hours the felt gag is removed from his mouth since he no longer has the strength left to scream. Warm rice pap is conducted into this electrically heated basin at the head of the Bed and the man can take as much of this as he likes and is able to get with just his tongue. Not one ever passes up this opportunity. I've never seen that happen, and my experience is quite extensive. Not until the sixth hour does he lose the desire to eat. I usually kneel down here then in order to see what happens. The man will very seldom swallow the last bite; instead he simply rolls it around in his mouth and then spits it out into the pit. I have to get out of the way rather quickly or he would spit it in my face. But how calm the man becomes at the sixth hour! Even the most stupid of them begins to understand. It is first noticeable around the eyes. From there it gradually spreads out and out. It is a moment when one is almost tempted to lie down under the Harrow himself. Actually, all that happens is that the man finally begins to decipher the inscription; he purses his lips as if listening to something. You have seen that it is not at all easy to make out the script with one's eyes—our man, however, deciphers it with his wounds. It's very hard work, to be sure; he requires six hours time fully to understand it all. At this point, however, the Harrow pierces him through and throws him down into the pit with the blood and water and cotton wool. Justice is then complete and we, the soldier and I, bury him."

The explorer had stood with his ear inclined toward the officer and his hands in the pockets of his jacket, watching the machine at work. The condemned man was watching too, but failed to comprehend what was happening. He bent forward a little to follow the wavering needles when, at a sign from the officer, the soldier took a knife and slit his pants and shirt up from the back so that they fell away altogether; he tried to grab hold of his falling clothes and cover himself, but the soldier lifted him into the air and shook the last of them off. The officer stopped the machine and, in the penetrating silence, the condemned man was laid underneath the

Harrow. His chains were removed and the straps fastened on in place of them; at first it seemed that this was almost a relief to the prisoner. But now the Harrow was lowered still further, since he was a thin man. As the points of the needles touched him, his skin quivered; he groped wildly with his left hand while the soldier busied himself with strapping down the right. The free hand was flung out in the direction of the explorer, and the officer kept watching him out of the corner of his eye, trying to see from his expression what sort of effect this execution was making upon someone who knew at least a little about the procedure. The wrist strap had broken; the soldier had probably pulled too hard on it. The officer had to go and help, the soldier showing him the broken strap. As the officer started over to him, his face still turned toward the explorer, he said: "The machine is quite intricately put together; one expects things to break or tear now and then, but one must never allow one's judgment to be swayed for this reason. Anyway, a substitute for this strap can easily be acquired; I'll just use the chains, even though it will interfere somewhat with the delicacy of movement for the right arm." As he attached the chains, he went on: "Means for keeping up the machine are very limited now. Under the former commandant I had a special fund which was entirely at my disposal for just this purpose. There was also a supply store which carried any spare part necessary. I must admit, I was almost prodigal with them; in the past, that is, not now, as the new commandant pretends, who never misses a chance to attack the old methods. Now he controls the money for the machine and if I send in an order for a new strap, he demands the broken one as proof and the new one doesn't get here until ten days later. Even then it turns out to be of shoddy workmanship and hardly any good at all. How I'm supposed to operate the machine without straps in the meantime, doesn't seem to concern anyone."

The explorer considered this a moment: It is always a precarious matter to intervene in others' affairs with any decisiveness. He was neither attached to the penal colony nor a citizen of the state to which it belonged. If he were to denounce this execution or actually try to stop it, one would be justified in saying to him: You are an outsider, this is none of your business. And he wouldn't really have an answer to that, unless perhaps to add that he himself found his attitude a bit ironic, for he traveled intending only to observe and never to change other people's judicial procedures. The matter at hand, however, was a source of strong temptation. The injustice of the procedure and inhumanity of the execution could not be ignored. No one could possibly accuse the explorer of any ulterior motive, for the condemned man was a complete stranger to him, neither a fellow countryman nor even a person who aroused much sympathy. Besides, the explorer had recommendations from important authorities and had been received here with the greatest courtesy; the very fact that he had been invited to this execution seemed reason enough to suppose that his opinion would be welcome. There was an even greater likelihood of this since the commandant was quite obviously not an advocate of the procedure and was hardly on friendly terms with the officer.

Suddenly the explorer heard a cry of rage from the officer. He had just gotten the piece of felt into the prisoner's mouth with much difficulty when the man was overcome with nausea, shut his eyes and vomited. The officer hurriedly pulled him away from the gag and tried to hold his head over the pit; but it was too late, vomit streamed all over the machine. "This is all the commandant's fault," yelled the officer and began aimlessly shaking the brass rods in front, "the machine is befouled like a pigsty." With trembling hands he showed the explorer what had happened. "Haven't I time and again tried to make the commandant realize how important it is that nothing be eaten for twenty-four hours prior to the execution. But this new lenient regime has other ideas. The commandant's ladies stuff the man with sweets just before he is led off. His whole life he has existed on stinking fish, and now he has to have candy! But it's still possible I wouldn't say anything in protest, but why can't they at least get me a new felt gag, as I've begged them to do for the last three months? How could anyone take that gag in his mouth without throwing up—the same gag that more than a hundred dying men have slobbered and gnawed on?"

The condemned man had put his head down and was looking very peaceful; the soldier was busy trying to wipe the machine off with the prisoner's shirt. The officer went over to the explorer, who in some vague premonition stepped back a little, but the officer grabbed his hand and pulled him aside. "I would like to tell you something in confidence," he said, "may I?" "Certainly," answered the explorer, and listened with downcast eyes.

"The procedure and method of execution which you are now having the opportunity to admire no longer has any professed advocates. I am its sole champion and at the same time the only upholder of our former commandant's traditions. It is no longer feasible to consider further improvements in the procedure; I need all my strength to maintain what's here. When the old commandant was alive, the colony was full of his adherents; to some extent I do possess his sureness of conviction, but his power is completely lacking in me; consequently the advocates have become cowardly— there are still quite a few of them but none will admit their true feelings. If you were to go into the teahouse now, on execution day, and listen to what the people there are saying, perhaps you would hear only some very ambiguous remarks. They are all adherents, actually, but with the present commandant and his existing attitude, they are of no use to me. But now I ask you: Should the work of a lifetime"—he pointed to the machine—"be destroyed because of this commandant and a few influential women? Can one allow that to happen? Even if one has only come to the island for a few days as a visitor? But there is no time to lose, they are already preparing some attack on my qualifications as a judge; even now there are dis- cussions going on in the commandant's office to which I was not invited; now your visit seems to me especially significant in view of the situation—they are cowards and are using you, a stranger, for their purposes.—How different an execution was in former times. Even on the day before, the whole valley overflowed with people; they all came just to see; the commandant would appear very early with his ladies; fanfares roused the entire camp; I reported that all was in readiness; the assembled company—none of the high officials dared be absent—gathered around the machine; this pile of cane chairs is the miserable relic of those times. The machine glit- tered, freshly cleaned; I had new parts for practically every execu- tion. Before a hundred eyes—the onlookers would be standing on tiptoe all the way to those heights—the condemned man was laid under the Harrow by the commandant himself. The duty given today to a lowly soldier was at that time my task; it belonged to the presiding judge, and was a great honor for me. And then the execution began! No disturbance of any kind interfered with the machine's progress. Many people averted their eyes at this point, lying in the sand, preferring not to watch; but they all knew: justice would be done now. In the silence only the sighs of the prisoner were audible, muffled by the felt gag. Today, the machine is no longer able to make a man sigh loud enough to be heard through the felt; formerly, acid was dropped from the needles as they wrote—but we're not allowed this any more. Well, now came the sixth hour! It was impossible to accommodate all those who requested permission to watch from nearby. With his usual foresight, the commandant ordered that all the children should be given first preference; naturally, I was always there because of my position in the colony; often I would crouch there with two small children on either side of me, my arms around them. How that transfigured expression on the tortured face affected us—our faces too would reflect the light of this justice, finally attained and too quickly dimmed! What times those were, my friend!" The officer had obviously forgotten to whom he spoke; he had embraced the explorer and now stood with his head on the man's shoulder. The explorer was greatly embarrassed and was looking nervously into the distance above the officer's head. The soldier had finished cleaning off the machine and was now shaking rice pap from a pot into the basin again. The prisoner had just become aware of this, as he now seemed to have completely recovered himself, and immediately began lapping at the rice with his tongue. The soldier kept pushing him away, since the rice was certainly meant for later, but it was hardly fitting either that the soldier himself had been digging in the stuff with his filthy hands and eating it in front of the other's miserable face.

The officer quickly recovered himself. "I didn't want to upset you," he said, "I know how impossible it is to make those times seem alive now. Anyway, the machine is still in operation, and is something just in itself. It is something even when it stands here in this valley all alone. And at the end the corpse still falls with an unbelievable gentleness into the pit, even though people don't any longer swarm about like so many hundreds of flies. Then it was necessary to build a strong fence around the pit; it was torn down a long time ago."

The explorer wanted to avert his face, and looked around at nothing in particular. The officer presumed he was struck by the desolation of the valley; he therefore grasped his hand, pulled him around to meet his gaze, and asked: "Do you see the scandal of it?"

But the explorer was silent. The officer left him for a moment; he stood with legs apart, his hands on his hips and stared at the ground. Then he smiled hopefully at the explorer and went on: "I stood very near you yesterday when the commandant gave his invitation. I heard what he said. I know the commandant well. I was instantly aware of the purpose of that invitation. Even though he might be powerful enough to oppose me, he wouldn't dare that quite yet, but he most certainly means to make use of you, as an illustrious foreigner, to secure your judgment against me. His logic is well thought out: You have been on the island for two days, you were not acquainted with the old commandant and his theories, you have been brought up with a European outlook, perhaps you oppose capital punishment on principle and especially when the procedure involves some sort of machine, on top of all this you have observed that the whole thing is carried out with no visible approval from the public and on a machine that is already in bad condition— in the light of all this (so thinks the commandant) isn't it easily possible that you do not approve of what I am doing? And if you don't approve of it, you most certainly would not conceal that fact (I am still speaking from the commandant's point of view), because you are sure to have faith in your own well-tried convictions. It's true, you have observed the peculiarities of many different people, and learned to respect them; for this reason you would probably not be inclined to oppose me in any drastic manner, as you might do in your own country. But the commandant doesn't need that sort of thing at all. A passing, even an unguarded remark, would suffice. It doesn't even have to betray your true feelings, if it just seems to be in accord with his desires. I am positive that he will question you very cautiously. And his ladies will sit around in a circle, keeping their ears open; you will say something like: 'The judicial procedure in our country is rather different,' or 'In our country death is not the only penalty given,' or 'In our country we haven't used torture since the Middle Ages.' These are all remarks that are quite fair since they seem natural to you, innocent comments which do not really reflect on my methods. But how will the commandant take them? Ah—I can see him, our good commandant —as he bolts from his chair and rushes to the balcony, the ladies trailing behind; and his voice, like a thunderclap (say the ladies), I can hear it now as he roars—'A truly great investigator from the West, whose duty it is to study various judicial systems all over the world, has just said that the methods we use, according to the old customs, are barbaric. Coming from such an esteemed personage, this judgment makes it impossible for me to have patience with the system a moment longer. Therefore, starting today, I am ordering —and so on.' You want to interrupt, to say that was not what you meant at all, you never called my methods barbaric; on the contrary, your extensive experience has shown them to be among the most humane and dignified of all systems, you also greatly admire this machine—but it is too late; you can't even get onto the balcony, which is packed with ladies; you want to draw attention to yourself, want to shout; but some lady holds her hand over your mouth—and I and the old commandant's work are lost for good."

The explorer had to suppress a smile; the job which he had expected to be so difficult had turned out to be quite simple after all. He said evasively: "You exaggerate the extent of my influence; the commandant read my letters of recommendation and is aware that I know nothing about judicial systems. If I were to express my opinion, it would only be the opinion of a private citizen, no more important than that of any other person, and in any case far *less* important than the commandant's ideas on the subject, especially since he exerts such a great amount of influence in this colony, I have been led to believe. If his attitude toward the system is as negative as you think, then the end seems to be approaching anyway, without any help from me."

Was it finally dawning on the officer? No, he hadn't grasped it yet. He vigorously nodded his head, stared back momentarily at the prisoner and the soldier, then came very near to the explorer, and, not looking into his eyes but somewhere on his coat, said more softly than before: "You don't know the commandant; you believe that as far as he and all of us are concerned—forgive the expression—you are comparatively harmless; but believe me, your influence cannot be overestimated. I was quite exuberant when I heard that you were to be the only one attending the execution. This little move on the commandant's part was supposed to be one more blow against me, but I shall use it to my distinct advantage. You have heard my explanations and been spared the inevitable whispered lies and disdainful looks from any large crowd attending the execution—you have seen the machine and are now about to witness the actual execution. You have doubtless already formed an opinion, but in case some small uncertainty remains, the sight of the execution will certainly take care of that. And so, now, I beg you: help me against the commandant!"

The explorer couldn't let him go on. "How could I do that," he cried in desperation, "it's absolutely impossible. I cannot help you any more than I could harm you."

"You can," said the officer. The explorer saw, with a bit of apprehension, that the officer had doubled his fists. "You can help me," he repeated more emphatically than before. "I have a plan that must succeed. You think that your influence won't suffice. I know that it will be enough. But even if you were right, even if it should prove insufficient, aren't we bound to try—in the interest of preserving this system? Listen to my plan, then. It is most important for its success that you say as little as possible in the colony today about your views on the system. Unless someone asks you about it directly, you must offer no comment; even then your remarks must be brief and noncommittal; it should be made obvious that you find it difficult to express an opinion, that you are embittered, that if you let yourself speak out, you would have to use some very strong language. I am not suggesting that you lie—not at all; it is just that you must answer as briefly as possible, like this: 'Yes, I saw the execution,' or 'Yes, everything was explained to me.' Nothing more than that. As for the embitterment you are supposed to display, there are grounds enough for that, even though not in the way the commandant would see it. Naturally he will misinterpret everything and distort it all to mean what he wants. This is exactly what my plan depends on. Tomorrow there will be an important conference in the commandant's office with all the high administrative officials present and the commandant himself presiding. The commandant, of course, has made a show out of these conferences. He has had a gallery built, which is always crowded with spectators. I will be forced to take part in this meeting, even though the idea turns my stomach. Now, it is quite certain that you will be invited to the conference too; if you carry out my plan today exactly as I told you, it will no longer be simply an invitation but a desperate plea. However, should you for some unforeseeable reason not receive an invitation, then you'll have to request it; it is impossible that you would then be refused. Now, tomorrow you'll be sitting in the commandant's box along with his ladies. He keeps looking up to assure himself that you're there. After all the many trivial, absurd matters which are introduced solely for the benefit of the audience (mostly concerning the harbor—always the harbor), the subject of our judicial procedure will be brought up for discussion. If the commandant doesn't get around to it, or doesn't mention it soon enough, I'll see to it that the subject is introduced. I will simply stand and report the day's execution. Very briefly, just a few words. It's true that such a statement is rather unusual, but I'll do it anyway. The commandant thanks me, as always, with the friendliest of smiles, and now, finding it impossible to resist, seizes upon the opportunity at hand. He says: 'We have just heard,' or something to that effect, 'the report that the execution has been carried out. I would only like to add to this that the distinguished explorer, who as you all know has so greatly honored our colony with his visit, attended this particular execution. His very presence gives this conference all the more dignity. Wouldn't it then be most fitting at this time to ask our honored guest his opinion on the traditional execution and its various preliminaries?' Naturally there is enthusiastic applause from all over the room, unanimous approval, and I am the most enthusiastic of all. The commandant bows to you and says, 'Then in the name of all those present, I ask you.' And you step to the front of the box. Keep your hands out where everyone can see them, or else the ladies will take hold of them and play with your fingers.—At last it comes time for your speech. I don't know how I'm going to be able to bear the tension of the long wait. In your speech nothing must be considered out-of-bounds, the truth must roar in their ears, you must lean out over the box, even shout, yes-yes, shout your true feelings, your unshakable convictions, at the commandant. But perhaps that sort of thing is not in keeping with your character; if in your own country one behaves differently in such a situation, that too is all right. It will be sufficient if you do not even stand up, if you say only a few words, whisper them so that the officials underneath can just catch what you say—that is enough. You won't even have to mention the lack of support for the execution, the creaking wheel, the broken straps, or the repulsive felt gag—no, I'll take over from there. And believe me, if my speech doesn't send him running from the room, it will force him to his knees, to acknowledge the truth: Old commandant—I bow down before you.—That is my plan; will you be my partner in it? But of course you will; what's more, you must!" And the officer grabbed the explorer by both arms and stared into his face, breathing heavily. He had shouted the last words so loudly that even the soldier and the prisoner had taken notice; though they couldn't understand a word, they had momentarily stopped eating and were now staring at the explorer, chewing all the while.

From the beginning, the explorer had known the answer he had to give; he had been through far too much in his lifetime to think of shrinking from this; he was basically honorable and courageous. But, nevertheless, he now hesitated before the gaze of the soldier and the prisoner for just a moment. After that second, however, he said as he knew he must: "No." The officer blinked his eyes several times, but never once looked away. "Do you want to know my reason?" asked the explorer. The officer nodded dumbly. "I cannot approve of this procedure," the explorer continued, "even before you took me into your confidence—I shall, of course, never under any circumstances reveal what you have told me—I had wondered whether or not I would be justified in denouncing the system and also if such a protest would have the slightest chance for success. It was obvious to whom I would have to go first: the commandant, of course. You have naturally made that fact even more obvious, but without having strengthened my original conviction in any way; on the contrary, your sincere enthusiasm has considerably impressed me, even though it could never change my feelings about the matter."

The officer remained silent, turned to the machine, took hold of a brass rod and then, bending slightly backwards, gazed up at the Designer as if to make sure everything was in order. The soldier and the prisoner seemed to have made friends with one another; the condemned man was motioning to the soldier, though this was a little difficult in view of the many straps holding him down; the soldier leaned over toward him; the prisoner whispered something in his ear, and the other nodded.

The explorer went over to the officer and said: "You don't know yet what I'm going to do. I am going to let the commandant know how I feel, not at a conference, but just between the two of us; I won't be here long enough anyway to get involved in any sort of meeting; I'll be leaving very early tomorrow, or at least boarding my ship."

The officer didn't seem to be listening. "Then the procedure did not impress you," he said to himself, and smiled in the way that an old man smiles at a child's nonsense, while behind the smile he pursues his own meditations.

"Then it is time," he said finally, and looked suddenly at the explorer with his bright eyes which seemed either to challenge or perhaps to ask for help.

"Time for what?" asked the explorer nervously, getting no answer.

"You're free to go," said the officer to the condemned man, speaking in his native tongue. The latter could hardly believe it at first. "I said that you're free," the officer repeated. For the first time real life showed itself on the prisoner's face. Was this the truth? Was it just one of the officer's little games that would end again? Had the foreign explorer asked him to show mercy? What was going on? His face seemed to ask all of this. But not for long. Whatever had happened, he wanted if he could to be really freed, and began to strain and tug as hard as possible under the confining straps.

"You're going to tear my straps," screamed the officer, "be still! We'll get you out soon enough." And motioning to the soldier to help, he set about doing so. The prisoner was laughing quietly to himself, turning his face to the officer on his left and now to the soldier on the right, also not forgetting the explorer.

"Pull him out," the officer ordered the soldier. Now some degree of caution was necessary because of the Harrow. The prisoner had already scratched himself on his back in several places because of his impatience.

However, from now on the officer didn't concern himself in the

least with the man. He went over to the explorer, pulled out the
leather wallet again, looked through the papers, finally coming to
the one he wanted, and showed it to the explorer. "Read this," he
said. "I can't," said the explorer, "I've already told you that it is
impossible for me." "Look at the paper very closely," said the
officer, and stood next to the explorer in order to read it with him.
Since that didn't help either, with his little finger he traced some
pattern in the air above the paper, as if the sheet of paper itself
must not be touched, but trying to make it easier for the explorer to
see what was there. The explorer did make an effort, if only out of
politeness to the officer, but it was still incomprehensible. At this
point the officer began to spell out what was written there and
then read it again in sequence. "BE JUST—that is what it says!"
he exclaimed. "Now you can surely read it." The explorer leaned
over so close to the paper that the officer pulled it back for fear
that it would be damaged; the explorer would say no more now,
but it was obvious that he still wasn't able to read it. "BE JUST
is written there," repeated the officer. "Well, perhaps so," said the
explorer, "I'll take your word for it." "Good, then," said the officer,
at least partly satisfied, and climbed up the ladder holding the
paper; he placed the sheet of paper in the Designer with great
caution and seemed to be completely reordering the cogwheels; it
was quite tedious work, apparently, involving the tiniest of wheels;
at times his head disappeared altogether within the Designer, while
he minutely inspected the cogs.

The explorer watched this process from underneath, never once
looking away; his neck grew stiff and his eyes began to burn from
the sun's glare. The soldier and the prisoner were now quite busy
together. The prisoner's shirt and pants, which were lying in the
pit, had been fished out on the point of the soldier's bayonet. The
shirt was disgustingly filthy and the prisoner began to wash it in
the water basin. As soon as he put them on, they both screamed
with laughter because the clothes were slit in two behind. For some
reason, the prisoner seemed to feel obliged to entertain the soldier;
he turned around and around displaying the tattered clothes for the
soldier, who squatted on the ground slapping his knees with
laughter. After a moment, however, they restrained their amusement out of respect for the two gentlemen present.

When the officer finally finished his work, he gazed once more over the entire apparatus with a little smile, shut the lid on the Designer, which had been open all this time, climbed down, looked in the pit, and then at the prisoner. He noticed with satisfaction that he had gotten his clothes out, and then went over to the pan of water to wash his hands, seeing too late how repulsively dirty it was. Upset now that he couldn't wash his hands, he decided finally to rub them in the sand, even though this alternative was not very satisfactory to him. He then stood up and began to unbutton the jacket to his uniform. As he did this, the two handkerchiefs he had stuffed down into his collar fell into his hands. "Here, take your handkerchiefs," he said and threw them over to the prisoner. And to the explorer, in explanation: "Gifts from the ladies."

In spite of the obvious haste with which he took off the jacket and finally all his clothes, he handled each piece with great care, stroking the silver lace on the jacket with his fingers and shaking a tassel into place. Strangely enough, despite this fastidiousness, as soon as he had finished with each piece, he immediately threw it roughly into the pit. The last thing remaining was his short sword and its belt. He pulled the sword out of the sheath, broke it to pieces, and then gathered everything together, the pieces of sword, the scabbard and the strap, and flung them clattering down into the pit.

He stood there completely naked. The explorer bit his lips and was silent. He knew, of course, what was going to happen, but he had no right to interfere with the officer. If the judicial procedure which was so important to the officer were really at its end—possibly because of the explorer's denunciation, which on his part he had felt compelled to give—then the officer was acting justly; the explorer himself would not have done otherwise.

At first, the soldier and the prisoner did not comprehend the situation; they hadn't even been watching. The prisoner was very pleased to have the handkerchiefs back, but he didn't have much time to enjoy them, because the soldier suddenly and unexpectedly jerked them away from him. Now the prisoner tried to get them back from the soldier, who had stuffed them into his belt, but the soldier guarded them well. They struggled, half in fun. It was only when the officer stood there nude that they began to take notice.

The prisoner, especially, seemed to notice suddenly that the situation had become very different. What had happened to him, was now going to happen to the officer. Perhaps it would even be fully carried out this time. The foreign explorer had probably given the order for this. So this was the revenge. Although he himself had not been made to suffer the whole thing, yet he would be revenged to the fullest extent. A huge, soundless laugh appeared on his face and did not go away.

The officer, however, had turned back to the machine. No matter how clear it had been before that he completely understood the machine, it was now almost astonishing to observe how he dealt with it and how sensitively it responded. He had only brought his hand close to the Harrow when it began to rise and fall again and again, until reaching the prescribed, exact position for receiving him; he touched only the edge of the Bed and it immediately began to quiver; the felt gag neared his mouth—one saw that the officer was not really willing to take it, but his hesitation lasted only a second before he managed to control himself and submit to it. Everything was in readiness and only the straps still hung at the sides, but they did not seem to be necessary—the officer didn't have to be strapped down. Then the prisoner noticed the dangling straps—to his mind the execution was not properly done if the straps were left unbuckled, and so he looked eagerly over to the soldier and they both hurried to strap the officer in. The latter had already put one foot out in order to kick the lever which would start the Designer; he saw the two coming toward him and pulled his foot back, allowing himself to be strapped down. Now it was impossible for him to reach the lever; neither the soldier nor the prisoner could ever find it; and the explorer was determined to stay strictly out of the matter. But it wasn't necessary; the straps were hardly brought into place when the machine started up; the Bed quivered, the needles danced over his skin, and the Harrow swayed up and down. The explorer had been staring at it for some time before remembering that a wheel in the Designer was supposed to creak; but everything was quiet, not the slightest hum reached their ears.

Because it worked so quietly, one was almost entirely unconscious of the machine's presence. The explorer looked over at the soldier and the prisoner. The prisoner was the livelier of the two. Everything about the machine fascinated him; he would bend down and then stand on tiptoe, always pointing here and there in order to bring something to the soldier's attention. The explorer found all this extremely painful. He had decided to stay until it was all over, but he couldn't stand the sight of these two much longer. "Go on back home," he said. The soldier might have complied willingly enough, but the prisoner seemed to consider the order a sort of punishment. He folded his hands and begged ardently that he might stay, and when the explorer shook his head, not willing to give in, the prisoner immediately got down on his knees. The explorer could see that his commands weren't going to have any effect, so he was tempted to go over and send them away by force. But it was then that he heard a noise coming from the Designer. He looked up. Was that cogwheel not working properly after all? But it was something else. Very slowly the lid to the Designer lifted up and then clicked wide open. The teeth of one cogwheel came into view, were lifted higher, until soon the entire wheel could be seen; it seemed as if some amazing force were pressing in on the Designer, so that there was no room left for this wheel—the wheel turned until it reached the edge of the Designer, fell off onto the ground, rolled waveringly upright through the sand a little way, and then lay still. But on top there was already another one rising up, to be followed by countless others, large ones, small ones, ones so tiny as to be hardly distinguishable. The same thing happened to each one of them, and it seemed impossible that the Designer was not already completely empty. But all of a sudden still another, especially complex system of wheels was lifted high, dropped off, rolled shakily away in the sand and fell over flat. With all this going on, the prisoner had completely forgotten about the explorer's command; he was entranced with the cogwheels. He was always trying to grab hold of one, at the same time motioning to the soldier to help him, but pulling his hand back in terror, because another wheel followed right behind, whose advance was enough each time to frighten him away momentarily.

The explorer, for his part, was becoming very uneasy; the apparatus was obviously falling apart entirely; its silent working was deceptive; he had the feeling that he was now going to have to stand by the officer, since he was no longer able to help himself. But all during this time he had been conscious of nothing but the falling cogwheels and had failed to pay attention to the rest of the machine. As he now bent over the Harrow (the last wheel had finally dropped off the Designer), he found a new and much more unpleasant surprise awaiting him. The Harrow was no longer writing, but simply jabbing, and the Bed was not turning the body over, but just lifting it, quivering, onto the needles. The explorer wanted to intervene, if possible to bring the whole thing to a standstill; this was hardly the kind of torture which the officer had desired, it was simply slaughter. He reached out with his hands. But the Harrow had already risen and now moved to one side with the body impaled on it, as was supposed to happen only after twelve hours. Blood flowed in a hundred directions, failing to mix with the water because the water jets, too, had stopped working. Now only one more thing was supposed to happen, and it too failed to go into operation; the body was not freed from the long needles, but simply hung there, swaying back and forth over the pit, blood streaming out, held fast by the needles. The Harrow was already attempting to return to its original position, but almost as if it were aware that it had not yet been freed of its burden, seemed finally content to remain hanging over the pit. "Help me," the explorer screamed to the prisoner and soldier, already taking hold of the officer's foot. He thought that he could push against the feet while the other two pulled from the opposite side at the head, and in this way lift him slowly off the needles. But the two couldn't seem to make up their minds to come; the prisoner actually turned all the way around; and the explorer had to go and forcibly drag them to a position at the officer's head. At this point, almost against his will, he looked into the face of the corpse. It was as it had been while alive; there was absolutely no sign of the assured deliverance; what everyone else had attained through the machine had been totally denied the officer; the lips were firmly pressed together, eyes wide open with their lifelong expression of peace and conviction; piercing the forehead was the tip of the huge, iron spike.

As the explorer came up to the first houses in the colony with the soldier and the prisoner, the soldier pointed one out and said, "There's the teahouse."

On the ground floor of the house there was a huge, low room like a cave, its ceiling and walls blackened from smoke. It was completely open on the street side. Although the teahouse stood out very little from the other houses of the colony, which, including the commandant's palatial residence, were all very dilapidated, still the explorer was struck somehow by its air of tradition, and felt in the place the power of the past. He came closer, and then, followed by his companions, made his way past the empty tables which stood in the street outside the teahouse; he stood there breathing in the cool, heavy air that came from inside. "The old man's buried here," said the soldier, "he was denied a place in the churchyard by the priests. For a long time nobody was sure where to bury him, but they finally decided to put him here. I'm sure the officer didn't tell you anything about that, because he's naturally quite ashamed of it. He even tried to dig the old man up a few times at night, but he always got chased away." "Where is the grave?" asked the explorer, not really believing what the soldier had told him. Both the soldier and the prisoner immediately ran ahead of him and indicated with outstretched hands where the grave was to be found. They led the explorer around to the back wall where a few guests sat eating. They probably worked along the harbor, muscular characters with short, gleaming black beards. None of them wore a coat, their shirts were torn, they were poor, humble men. As the explorer came closer, some of them stood up, pressed closely against the wall and stared at him. "A foreigner," the explorer heard whispered all around, "he wants to see the grave." They pushed one of the tables aside and there was, indeed, a gravestone underneath. It was a very plain stone, quite low so that it would not be noticed beneath the table. The inscription on it was in such tiny letters that the explorer had to kneel down in order to read it. "Here rests the old commandant. His adherents, who now go nameless, have dug this grave and placed this stone here. It is foretold that after a certain number of years the commandant will rise and lead his followers out of this house once more to reign over the colony. Abide, and keep faith!" When the explorer had read this and gotten back up, he saw the men all standing around him and smiling, as if they had been reading the inscription too, found it rather funny, and were waiting for him to agree with them. The explorer acted as if he hadn't noticed any of this, gave them a few coins, waited a bit until the table had been replaced over the grave, left the teahouse, and went down to the harbor.

The soldier and the prisoner had found some friends in the teahouse who detained them. They must have gotten away rather quickly, however, because the explorer had just reached the middle of the long steps which led to the boats, when they came running after him. Probably they intended to force him at the last minute into taking them along. While the explorer was down below bargaining with the ferryman about transportation out to the steamer, the two rushed up to the steps in silence, not daring to shout out. But by the time they got down, the explorer was already settled in the boat and the ferryman was just pulling away from the shore. They still could have leaped into the boat, but the explorer picked up a heavy, knotted rope from the bottom, threatening them with it so that they did not try to jump.

THOMAS MANN

Railway Accident

ELL YOU A STORY? But I don't know any. Well, yes, after all, here is something I might tell.

Once, two years ago now it is, I was in a railway accident; all the details are clear in my memory.

It was not really a first-class one—no wholesale telescoping or "heaps of unidentifiable dead"—not that sort of thing. Still, it was a proper accident, with all the trimmings, and on top of that it was at night. Not everybody has been through one, so I will describe it the best I can.

I was on my way to Dresden, whither I had been invited by some friends of letters: it was a literary and artistic pilgrimage, in short, such as, from time to time, I undertake not unwillingly. You make appearances, you attend functions, you show yourself to admiring crowds—not for nothing is one a subject of William II. And certainly Dresden is beautiful, especially the Zwinger; and afterwards I intended to go for ten days or a fortnight to the White Hart to rest, and if, thanks to the treatments, the spirit should come upon me, I might do a little work as well. To this end I had put my manuscript at the bottom of my trunk, together with my notes—a good stout bundle done up in brown paper and tied with string in the Bavarian colours. I like to travel in comfort, especially when my expenses are paid. So I patronized the sleeping-cars, reserving a place days ahead in a first-class compartment. All was in order; nevertheless I was excited, as I always am on such occasions, for a journey is still an adventure to me, and where travelling is con cerned I shall never manage to feel properly blasé. I perfectly well know that the night train for Dresden leaves the central station at Munich regularly every evening, and every morning is in Dresden. But when I am travelling with it, and linking my momentous destiny to its own, the matter assumes importance. I cannot rid myself of the notion that it is making a special trip today, just on my account, and the unreasoning and mistaken conviction sets up in me a deep and speechless unrest, which does not subside until all the formalities of departure are behind me—the packing, the drive in the loaded cab to the station, the arrival there, and the registration of luggage—and I can feel myself finally and securely bestowed. Then, indeed, a pleasing relaxation takes place, the mind turns to fresh concerns, the unknown unfolds itself beyond the expanse of window-pane, and I am consumed with joyful anticipations.

And so on this occasion. I had tipped my porter so liberally that he pulled his cap and gave me a pleasant journey; and I stood at the corridor window of my sleeping-car smoking my evening cigar

and watching the bustle on the platform. There were whistlings and
rumblings, hurryings and farewells, and the singsong of newspaper
and refreshment vendors, and over all the great electric moons
glowed through the mist of the October evening. Two stout fellows
pulled a hand-cart of large trunks along the platform to the baggage
car in front of the train. I easily identified, by certain unmistakable
features, my own trunk; one among many there it lay, and at the
bottom of it reposed my precious package. "There," thought I, "no
need to worry, it is in good hands. Look at that guard with the
leather cartridge-belt, the prodigious sergeant-major's moustache,
and the inhospitable eye. Watch him rebuking the old woman in the
threadbare black cape—for two pins she would have got into a
second-class carriage. He is security, he is authority, he is our parent,
he is the State. He is strict, not to say gruff, you would not care to
mingle with him; but reliability is writ large upon his brow, and in
his care your trunk reposes as in the bosom of Abraham."

A man was strolling up and down the platform in spats and a
yellow autumn coat, with a dog on a leash. Never have I seen a
handsomer dog: a small, stocky bull, smooth-coated, muscular, with
black spots; as well groomed and amusing as the dogs one sees in
circuses, who make the audience laugh by dashing round and
round the ring with all the energy of their small bodies. This dog
had a silver collar, with a plaited leather leash. But all this was not
surprising, considering his master, the gentleman in spats, who had
beyond a doubt the noblest origins. He wore a monocle, which
accentuated without distorting his general air; the defiant perch of
his moustache bore out the proud and stubborn expression of his
chin and the corners of his mouth. He addressed a question to the
martial guard, who knew perfectly well with whom he was dealing
and answered hand to cap. My gentleman strolled on, gratified with
the impression he had made. He strutted in his spats, his gaze was
cold, he regarded men and affairs with penetrating eye. Certainly
he was far above feeling journey-proud; travel by train was no
novelty to him. He was at home in life, without fear of authority
or regulations; he was an authority himself—in short, a nob. I could
not look at him enough. When he thought the time had come, he
got into the train (the guard had just turned his back). He came
along the corridor behind me, bumped into me, and did not apolo-

gize. What a man! But that was nothing to what followed. Without turning a hair he took his dog with him into the sleeping-compart ment! Surely it was forbidden to do that. When should I presume to take a dog with me into a sleeping-compartment? But he did it, on the strength of his prescriptive rights as a nob, and shut the door behind him.

There came a whistle outside, the locomotive whistled in response, gently the train began to move. I stayed awhile by the window watching the hand-waving and the shifting lights. . . . I retired inside the carriage.

The sleeping-car was not very full, a compartment next to mine was empty and had not been got ready for the night; I decided to make myself comfortable there for an hour's peaceful reading. I fetched my book and settled in. The sofa had a silky salmon-pink covering, an ash-tray stood on the folding table, the light burned bright. I read and smoked.

The sleeping-car attendant entered in pursuance of his duties and asked for my ticket for the night. I delivered it into his grimy hands. He was polite but entirely official, did not even vouchsafe me a good-night as from one human being to another, but went out at once and knocked on the door of the next compartment. He would better have left it alone, for my gentleman of the spats was inside; and perhaps because he did not wish anyone to discover his dog, but possibly because he had really gone to bed, he got furious at anyone daring to disturb him. Above the rumbling of the train I heard his immediate and elemental burst of rage. "What do you want?" he roared. "Leave me alone, you swine." He said "swine." It was a lordly epithet, the epithet of a cavalry officer— it did my heart good to hear it. But the sleeping-car attendant must have resorted to diplomacy—of course he had to have the man's ticket—for just as I stepped into the corridor to get a better view the door of the compartment abruptly opened a little way and the ticket flew out into the attendant's face; yes, it was flung with violence straight in his face. He picked it up with both hands, and though he had got the corner of it in one eye, so that the tears came, he thanked the man, saluting and clicking his heels together. Quite overcome, I returned to my book.

I considered whether there was anything against my smoking

another cigar and concluded that there was little or nothing. So I did it, rolling onward and reading; I felt full of contentment and good ideas. Time passed, it was ten o'clock, half past ten, all my fellow-travellers had gone to bed, at last I decided to follow them. I got up and went into my own compartment. A real little bedroom, most luxurious, with stamped leather wall hangings, clotheshooks, a nickel-plated wash-basin. The lower berth was snowily prepared, the covers invitingly turned back. Oh, triumph of modern times! I thought. One lies in this bed as though at home, it rocks a little all night, and the result is that next morning one is in Dresden. I took my suitcase out of the rack to get ready for bed; I was holding it above my head, with my arms stretched up.

It was at this moment that the railway accident occurred. I remember it like yesterday.

We gave a jerk—but jerk is a poor word for it. It was a jerk of deliberately foul intent, a jerk with a horrid reverberating crash, and so violent that my suitcase leaped out of my hands I knew not whither, while I was flung forcibly with my shoulder against the wall. I had no time to stop and think. But now followed a frightful rocking of the carriage, and while that went on, one had plenty of leisure to be frightened. A railway carriage rocks going over switches or on sharp curves, that we know; but this rocking would not let me stand up, I was thrown from one wall to the other as the carriage careened. I had only one simple thought, but I thought it with concentration, exclusively. I thought: "Something is the matter, something is the matter, something is *very much* the matter!" Just in those words. But later I thought: "Stop, stop, stop!" For I knew that it would be a great help if only the train could be brought to a halt. And lo, at this my unuttered but fervent behest, the train did stop.

Up to now a deathlike stillness had reigned in the carriage, but at this point terror found tongue. Shrill feminine screams mingled with deeper masculine cries of alarm. Next door someone was shouting "Help!" No doubt about it, this was the very same voice which, just previously, had uttered the lordly epithet—the voice of the man in spats, his very voice, though distorted by fear. "Help!" it cried; and just as I stepped into the corridor, where the passengers were collecting, he burst out of his compartment in a silk

sleeping-suit and halted, looking wildly round him. "Great God!"
he exclaimed, "Almighty God!" and then, as though to abase himself utterly, perhaps in hope to avert destruction, he added in a
deprecating tone: "*Dear* God!" But suddenly he thought of something else, of trying to help himself. He threw himself upon the
case on the wall where an axe and saw are kept for emergencies,
and broke the glass with his fist. But finding that he could not
release the tools at once, he abandoned them, buffeted his way
through the crowd of passengers, so that the half-dressed women
screamed afresh, and leaped out of the carriage.

All that was the work of a moment only. And then for the first
time I began to feel the shock: in a certain weakness of the spine,
a passing inability to swallow. The sleeping-car attendant, red-
eyed, grimy-handed, had just come up; we all pressed round him;
the women, with bare arms and shoulders, stood wringing their
hands.

The train, he explained, had been derailed, we had run off the
track. That, as it afterwards turned out, was not true. But behold,
the man in his excitement had become voluble, he abandoned his
official neutrality; events had loosened his tongue and he spoke to
us in confidence, about his wife. "I told her today, I did. 'Wife,'
I said, 'I feel in my bones somethin's goin' to happen.'" And sure
enough, hadn't something happened? We all felt how right he had
been. The carriage had begun to fill with smoke, a thick smudge;
nobody knew where it came from, but we all thought it best to get
out into the night.

That could only be done by quite a big jump from the foot-
board onto the line, for there was no platform of course, and besides our carriage was canted a good deal towards the opposite side.
But the ladies—they had hastily covered their nakedness—jumped
in desperation and soon we were all standing there between the
lines.

It was nearly dark, but from where we were we could see that
no damage had been done at the rear of the train, though all the
carriages stood at a slant. But further forward—fifteen or twenty
paces further forward! Not for nothing had the jerk we felt made
such a horrid crash. There lay a waste of wreckage; we could see

the margins of it, with the little lights of the guards' lanterns flickering across and to and fro.

Excited people came towards us, bringing reports of the situation. We were close by a small station not far beyond Regensburg, and as the result of a defective point our express had run onto the wrong line, had crashed at full speed into a stationary freight train, hurling it out of the station, annihilating its rear carriages, and itself sustaining serious damage. The great express engine from Maffei's in Munich lay smashed up and done for. Price seventy thousand marks. And in the forward coaches, themselves lying almost on one side, many of the seats were telescoped. No, thank goodness, there were no lives lost. There was talk of an old woman having been "taken out," but nobody had seen her. At least, people had been thrown in all directions, children buried under luggage, the shock had been great. The baggage car was demolished. Demolished—the baggage car? Demolished.

There I stood.

A bareheaded official came running along the track. The stationmaster. He issued wild and tearful commands to the passengers, to make them behave themselves and get back into the coaches. But nobody took any notice of him, he had no cap and no self-control. Poor wretch! Probably the responsibility was his. Perhaps this was the end of his career, the wreck of his prospects. I could not ask him about the baggage car—it would have been tactless.

Another official came up—he *limped* up. I recognized him by the sergeant-major's moustache: it was the stern and vigilant guard of the early evening—our Father, the State. He limped along, bent over with his hand on his knee, thinking about nothing else. "Oh, dear!" he said, "oh, dear, oh, dear me!" I asked him what was the matter. "I got stuck, sir, jammed me in the chest, I made my escape through the roof." This "made my escape through the roof" sounded like a newspaper report. Certainly the man would not have used the phrase in everyday life; he had experienced not so much an accident as a newspaper account of it—but what was that to me? He was in no state to give me news of my manuscript. So I accosted a young man who came up bustling and self-important from the waste of wreckage, and asked him about the heavy luggage.

"Well, sir, nobody can say anything as to that"—his tone implied that I ought to be grateful to have escaped unhurt. "Everything is all over the place. Women's shoes—" he said with a sweeping gesture to indicate the devastation, and wrinkled his nose. "When they start the clearing operations we shall see. . . . Women's shoes. . . ."

There I stood. All alone I stood there in the night and searched my heart. Clearing operations. Clearing operations were to be undertaken with my manuscript. Probably it was destroyed, then, torn up, demolished. My honeycomb, my spider-web, my nest, my earth, my pride and pain, my all, the best of me—what should I do if it were gone? I had no copy of what had been welded and forged, of what already was a living, speaking thing—to say nothing of my notes and drafts, all that I had saved and stored up and overheard and sweated over for years—my squirrel's hoard. What should I do? I inquired of my own soul and I knew that I should begin over again from the beginning. Yes, with animal patience, with the tenacity of a primitive creature the curious and complex product of whose little ingenuity and industry has been destroyed; after a moment of helpless bewilderment I should set to work again—and perhaps this time it would come easier!

But meanwhile a fire brigade had come up, their torches cast a red light over the wreck; when I went forward and looked for the baggage car, behold it was almost intact, the luggage quite unharmed. All the things that lay strewn about came out of the freight train: among the rest a quantity of balls of string—a perfect sea of string covered the ground far and wide.

A load was lifted from my heart. I mingled with the people who stood talking and fraternizing in misfortune—also showing off and being important. So much seemed clear, that the engine-driver had acted with great presence of mind. He had averted a great catastrophe by pulling the emergency brake at the last moment. Otherwise, it was said, there would have been a general smash and the whole train would have gone over the steep embankment on the left. Oh, praiseworthy engine-driver! He was not about, nobody had seen him, but his fame spread down the whole length of the train and we all lauded him in his absence. "That chap," said one man, and pointed with one hand somewhere off into the night, "that chap saved our lives." We all agreed.

But our train was standing on a track where it did not belong, and it behoved those in charge to guard it from behind so that another one did not run into it. Firemen perched on the rear carriage with torches of flaming pitch, and the excited young man who had given me such a fright with his "women's shoes" seized upon a torch too and began signalling with it, though no train was anywhere in sight.

Slowly and by degrees something like order was produced, the State our Father regained poise and presence. Steps had been taken, wires sent, presently a breakdown train from Regensburg steamed cautiously into the station and great gas flares with reflectors were set up about the wreck. We passengers were now turned off and told to go into the little station building to wait for our new conveyance. Laden with our hand luggage, some of the party with bandaged heads, we passed through a lane of inquisitive natives into the tiny waiting-room, where we herded together as best we could. And inside of an hour we were all stowed higgledy-piggledy into a special train.

I had my first-class ticket—my journey being paid for—but it availed me nothing, for everybody wanted to ride first and my carriage was more crowded than the others. But just as I found me a little niche, whom do I see diagonally opposite to me, huddled in the corner? My hero, the gentleman with the spats and the vocabulary of a cavalry officer. He did not have his dog, it had been taken away from him in defiance of his rights as a nob and now sat howling in a gloomy prison just behind the engine. His master, like myself, held a yellow ticket which was no good to him, and he was grumbling, he was trying to make head against this communistic levelling of rank in the face of general misfortune. But another man answered him in a virtuous tone: "You ought to be thankful that you can sit down." And with a sour smile my gentleman resigned himself to the crazy situation.

And now who got in, supported by two firemen? A wee little old grandmother in a tattered black cape, the very same who in Munich would for two pins have got into a second-class carriage. "Is this the first class?" she kept asking. And when we made room and assured her that it was, she sank down with a "God be praised!"

onto the plush cushions as though only now was she safe and sound.

By Hof it was already five o'clock and light. There we break-fasted; an express train picked me up and deposited me with my belongings, three hours late, in Dresden.

Well, that was the railway accident I went through. I suppose it had to happen once; but whatever mathematicians may say, I feel that I now have every chance of escaping another.

WILLA CATHER

A Wagner Matinée

RECEIVED ONE MORNING a letter, written in pale ink on glassy, blue-lined notepaper, and bearing the postmark of a little Nebraska village. This communication, worn and rubbed, look-ing as though it had been carried for some days in a coat pocket that was none too clean, was from my Uncle Howard and informed me that his wife had been left a small legacy by a bachelor relative who had recently died, and that it would be necessary for her to go to Boston to attend to the settling of the estate. He requested me to meet her at the station and render her whatever services might be necessary. On examining the date indicated as that of her arrival I found it no later than tomorrow. He had characteristically de-layed writing until, had I been away from home for a day, I must have missed the good woman altogether.

The name of my Aunt Georgiana called up not alone her own figure, at once pathetic and grotesque, but opened before my feet

a gulf of recollection so wide and deep that, as the letter dropped
from my hand, I felt suddenly a stranger to all the present conditions of my existence, wholly ill at ease and out of place amid the
familiar surroundings of my study. I became, in short, the gangling
farm boy my aunt had known, scourged with chilblains and bashfulness, my hands cracked and sore from the corn husking. I felt
the knuckles of my thumb tentatively, as though they were raw
again. I sat again before her parlor organ, fumbling the scales with
my stiff, red hands, while she, beside me, made canvas mittens for
the huskers.

The next morning, after preparing my landlady somewhat, I
set out for the station. When the train arrived I had some difficulty
in finding my aunt. She was the last of the passengers to alight, and
it was not until I got her into the carriage that she seemed really
to recognize me. She had come all the way in a day coach; her linen
duster had become black with soot, and her black bonnet gray with
dust, during the journey. When we arrived at my boardinghouse
the landlady put her to bed at once and I did not see her again
until the next morning.

Whatever shock Mrs. Springer experienced at my aunt's appearance she considerately concealed. As for myself, I saw my aunt's
misshapen figure with that feeling of awe and respect with which
we behold explorers who have left their ears and fingers north of
Franz Josef Land, or their health somewhere along the Upper
Congo. My Aunt Georgiana had been a music teacher at the Boston
Conservatory, somewhere back in the latter sixties. One summer,
while visiting in the little village among the Green Mountains
where her ancestors had dwelt for generations, she had kindled the
callow fancy of the most idle and shiftless of all the village lads,
and had conceived for this Howard Carpenter one of those extravagant passions which a handsome country boy of twenty-one sometimes inspires in an angular, spectacled woman of thirty. When
she returned to her duties in Boston Howard followed her, and the
upshot of this inexplicable infatuation was that she eloped with him,
eluding the reproaches of her family and the criticisms of her
friends by going with him to the Nebraska frontier. Carpenter, who,
of course, had no money, had taken a homestead in Red Willow
County, fifty miles from the railroad. There they had measured off

their quarter section themselves by driving across the prairie in a wagon, to the wheel of which they had tied a red cotton handkerchief, and counting off its revolutions. They built a dugout in the red hillside, one of those cave dwellings whose inmates so often reverted to primitive conditions. Their water they got from the lagoons where the buffalo drank, and their slender stock of provisions was always at the mercy of bands of roving Indians. For thirty years my aunt had not been further than fifty miles from the homestead.

But Mrs. Springer knew nothing of all this, and must have been considerably shocked at what was left of my kinswoman. Beneath the soiled linen duster which, on her arrival, was the most conspicuous feature of her costume, she wore a black stuff dress, whose ornamentation showed that she had surrendered herself unquestioningly into the hands of a country dressmaker. My poor aunt's figure, however, would have presented astonishing difficulties to any dressmaker. Originally stooped, her shoulders were now almost bent together over her sunken chest. She wore no stays, and her gown, which trailed unevenly behind, rose in a sort of peak over her abdomen. She wore ill-fitting false teeth, and her skin was as yellow as a Mongolian's from constant exposure to a pitiless wind and to the alkaline water which hardens the most transparent cuticle into a sort of flexible leather.

I owed to this woman most of the good that ever came my way in my boyhood, and had a reverential affection for her. During the years when I was riding herd for my uncle, my aunt, after cooking the three meals—the first of which was ready at six o'clock in the morning—and putting the six children to bed, would often stand until midnight at her ironing board, with me at the kitchen table beside her, hearing me recite Latin declensions and conjugations, gently shaking me when my drowsy head sank down over a page of irregular verbs. It was to her, at her ironing or mending, that I read my first Shakespeare, and her old textbook on mythology was the first that ever came into my empty hands. She taught me my scales and exercises, too—on the little parlor organ, which her husband had bought her after fifteen years, during which she had not so much as seen any instrument, but an accordion that belonged to one of the Norwegian farmhands. She would sit beside

me by the hour, darning and counting while I struggled with the
"Joyous Farmer," but she seldom talked to me about music, and I
understood why. She was a pious woman; she had the consolations
of religion and, to her at least, her martyrdom was not wholly
sordid. Once when I had been doggedly beating out some easy
passages from an old score of *Euryanthe* I had found among her
music books, she came up to me and, putting her hands over my
eyes, gently drew my head back upon her shoulder, saying
tremulously, "Don't love it so well, Clark, or it may be taken from
you. Oh, dear boy, pray that whatever your sacrifice may be, it be
not that."

When my aunt appeared on the morning after her arrival she
was still in a semisomnambulant state. She seemed not to realize
that she was in the city where she had spent her youth, the place
longed for hungrily half a lifetime. She had been so wretchedly
train-sick throughout the journey that she had no recollection of
anything but her discomfort, and, to all intents and purposes, there
were but a few hours of nightmare between the farm in Red
Willow County and my study on Newbury Street. I had planned
a little pleasure for her that afternoon, to repay her for some of the
glorious moments she had given me when we used to milk together
in the straw-thatched cowshed and she, because I was more than
usually tired, or because her husband had spoken sharply to me,
would tell me of the splendid performance of the *Huguenots* she
had seen in Paris, in her youth. At two o'clock the Symphony
Orchestra was to give a Wagner program, and I intended to take
my aunt; though, as I conversed with her I grew doubtful about
her enjoyment of it. Indeed, for her own sake, I could only wish her
taste for such things quite dead, and the long struggle mercifully
ended at last. I suggested our visiting the Conservatory and the
Common before lunch, but she seemed altogether too timid to wish
to venture out. She questioned me absently about various changes
in the city, but she was chiefly concerned that she had forgotten
to leave instructions about feeding half-skimmed milk to a certain
weakling calf, "old Maggie's calf, you know, Clark," she explained,
evidently having forgotten how long I had been away. She was
further troubled because she had neglected to tell her daughter

about the freshly opened kit of mackerel in the cellar, which would spoil if it were not used directly.

I asked her whether she had ever heard any of the Wagnerian operas and found that she had not, though she was perfectly familiar with their respective situations, and had once possessed the piano score of *The Flying Dutchman.* I began to think it would have been best to get her back to Red Willow County without waking her, and regretted having suggested the concert.

From the time we entered the concert hall, however, she was a trifle less passive and inert, and for the first time seemed to perceive her surroundings. I had felt some trepidation lest she might become aware of the absurdities of her attire, or might experience some painful embarrassment at stepping suddenly into the world to which she had been dead for a quarter of a century. But, again, I found how superficially I had judged her. She sat looking about her with eyes as impersonal, almost as stony, as those with which the granite Rameses in a museum watches the froth and fret that ebbs and flows about his pedestal—separated from it by the lonely stretch of centuries. I have seen this same aloofness in old miners who drift into the Brown Hotel at Denver, their pockets full of bullion, their linen soiled, their haggard faces unshaven; standing in the thronged corridors as solitary as though they were still in a frozen camp on the Yukon, conscious that certain experiences have isolated them from their fellows by a gulf no haberdasher could bridge.

We sat at the extreme left of the first balcony, facing the arc of our own and the balcony above us, veritable hanging gardens, brilliant as tulip beds. The matinée audience was made up chiefly of women. One lost the contour of faces and figures—indeed, any effect of line whatever—and there was only the color of bodices past counting, the shimmer of fabrics soft and firm, silky and sheer: red, mauve, pink, blue, lilac, purple, ecru, rose, yellow, cream, and white, all the colors that an impressionist finds in a sunlit landscape, with here and there the dead shadow of a frock coat. My Aunt Georgiana regarded them as though they had been so many daubs of tube-paint on a palette.

When the musicians came out and took their places, she gave a little stir of anticipation and looked with quickening interest down over the rail at that invariable grouping, perhaps the first wholly familiar thing that had greeted her eye since she had left old Maggie and her weakling calf. I could feel how all those details sank into her soul, for I had not forgotten how they had sunk into mine when I came fresh from plowing forever and forever between green aisles of corn, where, as in a treadmill, one might walk from daybreak to dusk without perceiving a shadow of change. The clean profiles of the musicians, the gloss of their linen, the dull black of their coats, the beloved shapes of the instruments, the patches of yellow light thrown by the green-shaded lamps on the smooth, varnished bellies of the cellos and the bass viols in the rear, the restless, wind-tossed forest of fiddle necks and bows—I recalled how, in the first orchestra I had ever heard, those long bow strokes seemed to draw the heart out of me, as a conjurer's stick reels out yards of paper ribbon from a hat.

The first number was the *Tannhäuser* overture. When the horns drew out the first strain of the Pilgrim's chorus my Aunt Georgiana clutched my coat sleeve. Then it was I first realized that for her this broke a silence of thirty years; the inconceivable silence of the plains. With the battle between the two motives, with the frenzy of the Venusberg theme and its ripping of strings, there came to me an overwhelming sense of the waste and wear we are so powerless to combat; and I saw again the tall, naked house on the prairie, black and grim as a wooden fortress; the black pond where I had learned to swim, its margin pitted with sun-dried cattle tracks; the rain-gullied clay banks about the naked house, the four dwarf ash seedlings where the dishcloths were always hung to dry before the kitchen door. The world there was the flat world of the ancients; to the east, a cornfield that stretched to daybreak; to the west, a corral that reached to sunset; between, the conquests of peace, dearer bought than those of war.

The overture closed; my aunt released my coat sleeve, but she said nothing. She sat staring at the orchestra through a dullness of thirty years, through the films made little by little by each of the three hundred and sixty-five days in every one of them. What, I wondered, did she get from it? She had been a good pianist in her day I knew, and her musical education had been broader than that of most music teachers of a quarter of a century ago. She had often told me of Mozart's operas and Meyerbeer's, and I could remember hearing her sing, years ago, certain melodies of Verdi's. When I had fallen ill with a fever in her house she used to sit by my cot in the evening—when the cool, night wind blew in through the faded mosquito netting tacked over the window, and I lay watching a certain bright star that burned red above the cornfield—and sing "Home to our mountains, O, let us return!" in a way fit to break the heart of a Vermont boy near dead of homesickness already.

I watched her closely through the prelude to *Tristan and Isolde*, trying vainly to conjecture what that seething turmoil of strings and winds might mean to her, but she sat mutely staring at the violin bows that drove obliquely downward, like the pelting streaks of rain in a summer shower. Had this music any message for her? Had she enough left to at all comprehend this power which had kindled the world since she had left it? I was in a fever of curiosity, but Aunt Georgiana sat silent upon her peak in Darien. She preserved this utter immobility throughout the number from *The Flying Dutchman*, though her fingers worked mechanically upon her black dress, as though, of themselves, they were recalling the piano score they had once played. Poor old hands! They had been stretched and twisted into mere tentacles to hold and lift and knead with; the palms unduly swollen, the fingers bent and knotted—on one of them a thin, worn band that had once been a wedding ring. As I pressed and gently quieted one of those groping hands I remembered with quivering eyelids their services for me in other days.

Soon after the tenor began the "Prize Song," I heard a quick drawn breath and turned to my aunt. Her eyes were closed, but the tears were glistening on her cheeks, and I think, in a moment more, they were in my eyes as well. It never really died, then—the soul that can suffer so excruciatingly and so interminably; it withers to the outward eye only; like that strange moss which can lie on a dusty shelf half a century and yet, if placed in water, grows green again. She wept so throughout the development and elaboration of the melody.

During the intermission before the second half of the concert, I questioned my aunt and found that the "Prize Song" was not new to her. Some years before there had drifted to the farm in Red

Willow County a young German, a tramp cowpuncher, who had
sung the chorus at Bayreuth, when he was a boy, along with the
other peasant boys and girls. Of a Sunday morning he used to sit on
his gingham-sheeted bed in the hands' bedroom which opened off
the kitchen, cleaning the leather of his boots and saddle, singing
the "Prize Song," while my aunt went about her work in the kitchen.
She had hovered about him until she had prevailed upon him to
join the country church, though his sole fitness for this step, insofar
as I could gather, lay in his boyish face and his possession of this
divine melody. Shortly afterward he had gone to town on the
Fourth of July, been drunk for several days, lost his money at a
faro table, ridden a saddled Texan steer on a bet, and disappeared
with a fractured collarbone. All this my aunt told me huskily,
wanderingly, as though she were talking in the weak lapses of
illness.

"Well, we have come to better things than the old *Trovatore*
at any rate, Aunt Georgie?" I queried, with a well-meant effort at
jocularity.

Her lip quivered and she hastily put her handkerchief up to her
mouth. From behind it she murmured, "And you have been hearing
this ever since you left me, Clark?" Her question was the gentlest
and saddest of reproaches.

The second half of the program consisted of four numbers
from the *Ring*, and closed with Siegfried's funeral march. My aunt
wept quietly, but almost continuously, as a shallow vessel over-
flows in a rainstorm. From time to time her dim eyes looked up at
the lights which studded the ceiling, burning softly under their dull
glass globes; doubtless they were stars in truth to her. I was still
perplexed as to what measure of musical comprehension was left
to her, she who had heard nothing but the singing of gospel hymns
at Methodist services in the square frame schoolhouse on Section
Thirteen for so many years. I was wholly unable to gauge how
much of it had been dissolved in soapsuds, or worked into bread,
or milked into the bottom of a pail.

The deluge of sound poured on and on; I never knew what she
found in the shining current of it; I never knew how far it bore
her, or past what happy islands. From the trembling of her face I
could well believe that before the last numbers she had been carried

out where the myriad graves are, into the gray, nameless burying grounds of the sea; or into some world of death vaster yet, where, from the beginning of the world, hope has lain down with hope and dream with dream and, renouncing, slept.

The concert was over; the people filed out of the hall chattering and laughing, glad to relax and find the living level again, but my kinswoman made no effort to rise. The harpist slipped its green felt cover over his instrument; the flute players shook the water from their mouthpieces; the men of the orchestra went out one by one, leaving the stage to the chairs and music stands, empty as a winter cornfield

I spoke to my aunt. She burst into tears and sobbed pleadingly. "I don't want to go, Clark, I don't want to go!"

I understood. For her, just outside the door of the concert hall, lay the black pond with the cattle-tracked bluffs; the tall, un-painted house, with weather-curled boards; naked as a tower, the crook-backed ash seedlings where the dishcloths hung to dry; the gaunt, molting turkeys picking up refuse about the kitchen door.

THE PILGRIM-ARTIST: *Willa Cather's "A Wagner Matinée"*

Willa Cather is frequently regarded as a writer who commemorates the nineteenth-century frontier and the pioneering spirit that conquered the hard and hostile forces set against human courage. This historical adventure, popular opinion would have it, is her "theme," and in that epoch with its special opportunities for heroism, opportunities now lost to us, we can locate her artistic loyalties. But these prevailing assumptions about Miss Cather's vision and work oversimplify her ambivalent attitude toward the frontier and her complex notion of heroism. Also, the conception of Willa Cather as a romantic, fictive historian has given us a false confidence about her topicality, a con-fidence which, in our reading of her fiction, encourages us to ignore her masterly craft and originality. One can, I judge, see something of Miss Cather's craftsmanship by examining a story that has been widely ap-preciated for its materials and that, at the same time, shows the other side of her attitude toward the Midwestern world with which she is so closely associated.

None of our romantic preconceptions about the glorious, rugged prairie applies to "A Wagner Matinée." Those who think of Willa Cather only in terms of *My Ántonia* or *O Pioneers!* and attempt to read this story by those terms will be either disappointed or irritated. One finds neither a nostalgic rendering of the untamed land nor an easy confidence in humanity's capacity to triumph over its cruel hardships. Instead, Willa Cather depicts here a defeat of human aspirations by the insuperable forces of nature. Though the defeat is without the conventional heroic trappings of combat or physical destruction, it is nevertheless one of final importance.

Essentially, "A Wagner Matinée" is a tragedy of the soul, a tragedy expressing the psychic loss a musician (the artistic counterpart of the pioneer in Willa Cather) experiences on the frontier. It is a story of effort and failure, a revelation of the shadows in the soul. Georgiana Carpenter was raised in Boston, spent some time in Paris, and eventually returned to Boston where she taught music at the Conservatory. At thirty, in the middle of her career, and undoubtedly apprehensive about marital prospects, she had abandoned the opportunities of pursuing music to marry a younger, twenty-one-year-old Westerner, Howard Carpenter, and to move to Red Willow County, Nebraska. At sixty, after three decades of exposure "to a pitiless wind and alkaline water" and being displaced from the cultural world of her natural affinities, she returns to Boston to settle a relative's estate. She is met and escorted about the city by her nephew Clark, whom she had taught "scales and exercises," and who is now studying music at the Conservatory. Back now in the city of cultural possibilities, she attends a Wagner matinée at the symphony; and this sudden confrontation with music stirs her dormant desire for the art she gave up and brings home the deprivations she has suffered these many years on the plains.

Aunt Georgiana's adjustment to prairie life during that time is a special and brave sort. She indulges her musical self at the same time that she suppresses these interests. After fifteen years she acquires "a little parlor organ," and with it she teaches her nephew the rudiments of music. Though she encourages Clark's musical training, she "seldom talked . . . about music." What is her true vocation becomes an avocation, and she tries to instill the same sense of music as hobby in the boy. Her reasons, one can see, are noble even if they are self-protective. "Don't love it so well, Clark, or it may be taken from you. Oh, dear boy, pray that whatever your sacrifice may be, it be not that." While not living the renunciatory life that art demands of its practitioners, she does speak in its behalf by acknowledging its great, personal importance. And in losing what is most sacred to her, Georgiana Carpenter achieves a renunciation of her own. We are given a clue as to what sustains her through the silent, prairie life; but this clue reveals less of the sustenance's succor than it tells us of the denial's intensity.

> She was a pious woman; she had the consolations of religion and, to her at least, her martyrdom was not really sordid.

If her martyrdom *is* "sordid," as Clark implies, it is because Aunt Georgiana was defeated in her struggle to preserve her music against the forces of the prairie. In the war between man's higher and lower instincts, the lower has won out.

At the concert hall, this struggle is explained through Miss Cather's handling of music. In fact, music defines the conflict in the story. Gradually, Georgiana Carpenter realizes her condition and the consequences of her choice. When she arrives in Boston she is altogether unaware of the world around her, but as she enters the hall, she becomes "a trifle less passive and inert." When the musicians come out and take their places, she gives "a stir of anticipation," and when they play the opening bars of Wagner, whom Aunt Georgiana is hearing for the first time (though she knew of his music before as a student), the rediscovery begins and the nature of her struggle is disclosed. The explanation is suggested in the leading motives of the overture to *Tannhäuser,* the first selection on the program, in which Wagner sets the symbolic struggle between the sacred and the profane in man. Willa Cather incorporates Wagner's opposing motives of man's higher and lower yearnings and gives them a special fictive immediacy and significance of her own.

The orchestra begins with the Pilgrim's Chant alone: it rises to a mighty outpour and finally passes away. In the operatic text this motive represents the ecstasy of sacred yearnings, and in "A Wagner Matinée" it represents those higher impulses of Georgiana Carpenter and of music and all art as well. The old woman intuitively apprehends Wagner's musical message though it has been many years since she thought of the composer:

> The first number was the *Tannhäuser* overture. When the horns drew out the first strains of the Pilgrim's chorus my Aunt Georgiana clutched my coat sleeve. Then it was I first realized that for her this broke a silence of thirty years; the inconceivable silence of the plains.

Then there rises the seductive spell of the Venusberg motive, the whirlings of the frightening tempting world created of man's profane desires. In the abstract, Willa Cather applies this Venusberg motive to the hostile world in which the artist must assert his higher drives and the world to which the artist occasionally succumbs. In the concrete, the profane world is the arid plains of Red Willow County, Nebraska, which destroyed Aunt Georgiana. (Also, the Venusberg motive suggests the woman's impetuous pursuit of physical love.) In the tug between "the inconceivable silence of the plains" and "the little parlor organ," silence won. Clark's associations with the Venusberg motive run:

> With the battle between the two motives, with the frenzy of the Venusberg theme and its ripping of strings, there came to me an overwhelming sense of the waste and wear we are so powerless to combat; and I saw again the tall, naked house on the prairie, black and grim as a wooden fortress; the black pond where I had learned to swim, its margin pitted with the sun-dried cattle tracks; the rain-gullied clay banks about the naked house, the four ash seedlings where the dishcloths were always hung to dry before the kitchen door. The world there was the flat world of the ancients; to the east, a cornfield that stretched to daybreak; to the west, a corral that reached to sunset; between, the conquests of peace, dearer bought than those of war.

The passage is a masterstroke of evocation: Willa Cather has given us Venusberg through Clark's musical consciousness. How could the delicate pilgrim-artist, Georgiana, defeat the powerful, ancient forces of such mysterious blackness and waste and aridity?

Aunt Georgiana is transfixed by the music. In answer to Clark's self-query, "had this music any message for her?," there are only the "quivering eyelids," expressing the anguish of discovery, and the fingers working upon her black dress in sympathy with the melodies of *The Flying Dutchman*, the piano score for which she owned when a student. Like the prelude to *Tristan und Isolde* which preceded it, *The Flying Dutchman* overture works through opposing motives (here, the tranquil Senta motive and the crashing Curse motive) and celebrates the eventual triumph of the higher, the Senta, over the lower, the Curse. The last piece before the intermission is the "Prize Song," and here the voice sings with the orchestra of the victory of the ideal. The *"Preislied"* is the musical summation of the contending themes presented earlier in the concert. Walthar's musical triumph, in Wagnerian terms, amounts to a victory for the noblest ideals of art, which were the particular purposes of the Mastersingers' Guild. And as Walthar wins Eva's hand with the mastersingers' emblem, Wagner celebrates the perfect union and the double triumph of art and life. That *Die Meistersinger* is a comic variation of the contest theme in *Tannhäuser* gives the first half of Willa Cather's Wagner matinée a thematic, as well as musical, balance.

Even Miss Cather's choice of a *Wagner* matinée has particular psychological relevance and historical suitability to the kind of awareness Georgiana Carpenter achieves. Clark explains that his aunt left the Boston Conservatory "somewhere back in the latter sixties." At that time Wagner's music was just coming into ascendency among the most knowledgeable musicians, and any performance of his operas would have been a rarity in the United States. Though there were scattered experimental presentations in the 1850s, it was not until the late 1880s that the Metropolitan Opera performed his works. Yet, Aunt Georgiana, whose musical education abruptly ended in the late 1860s, was "perfectly familiar with their respective situations." Moreover, she owned a piano score for *The Flying Dutchman*. So, when Clark, who by his own admission had judged his aunt "superficially," says that her musical training "had been broader than that of most music teachers of a quarter of a century ago," he is actually understating the range and depth of her musical sensitivity. She was, judging by her knowledge of Wagner, distinctly avant-garde.

Georgiana Carpenter's question to Clark during the intermission ("And have you been hearing this ever since you left me, Clark?") is, then, more than a sad and gentle reproach to the boy's taunt that "we have come to better things than *Trovatore*"; it is a self-measurement of her spiritual losses. Though the cultural world was once behind her in its admiration for Wagner, it is now she, hearing in the late 1890s what she loved in the 1860s, who has been left behind—and alone. Willa Cather has, then, in making Aunt Georgiana's concert a *Wagner* matinée, defined Georgiana's tragedy historically.

But as we have seen, Miss Cather's use of music goes deeper than a use of it as historical perspective. Thematically, the Wagnerian numbers serve as ironic comments on Aunt Georgiana's defeat; psychologically, they serve to heighten her tragedy of the soul by aligning her struggle with the legendary enactments of it.

> Soon after the tenor began the "Prize Song," I heard a quick drawn breath and turned to my aunt. Her eyes were closed, but the tears were glistening on her cheeks, and I think, in a moment

more, they were in my eyes as well. It never really died, then—the soul that can suffer so excruciatingly and so interminably; it withers to the outward eye only. . . . She wept so throughout the development of the melody.

After the intermission come four numbers from the *Ring* cycle. The first three are unspecified; the concluding selection is Siegfried's funeral march. In a general way, this simple but touching melody of heroic defeat anticipates Aunt Georgiana's taking leave of the concert hall and her return to Red Willow County, Nebraska. It signals the solemn procession to darkness and sadness. And with Siegfried's funeral music are mingled the Venusberg associations in Clark's mind:

The concert was over; the people filed out of the hall chattering and laughing, glad to relax and find the living level again, but my kinswoman made no effort to rise. . . .
I understood. For her, just outside the door of the concert hall, lay the black pond with the cattle-tracked bluffs; the tall unpainted house, with weather-curled boards; naked as a tower, the crook-backed ash seedlings where the dishcloths hung to dry; the gaunt, molting turkeys picking up refuse about the kitchen door.

Though she uses Wagnerian analogues, Willa Cather offers no Wagnerian conclusion to Georgiana Carpenter's pilgrimage in "A Wagner Matinée." There is no victory for the higher yearnings, no triumph of art, no redemption through love or even through renunciation. There is only defeat, the trek back to privation and hardship—to Venusberg and "the inconceivable silence of the plains."

                                              RICHARD GIANNONE

LUIGI PIRANDELLO

The Jar

HE OLIVE CROP WAS a bumper one that year: the trees had flowered luxuriantly the year before, and, though there had been a long spell of misty weather at the time, the fruit had set well. Lollo Zirafa had a fine plantation on his farm at Primosole. Reckoning that the five old jars of glazed earthenware which he had in his wine-cellar would not suffice to hold all the oil of that harvest, he had placed an order well beforehand at Santo Stefano Di Camastra, where they are made. His new jar was to be of greater capacity—breast-high and pot-bellied; it would be the mother-superior to the little community of five other jars.

I need scarcely say that Don Lollo Zirafa had had a dispute with the potter concerning this jar. It would indeed be hard to name anyone with whom he had not picked a quarrel: for every trifle—be it merely a stone that had fallen from his boundary wall, or a handful of straw—he would shout out to the servants to saddle his mule, so that he could hurry to the town and file a suit. He had half-ruined himself, because of the large sums he had had to spend on court fees and lawyers' bills, bringing actions against one person after another, which always ended in his having to pay the costs of both sides. People said that his legal adviser grew so tired of seeing him appear two or three times a week that he tried to reduce the frequency of his visits by making him a present of a volume which looked like a prayer-book: it contained the judicial code—the idea being that he should take the trouble to see for himself what the rights and wrongs of the case were before hurrying to bring a suit.

Previously, when anyone had a difference with him, they would

try to make him lose his temper by shouting out: "Saddle the mule!"
but now they changed it to "Go and look up your pocket-code!"
Don Lollo would reply: "That I will and I'll break the lot of you,
you sons of bitches!"

In course of time, the new jar, for which he had paid the goodly
sum of four florins, duly arrived; until room could be found for it
in the wine-cellar, it was lodged in the crushing-shed for a few days.
Never had there been a finer jar. It was quite distressing to see it
lodged in that foul den, which reeked of stale grape-juice and had
that musty smell of places deprived of light and air.

It was now two days since the harvesting of the olives had
begun, and Don Lollo was almost beside himself, having to super-
vise not only the men who were beating down the fruit from the
trees, but also a number of others who had come with mule-loads
of manure to be deposited in heaps on the hillside, where he had a
field in which he was going to sow beans for the next crop. He
felt that it was really more than one man could manage, he was at
his wits' ends whom to attend to: cursing like a trooper, he vowed
he would exterminate, first this man and then that, if an olive—
one single olive—was missing: he almost talked as if he had
counted them, one by one, on his trees; then he would turn to the
muleteers and utter the direst threats as to what would happen, if
any one heap of manure were not exactly the same size as the
others. A little white cap on his head, his sleeves rolled up and his
shirt open at the front, he rushed here, there and everywhere; his
face was a bright red and poured with sweat, his eyes glared about
him wolfishly, while his hands rubbed angrily at his shaven chin,
where a fresh growth of beard always sprouted the moment the
razor had left it.

At the close of the third day's work, three of the farm-hands—
rough fellows with dirty, brutish faces—went to the crushing-shed;
they had been beating the olive trees and went to replace their
ladders and poles in the shed. They stood aghast at the sight of the
fine new jar in two pieces, looking for all the world as if some one
had caught hold of the bulging front and cut it off with a sharp
sweep of the knife.

"Oh, my God! look! look!"

"How on earth has that happened?"

"My holy aunt! When Don Lollo hears of it! The new jar! What a pity, though!"

The first of the three, more frightened than his companions, proposed to shut the door again at once and to sneak away very quietly, leaving their ladders and poles outside leaning up against the wall; but the second took him up sharply.

"That's a stupid idea! You can't try that on Don Lollo. As like as not he'd believe we broke it ourselves. No, we all stay here!"

He went out of the shed and, using his hands as a trumpet, called out:—

"Don Lollo! Oh! Don LOLLOOOOO!"

When the farmer came up and saw the damage, he fell into a towering passion. First he vented his fury on the three men. He seized one of them by the throat, pinned him against the wall, and shouted:—

"By the Virgin's blood, you'll pay for that!"

The other two sprang forward in wild excitement, fell upon Don Lollo and pulled him away. Then his mad rage turned against himself: he stamped his feet, flung his cap on the ground, and slapped his cheeks, bewailing his loss with screams suited only for the death of a relation.

"The new jar! A four-florin jar! Brand new!"

Who could have broken it? Could it possibly have broken of itself? Certainly some one must have broken it, out of malice or from envy at his possession of such a beauty. But when? How? There was no sign of violence. Could it conceivably have come in a broken condition from the pottery? No, it rang like a bell on its arrival.

As soon as the farm-hands saw that their master's first outburst of rage was spent, they began to console him, saying that he should not take it so to heart, as the jar could be mended. After all, the break was not a bad one, for the front had come away all in one piece; a clever rivetter could repair it and make it as good as new. Zi' Dima Licasi was just the man for the job: he had invented a marvellous cement made of some composition which he kept a strict secret—miraculous stuff! Once it had set, you couldn't loosen it, even with a hammer. So they suggested that, if Don Lollo agreed, Zi' Dima Licasi should turn up at day-break and—as sure as eggs were eggs—the jar would be repaired and be even better than a new one.

For a long time Don Lollo turned a deaf ear to their advice—it was quite useless, there was no making good the damage—but in the end he allowed himself to be persuaded and punctually at daybreak Zi' Dima Licasi arrived at Primosole, with his outfit in a basket slung on his back. He turned out to be a misshapen old man with swollen, crooked joints, like the stem of an ancient Saracen olive tree. To extract a word from him, it looked as if you would have to use a pair of forceps on his mouth.

His ungraceful figure seemed to radiate discontent or gloom, due perhaps to his disappointment that no one had so far been found willing to do justice to his merits as an inventor. For Zi' Dima Licasi had not yet patented his discovery; he wanted to make a name for it first by its successful application. Meanwhile he felt it necessary to keep a sharp lookout, for fear lest some one steal the secret of his process.

"Let me see that cement of yours," began Don Lollo in a distrustful tone, after examining him from head to foot for several minutes.

Zi' Dima declined, with a dignified shake of the head.

"You'll see its results."

"But, will it hold?"

Zi' Dima put his basket on the ground and took out from it a red bundle composed of a large cotton handkerchief, much the worse for wear, wrapped round and round something. He began to unroll it very carefully, while they all stood round watching him with close attention. When at last, however, nothing came to light save a pair of spectacles with bridge and sides broken and tied up with string, there was a general laugh. Zi' Dima took no notice, but wiped his fingers before handling the spectacles, then put them on and, with much solemnity, began his examination of the jar, which had been brought outside on to the threshing-floor. Finally he said:

"It'll hold."

"But I can't trust cement alone," Don Lollo stipulated, "I must have rivets as well."

"I'm off," Zi' Dima promptly replied, standing up and replacing his basket on his back.

Don Lollo caught hold of his arm:—

"Off? Where to? You've got no more manners than a pig! . . . Just look at this pauper putting on an air of royalty! . . . Why! you wretched fool, I've got to put oil in that jar, and don't you know that oil oozes? Yards and yards to join together, and you talk of using cement alone! I want rivets—cement and rivets. It's for me to decide."

Zi' Dima shut his eyes, closed his lips tightly, and shook his head. People were all like that—they refused to give him the satisfaction of turning out a neat bit of work, performed with artistic thoroughness and proving the wonderful virtues of his cement.

"If," he said, "the jar doesn't ring as true as a bell once more. . . ."

"I won't listen to a word," Don Lollo broke in. "I want rivets! I'll pay you for cement and rivets. How much will it come to?"

"If I use cement only . . ."

"My God! what an obstinate fellow! What did I say? I told you I wanted rivets. We'll settle the terms after the work is done. I've no more time to waste on you."

And he went off to look after his men.

In a state of great indignation Zi' Dima started on the job and his temper continued to rise as he bored hole after hole in the jar and in its broken section—holes for his iron rivets. Along with the squeaking of his tool went a running accompaniment of grunts which grew steadily louder and more frequent; his fury made his eyes more piercing and bloodshot and his face became green with bile. When he had finished that first operation, he flung his borer angrily into the basket and held the detached portion up against the jar to satisfy himself that the holes were at equal distances and fitted one another; next he took his pliers and cut a length of iron wire into as many pieces as he needed rivets, and then called to one of the men who were beating the olive trees to come and help him.

"Cheer up, Zi' Dima!" said the labourer, seeing how upset the old man looked.

Zi' Dima raised his hand with a savage gesture. He opened the tin which contained the cement and held it up towards heaven, as if offering it to God, seeing that men refused to recognize its value. Then he began to spread it with his finger all round the detached portion and along the broken edge of the jar. Taking his pliers and the iron rivets he had prepared, he crept inside the open belly of the jar and instructed the farm-hand to hold the piece up, fitting it closely to the jar as he had himself done a short time previously. Before starting to put in the rivets, he spoke from inside the jar:—

"Pull! Pull! Tug at it with all your might! . . . You see it doesn't come loose. Curses on people who won't believe me! Knock it! Yes, knock it! . . . Doesn't it ring like a bell, even with me inside it? Go and tell your master that!"

"It's for the top-dog to give orders, Zi' Dima," said the man with a sigh, "and it's for the under-dog to carry them out. Put the rivets in. Put 'em in."

Zi' Dima began to pass the bits of iron through the adjacent holes, one on each side of the crack, twisting up the ends with his pliers. It took him an hour to put them all in, and he poured with sweat inside the jar. As he worked, he complained of his misfortune and the farm-hand stayed near, trying to console him.

"Now help me to get out," said Zi' Dima, when all was finished.

But large though its belly was, the jar had a distinctly narrow neck—a fact which Zi' Dima had overlooked, being so absorbed in his grievance. Now, try as he would, he could not manage to squeeze his way out. Instead of helping him, the farm-hand stood idly by, convulsed with laughter. So there was poor Zi' Dima, imprisoned in the jar which he had mended and—there was no use in blinking at the fact—in a jar which would have to be broken to let him out, and this time broken for good.

Hearing the laughter and shouts, Don Lollo came rushing up. Inside the jar Zi' Dima was spitting like an angry cat.

"Let me out," he screamed, "for God's sake! I want to get out! Be quick! Help!"

Don Lollo was quite taken aback and unable to believe his own ears.

"What? Inside there? He's riveted himself up inside?"

Then he went up to the jar and shouted out to Zi' Dima:—

"Help you? What help do you think I can give you? You stupid old dodderer, what d'you mean by it? Why couldn't you measure it first? Come, have a try! Put an arm out . . . that's it! Now the head! Up you come! . . . No, no, gently! . . . Down again. . . . Wait a bit! . . . Not that way. . . . Down, get down. . . . How on earth could you do such a thing? . . . What about my jar now? . . .

"Keep calm! Keep calm!" he recommended to all the onlookers, as if it was they who were becoming excited and not himself. . . . "My head's going round! Keep calm! This is quite a new point! Get me my mule!"

He rapped the jar with his knuckles. Yes, it really rang like a bell once again.

"Fine! Repaired as good as new. . . . You wait a bit!" he said to the prisoner; then instructed his man to be off and saddle the mule. He rubbed his forehead vigorously with his fingers, and continued:

"I wonder what's the best course. That's not a jar, it's a contrivance of the devil himself. . . . Keep still! Keep still!" he exclaimed, rushing up to steady the jar, in which Zi' Dima, now in a towering passion, was struggling like a wild animal in a trap.

"It's a new point, my good man, which the lawyer must settle. I can't rely on my own judgment. . . . Where's that mule? Hurry up with the mule! . . . I'll go straight there and back. You must wait patiently: it's in your own interest. . . . Meanwhile, keep quiet, be calm! I must look after my own rights. And, first of all, to put myself in the right, I fulfill my obligation. Here you are! I am paying you for your work, for a whole day's work. Here are your five lire. Is that enough?"

"I don't want anything," shouted Zi' Dima. "I want to get out!"

"You shall get out, but meanwhile I, for my part, am paying you. There they are—five lire."

He took the money out of his waistcoat pocket and tossed it into the jar, then enquired in a tone of great concern:—

"Have you had any lunch? . . . Bread and something to eat with it, at once! . . . What! You don't want it? Well, then, throw it to the dogs! I shall have done my duty when I've given it to you."

Having ordered the food, he mounted and set out for the town. His wild gesticulations made those who saw him galloping past think that he might well be hastening to shut himself up in a lunatic asylum.

As luck would have it, he did not have to spend much time in the ante-room before being admitted to the lawyer's study; he had, however, to wait a long while before the lawyer could finish laughing, after the matter had been related to him. Annoyed at the amusement he caused, Don Lollo said irritably:—

"Excuse me, but I don't see anything to laugh at. It's all very well for your Honour, who is not the sufferer, but the jar is my property."

The lawyer, however, continued to laugh and then made him tell the story all over again, just as it had happened, so that he could raise another laugh out of it.

"Inside, eh? So he'd rivetted himself inside?" And what did Don Lollo want to do? . . . "To ke . . . to ke . . . keep him there inside—ha! ha! ha! . . . keep him there inside, so as not to lose the jar?"

"Why should I lose it?" cried Don Lollo, clenching his fists. "Why should I put up with the loss of my money, and have people laughing at me?"

"But don't you know what that's called?" said the lawyer at last. "It's called 'wrongful confinement'."

"Confinement? Well, who's confined him? He's confined himself! What fault is that of mine?"

The lawyer then explained to him that the matter gave rise to two cases: on the one hand he, Don Lollo, must straightway liberate the prisoner, if he wished to escape from being prosecuted for wrongful confinement; while, on the other hand, the rivetter would be responsible for making good the loss resulting from his lack of skill or his stupidity.

"Ah!" said Don Lollo, with a sigh of relief. "So he'll have to pay me for my jar?"

"Wait a bit," remarked the lawyer. "Not as if it were a new jar, remember!"

"Why not?"

"Because it was a broken one, badly broken, too."

"Broken! No, Sir. Not broken. It's perfectly sound now and better than ever it was—he says so himself. And if I have to break it again, I shall not be able to have it mended. The jar will be ruined, Sir!"

The lawyer assured him that that point would be taken into account and that the rivetter would have to pay the value which the jar had in its present condition.

"Therefore," he counselled, "get the man himself to give you an estimate of its value first."

"I kiss your hands," Don Lollo murmured, and hurried away.

On his return home towards evening, he found all his labourers engaged in a celebration around the inhabited jar. The watch-dogs joined in the festivities with joyous barks and capers. Zi' Dima had not only calmed down, but had even come to enjoy his curious adventure and was able to laugh at it, with the melancholy humour of the unfortunate.

Don Lollo drove them all aside and bent down to look into the jar.

"Hallo! Getting along well?"

"Splendid! An open-air life for me!" replied the man. "It's better than in my own house."

"I'm glad to hear it. Meanwhile I'd just like you to know that that jar cost me four florins when it was new. How much do you think it is worth now?"

"With me inside it?" asked Zi' Dima.

The rustics laughed.

"Silence!" shouted Don Lollo. "Either your cement is of some use or it is of no use. There is no third possibility. If it is of no use, you are a fraud. If it is of some use, the jar, in its present condition, must have a value. What is that value? I ask for your estimate."

After a space for reflection, Zi' Dima said:—

"Here is my answer: if you had let me mend it with cement only—as I wanted to do—first of all I should not have been shut up inside it and the jar would have had its original value, without any doubt. But spoilt by these rivets, which had to be done from inside, it has lost most of its value. It's worth a third of its former price, more or less."

"One-third? That's one florin, thirty-three cents."

"Maybe less, but not more than that."

"Well," said Don Lollo. "Promise me that you'll pay me one florin thirty-three cents."

"What?" asked Zi' Dima, as if he did not grasp the point.

"I will break the jar to let you out," replied Don Lollo. "And—
the lawyer tells me—you are to pay me its value according to your
own estimate—one florin thirty-three."

"I? Pay?" laughed Zi' Dima, "I'd sooner stay here till I rot!"

With some difficulty he managed to extract from his pocket a
short and peculiarly foul pipe and lighted it, puffing out the smoke
through the neck of the jar.

Don Lollo stood there scowling: the possibility that Zi' Dima
would no longer be willing to leave the jar, had not been foreseen
either by himself or by the lawyer. What step should he take now?
He was on the point of ordering them to saddle the mule, but
reflected that it was already evening.

"Oh ho!" he said. "So you want to take up your abode in my jar!
I call upon all you men as witnesses to his statement. He refuses
to come out, in order to escape from paying. I am quite prepared to
break it. Well, as you insist on staying there, I shall take proceedings against you tomorrow for unlawful occupancy of the jar
and for preventing me from my rightful use of it."

Zi' Dima blew out another puff of smoke and answered
calmly:—

"No, your Honour. I don't want to prevent you at all. Do you
think I am here because I like it? Let me out and I'll go away
gladly enough. But as for paying, I wouldn't dream of it, your
Honour."

In a sudden access of fury Don Lollo made to give a kick at the
jar but stopped in time. Instead he seized it with both hands and
shook it violently, uttering a hoarse growl.

"You see what fine cement it is," Zi' Dima remarked from inside.

"You rascal!" roared Don Lollo. "Whose fault is it, yours or
mine? You expect me to pay for it, do you? You can starve to death
inside first. We'll see who'll win."

He went away, forgetting all about the five lire which he had
tossed into the jar that morning. But the first thing Zi' Dima thought
of doing was to spend that money in having a festive evening,
in company with the farm-hands, who had been delayed in their
work by that strange accident, and had decided to spend the night
at the farm, in the open air, sleeping on the threshing-floor. One of
them went to a neighboring tavern to make the necessary purchases.

The moon was so bright that it seemed almost day—a splendid night for their carousal.

Many hours later Don Lollo was awakened by an infernal din. Looking out from the farm-house balcony, he could see in the moonlight what looked like a gang of devils on his threshing-floor: his men, all roaring drunk, were holding hands and performing a dance around the jar, while Zi' Dima, inside it, was singing at the top of his voice.

This time Don Lollo could not restrain himself, but rushed down like a mad bull and, before they could stop him, gave the jar a push which started it rolling down the slope. It continued on its course, to the delight of the intoxicated company, until it hit an olive tree and cracked in pieces, leaving Zi' Dima the winner in the dispute.

F. SCOTT FITZGERALD

Winter Dreams

OME OF THE CADDIES were poor as sin and lived in one room houses with a neurasthenic cow in the front yard, but Dexter Green's father owned the second best grocery-store in Black Bear—the best one was "The Hub," patronized by the wealthy people from Sherry Island—and Dexter caddied only for pocket-money.

In the fall when the days became crisp and gray, and the long Minnesota winter shut down like the white lid of a box, Dexter's skis moved over the snow that hid the fairways of the golf course. At these times the country gave him a feeling of profound melancholy—it offended him that the links should lie in enforced fallowness, haunted by ragged sparrows for the long season. It was dreary, too, that on the tees where the gay colors fluttered in summer there were now only the desolate sand-boxes knee-deep in crusted ice. When he crossed the hills the wind blew cold as misery, and if the sun was out he tramped with his eyes squinted up against the hard dimensionless glare.

In April the winter ceased abruptly. The snow ran down into Black Bear Lake scarcely tarrying for the early golfers to brave the season with red and black balls. Without elation, without an interval of moist glory, the cold was gone.

Dexter knew that there was something dismal about this Northern spring, just as he knew there was something gorgeous about the fall. Fall made him clinch his hands and tremble and repeat idiotic sentences to himself, and make brisk abrupt gestures of command to imaginary audiences and armies. October filled him with hope which November raised to a sort of ecstatic triumph, and in this mood the fleeting brilliant impressions of the summer at Sherry Island were ready grist to his mill. He became a golf champion and defeated Mr. T. A. Hedrick in a marvellous match played a hundred times over the fairways of his imagination, a match each detail of which he changed about untiringly—sometimes he won with almost laughable ease, sometimes he came up magnificently from behind. Again, stepping from a Pierce-Arrow automobile, like Mr. Mortimer Jones, he strolled frigidly into the lounge of the Sherry Island Golf Club—or perhaps, surrounded by an admiring crowd, he gave an exhibition of fancy diving from the spring-board of the club raft. . . . Among those who watched him in open-mouthed wonder was Mr. Mortimer Jones.

And one day it came to pass that Mr. Jones—himself and not his ghost—came up to Dexter with tears in his eyes and said that Dexter was the — — best caddy in the club, and wouldn't he decide not to quit if Mr. Jones made it worth his while, because every other — — caddy in the club lost one ball a hole for him— regularly—

"No, sir," said Dexter decisively. "I don't want to caddy any more." Then, after a pause: "I'm too old."

"You're not more than fourteen. Why the devil did you decide just this morning that you wanted to quit? You promised that next week you'd go over to the state tournament with me."

"I decided I was too old."

Dexter handed in his "A Class" badge, collected what money was due him from the caddy master, and walked home to Black Bear Village.

"The best — — caddy I ever saw," shouted Mr. Mortimer Jones over a drink that afternoon. "Never lost a ball! Willing! Intelligent! Quiet! Honest! Grateful!"

The little girl who had done this was eleven—beautifully ugly as little girls are apt to be who are destined after a few years to be inexpressibly lovely and bring no end of misery to a great number of men. The spark, however, was perceptible. There was a general ungodliness in the way her lips twisted down at the corners when she smiled, and in the—Heaven help us!—in the almost passionate quality of her eyes. Vitality is born early in such women. It was utterly in evidence now, shining through her thin frame in a sort of glow.

She had come eagerly out on to the course at nine o'clock with a white linen nurse and five small new golf-clubs in a white canvas bag which the nurse was carrying. When Dexter first saw her she was standing by the caddy house, rather ill at ease and trying to conceal the fact by engaging her nurse in an obviously unnatural conversation graced by startling and irrelevant grimaces from herself.

"Well, it's certainly a nice day, Hilda," Dexter heard her say. She drew down the corners of her mouth, smiled, and glanced furtively around, her eyes in transit falling for an instant on Dexter.

Then to the nurse:

"Well, I guess there aren't very many people out here this morning, are there?"

The smile again—radiant, blatantly artificial—convincing.

"I don't know what we're supposed to do now," said the nurse, looking nowhere in particular.

"Oh, that's all right. I'll fix it up."

Dexter stood perfectly still, his mouth slightly ajar. He knew that if he moved forward a step his stare would be in her line of vision—if he moved backward he would lose his full view of her face. For a moment he had not realized how young she was. Now he remembered having seen her several times the year before—in bloomers.

Suddenly, involuntarily, he laughed, a short abrupt laugh—then, startled by himself, he turned and began to walk quickly away.

"Boy—"

Dexter stopped.

"Boy—"

Beyond question he was addressed. Not only that, but he was treated to that absurd smile, that preposterous smile—the memory of which at least a dozen men were to carry into middle age.

"Boy, do you know where the golf teacher is?"

"He's giving a lesson."

"Well, do you know where the caddy-master is?"

"He isn't here yet this morning."

"Oh." For a moment this baffled her. She stood alternately on her right and left foot.

"We'd like to get a caddy," said the nurse. "Mrs. Mortimer Jones sent us out to play golf, and we don't know how without we get a caddy."

Here she was stopped by an ominous glance from Miss Jones, followed immediately by the smile.

"There aren't any caddies here except me," said Dexter to the nurse, "and I got to stay here in charge until the caddy-master gets here."

"Oh."

Miss Jones and her retinue now withdrew, and at a proper distance from Dexter became involved in a heated conversation, which was concluded by Miss Jones taking one of the clubs and hitting it on the ground with violence. For further emphasis she raised it again and was about to bring it down smartly upon the nurse's bosom, when the nurse seized the club and twisted it from her hands.

"You damn little mean old *thing!*" cried Miss Jones wildly.

Another argument ensued. Realizing that the elements of the comedy were implied in the scene, Dexter several times began to laugh, but each time restrained the laugh before it reached audibility. He could not resist the monstrous conviction that the little girl was justified in beating the nurse.

The situation was resolved by the fortuitous appearance of the caddy-master, who was appealed to immediately by the nurse.

"Miss Jones is to have a little caddy, and this one says he can't go."

"Mr. McKenna said I was to wait here till you came," said Dexter quickly.

"Well, he's here now." Miss Jones smiled cheerfully at the caddy-master. Then she dropped her bag and set off at a haughty mince toward the first tee.

"Well?" The caddy-master turned to Dexter. "What you standing there like a dummy for? Go pick up the young lady's clubs."

"I don't think I'll go out to-day," said Dexter.

"You don't—"

"I think I'll quit."

The enormity of his decision frightened him. He was a favorite caddy, and the thirty dollars a month he earned through the summer were not to be made elsewhere around the lake. But he had received a strong emotional shock, and his perturbation required a violent and immediate outlet.

It is not so simple as that, either. As so frequently would be the case in the future, Dexter was unconsciously dictated to by his winter dreams.

II

Now, of course, the quality and the seasonability of these winter dreams varied, but the stuff of them remained. They persuaded Dexter several years later to pass up a business course at the state university—his father, prospering now, would have paid his way—for the precarious advantage of attending an older and more famous university in the East, where he was bothered by his scanty funds. But do not get the impression, because his winter dreams happened to be concerned at first with musings on the rich, that there was anything merely snobbish in the boy. He wanted not association with glittering things and glittering people

—he wanted the glittering things themselves. Often he reached out for the best without knowing why he wanted it—and sometimes he ran up against the mysterious denials and prohibitions in which life indulges. It is with one of those denials and not with his career as a whole that this story deals.

He made money. It was rather amazing. After college he went to the city from which Black Bear Lake draws its wealthy patrons. When he was only twenty-three and had been there not quite two years, there were already people who liked to say: "Now *there's* a boy—" All about him rich men's sons were peddling bonds precariously, or investing patrimonies precariously, or plodding through the two dozen volumes of the "George Washington Commercial Course," but Dexter borrowed a thousand dollars on his college degree and his confident mouth, and bought a partnership in a laundry.

It was a small laundry when he went into it, but Dexter made a specialty of learning how the English washed fine woolen golf-stockings without shrinking them, and within a year he was catering to the trade that wore knickerbockers. Men were insisting that their Shetland hose and sweaters go to his laundry, just as they had insisted on a caddy who could find golf-balls. A little later he was doing their wives' lingerie as well—and running five branches in different parts of the city. Before he was twenty-seven he owned the largest string of laundries in his section of the country. It was then that he sold out and went to New York. But the part of his story that concerns us goes back to the days when he was making his first big success.

When he was twenty-three Mr. Hart—one of the gray-haired men who like to say "Now there's a boy"—gave him a guest card to the Sherry Island Golf Club for a week-end. So he signed his name one day on the register, and that afternoon played golf in a foursome with Mr. Hart and Mr. Sandwood and Mr. T. A. Hedrick. He did not consider it necessary to remark that he had once carried Mr. Hart's bag over this same links, and that he knew every trap and gully with his eyes shut—but he found himself glancing at the four caddies who trailed them, trying to catch a gleam or gesture that would remind him of himself, that would lessen the gap which lay between his present and his past.

It was a curious day, slashed abruptly with fleeting, familiar impressions. One minute he had the sense of being a trespasser—in the next he was impressed by the tremendous superiority he felt toward Mr. T. A. Hedrick, who was a bore and not even a good golfer any more.

Then, because of a ball Mr. Hart lost near the fifteenth green, an enormous thing happened. While they were searching the stiff grasses of the rough there was a clear call of "Fore!" from behind a hill in their rear. And as they all turned abruptly from their search a bright new ball sliced abruptly over the hill and caught Mr. T. A. Hedrick in the abdomen.

"By Gad!" cried Mr. T. A. Hedrick, "they ought to put some of these crazy women off the course. It's getting to be outrageous."

A head and a voice came up together over the hill:

"Do you mind if we go through?"

"You hit me in the stomach!" declared Mr. Hedrick wildly.

"Did I?" The girl approached the group of men. "I'm sorry. I yelled 'Fore!'"

Her glance fell casually on each of the men—then scanned the fairway for her ball.

"Did I bounce into the rough?"

It was impossible to determine whether this question was ingenuous or malicious. In a moment, however, she left no doubt, for as her partner came up over the hill she called cheerfully:

"Here I am! I'd have gone on the green except that I hit something."

As she took her stance for a short mashie shot, Dexter looked at her closely. She wore a blue gingham dress, rimmed at throat and shoulders with a white edging that accentuated her tan. The quality of exaggeration, of thinness, which had made her passionate eyes and down-turning mouth absurd at eleven, was gone now. She was arrestingly beautiful. The color in her cheeks was centred like the color in a picture—it was not a "high" color, but a sort of fluctuating and feverish warmth, so shaded that it seemed at any moment it would recede and disappear. This color and the mobility of her mouth gave a continual impression of flux, of intense life, of passionate vitality—balanced only partially by the sad luxury of her eyes.

She swung her mashie impatiently and without interest, pitching the ball into a sand-pit on the other side of the green. With a quick, insincere smile and a careless "Thank you!" she went on after it.

"That Judy Jones!" remarked Mr. Hedrick on the next tee, as they waited—some moments—for her to play on ahead. "All she needs is to be turned up and spanked for six months and then to be married off to an old-fashioned cavalry captain."

"My God, she's good-looking!" said Mr. Sandwood, who was just over thirty.

"Good-looking!" cried Mr. Hedrick contemptuously, "she always looks as if she wanted to be kissed! Turning those big cow-eyes on every calf in town!"

It was doubtful if Mr. Hedrick intended a reference to the maternal instinct.

"She'd play pretty good golf if she'd try," said Mr. Sandwood.

"She has no form," said Mr. Hedrick solemnly.

"She has a nice figure," said Mr. Sandwood.

"Better thank the Lord she doesn't drive a swifter ball," said Mr. Hart, winking at Dexter.

Later in the afternoon the sun went down with a riotous swirl of gold and varying blues and scarlets, and left the dry, rustling night of Western summer. Dexter watched from the veranda of the Golf Club, watched the even overlap of the waters in the little wind, silver molasses under the harvest-moon. Then the moon held a finger to her lips and the lake became a clear pool, pale and quiet. Dexter put on his bathing-suit and swam out to the farthest raft, where he stretched dripping on the wet canvas of the springboard.

There was a fish jumping and a star shining and the lights around the lake were gleaming. Over on a dark peninsula a piano was playing the songs of last summer and of summers before that —songs from "Chin-Chin" and "The Count of Luxemburg" and "The Chocolate Soldier"—and because the sound of a piano over a stretch of water had always seemed beautiful to Dexter he lay perfectly quiet and listened.

The tune the piano was playing at that moment had been gay and new five years before when Dexter was a sophomore at college. They had played it at a prom once when he could not afford the luxury of proms, and he had stood outside the gymnasium and listened. The sound of the tune precipitated in him a sort of ecstasy and it was with that ecstasy he viewed what happened to him now. It was a mood of intense appreciation, a sense that, for once, he was magnificently attune to life and that everything about him was radiating a brightness and a glamour he might never know again.

A low, pale oblong detached itself suddenly from the darkness of the Island, spitting forth the reverberate sound of a racing motor-boat. Two white streamers of cleft water rolled themselves out behind it and almost immediately the boat was beside him, drowning out the hot tinkle of the piano in the drone of its spray. Dexter raising himself on his arms was aware of a figure standing at the wheel, of two dark eyes regarding him over the lengthening space of water—then the boat had gone by and was sweeping in an immense and purposeless circle of spray round and round in the middle of the lake. With equal eccentricity one of the circles flattened out and headed back toward the raft.

"Who's that?" she called, shutting off her motor. She was so near now that Dexter could see her bathing-suit, which consisted apparently of pink rompers.

The nose of the boat bumped the raft, and as the latter tilted rakishly he was precipitated toward her. With different degrees of interest they recognized each other.

"Aren't you one of those men we played through this afternoon?" she demanded.

He was.

"Well, do you know how to drive a motor-boat? Because if you do I wish you'd drive this one so I can ride on the surf-board behind. My name is Judy Jones"—she favored him with an absurd smirk—rather, what tried to be a smirk, for, twist her mouth as she might, it was not grotesque, it was merely beautiful—"and I live in a house over there on the Island, and in that house there is a man waiting for me. When he drove up at the door I drove out of the dock because he says I'm his ideal."

There was a fish jumping and a star shining and the lights around the lake were gleaming. Dexter sat beside Judy Jones and she explained how her boat was driven. Then she was in the water, swimming to the floating surfboard with a sinuous crawl. Watching her was without effort to the eye, watching a branch waving or a sea-gull flying. Her arms, burned to butternut, moved sinuously among the dull platinum ripples, elbow appearing first, casting the forearm back with a cadence of falling water, then reaching out and down, stabbing a path ahead.

They moved out into the lake; turning, Dexter saw that she was kneeling on the low rear of the now uptilted surfboard.

"Go faster," she called, "fast as it'll go."

Obediently he jammed the lever forward and the white spray mounted at the bow. When he looked around again the girl was standing up on the rushing board, her arms spread wide, her eyes lifted toward the moon.

"It's awful cold," she shouted. "What's your name?"

He told her.

"Well, why don't you come to dinner to-morrow night?" His heart turned over like the fly-wheel of the boat, and, for the second time, her casual whim gave a new direction to his life.

III

Next evening while he waited for her to come downstairs, Dexter peopled the soft deep summer room and the sun-porch that opened from it with the men who had already loved Judy Jones. He knew the sort of men they were—the men who when he first went to college had entered from the great prep schools with graceful clothes and the deep tan of healthy summers. He had seen that, in one sense, he was better than these men. He was newer and stronger. Yet in acknowledging to himself that he wished his children to be like them he was admitting that he was but the rough, strong stuff from which they eternally sprang.

When the time had come for him to wear good clothes, he had known who were the best tailors in America, and the best tailors in America had made him the suit he wore this evening. He had acquired that particular reserve peculiar to his university, that set it off from other universities. He recognized the value to him of such a mannerism and he had adopted it; he knew that to be careless in dress and manner required more confidence than to be careful. But carelessness was for his children. His mother's name had been Krimelich. She was a Bohemian of the peasant class and she had talked broken English to the end of her days. Her son must keep to the set patterns.

At a little after seven Judy Jones came down-stairs. She wore a blue silk afternoon dress, and he was disappointed at first that she had not put on something more elaborate. This feeling was accentuated when, after a brief greeting, she went to the door of a butler's pantry and pushing it open called: "You can serve dinner, Martha." He had rather expected that a butler would announce dinner, that there would be a cocktail. Then he put these thoughts behind him as they sat down side by side on a lounge and looked at each other.

"Father and mother won't be here," she said thoughtfully.

He remembered the last time he had seen her father, and he was glad the parents were not to be here to-night—they might wonder who he was. He had been born in Keeble, a Minnesota village fifty miles farther north, and he always gave Keeble as his home instead of Black Bear Village. Country towns were well enough to come from if they weren't inconveniently in sight and used as footstools by fashionable lakes.

They talked of his university, which she had visited frequently during the past two years, and of the near-by city which supplied Sherry Island with its patrons, and whither Dexter would return next day to his prospering laundries.

During dinner she slipped into a moody depression which gave Dexter a feeling of uneasiness. Whatever petulance she uttered in her throaty voice worried him. Whatever she smiled at—at him, at a chicken liver, at nothing—it disturbed him that her smile could have no root in mirth, or even in amusement. When the scarlet corners of her lips curved down, it was less a smile than an invitation to a kiss.

Then, after dinner, she led him out on the dark sun-porch and deliberately changed the atmosphere.

"Do you mind if I weep a little?" she said.

"I'm afraid I'm boring you," he responded quickly.

"You're not. I like you. But I've just had a terrible afternoon. There was a man I cared about, and this afternoon he told me out of a clear sky that he was poor as a church-mouse. He'd never even hinted it before. Does this sound horribly mundane?"

"Perhaps he was afraid to tell you."

"Suppose he was," she answered. "He didn't start right. You see, if I'd thought of him as poor—well, I've been mad about loads of poor men, and fully intended to marry them all. But in this case, I hadn't thought of him that way, and my interest in him wasn't strong enough to survive the shock. As if a girl calmly informed her fiancé that she was a widow. He might not object to widows, but—"

"Let's start right," she interrupted herself suddenly. "Who are you, anyhow?"

For a moment Dexter hesitated. Then:

"I'm nobody," he announced. "My career is largely a matter of futures."

"Are you poor?"

"No," he said frankly, "I'm probably making more money than any man my age in the Northwest. I know that's an obnoxious remark, but you advised me to start right."

There was a pause. Then she smiled and the corners of her mouth drooped and an almost imperceptible sway brought her closer to him, looking up into his eyes. A lump rose in Dexter's throat, and he waited breathless for the experiment, facing the unpredictable compound that would form mysteriously from the elements of their lips. Then he saw—she communicated her excitement to him, lavishly, deeply, with kisses that were not a promise but a fulfillment. They aroused in him not hunger demanding renewal but surfeit that would demand more surfeit . . . kisses that were like charity, creating want by holding back nothing at all.

It did not take him many hours to decide that he had wanted Judy Jones ever since he was a proud, desirous little boy.

IV

It began like that—and continued, with varying shades of intensity, on such a note right up to the dénouement. Dexter surrendered a part of himself to the most direct and unprincipled personality with which he had ever come in contact. Whatever Judy wanted, she went after with the full pressure of her charm. There was no divergence of method, no jockeying for position or premeditation of effects—there was a very little mental side to any of her affairs. She simply made men conscious to the highest degree of her physical loveliness. Dexter had no desire to change her. Her deficiencies were knit up with a passionate energy that transcended and justified them.

When, as Judy's head lay against his shoulder that first night, she whispered, "I don't know what's the matter with me. Last night I thought I was in love with a man and to-night I think I'm in love with you—"—it seemed to him a beautiful and romantic thing to say. It was the exquisite excitability that for the moment he controlled and owned. But a week later he was compelled to view this same quality in a different light. She took him in her roadster to a picnic supper, and after supper she disappeared, likewise in her roadster, with another man. Dexter became enormously upset and was scarcely able to be decently civil to the other people present. When she assured him that she had not kissed the other man, he knew she was lying—yet he was glad that she had taken the trouble to lie to him.

He was, as he found before the summer ended, one of a varying dozen who circulated about her. Each of them had at one time been favored above all others—about half of them still basked in the solace of occasional sentimental revivals. Whenever one showed signs of dropping out through long neglect, she granted him a brief honeyed hour, which encouraged him to tag along for a year or so longer. Judy made these forays upon the helpless and defeated without malice, indeed half unconscious that there was anything mischievous in what she did.

When a new man came to town every one dropped out—dates were automatically cancelled.

The helpless part of trying to do anything about it was that she did it all herself. She was not a girl who could be "won" in the kinetic sense—she was proof against cleverness, she was proof against charm; if any of these assailed her too strongly she would immediately resolve the affair to a physical basis, and under the magic of her physical splendor the strong as well as the brilliant played her game and not their own. She was entertained only by the gratification of her desires and by the direct exercise of her own charm. Perhaps from so much youthful love, so many youthful lovers, she had come, in self-defense, to nourish herself wholly from within.

Succeeding Dexter's first exhilaration came restlessness and dissatisfaction. The helpless ecstasy of losing himself in her was opiate rather than tonic. It was fortunate for his work during the winter that those moments of ecstasy came infrequently. Early in their acquaintance it had seemed for a while that there was a deep and spontaneous mutual attraction—that first August, for example—three days of long evenings on her dusky veranda, of strange wan kisses through the late afternoon, in shadowy alcoves or behind the protecting trellises of the garden arbors, of mornings when she was fresh as a dream and almost shy at meeting him in the clarity of the rising day. There was all the ecstasy of an engagement about it, sharpened by his realization that there was no engagement. It was during those three days that, for the first time, he had asked her to marry him. She said "maybe some day," she said "kiss me," she said "I'd like to marry you," she said "I love you"—she said—nothing.

The three days were interrupted by the arrival of a New York man who visited at her house for half September. To Dexter's agony, rumor engaged them. The man was the son of the president of a great trust company. But at the end of a month it was reported that Judy was yawning. At a dance one night she sat all evening in a motor-boat with a local beau, while the New Yorker searched the club for her frantically. She told the local beau that she was bored with her visitor, and two days later he left. She was seen with him at the station, and it was reported that he looked very mournful indeed.

On this note the summer ended. Dexter was twenty-four, and he found himself increasingly in a position to do as he wished. He joined two clubs in the city and lived at one of them. Though he was by no means an integral part of the stag-lines at these clubs, he managed to be on hand at dances where Judy Jones was likely to appear. He could have gone out socially as much as he liked—he was an eligible young man, now, and popular with down-town fathers. His confessed devotion to Judy Jones had rather solidified his position. But he had no social aspirations and rather despised the dancing men who were always on tap for the Thursday or

Saturday parties and who filled in at dinners with the younger married set. Already he was playing with the idea of going East to New York. He wanted to take Judy Jones with him. No disillusion as to the world in which she had grown up could cure his illusion as to her desirability.

Remember that—for only in the light of it can what he did for her be understood.

Eighteen months after he first met Judy Jones he became engaged to another girl. Her name was Irene Scheerer, and her father was one of the men who had always believed in Dexter. Irene was light-haired and sweet and honorable, and a little stout, and she had two suitors whom she pleasantly relinquished when Dexter formally asked her to marry him.

Summer, fall, winter, spring, another summer, another fall—so much he had given of his active life to the incorrigible lips of Judy Jones. She had treated him with interest, with encouragement, with malice, with indifference, with contempt. She had inflicted on him the innumerable little slights and indignities possible in such a case —as if in revenge for having ever cared for him at all. She had beckoned him and yawned at him and beckoned him again and he had responded often with bitterness and narrowed eyes. She had brought him ecstatic happiness and intolerable agony of spirit. She had caused him untold inconvenience and not a little trouble. She had insulted him, and she had ridden over him, and she had played his interest in her against his interest in his work—for fun. She had done everything to him except to criticise him—this she had not done—it seemed to him only because it might have sullied the utter indifference she manifested and sincerely felt toward him.

When autumn had come and gone again it occurred to him that he could not have Judy Jones. He had to beat this into his mind but he convinced himself at last. He lay awake at night for a while and argued it over. He told himself the trouble and the pain she had caused him, he enumerated her glaring deficiencies as a wife. Then he said to himself that he loved her, and after a while he fell asleep. For a week, lest he imagine her husky voice over the telephone or her eyes opposite him at lunch, he worked hard and late, and at night he went to his office and plotted out his years.

At the end of a week he went to a dance and cut in on her

once. For almost the first time since they had met he did not ask her
to sit out with him or tell her that she was lovely. It hurt him that
she did not miss these things—that was all. He was not jealous
when he saw that there was a new man to-night. He had been
hardened against jealousy long before.

He stayed late at the dance. He sat for an hour with Irene
Scheerer and talked about books and about music. He knew very
little about either. But he was beginning to be master of his own
time now, and he had a rather priggish notion that he—the young
and already fabulously successful Dexter Green—should know more
about such things.

That was in October, when he was twenty-five. In January,
Dexter and Irene became engaged. It was to be announced in June,
and they were to be married three months later.

The Minnesota winter prolonged itself interminably, and it was
almost May when the winds came soft and the snow ran down into
Black Bear Lake at last. For the first time in over a year Dexter was
enjoying a certain tranquillity of spirit. Judy Jones had been in
Florida, and afterward in Hot Springs, and somewhere she had been
engaged, and somewhere she had broken it off. At first, when Dexter
had definitely given her up, it had made him sad that people still
linked them together and asked for news of her, but when he began
to be placed at dinner next to Irene Scheerer people didn't ask him
about her any more—they told him about her. He ceased to be an
authority on her.

May at last. Dexter walked the streets at night when the darkness was damp as rain, wondering that so soon, with so little done,
so much of ecstasy had gone from him. May one year back had
been marked by Judy's poignant, unforgivable, yet forgiven
turbulence—it had been one of those rare times when he fancied
she had grown to care for him. That old penny's worth of happiness
he had spent for this bushel of content. He knew that Irene would
be no more than a curtain spread behind him, a hand moving
among gleaming teacups, a voice calling to children . . . fire and
loveliness were gone, the magic of nights and the wonder of the
varying hours and seasons . . . slender lips, down-turning, dropping
to his lips and bearing him up into a heaven of eyes. . . . The thing
was deep in him. He was too strong and alive for it to die lightly.

In the middle of May when the weather balanced for a few days on the thin bridge that led to deep summer he turned in one night at Irene's house. Their engagement was to be announced in a week now—no one would be surprised at it. And to-night they would sit together on the lounge at the University Club and look on for an hour at the dancers. It gave him a sense of solidity to go with her— she was so sturdily popular, so intensely "great."

He mounted the steps of the brownstone house and stepped inside.

"Irene," he called.

Mrs. Scheerer came out of the living-room to meet him.

"Dexter," she said, "Irene's gone up-stairs with a splitting head-ache. She wanted to go with you but I made her go to bed."

"Nothing serious, I—"

"Oh, no. She's going to play golf with you in the morning. You can spare her for just one night, can't you, Dexter?"

Her smile was kind. She and Dexter liked each other. In the living-room he talked for a moment before he said good-night.

Returning to the University Club, where he had rooms, he stood in the doorway for a moment and watched the dancers. He leaned against the door-post, nodded at a man or two—yawned.

"Hello, darling."

The familiar voice at his elbow startled him. Judy Jones had left a man and crossed the room to him—Judy Jones, a slender enamelled doll in cloth of gold: gold in a band at her head, gold in two slipper points at her dress's hem. The fragile glow of her face seemed to blossom as she smiled at him. A breeze of warmth and light blew through the room. His hands in the pockets of his dinner-jacket tightened spasmodically. He was filled with a sudden excitement.

"When did you get back?" he asked casually.

"Come here and I'll tell you about it."

She turned and he followed her. She had been away—he could have wept at the wonder of her return. She had passed through enchanted streets, doing things that were like provocative music. All mysterious happenings, all fresh and quickening hopes, had gone away with her, come back with her now.

She turned in the doorway.

"Have you a car here? If you haven't, I have."

"I have a coupé."

In then, with a rustle of golden cloth. He slammed the door. Into so many cars she had stepped—like this—like that—her back against the leather, so—her elbow resting on the door—waiting. She would have been soiled long since had there been anything to soil her—except herself—but this was her own self outpouring.

With an effort he forced himself to start the car and back into the street. This was nothing, he must remember. She had done this before, and he had put her behind him, as he would have crossed a bad account from his books.

He drove slowly down-town and, affecting abstraction, traversed the deserted streets of the business section, peopled here and there where a movie was giving out its crowd or where consumptive or pugilistic youth lounged in front of pool halls. The clink of glasses and the slap of hands on the bars issued from saloons, cloisters of glazed glass and dirty yellow light.

She was watching him closely and the silence was embarrassing, yet in this crisis he could find no casual word with which to profane the hour. At a convenient turning he began to zigzag back toward the University Club.

"Have you missed me?" she asked suddenly.

"Everybody missed you."

He wondered if she knew of Irene Scheerer. She had been back only a day—her absence had been almost contemporaneous with his engagement.

"What a remark!" Judy laughed sadly—without sadness. She looked at him searchingly. He became absorbed in the dashboard.

"You're handsomer than you used to be," she said thoughtfully. "Dexter, you have the most rememberable eyes."

He could have laughed at this, but he did not laugh. It was the sort of thing that was said to sophomores. Yet it stabbed at him.

"I'm awfully tired of everything, darling." She called everyone darling, endowing the endearment with careless, individual cama-raderie. "I wish you'd marry me."

The directness of this confused him. He should have told her now that he was going to marry another girl, but he could not tell her. He could as easily have sworn that he had never loved her.

"I think we'd get along," she continued, on the same note, "unless probably you've forgotten me and fallen in love with another girl."

Her confidence was obviously enormous. She had said, in effect, that she found such a thing impossible to believe, that if it were true he had merely committed a childish indiscretion—and probably to show off. She would forgive him, because it was not a matter of any moment but rather something to be brushed aside lightly.

"Of course you could never love anybody but me," she continued, "I like the way you love me. Oh, Dexter, have you forgotten last year?"

"No, I haven't forgotten."

"Neither have I!"

Was she sincerely moved—or was she carried along by the wave of her own acting?

"I wish we could be like that again," she said, and he forced himself to answer:

"I don't think we can."

"I suppose not. . . . I hear you're giving Irene Scheerer a violent rush."

There was not the faintest emphasis on the name, yet Dexter was suddenly ashamed.

"Oh, take me home," cried Judy suddenly; "I don't want to go back to that idiotic dance—with those children."

Then, as he turned up the street that led to the residence district, Judy began to cry quietly to herself. He had never seen her cry before.

The dark street lightened, the dwellings of the rich loomed up around them, he stopped his coupé in front of the great white bulk of the Mortimer Joneses' house, somnolent, gorgeous, drenched with the splendor of the damp moonlight. Its solidity startled him. The strong walls, the steel of the girders, the breadth and beam and pomp of it were there only to bring out the contrast with the young beauty beside him. It was sturdy to accentuate her slightness—as if to show what a breeze could be generated by a butterfly's wing.

He sat perfectly quiet, his nerves in wild clamor, afraid that if he moved he would find her irresistibly in his arms. Two tears had rolled down her wet face and trembled on her upper lip.

"I'm more beautiful than anybody else," she said brokenly, "why can't I be happy?" Her moist eyes tore at his stability—her mouth turned slowly downward with an exquisite sadness: "I'd like to marry you if you'll have me, Dexter. I suppose you think I'm not worth having, but I'll be so beautiful for you, Dexter."

A million phrases of anger, pride, passion, hatred, tenderness fought on his lips. Then a perfect wave of emotion washed over him, carrying off with it a sediment of wisdom, of convention, of doubt, of honor. This was his girl who was speaking, his own, his beautiful, his pride.

"Won't you come in?" He heard her draw in her breath sharply. Waiting.

"All right," his voice was trembling, "I'll come in."

V

It was strange that neither when it was over nor a long time afterward did he regret that night. Looking at it from the perspective of ten years, the fact that Judy's flare for him endured just one month seemed of little importance. Nor did it matter that by his yielding he subjected himself to a deeper agony in the end and gave serious hurt to Irene Scheerer and to Irene's parents, who had befriended him. There was nothing sufficiently pictorial about Irene's grief to stamp itself on his mind.

Dexter was at bottom hard-minded. The attitude of the city on his action was of no importance to him, not because he was going to leave the city, but because any outside attitude on the situation seemed superficial. He was completely indifferent to popular opinion. Nor, when he had seen that it was no use, that he did not possess in himself the power to move fundamentally or to hold Judy Jones, did he bear any malice toward her. He loved her, and he would love her until the day he was too old for loving—but he could not have her. So he tasted the deep pain that is reserved only for the strong, just as he had tasted for a little while the deep happiness.

Even the ultimate falsity of the grounds upon which Judy terminated the engagement that she did not want to "take him away" from Irene—Judy who had wanted nothing else—did not revolt him. He was beyond any revulsion or any amusement.

He went East in February with the intention of selling out his laundries and settling in New York—but the war came to America in March and changed his plans. He returned to the West, handed over the management of the business to his partner, and went into the first officers' training-camp in late April. He was one of those young thousands who greeted the war with a certain amount of relief, welcoming the liberation from webs of tangled emotion.

VI

This story is not his biography, remember, although things creep into it which have nothing to do with those dreams he had when he was young. We are almost done with them and with him now. There is only one more incident to be related here, and it happens seven years farther on.

It took place in New York, where he had done well—so well that there were no barriers too high for him. He was thirty-two years old, and, except for one flying trip immediately after the war, he had not been West in seven years. A man named Devlin from Detroit came into his office to see him in a business way, and then and there this incident occurred, and closed out, so to speak, this particular side of his life.

"So you're from the Middle West," said the man Devlin with careless curiosity. "That's funny—I thought men like you were probably born and raised on Wall Street. You know—wife of one of my best friends in Detroit came from your city. I was an usher at the wedding."

Dexter waited with no apprehension of what was coming.

"Judy Simms," said Devlin with no particular interest; "Judy Jones she was once."

"Yes, I knew her." A dull impatience spread over him. He had heard, of course, that she was married—perhaps deliberately he had heard no more.

"Awfully nice girl," brooded Devlin meaninglessly, "I'm sort of sorry for her."

"Why?" Something in Dexter was alert, receptive, at once.

"Oh, Lud Simms has gone to pieces in a way. I don't mean he ill-uses her, but he drinks and runs around—"

"Doesn't she run around?"

"No. Stays at home with her kids."

"Oh."

"She's a little too old for him," said Devlin.

"Too old!" cried Dexter. "Why, man, she's only twenty-seven."

He was possessed with a wild notion of rushing out into the streets and taking a train to Detroit. He rose to his feet spasmodically.

"I guess you're busy," Devlin apologized quickly. "I didn't realize—"

"No, I'm not busy," said Dexter, steadying his voice. "I'm not busy at all. Not busy at all. Did you say she was—twenty-seven? No, I said she was twenty-seven."

"Yes, you did," agreed Devlin dryly.

"Go on, then. Go on."

"What do you mean?"

"About Judy Jones."

Devlin looked at him helplessly.

"Well, that's—I told you all there is to it. He treats her like the devil. Oh, they're not going to get divorced or anything. When he's particularly outrageous she forgives him. In fact, I'm inclined to think she loves him. She was a pretty girl when she first came to Detroit."

A pretty girl! The phrase struck Dexter as ludicrous.

"Isn't she—a pretty girl, any more?"

"Oh, she's all right."

"Look here," said Dexter, sitting down suddenly. "I don't understand. You say she was a 'pretty girl' and now you say she's 'all right.' I don't understand what you mean—Judy Jones wasn't a pretty girl, at all. She was a great beauty. Why, I knew her, I knew her. She was—"

Devlin laughed pleasantly.

"I'm not trying to start a row," he said. "I think Judy's a nice girl and I like her. I can't understand how a man like Lud Simms could fall madly in love with her, but he did." Then he added: "Most of the women like her."

Dexter looked closely at Devlin, thinking wildly that there must be a reason for this, some insensitivity in the man or some private malice.

"Lots of women fade just like *that*," Devlin snapped his fingers. "You must have seen it happen. Perhaps I've forgotten how pretty she was at her wedding. I've seen her so much since then, you see. She has nice eyes."

A sort of dullness settled down upon Dexter. For the first time in his life he felt like getting very drunk. He knew that he was laughing loudly at something Devlin had said, but he did not know what it was or why it was funny. When, in a few minutes, Devlin went he lay down on his lounge and looked out the window at the New York sky-line into which the sun was sinking in dull lovely shades of pink and gold.

He had thought that having nothing else to lose he was invulnerable at last—but he knew that he had just lost something more, as surely as if he had married Judy Jones and seen her fade away before his eyes.

The dream was gone. Something had been taken from him. In a sort of panic he pushed the palms of his hands into his eyes and tried to bring up a picture of the waters lapping on Sherry Island and the moonlit veranda, and gingham on the golf-links and the dry sun and the gold color of her neck's soft down. And her mouth damp to his kisses and her eyes plaintive with melancholy and her freshness like new fine linen in the morning. Why, these things were no longer in the world! They had existed and they existed no longer.

For the first time in years the tears were streaming down his face. But they were for himself now. He did not care about mouth and eyes and moving hands. He wanted to care, and he could not care. For he had gone away and he could never go back any more. The gates were closed, the sun was gone down, and there was no beauty but the gray beauty of steel that withstands all time. Even the grief he could have borne was left behind in the country of illusion, of youth, of the richness of life, where his winter dreams had flourished.

"Long ago," he said, "long ago, there was something in me, but now that thing is gone. Now that thing is gone, that thing is gone. I cannot cry. I cannot care. That thing will come back no more."

WILLIAM FAULKNER

A Rose for Emily

HEN MISS EMILY GRIERSON died, our whole town went to her funeral: the men through a sort of respectful affection for a fallen monument, the women mostly out of curiosity to see the inside of her house, which no one save an old manservant—a combined gardener and cook—had seen in at least ten years.

It was a big, squarish frame house that had once been white, decorated with cupolas and spires and scrolled balconies in the heavily lightsome style of the seventies, set on what had once been our most select street. But garages and cotton gins had encroached and obliterated even the august names of that neighborhood; only Miss Emily's house was left, lifting its stubborn and coquettish decay above the cotton wagons and the gasoline pumps—an eyesore among eyesores. And now Miss Emily had gone to join the representatives of those august names where they lay in the cedar-bemused cemetery among the ranked and anonymous graves of Union and Confederate soldiers who fell at the battle of Jefferson.

Alive, Miss Emily had been a tradition, a duty, and a care; a sort of hereditary obligation upon the town, dating from that day in 1894 when Colonel Sartoris, the mayor—he who fathered the edict that no Negro woman should appear on the streets without an apron—remitted her taxes, the dispensation dating from the death of her father on into perpetuity. Not that Miss Emily would have accepted charity. Colonel Sartoris invented an involved tale to the effect that Miss Emily's father had loaned money to the town, which the town, as a matter of business, preferred this way of repaying. Only a man of Colonel Sartoris' generation and thought could have invented it, and only a woman could have believed it.

When the next generation, with its more modern ideas, became mayors and aldermen, this arrangement created some little dissatisfaction. On the first of the year they mailed her a tax notice. February came, and there was no reply. They wrote her a formal letter, asking her to call at the sheriff's office at her convenience. A week later the mayor wrote her himself, offering to call or to send his car for her, and received in reply a note on paper of an archaic shape, in a thin, flowing calligraphy in faded ink, to the effect that she no longer went out at all. The tax notice was also enclosed, without comment.

They called a special meeting of the Board of Aldermen. A deputation waited upon her, knocked at the door through which no visitor had passed since she ceased giving china-painting lessons eight or ten years earlier. They were admitted by the old Negro into a dim hall from which a stairway mounted into still more shadow. It smelled of dust and disuse—a close, dank smell. The Negro led them into the parlor. It was furnished in heavy, leather-covered furniture. When the Negro opened the blinds of one window, they could see that the leather was cracked; and when they sat down, a faint dust rose sluggishly about their thighs, spinning with slow motes in the single sun-ray. On a tarnished gilt easel before the fireplace stood a crayon portrait of Miss Emily's father.

They rose when she entered—a small, fat woman in black, with a thin gold chain descending to her waist and vanishing into her belt, leaning on an ebony cane with a tarnished gold head. Her skeleton was small and spare; perhaps that was why what would have been merely plumpness in another was obesity in her. She looked bloated, like a body long submerged in motionless water, and of that pallid hue. Her eyes, lost in the fatty ridges of her face, looked like two small pieces of coal pressed into a lump of dough as they moved from one face to another while the visitors stated their errand.

She did not ask them to sit. She just stood in the door and listened quietly until the spokesman came to a stumbling halt.

Then they could hear the invisible watch ticking at the end of the gold chain.

Her voice was dry and cold. "I have no taxes in Jefferson. Colonel Sartoris explained it to me. Perhaps one of you can gain access to the city records and satisfy yourselves."

"But we have. We are the city authorities, Miss Emily. Didn't you get a notice from the sheriff, signed by him?"

"I received a paper, yes," Miss Emily said. "Perhaps he considers himself the sheriff. . . . I have no taxes in Jefferson."

"But there is nothing on the books to show that, you see. We must go by the—"

"See Colonel Sartoris. I have no taxes in Jefferson."

"But, Miss Emily—"

"See Colonel Sartoris." (Colonel Sartoris had been dead almost ten years.) "I have no taxes in Jefferson. Tobe!" The Negro appeared. "Show these gentleman out."

II

So she vanquished them, horse and foot, just as she had vanquished their fathers thirty years before about the smell. That was two years after her father's death and a short time after her sweetheart—the one we believed would marry her—had deserted her. After her father's death she went out very little; after her sweetheart went away, people hardly saw her at all. A few of the ladies had the temerity to call, but were not received, and the only sign of life about the place was the Negro man—a young man then— going in and out with a market basket.

"Just as if a man—any man—could keep a kitchen properly," the ladies said; so they were not surprised when the smell developed. It was another link between the gross, teeming world and the high and mighty Griersons.

A neighbor, a woman, complained to the mayor, Judge Stevens, eighty years old.

"But what will you have me do about it, madam?" he said.

"Why, send her word to stop it," the woman said. "Isn't there a law?"

"I'm sure that won't be necessary," Judge Stevens said. "It's probably just a snake or a rat that nigger of hers killed in the yard. I'll speak to him about it."

The next day he received two more complaints, one from a man who came in diffident deprecation. "We really must do something about it, Judge. I'd be the last one in the world to bother Miss Emily, but we've got to do something." That night the Board of Aldermen met—three graybeards and one younger man, a member of the rising generation.

"It's simple enough," he said. "Send her word to have her place cleaned up. Give her a certain time to do it in, and if she don't . . ."

"Dammit, sir," Judge Stevens said, "will you accuse a lady to her face of smelling bad?"

So the next night, after midnight, four men crossed Miss Emily's lawn and slunk about the house like burglars, sniffing along the base of the brickwork and at the cellar openings while one of them performed a regular sowing motion with his hand out of a sack slung from his shoulder. They broke open the cellar door and sprinkled lime there, and in all the outbuildings. As they recrossed the lawn, a window that had been dark was lighted and Miss Emily sat in it, the light behind her, and her upright torso motionless as that of an idol. They crept quietly across the lawn and into the shadow of the locusts that lined the street. After a week or two the smell went away.

That was when people had begun to feel really sorry for her. People in our town, remembering how old lady Wyatt, her great-aunt, had gone completely crazy at last, believed that the Griersons held themselves a little too high for what they really were. None of the young men were quite good enough for Miss Emily and such. We had long thought of them as a tableau: Miss Emily a slender figure in white in the background, her father a spraddled silhouette in the foreground, his back to her and clutching a horsewhip, the two of them framed by the back-flung front door. So when she got to be thirty and was still single, we were not pleased exactly, but vindicated; even with insanity in the family she wouldn't have turned down all of her chances if they had really materialized.

When her father died, it got about that the house was all that was left to her; and in a way, people were glad. At last they could pity Miss Emily. Being left alone, and a pauper, she had become humanized. Now she too would know the old thrill and the old despair of a penny more or less.

The day after his death all the ladies prepared to call at the house and offer condolence and aid, as is our custom. Miss Emily met them at the door, dressed as usual and with no trace of grief on her face. She told them that her father was not dead. She did that for three days, with the ministers calling on her, and the doctors, trying to persuade her to let them dispose of the body. Just as they were about to resort to law and force, she broke down, and they buried her father quickly.

We did not say she was crazy then. We believed she had to do that. We remembered all the young men her father had driven away, and we knew that with nothing left, she would have to cling to that which had robbed her, as people will.

III

She was sick for a long time. When we saw her again, her hair was cut short, making her look like a girl, with a vague resemblance to those angels in colored church windows—sort of tragic and serene.

The town had just let the contracts for paving the sidewalks, and in the summer after her father's death they began the work. The construction company came with niggers and mules and machinery, and a foreman named Homer Barron, a Yankee—a big, dark, ready man, with a big voice and eyes lighter than his face. The little boys would follow in groups to hear him cuss the niggers, and the niggers singing in time to the rise and fall of picks. Pretty soon he knew everybody in town. Whenever you heard a lot of laughing anywhere about the square, Homer Barron would be in the center of the group. Presently we began to see him and Miss Emily on Sunday afternoons driving in the yellow-wheeled buggy and the matched team of bays from the livery stable.

At first we were glad that Miss Emily would have an interest, because the ladies all said, "Of course a Grierson would not think seriously of a Northerner, a day laborer." But there were still others, older people, who said that even grief could not cause a real lady to forget *noblesse oblige*—without calling it *noblesse oblige*. They just said, "Poor Emily. Her kinsfolk should come to her." She had some kin in Alabama; but years ago her father had fallen out with them over the estate of old lady Wyatt, the crazy woman, and there was no communication between the two families. They had not even been represented at the funeral.

And as soon as the old people said, "Poor Emily," the whispering began. "Do you suppose it's really so?" they said to one another. "Of course it is. What else could . . ." This behind their hands; rustling of craned silk and satin behind jalousies closed upon the sun of Sunday afternoon as the thin, swift clop-clop-clop of the matched team passed: "Poor Emily."

She carried her head high enough—even when we believed that she was fallen. It was as if she demanded more than ever the recognition of her dignity as the last Grierson; as if it had wanted that touch of earthiness to reaffirm her imperviousness. Like when she bought the rat poison, the arsenic. That was over a year after they had begun to say "Poor Emily," and while the two female cousins were visiting her.

"I want some poison," she said to the druggist. She was over thirty then, still a slight woman, though thinner than usual, with cold, haughty black eyes in a face the flesh of which was strained across the temples and about the eyesockets as you imagine a lighthouse-keeper's face ought to look. "I want some poison," she said.

"Yes, Miss Emily. What kind? For rats and such? I'd recom—"

"I want the best you have. I don't care what kind."

The druggist named several. "They'll kill anything up to an elephant. But what you want is—"

"Arsenic," Miss Emily said. "Is that a good one?"

"Is . . . arsenic? Yes, ma'am. But what you want—"

"I want arsenic."

The druggist looked down at her. She looked back at him, erect, her face like a strained flag. "Why, of course," the druggist said. "If that's what you want. But the law requires you to tell what you are going to use it for."

Miss Emily just stared at him, her head tilted back in order to look him eye for eye, until he looked away and went and got the arsenic and wrapped it up. The Negro delivery boy brought her the package; the druggist didn't come back. When she opened the package at home there was written on the box, under the skull and bones: "For rats."

IV

So the next day we all said, "She will kill herself"; and we said it would be the best thing. When she had first begun to be seen with Homer Barron, we had said, "She will marry him." Then we said, "She will persuade him yet," because Homer himself had remarked —he liked men, and it was known that he drank with the younger men in the Elks' Club—that he was not a marrying man. Later we said, "Poor Emily," behind the jalousies as they passed on Sunday afternoon in the glittering buggy, Miss Emily with her head high and Homer Barron with his hat cocked and a cigar in his teeth, reins and whip in a yellow glove.

Then some of the ladies began to say that it was a disgrace to the town and a bad example to the young people. The men did not want to interfere, but at last the ladies forced the Baptist minister —Miss Emily's people were Episcopal—to call upon her. He would never divulge what happened during that interview, but he refused to go back again. The next Sunday they again drove about the streets, and the following day the minister's wife wrote to Miss Emily's relations in Alabama.

So she had blood-kin under her roof again and we sat back to watch developments. At first nothing happened. Then we were sure that they were to be married. We learned that Miss Emily had been to the jeweler's and ordered a man's toilet set in silver, with the letters H.B. on each piece. Two days later we learned that she had bought a complete outfit of men's clothing, including a nightshirt, and we said, "They are married." We were really glad. We were glad because the two female cousins were even more Grierson than Miss Emily had ever been.

So we were not surprised when Homer Barron—the streets had been finished some time since—was gone. We were a little disappointed that there was not a public blowing-off, but we believed that he had gone on to prepare for Miss Emily's coming, or to give her a chance to get rid of the cousins. (By that time it was a cabal, and we were all Miss Emily's allies to help circumvent the cousins.) Sure enough, after another week they departed. And, as we had expected all along, within three days Homer Barron was back in town. A neighbor saw the Negro man admit him at the kitchen door at dusk one evening.

And that was the last we saw of Homer Barron. And of Miss Emily for some time. The Negro man went in and out with the market basket, but the front door remained closed. Now and then we would see her at a window for a moment, as the men did that night when they sprinkled the lime, but for almost six months she did not appear on the streets. Then we knew that this was to be expected too; as if that quality of her father which had thwarted her woman's life so many times had been too virulent and too furious to die.

When we next saw Miss Emily, she had grown fat and her hair was turning gray. During the next few years it grew grayer and grayer until it attained an even pepper-and-salt iron-gray, when it ceased turning. Up to the day of her death at seventy-four it was still that vigorous iron-gray, like the hair of an active man.

From that time on her front door remained closed, save for a period of six or seven years, when she was about forty, during which she gave lessons in china-painting. She fitted up a studio in one of the downstairs rooms, where the daughters and grand-daughters of Colonel Sartoris' contemporaries were sent to her with the same regularity and in the same spirit that they were sent on Sundays with a twenty-five cent piece for the collection plate. Meanwhile her taxes had been remitted.

Then the newer generation became the backbone and the spirit of the town, and the painting pupils grew up and fell away and did not send their children to her with boxes of color and tedious brushes and pictures cut from the ladies' magazines. The front door closed upon the last one and remained closed for good. When the town got free postal delivery Miss Emily alone refused to let them fasten the metal numbers above her door and attach a mailbox to it. She would not listen to them.

Daily, monthly, yearly we watched the Negro grow grayer and more stooped, going in and out with the market basket. Each

December we sent her a tax notice, which would be returned by
the post office a week later, unclaimed. Now and then we would see
her in one of the downstairs windows—she had evidently shut up
the top floor of the house—like the carven torso of an idol in a
niche, looking or not looking at us, we could never tell which. Thus
she passed from generation to generation—dear, inescapable, impervious, tranquil, and perverse.

And so she died. Fell ill in the house filled with dust and
shadows, with only a doddering Negro man to wait on her. We did
not even know she was sick; we had long since given up trying to
get any information from the Negro. He talked to no one, probably
not even to her, for his voice had grown harsh and rusty, as if from
disuse.

She died in one of the downstairs rooms, in a heavy walnut bed
with a curtain, her gray head propped on a pillow yellow and moldy
with age and lack of sunlight.

V

The Negro met the first of the ladies at the front door and let
them in, with their hushed, sibilant voices and their quick, curious
glances, and then he disappeared. He walked right through the
house and out the back and was not seen again.

The two female cousins came at once. They held the funeral on
the second day, with the town coming to look at Miss Emily beneath a mass of bought flowers, with the crayon face of her father
musing profoundly above the bier and the ladies sibilant and
macabre; and the very old men—some in their brushed Confederate
uniforms—on the porch and the lawn, talking of Miss Emily as if
she had been a contemporary of theirs, believing that they had
danced with her and courted her perhaps, confusing time with its
mathematical progression, as the old do, to whom all the past is
not a diminishing road, but, instead, a huge meadow which no
winter ever quite touches, divided from them now by the narrow
bottleneck of the most recent decade of years.

Already we knew that there was one room in that region above
stairs which no one had seen in forty years, and which would have

to be forced. They waited until Miss Emily was decently in the ground before they opened it.

The violence of breaking down the door seemed to fill this room with pervading dust. A thin, acrid pall as of the tomb seemed to lie everywhere upon this room decked and furnished as for a bridal: upon the valance curtain of faded rose color, upon the rose-shaded lights, upon the dressing table, upon the delicate array of crystal and the man's toilet things backed with tarnished silver, silver so tarnished that the monogram was obscured. Among them lay a collar and tie, as if they had just been removed, which, lifted, left upon the surface a pale crescent in the dust. Upon a chair hung the suit, carefully folded; beneath it the two mute shoes and the discarded socks.

The man himself lay in the bed.

For a long while we just stood there, looking down at the profound and fleshless grin. The body had apparently once lain in the attitude of an embrace, but now the long sleep that outlasts love, that conquers even the grimace of love, had cuckolded him. What was left of him, rotted beneath what was left of the nightshirt, had become inextricable from the bed in which he lay; and upon him and upon the pillow beside him lay that even coating of the patient and biding dust.

Then we noticed that in the second pillow was the indentation of a head. One of us lifted something from it, and leaning forward, that faint and invisible dust dry and acrid in the nostrils, we saw a long strand of iron-gray hair.

FRANK O'CONNOR

My Oedipus Complex

ATHER WAS IN THE army all through the war—the first war, I mean—so, up to the age of five, I never saw much of him, and what I saw did not worry me. Sometimes I woke and there was a big figure in khaki peering down at me in the candlelight. Sometimes in the early morning I heard the slamming of the front door and the clatter of nailed boots down the cobbles of the lane. These were Father's entrances and exits. Like Santa Claus he came and went mysteriously.

In fact, I rather liked his visits, though it was an uncomfortable squeeze between Mother and him when I got into the big bed in the early morning. He smoked, which gave him a pleasant musty smell, and shaved, an operation of astounding interest. Each time he left a trail of souvenirs—model tanks and Gurkha knives with handles made of bullet cases, and German helmets and cap badges and button-sticks, and all sorts of military equipment—carefully stowed away in a long box on top of the wardrobe, in case they ever came in handy. There was a bit of the magpie about Father; he expected everything to come in handy. When his back was turned, Mother let me get a chair and rummage through his treasures. She didn't seem to think so highly of them as he did.

The war was the most peaceful period of my life. The window of my attic faced southeast. My mother had curtained it, but that had small effect. I always woke with the first light and, with all the responsibilities of the previous day melted, feeling myself rather like the sun, ready to illumine and rejoice. Life never seemed so simple and clear and full of possibilities as then. I put my feet out from under the clothes—I called them Mrs. Left and Mrs. Right— and invented dramatic situations for them in which they discussed the problems of the day. At least Mrs. Right did; she was very demonstrative, but I hadn't the same control of Mrs. Left, so she mostly contented herself with nodding agreement.

They discussed what Mother and I should do during the day, what Santa Claus should give a fellow for Christmas, and what steps should be taken to brighten the home. There was that little matter of the baby, for instance. Mother and I could never agree about that. Ours was the only house in the terrace without a new baby, and Mother said we couldn't afford one till Father came back from the war because they cost seventeen and six. That showed how simple she was. The Geneys up the road had a baby, and everyone knew they couldn't afford seventeen and six. It was probably a cheap baby, and Mother wanted something really good, but I felt she was too exclusive. The Geneys' baby would have done us fine.

Having settled my plans for the day, I got up, put a chair under the attic window, and lifted the frame high enough to stick out my head. The window overlooked the front gardens of the terrace behind ours, and beyond these it looked over a deep valley to the tall, red-brick houses terraced up the opposite hillside, which were all still in shadow, while those at our side of the valley were all lit up, though with long strange shadows that made them seem unfamiliar; rigid and painted.

After that I went into Mother's room and climbed into the big bed. She woke and I began to tell her of my schemes. By this time, though I never seem to have noticed it, I was petrified in my nightshirt, and I thawed as I talked until, the last frost melted, I fell asleep beside her and woke again only when I heard her below in the kitchen, making the breakfast.

After breakfast we went into town; heard Mass at St. Augustine's and said a prayer for Father, and did the shopping. If the afternoon was fine we either went for a walk in the country or a visit to Mother's great friend in the convent, Mother St. Dominic. Mother had them all praying for Father, and every night, going to bed, I asked God to send him back safe from the war to us. Little, indeed, did I know what I was praying for!

One morning, I got into the big bed, and there, sure enough, was Father in his usual Santa Claus manner, but later, instead of uniform, he put on his best blue suit, and Mother was as pleased as anything. I saw nothing to be pleased about, because, out of uniform, Father was altogether less interesting, but she only beamed, and explained that our prayers had been answered, and off we went to Mass to thank God for having brought Father safely home.

The irony of it! That very day when he came in to dinner he took off his boots and put on his slippers, donned the dirty old cap he wore about the house to save him from colds, crossed his legs, and began to talk gravely to Mother, who looked anxious. Naturally, I disliked her looking anxious, because it destroyed her good looks, so I interrupted him.

"Just a moment, Larry!" she said gently.

This was only what she said when we had boring visitors, so I attached no importance to it and went on talking.

"Do be quiet, Larry!" she said impatiently. "Don't you hear me talking to Daddy?"

This was the first time I had heard those ominous words, "talking to Daddy," and I couldn't help feeling that if this was how God answered prayers, he couldn't listen to them very attentively.

"Why are you talking to Daddy?" I asked with as great a show of indifference as I could muster.

"Because Daddy and I have business to discuss. Now, don't interrupt again!"

In the afternoon, at Mother's request, Father took me for a walk. This time we went into town instead of out in the country, and I thought at first, in my usual optimistic way, that it might be an improvement. It was nothing of the sort. Father and I had quite different notions of a walk in town. He had no proper interest in trams, ships, and horses, and the only thing that seemed to divert him was talking to fellows as old as himself. When I wanted to stop he simply went on, dragging me behind him by the hand; when he wanted to stop I had no alternative but to do the same. I noticed that it seemed to be a sign that he wanted to stop for a

long time whenever he leaned against a wall. The second time I saw
him do it I got wild. He seemed to be settling himself forever. I
pulled him by the coat and trousers, but, unlike Mother who, if
you were too persistent, got into a wax and said: "Larry, if you
don't behave yourself, I'll give you a good slap," Father had an
extraordinary capacity for amiable inattention. I sized him up and
wondered would I cry, but he seemed to be too remote to be
annoyed even by that. Really, it was like going for a walk with a
mountain! He either ignored the wrenching and pummeling entirely,
or else glanced down with a grin of amusement from his peak. I
had never met anyone so absorbed in himself as he seemed.

At teatime, "talking to Daddy" began again, complicated this
time by the fact that he had an evening paper, and every few minutes he put it down and told Mother something new out of it. I felt
this was foul play. Man for man, I was prepared to compete with
him any time for Mother's attention, but when he had it all made
up for him by other people it left me no chance. Several times I
tried to change the subject without success.

"You must be quiet while Daddy is reading, Larry," Mother
said impatiently.

It was clear that she either genuinely liked talking to Father
better than talking to me, or else that he had some terrible hold on
her which made her afraid to admit the truth.

"Mummy," I said that night when she was tucking me up, "do
you think if I prayed hard God would send Daddy back to the
war?"

She seemed to think about that for a moment.

"No, dear," she said with a smile. "I don't think he would."

"Why wouldn't he, Mummy?"

"Because there isn't a war any longer, dear."

"But, Mummy, couldn't God make another war, if He liked?"

"He wouldn't like to, dear. It's not God who makes wars, but
bad people."

"Oh!" I said.

I was disappointed about that. I began to think that God
wasn't quite what he was cracked up to be.

Next morning I woke at my usual hour, feeling like a bottle of
champagne. I put out my feet and invented a long conversation in

which Mrs. Right talked of the trouble she had with her own father till she put him in the Home. I didn't quite know what the Home was but it sounded the right place for Father. Then I got my chair and stuck my head out of the attic window. Dawn was just breaking, with a guilty air that made me feel I had caught it in the act. My head bursting with stories and schemes, I stumbled in next door, and in the half-darkness scrambled into the big bed. There was no room at Mother's side so I had to get between her and Father. For the time being I had forgotten about him, and for several minutes I sat bolt upright, racking my brains to know what I could do with him. He was taking up more than his fair share of the bed, and I couldn't get comfortable, so I gave him several kicks that made him grunt and stretch. He made room all right, though. Mother waked and felt for me. I settled back comfortably in the warmth of the bed with my thumb in my mouth.

"Mummy!" I hummed, loudly and contentedly.

"Sssh! dear," she whispered. "Don't wake Daddy!"

This was a new development, which threatened to be even more serious than "talking to Daddy." Life without my early-morning conferences was unthinkable.

"Why?" I asked severely.

"Because poor Daddy is tired."

This seemed to me a quite inadequate reason, and I was sickened by the sentimentality of her "poor Daddy." I never liked that sort of gush; it always struck me as insincere.

"Oh!" I said lightly. Then in my most winning tone: "Do you know where I want to go with you today, Mummy?"

"No, dear," she sighed.

"I want to go down the Glen and fish for thornybacks with my new net, and then I want to go out to the Fox and Hounds, and—"

"Don't-wake-Daddy!" she hissed angrily, clapping her hand across my mouth.

But it was too late. He was awake, or nearly so. He grunted and reached for the matches. Then he stared incredulously at his watch.

"Like a cup of tea, dear?" asked Mother in a meek, hushed voice I had never heard her use before. It sounded almost as though she were afraid.

"Tea?" he exclaimed indignantly. "Do you know what the time is?"

"And after that I want to go up the Rathcooney Road," I said loudly, afraid I'd forget something in all those interruptions.

"Go to sleep at once, Larry!" she said sharply.

I began to snivel. I couldn't concentrate, the way that pair went on, and smothering my early-morning schemes was like burying a family from the cradle.

Father said nothing, but lit his pipe and sucked it, looking out into the shadows without minding Mother or me. I knew he was mad. Every time I made a remark Mother hushed me irritably. I was mortified. I felt it wasn't fair; there was even something sinister in it. Every time I had pointed out to her the waste of making two beds when we could both sleep in one, she had told me it was healthier like that, and now here was this man, this stranger, sleeping with her without the least regard for her health!

He got up early and made tea, but though he brought Mother a cup he brought none for me.

"Mummy," I shouted, "I want a cup of tea, too."

"Yes, dear," she said patiently. "You can drink from Mummy's saucer."

That settled it. Either Father or I would have to leave the house. I didn't want to drink from Mother's saucer; I wanted to be treated as an equal in my own home, so, just to spite her, I drank it all and left none for her. She took that quietly, too.

But that night when she was putting me to bed she said gently:

"Larry, I want you to promise me something."

"What is it?" I asked.

"Not to come in and disturb poor Daddy in the morning. Promise?"

"Poor Daddy" again! I was becoming suspicious of everything involving that quite impossible man.

"Why?" I asked.

"Because poor Daddy is worried and tired and he doesn't sleep well."

"Why doesn't he, Mummy?"

"Well, you know, don't you, that while he was at the war Mummy got the pennies from the Post Office?"

"From Miss MacCarthy?"

"That's right. But now, you see, Miss MacCarthy hasn't any

more pennies, so Daddy must go out and find us some. You know what would happen if he couldn't?"

"No," I said, "tell us."

"Well, I think we might have to go out and beg for them like the poor old woman on Fridays. We wouldn't like that, would we?"

"No," I agreed. "We wouldn't."

"So you'll promise not to come in and wake him?"

"Promise."

Mind you, I meant that. I knew pennies were a serious matter, and I was all against having to go out and beg like the old woman on Fridays. Mother laid out all my toys in a complete ring round the bed so that, whatever way I got out, I was bound to fall over one of them.

When I woke I remembered my promise all right. I got up and sat on the floor and played—for hours, it seemed to me. Then I got my chair and looked out the attic window for more hours. I wished it was time for Father to wake; I wished someone would make me a cup of tea. I didn't feel in the least like the sun; instead, I was bored and so very, very cold! I simply longed for the warmth and depth of the big featherbed.

At last I could stand it no longer. I went into the next room. As there was still no room at Mother's side I climbed over her and she woke with a start.

"Larry," she whispered, gripping my arm very tightly, "what did you promise?"

"But I did, Mummy," I wailed, caught in the very act. "I was quiet for ever so long."

"Oh, dear, and you're perished!" she said sadly, feeling me all over. "Now, if I let you stay will you promise not to talk?"

"But I want to talk, Mummy," I wailed.

"That has nothing to do with it," she said with a firmness that was new to me. "Daddy wants to sleep. Now, do you understand that?"

I understood it only too well. I wanted to talk, he wanted to sleep—whose house was it, anyway?

"Mummy," I said with equal firmness, "I think it would be healthier for Daddy to sleep in his own bed."

That seemed to stagger her, because she said nothing for a while.

"Now, once for all," she went on, "you're to be perfectly quiet or go back to your own bed. Which is it to be?"

The injustice of it got me down. I had convicted her out of her own mouth of inconsistency and unreasonableness, and she hadn't even attempted to reply. Full of spite, I gave Father a kick, which she didn't notice but which made him grunt and open his eyes in alarm.

"What time is it?" he asked in a panic-stricken voice, not looking at Mother but at the door, as if he saw someone there.

"It's early yet," she replied soothingly. "It's only the child. Go to sleep again. . . . Now, Larry," she added, getting out of bed, "you've wakened Daddy and you must go back."

This time, for all her quiet air, I knew she meant it, and knew that my principal rights and privileges were as good as lost unless I asserted them at once. As she lifted me, I gave a screech, enough to wake the dead, not to mind Father. He groaned.

"That damn child! Doesn't he ever sleep?"

"It's only a habit, dear," she said quietly, though I could see she was vexed.

"Well, it's time he got out of it," shouted Father, beginning to heave in the bed. He suddenly gathered all the bedclothes about him, turned to the wall, and then looked back over his shoulder with nothing showing only two small, spiteful, dark eyes. The man looked very wicked.

To open the bedroom door, Mother had to let me down, and I broke free and dashed for the farthest corner, screeching. Father sat bolt upright in bed.

"Shut up, you little puppy!" he said in a choking voice. I was so astonished that I stopped screeching. Never, never had anyone spoken to me in that tone before. I looked at him incredulously and saw his face convulsed with rage. It was only then that I fully realized how God had codded me, listening to my prayers for the safe return of this monster.

"Shut up, you!" I bawled, beside myself.

"What's that you said?" shouted Father, making a wild leap out of the bed.

"Mick, Mick!" cried Mother. "Don't you see the child isn't used to you?"

"I see he's better fed than taught," snarled Father, waving his arms wildly. "He wants his bottom smacked."

All his previous shouting was as nothing to these obscene words referring to my person. They really made my blood boil.

"Smack your own!" I screamed hysterically. "Smack your own! Shut up! Shut up!"

At this he lost his patience and let fly at me. He did it with the lack of conviction you'd expect of a man under Mother's horrified eyes, and it ended up as a mere tap, but the sheer indignity of being struck at all by a stranger, a total stranger who had cajoled his way back from the war into our big bed as a result of my innocent intercession, made me completely dotty. I shrieked and shrieked, and danced in my bare feet, and Father, looking awkward and hairy in nothing but a short grey army shirt, glared down at me like a mountain out for murder. I think it must have been then that I realized he was jealous too. And there stood Mother in her nightdress, looking as if her heart was broken between us. I hoped she felt as she looked. It seemed to me that she deserved it all.

From that morning out my life was a hell. Father and I were enemies, open and avowed. We conducted a series of skirmishes against one another, he trying to steal my time with Mother and I his. When she was sitting on my bed, telling me a story, he took to looking for some pair of old boots which he alleged he had left behind him at the beginning of the war. While he talked to Mother I played loudly with my toys to show my total lack of concern. He created a terrible scene one evening when he came in from work and found me at his box, playing with his regimental badges, Gurkha knives and button-sticks. Mother got up and took the box from me.

"You mustn't play with Daddy's toys unless he lets you, Larry," she said severely. "Daddy doesn't play with yours."

For some reason Father looked at her as if she had struck him and then turned away with a scowl.

"Those are not toys," he growled, taking down the box again to see had I lifted anything. "Some of those curios are very rare and valuable."

But as time went on I saw more and more how he managed to alienate Mother and me. What made it worse was that I couldn't grasp his method or see what attraction he had for Mother. In every possible way he was less winning than I. He had a common accent and made noises at his tea. I thought for a while that it might be the newspapers she was interested in, so I made up bits of news of my own to read to her. Then I thought it might be the smoking, which I personally thought attractive, and took his pipes and went round the house dribbling into them till he caught me. I even made noises at my tea, but Mother only told me I was disgusting. It all seemed to hinge round that unhealthy habit of sleeping together, so I made a point of dropping into their bedroom and nosing round, talking to myself, so that they wouldn't know I was watching them, but they were never up to anything that I could see. In the end it beat me. It seemed to depend on being grown-up and giving people rings, and I realized I'd have to wait.

But at the same time I wanted him to see that I was only waiting, not giving up the fight. One evening when he was being particularly obnoxious, chattering away well above my head, I let him have it.

"Mummy," I said, "do you know what I'm going to do when I grow up?"

"No, dear," she replied. "What?"

"I'm going to marry you," I said quietly.

Father gave a great guffaw out of him, but he didn't take me in. I knew it must only be pretence. And Mother, in spite of everything was pleased. I felt she was probably relieved to know that one day Father's hold on her would be broken.

"Won't that be nice?" she said with a smile.

"It'll be very nice," I said confidently. "Because we're going to have lots and lots of babies."

"That's right, dear," she said placidly. "I think we'll have one soon, and then you'll have plenty of company."

I was no end pleased about that because it showed that in spite of the way she gave in to Father she still considered my wishes. Besides, it would put the Geneys in their place.

It didn't turn out like that, though. To begin with, she was very preoccupied—I supposed about where she would get the seventeen

and six—and though Father took to staying out late in the evenings
it did me no particular good. She stopped taking me for walks,
became as touchy as blazes, and smacked me for nothing at all.
Sometimes I wished I'd never mentioned the confounded baby—I
seemed to have a genius for bringing calamity on myself.

And calamity it was! Sonny arrived in the most appalling hulla-
baloo—even that much he couldn't do without a fuss—and from
the first moment I disliked him. He was a difficult child—so far as
I was concerned he was always difficult—and demanded far too
much attention. Mother was simply silly about him, and couldn't
see when he was only showing off. As company he was worse than
useless. He slept all day, and I had to go round the house on tiptoe
to avoid waking him. It wasn't any longer a question of not waking
Father. The slogan now was "Don't-wake-Sonny!" I couldn't understand why the child wouldn't sleep at the proper time, so whenever Mother's back was turned I woke him. Sometimes to keep him
awake I pinched him as well. Mother caught me at it one day and
gave me a most unmerciful flaking.

One evening, when Father was coming in from work, I was
playing trains in the front garden. I let on not to notice him; instead,
I pretended to be talking to myself, and said in a loud voice: "If
another bloody baby comes into this house, I'm going out."

Father stopped dead and looked at me over his shoulder.

"What's that you said?" he asked sternly.

"I was only talking to myself," I replied, trying to conceal my
panic. "It's private."

He turned and went in without a word. Mind you, I intended
it as a solemn warning, but its effect was quite different. Father
started being quite nice to me. I could understand that, of course.
Mother was quite sickening about Sonny. Even at mealtimes she'd
get up and gawk at him in the cradle with an idiotic smile, and tell
Father to do the same. He was always polite about it, but he looked
so puzzled you could see he didn't know what she was talking
about. He complained of the way Sonny cried at night, but she only
got cross and said that Sonny never cried except when there was
something up with him—which was a flaming lie, because Sonny
never had anything up with him, and only cried for attention. It
was really painful to see how simple-minded she was. Father

wasn't attractive, but he had a fine intelligence. He saw through Sonny, and now he knew that I saw through him as well.

One night I woke with a start. There was someone beside me in the bed. For one wild moment I felt sure it must be Mother, having come to her senses and left Father for good, but then I heard Sonny in convulsions in the next room, and Mother saying: "There! There! There!" and I knew it wasn't she. It was Father. He was lying beside me, wide awake, breathing hard and apparently as mad as hell.

After a while it came to me what he was mad about. It was his turn now. After turning me out of the big bed, he had been turned out himself. Mother had no consideration now for anyone but that poisonous pup, Sonny. I couldn't help feeling sorry for Father. I had been through it all myself, and even at that age I was magnanimous. I began to stroke him down and say: "There! There!" He wasn't exactly responsive.

"Aren't you asleep either?" he snarled.

"Ah, come on and put your arm around us, can't you?" I said, and he did, in a sort of way. Gingerly, I suppose, is how you'd describe it. He was very bony but better than nothing.

At Christmas he went out of his way to buy me a really nice model railway.

ROBERT PENN WARREN

When the Light Gets Green

----

*M*Y GRANDFATHER HAD A long white beard and sat under the cedar tree. The beard, as a matter of fact, was not very long and not white, only gray, but when I was a child and was away from him at school during the winter, I would think of him, not seeing him in my mind's eye, and say: He has a long white beard. Therefore, it was a shock to me, on the first morning back home, to watch him lean over the dresser toward the wavy green mirror, which in his always shadowy room reflected things like deep water riffled by a little wind, and clip his gray beard to a point. It is gray and pointed, I would say then, remembering what I had thought before.

He turned his face to the green wavy glass, first one side and then the other in quarter profile, and lifted the long shears, which trembled a little, to cut the beard. His face being turned like that, with his good nose and pointed gray beard, he looked like General Robert E. Lee, without any white horse to ride. My grandfather had been a soldier, too, but now he wore blue-jean pants and when he leaned over like that toward the mirror, I couldn't help but notice how small his hips and backsides were. Only they weren't just small, they were shrunken. I noticed how the blue jeans hung loose from his suspenders and loose off his legs and down around his shoes.

And in the morning when I noticed all this about his legs and backsides, I felt a tight feeling in my stomach like when you walk behind
a woman and see the high heel of her shoe is worn and twisted and
jerks her ankle every time she takes a step.

Always before my grandfather had finished clipping his beard,
my Uncle Kirby came to the door and beat on it for breakfast. "I'll
be down in just a minute, thank you, sir," my grandfather said. My
uncle called him Mr. Barden. "Mr. Barden, breakfast is ready." It
was because my Uncle Kirby was not my real uncle, having
married my Aunt Lucy, who lived with my grandfather. Then my
grandfather put on a black vest and put his gold watch and chain
in the vest and picked up his cob pipe from the dresser top, and he
and I went down to breakfast, after Uncle Kirby was already downstairs.

When he came into the dining room, Aunt Lucy was sitting at
the foot of the table with the iron coffee pot on a plate beside her.
She said, "Good morning, Papa."

"Good morning, Lucy," he said, and sat down at the head of the
table, taking one more big puff off his pipe before laying it beside
his plate.

"You've brought that old pipe down to breakfast again," my
aunt said, while she poured the bright-looking coffee into the cups.

"Don't it stink," he always said.

My uncle never talked at breakfast, but when my grandfather
said that, my uncle always opened his lips to grin like a dog panting,
and showed his hooked teeth. His teeth were yellow because he
chewed tobacco, which my grandfather didn't do, although his
beard was yellow around the mouth from smoking. Aunt Lucy
didn't like my uncle to chew, that was the whole trouble. So she
rode my grandfather for bringing his pipe down, all in fun at first
before she got serious about it. But he always brought it down just
the same, and said to her, "Don't it stink."

After we ate, my uncle got up and said, "I got to get going,"
and went out through the kitchen where the cook was knocking
and sloshing around. If it had rained right and was a good tobacco-
setting season, my grandfather went off with me down to the stable
to get his mare, for he had to see the setting. We saddled up the
mare and went across the lot, where limestone bunched out of the

ground and cedar trees and blue grass grew out of the split rock. A branch of cold water with minnows in it went through the lot between rocks and under the cedar trees; it was where I used to play before I got big enough to go to the river with the niggers to swim.

My grandfather rode across the lot and over the rise back of the house. He sat up pretty straight for an old man, holding the bridle in his left hand, and in his right hand a long hickory tobacco stick whittled down to make a walking cane. I walked behind him and watched the big straw hat he wore waggle a little above his narrow neck, or how he held the stick in the middle, firm and straight up like something carried in a parade, or how smooth and slow the muscles in the mare's flanks worked as she put each hoof down in the ground, going up hill. Sassafras bushes and blackberry bushes grew thick along the lane over the rise. In summer, tufts of hay would catch and hang on the dry bushes and showed that the hay wagons had been that way; but when we went that way in setting time, just after breakfast, the blackberry blooms were hardly gone, only a few rusty patches of white left, and the sassafras leaves showed still wet with dew or maybe the rain.

From the rise we could look back on the house. The shingles were black with damp, and the whitewash grayish, except in spots where the sun already struck it and it was drying. The tops of the cedar trees, too, were below us, very dark green and quiet. When we crossed the rise, there were the fields going down toward the river, all checked off and ready for setting, very even, only for the gullies where brush was piled to stop the washing. The fields were reddish from the wet, not yet steaming. Across them, the green woods and the sycamores showing white far off told where the river was.

The hands were standing at the edge of the field under the trees when we got there. The little niggers were filling their baskets with the wet plants to drop, and I got me a basket and filled it. My Uncle Kirby gave me fifty cents for dropping plants, but he didn't give the little niggers that much, I remember. The hands and women stood around waiting a minute, watching Uncle Kirby, who always fumed around, waving his dibble, his blue shirt already sticking to his arms with sweat. "Get the lead out," he said. The little niggers filled faster, grinning with their teeth at him. "Goddam, get the lead out!" My grandfather sat on his mare under the trees, still holding the walking cane, and said, "Why don't you start 'em, sir?"

Then, all of a sudden, they all moved out into the field, scattering out down the rows, the droppers first, and after a minute the setters, who lurched along, never straightening up, down the rows toward the river. I walked down my row, separating out the plants and dropping them at the hills, while it got hotter and the ground steamed. The sun broke out now and then, making my shadow on the ground, then the cloud would come again, and I could see its shadow drifting at me on the red field.

My grandfather rode very slow along the edge of the field to watch the setting, or stayed still under the trees. After a while, maybe about ten o'clock, he would leave and go home. I could see him riding the mare up the rise and then go over the rise; or if I was working the other way toward the river, when I turned round at the end, the lane would be empty and nothing on top the rise, with the cloudy, blue-gray sky low behind it.

The tobacco was all he cared about, now we didn't have any horses that were any real good. He had some silver cups, only one real silver one though, that his horses won at fairs, but all that was before I was born. The real silver one, the one he kept on his dresser and kept string and old minnie balls and pins and things in, had *1859* on it because his horse won it then before the War, when he was a young man. Uncle Kirby said horses were foolishness, and Grandfather said, yes, he reckoned horses were foolishness, all right. So what he cared about now was the tobacco. One time he was a tobacco-buyer for three years, but after he bought a lot of tobacco and had it in his sheds, the sheds burned up on him. He didn't have enough insurance to do any good and he was a ruined man. After that all his children, he had all girls and his money was gone, said about him, "Papa's just visionary, he tried to be a tobacco-buyer but he's too visionary and not practical." But he always said, "All tobacco-buyers are sons-of-bitches, and three years is enough of a man's life for him to be a son-of-a-bitch, I reckon." Now he was old, the corn could get the rust or the hay get rained on for all he cared, it was Uncle Kirby's worry, but all summer, off and on, he had to go down to the tobacco field to watch them sucker or plow or worm, and sometimes he pulled a few suckers himself. And when a cloud would blow up black in summer, he got nervous as a cat, not knowing whether it was the rain they needed or maybe a hail storm coming that would cut the tobacco up bad.

Mornings he didn't go down to the field, he went out under the cedar tree where his chair was. Most of the time he took a book with him along with his pipe, for he was an inveterate reader. His being an inveterate reader was one of the things made his children say he was visionary. He read a lot until his eyes went bad the summer before he had his stroke, then after that, I read to him some, but not as much as I ought. He used to read out loud some from Macaulay's *History of England* or Gibbon's *Decline and Fall*, about Flodden Field or about how the Janizaries took Constantinople amid great slaughter and how the Turk surveyed the carnage and quoted from the Persian poet about the lizard keeping the courts of the mighty. My grandfather knew some poetry, too, and he said it to himself when he didn't have anything else to do. I lay on my back on the ground, feeling the grass cool and tickly on the back of my neck, and looked upside down into the cedar tree where the limbs were tangled and black-green like big hairy fern fronds with the sky blue all around, while he said some poetry. Like the "Isles of Greece, the Isles of Greece, where burning Sappho loved and sung." Or like "Roll on, thou deep and dark blue ocean, roll."

But he never read poetry, he just said what he already knew. He only read history and *Napoleon and His Marshals*, having been a soldier and fought in the War himself. He rode off and joined the cavalry, but he never told me whether he took the horse that won the real silver cup or not. He was with Forrest before Forrest was a general. He said Forrest was a great general, and if they had done what Forrest wanted and cleaned the country ahead of the Yankees, like the Russians beat Napoleon, they'd whipped the Yankees sure. He told me about Fort Donelson, how they fought in the winter woods, and how they got away with Forrest at night, splashing through the cold water. And how the dead men looked in the river bottoms in winter, and I lay on my back on the grass, looking up in the thick cedar limbs, and thought how it was to be dead.

After Shiloh was fought and they pushed the Yankees down in the river, my grandfather was a captain, for he raised a cavalry company of his own out of West Tennessee. He was a captain, but he never got promoted after the War; when I was a little boy everybody still called him Captain Barden, though they called lots of other people in our section Colonel and Major. One time I said to him: "Grandpa, did you ever kill any Yankees?" He said: "God-a-Mighty, how do I know?" So, being little, I thought he was just a captain because he never killed anybody, and I was ashamed. He talked about how they took Fort Pillow, and the drunk niggers under the bluff. And one time he said niggers couldn't stand a charge or stand the cold steel, so I thought maybe he killed some of them. But then I thought, Niggers don't count, maybe.

He only talked much in the morning. Almost every afternoon right after dinner, he went to sleep in his chair, with his hands curled up in his lap, one of them holding the pipe that still sent up a little smoke in the shadow, and his head propped back on the tree trunk. His mouth hung open, and under the hairs of his mustache, all yellow with nicotine, you could see his black teeth and his lips that were wet and pink like a baby's. Usually I remember him that way, asleep.

I remember him that way, or else trampling up and down the front porch, nervous as a cat, while a cloud blew up and the trees began to rustle. He tapped his walking cane on the boards and whistled through his teeth with his breath and kept looking off at the sky where the cloud and sometimes the lightning was. Then of a sudden it came, and if it was rain he used to go up to his room and lie down; but if it came hail on the tobacco, he stayed on the front porch, not trampling any more, and watched the hail rattle off the roof and bounce soft on the grass. "God-a-Mighty," he always said, "bigger'n minnie balls," even when it wasn't so big.

In 1914, just before the war began, it was a hot summer with the tobacco mighty good but needing rain. And when the dry spell broke and a cloud blew up, my grandfather came out on the front porch, watching it like that. It was mighty still, with lightning way off, so far you couldn't hardly hear the thunder. Then the leaves began to ruffle like they do when the light gets green, and my grandfather said to me, "Son, it's gonna hail." And he stood still. Down in the pasture, that far off, you could see the cattle bunching up and the white horse charging across the pasture, looking bright, for the sun was shining bright before the cloud struck it all at once. "It's gonna hail," my grandfather said. It was dark, with jagged lightning and the thunder high and steady. And there the hail was.

He just turned around and went in the house. I watched the hail bouncing, then I heard a noise and my aunt yelled. I ran back in the dining room where the noise was, and my grandfather was lying on the floor with the old silver pitcher he dropped and a broken glass. We tried to drag him, but he was too heavy; then my Uncle Kirby came up wet from the stable and we carried my grandfather upstairs and put him on his bed. My aunt tried to call the doctor even if the lightning might hit the telephone. I stayed back in the dining room and picked up the broken glass and the pitcher and wiped up the floor with a rag. After a while Dr. Blake came from town; then he went away.

When Dr. Blake was gone, I went upstairs to see my grandfather. I shut the door and went in his room, which was almost dark, like always, and quiet because the hail didn't beat on the roof any more. He was lying on his back in the featherbed, with a sheet pulled up over him, lying there in the dark. He had his hands curled loose on his stomach, like when he went to sleep in his chair holding the pipe. I sat on a splitbottom chair by the bed and looked at him: he had his eyes shut and his mouth hung loose, but you couldn't hear his breathing. Then I quit looking at him and looked round the room, my eyes getting used to the shadow. I could see his pants on the floor, and the silver cup on the dresser by the mirror, which was green and wavy like water.

When he said something, I almost jumped out of my skin, hearing his voice like that. He said, "Son, I'm gonna die." I tried to say something, but I couldn't. And he waited, then he said, "I'm on borrowed time, it's time to die." I said, "No!" so sudden and loud I jumped. He waited a long time and said, "It's time to die. Nobody loves me." I tried to say, "Grandpa, I love you." And then I did say it all right, feeling like it hadn't been me said it, and knowing all of a sudden it was a lie, because I didn't feel anything. He just lay there; and I went downstairs.

It was sunshiny in the yard, the clouds gone, but the grass was wet. I walked down toward the gate, rubbing my bare feet over the slick cold grass. A hen was in the yard and she kept trying to peck up a piece of hail, like a fool chicken will do after it hails; but every time she pecked, it bounced away from her over the green grass. I leaned against the gate, noticing the ground on one side the posts, close up, was still dry and dusty. I wondered if the tobacco was cut up bad, because Uncle Kirby had gone to see. And while I looked through the gate down across the pasture where everything in the sun was green and shiny with wet and the cattle grazed, I thought about my grandfather, not feeling anything. But I said out loud anyway, "Grandpa, I love you."

My grandfather lived four more years. The year after his stroke they sold the farm and moved away, so I didn't stay with them any more. My grandfather died in 1918, just before the news came that my Uncle Kirby was killed in France, and my aunt had to go to work in a store. I got the letter about my grandfather, who died of flu, but I thought about four years back, and it didn't matter much.

ROBERT PENN WARREN'S *"When the Light Gets Green"*

In telling this story, Mr. Warren has put the screen of two, though never entirely separable, fictive personalities between himself and his reader—one, that of the boy as boy, and the other that of the same person grown to be a man. We cannot say simply that the story is told from the boy's point of view. It is told, rather, from that point of view as recovered, or reconstructed, by the adult narrator through reminiscence.

This rather complicated technique has definite relevance to meaning. For the two central, intertwined themes of the story are the themes of self and of time. Looking back from the end of his narration—when the speaker tells us that the news of his grandfather's death "didn't matter much," because of what had happened the day of the hailstorm four years before—we see that the events of that day, on the other hand, did matter very much. They mattered so much, precisely, that it is implied *nothing* has mattered since. It is almost as if the speaker's own life, if not his grandfather's, or at any rate his desire and purpose to live, had ended that day; as if, like the grandfather for the four years after the stroke, he has continued since to "live" only in the minimal sense of physical existence. In other words, he has the feeling of having somehow lost his essential identity in the "lie" to the stricken old man. And the telling of the story is an effort to push back into the past before that day, the past in which his grandfather figured so prominently, in search of an explanation—or, indeed, in search of the lost self, which it would seem exists only in the past.

For the reader, at any rate—if not, even finally, for the narrator— the implications of the reconstruction are fairly clear. They have to do with another recurrent preoccupation of Warren's, the relationship of the real and the ideal. Actually, it is another aspect of the time-and-identity theme.

To support his own inadequate sense of status and self-esteem, the boy has begun very early in his life to construct an idealized image of his grandfather, and to associate himself with the old man in this role. Then, with that perversity which is characteristic of so many of Warren's heroes, when later the image fails to accommodate itself to his growing sense of reality, he turns on the grandfather as if it were he who had betrayed him.

It is the commonplace experience of children to feel that they are living "out of their time," that their existence is irrelevant in the world of practical, adult affairs. But his particular circumstances make this feeling more than usually intense for the boy in "When the Light Gets Green." For one thing, although we are never told what has happened to his parents, he is evidently an orphan—living (he calls it "staying") with his aunt and uncle—so that the sense of not belonging would be for him especially acute. Moreover, it would appear that the foster parents have no children of their own. The boy is alone in the family of adults, with no companions of his own age except the children of the Negro laborers—from whom, in the strictly class-structured Southern society, he inevitably feels more and more alienated as he grows older.

In this situation, and by temperament sensitive and impressionable, something of a daydreamer, the boy has turned instinctively to his grandfather for companionship. Besides simply having a good deal of free time, the old man is a glamorous figure, with his formal manner, his trophies, and his stories of the war, his grand bearing on horseback, his

history books and ringing recitations of poetry. In comparison, the aunt
and uncle are colorless and preoccupied.

But very gradually, we gather, as the child grows older, he is disillusioned in his hero worship. It becomes more and more difficult to
square the image with the reality. It is only when "not seeing him in his
mind's eye"—that is, not *permitting* himself to entertain a true mental
picture of the man—that he can paint him in the ideal character of
grandfatherly benignity, with "a long white beard." For a while, he can
salvage something. With the short gray beard, the old man still looks
like General Lee. And though it is painful to see his skinny shanks and
backside as he stands before the shaving mirror, still he cuts a proud
enough figure when riding out to the tobacco field.

But the incongruities, one by one, add up. The boy's mind is in-
capable of appreciating the subtle pride of the old soldier's rejecting—
deliberately, one must suppose—the spurious glory of the Confederate
veterans who "got promoted after the war," and preferring to keep only
his legitimate title of Captain. Nor is he prepared to understand that the
old man actually does not at all agree with Kirby that "horses are foolishness," but on the contrary gives up his stables because he cannot bear
having anything less than the best, and because he will not lower himself
to argue with someone like his son-in-law, who is simply blind to the
values of the gentleman and the sportsman.

It is one of the ironies of their relationship that the boy does not
realize how essentially alike he and his grandfather are. The paradoxical
combination of literal-mindedness and a love of idealistic fantasy is,
again, to a certain extent characteristic of all children. But, once more,
Warren has characterized the boy in this story as one who suffers with
more than common intensity the emotional conflict set up by these
opposing tendencies of mind. Essentially, both he and the grandfather
belong to a type frequently encountered among Warren's heroes of all
ages. They are idealists, but idealists who yearn to make the ideal real,
and are acutely aware of and embarrassed by temporal circumstances
that either prevent altogether their assuming the stance proper to the
heroic identity or that make it appear an idle posturing. But to the boy
his grandfather is simply the embodiment of an ideal, which must stand
or fall as such; he cannot see him as containing within himself the same,
full human drama, the clash of contraries, the pull of the real against the
ideal, which he knows as his own, shameful and bewildered, child's
experience.

The grandfather has been driven to last ditch in his efforts to find a
life role suiting the dignity of his self-conception. Although the farm

apparently in some sense belongs to him, he is financially ruined, so that we may surmise he is dependent on his daughter and her husband for making the place pay and holding onto the property. They treat him with great formal respect, but it is evident that he senses a condescension in it, the galling effect of which is only intensified by his equally evident feeling of superiority to Kirby. The younger man may be styleless, and a little absurd, with his nervousness and the stridently officious tone he takes with the grinning laborers; but it is he, nonetheless, as his father-in-law well knows, who is actually responsible for getting the tobacco planted. The old man's presence in the field is purely ceremonial.

But though the reader will understand and sympathize with him in his situation, perhaps even qualifiedly admire him, for the measure of quiet dignity he does manage in the face of his humiliating awareness —it would be the worst oversimplification of the story to see Warren as merely satirizing his idealism—such sympathy and admiration are beyond the scope of the boy's experience. It is evident that he does, in fact, to some extent sense his grandfather's likeness to himself. He senses, for example, that his own work in the field, along with the Negroes, is merely a form of play—valueless, precisely because he is overpaid for it. And it is implied that he vaguely associates this humiliation, of receiving a false reward, with that of his grandfather in his role of ceremonial overseer at the planting. But apprehensions of this kind, on the boy's part, are calculated only further to damage rather than to repair the image of his sometime hero.

The only likeness, in other words, that the boy is to any extent able to see, between his grandfather and himself, is that they are both childish. Ten or twelve years old at the most, one would judge, at the time of the main action of the story, he could not know that this is the inevitable fate of the very old, in a sense to live past maturity, and so come full circle back to childhood. Immature, and therefore still hopeful of maturity, despising, as all children do, his own status, he cannot know that in a certain measure such "childishness" is, indeed, the fate of *man,* young or old; that what we call maturity, the state in which the ideal is exactly commensurate with the possible, in which one's desire neither exceeds nor falls short of what he may reasonably hope to have, is achieved only briefly if ever in the course of any lifetime, every man living most or all of his life "out of his time" or "on borrowed time"; that the only possible heroism, therefore, defeat being inevitable, is in the struggle itself, in the proud refusal, which the grandfather has consistently made, knowingly to compromise either with his ideals or with his sense of reality. Unable to see his grandfather except with reference to himself, not in terms of the man's own life, the boy only feels betrayed by his final weakness.

To the young and healthy, even a purely physical infirmity, suffered by an elder upon whom they have depended, is unforgivable. Having only a vague notion of the psychological importance of the tobacco crop to the old man, and therefore unable to understand why the hailstorm should upset him so, the boy evidently feels betrayed, put off, simply by his succumbing to the stroke. It is excessive, embarrassingly histrionic, tending all too well to justify the implicit reproach in his observation about his grandfather's habit of exaggerating the size of the hailstones: " 'God-a-Mighty,' he always said, 'bigger'n minnie balls,' even when it wasn't so big." And then, on top of this, surprising the boy in the midst of the guilt feelings he would already and inevitably be entertaining for having been secretly ashamed of the old man, the startling appeal for love is the final and intolerable betrayal.

Once again, Warren is dealing with a universal characteristic of the young, especially of boys of this age, in representing the grandson's reaction to the name, the word, of love. It is not to be spoken, except by women and girls. But, besides being a man, the grandfather here is the one man to whom the boy himself has longest and most consistently looked for love. Love is what he, the boy, requires, of the man. It is an insufferable irony that the man should turn the tables in this way—again, turn child in his own right—and demand for himself, instead, what he is supposed to give.

In remarking that when he finally made the avowal of love, he felt it to be a "lie"—"feeling like it hadn't been me said it"—what the narrator is saying is that he became in that moment aware, without being precisely able to define it, of how he had always cast the grandfather in a role answerable simply to the needs of his own idealism. When the old man suddenly steps out of the role, asserting *his* need, the boy cannot truthfully respond—say whatever would truly reflect the affection he undoubtedly does feel (there would be no need, now, to tell the story, if he actually had not in some sense loved his grandfather)—without admitting that the role he himself has played has been all along somehow false. And that, of course, which would be to assume all of a sudden the burden of maturation, he cannot bring himself to do. He prefers to continue acting his customary part, to speak the expected line, even though he knows it to be a lie, can no longer identify himself with the one who says it—perhaps even suspecting, since the old man does not answer, that his grandfather himself is not deceived—rather than risk admitting that he is self-betrayed. He prefers, in other words, to tell a lie, even to repeat it to himself alone, rather than admit that he is a lie.

Or, we may say, he has "died," abandoned the old self in which he can no longer believe, without accepting the responsibility of a new identity. He prefers to feel nothing, which is to be dead, rather than come to terms with what it is possible for him to feel. And this is the state in which he still finds himself four years later, when the news of his grandfather's death reaches him.

We have so far concerned ourselves exclusively with the private, or personal, dimension of the story's significance. As usual in Warren's work, there is another dimension—the public, or historical. In so short a story, this range of meaning cannot be very fully developed. But, beyond and above the story of a personal experience, of events in the private life of a family, there is the clear outline of a reference to the history of the South.

Briefly, the implications are these. The grandfather, or as we should refer to him in this context, Captain Barden, is associated not only with his grandson's, the narrator's, past, but with the old order of Southern society. At the risk of oversimplification, it might be said that he *represents* the regional past, and the well-known Southern habit of idealizing the past. According to the suggested scheme, Uncle Kirby and his wife represent the succeeding generation of rather uneasy materialists, who dominate the fictive present. The boy, finally, is representative of the future—charged with the responsibility either of choosing between, or of somehow transcending, the opposed value systems of the two previous generations.

One would not, perhaps, want to push too hard along this line of analysis. It would certainly be an error to suggest that the personal story is devised primarily to support any superstructure of strict historical allegory. But, on the other hand, where the historical consciousness definitely penetrates the personal, as in the characterization of the grandfather—the "inveterate reader" mostly of history, who unquestionably conceives himself, in the deepest sense of self, according to an historical model—we are clearly obligated to accommodate the given facts.

And, finally, to return to my opening remarks on point of view, and the curious double self of the internal narrator, recognition of the historical dimension of meaning in the story would seem to be absolutely essential to the purpose of completing an analysis of Warren's narrative method. For this dimension is completely within the control of a third, tacit "voice," that of the author, as distinguished from the narrator's both as boy's and man's. The discovery of the second dimension should not at all tempt us to critical excursions into an "extra-literary" realm of historical concern. Rather, this is Warren's principal device, here, for keeping us within the story; for warning us, as it were, against the fundamental critical error of confusing the author with the hero. *J.E.H.*

JOHN STEINBECK

Flight

- -

*A*BOUT FIFTEEN MILES BELOW Monterey, on the wild coast, the Torres family had their farm, a few sloping acres above a cliff that dropped to the brown reefs and to the hissing white waters of the ocean. Behind the farm the stone mountains stood up against the sky. The farm buildings huddled like little clinging aphids on the mountain skirts, crouched low to the ground as though the wind might blow them into the sea. The little shack, the rattling, rotting barn were gray-bitten with sea salt, beaten by the damp wind until they had taken on the color of the granite hills. Two horses, a red cow and a red calf, half a dozen pigs and a flock of lean, multi-colored chickens stocked the place. A little corn was raised on the sterile slope, and it grew short and thick under the wind, and all the cobs formed on the landward sides of the stalks.

Mama Torres, a lean, dry woman with ancient eyes, had ruled the farm for ten years, ever since her husband tripped over a stone

From THE LONG VALLEY by John Steinbeck. Copyright 1938 by John Steinbeck. Reprinted by permission of The Viking Press, Inc.

in the field one day and fell full length on a rattlesnake. When one is bitten on the chest there is not much that can be done.

Mama Torres had three children, two undersized black ones of twelve and fourteen, Emilio and Rosy, whom Mama kept fishing on the rocks below the farm when the sea was kind and when the truant officer was in some distant part of Monterey County. And there was Pepé, the tall smiling son of nineteen, a gentle, affectionate boy, but very lazy. Pepé had a tall head, pointed at the top, and from its peak, coarse black hair grew down like a thatch all around. Over his smiling little eyes Mama cut a straight bang so he could see. Pepé had sharp Indian cheekbones and an eagle nose, but his mouth was as sweet and shapely as a girl's mouth, and his chin was fragile and chiseled. He was loose and gangling, all legs and feet and wrists, and he was very lazy. Mama thought him fine and brave, but she never told him so. She said, "Some lazy cow must have got into thy father's family, else how could I have a son like thee." And she said, "When I carried thee, a sneaking lazy coyote came out of the brush and looked at me one day. That must have made thee so."

Pepé smiled sheepishly and stabbed at the ground with his knife to keep the blade sharp and free from rust. It was his inheritance, that knife, his father's knife. The long heavy blade folded back into the black handle. There was a button on the handle. When Pepé pressed the button, the blade leaped out ready for use. The knife was with Pepé always, for it had been his father's knife.

One sunny morning when the sea below the cliff was glinting and blue and the white surf creamed on the reef, when even the stone mountains looked kindly, Mama Torres called out the door of the shack, "Pepé, I have a labor for thee."

There was no answer. Mama listened. From behind the barn she heard a burst of laughter. She lifted her full long skirt and walked in the direction of the noise.

Pepé was sitting on the ground with his back against a box. His white teeth glistened. On either side of him stood the two black ones, tense and expectant. Fifteen feet away a redwood post was set in the ground. Pepé's right hand lay limply in his lap, and in the palm the big black knife rested. The blade was closed back into the handle. Pepé looked smiling at the sky.

Suddenly Emilio cried, "Ya!"

Pepé's wrist flicked like the head of a snake. The blade seemed to fly open in mid-air, and with a thump the point dug into the redwood post, and the black handle quivered. The three burst into excited laughter. Rosy ran to the post and pulled out the knife and brought it back to Pepé. He closed the blade and settled the knife carefully in his listless palm again. He grinned self-consciously at the sky.

"Ya!"

The heavy knife lanced out and sunk into the post again. Mama moved forward like a ship and scattered the play.

"All day you do foolish things with the knife, like a toy-baby," she stormed. "Get up on thy huge feet that eat up shoes. Get up!" She took him by one loose shoulder and hoisted at him. Pepé grinned sheepishly and came half-heartedly to his feet. "Look!" Mama cried. "Big lazy, you must catch the horse and put on him thy father's saddle. You must ride to Monterey. The medicine bottle is empty. There is no salt. Go thou now, Peanut! Catch the horse."

A revolution took place in the relaxed figure of Pepé.

"To Monterey, me? Alone? Sí, Mama."

She scowled at him. "Do not think, big sheep, that you will buy candy. No, I will give you only enough for the medicine and the salt."

Pepé smiled. "Mama, you will put the hatband on the hat?"

She relented then. "Yes, Pepé. You may wear the hatband."

His voice grew insinuating, "And the green handkerchief, Mama?"

"Yes, if you go quickly and return with no trouble, the silk green handkerchief will go. If you make sure to take off the handkerchief when you eat so no spot may fall on it. . . ."

"Sí, Mama. I will be careful. I am a man."

"Thou? A man? Thou art a peanut."

He went into the rickety barn and brought out a rope, and he walked agilely enough up the hill to catch the horse.

When he was ready and mounted before the door, mounted on his father's saddle that was so old that the oaken frame showed through torn leather in many places, then Mama brought out the round black hat with the tooled leather band, and she reached up and knotted the green silk handkerchief about his neck. Pepé's blue denim coat was much darker than his jeans, for it had been washed much less often.

Mama handed up the big medicine bottle and the silver coins. "That for the medicine," she said, "and that for the salt. That for a candle to burn for the papa. That for *dulces* for the little ones. Our friend Mrs. Rodriguez will give you dinner and maybe a bed for the night. When you go to the church say only ten Paternosters and only twenty-five Ave Marias. Oh! I know, big coyote. You would sit there flapping your mouth over Aves all day while you looked at the candles and the holy pictures. That is not good devotion to stare at the pretty things."

The black hat, covering the high pointed head and black thatched hair of Pepé, gave him dignity and age. He sat the rangy horse well. Mama thought how handsome he was, dark and lean and tall. "I would not send thee now alone, thou little one, except for the medicine," she said softly. "It is not good to have no medicine, for who knows when the toothache will come, or the sadness of the stomach. These things are."

"Adios, Mama," Pepé cried. "I will come back soon. You may send me often alone. I am a man."

"Thou art a foolish chicken."

He straightened his shoulders, flipped the reins against the horse's shoulder and rode away. He turned once and saw that they still watched him, Emilio and Rosy and Mama. Pepé grinned with pride and gladness and lifted the tough buckskin horse to a trot.

When he had dropped out of sight over a little dip in the road, Mama turned to the black ones, but she spoke to herself. "He is nearly a man now," she said. "It will be a nice thing to have a man in the house again." Her eyes sharpened on the children. "Go to the rocks now. The tide is going out. There will be abalones to be found." She put the iron hooks into their hands and saw them down the steep trail to the reefs. She brought the smooth stone *metate* to the doorway and sat grinding her corn to flour and looking occasionally at the road over which Pepé had gone. The noonday came and then the afternoon, when the little ones beat the abalones on a rock to make them tender and Mama patted the tortillas to make them thin. They ate their dinner as the red sun was plunging down toward the ocean. They sat on the doorsteps and watched the big white moon come over the mountain tops.

Mama said, "He is now at the house of our friend Mrs. Rodriguez. She will give him nice things to eat and maybe a present."

Emilio said, "Some day I too will ride to Monterey for medicine. Did Pepé come to be a man today?"

Mama said wisely, "A boy gets to be a man when a man is needed. Remember this thing. I have known boys forty years old because there was no need for a man."

Soon afterwards they retired, Mama in her big oak bed on one side of the room, Emilio and Rosy in their boxes full of straw and sheepskins on the other side of the room.

The moon went over the sky and the surf roared on the rocks. The roosters crowed the first call. The surf subsided to a whispering surge against the reef. The moon dropped toward the sea. The roosters crowed again.

The moon was near down to the water when Pepé rode on a winded horse to his home flat. His dog bounced out and circled the horse yelping with pleasure. Pepé slid off the saddle to the ground. The weathered little shack was silver in the moonlight and the square shadow of it was black to the north and east. Against the east the piling mountains were misty with light; their tops melted into the sky.

Pepé walked wearily up the three steps and into the house. It was dark inside. There was a rustle in the corner.

Mama cried out from her bed. "Who comes? Pepé, is it thou?"

"Sí, Mama."

"Did you get the medicine?"

"Sí, Mama."

"Well, go to sleep, then. I thought you would be sleeping at the house of Mrs. Rodriguez." Pepé stood silently in the dark room. "Why do you stand there, Pepé? Did you drink wine?"

"Sí, Mama."

"Well, go to bed then and sleep out the wine."

His voice was tired and patient, but very firm. "Light the candle, Mama. I must go away into the mountains."

"What is this, Pepé? You are crazy." Mama struck a sulphur match and held the little blue burr until the flame spread up the stick. She set light to the candle on the floor beside her bed. "Now, Pepé, what is this you say?" She looked anxiously into his face.

He was changed. The fragile quality seemed to have gone from his chin. His mouth was less full than it had been, the lines of the lips were straighter, but in his eyes the greatest change had taken place. There was no laughter in them any more nor any bashfulness. They were sharp and bright and purposeful.

He told her in a tired monotone, told her everything just as it had happened. A few people came into the kitchen of Mrs. Rodriguez. There was wine to drink. Pepé drank wine. The little quarrel—the man started toward Pepé and then the knife—it went almost by itself. It flew, it darted before Pepé knew it. As he talked, Mama's face grew stern, and it seemed to grow more lean. Pepé finished. "I am a man now, Mama. The man said names to me I could not allow."

Mama nodded. "Yes, thou art a man, my poor little Pepé. Thou art a man. I have seen it coming on thee. I have watched you throwing the knife into the post, and I have been afraid." For a moment her face had softened, but now it grew stern again. "Come! We must get you ready. Go. Awaken Emilio and Rosy. Go quickly."

Pepé stepped over to the corner where his brother and sister slept among the sheepskins. He leaned down and shook them gently. "Come, Rosy! Come, Emilio! The mama says you must arise."

The little black ones sat up and rubbed their eyes in the candlelight. Mama was out of bed now, her long black skirt over her nightgown. "Emilio," she cried. "Go up and catch the other horse for Pepé. Quickly now! Quickly." Emilio put his legs in his overalls and stumbled sleepily out the door.

"You heard no one behind you on the road?" Mama demanded.

"No, Mama. I listened carefully. No one was on the road."

Mama darted like a bird about the room. From a nail on the wall she took a canvas water bag and threw it on the floor. She stripped a blanket from her bed and rolled it into a tight tube and tied the ends with string. From a box beside the stove she lifted a flour sack half full of black stringy jerky. "Your father's black coat, Pepé. Here, put it on."

Pepé stood in the middle of the floor watching her activity. She reached behind the door and brought out the rifle, a long 38-56, worn shiny the whole length of the barrel. Pepé took it from her and held it in the crook of his elbow. Mama brought a little leather bag and counted the cartridges into his hand. "Only ten left," she warned. "You must not waste them."

Emilio put his head in the door. "*'Qui 'st 'l caballo*, Mama."

"Put on the saddle from the other horse. Tie on the blanket. Here, tie the jerky to the saddle horn."

Still Pepé stood silently watching his mother's frantic activity. His chin looked hard, and his sweet mouth was drawn and thin. His little eyes followed Mama about the room almost suspiciously.

Rosy asked softly, "Where goes Pepé?"

Mama's eyes were fierce. "Pepé goes on a journey. Pepé is a man now. He has a man's thing to do."

Pepé straightened his shoulders. His mouth changed until he looked very much like Mama.

At last the preparation was finished. The loaded horse stood outside the door. The water bag dripped a line of moisture down the bay shoulder.

The moonlight was being thinned by the dawn and the big white moon was near down to the sea. The family stood by the shack. Mama confronted Pepé. "Look, my son! Do not stop until it is dark again. Do not sleep even though you are tired. Take care of the horse in order that he may not stop of weariness. Remember to be careful with the bullets—there are only ten. Do not fill thy stomach with jerky or it will make thee sick. Eat a little jerky and fill thy stomach with grass. When thou comest to the high mountains, if thou seest any of the dark watching men, go not near to them nor try to speak to them. And forget not thy prayers." She put her lean hands on Pepé's shoulders, stood on her toes and kissed him formally on both cheeks, and Pepé kissed her on both cheeks. Then he went to Emilio and Rosy and kissed both of their cheeks.

Pepé turned back to Mama. He seemed to look for a little softness, a little weakness in her. His eyes were searching, but Mama's face remained fierce. "Go now," she said. "Do not wait to be caught like a chicken."

Pepé pulled himself into the saddle. "I am a man," he said.

It was the first dawn when he rode up the hill toward the little canyon which let a trail into the mountains. Moonlight and daylight fought with each other, and the two warring qualities made it difficult to see. Before Pepé had gone a hundred yards, the outlines of his figure were misty; and long before he entered the canyon, he had become a gray, indefinite shadow.

Mama stood stiffly in front of her doorstep, and on either side of her stood Emilio and Rosy. They cast furtive glances at Mama now and then.

When the gray shape of Pepé melted into the hillside and disappeared, Mama relaxed. She began the high, whining keen of the death wail. "Our beautiful—our brave," she cried. "Our protector, our son is gone." Emilio and Rosy moaned beside her. "Our beautiful—our brave, he is gone." It was the formal wail. It rose to a high piercing whine and subsided to a moan. Mama raised it three times and then she turned and went into the house and shut the door.

Emilio and Rosy stood wondering in the dawn. They heard Mama whimpering in the house. They went out to sit on the cliff above the ocean. They touched shoulders. "When did Pepé come to be a man?" Emilio asked.

"Last night," said Rosy. "Last night in Monterey." The ocean clouds turned red with the sun that was behind the mountains.

"We will have no breakfast," said Emilio. "Mama will not want to cook." Rosy did not answer him. "Where is Pepé gone?" he asked.

Rosy looked around at him. She drew her knowledge from the quiet air. "He has gone on a journey. He will never come back."

"Is he dead? Do you think he is dead?"

Rosy looked back at the ocean again. A little steamer, drawing a line of smoke, sat on the edge of the horizon. "He is not dead," Rosy explained. "Not yet."

Pepé rested the big rifle across the saddle in front of him. He let the horse walk up the hill and he didn't look back. The stony slope took on a coat of short brush so that Pepé found the entrance to a trail and entered it.

When he came to the canyon opening, he swung once in his saddle and looked back, but the houses were swallowed in the misty light. Pepé jerked forward again. The high shoulder of the canyon closed in on him. His horse stretched out its neck and sighed and settled to the trail.

It was a well-worn path, dark soft leaf-mold earth strewn with broken pieces of sandstone. The trail rounded the shoulder of the canyon and dropped steeply into the bed of the stream. In the shallows the water ran smoothly, glinting in the first morning sun. Small round stones on the bottom were as brown as rust with sun moss. In the sand along the edges of the stream the tall, rich wild mint grew, while in the water itself the cress, old and tough, had gone to heavy seed.

The path went into the stream and emerged on the other side. The horse sloshed into the water and stopped. Pepé dropped his bridle and let the beast drink of the running water.

Soon the canyon sides became steep and the first giant sentinel redwoods guarded the trail, great round red trunks bearing foliage as green and lacy as ferns. Once Pepé was among the trees, the sun was lost. A perfumed and purple light lay in the pale green of the underbrush. Gooseberry bushes and blackberries and tall ferns lined the stream, and overhead the branches of the redwoods met and cut off the sky.

Pepé drank from the water bag, and he reached into the flour sack and brought out a black string of jerky. His white teeth gnawed at the string until the tough meat parted. He chewed slowly and drank occasionally from the water bag. His little eyes were slumberous and tired, but the muscles of his face were hard set. The earth of the trail was black now. It gave up a hollow sound under the walking hoofbeats.

The stream fell more sharply. Little waterfalls splashed on the stones. Five-fingered ferns hung over the water and dripped spray from their fingertips. Pepé rode half over in his saddle, dangling one leg loosely. He picked a bay leaf from a tree beside the way and put it into his mouth for a moment to flavor the dry jerky. He held the gun loosely across the pommel.

Suddenly he squared in his saddle, swung the horse from the trail and kicked it hurriedly up behind a big redwood tree. He pulled up the reins tight against the bit to keep the horse from whinnying. His face was intent and his nostrils quivered a little.

A hollow pounding came down the trail, and a horseman rode

by, a fat man with red cheeks and a white stubble beard. His horse put down its head and blubbered at the trail when it came to the place where Pepé had turned off. "Hold up!" said the man and he pulled up his horse's head.

When the last sound of the hoofs died away, Pepé came back into the trail again. He did not relax in the saddle any more. He lifted the big rifle and swung the lever to throw a shell into the chamber, and then he let down the hammer to half cock.

The trail grew very steep. Now the redwood trees were smaller and their tops were dead, bitten dead where the wind reached them. The horse plodded on; the sun went slowly overhead and started down toward the afternoon.

Where the stream came out of a side canyon, the trail left it. Pepé dismounted and watered his horse and filled up his water bag. As soon as the trail had parted from the stream, the trees were gone and only the thick brittle sage and manzanita and chaparral edged the trail. And the soft black earth was gone, too, leaving only the light tan broken rock for the trail bed. Lizards scampered away into the brush as the horse rattled over the little stones.

Pepé turned in his saddle and looked back. He was in the open now: he could be seen from a distance. As he ascended the trail the country grew more rough and terrible and dry. The way wound about the bases of great square rocks. Little gray rabbits skittered in the brush. A bird made a monotonous high creaking. Eastward the bare rock mountaintops were pale and powder-dry under the dropping sun. The horse plodded up and up the trail toward a little V in the ridge which was the pass.

Pepé looked suspiciously back every minute or so, and his eyes sought the tops of ridges ahead. Once, on a white barren spur, he saw a black figure for a moment, but he looked quickly away, for it was one of the dark watchers. No one knew who the watchers were, nor where they lived, but it was better to ignore them and never to show interest in them. They did not bother one who stayed on the trail and minded his own business.

The air was parched and full of light dust blown by the breeze from the eroding mountains. Pepé drank sparingly from his bag and corked it tightly and hung it on the horn again. The trail moved up the dry shale hillside, avoiding rocks, dropping under clefts, climbing in and out of old water scars. When he arrived at the little pass he stopped and looked back for a long time. No dark watchers were to be seen now. The trail behind was empty. Only the high tops of the redwoods indicated where the stream flowed.

Pepé rode on through the pass. His little eyes were nearly closed with weariness, but his face was stern, relentless and manly. The high mountain wind coasted sighing through the pass and whistled on the edges of the big blocks of broken granite. In the air, a red-tailed hawk sailed over close to the ridge and screamed angrily. Pepé went slowly through the broken jagged pass and looked down on the other side.

The trail dropped quickly, staggering among broken rock. At the bottom of the slope there was a dark crease, thick with brush, and on the other side of the crease a little flat, in which a grove of oak trees grew. A scar of green grass cut across the flat. And behind the flat another mountain rose, desolate with dead rocks and starving little black bushes. Pepé drank from the bag again for the air was so dry that it encrusted his nostrils and burned his lips. He put the horse down the trail. The hooves slipped and struggled on the steep way, starting little stones that rolled off into the brush. The sun was gone behind the westward mountain now, but still it glowed brilliantly on the oaks and on the grassy flat. The rocks and the hillsides still sent up waves of the heat they had gathered from the day's sun.

Pepé looked up to the top of the next dry withered ridge. He saw a dark form against the sky, a man's figure standing on top of a rock, and he glanced away quickly not to appear curious. When a moment later he looked up again, the figure was gone.

Downward the trail was quickly covered. Sometimes the horse floundered for footing, sometimes set his feet and slid a little way. They came at last to the bottom where the dark chaparral was higher than Pepé's head. He held up his rifle on one side and his arm on the other to shield his face from the sharp brittle fingers of the brush.

Up and out of the crease he rode, and up a little cliff. The grassy flat was before him, and the round comfortable oaks. For a moment he studied the trail down which he had come, but there was no movement and no sound from it. Finally he rode out over the flat, to the green streak, and at the upper end of the damp he found a little spring welling out of the earth and dropping into a dug basin before it seeped out over the flat.

Pepé filled his bag first, and then he let the thirsty horse drink out of the pool. He led the horse to the clump of oaks, and in the middle of the grove, fairly protected from sight on all sides, he took off the saddle and the bridle and laid them on the ground. The horse stretched his jaws sideways and yawned. Pepé knotted the lead rope about the horse's neck and tied him to a sapling among the oaks, where he could graze in a fairly large circle.

When the horse was gnawing hungrily at the dry grass, Pepé went to the saddle and took a black string of jerky from the sack and strolled to an oak tree on the edge of the grove, from under which he could watch the trail. He sat down in the crisp dry oak leaves and automatically felt for his big black knife to cut the jerky, but he had no knife. He leaned back on his elbow and gnawed at the tough strong meat. His face was blank, but it was a man's face.

The bright evening light washed the eastern ridge, but the valley was darkening. Doves flew down from the hills to the spring, and the quail came running out of the brush and joined them, calling clearly to one another.

Out of the corner of his eye Pepé saw a shadow grow out of the bushy crease. He turned his head slowly. A big spotted wildcat was creeping toward the spring, belly to the ground, moving like thought.

Pepé cocked his rifle and edged the muzzle slowly around. Then he looked apprehensively up the trail and dropped the hammer again. From the ground beside him he picked an oak twig and threw it toward the spring. The quail flew up with a roar and the doves whistled away. The big cat stood up: for a long moment he looked at Pepé with cold yellow eyes, and then fearlessly walked back into the gulch.

The dusk gathered quickly in the deep valley. Pepé muttered his prayers, put his head down on his arm and went instantly to sleep.

The moon came up and filled the valley with cold blue light, and the wind swept rustling down from the peaks. The owls worked up and down the slopes looking for rabbits. Down in the brush of the gulch a coyote gabbled. The oak trees whispered softly in the night breeze.

Pepé started up, listening. His horse had whinnied. The moon was just slipping behind the western ridge, leaving the valley in darkness behind it. Pepé sat tensely gripping his rifle. From far up the trail he heard an answering whinny and the crash of shod hooves on the broken rock. He jumped to his feet, ran to his horse and led it under the trees. He threw on the saddle and cinched it tight for the steep trail, caught the unwilling head and forced the bit into the mouth. He felt the saddle to make sure the water bag and the sack of jerky were there. Then he mounted and turned up the hill.

It was velvet dark. The horse found the entrance to the trail where it left the flat, and started up, stumbling and slipping on the rocks. Pepé's hand rose up to his head. His hat was gone. He had left it under the oak tree.

The horse had struggled far up the trail when the first change of dawn came into the air, a steel grayness as light mixed thoroughly with dark. Gradually the sharp snaggled edge of the ridge stood out above them, rotten granite tortured and eaten by the winds of time. Pepé had dropped his reins on the horn, leaving direction to the horse. The brush grabbed at his legs in the dark until one knee of his jeans was ripped.

Gradually the light flowed down over the ridge. The starved brush and rocks stood out in the half light, strange and lonely in high perspective. Then there came warmth into the light. Pepé drew up and looked back, but he could see nothing in the darker valley below. The sky turned blue over the coming sun. In the waste of the mountainside, the poor dry brush grew only three feet high. Here and there, big outcroppings of unrotted granite stood up like moldering houses. Pepé relaxed a little. He drank from his water bag and bit off a piece of jerky. A single eagle flew over, high in the light.

Without warning Pepé's horse screamed and fell on its side. He was almost down before the rifle crash echoed up from the valley. From a hole behind the struggling shoulder, a stream of bright crimson blood pumped and stopped and pumped and stopped. The hooves threshed on the ground. Pepé lay half stunned beside the horse. He looked slowly down the hill. A piece of sage clipped off beside his head and another crash echoed up from side to side of the canyon. Pepé flung himself frantically behind a bush.

He crawled up the hill on his knees and on one hand. His right hand held the rifle up off the ground and pushed it ahead of him. He moved with the instinctive care of an animal. Rapidly he wormed his way toward one of the big outcroppings of granite on the hill above him. Where the brush was high he doubled up and ran, but where the cover was slight he wriggled forward on his stomach, pushing the rifle ahead of him. In the last little distance there was no cover at all. Pepé poised and then he darted across the space and flashed around the corner of the rock.

He leaned panting against the stone. When his breath came easier he moved along behind the big rock until he came to a narrow split that offered a thin section of vision down the hill. Pepé lay on his stomach and pushed the rifle barrel through the slit and waited.

The sun reddened the western ridges now. Already the buzzards were settling down toward the place where the horse lay. A small brown bird scratched in the dead sage leaves directly in front of the rifle muzzle. The coasting eagle flew back toward the rising sun.

Pepé saw a little movement in the brush far below. His grip tightened on the gun. A little brown doe stepped daintily out on the trail and crossed it and disappeared into the brush again. For a long time Pepé waited. Far below he could see the little flat and the oak trees and the slash of green. Suddenly his eyes flashed back at the trail again. A quarter of a mile down there had been a quick movement in the chaparral. The rifle swung over. The front sight nestled in the V of the rear sight. Pepé studied for a moment and then raised the rear sight a notch. The little movement in the brush came again. The sight settled on it. Pepé squeezed the trigger. The explosion crashed down the mountain and up the other side, and came rattling back. The whole side of the slope grew still. No more movement. And then a white streak cut into the granite of the slit and a bullet whined away and a crash sounded up from below. Pepé felt a sharp pain in his right hand. A sliver of granite was sticking out from between his first and second knuckles and the

point protruded from his palm. Carefully he pulled out the sliver
of stone. The wound bled evenly and gently. No vein nor artery
was cut.

Pepé looked into a little dusty cave in the rock and gathered
a handful of spider web, and he pressed the mass into the cut,
plastering the soft web into the blood. The flow stopped almost
at once.

The rifle was on the ground. Pepé picked it up, levered a new
shell into the chamber. And then he slid into the brush on his
stomach. Far to the right he crawled, and then up the hill, moving
slowly and carefully, crawling to cover and resting and then crawling again.

In the mountains the sun is high in its arc before it penetrates
the gorges. The hot face looked over the hill and brought instant
heat with it. The white light beat on the rocks and reflected from
them and rose up quivering from the earth again, and the rocks
and bushes seemed to quiver behind the air.

Pepé crawled in the general direction of the ridge peak, zig-
zagging for cover. The deep cut between his knuckles began to
throb. He crawled close to a rattlesnake before he saw it, and when
it raised its dry head and made a soft beginning whirr, he backed
up and took another way. The quick gray lizards flashed in front
of him, raising a tiny line of dust. He found another mass of spider
web and pressed it against his throbbing hand.

Pepé was pushing the rifle with his left hand now. Little drops
of sweat ran to the ends of his coarse black hair and rolled down
his cheeks. His lips and tongue were growing thick and heavy. His
lips writhed to draw saliva into his mouth. His little dark eyes were
uneasy and suspicious. Once when a gray lizard paused in front of
him on the parched ground and turned its head sideways he crushed
it flat with a stone.

When the sun slid past noon he had not gone a mile. He
crawled exhaustedly a last hundred yards to a patch of high sharp
manzanita, crawled desperately, and when the patch was reached
he wriggled in among the tough gnarly trunks and dropped his head
on his left arm. There was little shade in the meager brush, but
there was cover and safety. Pepé went to sleep as he lay and the
sun beat on his back. A few little birds hopped close to him and

peered and hopped away. Pepé squirmed in his sleep and he
raised and dropped his wounded hand again and again.

The sun went down behind the peaks and the cool evening
came, and then the dark. A coyote yelled from the hillside, Pepé
started awake and looked about with misty eyes. His hand was
swollen and heavy; a little thread of pain ran up the inside of his
arm and settled in a pocket in his armpit. He peered about and
then stood up, for the mountains were black and the moon had
not yet risen. Pepé stood up in the dark. The coat of his father
pressed on his arm. His tongue was swollen until it nearly filled his
mouth. He wriggled out of the coat and dropped it in the brush,
and then he struggled up the hill, falling over rocks and tearing his
way through the brush. The rifle knocked against stones as he went.
Little dry avalanches of gravel and shattered stone went whispering
down the hill behind him.

After a while the old moon came up and showed the jagged
ridge top ahead of him. By moonlight Pepé traveled more easily.
He bent forward so that his throbbing arm hung away from his
body. The journey uphill was made in dashes and rests, a frantic
rush up a few yards and then a rest. The wind coasted down the
slope rattling the dry stems of the bushes.

The moon was at meridian when Pepé came at last to the sharp
backbone of the ridge top. On the last hundred yards of the rise no
soil had clung under the wearing winds. The way was on solid
rock. He clambered to the top and looked down on the other side.
There was a draw like the last below him, misty with moonlight,
brushed with dry struggling sage and chaparral. On the other side
the hill rose up sharply and at the top the jagged rotten teeth of the
mountain showed against the sky. At the bottom of the cut the
brush was thick and dark.

Pepé stumbled down the hill. His throat was almost closed with
thirst. At first he tried to run, but immediately he fell and rolled.
After that he went more carefully. The moon was just disappearing
behind the mountains when he came to the bottom. He crawled
into the heavy brush feeling with his fingers for water. There was
no water in the bed of the stream, only damp earth. Pepé laid his
gun down and scooped up a handful of mud and put it in his
mouth, and then he spluttered and scraped the earth from his

tongue with his finger, for the mud drew at his mouth like a poultice. He dug a hole in the stream bed with his fingers, dug a little basin to catch water; but before it was very deep his head fell forward on the damp ground and he slept.

The dawn came and the heat of the day fell on the earth, and still Pepé slept. Late in the afternoon his head jerked up. He looked slowly around. His eyes were slits of wariness. Twenty feet away in the heavy brush a big tawny mountain lion stood looking at him. Its long thick tail waved gracefully, its ears erect with interest, not laid back dangerously. The lion squatted down on its stomach and watched him.

Pepé looked at the hole he had dug in the earth. A half inch of muddy water had collected in the bottom. He tore the sleeve from his hurt arm, with his teeth ripped out a little square, soaked it in the water and put it in his mouth. Over and over he filled the cloth and sucked it.

Still the lion sat and watched him. The evening came down but there was no movement on the hills. No birds visited the dry bottom of the cut. Pepé looked occasionally at the lion. The eyes of the yellow beast drooped as though he were about to sleep. He yawned and his long thin red tongue curled out. Suddenly his head jerked around and his nostrils quivered. His big tail lashed. He stood up and slunk like a tawny shadow into the thick brush.

A moment later Pepé heard the sound, the faint far crash of horses' hooves on gravel. And he heard something else, a high whining yelp of a dog.

Pepé took his rifle in his left hand and he glided into the brush almost as quietly as the lion had. In the darkening evening he crouched up the hill toward the next ridge. Only when the dark came did he stand up. His energy was short. Once it was dark he fell over the rocks and slipped to his knees on the steep slope, but he moved on and on up the hill, climbing and scrabbling over the broken hillside.

When he was far up toward the top, he lay down and slept for a little while. The withered moon, shining on his face, awakened him. He stood up and moved up the hill. Fifty yards away he stopped and turned back, for he had forgotten his rifle. He walked heavily down and poked about in the brush, but he could not find his gun. At last he lay down to rest. The pocket of pain in his armpit had grown more sharp. His arm seemed to swell out and fall with every heartbeat. There was no position lying down where the heavy arm did not press against his armpit.

With the effort of a hurt beast, Pepé got up and moved again toward the top of the ridge. He held his swollen arm away from his body with his left hand. Up the steep hill he dragged himself, a few steps and a rest, and a few more steps. At last he was nearing the top. The moon showed the uneven sharp back of it against the sky.

Pepé's brain spun in a big spiral up and away from him. He slumped to the ground and lay still. The rock ridge top was only a hundred feet above him.

The moon moved over the sky. Pepé half turned on his back. His tongue tried to make words, but only a thick hissing came from between his lips.

When the dawn came, Pepé pulled himself up. His eyes were sane again. He drew his great puffed arm in front of him and looked at the angry wound. The black line ran up from his wrist to his armpit. Automatically he reached in his pocket for the big black knife, but it was not there. His eyes searched the ground. He picked up a sharp blade of stone and scraped at the wound, sawed at the proud flesh and then squeezed the green juice out in big drops. Instantly he threw back his head and whined like a dog. His whole right side shuddered at the pain, but the pain cleared his head.

In the gray light he struggled up the last slope to the ridge and crawled over and lay down behind a line of rocks. Below him lay a deep canyon exactly like the last, waterless and desolate. There was no flat, no oak trees, not even heavy brush in the bottom of it. And on the other side a sharp ridge stood up, thinly brushed with starving sage, littered with broken granite. Strewn over the hill there were giant outcroppings, and on the top the granite teeth stood out against the sky.

The new day was light now. The flame of sun came over the ridge and fell on Pepé where he lay on the ground. His coarse black hair was littered with twigs and bits of spider web. His eyes had retreated back into his head. Between his lips the tip of his black tongue showed.

He sat up and dragged his great arm into his lap and nursed it, rocking his body and moaning in his throat. He threw back his head and looked up into the pale sky. A big black bird circled nearly out of sight, and far to the left another was sailing near.

He lifted his head to listen, for a familiar sound had come to him from the valley he had climbed out of; it was the crying yelp of hounds, excited and feverish, on a trail.

Pepé bowed his head quickly. He tried to speak rapid words but only a thick hiss came from his lips. He drew a shaky cross on his breast with his left hand. It was a long struggle to get to his feet. He crawled slowly and mechanically to the top of a big rock on the ridge peak. Once there, he arose slowly, swaying to his feet, and stood erect. Far below he could see the dark brush where he had slept. He braced his feet and stood there, black against the morning sky.

There came a ripping sound at his feet. A piece of stone flew up and a bullet droned off into the next gorge. The hollow crash echoed up from below. Pepé looked down for a moment and then pulled himself straight again.

His body jarred back. His left hand fluttered helplessly toward his breast. The second crash sounded from below. Pepé swung forward and toppled from the rock. His body struck and rolled over and over, starting a little avalanche. And when at last he stopped against a bush, the avalanche slid slowly down and covered up his head.

CAROLINE GORDON

Mr. Powers

ACK AND ELLEN had been living at the hill farm a little over a year when a strange man came up the path one morning, a well-set-up young man with blue eyes in a wind-burned country face. He and Jack talked together a few minutes on the porch, then they stepped down on the path and walked slowly over the lawn and out to the brow of the hill. They stood there a while, talking, gesticulating occasionally toward the green wooded hill that rose up sharply from the river bottom just opposite the Cromlie house. Ellen watched the two figures poised there against the bright sky and thought that they seemed to belong to the landscape: Jack, slouching and relaxed in his old corduroys and the sweater that was already weathering to the color of the hillside; the young country-man, more composed, erect except for the stoop of the shoulders that she had come to recognize as the mark of a teamster.

When Jack came back he said that the man had made him a proposition: he wanted to go through the woods and get the fallen trees and the trees that were dying out "on shares." He would saw them up into the right lengths for stove and fireplace, giving the Cromlies a half of all the wood he handled and selling his own share in Gloversville.

"He wants to rent the old cabin too," Jack said. "He's going to give me five dollars a month for it."

"Hadn't you better find out something about him first?" Ellen asked, and then pretended that she hadn't spoken, seeing by Jack's face that the trade was already made.

"Powers," she said, musing, "Powers. That's a good country name. I reckon he's all right."

At lunch they were very gay, saying that now they had a settled income from the place. "Sixty dollars a year for that old cabin," Jack said, "and without turning your hand over to get it. That's not bad."

"It'll pay the milk bill," Ellen said.

Early in the afternoon Mr. Powers's little dun-colored mules drew up before the cabin that was set in the hollow just below the Cromlie house. Mrs. Powers sat beside Mr. Powers on the driver's seat, holding a child in her lap. Their household goods were stacked behind them in the rickety wagon. Ellen, in the swing with Lucy, watched them unloading. There was not much to carry into the house. A little, rusty stove, a bed, a roll of quilts and blankets, and a bushel basket heaped with pots and pans and skillets.

Lucy pulled at her mother's arm. "Where does the baby sleep?" she asked. "Mama, where does the *baby* sleep?"

Ellen was thinking of some plates, flowered plates with gold rims that she never used. There were two or three tablecloths, too, that didn't fit either the dining-table or the small table in the window nook. "I have no idea," she said absently.

She decided that she would not offer the plates or the tablecloths to Mrs. Powers, not just yet anyhow. They all said it was better not to start off being too intimate with your tenants. Aunt Molly was always having trouble with hers. Tom Potter had actually stolen three loads of tobacco out of her barn. Took them to a loose floor in Springfield and sold them as his own crop and never gave her any account of them. Cousin Sarah thought that Aunt Molly had started Potter off on the wrong track by being too kind to him. "I'm going to be Christian. I hope I'll always be Christian to people, but I'm going to stand on my dignity. I believe it pays, with tenants."

At three o'clock Ellen and Lucy took a basket of butter beans out under the trees to shell. They had not been sitting there long before Mrs. Foster came toiling up the path, leaning on her blackthorn stick. Ellen brought a chair for her and then went into the kitchen and fixed a tray with a plate of ginger cookies for Lucy and a decanter of blackberry wine for Mrs. Foster and herself. They sat there all afternoon talking and drinking their wine and looking

out over the valley that was already beginning to shimmer with
blue haze. It was five o'clock when Mrs. Foster moved nearer to
Ellen and laid her hand on her knee. Her eyes were sparkling and
her mouth made a straight line across her tanned face. "I told Ed
I was just coming up here and see you myself," she said. "I told
him you was new people here and it wasn't reasonable to expect you
to know everybody in the country . . ."

Ellen had been looking at the fields on the other side of the
river, thinking that it was strange that one patch of ground should
be in deep shade and the one adjoining it in brilliant sunshine.
She raised her eyes to the horizon now and saw that it was filled
with thick, scudding white clouds.

"It's something about our new tenant," she said.

She was waiting at the gate when Jack came home that night.

"Do you know who our new tenant is?" she cried. "Do you
know who he is?"

Jack waited until he had put the car in the garage before he
answered. "He's Bill Powers's brother," he said then. "They're both
sons of that old Albert Powers who used to be miller."

"If you'd read the paper once in a while you wouldn't be so
ignorant," Ellen told him. "Everybody in the whole country read
about it except us."

She gave him Mrs. Foster's account of Mr. Powers. He was the
Powers—the Jim Powers—that had killed his little boy over in the
Brush Run community in a fight with the hired man over his wife.
They had had a new hired man all summer, "a mean feller named
Shell, from over in Trigg County." Jim had been down guarding
his watermelon patch and had come back to the house around midnight to find his wife out in the grape arbor with the hired man.
There had been a good deal of shouting back and forth and calling
of names. Jim's sister and his six-year-old son had come downstairs
in their night clothes to find out what it was all about. Jim finally
picked up an axe and went after the feller with that. Shell had
dodged in time, but the double-bladed axe, swinging backward,
had caught the little boy in the side of the head and felled him to
the ground. Shell had run off down the road while they were all
going on over the child, who had never regained consciousness and

had died in a few minutes. Jim had stayed right with him, holding his hand.

Ellen was laughing hysterically when she finished.

"I asked him yesterday if he had any children and he said, 'Just one. She's mighty spoiled!'"

"Cool feller, isn't he?" Jack said. He had been standing looking straight ahead while she talked. He started up the walk now. Ellen hurried to catch up with him.

"Mrs. Foster couldn't understand why we hadn't heard about it." She imitated Mrs. Foster's high-pitched country drawl: "I told Ed I didn't see why they didn't know about it. They git the paper every day and both of 'em can read . . ."

"Can't Mrs. Foster read?" Jack asked.

"No. She has to wait for things like this to happen. She seemed to think Mr. Powers had taken an unfair advantage of our innocence. She kept saying, 'An' him comin' and settin' down on y'all just 'cause you was new here!'"

"I reckon the poor devil was up against it," Jack said. "I reckon we were the only people in the country who would take him in."

"We are going to let him stay," Ellen said. "Jack, we *are* going to let him stay, aren't we?"

Jack laughed. "*You* put him out," he said.

The Cromlies could look down from their high porch almost into the back windows of the Powers's cabin. When the white curtains were pushed aside they could see Mrs. Powers preparing the meals in the small room that was used as a kitchen. A small woman, with an untidy mass of blond hair, she moved slowly about from kitchen to porch and back again, wearing always a faint, excited smile.

"It's the most extraordinary expression," Ellen said, "a sort of smirk. You know, the way people look when they're so pleased with themselves that they simply can't hide it! What *I* can't understand, though, is why she's stuck to him through all this."

Jack said that he thought Mrs. Powers's situation must be in some ways highly satisfactory. "Probably the first time in her life she's ever had the upper hand of him, morally, I mean. They've changed places at one fell swoop. Whatever her sins have been in the past, his are greater . . . since this killing. Must leave 'em both a little dazed."

"It's terrible," Ellen said. "It's terrible to think of them being there together. What do you suppose they can find to say to each other?"

"Well, talking things over is hardly in Powers's line," Jack observed. "He's a man of deeds. I was talking to Judge Pryor about him the other day. He lived on his place five years. The judge thinks a lot of him. Says he's always had this quick temper, like all the Powerses, but he's all right if you handle him properly. He's a hustler, too. Got nine hundred dollars for his share of the tobacco crop the last year he lived on the judge's place."

"Does the judge think he's got any chance to get off?" Ellen asked.

"Oh, they all think Scott'll get him off with a light sentence. Ten to twenty years. He could hardly expect to get off with less than that."

"Twenty years is a long time," Ellen said. "Ten years is a long time."

"It's a hell of a long time," Jack said.

People who came out from town were very much interested in the Powers family. They peered fearfully over the balcony railings, speculating on what sort of mood Mr. Powers was likely to be in that day and discussed his chances for escaping the pen. Tom Eliott suggested that he and Jack fight a duel, with hatchets, at twenty paces. Jack said that he was thinking of putting a machine-gun in the crape myrtle bushes.

"You could do a lot of damage from this hill with a machine-gun," he said.

Nobody at the Cromlie house was ever up in time to see Mr. Powers go off to work in the morning. They could hear the sound of his axe ringing out in the woods, though, all during the day, and occasionally the great crash of a falling tree shook the whole valley. When this happened Ellen stopped whatever she was doing and a little chill went over her as she thought of Mr. Powers moving about in the dim light among the fallen green boughs. She thought, too, of what Jack had said, that he would certainly go to the penitentiary, and tried to imagine the tall, red-faced countryman in prison.

"I hope they let him drive a team or something like that," she told Jack. "They do have wagons and teams at the penitentiary, don't they?"

"No," Jack said. "They're progressive up there. Use trucks."

One afternoon when they came back from town they saw Mr. Powers's wagon standing beside the drive, filled with logs. Mr. Powers was stooping beside the off mule, mending a trace chain with a length of wire.

Jack came to a halt opposite the wagon. "You got some nice logs there," he said.

Mr. Powers straightened up. Standing with his arm lying along the mule's back he pointed to the strip of woods that lay next to the cornfield. "I aim to get down in the bottom tomorrow," he said. "Thar's some timber in thar needs takin' out."

"What kind of wood is it?" Ellen asked.

He pushed aside the black lock that overhung his forehead. His eyes—very blue eyes with wrinkles raying out from the corners—rested on her face for a moment. "Hickory, mostly," he said. His gaze shifted to Jack. "You don't want to burn up all your barn wood, but them saplings is too thick in thar. Won't hurt to clean 'em out a little."

"Well, hickory's fine to burn," Jack said.

Mr. Powers nodded. "Ain't nothin' better than a hickory fire," he said.

They did not see Mr. Powers again for several days. When he appeared then he said that he and his wife found that the cabin was too small, after all. They were moving back to his father-in-law's that afternoon. He would be glad, though, if Mr. Cromlie would let him keep his mules in the stable that was across the road from the cabin a few days longer. His father-in-law didn't have any more stable room than he needed himself.

Ellen was waiting in the living-room when Jack came back into the house. "Did he say anything about the wood?" she demanded.

Jack lit a cigarette. "We didn't get around to that," he said.

"Then I wouldn't let him keep his mules in our stable," Ellen said. "I wouldn't let him get away with it. I just would not do it."

"Oh, he'll be all right," Jack said. "That first load was his, anyhow, according to the trade. He probably took it off to town and
sold it on the spot. Needs cash, I expect." He grinned. "You have
to excuse him for being a little absent-minded. He has important
business on his hands."

Ellen reflected that Mr. Powers's hearing was set for Monday
week and said no more about the wood.

At the preliminary hearing Jim Powers was charged with
murder and released after he had executed bond for a thousand
dollars. Ellen was aghast when she heard the news.

"But they *can't* accuse him of murder," she said. "The most they
can accuse him of is involuntary manslaughter."

"Manslaughter and assault and battery with intent to kill," Jack
said. "He could get life for that."

They saw Mr. Powers occasionally at a distance, taking his
mules in or out of the old stable, but they had no conversation with
him. He was reported by Mrs. Foster to be living in a cabin that
belonged to his father-in-law, Nate Dockery. The Dockery place
joined the hill farm. Ellen speculated as to whether the trees that
were heard to fall occasionally in the woods belonged to Mr.
Dockery or to the hill farm.

Jack was irritable when she suggested that he walk over in the
woods and see if the cutting was being done on their line.

"There are fully ten thousand trees in that piece of woods," he
said, "and not more than twenty of them are worth a damn. And
those twenty are red oaks, worth, say, four dollars apiece, board
measure. Well, I hotfoot it over there this afternoon and save two
trees. What do I get for my afternoon's work? Eight dollars. I can
make two hundred if I get on in the house and finish that article.
Miller's wired for it twice now."

"Oh, all right if you feel that way about it," Ellen said. "I just
hate for him to think we're soft. Everybody in this country thinks
we're soft because we're city people."

She did not mention the matter to Jack again, however, seeing
that he so disliked the idea of talking to Powers about the wood.
It was not long after that that Mr. Powers took his mules out of the
old stable. Shortly afterward the axe strokes ceased to ring out in

the woods. Mr. Powers, Mrs. Foster said, had moved again. He and his father-in-law had never gotten on any too well and it stood to reason that they wouldn't get on no better after what had happened. He was working now for a Mr. Mason out on the Jasper road. He and Mrs. Powers were still living together. Ellen was curious about the character of the woman who had been the cause of the affray.

"Has she had a bad character before this, Mrs. Foster?" she asked.

Mrs. Foster compressed her lips. "Ever since she was big enough, Miz Cromlie," she said. "But you can't tell Jim nothin'. All them Powerses is hard-headed and he's the hard-headedest of all of 'em."

Mrs. Powers's name was mentioned less and less often in the Cromlie household from that time forward. Ellen remarked once that he had to pass their house every time he went to town. "If I ever meet him in the big road I'm going to ask him about that wood," she said. "I swear I am!"

" 'Twon't do you any good," Jack said. "He'll just tell you what he told me."

"Well, what *did* he tell you?" Ellen asked.

"Just smiled and said he'd been aimin' to get at it now for two, three days. He means it too. He'll get us up a load one day."

"Unless he goes to the pen first," Ellen said.

The season turned slowly toward fall. The trees on the hill had not begun to turn, but their green was softened, verging already toward yellow And yellow leaves from the willows fell occasionally into the green water of the swimming-hole. The air was clear and bright, touched faintly with cold in the early morning.

The Negro boy, Chap, spaded up wide beds of earth in front of the house and on either side of the brick walk and set out iris and tulip and jonquil bulbs and scattered larkspur and delphinium seed among them. The Cromlies walked around in the yard or out from the shade of the beech trees and down the slope. Sometimes Ellen, standing on the walk, would look back into the hall and think how the house that was spread out now, with all its doors and windows open to the sunshine, would contract and darken soon with winter.

One evening at sunset she and Lucy walked out on the brow

of the hill and sat down on the bench that was fixed around the big beech tree. Sitting there they had the whole valley spread out before them, the wooded hill that rose steeply on the right, with the Jasper road curving between it and the river, and stretching away on the other side of the river beyond the old covered bridge the flat fields that were still covered with late corn and tobacco. Some of the blue haze that had been over the whole country all day still lingered in these far fields, but the rest of the valley was bathed in bright, flickering light.

A wagon drawn by two mules came up over the hill and began the long descent to the bridge. Ellen watched the mules hold back at first and then put their feet down faster and faster as the driver eased his brake on. A tall young man in blue shirt and pants, he sat sidewise on the high driver's seat with his face turned toward the river.

Ellen looked away and then back again, trying to fix the scene in her memory. The broad valley, the turning green river, and the long line of the old covered bridge would stay, she knew, in her memory, but the bright, flickering light that was so much a part of it all would grow dimmer and more unreal until finally it would vanish entirely. You could not prison light in the memory.

The team of mules and the wagon were directly beneath the bench now. The driver had taken his hat off and flung it in the bottom of the wagon. His head bared to the evening air, he sat whistling, breaking off occasionally to call to his mules in a loud, clear voice.

Lucy had got up and was standing on the brow of the hill looking down at him.

"Mama," she cried out suddenly, "it's Mr. Powers! It's Mr. Powers, mama!"

"Hush!" Ellen said. "He'll hear you."

She watched the mules round the curve and approach the bridge. Mr. Powers's figure was bright for a moment against the black shed, then it disappeared into the dark. His whistle could be heard for a little while, mixed with the rattling of the mules' feet on the wooden flooring; then that too died away. Ellen stood up. Most of the color was gone from the west by this time, but the east still held a reflected glow, soft lavenders and pinks and here and there a streak of azure.

Lucy was tugging at her mother's hand.

"Didn't you want to speak to him, mama? You said you wanted to speak to him."

Ellen shook her head. "No," she said, "I don't want to speak to him."

GRAHAM GREENE

The Hint of an Explanation

LONG TRAIN JOURNEY on a late December evening, in this new version of peace, is a dreary experience. I suppose that my fellow traveller and I could consider ourselves lucky to have a compartment to ourselves, even though the heating apparatus was not working, even though the lights went out entirely in the frequent Pennine tunnels and were too dim anyway for us to read our books without straining our eyes, and though there was no restaurant car to give at least a change of scene. It was when we were trying simultaneously to chew the same kind of dry bun bought at the same station buffet that my companion and I came together.

Before that we had sat at opposite ends of the carriage, both muffled to the chin in overcoats, both bent low over type we could barely make out, but as I threw the remains of my cake under the seat our eyes met, and he laid his book down.

By the time we were half-way to Bedwell Junction we had found an enormous range of subjects for discussion; starting with buns and the weather, we had gone on to politics, the government, foreign affairs, the atom bomb, and, by an inevitable progression, God. We had not, however, become either shrill or acid. My companion, who now sat opposite me, leaning a little forward, so that our knees nearly touched, gave such an impression of serenity that it would have been impossible to quarrel with him, however much our views differed, and differ they did profoundly.

I had soon realized I was speaking to a Catholic, to someone who believed—how do they put it?—in an omnipotent and omniscient Deity, while I was what is loosely called an Agnostic. I have a certain intuition (which I do not trust, founded as it may well be on childish experiences and needs) that a God exists, and I am surprised occasionally into belief by the extraordinary coincidences that beset our path like the traps set for leopards in the jungle, but intellectually I am revolted at the whole notion of such a God who can so abandon his creatures to the enormities of Free Will. I found myself expressing this view to my companion, who listened quietly and with respect. He made no attempt to interrupt: he showed none of the impatience or the intellectual arrogance I have grown to expect from Catholics; when the lights of a wayside station flashed across his face that had escaped hitherto the rays of the one globe working in the compartment, I caught a glimpse suddenly of— what? I stopped speaking, so strong was the impression. I was carried back ten years, to the other side of the great useless conflict, to a small town, Gisors in Normandy. I was again, for a moment, walking on the ancient battlements and looking down across the grey roofs, until my eyes for some reason lit on one grey stony "back" out of the many, where the face of a middle-aged man was pressed against a windowpane (I suppose that face has ceased to exist now, just as I believe the whole town with its medieval memories has been reduced to rubble). I remembered saying to myself with astonishment, "That man is happy—completely happy."

I looked across the compartment at my fellow traveller, but his face was already again in shadow. I said weakly, "When you think what God—if there is a God—allows. It's not merely the physical agonies, but think of the corruption, even of children. . . ."

He said, "Our view is so limited," and I was disappointed at the conventionality of his reply. He must have been aware of my disappointment (it was as though our thoughts were huddled as closely as ourselves for warmth), for he went on, "Of course there is no answer here. We catch hints . . ." and then the train roared into another tunnel and the lights again went out. It was the longest tunnel yet; we went rocking down it, and the cold seemed to become more intense with the darkness like an icy fog (perhaps when one sense—of sight—is robbed of sensation, the others grow more sensitive). When we emerged into the mere grey of night and the globe lit up once more, I could see that my companion was leaning back on his seat.

I repeated his last words as a question, "Hints?"

"Oh, they mean very little in cold print—or cold speech," he said, shivering in his overcoat. "And they mean nothing at all to a human being other than the man who catches them. They are not scientific evidence—or evidence at all for that matter. Events that don't somehow, turn out as they were intended—by the human actors I mean, or by the thing behind the human actors."

"The thing?"

"The word Satan is so anthropomorphic."

I had to lean forward now: I wanted to hear what he had to say. I am—I really am, God knows—open to conviction.

He said, "One's words are so crude, but I sometimes feel pity for that thing. It is so continually finding the right weapon to use against its Enemy and the weapon breaks in its own breast. It sometimes seems to me so—powerless. You said something just now about the corruption of children. It reminded me of something in my own childhood. You are the first person—except for one—that I have thought of telling it to, perhaps because you are anonymous. It's not a very long story, and in a way it's relevant."

I said, "I'd like to hear it."

"You mustn't expect too much meaning. But to me there seems to be a hint. That's all. A hint."

He went slowly on, turning his face to the pane, though he could have seen nothing real in the whirling world outside except an occasional signal lamp, a light in a window, a small country station torn backwards by our rush, picking his words with precision. He said, "When I was a child they taught me to serve at Mass. The church was a small one, for there were very few Catholics where I lived. It was a market town in East Anglia, surrounded by flat, chalky fields and ditches—so many ditches. I don't suppose there were fifty Catholics all told, and for some reason there was a tradition of hostility to us. Perhaps it went back to the burning of a Protestant martyr in the sixteenth century—there was a stone marking the place near where the meat stalls stood on Wednesdays. I was only half aware of the enmity, though I know that my school nickname of Popey Martin had something to do with my religion, and I had heard that my father was nearly excluded from the Constitutional Club when he first came to the town.

"Every Sunday I had to dress up in my surplice and serve Mass. I hated it—I have always hated dressing up in any way (which is funny when you come to think of it), and I never ceased to be afraid of losing my place in the service and doing something which would put me to ridicule. Our services were at a different hour from the Anglican, and as our small, far-from-select band trudged out of the hideous chapel the whole of the townsfolk seemed to be on the way past to the proper church—I always thought of it as the proper church. We had to pass the parade of their eyes, indifferent, supercilious, mocking; you can't imagine how seriously religion can be taken in a small town, if only for social reasons.

"There was one man in particular; he was one of the two bakers in the town, the one my family did not patronize. I don't think any of the Catholics patronized him because he was called a free-thinker —an odd title, for, poor man, no one's thoughts were less free than his. He was hemmed in by his hatred—his hatred of us. He was very ugly to look at, with one wall-eye and a head the shape of a turnip, with the hair gone on the crown, and he was unmarried. He had no interests, apparently, but his baking and his hatred, though now that I am older I begin to see other sides to his nature—it did contain, perhaps, a certain furtive love. One would come across him suddenly sometimes on a country walk, especially if one were alone and

it was Sunday. It was as if he rose from the ditches, and the smear
of chalk on his clothes reminded one of the flour on his working
overalls. He would have a stick in his hand and stab at the hedges,
and if his mood were very black he would call out after one strange
abrupt words like a foreign tongue—I know the meaning of those
words, of course, now. Once the police went to his house because
of what a boy said he'd seen, but nothing came of it except that the
hate shackled him closer. His name was Blacker and he terrified me.

"I think he had a particular hatred of my father—I don't know
why. My father was manager of the Midland Bank, and it's possible
that at some time Blacker may have had unsatisfactory dealings
with the bank; my father was a very cautious man who suffered all
his life from anxiety about money—his own and other people's. If
I try and picture Blacker now I see him walking along a narrow
path between high windowless walls, and at the end of the path
stands a small boy of ten—me. I don't know whether it's a symbolic
picture or the memory of one of our encounters—our encounters
somehow got more and more frequent. You talked just now about
the corruption of children. That poor man was preparing to revenge
himself on everything he hated—my father, the Catholics, the God
whom people persisted in crediting—and that by corrupting me. He
had evolved a horrible and ingenious plan.

"I remember the first time I had a friendly word from him. I
was passing his shop as rapidly as I could when I heard his voice
call out with a kind of sly subservience as though he were an under
servant. 'Master David,' he called, 'Master David,' and I hurried on.
But the next time I passed that way he was at his door (he must
have seen me coming) with one of those curly cakes in his hand that
we called Chelsea buns. I didn't want to take it, but he made me,
and then I couldn't be other than polite when he asked me to come
into his parlour behind the shop and see something very special.

"It was a small electric railway—a rare sight in those days, and
he insisted on showing me how it worked. He made me turn the
switches and stop and start it, and he told me that I could come in
any morning and have a game with it. He used the word 'game' as
though it were something secret, and it's true that I never told my
family of this invitation and of how, perhaps twice a week those
holidays, the desire to control that little railway became overpower-

ing, and looking up and down the street to see if I were observed, I would dive into the shop."

Our larger, dirtier, adult train drove into a tunnel and the light went out. We sat in darkness and silence, with the noise of the train blocking our ears like wax. When we were through we didn't speak at once and I had to prick him into continuing. "An elaborate seduction," I said.

"Don't think his plans were as simple as that," my companion said, "or as crude. There was much more hate than love, poor man, in his make-up. Can you hate something you don't believe in? And yet he called himself a free-thinker. What an impossible paradox, to be free and to be so obsessed. Day by day all through those holidays his obsession must have grown, but he kept a grip; he bided his time. Perhaps that thing I spoke of gave him the strength and the wisdom. It was only a week from the end of the holidays that he spoke to me on what concerned him so deeply.

"I heard him behind me as I knelt on the floor, coupling two coaches. He said, 'You won't be able to do this, Master David, when school starts.' It wasn't a sentence that needed any comment from me any more than the one that followed. 'You ought to have it for your own, you ought,' but how skilfully and unemphatically he had sowed the longing, the idea of a possibility. . . . I was coming to his parlour every day now; you see, I had to cram every opportunity in before the hated term started again, and I suppose I was becoming accustomed to Blacker, to that wall-eye, that turnip head, that nauseating subservience. The Pope, you know, describes himself as 'the servant of the servants of God,' and Blacker—I sometimes think that Blacker was 'the servant of the servants of . . . .' well, let it be.

"The very next day, standing in the doorway watching me play, he began to talk to me about religion. He said, with what untruth even I recognized, how much he admired the Catholics; he wished he could believe like that, but how could a baker believe? He accented 'a baker' as one might say a biologist, and the tiny train spun round the gauge 0 track. He said, 'I can bake the things you eat just as well as any Catholic can,' and disappeared into his shop. I hadn't the faintest idea what he meant. Presently he emerged again, holding in his hand a little wafer. 'Here,' he said, 'eat that and tell me. . . .' When I put it in my mouth I could tell that it was made in the same way as our wafers for communion—he had got the shape a little wrong, that was all—and I felt guilty and irrationally scared. 'Tell me,' he said, 'what's the difference?'

" 'Difference?' I asked.

" 'Isn't that just the same as you eat in church?'

"I said smugly, 'It hasn't been consecrated.'

"He said, 'Do you think, if I put the two of them under a microscope, you could tell the difference?'

"But even at ten I had the answer to that question. 'No,' I said, 'the—accidents don't change,' stumbling a little on the word 'accidents' which had suddenly conveyed to me the idea of death and wounds.

"Blacker said with sudden intensity, 'How I'd like to get one of your ones in my mouth—just to see. . . .'

"It may seem odd to you, but this was the first time that the idea of transsubstantiation really lodged in my mind. I had learned it all by rote; I had grown up with the idea. The Mass was as lifeless to me as the sentences in *De Bello Gallico;* communion a routine like drill in the school-yard, but here suddenly I was in the presence of a man who took it seriously, as seriously as the priest whom naturally one didn't count—it was his job. I felt more scared than ever.

"He said, 'It's all nonsense, but I'd just like to have it in my mouth.'

" 'You could if you were a Catholic,' I said naïvely.

"He gazed at me with his one good eye, like a Cyclops. He said, 'You serve at Mass, don't you? It would be easy for you to get at one of those things. I tell you what I'd do—I'd swap this electric train for one of your wafers—consecrated, mind. It's got to be consecrated.'

" 'I could get you one out of the box,' I said. I think I still imagined that his interest was a baker's interest—to see how they were made.

" 'Oh, no,' he said, 'I want to see what your God tastes like.'

" 'I couldn't do that.'

" 'Not for a whole electric train, just for yourself? You wouldn't have any trouble at home. I'd pack it up and put a label inside that your dad could see: "For my bank manager's little boy from a grateful client." He'd be pleased as punch with that.'

"Now that we are grown men it seems a trivial temptation, doesn't it? But try to think back to your own childhood. There was a whole circuit of rails there on the floor at our feet, straight rails and curved, and a little station with porters and passengers, a tunnel, a foot-bridge, a level crossing, two signals, buffers, of course —and, above all, a turntable. The tears of longing came into my eyes when I looked at the turntable. It was my favorite piece—it looked so ugly and practical and true. I said weakly, 'I wouldn't know how.'

"How carefully he had been studying the ground! He must have slipped several times into Mass at the back of the church. It would have been no good, you understand, in a little town like that, presenting himself for communion. Everybody there knew him for what he was. He said to me, 'When you've been given communion you could just put it under your tongue a moment. He serves you and the other boy first, and I saw you once go out behind the curtain straight afterwards. You'd forgotten one of those little bottles.'

" 'The cruet,' I said.

" 'Pepper and salt.' He grinned at me jovially, and I—well, I looked at the little railway which I could no longer come and play with when term started. I said, 'You'd just swallow it, wouldn't you?'

" 'Oh, yes,' he said. 'I'd just swallow it.'

"Somehow I didn't want to play with the train any more that day. I got up and made for the door, but he detained me, gripping my lapel. He said, 'This will be a secret between you and me. Tomorrow's Sunday. You come along here in the afternoon. Put it in an envelope and post it me. Monday morning the train will be delivered bright and early.'

" 'Not tomorrow,' I implored him.

" 'I'm not interested in any other Sunday,' he said. 'It's your only chance.' He shook me gently backwards and forwards. 'It will always have to be a secret between you and me,' he said. 'Why, if anyone knew they'd take away the train and there'd be me to reckon with. I'd bleed you something awful. You know how I'm always about on Sunday walks. You can't avoid a man like me. I crop up. You wouldn't ever be safe in your own house. I know ways to get into houses when people are asleep.' He pulled me into the shop after him and opened a drawer. In the drawer was an odd

looking key and a cut-throat razor. He said, "That's a master key
that opens all locks and that—that's what I bleed people with.'
Then he patted my cheek with his plump floury fingers and said,
'Forget it. You and me are friends.'

"That Sunday Mass stays in my head, every detail of it, as
though it had happened only a week ago. From the moment of the
Confession to the moment of Consecration it had a terrible importance; only one other Mass has ever been so important to me—
perhaps not even one, for this was a solitary Mass which would
never happen again. It seemed as final as the last Sacrament when
the priest bent down and put the wafer in my mouth where I knelt
before the altar with my fellow server.

"I suppose I had made up my mind to commit this awful act—
for, you know, to us it must always seem an awful act—from the
moment when I saw Blacker watching from the back of the church.
He had put on his best black Sunday clothes and, as though he
could never quite escape the smear of his profession, he had a dab
of dried talcum on his cheek, which he had presumably applied
after using that cut-throat of his. He was watching me closely all
the time, and I think it was fear—fear of that terrible undefined
thing called bleeding—as much as covetousness that drove me to
carry out my instructions.

"My fellow server got briskly up and, taking the paten, preceded Father Carey to the altar rail where the other communicants
knelt. I had the Host lodged under my tongue: it felt like a blister.
I got up and made for the curtain to get the cruet that I had purposely left in the sacristy. When I was there I looked quickly round
for a hiding place and saw an old copy of the *Universe* lying on a
chair. I took the Host from my mouth and inserted it between two
sheets—a little damp mess of pulp. Then I thought: perhaps Father
Carey has put out the paper for a particular purpose and he will
find the Host before I have time to remove it, and the enormity of
my act began to come home to me when I tried to imagine what
punishment I should incur. Murder is sufficiently trivial to have its
appropriate punishment, but for this act the mind boggled at the
thought of any retribution at all. I tried to remove the Host, but it
stuck clammily between the pages, and in desperation I tore out a
piece of the newspaper and, screwing the whole thing up, stuck it

in my trousers pocket. When I came back through the curtain carrying the cruet my eyes met Blacker's. He gave me a grin of encouragement and unhappiness—yes, I am sure, unhappiness. Was it
perhaps that the poor man was all the time seeking something
incorruptible?

"I can remember little more of that day. I think my mind was
shocked and stunned, and I was caught up too in the family bustle
of Sunday. Sunday in a provincial town is the day for relations. All
the family are at home, and unfamiliar cousins and uncles are apt to
arrive, packed in the back seats of other people's cars. I remember
that some crowd of the kind descended on us and pushed Blacker
temporarily out of the foreground of my mind. There was somebody
called Aunt Lucy, with a loud hollow laugh that filled the house
with mechanical merriment like the sound of recorded laughter from
inside a hall of mirrors, and I had no opportunity to go out alone
even if I had wished to. When six o'clock came and Aunt Lucy and
the cousins departed and peace returned, it was too late to go to
Blacker's, and at eight it was my own bed-time.

"I think I had half forgotten what I had in my pocket. As I
emptied my pocket the little screw of newspaper brought quickly
back the Mass, the priest bending over me, Blacker's grin. I laid the
packet on the chair by my bed and tried to go to sleep, but I was
haunted by the shadows on the wall where the curtains blew, the
squeak of furniture, the rustle in the chimney, haunted by the
presence of God there on the chair. The Host had always been to
me—well, the Host. I knew theoretically, as I have said, what I had
to believe, but suddenly, as someone whistled in the road outside,
whistled secretively, knowingly, to me, I knew that this which I had
beside my bed was something of infinite value—something a man
would pay for with his whole peace of mind, something that was
so hated one could love it as one loves an outcast or a bullied child.
These are adult words, and it was a child of ten who lay scared in
bed, listening to the whistle from the road, Blacker's whistle, but I
think he felt fairly clearly what I am describing now. That is what
I meant when I said this Thing, whatever it is, that seizes every possible weapon against God, is always, everywhere, disappointed at
the moment of success. It must have felt as certain of me as Blacker
did. It must have felt certain too of Blacker. But I wonder, if one

knew what happened later to that poor man, whether one would not find again that the weapon had been turned against its own breast.

"At last I couldn't bear that whistle any more and got out of bed. I opened the curtains a little way, and there right under my window, the moonlight on his face, was Blacker. If I had stretched my hand down, his fingers reaching up could almost have touched mine. He looked up at me, flashing the one good eye, with hunger— I realize now that near-success must have developed his obsession almost to the point of madness. Desperation had driven him to the house. He whispered up at me. 'David, where is it?'

"I jerked my head back at the room. 'Give it me,' he said. 'Quick. You shall have the train in the morning.'

"I shook my head. He said, 'I've got the bleeder here, and the key. You'd better toss it down.'

" 'Go away,' I said, but I could hardly speak for fear.

" 'I'll bleed you first and then I'll have it just the same.'

" 'Oh, no, you won't,' I said. I went to the chair and picked it —Him—up. There was only one place where He was safe. I couldn't separate the Host from the paper, so I swallowed both. The newsprint stuck like a prune skin to the back of my throat, but I rinsed it down with water from the ewer. Then I went back to the window and looked down at Blacker. He began to wheedle me. 'What have you done with it, David? What's the fuss? It's only a bit of bread,' looking so longingly and pleadingly up at me that even as a child I wondered whether he could really think that, and yet desire it so much.

" 'I swallowed it,' I said.

" 'Swallowed it?'

" 'Yes,' I said. 'Go away.'

"Then something happened which seems to me now more terrible than his desire to corrupt or my thoughtless act: he began to weep—the tears ran lopsidedly out of the one good eye and his shoulders shook. I only saw his face for a moment before he bent his head and strode off, the bald turnip head shaking, into the dark. When I think of it now, it's almost as if I had seen that Thing weeping for its inevitable defeat. It had tried to use me as a weapon, and now I had broken in its hands and it wept its hopeless tears through one of Blacker's eyes."

The black furnaces of Bedwell Junction gathered around the line. The points switched and we were tossed from one set of rails to another. A spray of sparks, a signal light changing to red, tall chimneys jetting into the grey night sky, the fumes of steam from stationary engines—half the cold journey was over, and now remained the long wait for the slow cross-country train. I said, "It's an interesting story. I think I should have given Blacker what he wanted. I wonder what he would have done with it."

"I really believe," my companion said, "that he would first of all have put it under his microscope—before he did all the other things I expect he had planned."

"And the hints," I said. "I don't quite see what you mean by that."

"Oh, well," he said vaguely, "you know for me it was an odd beginning, that affair, when you come to think of it," but I never should have known what he meant had not his coat, when he rose to take the bag from the rack, come open and disclosed the collar of a priest.

I said, "I suppose you think you owe a lot to Blacker."

"Yes," he said, "you see, I am a very happy man."

HEINRICH BÖLL

A Crate for Kop

Translated by John Edward Hardy
and Leonore Hardy

HEN HE CAME BACK from the train station,
Lasnow brought with him the news that a crate had arrived for
Kop. Every morning, Lasnow went to meet the train from Odessa,
and tried to do business with the soldiers. During the first year,
he had paid for socks, saccharine, salt, and matches and flints with
butter and oil, and had enjoyed the generous profits which are
common when barter is used; later, the rate of exchange fell, and
it was a hard fight to do anything with the money, which became
more and more worthless as the war situation got worse. There
was no more butter to trade, and for a long time now, there had
been none of the rich sides of bacon, for which you used to be able
to get a French double-bed mattress. The trading had become
sharp, sour, and grinding since the soldiers had begun to despise
their own money. They laughed when Lasnow ran alongside the
train with his packets of banknotes, calling in at the windows in a
nervous sing-song: "I pay the highest prices for everything. The
highest prices for everything."

Very seldom, someone new came along, who could be fooled
by the money and let himself be talked out of a coat or an undershirt. And rare indeed were the days on which Lasnow had to
argue so long over something big—a pistol, a watch, or a telescope

—that he must bribe the stationmaster to increase the stopover time of the trains until he had finished his business. At first, each minute had cost only a mark, but the greedy, drunken station-master had long ago raised the charge per minute to six marks.

On this particular morning, there had been no business at all. A military policeman, on patrol beside the motionless train, checked his watch against the station clock, and scolded the ragged boy who ran along by the train searching for cigarette stubs. But the soldiers had long since stopped throwing away the butts; they greedily scratched off the black ashes and put the precious remnants into their tobacco pouches. They were even tight with bread, and the boy, when he had found no tobacco, ran beside the train, waving his arms and singing out dramatically: "Bread, bread—bread, friends." He got only a kick from the MP, and sprang onto the fence as the train rolled away. But a paper bag rolled up to his feet. It contained a piece of bread and an apple. The boy grinned as Lasnow went past into the waiting room. The waiting room was empty and cold. Lasnow went to the vestibule and stood still, hesitating. It seemed to him that the train hadn't come yet; it had gone too quickly, correctly, on time; but he heard the rusty scraping: the signal-arm slid to a halt again.

Lasnow started when he felt a hand on his shoulder—too light to be the stationmaster's. It was the hand of the boy, who held out to Lasnow the partly-eaten apple and murmured, "Sour, the little apple is so sour—but what will you give me for this?" He pulled from his left pocket a red toothbrush, and held it out to Lasnow. Lasnow opened his mouth and ran his forefinger mechanically over his strong teeth, on which there lay a thin fur. He closed his mouth again, took the toothbrush from the boy, and looked at it; its red handle was transparent, and the bristles were white and hard.

"A nice Christmas present for your wife," said the boy. "She has such beautiful white teeth."

"You fool," said Lasnow quietly, "what concern of yours are my wife's teeth?"

"Or for your children," said the boy. "You can look through it—like this." He took the brush from Lasnow, held it before his eyes, looked at Lasnow, the train station, the trees, the dilapidated

sugar refinery, and gave the brush back to Lasnow. "Try it," he said. "It's pretty." Lasnow took the brush and held it before his eyes; in the inside of the handle the light refractions were broken: the train station looked like a stretched-out barn, the trees like broken brooms, the boy's face was distorted into a flat grimace, the apple, which he held before his face, looked like a reddish sponge. Lasnow gave the brush back to the boy. "Well, well," he said. "Really very pretty."

"Ten," said the boy.

"Two."

"No," said the boy, whining, "no, it's so pretty."

Lasnow turned away.—

"Give me at least five."

"Well, all right," said Lasnow, "come on, I'll give you five." He took the brush and gave the boy the bill. The boy ran back into the waiting room, and Lasnow saw him carefully and systematically search with a stick for cigarette butts in the ashes of the stove; a grey cloud of dust arose, and the boy murmured something to himself in his sing-song which Lasnow did not understand.

The stationmaster came up just as Lasnow had decided to roll a cigarette and was surveying his supply of tobacco, sorting the dust from the flakes. "Well, now," said the stationmaster, "that looks like it would just be enough for two." He reached out without asking permission, and the two men stood smoking in the corner of the station and looked into the street, on which booths, stands, and dirty tents were set up: everything was gray, brown, or dirt-colored; there was no color even on the children's carousel.

"My children," said the stationmaster, "once got coloring books as presents from someone; on the one side, you could see the finished picture, colored, on the other side the sketch, which you had to color in. But I didn't have any paints, not even any colored pencils, and my children scribbled in everything with pencil—I think about that when I look at this market place. No more paint, just pencil—gray, dirty, dark. . . ."

"Yes," said Lasnow, "there's no business; the only things to eat are Ruchew's corncakes, and you know how he makes them."

"Raw corn kernels, pressed together—I know," said the sta-

tionmaster. "Then smeared with dark oil, so that you're supposed
to think they're baked in oil."

"Oh, well," said Lasnow, "I want to go see if anything at all
is going on."

"If you see Kop, tell him that a crate arrived for him."

"A crate? What's in it?"

"I don't know. Came from Odessa. I'll send the boy with my
wheelbarrow up to Kop. Will you tell him?"

"Yes," said Lasnow.

Again and again, as he strolled around the market place, he
glanced down to the train station, to see whether the boy with the
crate was coming yet. And he told everyone that a crate for Kop
had come from Odessa. The news went around the market place
quickly, overtook Lasnow, and, while he walked slowly to Kop's
booth, came back to him from the other side of the street.

As he came up to the children's carousel, the owner was just
harnessing the horse: the horse's face was thin and dark, made
noble from hunger; it reminded Lasnow of the Nun of Nowgorod,
whom he had once seen when he was a child. Her face, too, had
been thin and dark, noble from abstinence; she had put herself
on display in a dark green tent at the annual fair, and it hadn't cost
any money to see her; the viewers were only asked for contribu-
tions as they left the tent.

The owner of the carousel came up to Lasnow, bowed to him,
and whispered: "Have you heard about the crate yet, which is
suposed to have come for Kop?"

"No," said Lasnow.

"There are supposed to be toys in it—little cars you wind up."

"No," said Lasnow, "I've heard that it's toothbrushes."

"No, no," said the carousel owner, "toys."

Lasnow stroked the horse's nose softly, went on tiredly, and
thought bitterly about the business he had formerly done. He had
bought and sold enough clothes to outfit a whole army, and now
he had fallen so low that he had allowed himself to be talked into
buying a toothbrush from that fool boy. He had sold jugs of oil,
butter, and bacon, and during Christmas he had had a little stand
full of candy sticks for the children. The colors of the candy sticks
had been as glaring as the joys and sufferings of the poor: red like

love, which one celebrates in vestibules, or at the factory wall, while the bittersweet scent of molasses comes over the wall; yellow like the flames in the brain of a drunkard; or as light green as the pain with which one awakes in the morning and looks at the face of his sleeping wife, a child's face, whose only protection against the light are those weak, reddish lids, frail coverings that have to open when the children begin to scream. But this year, there were no candy sticks, and they would sit at home, spoon their soup, and look by turns through the handle of the toothbrush.

An old woman had set two chairs side by side next to the carousel and had opened a shop there; she had two mattresses to sell, on which the words *Magasin du Louvre* could still be read, a well-thumbed book with the title *Left and Right of the Train, Gelsenkirchen to Essen*, a 1938 issue of an English magazine, and a little tin box, on which there had once been a colored ribbon.

"Beautiful things," said the old woman, as Lasnow stopped.

"Pretty things," he said, and as he started to move away, the woman rushed up to him, pulled him nearer by his sleeve, and whispered:

"A crate has arrived from Odessa for Kop. With Christmas things."

"Oh?" he said. "What?"

"Candies, all colors, and rubber animals that squeak—that'll be nice."

"Yes," said Lasnow, "that will be nice."

When he finally reached Kop's booth, the man had just begun to unload and set up his wares: fire pokers, cooking pots, stoves, rusty nails which he was always sorting and hammering straight. Almost everyone had gathered by Kop's stand, and stood silent with anticipation and looked down the street. As Lasnow came up to Kop, Kop was just unloading a fire screen, on which there were painted golden flowers and a Chinese girl.

"I'm supposed to tell you," said Lasnow, "that a crate has arrived for you. The boy who always hangs around the station will bring it to you."

Kop looked up, sighing, and said softly: "You're starting too, you're starting too."

"Why me too?" said Lasnow. "I came straight from the train station to tell you about it."

Kop ducked anxiously; he was elegant, he wore a clean gray fur cap, always carried a stick, with which, while walking, he knocked holes in the earth, and, as the only memory of his better days, he held a cigarette in his mouth, a cigarette which almost never burned, because he seldom had enough money for tobacco. Twenty-seven years before, when Lasnow had returned to the village, a deserter, and had brought the news of the revolution, Kop had been an ensign, railroad commander, and when Lasnow had come to the front of the revolutionary soldiers' council in the railroad station, to arrest Kop, Kop had been prepared to let a movement of his lips, the position of his cigarette, cost his life. In any case, everyone had watched the angle of his mouth, and he had been certain that they would shoot him, but he had not taken the cigarette from his mouth as Lasnow came up to him. But Lasnow had only struck him, the cigarette had fallen from his mouth, and, without it, he had looked like a boy who has forgotten his school lessons. They had left him in peace; he had at first become a teacher, then a merchant, but still, whenever he met Lasnow, he was afraid that he would strike the cigarette from his mouth. He lifted his head fearfully, pushed the fire screen upright, and said:

"If you only knew how often I've heard that already."

"A fire screen," said a woman. "If you only had heat enough to have to protect yourself from it with a fire screen."

Kop looked at her contemptuously.

"You don't have any sense of beauty, anyway."

"No," said the woman, laughing, "I am beautiful enough myself, and look how many pretty children I have." She ran her hand quickly over the heads of the four children who stood around her. "You need . . ." Startled, she looked around at her offspring when they suddenly ran off after the other children toward the railroad station, to meet the boy who was bringing Kop's crate in the stationmaster's wheelbarrow.

Everyone came running from their stands; the children sprang from the carousel.

"My God," said Kop softly to Lasnow, who was the only one

still standing near him, "I almost wish the crate hadn't come. They'll tear me apart."

"Don't you know what's in it?"

"Don't have any idea," said Kop. "I only know that it has to be made of tin."

"Lots of things can be made out of tin—cans, toys, spoons."

"Toy drums, that you wind up."

"Yes—oh, God."

Together with Lasnow, Kop helped the boy lift the crate from the cart; the crate was white, made of fresh, smooth boards, and it was almost as high as the table on which Kop had spread out his rusty nails, fire pokers, and scissors.

Everyone was silent as Kop pushed an old poker under the top of the crate and slowly lifted; you could hear the soft screak of the nails. Lasnow wondered where all the people had come from so quickly; he started as the boy suddenly said: "I can tell you what's in it."

No one asked; everyone looked at him in expectation, and the boy looked silently into the excited faces; sweat broke out on him, and he said softly: "Nothing—nothing's in there."

Had he said it a moment sooner, they would have leapt upon him and fought with him in their disappointment, but now, Kop had taken off the cover, and was rummaging about with his hand in the excelsior, and lifted out a whole layer of it, then another, then wadded-up paper—then he held up two handfuls of the things which he had found in the middle of the crate. "Pincers," cried a woman. But it wasn't that.

"What is it, then?" said a little boy.

"It's sugar tongs," said the carousel owner in a dry voice. Then he suddenly laughed angrily, threw his arms over his head, and ran back to his carousel, laughing loudly.

"It really is," said Kop, "it *is* sugar tongs—lots of them." He threw the tongs which he held in his hands back into the crate, rummaged around inside, and, although they couldn't see his face, they all knew that he wasn't laughing. He rummaged around in the clattering sugar tongs, as misers in paintings rummage around in their treasures.

"That's just like them," said a woman, "sugar tongs . . . I guess

if there were any sugar at all, I could bring myself to pick it up
with my fingers, eh?"

"I had a grandmother," said Lasnow, "who always picked up
sugar with her fingers—but she was just a dirty peasant woman."

"I guess I could bring myself to do it, too."

"You always were a slob, anyway—taking sugar with your
fingers. Never."

"You could," said Lasnow, "fish tomatoes out of jars with
them."

"If you had any," said the woman who had called herself
beautiful. Lasnow looked at her in interest. She was indeed beautiful. She had strong, blond hair, a straight nose, and dark,
beautiful eyes.

"You could," said Lasnow, "also pick up cucumbers with
them."

"If you had any," said the woman.

"You can pinch yourself on the behind with them."

"If you still have one," said the woman coldly. Her face was
becoming more and more angry and beautiful.

"You can pick up coal with them."

"If you have any."

"You can use them as cigarette holders."

"If you have anything to smoke."

Whenever Lasnow spoke, everyone looked at him, and as soon
as he finished, the people all turned to the woman, and as the
sugar tongs in this dialogue became more and more senseless, the
faces of the children and parents became more and more empty
and pitiful. I must make them laugh, thought Lasnow. I had feared
that there would be toothbrushes in there, but sugar tongs are even
worse. He reddened under the triumphant gaze of the woman, and
said loudly: "You can pick apart boiled fish with them."

"If you had any," said the woman.

"The children can play with them," said Lasnow softly.

"If you . . ." the woman began, then she suddenly laughed
loudly, and everyone else laughed too, because they all had children enough.

"Come here," said Lasnow to Kop, "give me three. What do
they cost?"

"Twelve," said Kop.

"Twelve," said Lasnow, and threw the money on Kop's table, "that's a gift."

"It's really not very much," said Kop shyly.

Ten minutes later, all the children were running around the market place with shining sugar tongs. They sat on the carousel poking them in their noses, ran about whacking the adults with them.

Even the boy, the one who had brought the crate, had gotten one. He sat on the stone steps of the train station and hammered his tongs flat. At last, he thought, I have something that I can reach between the cracks of the floor with. He had tried it with fire pokers, with wires, and with scissors, but he had never been able to do it. He was sure that he would succeed with this implement.

Kop counted his money, gathered it up, and stuffed it contentedly into his brief case. He looked at Lasnow, who was standing next to him and dismally watching the action in the marketplace.

"You could do me a favor," said Kop.

"What?" said Lasnow distantly, without looking at Kop.

"Hit me in the face," said Kop, "so hard that my cigarette falls out of my mouth."

Lasnow, still without looking at Kop, shook his head thoughtfully.

"Do it," said Kop. "Please, do it. Don't you remember anymore?"

"I still remember," said Lasnow, "but I don't have any desire to do it again."

"Really?"

"No," said Lasnow, "I really don't; I've never thought of doing it again."

"Damn," said Kop, "and for twenty-seven years I've been afraid of being hit."

"You didn't have to be," said Lasnow. He went to the train station, shaking his head. Perhaps, he thought, a special train will come, with vacationists, or wounded men; special trains very seldom came. He played thoughtfully with the toothbrush and the

three pairs of sugar tongs in his pocket. It has happened, he
thought, that three special trains came in one day.

He leaned against the lantern post in front of the train station
and scratched together his last bits of tobacco . . .

PETER TAYLOR

What You Hear from 'Em?

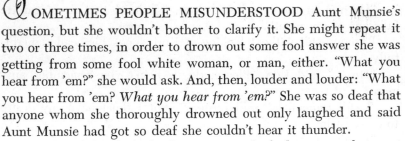

OMETIMES PEOPLE MISUNDERSTOOD Aunt Munsie's
question, but she wouldn't bother to clarify it. She might repeat it
two or three times, in order to drown out some fool answer she was
getting from some fool white woman, or man, either. "What you
hear from 'em?" she would ask. And, then, louder and louder: "What
you hear from 'em? *What you hear from 'em?*" She was so deaf that
anyone whom she thoroughly drowned out only laughed and said
Aunt Munsie had got so deaf she couldn't hear it thunder.

It was, of course, only the most utterly fool answers that ever
received Aunt Munsie's drowning-out treatment. She was, for a
number of years at least, willing to listen to those who mistook
her " 'em" to mean any and all of the Dr. Tolliver children. And
for more years than that she was willing to listen to those who
thought she wanted just *any* news of her two favorites among the
Tolliver children—Thad and Will. But later on she stopped putting

Reprinted by permission of Peter Taylor.

the question to all insensitive and frivolous souls who didn't understand that what she was interested in hearing—and *all* she was interested in hearing—was when Mr. Thad Tolliver and Mr. Will Tolliver were going to pack up their families and come back to Thornton for good.

They had always promised her to come back—to come back sure enough, once and for all. On separate occasions, both Thad and Will had actually given her their word. She had not seen them together for ten years, but each of them had made visits to Thornton now and then with his own family. She would see a big car stopping in front of her house on a Sunday afternoon and see either Will or Thad with his wife and children piling out into the dusty street—it was nearly always summer when they came—and then see them filing across the street, jumping the ditch, and unlatching the gate to her yard. She always met them in that pen of a yard, but long before they had jumped the ditch she was clapping her hands and calling out, "Hai-ee! Hai-ee, now! Look-a-here! Whee! Whee! Look-a-here!" She had got so blind that she was never sure whether it was Mr. Thad or Mr. Will until she had her arms around his waist. They had always looked a good deal alike, and their city clothes made them look even more alike nowadays. Aunt Munsie's eyes were so bad, besides being so full of moisture on those occasions, that she really recognized them by their girth. Will had grown a regular wash pot of a stomach and Thad was still thin as a rail. They would sit on her porch for twenty or thirty minutes—whichever one it was and his family—and then they would be gone again.

Aunt Munsie would never try to detain them—not seriously. Those short little old visits didn't mean a thing to her. He—Thad or Will—would lean against the banister rail and tell her how well his children were doing in school or college, and she would make each child in turn come and sit beside her on the swing for a minute and receive a hug around the waist or shoulders. They were timid with her, not seeing her any more than they did, but she could tell from their big Tolliver smiles that they liked her to hug them and make over them. Usually, she would lead them all out to her back yard and show them her pigs and dogs and chickens. (She always had at least one frizzly chicken to show the

children.) They would traipse through her house to the back yard
and then traipse through again to the front porch. It would be
time for them to go when they came back, and Aunt Munsie
would look up at *him*—Mr. Thad or Mr. Will (she had begun
calling them "Mr." the day they married)—and say, "Now, look-a-
here. When you comin' back?"

Both Thad and Will knew what she meant, of course, and
whichever it was would tell her he was making definite plans to
wind up his business and that he was going to buy a certain piece
of property, "a mile north of town" or "on the old River Road,"
and build a jim-dandy house there. He would say, too, how good
Aunt Munsie's own house was looking, and his wife would say how
grand the zinnias and cannas looked in the yard. (The yard was
all flowers—not a blade of grass, and the ground packed hard in
little paths between the flower beds.) The visit was almost over
then. There remained only the exchange of presents. One of the
children would hand Aunt Munsie a paper bag containing a pint
of whisky or a carton of cigarettes. Aunt Munsie would go to her
back porch or to the pit in the yard and get a fern or a Wandering
Jew, potted in a rusty lard bucket, and make Mrs. Thad or Mrs.
Will take it along. Then the visit was over, and they would leave.
From the porch Aunt Munsie would wave good-by with one hand
and lay the other hand, trembling slightly, on the banister rail.
And sometimes her departing guests, looking back from the yard,
would observe that the banisters themselves were trembling under
her hand—so insecurely were those knobby banisters attached to
the knobby porch pillars. Often as not Thad or Will, observing
this, would remind his wife that Aunt Munsie's porch banisters
and pillars had come off a porch of the house where he had grown
up. (Their father, Dr. Tolliver, had been one of the first to widen
his porches and remove the gingerbread from his house.) The
children and their mother would wave to Aunt Munsie from the
street. Their father would close the gate, resting his hand a
moment on its familiar wrought-iron frame, and wave to her before
he jumped the ditch. If the children had not gone too far ahead,
he might even draw their attention to the iron fence which, with
its iron gate, had been around the yard at the Tolliver place till
Dr. Tolliver took it down and set out a hedge, just a few weeks
before he died.

But such paltry little visits meant nothing to Aunt Munsie. No more did the letters that came with "her things" at Christmas. She was supposed to get her daughter, Lucrecie, who lived next door, to read the letters, but in late years she had taken to putting them away unopened, and some of the presents, too. All she wanted to hear from *them* was when they were coming back for good, and she had learned that the Christmas letters never told her that. On her daily route with her slop wagon through the Square, up Jackson Street, and down Jefferson, there were only four or five houses left where she asked her question. These were houses where the amount of pig slop was not worth stopping for, houses where one old maid, or maybe two, lived, or a widow with one old bachelor son who had never amounted to anything and ate no more than a woman. And so—in the summertime, anyway—she took to calling out at the top of her lungs, when she approached the house of one of the elect, "What you hear from 'em?" Sometimes a Miss Patty or a Miss Lucille or a Mr. Ralph would get up out of a porch chair and come down the brick walk to converse with Aunt Munsie. Or sometimes one of them would just lean out over the shrubbery planted around the porch and call, "Not a thing, Munsie. Not a thing lately."

She would shake her head and call back, "Naw. Naw. Not a thing. Nobody don't hear from 'em. Too busy, they be."

Aunt Munsie's skin was the color of a faded tow sack. She was hardly four feet tall. She was generally believed to be totally bald, and on her head she always wore a white dust cap with an elastic band. She wore an apron, too, while making her rounds with her slop wagon. Even when the weather got bad and she tied a wool scarf about her head and wore an overcoat, she put on an apron over the coat. Her hands and feet were delicately small, which made the old-timers sure she was of Guinea stock that had come to Tennessee out of South Carolina. What most touched the hearts of old ladies on Jackson and Jefferson Streets were her little feet. The sight of her feet "took them back to the old days," they said, because Aunt Munsie still wore flat-heeled, high button shoes. Where ever did Munsie find such shoes any more?

She walked down the street, down the very center of the street, with a spry step, and she was continually turning her head from side to side, as though looking at the old houses and trees for the first time. If her sight was as bad as she sometimes let on it was, she probably recognized the houses only by their roof lines against the Thornton sky. Since this was nearly thirty years ago, most of the big Victorian and ante-bellum houses were still standing, though with their lovely gingerbread work beginning to go. (It went first from houses where there was someone, like Dr. Tolliver, with a special eye for style and for keeping up with the times.) The streets hadn't yet been broadened—or only Nashville Street had—and the maples and elms met above the streets. In the autumn, their leaves covered the high banks and filled the deep ditches on either side. The dark macadam surfacing itself was barely wide enough for two automobiles to pass. Aunt Munsie, pulling her slop wagon, which was a long, low, four-wheeled vehicle about the size and shape of a coffin, paraded down the center of the street without any regard for, if with any awareness of, the traffic problems she sometimes made. Seizing the wagon's heavy, sawed-off-looking tongue, she hauled it after her with a series of impatient jerks, just as though that tongue were the arm of some very stubborn, overgrown white child she had to nurse in her old age. Strangers in town or trifling high-school boys would blow their horns at her, but she was never known to so much as glance over her shoulder at the sound of a horn. Now and then a pedestrian on the sidewalk would call out to the driver of an automobile, "She's so deaf she can't hear it thunder."

It wouldn't have occurred to anyone in Thornton—not in those days—that something ought to be done about Aunt Munsie and her wagon for the sake of the public good. In those days, everyone had equal rights on the streets of Thornton. A vehicle was a vehicle, and a person was a person, each with the right to move as slowly as he pleased and to stop where and as often as he pleased. In the Thornton mind, there was no imaginary line down the middle of the street, and, indeed, no one there at that time had heard of drawing a real line on *any* street. It was merely out of politeness that you made room for others to pass. Nobody would have blown a horn at an old colored woman with her slop wagon—nobody but some Yankee stranger or a trifling high-school boy or maybe old Mr. Ralph Hadley in a special fit of temper. When citizens of Thornton were in a particular hurry and got caught behind Aunt Munsie, they leaned out their car windows and shouted: "Aunt

Munsie, can you make a little room?" And Aunt Munsie didn't fail
to hear *them*. She would holler, "Hai-ee, now! Whee! Look-a-here!"
and jerk her wagon to one side. As they passed her, she would
wave her little hand and grin a toothless, pink-gummed grin.

Yet, without any concern for the public good, Aunt Munsie's
friends and connections among the white women began to worry
more and more about the danger of her being run down by an
automobile. They talked among themselves and they talked to her
about it. They wanted her to give up collecting slop, now she had
got so blind and deaf. "Pshaw," said Aunt Munsie, closing her eyes
contemptuously. "Not me." She meant by that that no one would
dare run into her or her wagon. Sometimes when she crossed the
Square on a busy Saturday morning or on a first Monday, she would
hold up one hand with the palm turned outward and stop all traffic
until she was safely across and in the alley beside the hotel.

Thornton wasn't even then what it had been before the Great
World War. In every other house there was a stranger or a mill
hand who had moved up from Factory Town. Some of the biggest
old places stood empty, the way Dr. Tolliver's had until it burned.
They stood empty not because nobody wanted to rent them or buy
them but because the heirs who had gone off somewhere making
money could never be got to part with "the home place." The
story was that Thad Tolliver nearly went crazy when he heard their
old house had burned, and wanted to sue the town, and even said
he was going to help get the Republicans into office. Yet Thad had
hardly put foot in the house since the day his daddy died. It was
said the Tolliver house had caught fire from the Major Pettigru
house, which had burned two nights before. And no doubt it had.
Sparks could have smoldered in that roof of rotten shingles for a
long time before bursting into flame. Some even said the Pettigru
house might have caught from the Johnston house, which had
burned earlier that same fall. But Thad knew and Will knew and
everybody knew the town wasn't to blame, and knew there was no
firebug. Why, those old houses stood there empty year after year,
and in the fall the leaves fell from the trees and settled around the
porches and stoops, and who was there to rake the leaves? Maybe
it was a good thing those houses burned, and maybe it would have
been as well if some of the houses that still had people in them

burned, too. There were houses in Thornton the heirs had never left
that looked far worse than the Tolliver or the Pettigru or the
Johnston house ever had. The people who lived in them were the
ones who gave Aunt Munsie the biggest fool answers to her question, the people whom she soon quit asking her question of or even
passing the time of day with, except when she couldn't help it, out
of politeness. For, truly, to Aunt Munsie there were things under
the sun worse than going off and getting rich in Nashville or in
Memphis or even in Washington, D.C. It was a subject she and
her daughter Lucrecie sometimes mouthed at each other about
across their back fence. Lucrecie was shiftless, and she liked shiftless
white people like the ones who didn't have the ambition to leave
Thornton. She thought their shiftlessness showed they were *quality*.
"Quality?" Aunt Munsie would echo, her voice full of sarcasm.
"Whee! Hai-ee! You talk like *you* was *my* mammy, Crecie. Well, if
there be quality, there be quality *and* quality. There's quality and
there's *has-been* quality, Crecie." There was no end to that argument Aunt Munsie had with Crecie, and it wasn't at all important
to Aunt Munsie. The people who still lived in those houses—the
ones she called has-been quality—meant little more to her than the
mill hands, or the strangers from up North who ran the Piggly
Wiggly, the five-and-ten-cent store, and the roller-skating rink.
    There was this to be said, though, for the has-been quality:
They knew *who* Aunt Munsie was, and in a limited, literal way they
understood what she said. But those *others*—why, they thought
Aunt Munsie a beggar, and she knew they did. They spoke of her
as Old What You Have for Mom, because that's what they thought
she was saying when she called out, "What you hear from 'em?"
Their ears were not attuned to that soft "r" she put in "from" or
the elision that made "from 'em" sound to them like "for Mom."
Many's the time Aunt Munsie had seen or sensed the presence of
one of those *other* people, watching from next door, when Miss
Leonora Lovell, say, came down her front walk and handed her a
little parcel of scraps across the ditch. Aunt Munsie knew what they
thought of her—how they laughed at her and felt sorry for her
and despised her all at once. But, like the has-been quality, they
didn't matter, never had, never would. Not ever.
    Oh, they mattered in a way to Lucrecie. Lucrecie thought about

them and talked about them a lot. She called them "white trash" and even "radical Republicans." It made Aunt Munsie grin to hear Crecie go on, because she knew Crecie got all her notions from her own has-been-quality people. And so it didn't matter, except that Aunt Munsie knew that Crecie truly had all sorts of good sense and had only been carried away and spoiled by such folks as she had worked for, such folks as had really raised Crecie from the time she was big enough to run errands for them, fifty years back. In her heart, Aunt Munsie knew that even Lucrecie didn't matter to her the way a daughter might. It was because while Aunt Munsie had been raising a family of white children, a different sort of white people from hers had been raising her own child, Crecie. Sometimes, if Aunt Munsie was in her chicken yard or out in her little patch of cotton when Mr. Thad or Mr. Will arrived, Crecie would come out to the fence and say, "Mama, some of your chillun's out front."

Miss Leonora Lovell and Miss Patty Bean, and especially Miss Lucille Satterfield, were all the time after Aunt Munsie to give up collecting slop. "You're going to get run over by one of those crazy drivers, Munsie," they said. Miss Lucille was the widow of old Judge Satterfield. "If the Judge were alive, Munsie," she said, "I'd make him find a way to stop you. But the men down at the courthouse don't listen to the women in this town any more. Not since we got the vote. And I think they'd be most too scared of you to do what I want them to do." Aunt Munsie wouldn't listen to any of that. She knew that if Miss Lucille had come out there to her gate, she must have *something* she was going to say about Mr. Thad or Mr. Will. Miss Lucille had two brothers and a son of her own who were lawyers in Memphis, and who lived in style down there and kept Miss Lucille in style here in Thornton. Memphis was where Thad Tolliver had his Ford and Lincoln agency, and so Miss Lucille always had news about Thad, and indirectly about Will, too.

"Is they doin' any good? What you hear from 'em?" Aunt Munsie asked Miss Lucille one afternoon in early spring. She had come along just when Miss Lucille was out picking some of the jonquils that grew in profusion on the steep bank between the sidewalk and the ditch in front of her house.

"Mr. Thad and his folks will be up one day in April, Munsie," Miss Lucille said in her pleasantly hoarse voice. "I understand Mr. Will and his crowd may come for Easter Sunday."

"One day, and gone again!" said Aunt Munsie.

"We always try to get them to stay at least one night, but they're busy folks, Munsie."

"When they comin' back sure enough, Miss Lucille?"

"Goodness knows, Munsie. Goodness knows. Goodness knows when any of them are coming back to stay." Miss Lucille took three quick little steps down the bank and hopped lightly across the ditch. "They're prospering so, Munsie," she said, throwing her chin up and smiling proudly. This fragile lady, this daughter, wife, sister, mother of lawyers (and, of course, the darling of all their hearts), stood there in the street with her pretty little feet and shapely ankles close together, and holding a handful of jonquils before her as if it were her bridal bouquet. "They're *all* prospering so, Munsie. Mine *and* yours. You ought to go down to Memphis to see them now and then, the way I do. Or go up to Nashville to see Mr. Will. I understand he's got an even finer establishment than Thad. They've done well, Munsie—yours *and* mine—and we can be proud of them. You owe it to yourself to go and see how well they're fixed. They're rich men by our standards in Thornton, and they're going farther—*all* of them."

Aunt Munsie dropped the tongue of her wagon noisily on the pavement. "What I want to go see 'em for?" she said angrily and with a lowering brow. Then she stooped and, picking up the wagon tongue again, she wheeled her vehicle toward the middle of the street, to get by Miss Lucille, and started off toward the Square. As she turned out into the street, the brakes of a car, as so often, screeched behind her. Presently everyone in the neighborhood could hear Mr. Ralph Hadley tooting the insignificant little horn on his mama's coupé and shouting at Aunt Munsie in his own tooty voice, above the sound of the horn. Aunt Munsie pulled over, making just enough room to let poor old Mr. Ralph get by but without once looking back at him. Then, before Mr. Ralph could get his car started again, Miss Lucille was running along beside Aunt Munsie, saying, "Munsie, you be careful! You're going to meet your death on the streets of Thornton, Tennessee!"

"Let 'em," said Aunt Munsie.

Miss Lucille didn't know whether Munsie meant "Let 'em run over me; I don't care" or meant "Let 'em just dare!" Miss Lucille soon turned back, without Aunt Munsie's ever looking at her. And when Mr. Ralph Hadley did get his motor started, and sailed past in his mama's coupé, Aunt Munsie didn't give him a look, either. Nor did Mr. Ralph bother to turn his face to look at Aunt Munsie. He was on his way to the drugstore, to pick up his mama's prescriptions, and he was too entirely put out, peeved, and upset to endure even the briefest exchange with that ugly, uppity old Munsie of the Tollivers.

Aunt Munsie continued to tug her slop wagon on toward the Square. There was a more animated expression on her face than usual, and every so often her lips would move rapidly and emphatically over a phrase or sentence. Why should she go to Memphis and Nashville and see how rich they were? No matter how rich they were, what difference did it make; they didn't own any land, did they? Or at least none in Cameron County. She had heard the old Doctor tell them—tell his boys and tell his girls, and tell the old lady, too, in her day—that nobody was rich who didn't own land, and nobody stayed rich who didn't see after his land firsthand. But of course Aunt Munsie had herself mocked the old Doctor to his face for going on about land so much. She knew it was only something he had heard his own daddy go on about. She would say right to his face that she hadn't ever seen *him* behind a plow. And was there ever anybody more scared of a mule than Dr. Tolliver was? Mules or horses, either? Aunt Munsie had heard him say that the happiest day of his life was the day he first learned that the horseless carriage was a reality.

No, it was not really to own land that Thad and Will ought to come back to Thornton. It was more that if they were going to be rich, they ought to come home, where their granddaddy had owned land and where their money counted for something. How could they ever be rich anywhere else? They could have a lot of money in the bank and a fine house, that was all—like that mill manager from Chi. The mill manager could have a yard full of big

cars and a stucco house as big as you like, but who would ever take
him for rich? Aunt Munsie would sometimes say all these things to
Crecie, or something as nearly like them as she could find words
for. Crecie might nod her head in agreement or she might be in a
mood to say being rich wasn't any good for anybody and didn't
matter, and that you could live on just being quality better than on
being rich in Thornton. "Quality's better than land or better than
money in the bank here," Crecie would say.

Aunt Munsie would sneer at her and say, "It never were."

Lucrecie could talk all she wanted about the old times. Aunt
Munsie knew too much about what they were like, for both the
richest white folks and the blackest field hands. Nothing about the
old times was as good as these days, and there were going to be
better times yet when Mr. Thad and Mr. Will Tolliver came back.
Everybody lived easier now than they used to, and were better off.
She could never be got to reminisce about her childhood in slavery,
or her life with her husband, or even about those halcyon days after
the old Mizziz had died and Aunt Munsie's word had become law
in the Tolliver household. Without being able to book-read or even
to make numbers, she had finished raising the whole pack of tow-
headed Tollivers just as the Mizziz would have wanted it done. The
Doctor told her she *had* to—he didn't ever once think about getting
another wife, or taking in some cousin, not after his "Molly darling"
—and Aunt Munsie *did*. But, as Crecie said, when a time was past
in her mama's life, it seemed to be gone and done with in her head,
too.

Lucrecie would say frankly she thought her mama was "hard
about people and things in the world." She talked about her mama
not only to the Blalocks, for whom she had worked all her life, but
to anybody else who gave her an opening. It wasn't just about her
mama, though, that she would talk to anybody. She liked to talk,
and she talked about Aunt Munsie not in any ugly, resentful way
but as she would about when the sheep-rains would begin or where
the fire was last night. (Crecie was twice the size of her mama, and
black the way her old daddy had been, and loud and good-natured
the way he was—or at least the way Aunt Munsie wasn't. You
wouldn't have known they were mother and daughter, and not

many of the young people in town did realize it. Only by accident did they live next door to each other; Mr. Thad and Mr. Will had bought Munsie her house, and Crecie had heired hers from her second husband.) *That* was how she talked about her mama—as she would have about any lonely, eccentric, harmless neighbor. "I may be dead wrong, but I think Mama's kind of hardhearted," she would say. "Mama's a good old soul, I reckon, but when something's past, it's gone and done with for Mama. She don't think about day before yestiddy—yestiddy, either. I don't know, maybe that's the way to be. Maybe that's why the old soul's gonna outlive us all." Then, obviously thinking about what a picture of health she herself was at sixty, Crecie would toss her head about and laugh so loud you might hear her all the way out to the fair grounds.

Crecie, however, knew her mama was not honest-to-God mean and hadn't ever been mean to the Tolliver children, the way the Blalocks liked to make out she had. All the Tolliver children but Mr. Thad and Mr. Will had quarreled with her for good by the time they were grown, but they had quarreled with the old Doctor, too (and as if they were the only ones who shook off their old folks this day and time). When Crecie talked about her mama, she didn't spare her anything, but she was fair to her, too. And it was in no hateful or disloyal spirit that she took part in the conspiracy that finally got Aunt Munsie and her slop wagon off the streets of Thornton. Crecie would have done the same for any neighbor. She had small part enough, actually, in that conspiracy. Her part was merely to break the news to Aunt Munsie that there was now a law against keeping pigs within the city limits. It was a small part but one that no one else quite dared to take.

"They ain't no such law!" Aunt Munsie roared back at Crecie. She was slopping her pigs when Crecie came to the fence and told her about the law. It had seemed the most appropriate time to Lucrecie. "They ain't never been such a law, Crecie," Aunt Munsie said. "Every house on Jackson and Jefferson used to keep pigs."

"It's a brand-new law, Mama."

Aunt Munsie finished bailing out the last of the slop from her wagon. It was just before twilight. The last, weak rays of the sun colored the clouds behind the mock orange tree in Crecie's yard. When Aunt Munsie turned around from the sty, she pretended that

that little bit of light in the clouds hurt her eyes, and turned away her head. And when Lucrecie said that everybody had until the first of the year to get rid of their pigs, Aunt Munsie was in a spell of deafness. She headed out toward the crib to get some corn for the chickens. She was trying to think whether anybody else inside the town still kept pigs. Herb Mallory did—two doors beyond Crecie. Then Aunt Munsie remembered Herb didn't pay town taxes. The town line ran between him and Shad Willis.

That was sometime in June, and before July came, Aunt Munsie knew all there was worth knowing about the conspiracy. Mr. Thad and Mr. Will had each been in town for a day during the spring. They and their families had been to her house and sat on the porch; the children had gone back to look at her half-grown collie dog and the two hounds, at the old sow and her farrow of new pigs, and at the frizzliest frizzly chicken Aunt Munsie had ever had. And on those visits to Thornton, Mr. Thad and Mr. Will had also made their usual round among their distant kin and close friends. Everywhere they went, they had heard of the near-accidents Aunt Munsie was causing with her slop wagon and the real danger there was of her being run over. Miss Lucille Satterfield and Miss Patty Bean had both been to the mayor's office and also to see Judge Lawrence to try to get Aunt Munsie "ruled" off the streets, but the men in the courthouse and in the mayor's office didn't listen to the women in Thornton any more. And so either Mr. Thad or Mr. Will—how would which one of them it was matter to Munsie?—had been prevailed upon to stop by Mayor Lunt's office, and in a few seconds' time had set the wheels of conspiracy in motion. Soon a general inquiry had been made in the town as to how many citizens still kept pigs. Only two property owners besides Aunt Munsie had been found to have pigs on their premises, and they, being men, had been docile and reasonable enough to sell what they had on hand to Mr. Will or Mr. Thad Tolliver. Immediately afterward—within a matter of weeks, that is—a town ordinance had been passed forbidding the possession of swine within the corporate limits of Thornton. Aunt Munsie had got the story bit by bit from Miss Leonora and Miss Patty and Miss Lucille and others, including the constable himself, whom she did not hesitate to stop right in the middle of the Square on a Saturday noon. Whether it was Mr. Thad or Mr. Will who had been prevailed upon by the ladies she never ferreted out, but that was only because she did not wish to do so.

The constable's word was the last word for her. The constable said yes, it was the law, and he admitted yes, he had sold his own pigs—for the constable was one of those two reasonable souls—to Mr. Thad or Mr. Will. He didn't say which of them it was, or if he did, Aunt Munsie didn't bother to remember it. And after her interview with the constable, Aunt Munsie never again exchanged words with any human being about the ordinance against pigs. That afternoon, she took a fishing pole from under her house and drove the old sow and the nine shoats down to Herb Mallory's, on the outside of town. They were his, she said, if he wanted them, and he could pay her at killing time.

It was literally true that Aunt Munsie never again exchanged words with anyone about the ordinance against pigs or about the conspiracy she had discovered against herself. But her daughter Lucrecie had a tale to tell about what Aunt Munsie did that afternoon after she had seen the constable and before she drove the pigs over to Herb Mallory's. It was mostly a tale of what Aunt Munsie said to her pigs and to her dogs and her chickens.

Crecie was in her own back yard washing her hair when her mama came down the rickety porch steps and into the yard next door. Crecie had her head in the pot of suds, and so she couldn't look up, but she knew by the way Mama flew down the steps that there was trouble. "She come down them steps like she was wasp-nest bit, or like some youngun who's got hisself wasp-nest bit—and her all of eighty, I reckon!" Then, as Crecie told it, her mama scurried around in the yard for a minute or so like she thought Judgment was about to catch up with her, and pretty soon she commenced slamming at something. Crecie wrapped a towel about her soapy head, squatted low, and edged over toward the plank fence. She peered between the planks and saw what her mama was up to. Since there never had been a gate to the fence around the pigsty, Mama had taken the wood ax and was knocking a hole in it. But directly, just after Crecie had taken her place by the plank fence, her mama had left off her slamming at the sty and turned

about so quickly and so exactly toward Crecie that Crecie thought
the poor, blind old soul had managed to spy her squatting there.
Right away, though, Crecie realized it was not *her* that Mama was
staring at. She saw that all Aunt Munsie's chickens and those three
dogs of hers had come up behind her, and were all clucking and
whining to know why she didn't stop that infernal racket and put
out some feed for them.

Crecie's mama set one hand on her hip and rested the ax on the
ground. "Just look at yuh!" she said, and then she let the chickens
and the dogs—and the pigs, too—have it. She told them what a
miserable bunch of creatures they were, and asked them what right
they had to always be looking for handouts from her. She sounded
like the boss-man who's caught all his pickers laying off before sundown, and she sounded, too, like the preacher giving his sinners
Hail Columbia at camp meeting. Finally, shouting at the top of her
voice and swinging the ax wide and broad above their heads, she
sent the dogs howling under the house and the chickens scattering
in every direction. "Now, g'wine! G'wine widja!" she shouted after
them. Only the collie pup, of the three dogs, didn't scamper to the
farthest corner underneath the house. He stopped under the porch
steps, and not two seconds later he was poking his long head out
again and showing the whites of his doleful brown eyes. Crecie's
mama took a step toward him and then she halted. "You want to
know what's the commotion about? I reckoned you would," she
said with profound contempt, as though the collie were a more
reasonable soul than the other animals, and as though there were
nothing she held in such thorough disrespect as reason. "I tell you
what the commotion's about," she said. "They *ain't* comin' back.
They ain't never comin' back. They ain't never had no notion of
comin' back." She turned her head to one side, and the only explanation Crecie could find for her mama's next words was that
that collie pup did look so much like Miss Lucille Satterfield.

"Why don't I go down to Memphis or up to Nashville and see
'em sometime, like *you* does?" Aunt Munsie asked the collie. "I tell
you why. Becaze I ain't nothin' to 'em in Memphis, and they ain't
nothin' to me in Nashville. *You* can go!" she said, advancing and
shaking the big ax at the dog. "A collie dog's a collie dog anywhar.
But Aunt Munsie, she's just their Aunt Munsie here in Thornton. I

got mind enough to see *that*." The collie slowly pulled his head back
under the steps, and Aunt Munsie watched for a minute to see if
he would show himself again. When he didn't, she went and jerked
the fishing pole out from under the house and headed toward the
pigsty. Crecie remained squatting beside the fence until her mama
and the pigs were out in the street and on their way to Herb
Mallory's.

That was the end of Aunt Munsie's keeping pigs and the end of
her daily rounds with her slop wagon, but it was not the end of
Aunt Munsie. She lived on for nearly twenty years after that, till
long after Lucrecie had been put away, in fine style, by the
Blalocks. Ever afterward, though, Aunt Munsie seemed different to
people. They said she softened, and everybody said it was a change
for the better. She would take paper money from under her carpet,
or out of the chinks in her walls, and buy things for up at the
church, or buy her own whisky when she got sick, instead of
making somebody bring her a nip. On the Square she would laugh
and holler with the white folks the way they liked her to and the
way Crecie and all the other old-timers did, and she even took to
tying a bandanna about her head—took to talking old-nigger foolishness, too, about the Bell Witch, and claiming she remembered the
day General N. B. Forrest rode into town and saved all the cotton
from the Yankees at the depot. When Mr. Will and Mr. Thad came
to see her with their families, she got so she would reminisce with
them about their daddy and tease them about all the silly little
things they had done when they were growing up: "Mr. Thad—him
still in kilts, too—he says, 'Aunt Munsie, reach down in yo' stockin'
and git me a copper cent. I want some store candy.'" She told them
about how Miss Yola Ewing, the sewing woman, heard her threatening to bust Will's back wide open when he broke the lamp chimney,
and how Miss Yola went to the Doctor and told him he ought to run
Aunt Munsie off. Then Aunt Munsie and the Doctor had had a big
laugh about it out in the kitchen, and Miss Yola must have eaves-
dropped on them, because she left without finishing the girls' Easter
dresses.

Indeed, these visits from Mr. Thad and Mr. Will continued as
long as Aunt Munsie lived, but she never asked them any more

about when they were sure enough coming back. And the children, though she hugged them more than ever—and, toward the last, there were the children's children to be hugged—never again set foot in her back yard. Aunt Munsie lived on for nearly twenty years, and when they finally buried her, they put on her tombstone that she was aged one hundred years, though nobody knew how old she was. There was no record of when she was born. All anyone knew was that in her last years she had said she was a girl helping about the big house when freedom came. That would have made her probably about twelve years old in 1865, according to her statements and depictions. But all agreed that in her extreme old age Aunt Munsie, like other old darkies, was not very reliable about dates and such things. Her spirit softened, even her voice lost some of the rasping quality that it had always had, and in general she became not very reliable about facts.

TRUMAN CAPOTE

A Diamond Guitar

HE NEAREST TOWN to the prison farm is twenty miles away. Many forests of pine trees stand between the farm and the town, and it is in these forests that the convicts work; they tap for turpentine. The prison itself is in a forest. You will find it there at the end of a red rutted road, barbed wire sprawling like a vine over its walls. Inside, there live one hundred and nine white men,

ninety-seven Negroes and one Chinese. There are two sleep houses
—great green wooden buildings with tar-paper roofs. The white
men occupy one, the Negroes and the Chinese the other. In each
sleep house there is one large pot-bellied stove, but the winters are
cold here, and at night with the pines waving frostily and a freezing
light falling from the moon the men, stretched on their iron cots,
lie awake with the fire colors of the stove playing in their eyes.

The men whose cots are nearest the stove are the important
men—those who are looked up to or feared. Mr. Schaeffer is one
of these. Mr. Schaeffer—for that is what he is called, a mark of
special respect—is a lanky, pulled-out man. He has reddish, silver-
ing hair, and his face is attenuated, religious; there is no flesh to
him; you can see the workings of his bones, and his eyes are a poor,
dull color. He can read and he can write, he can add a column of
figures. When another man receives a letter, he brings it to Mr.
Schaeffer. Most of these letters are sad and complaining; very often
Mr. Schaeffer improvises more cheerful messages and does not read
what is written on the page. In the sleep house there are two other
men who can read. Even so, one of them brings his letters to Mr.
Schaeffer, who obliges by never reading the truth. Mr. Schaeffer
himself does not receive mail, not even at Christmas; he seems to
have no friends beyond the prison, and actually he has none there
—that is, no particular friend. This was not always true.

One winter Sunday some winters ago Mr. Schaeffer was sitting
on the steps of the sleep house carving a doll. He is quite talented
at this. His dolls are carved in separate sections, then put together
with bits of spring wire; the arms and legs move, the head rolls.
When he has finished a dozen or so of these dolls, the Captain of
the farm takes them into town, and there they are sold in a general
store. In this way Mr. Schaeffer earns money for candy and tobacco.

That Sunday, as he sat cutting out the fingers for a little hand,
a truck pulled into the prison yard. A young boy, handcuffed to the
Captain of the farm, climbed out of the truck and stood blinking at
the ghostly winter sun. Mr. Schaeffer only glanced at him. He was
then a man of fifty, and seventeen of those years he'd lived at the
farm. The arrival of a new prisoner could not arouse him. Sunday
is a free day at the farm, and other men who were moping around
the yard crowded down to the truck. Afterward, Pick Axe and
Goober stopped by to speak with Mr. Schaeffer.

Pick Axe said, "He's a foreigner, the new one is. From Cuba. But with yellow hair."

"A knifer, Cap'n says," said Goober, who was a knifer himself. "Cut up a sailor in Mobile."

"Two sailors," said Pick Axe. "But just a café fight. He didn't hurt them boys none."

"To cut off a man's ear? You call that not hurtin' him? They give him two years, Cap'n says."

Pick Axe said, "He's got a guitar with jewels all over it."

It was getting too dark to work. Mr. Schaeffer fitted the pieces of his doll together and, holding its little hands, set it on his knee. He rolled a cigarette; the pines were blue in the sundown light, and the smoke from his cigarette lingered in the cold, darkening air. He could see the Captain coming across the yard. The new prisoner, a blond young boy, lagged a pace behind. He was carrying a guitar studded with glass diamonds that cast a starry twinkle, and his new uniform was too big for him; it looked like a Halloween suit.

"Somebody for you, Schaeffer," said the Captain, pausing on the steps of the sleep house. The Captain was not a hard man; occasionally he invited Mr. Schaeffer into his office, and they would talk together about things they had read in the newspaper. "Tico Feo," he said as though it were the name of a bird or a song, "this is Mr. Schaeffer. Do like him, and you'll do right."

Mr. Schaeffer glanced up at the boy and smiled. He smiled at him longer than he meant to, for the boy had eyes like strips of sky—blue as the winter evening—and his hair was as gold as the Captain's teeth. He had a fun-loving face, nimble, clever; and, looking at him, Mr. Schaeffer thought of holidays and good times.

"Is like my baby sister," said Tico Feo, touching Mr. Schaeffer's doll. His voice with its Cuban accent was soft and sweet as a banana. "She sit on my knee also."

Mr. Schaeffer was suddenly shy. Bowing to the Captain, he walked off into the shadows of the yard. He stood there whispering the names of the evening stars as they opened in flower above him. The stars were his pleasure, but tonight they did not comfort him; they did not make him remember that what happens to us on earth is lost in the endless shine of eternity. Gazing at them—the stars— he thought of the jeweled guitar and its worldly glitter.

It could be said of Mr. Schaeffer that in his life he'd done only

one really bad thing: he'd killed a man. The circumstances of that
deed are unimportant, except to say that the man deserved to die
and that for it Mr. Schaeffer was sentenced to ninety-nine years and
a day. For a long while—for many years, in fact—he had not
thought of how it was before he came to the farm. His memory of
those times was like a house where no one lives and where the
furniture has rotted away. But tonight it was as if lamps had been
lighted through all the gloomy dead rooms. It had begun to happen
when he saw Tico Feo coming through the dusk with his splendid
guitar. Until that moment he had not been lonesome. Now, recog-
nizing his loneliness, he felt alive. He had not wanted to be alive.
To be alive was to remember brown rivers where the fish run, and
sunlight on a lady's hair.

Mr. Schaeffer hung his head. The glare of the stars had made
his eyes water.

The sleep house usually is a glum place, stale with the smell of
men and stark in the light of two unshaded electric bulbs. But with
the advent of Tico Feo it was as though a tropic occurrence had
happened in the cold room, for when Mr. Schaeffer returned from
his observance of the stars he came upon a savage and garish scene.
Sitting cross-legged on a cot, Tico Feo was picking at his guitar
with long swaying fingers and singing a song that sounded as jolly
as jingling coins. Though the song was in Spanish, some of the men
tried to sing it with him, and Pick Axe and Goober were dancing
together. Charlie and Wink were dancing too, but separately. It
was nice to hear the men laughing, and when Tico Feo finally put
aside his guitar, Mr. Schaeffer was among those who congratulated
him.

"You deserve such a fine guitar," he said.

"Is diamond guitar," said Tico Feo, drawing his hand over its
vaudeville dazzle. "Once I have a one with rubies. But that one is
stole. In Havana my sister work in a, how you say, where make
guitar; is how I have this one."

Mr. Schaeffer asked him if he had many sisters, and Tico Feo,
grinning, held up four fingers. Then, his blue eyes narrowing
greedily, he said, "Please, Mister, you give me doll for my two
little sister?"

The next evening Mr. Schaeffer brought him the dolls. After

that he was Tico Feo's best friend and they were always together. At all times they considered each other.

Tico Feo was eighteen years old and for two years had worked on a freighter in the Caribbean. As a child he'd gone to school with nuns, and he wore a gold crucifix around his neck. He had a rosary too. The rosary he kept wrapped in a green silk scarf that also held three other treasures: a bottle of Evening in Paris cologne, a pocket mirror and a Rand McNally map of the world. These and the guitar were his only possessions, and he would not allow anyone to touch them. Perhaps he prized his map the most. At night, before the lights were turned off, he would shake out his map and show Mr. Schaeffer the places he'd been—Galveston, Miami, New Orleans, Mobile, Cuba, Haiti, Jamaica, Puerto Rico, the Virgin Islands—and the places he wanted to go to. He wanted to go almost everywhere, especially Madrid, especially the North Pole. This both charmed and frightened Mr. Schaeffer. It hurt him to think of Tico Feo on the seas and in far places. He sometimes looked defensively at his friend and thought, "You are just a lazy dreamer."

It is true that Tico Feo was a lazy fellow. After that first evening he had to be urged even to play his guitar. At daybreak when the guard came to rouse the men, which he did by banging a hammer on the stove, Tico Feo would whimper like a child. Sometimes he pretended to be ill, moaned and rubbed his stomach; but he never got away with this, for the Captain would send him out to work with the rest of the men. He and Mr. Schaeffer were put together on a highway gang. It was hard work, digging at frozen clay and carrying croker sacks filled with broken stone. The guard had always to be shouting at Tico Feo, for he spent most of the time trying to lean on things.

Each noon, when the dinner buckets were passed around, the two friends sat together. There were some good things in Mr. Schaeffer's bucket, as he could afford apples and candy bars from the town. He liked giving these things to his friend, for his friend enjoyed them so much, and he thought, "You are growing; it will be a long time until you are a grown man."

Not all the men liked Tico Feo. Because they were jealous, or for more subtle reasons, some of them told ugly stories about him. Tico Feo himself seemed unaware of this. When the men gathered around him, and he played his guitar and sang his songs, you could see that he felt he was loved. Most of the men did feel a love for him; they waited for and depended upon the hour between supper and lights out. "Tico, play your box," they would say. They did not notice that afterward there was a deeper sadness than there had ever been. Sleep jumped beyond them like a jack rabbit, and their eyes lingered ponderingly on the firelight that creaked behind the grating of the stove. Mr. Schaeffer was the only one who understood their troubled feeling, for he felt it too. It was that his friend had revived the brown rivers where the fish run, and ladies with sunlight in their hair.

Soon Tico Feo was allowed the honor of having a bed near the stove and next to Mr. Schaeffer. Mr. Schaeffer had always known that his friend was a terrible liar. He did not listen for the truth in Tico Feo's tales of adventure, of conquests and encounters with famous people. Rather, he took pleasure in them as plain stories, such as you would read in a magazine, and it warmed him to hear his friend's tropic voice whispering in the dark.

Except that they did not combine their bodies or think to do so, though such things were not unknown at the farm, they were as lovers. Of the seasons, spring is the most shattering: stalks thrusting through the earth's winter-stiffened crust, young leaves cracking out on old left-to-die branches, the falling-asleep wind cruising through all the newborn green. And with Mr. Schaeffer it was the same, a breaking up, a flexing of muscles that had hardened.

It was late January. The friends were sitting on the steps of the sleep house, each with a cigarette in his hand. A moon thin and yellow as a piece of lemon rind curved above them, and under its light, threads of ground frost glistened like silver snail trails. For many days Tico Feo had been drawn into himself—silent as a robber waiting in the shadows. It was no good to say to him, "Tico, play your box." He would only look at you with smooth, under-ether eyes.

"Tell a story," said Mr. Schaeffer, who felt nervous and helpless when he could not reach his friend. "Tell about when you went to the race track in Miami."

"I not ever go to no race track," said Tico Feo, thereby admitting to his wildest lie, one involving hundreds of dollars and a meeting with Bing Crosby. He did not seem to care. He produced a comb and pulled it sulkily through his hair. A few days before this comb had been the cause of a fierce quarrel. One of the men, Wink, claimed that Tico Feo had stolen the comb from him, to which the accused replied by spitting in his face. They had wrestled around until Mr. Schaeffer and another man got them separated. "Is my comb. You tell him!" Tico Feo had demanded of Mr. Schaeffer. But Mr. Schaeffer with quiet firmness had said no, it was not his friend's comb—an answer that seemed to defeat all concerned. "Aw," said Wink, "if he wants it so much, Christ's sake, let the sonofabitch keep it." And later, in a puzzled, uncertain voice, Tico Feo had said, "I thought you was my friend." "I am," Mr. Schaeffer had thought, though he said nothing.

"I not go to no race track, and what I said about the widow woman, that is not true also." He puffed up his cigarette to a furious glow and looked at Mr. Schaeffer with a speculating expression. "Say, you have money, Mister?"

"Maybe twenty dollars," said Mr. Schaeffer hesitantly, afraid of where this was leading.

"Not so good, twenty dollar," Tico said, but without disappointment. "No important, we work our way. In Mobile I have my friend Frederico. He will put us on a boat. There will not be trouble," and it was as though he were saying that the weather had turned colder.

There was a squeezing in Mr. Schaeffer's heart; he could not speak.

"Nobody here can run to catch Tico. He run the fastest."

"Shotguns run faster," said Mr. Schaeffer in a voice hardly alive. "I'm too old," he said, with the knowledge of age churning like nausea inside him.

Tico Feo was not listening. "Then, the world. The world, *el mundo*, my friend." Standing up, he quivered like a young horse; everything seemed to draw close to him—the moon, the callings of screech owls. His breath came quickly and turned to smoke in the air. "Should we go to Madrid? Maybe someone teach me to bullfight. You think so, Mister?"

Mr. Schaeffer was not listening either. "I'm too old," he said. "I'm too damned old."

For the next several weeks Tico Feo kept after him—the world, *el mundo*, my friend; and he wanted to hide. He would shut himself in the toilet and hold his head. Nevertheless, he was excited, tantalized. What if it could come true, the race with Tico across the forests and to the sea? And he imagined himself on a boat, he who had never seen the sea, whose whole life had been land-rooted. During this time one of the convicts died, and in the yard you could hear the coffin being made. As each nail thudded into place, Mr. Schaeffer thought, "This is for me, it is mine."

Tico Feo himself was never in better spirits; he sauntered about with a dancer's snappy, gigolo grace, and had a joke for everyone. In the sleep house after supper his fingers popped at the guitar like firecrackers. He taught the men to cry *olé*, and some of them sailed their caps through the air.

When work on the road was finished, Mr. Schaeffer and Tico Feo were moved back into the forests. On Valentine's Day they ate their lunch under a pine tree. Mr. Schaeffer had ordered a dozen oranges from the town and he peeled them slowly, the skins unraveling in a spiral; the juicier slices he gave to his friend, who was proud of how far he could spit the seeds—a good ten feet.

It was a cold beautiful day, scraps of sunlight blew about them like butterflies, and Mr. Schaeffer, who liked working with the trees, felt dim and happy. Then Tico Feo said, "That one, he no could catch a fly in his mouth." He meant Armstrong, a hog-jowled man sitting with a shotgun propped between his legs. He was the youngest of the guards and new at the farm.

"I don't know," said Mr. Schaeffer. He'd watched Armstrong and noticed that, like many people who are both heavy and vain, the new guard moved with a skimming lightness. "He might could fool you."

"I fool him, maybe," said Tico Feo, and spit an orange seed in Armstrong's direction. The guard scowled at him, then blew a whistle. It was the signal for work to begin.

Sometime during the afternoon the two friends came together again; that is, they were nailing turpentine buckets onto trees that stood next to each other. At a distance below them a shallow bouncing creek branched through the woods. "In water no smell," said Tico Feo meticulously, as though remembering something he'd heard. "We run in the water; until dark we climb a tree. Yes, Mister?"

Mr. Schaeffer went on hammering, but his hand was shaking, and the hammer came down on his thumb. He looked around dazedly at his friend. His face showed no reflection of pain, and he did not put the thumb in his mouth, the way a man ordinarily might.

Tico Feo's blue eyes seemed to swell like bubbles, and when in a voice quieter than the wind sounds in the pinetops he said, "Tomorrow," these eyes were all that Mr. Schaeffer could see.

"Tomorrow, Mister?"

"Tomorrow," said Mr. Schaeffer.

The first colors of morning fell upon the walls of the sleep house, and Mr. Schaeffer, who had rested little, knew that Tico Feo was awake too. With the weary eyes of a crocodile he observed the movements of his friend in the next cot. Tico Feo was unknotting the scarf that contained his treasures. First he took the pocket mirror. Its jellyfish light trembled on his face. For a while he admired himself with serious delight, and combed and slicked his hair as though he were preparing to step out to a party. Then he hung the rosary about his neck. The cologne he never opened, nor the map. The last thing he did was to tune his guitar. While the other men were dressing, he sat on the edge of his cot and tuned the guitar. It was strange, for he must have known he would never play it again.

Bird shrills followed the men through the smoky morning woods. They walked single file, fifteen men to a group, and a guard bringing up the rear of each line. Mr. Schaeffer was sweating as though it were a hot day, and he could not keep in marching step with his friend, who walked ahead, snapping his fingers and whistling at the birds.

A signal had been set. Tico Feo was to call, "Time out," and pretend to go behind a tree. But Mr. Schaeffer did not know when it would happen.

The guard named Armstrong blew a whistle, and his men dropped from the line and separated to their various stations. Mr. Schaeffer, though going about his work as best he could, took care always to be in a position where he could keep an eye on both Tico Feo and the guard. Armstrong sat on a stump, a chew of tobacco lopsiding his face, and his gun pointing into the sun. He had the tricky eyes of a cardsharp; you could not really tell where he was looking.

Once another man gave the signal. Although Mr. Schaeffer had known at once that it was not the voice of his friend, panic had pulled at his throat like a rope. As the morning wore on there was such a drumming in his ears he was afraid he would not hear the signal when it came.

The sun climbed to the center of the sky. "He is just a lazy dreamer. It will never happen," thought Mr. Schaeffer, daring a moment to believe this. But "First we eat," said Tico Feo with a practical air as they set their dinner pails on the bank above the creek. They ate in silence, almost as though each bore the other a grudge, but at the end of it Mr. Schaeffer felt his friend's hand close over his own and hold it with a tender pressure.

"Mister Armstrong, time out . . ."

Near the creek Mr. Schaeffer had seen a sweet gum tree, and he was thinking it would soon be spring and the sweet gum ready to chew. A razory stone ripped open the palm of his hand as he slid off the slippery embankment into the water. He straightened up and began to run; his legs were long, he kept almost abreast of Tico Feo, and icy geysers sprayed around them. Back and forth through the woods the shouts of men boomed hollowly like voices in a cavern, and there were three shots, all highflying, as though the guard were shooting at a cloud of geese.

Mr. Schaeffer did not see the log that lay across the creek. He thought he was still running, and his legs thrashed about him; it was as though he were a turtle stranded on its back.

While he struggled there, it seemed to him that the face of his friend, suspended above him, was part of the white winter sky— it was so distant, judging. It hung there but an instant, like a hummingbird, yet in that time he'd seen that Tico Feo had not wanted him to make it, had never thought he would, and he remembered once thinking that it would be a long time before his friend was a grown man. When they found him, he was still lying in the ankle-deep water as though it were a summer afternoon and he were idly floating on the stream.

Since then three winters have gone by, and each has been said to be the coldest, the longest. Two recent months of rain washed deeper ruts in the clay road leading to the farm, and it is harder than ever to get there, harder to leave. A pair of searchlights has

been added to the walls, and they burn there through the night
like the eyes of a giant owl. Otherwise, there have not been many
changes. Mr. Schaeffer, for instance, looks much the same, except
that there is a thicker frost of white in his hair, and as the result of
a broken ankle he walks with a limp. It was the Captain himself
who said that Mr. Schaeffer had broken his ankle attempting to
capture Tico Feo. There was even a picture of Mr. Schaeffer in
the newspaper, and under it this caption: "Tried to Prevent Escape."
At the time he was deeply mortified, not because he knew the other
men were laughing, but because he thought of Tico Feo seeing it.
But he cut it out of the paper anyway, and keeps it in an envelope
along with several clippings pertaining to his friend: a spinster
woman told the authorities he'd entered her home and kissed her,
twice he was reported seen in the Mobile vicinity, finally it was
believed that he had left the country.

No one has ever disputed Mr. Schaeffer's claim to the guitar.
Several months ago a new prisoner was moved into the sleep
house. He was said to be a fine player, and Mr. Schaeffer was
persuaded to lend him the guitar. But all the man's tunes came out
sour, for it was as though Tico Feo, tuning his guitar that last
morning, had put a curse upon it. Now it lies under Mr. Schaeffer's
cot, where its glass diamonds are turning yellow; in the night his
hand sometimes searches it out, and his fingers drift across the
strings: then, the world.

TRUMAN CAPOTE'S *"A Diamond Guitar"*

Mr. Capote specializes in the atmosphere of the waking
dream. I do not mean, in the ordinary sense, the "daydream"—the idle
but still loosely controlled and conscious, wishful fantasy. Rather, in
almost all of Capote's stories, the central figure—the one through whose
eyes we see the events—has something of the character of a sleepwalker,
or of a person whose consciousness is permanently suspended somewhere between sleep and full wakefulness.

From COMMENTARIES ON FIVE MODERN AMERICAN SHORT STORIES, by
John Edward Hardy, Verlag Moritz Diesterweg. Frankfurt/Main. Copyright
1962 by Moritz Diesterweg.

There is almost never any clear sense of contrast between waking reality and the dream state. In some of Capote's stories, the people are directly spoken of as being at one time awake and at another time asleep and dreaming. But between the account of the dream and the account of waking action, it is difficult to see any great difference. From beginning to end, all things (persons, places, events, objects) appear to us in the manner of dream images. It is a world now and then oddly delightful, with moments of tenderness and even cheerfulness, but for the most part sad and terrible—intense and vivid, but hopelessly distorted, completely irrational and completely uncontrolled. There is, as in dreams, a strange sense of attraction, even to images that in waking reality we might find repulsive, and a strangely and intensely *felt* significance. But it is a significance never to be entirely grasped by the reason, mocking and elusive. The characters—and, when Mr. Capote is successful in carrying out his intention, we—are compelled by the action of the story. We are "led on," simply. We have no choice in the matter. And we are promised nothing, either, in the way of final understanding of what we experience.

But I have been speaking so far only of an effect aimed at and sometimes achieved. Behind the effect, there is an art, which is fully conscious and explicable. Mr. Capote is not a magician. Neither is he simply telling us his own dreams. He is telling us stories, rather. And his art, as storyteller, the means by which he seeks to establish the dreamlike effect, is just as easily subject to analysis as that of any other writer. The analysis, to be sure, is possible only upon second or third reading of the story—only after we have thoroughly "experienced" the story, allowed it to have its effect upon us, and (as I have, in a general fashion, attempted above) made some effort at least to describe that effect, if not to render it fully intelligible. But this, again, is true of all fiction that we propose to study and not simply to use as a means of entertaining ourselves.

Let us, then, see what Capote is doing in "A Diamond Guitar." There is, I have meant to suggest, almost nowhere in his fiction a sense of the "normality" of life. One of the means by which he seeks to establish the consistent dream atmosphere is that he deals with the experience of "outcasts" of one sort or another, people who live somehow on the fringes of society: the very young or the very old, the widowed, the orphaned, the poor, those deformed in body or mind, vagabonds and carnival entertainers, exiles, Negroes, writers. In "A Diamond Guitar," it is the life of prisoners on a Southern penal farm. And with the establishment of this setting in the opening paragraph of the story, we have already taken the first step away from the realm of workaday normality. For we must always think of a prison as "another world," a world apart, complete and whole unto itself—in which the ordinary laws of human behavior, if not of human nature, are radically altered. This theme, in one version or another, is the common property of all prison stories in all literatures.

But it is important to note the particular details of Capote's adaptation of the convention. First, it is significant that it is a penal *farm*, not a city prison: "the nearest town . . . twenty miles away," with "many forests of pine trees between the farm and the town," and "the prison itself in a forest." With all this—and many other things such as the account of Mr. Schaeffer's reading their mail to the other prisoners, altering "the sad and complaining" truth of the letters to save the men from concern with troubles in the outside world they cannot help—the author is, of course, simply emphasizing the remoteness and separateness of the prison, as prison. But his intention, it seems to me, is finally somewhat more complex.

Subtly, as an undertone to the straightforward, realistic description of the place, and the introduction of Mr. Schaeffer, he has begun to build up an atmosphere of *enchantment*. The prisoners, especially Mr. Schaeffer, are not so much prisoners of the law, and of walls and bars and chains, as prisoners of a dream. There is a wall, to be sure, and with barbed wire upon it. But this, except for the guard's shotgun, is all that is ever mentioned of the ordinary restraining devices of a prison. Even the barbed wire is spoken of as "sprawling *like a vine* over (the) walls"—a simile that tends to de-emphasize its simple, realistic function. The men, as if entranced by the cold of the winter nights, "lie awake with the fire colors of the stove playing in their eyes." And so on. Everywhere, the language throws over things a light of the preternatural or surrealistic.

Mr. Shaeffer's, of course, is the central consciousness of the narrative. It is "his story," as we say. We may see him, at first glance, simply as the principal victim of the evil enchantment of the place—to whom the young Cuban, Tico Feo, comes pathetically too late with his offer of "el mundo," of escape to the real world outside, with its treasures and its joys, its promise of journeys to lands with "brown rivers where the fish run, and ladies with sunlight in their hair," to freedom. The outcome is pathetic, because it is too late; because Mr. Schaeffer is simply too old, now, to run fast and far enough; because, more profoundly, his imagination is paralyzed by the long years in the prison and he cannot, against the "nausea" of his consciousness of age, believe in himself as a part of "el mundo," "the world." He has developed, as long-term prisoners commonly do, a kind of contentment with his environment, and is indeed reluctant to give it up. This contentment is the principal effect of what I have called the "enchantment."

But there is yet a further level of irony. For Tico Feo himself is a dream. Everything about him (this representative of "the world," of "reality") is *un*real, fake, false, a cheap and gaudy magic. His guitar, of course, with its glass "diamonds," is the principal symbol of this falsity of his appeal. But there is something improbable about the man himself—even to the coloring of his eyes and hair. A blond and blue-eyed Cuban! Moreover, he is a terrible liar, and not simply at the level of "embroidering" his stories of adventure, which would be harmless enough, but at the level of cheating, thievery, and betrayal. Mr. Schaeffer realizes at the last moment—when he has fallen against the log in the stream, and the boy's face hovers above him a moment, dreamlike, "suspended . . . [like] a part of the winter sky . . . like a hummingbird" —that Tico Feo "had not wanted him to make it, had never thought he would."

This is the final cruelty and falsity, then, of his "friend," and final, pathetic irony of Mr. Schaeffer's situation. He is caught, in fact, between *two* dreams—that of the prison, this "enchanted forest," and that of freedom outside, of "the world." Both are equally unreal; and both— once they have touched, once been seen in the light of each other— equally unattainable, equally not to be believed in. Mr. Schaeffer cannot escape, and he can never again, after Tico Feo's visit, recover his old contentment with the life of the prison. The guitar will no longer play in tune—"it was as though . . . Tico Feo had put a curse upon it"—and its diamonds have long since turned dull and yellow; but the old man, three years after the disappearance of the Cuban, continues hopelessly to let his hand stray over the strings in the darkness.

In this as in all his fiction, what Mr. Capote seems to be saying is not only, with T. S. Eliot, that man cannot bear very much reality, but that no reality is available to him. Any and every world is equally false; and the sum of man's experience is the shadow of sense impressions. *J.E.H.*

SHIRLEY JACKSON

The Lottery

HE MORNING OF JUNE 27th was clear and sunny, with the fresh warmth of a full-summer day; the flowers were blossoming profusely and the grass was richly green. The people of the village began to gather in the square, between the post office and the bank, around ten o'clock; in some towns there were so many people that the lottery took two days and had to be started on June 26th, but in this village, where there were only about three hundred people, the whole lottery took only about two hours, so it could begin at ten o'clock in the morning and still be through in time to allow the villagers to get home for noon dinner.

The children assembled first, of course. School was recently over for the summer, and the feeling of liberty sat uneasily on most of them; they tended to gather together quietly for a while before they broke into boisterous play, and their talk was still of the classroom and the teacher, of books and reprimands. Bobby Martin had already stuffed his pockets full of stones, and the other boys soon followed his example, selecting the smoothest and roundest stones; Bobby and Harry Jones and Dickie Delacroix—the villagers pronounced this name "Dellacroy"—eventually made a great pile of stones in one corner of the square and guarded it against the raids of the other boys. The girls stood aside, talking among themselves, looking over their shoulders at the boys, and the very small children rolled in the dust or clung to the hands of their older brothers or sisters.

Reprinted from THE LOTTERY by Shirley Jackson, by permission of Farrar, Straus & Company, Inc. Copyright 1948 by The New Yorker Magazine, 1949 by Shirley Jackson.

Soon the men began to gather, surveying their own children, speaking of planting and rain, tractors and taxes. They stood together, away from the pile of stones in the corner, and their jokes were quiet and they smiled rather than laughed. The women, wearing faded house dresses and sweaters, came shortly after their menfolk. They greeted one another and exchanged bits of gossip as they went to join their husbands. Soon the women, standing by their husbands, began to call to their children, and the children came reluctantly, having to be called four or five times. Bobby Martin ducked under his mother's grasping hand and ran, laughing, back to the pile of stones. His father spoke up sharply, and Bobby came quickly and took his place between his father and his oldest brother.

The lottery was conducted—as were the square dances, the teen-age club, the Halloween program—by Mr. Summers, who had time and energy to devote to civic activities. He was a round-faced, jovial man and he ran the coal business, and people were sorry for him, because he had no children and his wife was a scold. When he arrived in the square, carrying the black wooden box, there was a murmur of conversation among the villagers, and he waved and called, "Little late today, folks." The postmaster, Mr. Graves, followed him, carrying a three-legged stool, and the stool was put in the center of the square and Mr. Summers set the black box down on it. The villagers kept their distance, leaving a space between themselves and the stool, and when Mr. Summers said, "Some of you fellows want to give me a hand?" there was a hesitation before two men, Mr. Martin and his oldest son, Baxter, came forward to hold the box steady on the stool while Mr. Summers stirred up the papers inside it.

The original paraphernalia for the lottery had been lost long ago, and the black box now resting on the stool had been put into use even before Old Man Warner, the oldest man in town, was born. Mr. Summers spoke frequently to the villagers about making a new box, but no one liked to upset even as much tradition as was represented by the black box. There was a story that the present box had been made with some pieces of the box that had preceded it, the one that had been constructed when the first people settled down to make a village here. Every year, after the lottery, Mr. Summers began talking again about a new box, but every year the subject was allowed to fade off without anything's being done. The black box grew shabbier each year; by now it was no longer completely black but splintered badly along one side to show the original wood color, and in some places faded or stained.

Mr. Martin and his oldest son, Baxter, held the black box securely on the stool until Mr. Summers had stirred the papers thoroughly with his hand. Because so much of the ritual had been forgotten or discarded, Mr. Summers had been successful in having slips of paper substituted for the chips of wood that had been used for generations. Chips of wood, Mr. Summers had argued, had been all very well when the village was tiny, but now that the population was more than three hundred and likely to keep on growing, it was necessary to use something that would fit more easily into the black box. The night before the lottery, Mr. Summers and Mr. Graves made up the slips of paper and put them into the box, and it was then taken to the safe of Mr. Summers' coal company and locked up until Mr. Summers was ready to take it to the square next morning. The rest of the year, the box was put away, sometimes one place, sometimes another; it had spent one year in Mr. Graves' barn and another year underfoot in the post office, and sometimes it was set on a shelf in the Martin grocery and left there.

There was a great deal of fussing to be done before Mr. Summers declared the lottery open. There were the lists to make up —of heads of families, heads of households in each family, members of each household in each family. There was the proper swearing-in of Mr. Summers by the postmaster, as the official of the lottery; at one time, some people remembered, there had been a recital of some sort, performed by the official of the lottery, a perfunctory, tuneless chant that had been rattled off duly each year; some people believed that the official of the lottery used to stand just so when he said or sang it, others believed that he was supposed to walk among the people, but years and years ago this part of the ritual had been allowed to lapse. There had been, also, a ritual salute, which the official of the lottery had had to use in addressing each person who came up to draw from the box, but this also had changed with time, until now it was felt necessary only for the official to speak to each person approaching. Mr. Summers was very good at all this; in his clean white shirt and blue jeans, with one hand resting carelessly on the black box, he seemed very proper and important as he talked interminably to Mr. Graves and the Martins.

Just as Mr. Summers finally left off talking and turned to the assembled villagers, Mrs. Hutchinson came hurriedly along the path to the square, her sweater thrown over her shoulders, and slid into place in the back of the crowd. "Clean forgot what day it was," she said to Mrs. Delacroix, who stood next to her, and they both laughed softly. "Thought my old man was out back stacking wood," Mrs. Hutchinson went on, "and then I looked out the window and the kids was gone, and then I remembered it was the twenty-seventh and came a-running." She dried her hands on her apron, and Mrs. Delacroix said, "You're in time, though. They're still talking away up there."

Mrs. Hutchinson craned her neck to see through the crowd and found her husband and children standing near the front. She tapped Mrs. Delacroix on the arm as a farewell and began to make her way through the crowd. The people separated good-humoredly to let her through; two or three people said, in voices just loud enough to be heard across the crowd, "Here comes your Mrs., Hutchinson," and "Bill, she made it after all." Mrs. Hutchinson reached her husband, and Mr. Summers, who had been waiting, said cheerfully, "Thought we were going to have to get on without you, Tessie." Mrs. Hutchinson said, grinning, "Wouldn't have me leave m'dishes in the sink, now, would you, Joe?" and soft laughter ran through the crowd as the people stirred back into position after Mrs. Hutchinson's arrival.

"Well, now," Mr. Summers said soberly, "guess we better get started, get this over with, so's we can go back to work. Anybody ain't here?"

"Dunbar," several people said. "Dunbar, Dunbar."

Mr. Summers consulted his list. "Clyde Dunbar," he said. "That's right. He's broke his leg, hasn't he? Who's drawing for him?"

"Me, I guess," a woman said, and Mr. Summers turned to look at her. "Wife draws for her husband," Mr. Summers said. "Don't you have a grown boy to do it for you, Janey?" Although Mr.

Summers and everyone else in the village knew the answer perfectly well, it was the business of the official of the lottery to ask such questions formally. Mr. Summers waited with an expression of polite interest while Mrs. Dunbar answered.

"Horace's not but sixteen yet," Mrs. Dunbar said regretfully. "Guess I gotta fill in for the old man this year."

"Right," Mr. Summers said. He made a note on the list he was holding. Then he asked, "Watson boy drawing this year?"

A tall boy in the crowd raised his hand. "Here," he said. "I'm drawing for m'mother and me." He blinked his eyes nervously and ducked his head as several voices in the crowd said things like "Good fellow, Jack," and "Glad to see your mother's got a man to do it."

"Well," Mr. Summers said, "guess that's everyone. Old Man Warner make it?"

"Here," a voice said, and Mr. Summers nodded.

A sudden hush fell on the crowd as Mr. Summers cleared his throat and looked at the list. "All ready?" he called. "Now, I'll read the names—heads of families first—and the men come up and take a paper out of the box. Keep the paper folded in your hand without looking at it until everyone has had a turn. Everything clear?"

The people had done it so many times that they only half listened to the directions; most of them were quiet, wetting their lips, not looking around. Then Mr. Summers raised one hand high and said, "Adams." A man disengaged himself from the crowd and came forward. "Hi, Steve," Mr. Summers said, and Mr. Adams said, "Hi, Joe." They grinned at one another humorlessly and nervously. Then Mr. Adams reached into the black box and took out a folded paper. He held it firmly by one corner as he turned and went hastily back to his place in the crowd, where he stood a little apart from his family, not looking down at his hand.

"Allen," Mr. Summers said. "Anderson. . . . Bentham."

"Seems like there's no time at all between lotteries any more," Mrs. Delacroix said to Mrs. Graves in the back row. "Seems like we got through with the last one only last week."

"Time sure goes fast," Mrs. Graves said.

"Clark. . . . Delacroix."

"There goes my old man," Mrs. Delacroix said. She held her breath while her husband went forward.

"Dunbar," Mr. Summers said, and Mrs. Dunbar went steadily to the box while one of the women said, "Go on, Janey," and another said, "There she goes."

"We're next," Mrs. Graves said. She watched while Mr. Graves came around from the side of the box, greeted Mr. Summers gravely, and selected a slip of paper from the box. By now, all through the crowd there were men holding the small folded papers in their large hands, turning them over and over nervously. Mrs. Dunbar and her two sons stood together, Mrs. Dunbar holding the slip of paper.

"Harburt. . . . Hutchinson."

"Get up there, Bill," Mrs. Hutchinson said, and the people near her laughed.

"Jones."

"They do say," Mr. Adams said to Old Man Warner, who stood next to him, "that over in the north village they're talking of giving up the lottery."

Old Man Warner snorted. "Pack of crazy fools," he said. "Listening to the young folks, nothing's good enough for *them*. Next thing you know, they'll be wanting to go back to living in caves, nobody work any more, live *that* way for a while. Used to be a saying about 'Lottery in June, corn be heavy soon.' First thing you know, we'd all be eating stewed chickenweed and acorns. There's *always* been a lottery," he added petulantly. "Bad enough to see young Joe Summers up there joking with everybody."

"Some places have already quit lotteries," Mrs. Adams said.

"Nothing but trouble in *that*," Old Man Warner said stoutly. "Pack of young fools."

"Martin." And Bobby Martin watched his father go forward. "Overdyke. . . . Percy."

"I wish they'd hurry," Mrs. Dunbar said to her older son. "I wish they'd hurry."

"They're almost through," her son said.

"You get ready to run tell Dad," Mrs. Dunbar said.

Mr. Summers called his own name and then stepped forward

precisely and selected a slip from the box. Then he called, "Warner."

"Seventy-seventh year I been in the lottery," Old Man Warner said as he went through the crowd. "Seventy-seventh time."

"Watson." The tall boy came awkwardly through the crowd. Someone said, "Don't be nervous, Jack," and Mr. Summers said, "Take your time, son."

"Zanini."

After that, there was a long pause, a breathless pause, until Mr. Summers, holding his slip of paper in the air, said, "All right, fellows." For a minute, no one moved, and then all the slips of paper were opened. Suddenly, all the women began to speak at once, saying, "Who is it?" "Who's got it?" "Is it the Dunbars?" "Is it the Watsons?" Then the voices began to say, "It's Hutchinson. It's Bill," "Bill Hutchinson's got it."

"Go tell your father," Mrs. Dunbar said to her older son.

People began to look around to see the Hutchinsons. Bill Hutchinson was standing quiet, staring down at the paper in his hand. Suddenly, Tessie Hutchinson shouted to Mr. Summers, "You didn't give him time enough to take any paper he wanted. I saw you. It wasn't fair!"

"Be a good sport, Tessie," Mrs. Delacroix called, and Mrs. Graves said, "All of us took the same chance."

"Shut up, Tessie," Bill Hutchinson said.

"Well, everyone," Mr. Summers said, "that was done pretty fast, and now we've got to be hurrying a little more to get done in time." He consulted his next list. "Bill," he said, "you draw for the Hutchinson family. You got any other households in the Hutchinsons?"

"There's Don and Eva," Mrs. Hutchinson yelled. "Make *them* take their chance!"

"Daughters draw with their husbands' families, Tessie," Mr. Summers said gently. "You know that as well as anyone else."

"It wasn't *fair*," Tessie said.

"I guess not, Joe," Bill Hutchinson said regretfully. "My daughter draws with her husband's family, that's only fair. And I've got no other family except the kids."

"Then, as far as drawing for families is concerned, it's you," Mr.

Summers said in explanation, "and as far as drawing for households is concerned, that's you, too. Right?"

"Right," Bill Hutchinson said.

"How many kids, Bill?" Mr. Summers asked formally.

"Three," Bill Hutchinson said. "There's Bill, Jr., and Nancy, and
little Dave. And Tessie and me."

"All right, then," Mr. Summers said. "Harry, you got their
tickets back?"

Mr. Graves nodded and held up the slips of paper. "Put them
in the box, then," Mr. Summers directed. "Take Bill's and put it in."

"I think we ought to start over," Mrs. Hutchinson said, as
quietly as she could. "I tell you it wasn't *fair*. You didn't give him
time enough to choose. *Every*body saw that."

Mr. Graves had selected the five slips and put them in the box,
and he dropped all the papers but those onto the ground, where
the breeze caught them and lifted them off.

"Listen, everybody," Mrs. Hutchinson was saying to the people
around her.

"Ready, Bill?" Mr. Summers asked, and Bill Hutchinson, with
one quick glance around at his wife and children, nodded.

"Remember," Mr. Summers said, "take the slips and keep them
folded until each person has taken one. Harry, you help little
Dave." Mr. Graves took the hand of the little boy, who came
willingly with him up to the box. "Take a paper out of the box,
Davy," Mr. Summers said. Davy put his hand into the box and
laughed. "Take just *one* paper," Mr. Summers said. "Harry, you
hold it for him." Mr. Graves took the child's hand and removed
the folded paper from the tight fist and held it while little Dave
stood next to him and looked up at him wonderingly.

"Nancy next," Mr. Summers said. Nancy was twelve, and her
school friends breathed heavily as she went forward, switching her
skirt, and took a slip daintily from the box. "Bill, Jr.," Mr. Summers said, and Billy, his face red and his feet overlarge, nearly
knocked the box over as he got a paper out. "Tessie," Mr. Summers
said. She hesitated for a minute, looking around defiantly, and then
set her lips and went up to the box. She snatched a paper out and
held it behind her.

"Bill," Mr. Summers said, and Bill Hutchinson reached into the box and felt around, bringing his hand out at last with the slip of paper in it.

The crowd was quiet. A girl whispered, "I hope it's not Nancy," and the sound of the whisper reached the edges of the crowd.

"It's not the way it used to be," Old Man Warner said clearly. "People ain't the way they used to be."

"All right," Mr. Summers said. "Open the papers. Harry, you open little Dave's."

Mr. Graves opened the slip of paper and there was a general sigh through the crowd as he held it up and everyone could see that it was blank. Nancy and Bill, Jr., opened theirs at the same time, and both beamed and laughed, turning around to the crowd and holding their slips of paper above their heads.

"Tessie," Mr. Summers said. There was a pause, and then Mr. Summers looked at Bill Hutchinson, and Bill unfolded his paper and showed it. It was blank.

"It's Tessie," Mr. Summers said, and his voice was hushed. "Show us her paper, Bill."

Bill Hutchinson went over to his wife and forced the slip of paper out of her hand. It had a black spot on it, the black spot Mr. Summers had made the night before with the heavy pencil in the coal-company office. Bill Hutchinson held it up, and there was a stir in the crowd.

"All right, folks," Mr. Summers said. "Let's finish quickly."

Although the villagers had forgotten the ritual and lost the original black box, they still remembered to use stones. The pile of stones the boys had made earlier was ready; there were stones on the ground with the blowing scraps of paper that had come out of the box. Mrs. Delacroix selected a stone so large she had to pick it up with both hands and turned to Mrs. Dunbar. "Come on," she said. "Hurry up."

Mrs. Dunbar had small stones in both hands, and she said, gasping for breath, "I can't run at all. You'll have to go ahead and I'll catch up with you."

The children had stones already, and someone gave little Davy Hutchinson a few pebbles.

Tessie Hutchinson was in the center of a cleared space by now, and she held her hands out desperately as the villagers moved in on her. "It isn't fair," she said. A stone hit her on the side of the head.

Old Man Warner was saying, "Come on, come on, everyone." Steve Adams was in the front of the crowd of villagers, with Mrs. Graves beside him.

"It isn't fair, it isn't right," Mrs. Hutchinson screamed, and then they were upon her.

ELLINGTON WHITE

The Sergeant's Good Friend

HE SERGEANT AND MRS. Williams rented the vacant half of a duplex house directly across the street from us. This was at a time when everyone on Vine Street was known to me by his first name. I don't mean that I called old Dr. Rogers "Bob," as my father did, or that Dr. Rogers would have answered me if I had. All I mean is that I knew the people my father and mother were talking about when they spoke of Dave and Miss Ellen or Judith and Tom. Eventually this changed. But the day my father came home with the news that Bob had finally got around to having his sign made, I knew without asking him that he meant Dr. Rogers. My mother, however, was not so sure.

First printed in THE SEWANEE REVIEW, Winter 1957. Copyright © 1957 by The University of the South.

"I don't believe you," she said to my father.

"Then go down there and look for yourselves."

We found the sign hanging from a dusky metal arrow that looked as though it were just then leaving one of the holes in the high stone wall that fortressed Dr. Rogers' corner house, made too of stone. *Ye Vinne Street.*

"I still don't believe it," my mother said. "What do you see?"

"Ye Vinne Street," I told her.

She laughed and shook her head. "Well, who'd have thought it? After all these years he finally worked up the nerve!"

Off and on for as long as I could remember Dr. Rogers had talked about hanging such a sign, but no one ever thought he would because he also talked about having the asphalt pulled off the street in order to expose for further use the cobblestones underneath. Then over night the sign appeared. Would the cobblestones be next? My father didn't think so. "If all that stuff about the Sergeant hadn't gotten in the newspapers," he said, "the sign wouldn't be there, you can bet on that." Myself, I thought it was a beautiful sign. The wood was so richly polished that it seemed to glow from within, as though a red light bulb had been turned on inside, and such fine flourishes grew out of each silver letter that I felt sure they had been copied after the nocturnal script that I had often seen snails leave behind them, scrawled across stone ledges and the smooth surface of riverjacks.

Soon, however, a producer of safety razors built a large factory in town, following which many of the big homes on Ye Vinne Street were converted into apartments, sometimes as many as four to a house, and the sign was stolen. Dr. Rogers had it replaced by another, smaller and less eye-catching in design, but when that one too disappeared, he gave it up for good and we awoke one morning to find ourselves back on Vine Street. By then, however, Dr. Rogers' "folly," as we called it, had become a fixture in my mother's mind, and often since then I have heard her using it to place some past event whose date she is no longer sure of. "The razor factory? Why, well as I recall it was built during the time we lived on Ye Vinne Street." But of the Sergeant and Mrs. Williams—"Oh, yes," she will say, "let me see now. . . . I think they were here up until a month or so before Bob Rogers put up that old sign of his." Then (how often have I seen her do this?) she will shake her head and look confidingly at the person to whom she is speaking—"The poor Sergeant! He and my son, David, were very close friends, you know."

Before the Sergeant and Mrs. Williams arrived I don't believe I had formed any strong impression of what either of them would look like, although the real estate agent who arranged for their tenancy, a short, fat man who wore his belt hitched under his stomach like a sling, saw to it that their shadowy outlines reached Vine Street well ahead of them. Rant Thompson he was called. "Couldn't nobody ask for a woman any finer than that little lady is," he said, "and when I say lady, that's what I mean. The real item, the kind a man hankers to get up next to once in a while for all the pleasure it brings him. Been around the world a couple of times, she has, and got outfittin's for a house the likes of which this town's not liable to lay its eyes on again. You wait and see. 'Listen,' I says, speakin' to yours truly, 'all those good people up there on Vine Street are goin' to be mighty much obliged when they see who it is old Rant Thompson's brought up there for 'em to live along side of.' The other one now, the one she calls Sergeant—him I didn't off hand take to. A big beef of a fellow what's gone soft around the middle. Does her house work for her and some nursin' too, I guess, judgin' from the looks of things. But . . . I don't know, he just don't seem right to me. Like there was somethin' all kind of hunkered up inside him. You know what I mean?" The Sergeant, as it turned out, had been General Williams' orderly for thirty years, and after the General's death, had left the Army in order to take care of Mrs. Williams. For a while they settled in New York where Mrs. Williams ran an antique shop, but there she had a minor stroke, and on the advice of her doctor, they decided to look for a warmer climate. Why she chose Virginia instead of Georgia, where her daughter lived, no one bothered to inquire because at that time we had living around us a good many elderly people whose health had drawn them to the mountains.

The chances are that the day they arrived would have gone by completely unnoticed in my mind had not something happened which gave it a place there forever. I saw one of the men unloading Mrs. Williams' furniture fall off the tail gate of the moving van. He fell backwards under a wooden crate that slammed down on top of him, and the thudding sound his head made as it hit the street filled me with such fear that I wanted to pretend I had not seen it and run the other way, but my desire to do this was so strong that I felt it was a product of childhood weakness and stayed there with my eyes closed, hoping that no one, least of all the Sergeant, would notice me. I had made up my mind beforehand that I would not be taken for a child by him, yet this decision was in conflict with an even stronger yearning on my part to see something of a general's possessions—a yearning that I felt might come out in the form of a long, open-mouthed gape. And to whom if not to a child did such a gape belong? So by way of a solution I arranged to spend that morning uprooting some weeds that were wedged in between the bricks of the sidewalk in front of our house. From there I could observe what was going on without giving anyone to believe that I was interested in such matters, and it was from there, as I tugged away on my knees with the sun bearing down from a cloudless sky, that I saw the man fall. A sudden scream—and when I opened my eyes, the first person I saw was the Sergeant jerking awkwardly down the front porch steps with a broom in one hand. Rant Thompson was right: he was huge. The steps sagged under him, and as he lumbered down them, muttering, "Good God, don't move him!" I was unable to decide whether the stricken look on his face—his painfully wide eyes and gaping mouth—was due to the sight of the poor man lying crumpled up in the street or to some difficulty he had walking, which caused his round, butcher's-like bald head to swing comically in front of him like a counterbalance to the great weight he carried above his hips. And I remember how surprised I was to see that he wore over his trousers a long white apron tucked first under his belt then tied behind him in a big, flaring white bow. "Everything's going to be all right," I heard him say as he pushed in between two other workers who were kneeling helplessly beside their companion and, bending over, peered into the injured man's face. "Just lie quiet," he said. I watched his hand go out to the man's forehead and slide from there down one arm. It moved gently with great care. Then he straightened up and spoke directly to me.

"Tell your mother to call an ambulance."

Me? Was he speaking to me? His eyes said yes, but I could not believe them.

"What?" I said.

"We need an ambulance quick!"

"But she's not home."

"Who isn't?"

"My mother," I said.

"Then call one yourself."

"I don't think we have an ambulance."

"Certainly you have an ambulance!" he shouted. "If not, get a taxi. But don't just stand there!"

At that moment, however, I saw old Dr. Rogers come hurrying across the street, and pointing to him, I said with great relief, "He's a doctor," as though this would take care of everything. And so far as I was concerned it did, for after Dr. Rogers had looked the man over, he told me not to bother about an ambulance.

"We'll take him in my car," he said.

I held open the door while the Sergeant and the two other workers laid the man on the back seat, and as they were about to drive off, the Sergeant leaned out of the window and asked me to tell Mrs. Williams where he had gone.

"And if you wouldn't mind staying with her until I get back," he said, "I'd appreciate it."

I had a vision of the only sick person I knew, my grandmother. Her sour bed, soiled handkerchiefs, brown-stained apple cores, bed pans and the tedious hours I had to spend with her on Sunday afternoons, all of these passed darkly across my mind, and I was on the point of telling the Sergeant I had something else to do when the idea reached me that here was a chance to see at first hand the fabulous things with which I imagined a general as surrounding his life, and I nodded my head. The Sergeant tried to smile back, but I could tell that his thoughts were divided between Mrs. Williams and the man on the back seat.

"You'll find her downstairs in the rear room," he said. "Tell her I'll be back as soon as possible."

Eventually this room became the Sergeant's. About the size of a large pantry, it was jammed between the dining room and the kitchen with doors exposing it to both, quite dark, public and bare

that morning except for some unopened boxes and the bed on which
Mrs. Williams was lying, anxiously propped on one elbow when I
entered.

"That poor man!" she said. "Is he all right?"

The way her eyes were turned on me, full of grave, earnest
concern, combined with the urgency in her voice, made me stop.

"I don't know," I said. "They've taken him to the hospital.
Your cook told me to tell you."

I didn't know what else to call the Sergeant, but that "cook"
was not right either I knew also, yet Mrs. Williams made no
reference to it and fell back on her pillow, as though she were
suddenly exhausted, and closed her eyes. I stood by her bed. The
only sound other than her breathing came from the kitchen where
a faucet was leaking into an empty sink. I looked around for something to connect Mrs. Williams to my grandmother, but no connections were in sight: no bed pans, no sour odors, no dishevelled
bed clothes, as though all things associated with sickness, including
flowers, medicines and visitors, had been purposely removed from
the room. She was a tall woman with fair skin and a wealth of
thick grey hair pulled behind her ears to form a knot at the base
of her head. Her face was slender. There were wrinkles over and
beneath her eyes but nowhere else, and unlike my grandmother,
who represented both sickness and age in my mind, her mouth was
still full and strong, untouched as yet by the disfigurements of pain.
One arm, I noticed, she kept pressed to her side like a dead
weight.

"Do you know what's the worst part of being sick?" she said to
me, her eyes still closed. "It's that everything has to reach you in
pieces. A voice here, a sound there, a familiar word—and if you
listen to them long enough, close enough, you're sometimes able to
piece together a halfway dim picture of the simplest little thing
that's happening under your window." She opened her eyes and
looked at me, smiling. "That is, unless some nice person comes along
and does the work for you. And what does that nice person get in
return? Nothing but an old woman going on about nothing. It
isn't fair, is it? But come here so I can see you. . . . What's your
name?"

"David Ledbetter," I said.

"That's a nice name. You live on Vine Street, don't you?"

I nodded my head.

"That's nice too. Next time you bring your sister to see me."

"I don't have a sister."

"No sister?" Her eyes were heavy, and I was not altogether sure she was keeping track of what she had said. "Shucks, and I so much prefer sisters to brothers myself. But then I bet you prefer the Sergeant to me, don't you?"

"I don't know him well enough to say."

"You will someday. Then you can come back and tell me how much better you like him than me. Will you do that?"

I said I would.

"It's a promise then."

"I guess so."

"Good." She sighed heavily. "Now if nothing's wrong with that poor man, everything'll be all right."

"He was bleeding," I said.

"Bleeding?" She sat up in bed. "You didn't tell me that! Where?"

"From a hole above his ear."

"Oh. . . .

"His neck was covered with blood, and it was pouring out of his mouth, and. . . ."

"Why are you saying all this? It isn't true, is it?"

I had no way of answering her. After a moment of saying nothing, of only looking at me, she settled back against her pillow and fixed her red shawl closer around her neck while I stared at her lifeless arm. Then she smiled. "Listen to that awful leak in the kitchen. I've been hearing it all morning. Do you think you could stop it on your way out?"

In the morning the Sergeant came over to thank me for staying with Mrs. Williams. He was in high spirits. I wasn't. I was raking leaves from under the rose bushes in front of our house—a messy job because the leaves had decayed and turned black and soggy. And the sight of the Sergeant in an equally black suit only increased my general glumness.

"I didn't stay with her very long," I said.

"Long enough to give her a good deal of pleasure."

He was standing on the sidewalk several feet under the height of our yard so that I could look down on top of his bald head sweating in the sunshine.

"You won't believe this," he said, "but I've seen leaves turn
so red they set themselves on fire."

"Well, these aren't the ones."

"No. They're in another country."

"Where's that?"

"A long way from here. Where the people wear dirt for clothes.
You don't believe that either, do you? That people could dress that
way. Well, they do. I've seen the dirt get so thick on some of them
that grass is coming out of their legs, weeds six inches long."

A laugh rang out, and turning around, I saw that my mother
had come out on the front porch.

"That's a lot of dirt," she said.

"A lot of it, yes mam," the Sergeant answered, reaching for
his hat, then bowing to her when he found it was not there. "I
trust the boy here has told you of the hand he gave me yesterday
when I was needing it?"

"He did."

"Good for him. If he hadn't, I was going to tell you m'self."

"It's true then—a man did fall?"

"That a man did! A double back jack as sure as it's you I'm
talkin' to, mam, and struck this street here a powerful wallop.
'Ah!' I said, 'he's a goner for sure.' But such a roughneck he was!
Why, you'll never be guessin' who he took me for."

"You?"

"Me, mam—the Sergeant. He thought I was The Christ, he
did. He opened his eyes and looked me over and that's what he
said—'Jesus Christ!' And you know what I told him? I said, 'Not
quite, my boy, but I'll do my best.' And damned if I didn't, and
damned if the doctors don't tell me the damage'll mend. Now what
do you think of that? But maybe it's the boy you'd like to send to
him with a word of cheer? I'm off that way and would call his
company a pleasure m'self."

But before either of us could answer, he had turned around
and was pointing to the two green hills—Betsy Bell and Mary
Gray, they were called—that stood on the outskirts of town, lifting
over the roof tops an acre apiece of thick, unbroken woodland.

"Then," he said, "if it's all the same to you, and the boy's
willin', I'd like to have a look at them. Such a pretty pair!"

My mother was charmed.

"Well"—and looking at me, she smiled.

Walking anywhere with the Sergeant was not my idea of a good time, but neither was raking leaves, and so long as I had to choose between the two, I took him.

"I guess so," I said.

The Sergeant grinned, and grinning myself—this because my mother insisted upon seeing us off from the corner, waving heartily —we set out.

It was the first of many walks. Of these only a few things, a few possessions, are around today: several water marked stones; the Sergeant's black rubber boots that my father recovered from a trash can when Mrs. Williams was taken away; the sound of his boots sloshing through mud, through boggy underbrush; the picture of his heavy thighs rolling from side to side like a heavy old bull sludging riverward to drink—they all draw together, merge, and here is the Sergeant standing before a hump of rocks piled one on top of the other in the middle of an empty field. "Any explanation for this?" he asks.

"I don't know of any."

"You don't say? Then maybe we ought to find one."

"What difference does it make?"

I was hot and tired. I wanted to get home. I had had enough of him for that day. He was always on the point of some great discovery, always talking.

"Butterflies only fly southeast. Did you know that?"

No, I didn't know that.

"Well, it's a fact."

Or, "Look at the sky," he would say. "What a grand sight—that one white cloud polishing it fine for tomorrow."

And tomorrow under a clear blue sky we would view the mountains breaking green against the far horizon, or climb Betsy Bell for the tenth time, or hunt for fossils under the damp granite shelves that cropped out of its side. These sunless, cobwebbed places crawling with slithering fat slugs were loathsome to me, but forth from one would come the roundabout path of a snail, and "Ay," the Sergeant would say, shaking his head, "but it's a terrible shame we haven't the knowledge to read this."

You fool, I thought.

Once we found brim full of water a small abandoned rock

quarry opened in the slope of a hill. It had taken us most of the morning to get there, walking through fields of scrub pine where no air moved and the sun bore down on the swarms of grasshoppers that crowded before our feet. The Sergeant was flushed and sweating when we arrived, but once he saw the water and the large oak trees shading it, his eyes drew in some of the sunlight, and he sat down on a rock and pulled off his boots.

"Get a move on," he shouted, "or I'll throw you in!"

The quarry fell off into wide, mushy quagmire of dead leaves that had collected around the edge, and pointing to this, I said, "How you going to get through that stuff?"

He shrugged it off.

"There's always a way for a man to get his body wet."

"Maybe for you there is," I said and sat down beside him.

He dropped one of his boots and looked at me.

"You're not goin' in?"

"I'm not going to wade through that slop."

"Then," he smiled, "we'll have to find some other way."

"There isn't any other way."

"You've looked, have you?"

"Lots of times," I lied.

"Then I'll have to carry you in. What about that?"

"It wouldn't work."

"And why not?"

"The water's too deep."

"Oh"—and he laughed.

"It's too deep," I said.

"But there's bound to be some way! Won't you look once more? . . . Ay, there's the spirit!"

"What for?" I said. "It's the same all around."

The truth was, I dreaded the sight of his slug-colored, fat body, and this he must have sensed, for after a moment he turned away and gazed emptily across the water. A minute went by, two. Then he put on his boots and stood up wearily. Then he smiled.

"A man was tellin' me about an Indian mound in here somewhere. What do you say we have a look for it?"

He was always hearing about Indian mounds and unexplored caves, even caches of buried silver—a deserted house at the con-

fluence of two rivers, a solitary, lightning-struck tree whose roots
hold within them a flat stone, and on this stone will be scratched
. . . what fantastic directions this time?

As separate streamers I see them now, these walks, all attached
to a single cord, and this the Sergeant is holding, all tossing in the
wind, so willful and childishly colored, so wildly flying, that many
of them I was afraid to take home. I was afraid to display them.
I was afraid of what they would do to the profitable prestige that
becoming the Sergeant's friend had endowed me with in the eyes
of my mother and father. On his account I was awarded adult
liberties hitherto undreamed of. People said I was the Sergeant's
good friend—"He is, you know. They're practically never apart."
And my mother and father took pride in this. They let me buy my
own clothes and go to the movies alone, and to preserve these
liberties, I tolerated a tiresome situation. Our friendship had begun
as a chore less painful and more profitable than raking leaves, and
as a chore it remained. I thought the Sergeant was a fool. But my
mother and father thought he was someone good for me to know,
a man who had experienced the world and would impart some of it
to me, so I kept my feelings to myself and the months went by.

Except on rare occasions our week day walks never took us any
further from town than Betsy Bell, but often on Saturdays we went
on longer trips into the mountains. These were elaborately prepared
for. The Sergeant produced maps of the forests and made a game of
deciding to which we ought to go. They were never idle decisions.
He always had something in mind—an Indian mound or a rock for-
mation he heard about. Saturday arrived and I would see him
sitting on the front porch with a lunch bag under his arm, waiting
for me to appear. Maybe I would open and close the door several
times before going out. Each time he would bounce up; then, when
the door shut, slowly sit down again. My mother caught me at this
once and asked me what I was doing. I told her something about
the door being stuck and hurried out into the street where the
Sergeant met me, heartily as usual, and off we went—like father
and son, people said.

One Saturday we took a rusty old bus that clanked over the
mountains to a small hilled-in village where a saw mill made up the

public square. Plumb Nearly it was called: plumb out of the world, nearly out of civilization. And when we were half way there, the driver stopped to let us out and the Sergeant told him to pick us up on his return trip.

"It might be late evenin' by then," the driver said, "dependin' on what time the mill pays off and I collect my fares." He was a short, sunken-mouthed, chinless little man who spit tobacco juice into a lard pail between his legs and talked about the Tabernickle Babtist Church. "What you want off here for anyway? It ain't no stop."

"Just walkin'," the Sergeant said.

"Walkin'!" The driver eyed us suspiciously. "Where to?"

"Up here somewhere."

"Any particular place?"

"Not exactly."

"Jest out for the exercise, huh?"

"That's right. Would you mind opening the door?"

The Sergeant said this impatiently. I stood behind him, squirming under the eyes of the other passengers.

"Exercisin's good for a man. Wish I did more of it myself. What direction you intend to go?"

"In whatever direction," the Sergeant said, "those elephants are that broke loose last night from the Tabernickle Babtist Church."

The driver jumped.

"What's that!"

By then the door had swung open and the Sergeant stepped off. I followed.

"What's that you say?"

"Come on, David."

"A wise guy, huh! What likes to go out walkin' with little boys! Well, I know your kind, buster!"

Then he slammed the door and the bus roared off, clouding us with fumes. I watched it go around a curve with the sinking thought that we were stranded for the night.

"What did you say that for? Now he'll never stop!"

I didn't think the Sergeant heard me, although he was looking straight at me, pale and tense. His eyes were worried.

"What's the matter?" I said.

"What? . . . Oh, nothing." He smiled and turned away. "Nothing's the matter."

"Did you hear what I said?"

"About the bus, you mean?"

"What if it doesn't stop? Then what'll we do?"

"Oh, it'll stop. Don't worry about that."

I wasn't as sure myself, and the vision of us huddled around a fire waiting for someone to come looking for us was so strong that for a while I noticed nothing else. The Sergeant led the way. All I did was follow.

Grey clouds hovered overhead. It had rained nearly every day that fall, and the leaves looked as though they had been soaked overnight, then hung out to dry, heavy and limp, on twisted black limbs. The air was damp with mist. In front of us a deep hollow opened back into the mountains, and from this gushed a white-water stream, swept by low-hanging spruce and hemlock as it thrashed down between the rock shoulders of two wooded spurs. A path accompanied it, narrow and steep for a while, but gradually widening out into an open space where the ground levelled off under a thick mossy blanket beneath which stumps and fallen limbs had been stuffed tidily out of sight. Near the center stood the hollow shell of a dead tree with a spring pumping out of its middle, forming a pool among the roots. White flowers were clumped around it.

The walk had tired the Sergeant. He was still pale and breathing hard and I noticed for the first time that his hands trembled as he let himself down beside the tree and rested his back against it. He looked around him, then up into the sky—still grave and threatening.

"Ay, not what you'd call a Hellenic day, is it?"

"I don't know what you mean."

"I mean when the sky's blue and full of friendly white clouds." He smiled. "The way it was in the Phillipines, back in the old Constabulary day, when the General was a little shavetail of a captain and we first took up together. Those were Hellenic days. For me they were. For him too, I think."

I had seen the General's portrait hanging over Mrs. Williams' mantel: a mild, pleasant face with a pug nose. I found it disappointing, but more disappointing still was the absence of anything else belonging to him.

"Where do you keep his things?" I said.

"What things?"

"His uniform? He must have owned a sword?" I didn't know what else I expected.

The Sergeant grinned.

"Mrs. Williams has them. Ask her to show 'em to you some day. She'd like that."

He seemed to doze for a moment with his eyes open. Then he said, "Ay, he was a grand one, the General, the type of man you meet once and never forget. You'd have liked him, David. Young people did. He was all light inside and full of the devil's own fire when it was needed. Ask Mrs. Williams to show you the blanket of his with all the bullet holes in it. Only," he laughed, "don't tell her it was the General himself who put 'em there."

"She doesn't know?"

The Sergeant shook his head.

"The General was a kind of peace officer in northern Luzon— a mean job in those days because the islands were full of half-civilized people. They had learned how to steal but not how to look the other way while they were about it, so they were always being caught, and it was the General who had to make up for them. Here would come a party of Malays out of the hills to trade, and to a man the villagers would cheat them, and to a man the Malays would catch them at it. Then the villagers would run to the General for protection, because they knew in a day or so the Malays would be back, only this time with their spears. They fairly ran our legs off. It finally go so bad that the General had to teach the Malays themselves how to steal so they would have something other than murder to think about, and it worked: we had peace. But being a rather delicate matter—I mean how the General had brought it off —he couldn't take any credit for it, although he did take a leave. He went home. And when he came back, Mrs. Williams was with him. She gave him a pair of blankets as a wedding gift. Brought them with her from the States and made the General, I remember, take one of them on our next inspection tour. I told him to leave it off somewhere, it was much too fine for that, but he took it anyway, and what should happen our first night out, but his arm goes to sleep, and waking up, he feels it laying there beside him, thinks it's a snake crawled in bed with him, leaps up and blows the blanket full of holes. Oh, the lies we made up going back! And all of them because of that blanket! We finally told Mrs. Williams something about being potted at from the bush by an outlaw tribe, and she believed it. So don't you give us away, David. The General swore me to an oath of faithfulness, and it's faithful I've always been to him. You remember that."

Remember it? "Why?" I asked.

"Oh"—he drew a long breath—"no particular reason. I'm talking too much."

He slumped against the tree, as though overcome by a heavy weariness. I got up and walked around the damp fringes of the forest. There was nothing else to do, nowhere else to go. Once I looked back and saw the Sergeant shaking his head at nothing. Or was he shaking it at the few bird songs that now and then fell out of the trees? A thin offering this must have seemed compared to the abundance of song that fell over the Philippines, where the sun shone perpetually and friendly white clouds drifted in from the sea.

As he predicted, the bus driver stopped for us on his way back to town. Either darkness obscured his anger, or the sound of our fares jingling all that distance in his head had taken the edge off. In any case, I was thankful and relieved when we climbed aboard. "That's the one," I heard a passenger say, and I saw another blocking the aisle with his foot. But the Sergeant took a seat closer to the front, and I sat down beside him. Soon he was asleep. His head rolled over on my shoulder. His mouth fell open, and to my horror, he began to snore with the coarse labors of a heavy animal. Laughter sprang up behind me. I shoved him away, feeling miserable and cursing him with all my heart, he looked like such an ordinary fool sitting there.

II

"What's the matter," my father said. "You and the Sergeant have a falling out?"

"Not in particular."

"I don't see you together as much."

"It's school," I said. "I don't have as much time."

"Well, the holidays'll soon be here."

They didn't change things however. I still avoided him. Several times a week he went to town for groceries, carrying a black leather satchel, the kind doctors use, and on these mornings he usually waited until I came out of the house and walked part of the way with me. Otherwise I saw little of him.

"Wouldn't it be nice," my mother often said, "if we had more neighbors like them. They live such quiet lives."

Sometimes in the late evenings, shortly before the street lights were turned on, we would see Mrs. Williams, bundled in a fur coat, walking up and down the front porch on the Sergeant's arm. But except for these brief outings she seldom left her room—a confinement, I remember, which seemed a terrible pity to my mother. "Think of owning a coat like that," she would say, "and not being able to wear it someplace that counts."

After dark Mrs. Williams' bedroom windows, facing the street, rarely showed any light, and I used to imagine her lying up there alone with the General's trunk near her bed. She never came downstairs for her meals. The Sergeant carried them up to her on a tray. He slept off the kitchen in the little room in which I had first seen Mrs. Williams. It was thinly furnished: a foot locker, a desk, a book rack, two chairs, a bed, although the bed, as it turned out, was for appearance only. Due to a back injury, he used a cotton pallet rolled out on the floor to sleep on—something that not even Mrs. Williams knew about. It was Dr. Rogers who told us. The Sergeant had gone to see him about a breaking out on his hands. "He's far from being well," Dr. Rogers said. "If you ask me, she expects too much of him. All that house to look after and her meals to get. I told him so too, but he's a stubborn man." My father thought his coloring looked bad, and when summer arrived and he said nothing to me about a walk, I knew that something was wrong.

I can't say that I was sorry. The prestige he had given me was still mine while the effort I had to pay for it had now disappeared. I suppose it was for this reason that I began to think of him anew, as the weeks passed, as not such a bad guy after all. The mornings I spent swimming in the park, I played baseball, and went often to the movies, but the hours between were nevertheless many and much of the time I had nothing to do. He asked me once to go with him to the top of Betsy Bell, and I went gladly. But halfway there he stumbled and fell against a tree, and looking into his face, I knew that he would never make it. It was pale and worn and his eyes looked bruised and hurt. His skin was dry, and he breathed hard. "I guess," he said, "we'd better turn back."

At supper that night I told my mother and father what had happened. They both shook their heads. "It seems to me," my father said, "that if Mrs. Williams hasn't got enough sense to see that something's the matter with him, then somebody ought to get in touch with her daughter and ask her to come up here. Why don't they?"

"Because it's nobody's business, that's why," my mother said.

"Then maybe we ought to make it our business."

But we didn't. Summer wore on. I wandered around the house or sat on the porch steps, vaguely wondering what was going on in the shuttered, quiet house across the street. The Sergeant no longer walked to town for groceries; a delivery boy brought them instead. Nowadays the front door was always shut, and I could imagine the oppressive, unaired heat closed up inside.

For two weeks in September no rain fell. We watched the grass in the Sergeant's yard wither and turn brown. I remembered what he had said about leaves, that he had known some to turn so red they set themselves on fire. There was no fire here, only a slow, brown death.

"Why don't you go over there and ask him to let you water the lawn," my mother said to me one day while I was drifting aimlessly from room to room.

I had nothing else to do—nothing at least any better. Besides I was curious to see the Sergeant.

There was no answer when I knocked on the front door, so I went around to the back and called to him underneath his window. I called several times without a reply. Then I heard Mrs. Williams answer from the front of the house.

"It's me, Mrs. Williams," I yelled, "David Ledbetter. I came to see if you wanted your lawn watered."

"Come up here a moment, David."

"I can't. The doors are locked."

"The back door isn't."

I didn't want to go, but I didn't see either how I could refuse, now that I had answered her. The house was hushed and dark. I had to pass through the Sergeant's room in order to reach the stairs which led off the parlor. His pallet was rolled out on the floor, a sheet balled up at the foot. It was the first time I had seen it, like something come to light out of the unknown part of his life. Dust had gathered in the corners. A spider web dangled from a parlor lamp. Climbing the stairs I had the feeling that I had gone much further than simply across the street. So strong was this feeling that the first thing I did on entering Mrs. Williams' room was look out of the window to make sure our house was where it was supposed to be.

"David," Mrs. Williams said, "you're much nicer I'm sure than your sister would have been."

She was smiling, her head propped on a pillow with a sheet folded down over her waist. She looked very fragile, composed, smiling in a light blue bed jacket flowered around the collar with pink roses.

I said, "If you'd tell me where the hose is, I'd water the grass."

"We have a hose, do we?"

"I think so."

"You must think I'm an awful idiot. But the poor Sergeant has looked after things for so long now. . . . You'll have to ask him."

"Where is he?"

"He'll be back soon. But it would be nice, wouldn't it, if now and then you'd do things for him like watering the grass and putting out the trash. That would be such a help. He isn't as strong as he used to be, and . . . Well, look at me. I'm no good. Do you think you could do that? It would be something like a summer job, just between you and me."

"Summer's over," I said.

She laughed. "Then a winter job. People do have winter jobs."

"I know they do."

"Of course, I'll pay you," she said.

"I don't think I could take a job in the winter."

"Why not?"

"My mother wouldn't let me."

"But this would be such a small job."

"I'll have to ask her. But I don't think. . . ."

"David," she said, "you like the Sergeant, don't you."

"Yes."

"Then we've got to do something to help him. We've got to—he's so ill!"

And before I knew it she was crying. Her head slipped off the pillow, pulling her jacket to one side so that it drew tight around her neck, and lying so, disheveled and shaken, hiding her wet eyes, she lapsed into a helpless old woman not unlike my grandmother. Surprised and frightened, I said the first thing that came into my mind.

"My father says it's up to your daughter to do something."

At first I didn't believe she had heard me. Then, when she looked at me, her eyes full of suspicion and fear, I knew that she had. Dimly I was aware of something terrible that had come into the room.

"My daughter? What do you know about my daughter?"

There was nothing I could say.

"What does your father know about her?"

"Nothing. I. . . ."

"How dare he know anything about her. What right has he?"

I mumbled something about Rant Thompson: that it was he who had told us.

"That fool!" she said, pulling nervously at the sheet. Her other arm, the dead one, lay beside her, as though it had gone to sleep, like the General's arm when he shot his blanket full of holes. She shook her head.

"But this is absurd! A mere child. . . . He's only a child. You!" she said. "You and your father, both children. Well, I'm tired of children!"

Wearily she turned away from me. I started to leave.

Then: "I suppose your father has written to my daughter. That would be the proper thing for him to do."

"I don't think he has."

"You're sure?"

"Not positive."

"Find out. Tell your father I'd like to see him. Tell him that if my daughter comes up here, that will be the end of the Sergeant.

He'll be thrown out on the street. Do you understand that?"

I nodded.

"Then go. Please go."

I had reached the foot of the stairs when I saw the Sergeant. It was only for a second. He was standing in the door to his room, coldly watching me—a grave figure framed against the light. "Tell your father," he said quietly, "that Mrs. Williams' daughter will be here tomorrow night." Then the door closed.

I told my father nothing. I was far too ashamed. It was clear that the Sergeant had overheard what I had said to Mrs. Williams, and for some reason, in my mind, this amounted to the same thing as a window through which he had looked at last into my real feelings. How many times that night did I wake with the impression that he was standing on our front porch, trying to get in? Once I even went downstairs to make certain the door had been locked. The street was quiet and dark. Trees swung in the wind: shifting shadows and long, distant, rolling thunder; then a light suddenly thrust into the darkness from the Sergeant's window. I tried to imagine what he was doing at this hour. But it was as though strangers now lived there. Shivering I told myself that tomorrow I would water their grass and put out their trash both, as though this could make up for what the Sergeant had seen.

But by morning a mass of grey clouds had lowered the sky until it touched the twin mountains and a cold rain swept up the street, watering the grass ahead of me. I felt cheated and even conspired against when I walked across the street before breakfast and found that sometime during the night the Sergeant had put out his own trash. But why? It would not be collected until the following day. Disappointed and wet, I turned to the house, certain that it was aware of my distress and would provide me with some other chore.

And it did. Mrs. Williams was standing on the front porch. I had not heard her over the rain.

"Is your father at home?" she called.

I could see that she was frantic. Her hair was down, and the wind caught it, whipping it in front of her face; whipping too her kimono and pushing her against the screen door.

She said, "Please get your father!"

"He's already gone," I shouted.

"No!" Despairingly she looked up and down the street. No one was in sight. "Then you will have to do something for me," she said.

Excuses thronged into my mind: the weather, other errands, school. . . .

"Please go around the back way and see if anything has happened to the Sergeant. He's locked his door and doesn't answer me!" Her voice trailed off.

"What about Dr. Rogers?"

"IIis phone won't answer. Hurry! Please hurry!"

The idea accompanied me around the house that certainly the back door would be locked, in which case I had nothing to fear. I stopped under the Sergeant's window, where a lone curtain billowed within, and called to him. There was no answer. I won't be able to get in, I said. But the back door was not locked. It opened of its own accord when I turned the knob. Stupefied, I found myself in the kitchen. Still I could tell her it was locked, I said; she would never know. . . . But here the issue was decided for me: a strong gust of wind suddenly slammed the door behind me; another gust followed, and slowly the door to the Sergeant's room swung open. I almost fell to the floor. He was crumpled up beside a little stool, this surrounded by a square of newspapers on which he had fallen, his neck twisted to one side so that I could see the wound through which his life had poured—like a door itself unlocked by the razor that lay by his head. IIow calculated, how well the newspapers had protected the floor! And the trash carried out during the night. . . . Such were my thoughts. Then, hearing Mrs. Williams, I realized that the door was locked so that she would not be the first to find him. A note was wedged in the jamb. "I've built a fire in the furnace. Will Mr. Ledbetter kindly see to it that the house is kept warm while Mrs. Williams' daughter is here." I turned the key and flung the door open.

She had pulled a chair in front of it and was sitting there, resigned, her eyes on the floor. I did not wait for her to raise them; she more than the Sergeant terrified me, this old woman, whose voice followed me into the street: "My dearest, my dearest, my dearest."

III

Among the curious who were drawn that morning to Mrs. Williams' porch, and stayed hours after the ambulances had departed—there turned out to be three of these, besides a rescue squad from the Fire Department, all of which arrived simultaneously—were two men who belonged there even less than the others: Rant Thompson and a person I had some trouble at first identifying, the bus driver with whom the Sergeant had had the rude encounter I but dimly now remembered. Each in his own way had formed a connection with the Sergeant, one through business, the other through hate. Or was the bus driver simply killing time? In any case, rosy and talkative, Rant bounced from person to person, noisily acclaiming his priority over the Sergeant—hadn't he been the first in town to know him?—while the bus driver remained aloof, solemn and deaconish, as though this were Sunday and the front stoop of the Tabernickle Babtist Church. Eventually they found one another.

"You know him?" I heard Rant ask, piously nodding his head, as much as to say, Of course you did.

"Some," the driver replied. "Took him and that boy there to the mountains once."

"They were great pals."

"That's what I hear."

"A likeable fellow, wa'n't he?"

"I guess there's some who'd call him that."

Rant's head perked up. Apparently this was what he had been looking for—a hint of doubt. Wetting his lips, he edged closer.

"Say, what's your name?"

"Sonny's what they call me."

"Rant Thompson here."

"Glad to know you."

"Look here, Sonny. . . ." Rant cleared his throat and looked around him. "Mind you, I'm not one to talk loose, but speakin' man to man now, do you reckon there was anything between him and the old lady, I mean what'd make a fellow do a thing like that?"

Sonny smiled and made a vigorous sign with his head, "Come

here." He led Rant to a less crowded corner of the porch and there, behind a glider, fell upon his ears with an eager hiss.

As eagerly, I remembered, the Sergeant had once confided in me, and now that he would never do so again, feeling hurt and miserable, I thought anew of our many walks in the mountains. Warm golden days broke over the horizon of my memory. Here the Sergeant, like Sonny, but how different! how different! had found someone in whom he could confide.

"So that's the way it was," I heard Rant say glancing at me. Then again: "The slimy son-of-a-bitch!"

But his words made no real impression. Two policemen had arrived, shedding their black rubber coats and stamping their feet. A tremor of excitement shivered through me. The Sergeant's note was still in my pocket; as yet no one had seen it. Dr. Rogers greeted them at the door and with great solemnity showed them the way to the Sergeant's room. All that morning he had been trying to get in touch with Mrs. Williams' daughter, only it seemed that the Sergeant had reached her first, by telegraph the previous afternoon, and she had already taken a train.

"It's so morbid!" my mother had said, shuddering.

"He was a sick man," Dr. Rogers told her, "and sick men do curious things."

"Curious may be your word."

"It isn't yours?"

"Not when it had to be my son who found one of those things. Then I call it selfish. Yes, and I call her that too! Asking a child to do such a thing. It's enough to make your blood boil!"

Dr. Rogers had nothing more to say. He came to the door now and called me inside. My mother was there too.

"They'll want you to tell them everything," she said, putting her arm around me, "then we'll be done with the whole terrible mess."

I told them as much as I cared to. One of the policemen took it down with a pencil while the other climbed the stairs to speak with Mrs. Williams. Dr. Rogers remained behind. Other people crowded in from the porch, among them Rant Thompson and Sonny, and formed a circle around us. It was a grave, serious moment whose importance no one felt more keenly than I—nor enjoyed. Indeed my feelings were such that at any moment they could have broken through and altogether spoiled the horror of what I had to relate. But they did not. And when I had finished, there was much sighing and shuffling of feet.

"How awful!"

"The poor kid!"

All of this quite unnerved the policeman, who fumbled with his notebook and glanced at my mother as though he were ashamed of himself.

"One more question," he said. "Do you think maybe you can remember what time it was?"

"Oh," someone grumbled, "leave off!"

"Yeah, let the boy alone."

That was sufficient. The policeman slapped his book closed— "Never mind. This'll do," he said.

However, there was still the matter of the Sergeant's note, and before the crowd had a chance to get away, I took it out of my pocket and gave it to him.

He seemed reluctant at first to take it.

"That was in the door," I said.

"David!" my mother exclaimed, hurt. "You didn't tell me about that."

I felt hot and breathless. My heart pounded. He was certain to see the smudge on the paper, which after all could have been made by the Sergeant, but would he dare ask any questions about it? Apparently not, he was taking it down: "I've built a fire in the furnace. Will David Ledbetter kindly see to it. . . ." It was not as though I had made a serious change. Many times I could remember the Sergeant's having called me Mr. Ledbetter, but fools like Dr. Rogers, unfamiliar with army customs, might think he meant my father.

There was a little murmur among the crowd as the contents of the note drifted about. My mother's eyes flooded with tears. Old Dr. Rogers muttered something under his breath and patted me clumsily on the back. A man stepped forward, a woman, both of whom wanted me to know how sorry they were over the loss of my friend. For the moment Mrs. Williams was quite forgotten. Even the policeman coughed. But back in the room stood one untouched by sentiment, and in the instant that our eyes chanced to meet, he displayed a row of strong, china-white teeth and winked. That person was Sonny.

I kept the furnace blazing while Mrs. Williams' daughter was there. She was a brisk, angular woman with the unmistakable pug nose of her father, whose portrait was the first thing she took down from the wall and ordered to be packed. Not once did she mention the Sergeant by name. *Him* was as close as she would get. For my services she gave me ten dollars and told me to take anything I wanted from *his* room, a painful temptation. But so as not to appear greedy, I chose objects with a sentimental value only: a book, a broken pen knife, a little teakwood box containing his service ribbons. His other things she either gave to the Salvation Army or discarded when the moving vans arrived.

I saw Mrs. Williams only once. This was from across the street on the morning of the Sergeant's funeral, when a feeble old woman was bundled into a taxi and driven off to catch a train for Georgia.

A place was found for the Sergeant in a Federal Cemetery left by the Civil War on the outskirts of town. The chaplain whom the Army sent to conduct the service asked my mother and me if we would mind standing in the area roped off for the family: no one else stood there, although a surprising number of people had assembled around it. Among them, however, I wonder if there was one who did not ask the same question that my mother did as we drove home: "Had you ever before heard the Sergeant's last name?"

What else could his good friend say but yes?

EUDORA WELTY

A Curtain of Green

VERY DAY ONE SUMMER in Larkin's Hill, it rained a little.
The rain was a regular thing, and would come about two o'clock in
the afternoon.

One day, almost as late as five o'clock, the sun was still shining.
It seemed almost to spin in a tiny groove in the polished sky, and
down below, in the trees along the street and in the rows of
flower gardens in the town, every leaf reflected the sun from a
hardness like a mirror surface. Nearly all the woman sat in the
windows of their houses, fanning and sighing, waiting for the rain.

Mrs. Larkin's garden was a large, densely grown plot running
downhill behind the small white house where she lived alone now,
since the death of her husband. The sun and the rain that beat down
so heavily that summer had not kept her from working there daily.
Now the intense light like a tweezers picked out her clumsy, small
figure in its old pair of men's overalls rolled up at the sleeves and
trousers, separated it from the thick leaves, and made it look
strange and yellow as she worked with a hoe—over-vigorous, disreputable, and heedless.

Within its border of hedge, high like a wall, and visible only
from the upstairs windows of the neighbors, this slanting, tangled
garden, more and more over-abundant and confusing, must have
become so familiar to Mrs. Larkin that quite possibly by now she
was unable to conceive of any other place. Since the accident in
which her husband was killed, she had never once been seen any-

where else. Every morning she might be observed walking slowly, almost timidly, out of the white house, wearing a pair of the untidy overalls, often with her hair streaming and tangled where she had neglected to comb it. She would wander about for a little while at first, uncertainly, deep among the plants and wet with their dew, and yet not quite putting out her hand to touch anything. And then a sort of sturdiness would possess her—stabilize her; she would stand still for a moment, as if a blindfold were being removed; and then she would kneel in the flowers and begin to work.

She worked without stopping, almost invisibly, submerged all day among the thick, irregular, sloping beds of plants. The servant would call her at dinnertime, and she would obey; but it was not until it was completely dark that she would truthfully give up her labor and with a drooping, submissive walk appear at the house, slowly opening the small low door at the back. Even the rain would bring only a pause to her. She would move to the shelter of the pear tree, which in mid-April hung heavily almost to the ground in brilliant full leaf, in the center of the garden.

It might seem that the extreme fertility of her garden formed at once a preoccupation and a challenge to Mrs. Larkin. Only by ceaseless activity could she cope with the rich blackness of this soil. Only by cutting, separating, thinning and tying back in the clumps of flowers and bushes and vines could she have kept them from over-reaching their boundaries and multiplying out of all reason. The daily summer rains could only increase her vigilance and her already excessive energy. And yet, Mrs. Larkin rarely cut, separated, tied back. . . . To a certain extent, she seemed not to seek for order, but to allow an over-flowering, as if she consciously ventured forever a little farther, a little deeper, into her life in the garden.

She planted every kind of flower that she could find or order from a catalogue—planted thickly and hastily, without stopping to think, without any regard for the ideas that her neighbors might elect in their club as to what constituted an appropriate vista, or an effect of restfulness, or even harmony of color. Just to what end Mrs. Larkin worked so strenuously in her garden, her neighbors could not see. She certainly never sent a single one of her fine flowers to any of them. They might get sick and die, and she would never send a flower. And if she thought of *beauty* at all (they regarded her stained overalls, now almost of a color with the leaves), she certainly did not strive for it in her garden. It was impossible to enjoy looking at such a place. To the neighbors gazing down from their upstairs windows it had the appearance of a sort of jungle, in which the slight, heedless form of its owner daily lost itself.

At first, after the death of Mr. Larkin—for whose father, after all, the town had been named—they had called upon the widow with decent frequency. But she had not appreciated it, they said to one another. Now, occasionally, they looked down from their bedroom windows as they brushed studiously at their hair in the morning; they found her place in the garden, as they might have run their fingers toward a city on a map of a foreign country, located her from their distance almost in curiosity, and then forgot her.

Early that morning they had heard whistling in the Larkin garden. They had recognized Jamey's tune, and had seen him kneeling in the flowers at Mrs. Larkin's side. He was only the colored boy who worked in the neighborhood by the day. Even Jamey, it was said, Mrs. Larkin would tolerate only now and then. . . .

Throughout the afternoon she had raised her head at intervals to see how fast he was getting along in his transplanting. She had to make him finish before it began to rain. She was busy with the hoe, clearing one of the last patches of uncultivated ground for some new shrubs. She bent under the sunlight, chopping in blunt, rapid, tireless strokes. Once she raised her head far back to stare at the flashing sky. Her eyes were dull and puckered, as if from long impatience or bewilderment. Her mouth was a sharp line. People said she never spoke.

But memory tightened about her easily, without any prelude of warning or even despair. She would see promptly, as if a curtain had been jerked quite unceremoniously away from a little scene, the front porch of the white house, the shady street in front, and the blue automobile in which her husband approached, driving home from work. It was a summer day, a day from the summer before. In the freedom of gaily turning her head, a motion she was now forced by memory to repeat as she hoed the ground, she could see again the tree that was going to fall. There had been no warning. But there was the enormous tree, the fragrant chinaberry tree, suddenly tilting, dark and slow like a cloud, leaning down to her husband. From her place on the front porch she had spoken in a soft voice to him, never so intimate as at that moment, "You can't be hurt." But the tree had fallen, had struck the car exactly so as to crush him to death. She had waited there on the porch for a time afterward, not moving at all—in a sort of recollection—as if to reach under and bring out from obliteration her protective words and to try them once again . . . so as to change the whole happening. It was accident that was incredible, when her love for her husband was keeping him safe.

She continued to hoe the breaking ground, to beat down the juicy weeds. Presently she became aware that hers was the only motion to continue in the whole slackened place. There was no wind at all now. The cries of the birds had hushed. The sun seemed clamped to the side of the sky. Everything had stopped once again, the stillness had mesmerized the stems of the plants, and all the leaves went suddenly into thickness. The shadow of the pear tree in the center of the garden lay callous on the ground. Across the yard, Jamey knelt, motionless.

"Jamey!" she called angrily.

But her voice hardly carried in the dense garden. She felt all at once terrified, as though her loneliness had been pointed out by some outside force whose finger parted the hedge. She drew her hand for an instant to her breast. An obscure fluttering there frightened her, as though the force babbled to her, The bird that flies within your heart could not divide this cloudy air . . . She stared without expression at the garden. She was clinging to the hoe, and she stared across the green leaves toward Jamey.

A look of docility in the Negro's back as he knelt in the plants began to infuriate her. She started to walk toward him, dragging the hoe vaguely through the flowers behind her. She forced herself to look at him, and noticed him closely for the first time—the way he looked like a child. As he turned his head a little to one side and negligently stirred the dirt with his yellow finger, she saw, with a sort of helpless suspicion and hunger, a soft, rather deprecating smile on his face; he was lost in some impossible dream of his own while he was transplanting the little shoots. He was not even whistling; even that sound was gone.

She walked nearer to him—he must have been deaf!—almost stealthily bearing down upon his laxity and his absorption, as if that glimpse of the side of his face, that turned-away smile, were a teasing, innocent, flickering and beautiful vision—some mirage to her strained and wandering eyes.

Yet a feeling of stricture, of a responding hopelessness almost approaching ferocity, grew with alarming quickness about her. When she was directly behind him she stood quite still for a moment, in the queer sheathed manner she had before beginning her gardening in the morning. Then she raised the hoe above her head; the clumsy sleeves both fell back, exposing the thin, unsunburned whiteness of her arms, the shocking fact of their youth.

She gripped the handle tightly, tightly, as though convinced that the wood of the handle could feel, and that all her strength could indent its surface with pain. The head of Jamey, bent there below her, seemed witless, terrifying, wonderful, almost inaccessible to her, and yet in its explicit nearness meant surely for destruction, with its clustered hot woolly hair, its intricate, glistening ears, its small brown branching streams of sweat, the bowed head holding so obviously and so deadly its ridiculous dream.

Such a head she could strike off, intentionally, so deeply did she know, from the effect of a man's danger and death, its cause in oblivion; and so helpless was she, too helpless to defy the workings of accident, of life and death, of unaccountability. . . . Life and death, she thought, gripping the heavy hoe, life and death, which now meant nothing to her but which she was compelled continually to wield with both her hands, ceaselessly asking, Was it not possible to compensate? to punish? to protest? Pale darkness turned for a moment through the sunlight, like a narrow leaf blown through the garden in a wind.

In that moment, the rain came. The first drop touched her upraised arm. Small, close sounds and coolness touched her.

Sighing, Mrs. Larkin lowered the hoe to the ground and laid it carefully among the growing plants. She stood still where she was, close to Jamey, and listened to the rain falling. It was so gentle. It was so full—the sound of the end of waiting.

In the light from the rain, different from sunlight, everything appeared to gleam unreflecting from within itself in its quiet arcade of identity. The green of the small zinnia shoots was very pure, almost burning. One by one, as the rain reached them, all the individual little plants shone out, and then the branching vines. The pear tree gave a soft rushing noise, like the wings of a bird alighting. She could sense behind her, as if a lamp were lighted in the night, the signal-like whiteness of the house. Then Jamey, as if in the shock of realizing the rain had come, turned his full face toward her, questions and delight intensifying his smile, gathering up his aroused, stretching body. He stammered some disconnected words, shyly.

She did not answer Jamey or move at all. She would not feel anything now except the rain falling. She listened for its scattered soft drops between Jamey's words, its quiet touching of the spears of the iris leaves, and a clear sound like a bell as it began to fall into a pitcher the cook had set on the doorstep.

Finally, Jamey stood there quietly, as if waiting for his money, with his hand trying to brush his confusion away from before his face. The rain fell steadily. A wind of deep wet fragrance beat against her.

Then as if it had swelled and broken over a daily levee, tenderness tore and spun through her sagging body.

It has come, she thought senselessly, her head lifting and her eyes looking without understanding at the sky which had begun to move, to fold nearer in softening, dissolving clouds. It was almost dark. Soon the loud and gentle night of rain would come. It would pound upon the steep roof of the white house. Within, she would lie in her bed and hear the rain. On and on it would fall, beat and fall. The day's work would be over in the garden. She would lie in bed, her arms tired at her sides and in motionless peace: against that which was inexhaustible, there was no defense.

Then Mrs. Larkin sank in one motion down into the flowers and lay there, fainting and streaked with rain. Her face was fully upturned, down among the plants, with the hair beaten away from her forehead and her open eyes closing at once when the rain touched them. Slowly her lips began to part. She seemed to move slightly, in the sad adjustment of a sleeper.

Jamey ran jumping and crouching about her, drawing in his breath alternately at the flowers breaking under his feet and at the shapeless, passive figure on the ground. Then he became quiet, and stood back at a little distance and looked in awe at the unknowing face, white and rested under its bombardment. He remembered how something had filled him with stillness when he felt her standing there behind him looking down at him, and he would not have turned around at that moment for anything in the world. He remembered all the while the oblivious crash of the windows next door being shut when the rain started. . . . But now, in this unseen place, it was he who stood looking at poor Mrs. Larkin.

He bent down and in a horrified, piteous, beseeching voice he began to call her name until she stirred.

"Miss Lark'! Miss Lark'!"

Then he jumped nimbly to his feet and ran out of the garden.

EUDORA WELTY'S "*A Curtain of Green*"

At first glance, through the curtain of green, we might regard Mrs. Larkin merely as a small and lonely woman, isolated by grief from the normal life of the community. We look at her, in other words, much as her neighbors do, from the high windows of their community complacency. With her overexuberant garden and her shapeless work clothes, her indifference to the heat which prostrates all the other women, she is a mere eccentric—whom her neighbors, at first dutifully sympathetic but then a little impatient with her when she unhealthily, as it were almost indecently, prolongs her mourning, have decided discreetly to ignore.

But this viewpoint is one from which interest in a story with Mrs. Larkin as heroine could hardly be sustained. Larkin's Hill is a Southern town, of course; and Miss Welty has entirely captured the tone of the peculiar Southern "tolerance" for the eccentric, especially for the eccentric of patrician family. "At first, after the death of Mr. Larkin —for whose father, after all, the town had been named—they had called on her with decent frequency." The phrase "after all"—with the following sentence, "But she had not appreciated it, they said to one another"—exactly defines the limits of that tolerance. It is a tolerance that is based exclusively upon a traditional sense of decency, or decorum, assigning certain standards of conduct according to social class, and that simply does not recognize, except as the object of a detached curiosity, any mode of personal behavior which escapes the received categories. Mrs. Larkin's neighbors are not bad neighbors, not hostile or vicious. They would not think of retaliating against her, with open ostracism, for her failure to "appreciate" their courtesies. But, precisely, they let her alone. They are simply people who don't and can't "see" the little widow in any deeply personal way, who don't, as we say, "get" her.

And it is just for the sake of this incapacity of theirs that Miss Welty has put them in the story. They are there, finally, to indicate what the story is *not* about, to set up the point of view from which we are *not* to regard the heroine. We are given negatively to understand, that the story is concerned neither with tolerance nor intolerance. Mrs. Larkin is the victim of neither and practices neither. The story has no essential social dimension. It concerns, rather, an existential situation and existential sensibilities.

The garden is both the actual and the symbolic setting for this situation and for the action of sensibility. It provides a little enclosed world, apart from the concerns of the social community. The other women of the neighborhood also keep gardens. But their gardening is notably a club activity. It is done according to the ideas which the garden-club members "elect" each year. And, though they implicitly recognize some distinction between standards of "appropriateness" thus defined and possibly higher considerations of "beauty" to which the nonclub gardener might defer, still it is obvious that their conception of beauty, too, is ultimately conventional. Mrs. Larkin's activity, on the other hand, subscribes to no discernible convention, local or universal. Traditionally, gardening is by definition an art whereby man asserts his human superiority over the forces of external nature. It is an art, above all, of control—an art of "cutting, separating, thinning and tying back" —an art of order, which symbolically reflects the social order. But "Mrs. Larkin rarely cut, separated, tied back. . . . To a certain extent, she seemed not to seek for order, but to allow an over-flowering, as if she consciously ventured forever a little farther, a little deeper, into her life in the garden." It is gradually impressed upon us that this garden, in a sense, *is* its owner's life. It is, to repeat, her whole world. It is not something which she is using to "express herself," vis-a-vis the community, the world of civilization. Rather—and here Miss Welty employs a word which conveys the tone of the community attitude, but which also, in the full context of the story, will be significant to the reader beyond the intention of the neighbors who might use it—rather, Mrs. Larkin's garden is "a sort of jungle," and a jungle "in which the slight, heedless form of its owner daily lost itself." We are soon to discover that it is in no innocently figurative sense that the place is a jungle and that Mrs. Larkin is lost in it.

In the description of the garden, and of Mrs. Larkin's emotions as she moves about within its fastness, there is a sense of first things, and of last. What is the source of the peculiar terror she feels "as though her loneliness had been pointed out by some outside force whose finger parted the hedge"? As we have observed, the loneliness is not a matter simply of her being cut off, by her widowhood, from the normal life of the community. Further, it is not in any usual way the loneliness of personal bereavement, what she might be expected to feel simply in the loss of her beloved husband.

In the first place, we should note, not only has she lost a mate, but, as a consequence of that, she is all but entirely bereft of her sexual character. Her habitual costume, the old pair of men's overalls, obscures her womanliness. It makes her strangely sexless—and strangely ageless. We are startled to discover, late in the story, that she is a *young* woman. When she raises the hoe above Jamey's head, the "clumsy sleeves" of the overalls fall back, "exposing the thin, unsunburned whiteness of her arms, the shocking fact of their youth." But what all this finally points toward is the loss of her specifically *human* character, her human consciousness. The neighbors, regarding her stained overalls, note that they have become "almost of a color with the leaves." The garden becomes a strangely inverted image of the garden of creation, in which she moves like an Eve made before the Adam, with no rational companion to secure her sense of creaturely differentiation from the plants and birds.

Her terror is the terror of a radical dumbness. What essentially distinguishes man from the rest of nature, the prime mark of his rationality, is his power of intelligible speech. And Mrs. Larkin is bereft of speech. The dominant effect in the entire description of the garden is of an all-pervasive, as if primordial, silence. The intense heat, of course, accounts for the kind of delirium into which the woman falls when she is about to attack Jamey, and perhaps for the corresponding, strangely conscious oblivion into which he too lapses as he senses her presence and would let her kill him. But in one sense the heat merely reinforces, adds weight, to the silence. Above all, she cannot speak to Jamey, nor he to her.

Speechless, she is deprived of will—and of the power of moral recognition. We assume that this paralysis of the will has been coming on her for some time, ever since the moment of her husband's death, when she discovered that her love had no power in the realm of external nature, and could not stay the fall of the tree, the fatal colliding of its body with his body. She has suspected, for a long time, that vast numbers of created things exist apart from any consideration of human intention. And, cultivating the garden, this riot of vegetation which most prominently embodies the indifference of nature, she herself has become more and more "heedless." But the heedlessness reaches its supreme intensity, she is finally and wholly taken by it, on this hot afternoon when Jamey does not answer her call, and in a terrible, violent passivity she lifts the hoe over his head to strike him.

The passage repeatedly emphasizes the silence and, in and of it, the unutterable helplessness of the woman. ". . . so helpless was she, too helpless to defy the workings of accident, of life and death, of unaccountability." She would "punish," "protest." And yet, the very proposed act, of striking off the Negro's head, is not so much an effort of protest or punishment, as itself the final and despairing acceptance of her incapacity to act—that is, to act humanly, as a consequence of moral intent, and in a context of human recognition. The normal implications of the word "intentionally"—in her thought that "such a head she could strike off, intentionally"—are deliberately contradicted in the clause that follows: "so deeply did she know, from the effect of a man's danger and death, its cause in oblivion."

The description of Jamey's head as, holding the hoe to strike, she sees it in her moment of paralyzed surprise, is profoundly instructive. "With its clustered hot woolly hair, its intricate, glistening ears, its small brown branching streams of sweat," the head is merest organic work of the creator's wholly unintelligible art. It is precisely as if Mrs. Larkin were seeing such a head for the first time, regarding this human thing much, but more intensely, as she might look at some fantastic caterpillar, of a species previously unknown to her, which she had come upon among the flowers.

It is the incredible separacy, otherness, of the thing that overwhelms her, its unbelievable self-containment—"the bowed head holding so obviously and so deadly its ridiculous dream." In the crucial moment, Jamey "responds" to the danger of her dumb and will-less presence only with his own oblivion.

And though the coming of the rain stays her, breaks the murderous spell, brings a kind of release or relief of tension—the description of her swoon under the falling rain is of an orgasmic surrender—yet the transition is only from a violent to a gentle passivity. There is no escape from the prison of separacy, no establishment of communication, or communion. Jamey finally speaks, but at first she does not understand him, and then, when she has fainted and fallen, no longer even hears him. Paradoxically, the rain only confirms what the still heat has promised; in this new light, "the light from the rain," although it is "different from sunlight," "everything appeared to gleam unreflecting from within itself in its quiet arcade of identity." Each thing, each consciousness, is more than ever impenetrable, though surrendered and open. And we see that it is a matter of utter indifference whether the hoe is lifted or let fall, the choice between striking or desisting, between death and "life," decided for Mrs. Larkin by the merest accident of time, when "the first drop touched her upraised arm." The rain falls as the tree fell on her husband's car. Love and hate, the intent of affection, the lust of malice, decide nothing and explain nothing.   *J.E.H.*

DYLAN THOMAS

The Peaches

HE GRASS-GREEN CART, with 'J. Jones, Gorsehill' painted shakily on it, stopped in the cobblestone passage between 'The Hare's Foot' and 'The Pure Drop.' It was late on an April evening. Uncle Jim, in his black market suit with a stiff white shirt and no collar, loud new boots, and a plaid cap, creaked and climbed down. He dragged out a thick wicker basket from a heap of straw in the corner of the cart and swung it over his shoulder. I heard a squeal from the basket and saw the tip of a pink tail curling out as Uncle Jim opened the public door of 'The Pure Drop.'

'I won't be two minutes,' he said to me. The bar was full; two fat women in bright dresses sat near the door, one with a small, dark child on her knee; they saw Uncle Jim and nudged up on the bench.

'I'll be out straight away,' he said fiercely, as though I had contradicted him, 'you stay there quiet.'

The woman without the child raised up her hands. 'Oh, Mr Jones,' she said in a high laughing voice. She shook like a jelly.

Then the door closed and the voices were muffled.

I sat alone on the shaft of the cart in the narrow passage, staring through a side window of 'The Hare's Foot.' A stained blind was drawn half over it. I could see into half of a smoky, secret room, where four men were playing cards. One man was huge and swarthy, with a handlebar moustache and a love-curl on his forehead; seated by his side was a thin, bald, pale old man with his cheeks in his mouth; the faces of the other two were in shadow. They all drank out of brown pint tankards and never spoke, laying the cards down with a smack, scraping at their matchboxes, puffing at their pipes, swallowing unhappily, ringing the brass bell, ordering more, by a sign of the fingers, from a sour woman with a flowered blouse and a man's cap.

The passage grew dark too suddenly, the walls crowded in, and the roofs crouched down. To me, staring timidly there in a dark passage in a strange town, the swarthy man appeared like a giant in a cage surrounded by clouds, and the bald old man withered into a black hump with a white top; two white hands darted out of the corner with invisible cards. A man with spring-heeled boots and a two-edged knife might be bouncing towards me from Union Street.

I called, 'Uncle Jim, Uncle Jim,' softly so that he should not hear.

I began to whistle between my teeth, but when I stopped I thought the sound went hissing on behind me. I climbed down from the shaft and stepped close to the half-blind window; a hand clawed up the pane to the tassel of the blind; in the little, packed space be-

tween me on the cobbles and the card-players at the table, I could
not tell which side of the glass was the hand that dragged the blind
down slowly. I was cut from the night by a stained square. A story
I had made in the warm, safe island of my bed, with sleepy midnight Swansea flowing and rolling round outside the house, came
blowing down to me then with a noise on the cobbles. I remembered the demon in the story, with his wings and hooks, who clung
like a bat to my hair as I battled up and down Wales after a tall,
wise, golden, royal girl from Swansea Convent. I tried to remember
her true name, her proper, long, black-stockinged legs, her giggle
and paper curls, but the hooked wings tore at me and the colour of
her hair and eyes faded and vanished like the grass-green of the cart
that was a dark, grey mountain now standing between the passage
walls.

And all this time the old, broad, patient, nameless mare stood
without stirring, not stamping once on the cobbles or shaking her
reins. I called her a good girl and stood on tiptoe to try to stroke
her ears as the door of 'The Pure Drop' swung open and the warm
lamplight from the bar dazzled me and burned my story up. I felt
frightened no longer, only angry and hungry. The two fat women
near the door giggled 'Good night, Mr Jones' out of the rich noise
and the comfortable smells. The child lay curled asleep under the
bench. Uncle Jim kissed the two women on the lips.

'Good night.'

'Good night.'

'Good night.'

Then the passage was dark again.

He backed the mare into Union Street, lurching against her side,
cursing her patience and patting her nose, and we both climbed into
the cart.

'There are too many drunken gipsies,' he said as we rolled and
rattled through the flickering, lamp-lit town.

He sang hymns all the way to Gorsehill in an affectionate bass
voice, and conducted the wind with his whip. He did not need to
touch the reins. Once on the rough road, between hedges twisting
out to twig the mare by the bridle and poke our caps, we stopped,
at a whispered 'Whoa,' for uncle to light his pipe and set the darkness on fire and show his long, red, drunken, fox's face to me, with

its bristling side-bushes and wet, sensitive nose. A white house with a light in one bedroom window shone in a field on a short hill beyond the road.

Uncle whispered, 'Easy, easy, girl,' to the mare, though she was standing calmly, and said to me over his shoulder in a suddenly loud voice: 'A hangman lived there.'

He stamped on the shaft, and we rattled on through a cutting wind. Uncle shivered, pulling down his cap to hide his ears; but the mare was like a clumsy statue trotting, and all the demons of my stories, if they trotted by her side or crowded together and grinned into her eyes, would not make her shake her head or hurry.

'I wish he'd have hung Mrs Jesus,' uncle said.

Between hymns he cursed the mare in Welsh. The white house was left behind, the light and the hill were swallowed up.

'Nobody lives there now,' he said.

We drove into the farm-yard of Gorsehill, where the cobbles rang and the black, empty stables took up the ringing and hollowed it so that we drew up in a hollow circle of darkness and the mare was a hollow animal and nothing lived in the hollow house at the end of the yard but two sticks with faces scooped out of turnips.

'You run and see Annie,' said uncle. 'There'll be hot broth and potatoes.'

He led the hollow, shaggy statue towards the stable; clop, clop to the mice-house. I heard locks rattle as I ran to the farm-house door.

The front of the house was the single side of a black shell, and the arched door was the listening ear. I pushed the door open and walked into the passage out of the wind. I might have been walk-into the hollow night and the wind, passing through a tall vertical shell on an inland sea-shore. Then a door at the end of the passage opened; I saw the plates on the shelves, the lighted lamp on the long, oil-clothed table, 'Prepare to Meet Thy God' knitted over the fire-place, the smiling china dogs, the brown-stained settle, the grandmother clock, and I ran into the kitchen and into Annie's arms.

There was a welcome, then. The clock struck twelve as she kissed me, and I stood among the shining and striking like a prince taking off his disguise. One minute I was small and cold, skulking dead-scared down a black passage in my stiff, best suit, with my hollow belly thumping and my heart like a time bomb, clutching my grammar school cap, unfamiliar to myself, a snub-nosed story-teller lost in his own adventures and longing to be home; the next I was a royal nephew in smart town clothes, embraced and wel-comed, standing in the snug centre of my stories and listening to the clock announcing me. She hurried me to the seat in the side of the cavernous fire-place and took off my shoes. The bright lamps and the ceremonial gongs blazed and rang for me.

She made a mustard bath and strong tea, told me to put on a pair of my cousin Gwilym's socks and an old coat of uncle's that smelt of rabbit and tobacco. She fussed and clucked and nodded and told me, as she cut bread and butter, how Gwilym was still studying to be a minister, and how Aunt Rach Morgan, who was ninety years old, had fallen on her belly on a scythe.

Then Uncle Jim came in like the devil with a red face and a wet nose and trembling, hairy hands. His walk was thick. He stumbled against the dresser and shook the coronation plates, and a lean cat shot booted out from the settle corner. Uncle looked nearly twice as tall as Annie. He could have carried her about under his coat and brought her out suddenly, a little, brown-skinned, toothless, hunchbacked woman with a cracked, sing-song voice.

'You shouldn't have kept him out so long,' she said, angry and timid.

He sat down in his special chair, which was the broken throne of a bankrupt bard, and lit his pipe and stretched his legs and puffed clouds at the ceiling.

'He might catch his death of cold,' she said.

She talked at the back of his head while he wrapped himself in clouds. The cat slunk back. I sat at the table with my supper finished, and found a little empty bottle and a white balloon in the pockets of my coat.

'Run off to bed, there's a dear,' Annie whispered.

'Can I go and look at the pigs?'

'In the morning, dear,' she said.

So I said good night to Uncle Jim, who turned and smiled at me and winked through the smoke, and I kissed Annie and lit my candle.

'Good night.'
'Good night.'
'Good night.'

I climbed the stairs; each had a different voice. The house smelt of rotten wood and damp and animals. I thought that I had been walking long, damp passages all my life, and climbing stairs in the dark, alone. I stopped outside Gwilym's door on the draughty landing.

'Good night.'

The candle flame jumped in my bedroom where a lamp was burning very low, and the curtains waved; the water in a glass on a round table by the bed stirred, I thought, as the door closed, and lapped against the sides. There was a stream below the window; I thought it lapped against the house all night until I slept.

'Can I go and see the pigs?' I asked Gwilym next morning. The hollow fear of the house was gone, and, running downstairs to my breakfast, I smelt the sweetness of wood and the fresh spring grass and the quiet untidy farm-yard, with its tumbledown dirty-white cow-house and empty stables open.

Gwilym was a tall young man aged nearly twenty, with a thin stick of a body and spade-shaped face. You could dig the garden with him. He had a deep voice that cracked in half when he was excited, and he sang songs to himself, treble and bass, with the same sad hymn tune, and wrote hymns in the barn. He told me stories about girls who died for love. 'And she put a rope round a tree but it was too short,' he said; 'she stuck a penknife in her bosom but it was too blunt.' We were sitting together on the straw heaps that day in the half-dark of the shuttered stable. He twisted and leaned near me, raising his big finger, and the straw creaked.

'She jumped in the cold river, she jumped,' he said, his mouth against my ear, 'arse over tip and, Diu, she was dead.' He squeaked like a bat.

The pigsties were at the far end of the yard. We walked towards them, Gwilym dressed in minister's black, though it was a weekday morning, and me in a serge suit with a darned bottom, past three hens scrabbling the muddy cobbles and a collie with one eye, sleeping with it open. The ramshackle outhouses had tumbling, rotten roofs, jagged holes in their sides, broken shutters, and peeling whitewash; rusty screws ripped out from the dangling, crooked boards; the lean cat of the night before sat snugly between the splintered jaws of bottles, cleaning its face, on the tip of the rubbish pile that rose triangular and smelling sweet and strong to the level of the riddled cart-house roof. There was nowhere like that farm-yard in all the slap dash county, nowhere so poor and grand and dirty as that square of mud and rubbish and bad wood and falling stone, where a bucketful of old and bedraggled hens scratched and laid small eggs. A duck quacked out of the trough in one deserted sty. Now a young man and a curly boy stood staring and sniffing over a wall at a sow, with its tits on the mud, giving suck.

'How many pigs are there?'

'Five. The bitch ate one,' said Gwilym.

We counted them as they squirmed and wriggled, rolled on their backs and bellies, edged and pinched and pushed and squealed about their mother. There were four. We counted again. Four pigs, four naked pink tails curling up as their mouths guzzled down and the sow grunted with pain and joy.

'She must have ate another,' I said, and picked up a scratching stick and prodded the grunting sow and rubbed her crusted bristles backwards. 'Or a fox jumped over the wall,' I said.

'It wasn't the sow or the fox,' said Gwilym. 'It was father.'

I could see uncle, tall and sly and red, holding the writhing pig in his two hairy hands, sinking his teeth in its thigh, crunching its trotters up; I could see him leaning over the wall of the sty with the pig's legs sticking out of his mouth. 'Did Uncle Jim eat the pig?'

Now, at this minute, behind the rotting sheds, he was standing, knee-deep in feathers, chewing off the live heads of the poultry.

'He sold it to go on the drink,' said Gwilym in his deepest rebuking whisper, his eyes fixed on the sky. 'Last Christmas he took a sheep over his shoulder, and he was pissed for ten days.'

The sow rolled nearer the scratching stick, and the small pigs sucking at her, lost and squealing in the sudden darkness, struggled under her folds and pouches.

'Come and see my chapel,' said Gwilym. He forgot the lost pig at once and began to talk about the towns he had visited on a religious tour, Neath and Bridgend and Bristol and Newport, with their lakes and luxury gardens, their bright, coloured streets roaring with temptation. We walked away from the sty and the disappointed sow.

'I met actress after actress,' he said.

Gwilym's chapel was the last old barn before the field that led down to the river; it stood well above the farm-yard, on a mucky hill. There was one whole door with a heavy padlock, but you could get in easily through the holes on either side of it. He took out a ring of keys and shook them gently and tried each one in the lock. 'Very posh,' he said; 'I bought them from the junk-shop in Carmarthen.' We climbed into the chapel through a hole.

A dusty wagon with the name painted out and a whitewash cross on its side stood in the middle. 'My pulpit cart,' he said, and walked solemnly into it up the broken shaft. 'You sit on the hay; mind the mice,' he said. Then he brought out his deepest voice again, and cried to the heavens and the batlined rafters and the hanging webs: 'Bless us this holy day, O Lord, bless me and Dylan and this Thy little chapel for ever and ever, Amen. I've done a lot of improvements to this place.'

I sat on the hay and stared at Gwilym preaching, and heard his voice rise and crack and sink to a whisper and break into singing and Welsh and ring triumphantly and be wild and meek. The sun, through a hole, shone on his praying shoulders, and he said: 'O God, Thou art everywhere all the time, in the dew of the morning, in the frost of the evening, in the field and the town, in the preacher and the sinner, in the sparrow and the big buzzard. Thou canst see everything, right down deep in our hearts; Thou canst see us when the sun is gone; Thou canst see us when there aren't any stars, in the gravy blackness, in the deep, deep, deep, deep pit; Thou canst see and spy and watch us all the time, in the little black corners, in the big cowboys' prairies, under the blankets when we 're snoring fast, in the terrible shadows, pitch black, pitch black; Thou canst see everything we do, in the night and the day, in the day and the night, everything, everything; Thou canst see all the time. O God mun, you're like a bloody cat.'

He let his clasped hands fall. The chapel in the barn was still, and shafted with sunlight. There was nobody to cry Hallelujah or God-bless; I was too small and enamoured in the silence. The one duck quacked outside.

'Now I take a collection,' Gwilym said.

He stepped down from the cart and groped about in the hay beneath it and held out a battered tin to me.

'I haven't got a proper box,' he said.

I put two pennies in the tin.

'It 's time for dinner,' he said, and we went back to the house without a word.

Annie said, when we had finished dinner: 'Put on your nice suit for this afternoon. The one with stripes.'

It was to be a special afternoon, for my best friend, Jack Williams, from Swansea, was coming down with his rich mother in a motor car, and Jack was to spend a fortnight's holiday with me.

'Where 's Uncle Jim?'

'He 's gone to market,' said Annie.

Gwilym made a small pig's noise. We knew where uncle was; he was sitting in a public house with a heifer over his shoulder and two pigs nosing out of his pockets, and his lips were wet with bull's blood.

'Is Mrs. Williams very rich?' asked Gwilym.

I told him she had three motor cars and two houses, which was a lie. 'She 's the richest woman in Wales, and once she was a mayoress,' I said. 'Are we going to have tea in the best room?'

Annie nodded. 'And a large tin of peaches,' she said.

'That old tin's been in the cupboard since Christmas,' said Gwilym, 'mother's been keeping it for a day like this.'

'They 're lovely peaches,' Annie said. She went upstairs to dress like Sunday.

The best room smelt of moth-balls and fur and damp and dead plants and stale, sour air. Two glass cases on wooden coffin-boxes lined the window wall. You looked at the weed-grown vegetable garden through a stuffed fox's legs, over a partridge's head, along the red-paint-stained breast of a stiff wild duck. A case of china and pewter, trinkets, teeth, family brooches, stood beyond the bandy table; there was a large oil lamp on the patchwork table-cloth, a Bible with a clasp, a tall vase with a draped woman about to bathe on it, and a framed photograph of Annie, Uncle Jim, and Gwilym smiling in front of a fern-pot. On the mantelpiece were two clocks, some dogs, brass candlesticks, a shepherdess, a man in a kilt, and a tinted photograph of Annie, with high hair and her breasts coming out. There were chairs around the table and in each corner, straight, curved, stained, padded, all with lace cloths hanging over their backs. A patched white sheet shrouded the harmonium. The fireplace was full of brass tongs, shovels, and pokers. The best room was rarely used. Annie dusted and brushed and polished there once a week, but the carpet still sent up a grey cloud when you trod on it, and dust lay evenly on the seats of the chairs, and balls of cotton and dirt and black stuffing and long black horse hairs were wedged in the cracks of the sofa. I blew on the glass to see the pictures. Gwilym and castles and cattle.

'Change your suit now,' said Gwilym.

I wanted to wear my old suit, to look like a proper farm boy and have manure in my shoes and hear it squelch as I walked, to see a cow have calves and a bull on top of a cow, to run down in the dingle and wet my stockings, to go out and shout, 'Come on, you bugger,' and pelt the hens and talk in a proper voice. But I went upstairs to put my striped suit on.

From my bedroom I heard the noise of a motor car drawing up in the yard. It was Jack Williams and his mother.

Gwilym shouted, 'They're here, in a Daimler!' from the foot of the stairs, and I ran down to meet them with my tie undone and my hair uncombed.

Annie was saying at the door: 'Good afternoon, Mrs Williams, good afternoon. Come right in, it's a lovely day, Mrs Williams. Did you have a nice journey then? This way, Mrs Williams, mind the step.'

Annie wore a black, shining dress that smelt of mothballs, like the chair covers in the best room; she had forgotten to change her gym-shoes, which were caked with mud and all holes. She fussed on before Mrs Williams down the stone passage, darting her head round, clucking, fidgetting, excusing the small house, anxiously tidying her hair with one rough, stubby hand.

Mrs Williams was tall and stout, with a jutting bosom and thick legs, her ankles swollen over her pointed shoes; she was fitted out like a mayoress or a ship, and she swayed after Annie into the best room.

She said: 'Please don't put yourself out for me, Mrs Jones,

there 's a dear.' She dusted the seat of a chair with a lace handkerchief from her bag before sitting down.

'I can't stop, you know,' she said.

'Oh, you must stay for a cup of tea,' said Annie, shifting and scraping the chairs away from the table so that nobody could move and Mrs Williams was hemmed in fast with her bosom and her rings and her bag, opening the china cupboard, upsetting the Bible on the floor, picking it up, dusting it hurriedly with her sleeve.

'And peaches,' Gwilym said. He was standing in the passage with his hat on.

Annie said, 'Take your hat off, Gwilym, make Mrs Williams comfortable,' and she put the lamp on the shrouded harmonium and spread out a white tablecloth that had a tea stain in the centre, and brought out the china and laid knives and cups for five.

'Don't bother about me, there 's a dear,' said Mrs Williams. 'There 's a lovely fox!' She flashed a finger of rings at the glass case.

'It 's real blood,' I told Jack, and we climbed over the sofa to the table.

'No it isn't,' he said, 'it 's red ink.'

'Oh, your shoes!' said Annie.

'Don't tread on the sofa, Jack, there 's a dear.'

'If it isn't ink it 's paint then.'

Gwilym said: 'Shall I get you a bit of cake, Mrs Williams?'

Annie rattled the tea-cups. 'There isn't a single bit of cake in the house,' she said; 'we forgot to order it from the shop; not a single bit. Oh, Mrs Williams!'

Mrs Williams said: 'Just a cup of tea, thanks.' She was still sweating because she had walked all the way from the car. It spoiled her powder. She sparkled her rings and dabbed at her face.

'Three lumps,' she said. 'And I'm sure Jack will be very happy here.'

'Happy as sandboys.' Gwilym sat down.

'Now, you must have some peaches, Mrs Williams, they're lovely.'

'They should be, they 've been here long enough,' said Gwilym.

Annie rattled the tea-cups at him again.

'No peaches, thanks,' Mrs Williams said.

'Oh, you must, Mrs Williams, just one. With cream.'

'No, no, Mrs Jones, thanks the same,' she said. 'I don't mind pears or chunks, but I can't bear peaches.'

Jack and I had stopped talking. Annie stared down at her gym-shoes. One of the two clocks on the mantelpiece coughed, and struck. Mrs Williams struggled from her chair.

'There, time flies!' she said.

She pushed her way past the furniture, jostled against the cup-board, rattled the trinkets and brooches, and kissed Jack on the forehead.

'You 've got scent on,' he said.

She patted my head.

'Now, behave yourselves.'

To Annie, she said in a whisper: 'And remember, Mrs Jones, just good plain food. No spoiling his appetite.'

Annie followed her out of the room. She moved slowly now. 'I'll do my very best, Mrs Williams.'

We heard her say, 'Good-bye then, Mrs Williams,' and go down the steps of the kitchen and close the door. The motor car roared in the yard, then the noise grew softer and died.

Down the thick dingle Jack and I ran shouting, scalping the brambles with our thin stick-hatchets, dancing, hallooing. We skidded to a stop and prowled on the bushy banks of the stream. Up above, sat one-eyed, dead-eyed, sinister, slim, ten-notched Gwilym, loading his guns in Gallows Farm. We crawled and rat-tatted through the bushes, hid, at a whistled signal, in the deep grass, and crouched there, waiting for the crack of a twig or the secret break-ing of boughs.

On my haunches, eager and alone, casting an ebony shadow, with the Gorsehill jungle swarming, the violent, impossible birds and fishes leaping, hidden under four-stemmed flowers the height of horses, in the early evening in a dingle near Carmarthen, my friend Jack Williams invisibly near me, I felt all my young body like an excited animal surrounding me, the torn knees bent, the bumping heart, the long heat and depth between the legs, the sweat prickling in the hands, the tunnels down to the eardrums, the little balls of dirt between the toes, the eyes in the sockets, the tucked-up voice, the blood racing, the memory around and within flying, jumping, swimming, and waiting to pounce. There, playing Indians

in the evening, I was aware of me myself in the exact middle of a
living story, and my body was my adventure and my name. I
sprang with excitement and scrambled up through the scratching
brambles again.

Jack cried: 'I see you! I see you!' He scampered after me.
'Bang! bang! you're dead!'

But I was young and loud and alive, though I lay down
obediently.

'Now you try and kill me,' said Jack. 'Count a hundred.'

I closed one eye, saw him rush and stamp towards the upper
field, then tiptoe back and begin to climb a tree, and I counted
fifty and ran to the foot of the tree and killed him as he climbed.
'You fall down,' I said.

He refused to fall, so I climbed too, and we clung to the top
branches and stared down at the lavatory in the corner of the field.
Gwilym was sitting on the seat with his trousers down. He looked
small and black. He was reading a book and moving his hands.

'We can see you!' we shouted.

He snatched his trousers up and put the book in his pocket.

'We can see you, Gwilym!'

He came out into the field. 'Where are you, then?'

We waved our caps at him.

'In the sky!' Jack shouted.

'Flying!' I shouted.

We stretched our arms out like wings.

'Fly down here.'

We swung and laughed on the branches.

'There 's birds!' cried Gwilym.

Our jackets were torn and our stockings were wet and our
shoes were sticky; we had green moss and brown bark on our
hands and faces when we went in for supper and a scolding. Annie
was quiet that night, though she called me a ragamuffin and said
she didn't know what Mrs Williams would think and told Gwilym
he should know better. We made faces at Gwilym and put salt
in his tea, but after supper he said: 'You can come to chapel if you
like. Just before bed.'

He lit a candle on the top of the pulpit cart. It was a small light
in the big barn. The bats were gone. Shadows still clung upside

down along the roof. Gwilym was no longer my cousin in a Sunday suit, but a tall stranger shaped like a spade in a cloak, and his voice grew too deep. The straw heaps were lively. I thought of the sermon on the cart: we were watched, Jack's heart was watched, Gwilym's tongue was marked down, my whisper, 'Look at the little eyes,' was remembered always.

'Now I take confessions,' said Gwilym from the cart.

Jack and I stood bareheaded in the circle of the candle, and I could feel the trembling of Jack's body.

'You first.' Gwilym's finger, as bright as though he had held it in the candle flame until it burned, pointed me out, and I took a step towards the pulpit cart, raising my head.

'Now you confess,' said Gwilym.

'What have I got to confess?'

'The worst thing you 've done.'

I let Edgar Reynolds be whipped because I had taken his homework; I stole from my mother's bag; I stole from Gwyneth's bag; I stole twelve books in three visits from the library, and threw them away in the park; I drank a cup of my water to see what it tasted like; I beat a dog with a stick so that it would roll over and lick my hand afterwards; I looked with Dan Jones through the key-hole while his maid had a bath; I cut my knee with a penknife, and put the blood on my handkerchief and said it had come out of my ears so that I could pretend I was ill and frighten my mother; I pulled my trousers down and showed Jack Williams; I saw Billy Jones beat a pigeon to death with a fire-shovel, and laughed and got sick; Cedric Williams and I broke into Mrs Samuel's house and poured ink over the bedclothes.

I said: 'I haven't done anything bad.'

'Go on, confess!' said Gwilym. He was frowning down at me.

'I can't! I can't!' I said. 'I haven't done anything bad.'

'Go on, confess!'

'I won't! I won't!'

Jack began to cry. 'I want to go home,' he said.

Gwilym opened the chapel door and we followed him into the yard, down past the black, humped sheds, towards the house, and Jack sobbed all the way.

In bed together, Jack and I confessed our sins.

'I steal from my mother's bag, too; there are pounds and pounds.'

'How much do you steal?'

'Threepence.'

'I killed a man once.'

'No you didn't then.'

'Honest to Christ, I shot him through the heart.'

'What was his name?'

'Williams.'

'Did he bleed?'

I thought the stream was lapping against the house.

'Like a bloody pig,' I said.

Jack's tears had dried. 'I don't like Gwilym, he 's barmy.'

'No, he isn't. I found a lot of poems in his bedroom once. They were all written to girls. And he showed them to me afterwards, and he 'd changed all the girls' names to God.'

'He 's religious.'

'No he isn't, he goes with actresses. He knows Corinne Griffith.'

Our door was open. I like the door locked at night, because I would rather have a ghost in the bedroom than think of one coming in; but Jack liked it open, and we tossed and he won. We heard the front door rattle and footsteps in the kitchen passage.

'That 's Uncle Jim.'

'What 's he like?'

'He 's like a fox, he eats pigs and chickens.'

The ceiling was thin and we heard every sound, the creaking of the bard's chair, the clatter of plates, Annie's voice saying: 'Midnight!'

'He 's drunk,' I said. We lay quite still, hoping to hear a quarrel.

'Perhaps he 'll throw plates,' I said.

But Annie scolded him softly: 'There 's a fine state, Jim.'

He murmured to her.

'There 's one pig gone,' she said. 'Oh, why do you have to do it, Jim? There 's nothing left now. We 'll never be able to carry on.'

'Money! money! money!' he said. I knew he would be lighting his pipe.

Then Annie's voice grew so soft we could not hear the words, and uncle said: 'Did she pay you the thirty shillings?'

'They 're talking about your mother,' I told Jack.

For a long time Annie spoke in a low voice, and we waited for words. 'Mrs Williams,' she said, and 'motor car,' and 'Jack,' and 'peaches.' I thought she was crying, for her voice broke on the last word.

Uncle Jim's chair creaked again, he might have struck his fist on the table, and we heard him shout: 'I 'll give her peaches! Peaches, peaches! Who does she think she is? Aren't peaches good enough for her? To hell with her bloody motor car and her bloody son! Making us small.'

'Don't, don't, Jim!' Annie said, 'you 'll wake the boys.'

'I 'll wake them and whip the hell out of them, too!'

'Please, please, Jim!'

'You send the boy away,' he said, 'or I 'll do it myself. Back to his three bloody houses.'

Jack pulled the bedclothes over his head and sobbed into the pillow: 'I don't want to hear, I don't want to hear. I 'll write to my mother. She 'll take me away.'

I climbed out to close the door. Jack would not talk to me again, and I fell asleep to the noise of the voices below, which soon grew gentle.

Uncle Jim was not at breakfast. When we came down, Jack's shoes were cleaned for him and his jacket was darned and pressed. Annie gave two boiled eggs to Jack and one to me. She forgave me when I drank tea from the saucer.

After breakfast, Jack walked to the post office. I took the one-eyed collie to chase rabbits in the upper fields, but it barked at ducks and brought me a tramp's shoe from a hedge, and lay down with its tail wagging in a rabbit hole. I threw stones at the deserted duck pond, and the collie ambled back with sticks.

Jack went sulking into the damp dingle, his hands in his pockets, his cap over one eye. I left the collie sniffing at a molehill, and climbed to the tree-top in the corner of the lavatory field. Below me, Jack was playing Indians all alone, scalping through the bushes, surprising himself round a tree, hiding from himself in the grass. I called to him once, but he pretended not to hear. He played alone, silently and savagely. I saw him standing with his hands in his pockets, swaying like a Kelly, on the mud-bank by the stream at the foot of the dingle. My bough lurched, the heads of the dingle bushes spun up towards me like green tops, 'I 'm falling!' I cried, my trousers saved me, I swung and grasped, this was one minute of wild adventure, but Jack did not look up and the minute was lost. I climbed, without dignity, to the ground.

Early in the afternoon, after a silent meal, when Gwilym was reading the scriptures or writing hymns to girls or sleeping in his chapel, Annie was baking bread, and I was cutting a wooden whistle in the loft over the stable, the motor car drove up in the yard again.

Out of the house Jack, in his best suit, ran to meet his mother, and I heard him say as she stepped, raising her short skirts, on to the cobbles: 'And he called you a bloody cow, and he said he 'd whip the hell out of me, and Gwilym took me to the barn in the dark and let the mice run over me, and Dylan 's a thief, and that old woman 's spoilt my jacket.'

Mrs Williams sent the chauffeur for Jack's luggage. Annie came to the door, trying to smile and curtsy, tidying her hair, wiping her hands on her pinafore.

Mrs Williams said, 'Good afternoon,' and sat with Jack in the back of the car and stared at the ruin of Gorsehill.

The chauffeur came back. The car drove off, scattering the hens. I ran out of the stable to wave to Jack. He sat still and stiff by his mother's side. I waved my handkerchief.

JOHN CHEEVER

The Enormous Radio

IM AND IRENE WESTCOTT were the kind of people who seem to strike that satisfactory average of income, endeavor, and respectability that is reached by the statistical reports in college bulletins. They were the parents of two young children, they had been married nine years, they lived on the twelfth floor of an apartment house in the East Seventies between Fifth and Madison Avenues, they went to the theatre on an average of 10.3 times a year, and they hoped someday to live in Westchester. Irene Westcott was a pleasant, rather plain girl with soft brown hair and a wide, fine forehead upon which nothing at all had been written, and in the cold weather she wore a coat of fitch skins dyed to resemble mink. You could not say that Jim Westcott, at thirty-seven, looked younger than he was, but you could at least say of him that he seemed to feel younger. He wore his graying hair cut very short, he dressed in the kind of clothes his class had worn at Andover, and his manner was earnest, vehement, and intentionally naïve. The Westcotts differed from their friends, their classmates, and their neighbors only in an interest they shared in serious music. They went to a great many concerts—although they seldom mentioned this to anyone—and they spent a good deal of time listening to music on the radio.

Their radio was an old instrument, sensitive, unpredictable, and beyond repair. Neither of them understood the mechanics of radio —or any of the other appliances that surrounded them—and when the instrument faltered, Jim would strike the side of the cabinet

Reprinted from THE ENORMOUS RADIO AND OTHER STORIES by John Cheever. By permission of the publishers, Funk & Wagnalls, N.Y.

with his hand. This sometimes helped. One Sunday afternoon, in the middle of a Schubert quartet, the music faded away altogether. Jim struck the cabinet repeatedly, but there was no response; the Schubert was lost to them forever. He promised to buy Irene a new radio, and on Monday when he came home from work he told her that he had got one. He refused to describe it, and said it would be a surprise for her when it came.

The radio was delivered at the kitchen door the following afternoon, and with the assistance of her maid and the handyman Irene uncrated it and brought it into the living room. She was struck at once with the physical ugliness of the large gumwood cabinet. Irene was proud of her living room, she had chosen its furnishings and colors as carefully as she chose her clothes, and now it seemed to her that the new radio stood among her intimate possessions like an aggressive intruder. She was confounded by the number of dials and switches on the instrument panel, and she studied them thoroughly before she put the plug into a wall socket and turned the radio on. The dials flooded with a malevolent green light, and in the distance she heard the music of a piano quintet. The quintet was in the distance for only an instant; it bore down upon her with a speed greater than light and filled the apartment with the noise of music amplified so mightily that it knocked a china ornament from a table to the floor. She rushed to the instrument and reduced the volume. The violent forces that were snared in the ugly gumwood cabinet made her uneasy. Her children came home from school then, and she took them to the Park. It was not until later in the afternoon that she was able to return to the radio.

The maid had given the children their suppers and was supervising their baths when Irene turned on the radio, reduced the volume, and sat down to listen to a Mozart quintet that she knew and enjoyed. The music came through clearly. The new instrument had much purer tone, she thought, than the old one. She decided that tone was most important and that she could conceal the cabinet behind a sofa. But as soon as she had made her peace with the radio, the interference began. A crackling sound like the noise of a burning powder fuse began to accompany the singing of the strings. Beyond the music, there was a rustling that reminded Irene unpleasantly of the sea, and as the quintet progressed, these noises were joined by many others. She tried all the dials and switches but nothing dimmed the interference, and she sat down, disappointed and bewildered, and tried to trace the flight of the melody. The elevator shaft in her building ran beside the living-room wall, and it was the noise of the elevator that gave her a clue to the character of the static. The rattling of the elevator cables and the opening and closing of the elevator doors were reproduced in her loudspeaker, and, realizing that the radio was sensitive to electrical currents of all sorts, she began to discern through the Mozart the ringing of telephone bells, the dialing of phones, and the lamentation of a vacuum cleaner. By listening more carefully, she was able to distinguish doorbells, elevator bells, electric razors, and Waring mixers, whose sounds had been picked up from the apartments that surrounded hers and transmitted through her loudspeaker. The powerful and ugly instrument, with its mistaken sensitivity to discord, was more than she could hope to master, so she turned the thing off and went into the nursery to see her children.

When Jim Westcott came home that night, he went to the radio confidently and worked the controls. He had the same sort of experience Irene had had. A man was speaking on the station Jim had chosen, and his voice swung instantly from the distance into a force so powerful that it shook the apartment. Jim turned the volume control and reduced the voice. Then, a minute or two later, the interference began. The ringing of telephones and doorbells set in, joined by the rasp of the elevator doors and the whir of cooking appliances. The character of the noise had changed since Irene had tried the radio earlier; the last of the electric razors was being unplugged, the vacuum cleaners had all been returned to their closets, and the static reflected that change in pace that overtakes the city after the sun goes down. He fiddled with the knobs but couldn't get rid of the noises, so he turned the radio off and told Irene that in the morning he'd call the people who had sold it to him and give them hell.

The following afternoon, when Irene returned to the apartment from a luncheon date, the maid told her that a man had come and fixed the radio. Irene went into the living room before she took off her hat or her furs and tried the instrument. From the loudspeaker came a recording of the 'Missouri Waltz.' It reminded her of the thin, scratchy music from an old-fashioned phonograph that she sometimes heard across the lake where she spent her summers. She waited until the waltz had finished, expecting an explanation of the recording, but there was none. The music was followed by silence, and then the plaintive and scratchy record was repeated. She turned the dial and got a satisfactory burst of Caucasian music —the thump of bare feet in the dust and the rattle of coin jewelry— but in the background she could hear the ringing of bells and a confusion of voices. Her children came home from school then, and she turned off the radio and went to the nursery.

When Jim came home that night, he was tired, and he took a bath and changed his clothes. Then he joined Irene in the living room. He had just turned on the radio when the maid announced dinner, so he left it on, and he and Irene went to the table.

Jim was too tired to make even a pretense of sociability, and there was nothing about the dinner to hold Irene's interest, so her attention wandered from the food to the deposits of silver polish on the candlesticks and from there to the music in the other room. She listened for a few moments to a Chopin prelude and then was surprised to hear a man's voice break in. 'For Christ's sake, Kathy,' he said, 'do you always have to play the piano when I get home?' The music stopped abruptly. 'It's the only chance I have,' a woman said. 'I'm at the office all day.' 'So am I,' the man said. He added something obscene about an upright piano, and slammed a door. The passionate and melancholy music began again.

'Did you hear that?' Irene asked.

'What?' Jim was eating his dessert.

'The radio. A man said something while the music was still going on—something dirty.'

'It's probably a play.'

'I don't think it *is* a play,' Irene said.

They left the table and took their coffee into the living room. Irene asked Jim to try another station. He turned the knob. 'Have you seen my garters?' a man asked. 'Button me up,' a woman said. 'Have you seen my garters?' the man said again. 'Just button me up and I'll find your garters,' the woman said. Jim shifted to another station. 'I wish you wouldn't leave apple cores in the ashtrays,' a man said. 'I hate the smell.'

'This is strange,' Jim said.

'Isn't it?' Irene said.

Jim turned the knob again. ' "On the coast of Coromandel where the early pumpkins blow," ' a woman with a pronounced English accent said, ' "in the middle of the woods lived the Yonghy-Bonghy-Bò. Two old chairs, and half a candle, one old jug without a handle . . . " '

'My God!' Irene cried. 'That's the Sweeneys' nurse.'

' "These were all his worldly goods," ' the British voice continued.

'Turn that thing off,' Irene said. 'Maybe they can hear *us*.' Jim switched the radio off. 'That was Miss Armstrong, the Sweeneys' nurse,' Irene said. 'She must be reading to the little girl. They live in 17-B. I've talked with Miss Armstrong in the Park. I know her voice very well. We must be getting other people's apartments.'

'That's impossible,' Jim said.

'Well, that was the Sweeneys' nurse,' Irene said hotly. 'I know her voice. I know it very well. I'm wondering if they can hear us.'

Jim turned the switch. First from a distance and then nearer, nearer, as if borne on the wind, came the pure accents of the Sweeneys' nurse again: ' "Lady Jingly! Lady Jingly!" ' she said, ' "Sitting where the pumpkins blow, will you come and be my wife,' said the Yonghy-Bonghy-Bò . . . " '

Jim went over to the radio and said 'Hello' loudly into the speaker.

' "I am tired of living singly," ' the nurse went on, ' "on this coast so wild and shingly, I'm a-weary of my life; if you'll come and be my wife, quite serene would be my life . . ." '

'I guess she can't hear us,' Irene said. 'Try something else.'

Jim turned to another station, and the living room was filled with the uproar of a cocktail party that had overshot its mark. Someone was playing the piano and singing the Whiffenpoof Song, and the voices that surrounded the piano were vehement and happy. 'Eat some more sandwiches,' a woman shrieked. There were screams of laughter and a dish of some sort crashed to the floor.

'Those must be the Hutchinsons, in 15-B,' Irene said. 'I knew they were giving a party this afternoon. I saw her in the liquor store. Isn't this too divine? Try something else. See if you can get those people in 18-C.'

The Westcotts overheard that evening a monologue on salmon fishing in Canada, a bridge game, running comments on home movies of what had apparently been a fortnight at Sea Island, and a bitter family quarrel about an overdraft at the bank. They turned off the radio at midnight and went to bed, weak with laughter. Sometime in the night, their son began to call for a glass of water and Irene got one and took it to his room. It was very early. All the lights in the neighborhood were extinguished, and from the boy's window she could see the empty street. She went into the living room and tried the radio. There was some faint coughing, a moan, and then a man spoke. 'Are you all right, darling?' he asked. 'Yes,' a woman said wearily. 'Yes, I'm all right, I guess,' and then she added with great feeling, 'But, you know, Charlie, I don't feel like myself any more. Sometimes there are about fifteen or twenty minutes in the week when I feel like myself. I don't like to go to another doctor, because the doctor's bills are so awful already, but I just don't feel like myself, Charlie. I just never feel like myself.' They were not young, Irene thought. She guessed from the timbre of their voices that they were middle-aged. The restrained melancholy of the dialogue and the draft from the bedroom window made her shiver, and she went back to bed.

The following morning, Irene cooked breakfast for the family— the maid didn't come up from her room in the basement until ten —braided her daughter's hair, and waited at the door until her children and her husband had been carried away in the elevator. Then she went into the living room and tried the radio. 'I don't want to go to school,' a child screamed. 'I hate school. I won't go to school. I hate school.' 'You will go to school,' an enraged woman said. 'We paid eight hundred dollars to get you into that school and you'll go if it kills you.' The next number on the dial produced the worn record of the 'Missouri Waltz.' Irene shifted the control and invaded the privacy of several breakfast tables. She overheard demonstrations of indigestion, carnal love, abysmal vanity, faith, and despair. Irene's life was nearly as simple and sheltered as it appeared to be, and the forthright and sometimes brutal language that came from the loudspeaker that morning astonished and troubled her. She continued to listen until her maid came in. Then she turned off the radio quickly, since this insight, she realized, was a furtive one.

Irene had a luncheon date with a friend that day, and she left her apartment at a little after twelve. There were a number of women in the elevator when it stopped at her floor. She stared at their handsome and impassive faces, their furs, and the cloth flowers in their hats. Which one of them had been to Sea Island, she wondered. Which one had overdrawn her bank account? The elevator stopped at the tenth floor and a woman with a pair of Skye terriers joined them. Her hair was rigged high on her head and she wore a mink cape. She was humming the 'Missouri Waltz.'

Irene had two Martinis at lunch, and she looked searchingly at her friend and wondered what her secrets were. They had intended to go shopping after lunch, but Irene excused herself and went home. She told the maid that she was not to be disturbed; then she went into the living room, closed the doors, and switched on the radio. She heard, in the course of the afternoon, the halting conversation of a woman entertaining her aunt, the hysterical conclusion of a luncheon party, and a hostess briefing her maid about some cocktail guests. 'Don't give the best Scotch to anyone who hasn't white hair,' the hostess said. 'See if you can get rid of that liver paste before you pass those hot things, and could you lend me five dollars? I want to tip the elevator man.'

As the afternoon waned, the conversations increased in intensity. From where Irene sat, she could see the open sky above Central Park. There were hundreds of clouds in the sky, as though the south wind had broken the winter into pieces and were blowing it north, and on her radio she could hear the arrival of cocktail guests and the return of children and businessmen from their schools and offices. 'I found a good-sized diamond on the bathroom floor this morning,' a woman said. 'It must have fallen out of that bracelet Mrs. Dunston was wearing last night.' 'We'll sell it,' a man said. 'Take it down to the jeweller on Madison Avenue and sell it. Mrs. Dunston won't know the difference, and we could use a couple of hundred bucks . . .' ' "Oranges and lemons, say the bells of St. Clement's," ' the Sweeneys' nurse sang. ' "Half-pence and farthings, say the bells of St. Martin's. When will you pay me? say the

bells at old Bailey . . ." ' 'It's not a hat,' a woman cried, and at her
back roared a cocktail party. 'It's not a hat, it's a love affair. That's
what Walter Florell said. He said it's not a hat, it's a love affair,' and
then, in a lower voice, the same woman added, 'Talk to somebody,
for Christ's sake, honey, talk to somebody. If she catches you standing here not talking to anybody, she'll take us off her invitation list,
and I love these parties.'

The Westcotts were going out for dinner that night, and when
Jim came home, Irene was dressing. She seemed sad and vague, and
he brought her a drink. They were dining with friends in the neighborhood, and they walked to where they were going. The sky was
broad and filled with light. It was one of those splendid spring evenings that excite memory and desire, and the air that touched their
hands and faces felt very soft. A Salvation Army band was on the
corner playing 'Jesus Is Sweeter.' Irene drew on her husband's arm
and held him there for a minute, to hear the music. 'They're really
such nice people, aren't they?' she said. 'They have such nice faces.
Actually, they're so much nicer than a lot of the people we know.'
She took a bill from her purse and walked over and dropped it into
the tambourine. There was in her face, when she returned to her
husband, a look of radiant melancholy that he was not familiar
with. And her conduct at the dinner party that night seemed strange
to him, too. She interrupted her hostess rudely and stared at the
people across the table from her with an intensity for which she
would have punished her children.

It was still mild when they walked home from the party, and
Irene looked up at the spring stars. ' "How far that little candle
throws its beams," ' she exclaimed. ' "So shines a good deed in a
naughty world." ' She waited that night until Jim had fallen asleep,
and then went into the living room and turned on the radio.

Jim came home at about six the next night. Emma, the maid, let
him in, and he had taken off his hat and was taking off his coat
when Irene ran into the hall. Her face was shining with tears and
her hair was disordered. 'Go up to 16-C, Jim!' she screamed. 'Don't
take off your coat. Go up to 16-C. Mr. Osborn's beating his wife.
They've been quarrelling since four o'clock, and now he's hitting
her. Go up there and stop him.'

From the radio in the living room, Jim heard screams, obscenitics, and thuds. 'You know you don't have to listen to this sort of thing,' he said. He strode into the living room and turned the switch. 'It's indecent,' he said. 'It's like looking in windows. You know you don't have to listen to this sort of thing. You can turn it off.'

'Oh, it's so horrible, it's so dreadful,' Irene was sobbing. 'I've been listening all day, and it's so depressing.'

'Well, if it's so depressing, why do you listen to it? I bought this damned radio to give you some pleasure,' he said. 'I paid a great deal of money for it. I thought it might make you happy. I wanted to make you happy.'

'Don't, don't, don't, don't quarrel with me,' she moaned, and laid her head on his shoulder. 'All the others have been quarrelling all day. Everybody's been quarrelling. They're all worried about money. Mrs. Hutchinson's mother is dying of cancer in Florida and they don't have enough money to send her to the Mayo Clinic. At least, Mr. Hutchinson says they don't have enough money. And some woman in this building is having an affair with the superintendent —with that hideous superintendent. It's too disgusting. And Mrs. Melville has heart trouble and Mr. Hendricks is going to lose his job in April and Mrs. Hendricks is horrid about the whole thing and that girl who plays the 'Missouri Waltz' is a whore, a common whore, and the elevator man has tuberculosis and Mr. Osborn has been beating Mrs. Osborn.' She wailed, she trembled with grief and checked the stream of tears down her face with the heel of her palm.

'Well, why do you have to listen?' Jim asked again. 'Why do you have to listen to this stuff if it makes you so miserable?'

'Oh, don't don't don't,' she cried. 'Life is too terrible, too sordid and awful. But we've never been like that, have we, darling? Have we? I mean we've always been good and decent and loving to one another, haven't we? And we have two children, two beautiful children. Our lives aren't sordid, are they, darling? Are they?' She flung her arms around his neck and drew his face down to hers. 'We're happy, aren't we, darling? We are happy, aren't we?'

'Of course we're happy,' he said tiredly. He began to surrender his resentment. 'Of course we're happy. I'll have that damned radio fixed or taken away tomorrow.' He stroked her soft hair. 'My poor girl,' he said.

'You love me, don't you?' she asked. 'And we're not hypercritical or worried about money or dishonest, are we?'

'No, darling,' he said.

A man came in the morning and fixed the radio. Irene turned it on cautiously and was happy to hear a California-wine commercial and a recording of Beethoven's Ninth Symphony, including Schiller's 'Ode to Joy.' She kept the radio on all day and nothing untoward came from the speaker.

A Spanish suite was being played when Jim came home. 'Is everything all right?' he asked. His face was pale, she thought. They had some cocktails and went in to dinner to the 'Anvil Chorus' from 'Il Trovatore.' This was followed by Debussy's 'La Mer.'

'I paid the bill for the radio today,' Jim said. 'It cost four hundred dollars. I hope you'll get some enjoyment out of it.'

'Oh, I'm sure I will,' Irene said.

'Four hundred dollars is a good deal more than I can afford,' he went on. 'I wanted to get something that you'd enjoy. It's the last extravagance we'll be able to indulge in this year. I see that you haven't paid your clothing bills yet. I saw them on your dressing table.' He looked directly at her. 'Why did you tell me you'd paid them? Why did you lie to me?'

'I just didn't want you to worry, Jim,' she said. She drank some water. 'I'll be able to pay my bills out of this month's allowance. There were the slipcovers last month, and that party.'

'You've got to learn to handle the money I give you a little more intelligently, Irene,' he said. 'You've got to understand that we won't have as much money this year as we had last. I had a very sobering talk with Mitchell today. No one is buying anything. We're spending all our time promoting new issues, and you know how long that takes. I'm not getting any younger, you know. I'm thirty-seven. My hair will be gray next year. I haven't done as well as I'd hoped to do. And I don't suppose things will get any better.'

'Yes, dear,' she said.

'We've got to start cutting down,' Jim said. 'We've got to think of the children. To be perfectly frank with you, I worry about money a great deal. I'm not at all sure of the future. No one is. If anything should happen to me, there's the insurance, but that wouldn't go very far today. I've worked awfully hard to give you and the children a comfortable life,' he said bitterly. 'I don't like to see all of my energies, all of my youth, wasted in fur coats and radios and slipcovers and—'

'Please, Jim,' she said. 'Please. They'll hear us.'

'*Who'll* hear us? Emma can't hear us.'

'The radio.'

'Oh, I'm sick!' he shouted. 'I'm sick to death of your apprehensiveness. The radio can't hear us. Nobody can hear us. And what if they can hear us? Who cares?'

Irene got up from the table and went into the living room. Jim went to the door and shouted at her from there. 'Why are you so Christly all of a sudden? What's turned you overnight into a convent girl? You stole your mother's jewelry before they probated her will. You never gave your sister a cent of that money that was intended for her—not even when she needed it. You made Grace Howland's life miserable, and where was all your piety and your virtue when you went to that abortionist? I'll never forget how cool you were. You packed your bag and went off to have that child murdered as if you were going to Nassau. If you'd had any reasons, if you'd had any good reasons——'

Irene stood for a minute before the hideous cabinet, disgraced and sickened, but she held her hand on the switch before she extinguished the music and the voices, hoping that the instrument might speak to her kindly, that she might hear the Sweeneys' nurse. Jim continued to shout at her from the door. The voice on the radio was suave and noncommittal. 'An early-morning railroad disaster in Tokyo,' the loudspeaker said, 'killed twenty-nine people. A fire in a Catholic hospital near Buffalo for the care of blind children was extinguished early this morning by nuns. The temperature is forty-seven. The humidity is eighty-nine.'

J. F. POWERS

The Forks

- •- -

HAT SUMMER WHEN Father Eudex got back from saying Mass at the orphanage in the morning, he would park Monsignor's car, which was long and black and new like a politician's, and sit down in the cool of the porch to read his office. If Monsignor was not already standing in the door, he would immediately appear there, seeing that his car had safely returned, and inquire:

"Did you have any trouble with her?"

Father Eudex knew too well the question meant, Did you mistreat my car?

"No trouble, Monsignor."

"Good," Monsignor said, with imperfect faith in his curate, who was not a car owner. For a moment Monsignor stood framed in the screen door, fumbling his watch fob as for a full-length portrait, and then he was suddenly not there.

"Monsignor," Father Eudex said, rising nervously, "I've got a chance to pick up a car."

At the door Monsignor slid into his frame again. His face expressed what was for him intense interest.

"Yes? Go on."

"I don't want to have to use yours every morning."

"It's all right."

"And there are other times." Father Eudex decided not to be maudlin and mention sick calls, nor be entirely honest and admit

From Prince of Darkness and Other Stories by J. F. Powers. Copyright 1947 by J. F. Powers. Reprinted by permission of Doubleday & Company, Inc.

he was tired of busses and bumming rides from parishioners. "And now I've got a chance to get one—cheap."

Monsignor, smiling, came alert at *cheap*.

"New?"

"No, I wouldn't say it's new."

Monsignor was openly suspicious now. "What kind?"

"It's a Ford."

"And not new?"

"Not new, Monsignor—but in good condition. It was owned by a retired farmer and had good care."

Monsignor sniffed. He *knew* cars. "V-Eight, Father?"

"No," Father Eudex confessed. "It's a Model A."

Monsignor chuckled as though this were indeed the damnedest thing he had ever heard.

"But in very good condition, Monsignor."

"You said that."

"Yes. And I could take it apart if anything went wrong. My uncle had one."

"No doubt." Monsignor uttered a laugh at Father Eudex's rural origins. Then he delivered the final word, long delayed out of amusement. "It wouldn't be prudent, Father. After all, this isn't a country parish. You know the class of people we get here."

Monsignor put on his Panama hat. Then, apparently mistaking the obstinacy in his curate's face for plain ignorance, he shed a little more light. "People watch a priest, Father. *Damnant quod non intelligunt.* It would never do. You'll have to watch your tendencies."

Monsignor's eyes tripped and fell hard on the morning paper lying on the swing where he had finished it.

"Another flattering piece about that crazy fellow. . . . There's a man who might have gone places if it weren't for his mouth! A bishop doesn't have to get mixed up in all that stuff!"

Monsignor, as Father Eudex knew, meant unions, strikes, race riots—all that stuff.

"A parishioner was saying to me only yesterday it's getting so you can't tell the Catholics from the Communists, with the priests as bad as any. Yes, and this fellow is the worst. He reminds me of that bishop a few years back—at least he called himself a bishop, a Protestant—that was advocating companionate marriages. It's not that bad, maybe, but if you listened to some of them you'd think that Catholicity and capitalism were incompatible!"

"The Holy Father——"

"The Holy Father's in Europe, Father. Mr. Memmers lives in this parish. I'm his priest. What can I tell him?"

"Is it Mr. Memmers of the First National, Monsignor?"

"It is, Father. And there's damned little cheer I can give a man like Memmers. Catholics, priests, and laity alike—yes, and princes of the Church, all talking atheistic communism!"

This was the substance of their conversation, always, the deadly routine in which Father Eudex played straight man. Each time it happened he seemed to participate, and though he should have known better he justified his participation by hoping that it would not happen again, or in quite the same way. But it did, it always did, the same way, and Monsignor, for all his alarums, had nothing to say really and meant one thing only, the thing he never said— that he dearly wanted to be, and was not, a bishop.

Father Eudex could imagine just what kind of bishop Monsignor would be. His reign would be a wise one, excessively so. His mind was made up on everything, excessively so. He would know how to avoid the snares set in the path of the just man, avoid them, too, in good taste and good conscience. He would not be trapped as so many good shepherds before him had been trapped, poor souls— caught in fair-seeming dilemmas of justice that were best left alone, like the first apple. It grieved him, he said, to think of those great hearts broken in silence and solitude. It was the worst kind of exile, alas! But just give him the chance and he would know what to do, what to say, and, more important, what not to do, not to say—neither yea nor nay for him. He had not gone to Rome for nothing. For him the dark forest of decisions would not exist; for him, thanks to hours spent in prayer and meditation, the forest would vanish as dry grass before fire, his fire. He knew the mask of evil already—birth control, indecent movies, salacious books—and would call these things by their right names and dare to deal with them for what they were, these new occasions for the old sins of the cities of the plains.

But in the meantime—oh, to have a particle of the faith that

God had in humanity! Dear, trusting God forever trying them
beyond their feeble powers, ordering terrible tests, fatal trials by
nonsense (the crazy bishop). And keeping Monsignor steadily
warming up on the side lines, ready to rush in, primed for the day
that would perhaps never dawn.

At one time, so the talk went, there had been reason to think
that Monsignor was headed for a bishopric. Now it was too late;
Monsignor's intercessors were all dead; the cupboard was bare; he
knew it at heart, and it galled him to see another man, this *crazy*
man, given the opportunity, and making such a mess of it.

Father Eudex searched for and found a little salt for Monsignor's wound. "The word's going around he'll be the next archbishop," he said.

"I won't believe it," Monsignor countered hoarsely. He glanced
at the newspaper on the swing and renewed his horror. "If that
fellow's right, Father, I'm"—his voice cracked at the idea—"*wrong!*"

Father Eudex waited until Monsignor had started down the
steps to the car before he said, "It could be."

"I'll be back for lunch, Father. I'm taking her for a little spin."

Monsignor stopped in admiration a few feet from the car—her.
He was as helpless before her beauty as a boy with a birthday
bicycle. He could not leave her alone. He had her out every morning and afternoon and evening. He was indiscriminate about picking people up for a ride in her. He kept her on a special diet—
only the best of gas and oil and grease, with daily rubdowns. He
would run her only on the smoothest roads and at so many miles
an hour. That was to have stopped at the first five hundred, but
only now, nearing the thousand mark, was he able to bring himself
to increase her speed, and it seemed to hurt him more than it did
her.

Now he was walking around behind her to inspect the tires.
Apparently O.K. He gave the left rear fender an amorous chuck
and eased into the front seat. Then they drove off, the car and he,
to see the world, to explore each other further on the honeymoon.

Father Eudex watched the car slide into the traffic, and waited,
on edge. The corner cop, fulfilling Father Eudex's fears, blew his
whistle and waved his arms up in all four directions, bringing
traffic to a standstill. Monsignor pulled expertly out of line and

drove down Clover Boulevard in a one-car parade; all others stalled respectfully. The cop, as Monsignor passed, tipped his cap, showing a bald head. Monsignor, in the circumstances, could not acknowledge him, though he knew the man well—a parishioner. He was occupied with keeping his countenance kindly, grim, and exalted, that the cop's faith remain whole, for it was evidently inconceivable to him that Monsignor should ever venture abroad unless to bear the Holy Viaticum, always racing with death.

Father Eudex, eyes baleful but following the progress of the big black car, saw a hand dart out of the driver's window in a wave. Monsignor would combine a lot of business with pleasure that morning, creating what he called "good will for the Church"—all morning in the driver's seat toasting passers-by with a wave that was better than a blessing. How he loved waving to people!

Father Eudex overcame his inclination to sit and stew about things by going down the steps to meet the mailman. He got the usual handful for the Monsignor—advertisements and amazing offers, the unfailing crop of chaff from dealers in church goods, organs, collection schemes, insurance, and sacramental wines. There were two envelopes addressed to Father Eudex, one a mimeographed plea from a missionary society which he might or might not acknowledge with a contribution, depending upon what he thought of the cause—if it was really lost enough to justify a levy on his poverty—and the other a check for a hundred dollars.

The check came in an eggshell envelope with no explanation except a tiny card, "Compliments of the Rival Tractor Company," but even that was needless. All over town clergymen had known for days that the checks were on the way again. Some, rejoicing, could hardly wait. Father Eudex, however, was one of those who could.

With the passing of hard times and the coming of the fruitful war years, the Rival Company, which was a great one for public relations, had found the best solution to the excess-profits problem to be giving. Ministers and even rabbis shared in the annual jack pot, but Rival employees were largely Catholic and it was the checks to the priests that paid off. Again, some thought it was a wonderful idea, and others thought that Rival, plagued by strikes and justly so, had put their alms to work.

There was another eggshell envelope, Father Eudex saw, among the letters for Monsignor, and knew his check would be for two hundred, the premium for pastors.

Father Eudex left Monsignor's mail on the porch table by his cigars. His own he stuck in his back pocket, wanting to forget it, and went down the steps into the yard. Walking back and forth on the shady side of the rectory where the lilies of the valley grew and reading his office, he gradually drifted into the back yard, lured by a noise. He came upon Whalen, the janitor, pounding pegs into the ground.

Father Eudex closed the breviary on a finger. "What's it all about, Joe?"

Joe Whalen snatched a piece of paper from his shirt and handed it to Father Eudex. "He gave it to me this morning."

He—it was the word for Monsignor among them. A docile pronoun only, and yet when it meant the Monsignor it said, and concealed, nameless things.

The paper was a plan for a garden drawn up by the Monsignor in his fine hand. It called for a huge fleur-de-lis bounded by smaller crosses—and these Maltese—a fountain, a sundial, and a cloister walk running from the rectory to the garage. Later there would be birdhouses and a ten-foot wall of thick gray stones, acting as a moat against the eyes of the world. The whole scheme struck Father Eudex as expensive and, in this country, Presbyterian.

When Monsignor drew the plan, however, he must have been in his medieval mood. A spouting whale jostled with Neptune in the choppy waters of the fountain. North was indicated in the legend by a winged cherub huffing and puffing.

Father Eudex held the plan up against the sun to see the watermark. The stationery was new to him, heavy, simulated parchment, with the Church of the Holy Redeemer and Monsignor's name embossed, three initials, W. F. X., William Francis Xavier. With all those initials the man could pass for a radio station, a chancery wit had observed, or if his last name had not been Sweeney, Father Eudex added now, for high Anglican.

Father Eudex returned the plan to Whalen, feeling sorry for him and to an extent guilty before him—if only because he was a priest like Monsignor (now turned architect) whose dream of a monastery garden included the overworked janitor under the head of "labor."

Father Eudex asked Whalen to bring another shovel. Together, almost without words, they worked all morning spading up crosses, leaving the big fleur-de-lis to the last. Father Eudex removed his coat first, then his collar, and finally was down to his undershirt.

Toward noon Monsignor rolled into the driveway.

He stayed in the car, getting red in the face, recovering from the pleasure of seeing so much accomplished as he slowly recognized his curate in Whalen's helper. In a still, appalled voice he called across the lawn, "Father," and waited as for a beast that might or might not have sense enough to come.

Father Eudex dropped his shovel and went over to the car, shirtless.

Monsignor waited a moment before he spoke, as though annoyed by the everlasting necessity, where this person was concerned, to explain. "Father," he said quietly at last, "I wouldn't do any more of that—if I were you. Rather, in any event, I wouldn't."

"All right, Monsignor."

"To say the least, it's not prudent. If necessary"—he paused as Whalen came over to dig a cross within earshot—"I'll explain later. It's time for lunch now."

The car, black, beautiful, fierce with chromium, was quiet as Monsignor dismounted, knowing her master. Monsignor went around to the rear, felt a tire, and probed a nasty cinder in the tread.

"Look at that," he said, removing the cinder.

Father Eudex thought he saw the car lift a hoof, gaze around, and thank Monsignor with her headlights.

Monsignor proceeded at a precise pace to the back door of the rectory. There he held the screen open momentarily, as if remembering something or reluctant to enter before himself—such was his humility—but then called to Whalen with an intimacy that could never exist between them.

"Better knock off now, Joe."

Whalen turned in on himself. "*Joe*—is it!"

Father Eudex removed his clothes from the grass. His hands were all blisters, but in them he found a little absolution. He apologized to Joe for having to take the afternoon off. "I can't make it, Joe. Something turned up."

"Sure, Father."

Father Eudex could hear Joe telling his wife about it that night —yeah, the young one got in wrong with the old one again. Yeah, the old one, he don't believe in it, work, for them.

Father Eudex paused in the kitchen to remember he knew not what. It was in his head, asking to be let in, but he did not place it until he heard Monsignor in the next room complaining about the salad to the housekeeper. It was the voice of dear, dead Aunt Hazel, coming from the summer he was ten. He translated the past into the present: I can't come out and play this afternoon, Joe, on account of my monsignor won't let me.

In the dining room Father Eudex sat down at the table and said grace. He helped himself to a chop, creamed new potatoes, pickled beets, jelly, and bread. He liked jelly. Monsignor passed the butter.

"That's supposed to be a tutti-frutti salad," Monsignor said, grimacing at his. "But she used green olives."

Father Eudex said nothing.

"I said she used green olives."

"I like green olives all right."

"*I* like green olives, but *not* in tutti-frutti salad."

Father Eudex replied by eating a green olive, but he knew it could not end there.

"Father," Monsignor said in a new tone. "How would you like to go away and study for a year?"

"Don't think I'd care for it, Monsignor. I'm not the type."

"You're no canonist, you mean?"

"That's one thing."

"Yes. Well, there are other things it might not hurt you to know. To be quite frank with you, Father, I think you need broadening."

"I guess so," Father Eudex said thickly.

"And still, with your tendencies . . . and with the universities honeycombed with Communists. No, that would never do. I think I meant seasoning, not broadening."

"Oh."

"No offense?"

"No offense."

Who would have thought a little thing like an olive could lead to all this, Father Eudex mused—who but himself, that is, for his association with Monsignor had shown him that anything could lead to everything. Monsignor was a master at making points. Nothing had changed since the day Father Eudex walked into the rectory saying he was the new assistant. Monsignor had evaded Father Eudex's hand in greeting, and a few days later, after he began to get the range, he delivered a lecture on the whole subject of handshaking. It was Middle West to shake hands, or South West, or West in any case, and it was not done where he came from, and—why had he ever come from where he came from? Not to be reduced to shaking hands, you could bet! Handshaking was worse than foot washing and unlike that pious practice there was nothing to support it. And from handshaking Monsignor might go into a general discussion of Father Eudex's failings. He used the open forum method, but he was the only speaker and there was never time enough for questions from the audience. Monsignor seized his examples at random from life. He saw Father Eudex coming out of his bedroom in pajama bottoms only and so told him about the dressing gown, its purpose, something of its history. He advised Father Eudex to barber his armpits, for it was being done all over now. He let Father Eudex see his bottle of cologne, "Steeple," special for clergymen, and said he should not be afraid of it. He suggested that Father Eudex shave his face oftener, too. He loaned him his Rogers Peet catalogue, which had sketches of clerical blades togged out in the latest, and prayed that he would stop going around looking like a rabbinical student.

He found Father Eudex reading *The Catholic Worker* one day and had not trusted him since. Father Eudex's conception of the priesthood was evangelical in the worse sense, barbaric, gross, foreign to the mind of the Church, which was one of two terms he used as sticks to beat him with. The other was taste. The air of the rectory was often heavy with The Mind of the Church and Taste.

Another thing. Father Eudex could not conduct a civil conversation. Monsignor doubted that Father Eudex could even think to himself with anything like agreement. Certainly any discussion with Father Eudex ended inevitably in argument or sighing. Sighing! Why didn't people talk up if they had anything to say? No, they'd rather sigh! Father, don't ever, ever sigh at me again!

Finally, Monsignor did not like Father Eudex's table manners. This came to a head one night when Monsignor, seeing his curate's plate empty and all the silverware at his place unused except for a single knife, fork, and spoon, exploded altogether, saying it had been on his mind for weeks, and then descending into the vernacular he declared that Father Eudex did not know the forks—now perhaps he could understand that! Meals, unless Monsignor had guests or other things to struggle with, were always occasions of instruction for Father Eudex, and sometimes of chastisement.

And now he knew the worst—if Monsignor was thinking of recommending him for a year of study, in a Sulpician seminary probably, to learn the forks. So this was what it meant to be a priest. *Come, follow me. Going forth, teach ye all nations. Heal the sick, raise the dead, cleanse the lepers, cast out devils.* Teach the class of people we get here? Teach Mr. Memmers? Teach Communists? Teach Monsignors? And where were the poor? The lepers of old? The lepers were in their colonies with nuns to nurse them. The poor were in their holes and would not come out. Mr. Memmers was in his bank, without cheer. The Communists were in their universities, awaiting a sign. And he was at table with Monsignor, and it was enough for the disciple to be as his master, but the housekeeper had used green olives.

Monsignor inquired, "Did you get your check today?"

Father Eudex, looking up, considered. "I got *a* check," he said.

"From the Rival people, I mean?"

"Yes."

"Good. Well, I think you might apply it on the car you're wanting. A decent car. That's a worthy cause." Monsignor noticed that he was not taking it well. "Not that I mean to dictate what you shall do with your little windfall, Father. It's just that I don't like to see you mortifying yourself with a Model A—and disgracing the Church."

"Yes," Father Eudex said, suffering.

"Yes. I dare say you don't see the danger, just as you didn't a while ago when I found you making a spectacle of yourself with

Whalen. You just don't see the danger because you just don't think. Not to dwell on it, but I seem to remember some overshoes."

The overshoes! Monsignor referred to them as to the Fall. Last winter Father Eudex had given his overshoes to a freezing picket. It had got back to Monsignor and—good Lord, a man could have his sympathies, but he had no right clad in the cloth to endanger the prestige of the Church by siding in these wretched squabbles. Monsignor said he hated to think of all the evil done by people doing good! Had Father Eudex ever heard of the Albigensian heresy, or didn't the seminary teach that any more?

Father Eudex declined dessert. It was strawberry mousse.

"Delicious," Monsignor said. "I think I'll let her stay."

At that moment Father Eudex decided that he had nothing to lose. He placed his knife next to his fork on the plate, adjusted them this way and that until they seemed to work a combination in his mind, to spring a lock which in turn enabled him to speak out.

"Monsignor," he said. "I think I ought to tell you I don't intend to make use of that money. In fact—to show you how my mind works—I have even considered endorsing the check to the striker's relief fund."

"So," Monsignor said calmly—years in the confessional had prepared him for anything.

"I'll admit I don't know whether I can in justice. And even if I could I don't know that I would. I don't know why . . . I guess hush money, no matter what you do with it, is lousy."

Monsignor regarded him with piercing baby blue eyes. "You'd find it pretty hard to prove, Father, that *any* money *in se* is . . . what you say it is. I would quarrel further with the definition 'hush money.' It seems to me nothing if not rash that you would presume to impugn the motive of the Rival company in sending out these checks. You would seem to challenge the whole concept of good works—not that I am ignorant of the misuses to which money can be put." Monsignor, changing tack, tucked it all into a sigh. "Perhaps I'm just a simple soul, and it's enough for me to know personally some of the people in the Rival company and to know them good people. Many of them Catholic . . ." A throb had crept into Monsignor's voice. He shut it off.

"I don't mean anything that subtle, Monsignor," Father Eudex said. "I'm just telling you, as my pastor, what I'm going to do with the check. Or what I'm not going to do with it. I don't know what I'm going to do with it. Maybe send it back."

Monsignor rose from the table, slightly smiling. "Very well, Father. But there's always the poor."

Monsignor took leave of Father Eudex with a laugh. Father Eudex felt it was supposed to fool him into thinking that nothing he had said would be used against him. It showed, rather, that Monsignor was not winded, that he had broken wild curates before, plenty of them, and that he would ride again.

Father Eudex sought the shade of the porch. He tried to read his office, but was drowsy. He got up for a glass of water. The saints in Ireland used to stand up to their necks in cold water, but not for drowsiness. When he came back to the porch a woman was ringing the doorbell. She looked like a customer for rosary beads.

"Hello," he said.

"I'm Mrs. Klein, Father, and I was wondering if you could help me out."

Father Eudex straightened a porch chair for her. "Please sit down."

"It's a German name, Father. Klein was German descent," she said, and added with a silly grin, "It ain't what you think, Father."

"I beg your pardon."

"Klein. Some think it's a Jew name. But they stole it from Klein."

Father Eudex decided to come back to that later. "You were wondering if I could help you?"

"Yes, Father. It's personal."

"Is it matter for confession?"

"Oh no, Father." He had made her blush.

"Then go ahead."

Mrs. Klein peered into the honeysuckle vines on either side of the porch for alien ears.

"No one can hear you, Mrs. Klein."

"Father—I'm just a poor widow," she said, and continued as

though Father Eudex had just slandered the man. "Klein was awful good to me, Father."

"I'm sure he was."

"So good . . . and he went and left me all he had." She had begun to cry a little.

Father Eudex nodded gently. She was after something, probably not money, always the best bet—either that or a drunk in the family—but this one was not Irish. Perhaps just sympathy.

"I come to get your advice, Father. Klein always said, 'If you got a problem, Freda, see the priest.' "

"Do you need money?"

"I got more than I can use from the bakery."

"You have a bakery?"

Mrs. Klein nodded down the street. "That's my bakery. It was Klein's. The Purity."

"I go by there all the time," Father Eudex said, abandoning himself to her. He must stop trying to shape the conversation and let her work it out.

"Will you give me your advice, Father?" He felt that she sensed his indifference and interpreted it as his way of rejecting her. She either had no idea how little sense she made or else supreme faith in him, as a priest, to see into her heart.

"Just what is it you're after, Mrs. Klein?"

"He left me all he had, Father, but it's just laying in the bank."

"And you want me to tell you what to do with it?"

"Yes, Father."

Father Eudex thought this might be interesting, certainly a change. He went back in his mind to the seminary and the class in which they had considered the problem of inheritances. Do we have any unfulfilled obligations? Are we sure? . . . Are there any impedimenta? . . .

"Do you have any dependents, Mrs. Klein—any children?"

"One boy, Father. I got him running the bakery. I pay him good—too much, Father."

"Is 'too much' a living wage?"

"Yes, Father. He ain't got a family."

"A living wage is not too much," Father Eudex handed down, sailing into the encyclical style without knowing it.

Mrs. Klein was smiling over having done something good without knowing precisely what it was.

"How old is your son?"

"He's thirty-six, Father."

"Not married?"

"No, Father, but he's got him a girl." She giggled, and Father Eudex, embarrassed, retied his shoe.

"But you don't care to make a will and leave this money to your son in the usual way?"

"I guess I'll have to . . . if I die." Mrs. Klein was suddenly crushed and haunted, but whether by death or charity, Father Eudex did not know.

"You don't have to, Mrs. Klein. There are many worthy causes. And the worthiest is the cause of the poor. My advice to you, if I understand your problem, is to give what you have to someone who needs it."

Mrs. Klein just stared at him.

"You could even leave it to the archdiocese," he said, completing the sentence to himself: but I don't recommend it in your case . . . with your tendencies. You look like an Indian giver to me.

But Mrs. Klein had got enough. "Huh!" she said, rising. "Well! You *are* a funny one!"

And then Father Eudex realized that she had come to him for a broker's tip. It was in the eyes. The hat. The dress. The shoes. "If you'd like to speak to the pastor," he said, "come back in the evening."

"You're a nice young man," Mrs. Klein said, rather bitter now and bent on getting away from him. "But I got to say this—you ain't much of a priest. And Klein said if I got a problem, see the priest—huh! You ain't much of a priest! What time's your boss come in?"

"In the evening," Father Eudex said. "Come any time in the evening."

Mrs. Klein was already down the steps and making for the street.

"You might try Mr. Memmers at the First National," Father Eudex called, actually trying to help her, but she must have thought it was just some more of his nonsense and did not reply.

After Mrs. Klein had disappeared Father Eudex went to his room. In the hallway upstairs Monsignor's voice, coming from the depths of the clerical nap, halted him.

"Who was it?"

"A woman," Father Eudex said. "A woman seeking good counsel."

He waited a moment to be questioned, but Monsignor was not awake enough to see anything wrong with that, and there came only a sigh and a shifting of weight that told Father Eudex he was simply turning over in bed.

Father Eudex walked into the bathroom. He took the Rival check from his pocket. He tore it into little squares. He let them flutter into the toilet. He pulled the chain—hard.

He went to his room and stood looking out the window at nothing. He could hear the others already giving an account of their stewardship, but could not judge them. I bought baseball uniforms for the school. I bought the nuns a new washing machine. I purchased a Mass kit for a Chinese missionary. I bought a set of matched irons. Mine helped pay for keeping my mother in a rest home upstate. I gave mine to the poor.

And you, Father?

JOHN R. MARVIN

The Wrath-Bearing Tree

NORTH OF CHEYENNE the country was broken and eroded in long arroyos and flat mesas, and there were few settlers in these badlands, though there were beginnings, small ranches, homesteads and farms on the greener upglades. The silver rush had passed, though the mines still held a trace of lucre, and there were a few small strikes, but the settlers who remained were migratory, waiting to go somewhere better, except for a handful of ranchers and those for whom (lust, poverty, and terror having run their course) this was somewhere near the end of the string. The day was keen, cold, with a threat of snow. A wind like a diminutive cyclone whirled away into the distance, a diminishing skirl over the light dust of snow, soon vitiated by the broken contours of the land. Where the two riders had just topped one of the mesquite knolls there was a momentary view of the uneroded uplands beyond, which led finally to the steep wall of the mountains, now only a blue surge on the horizon, not real in distance or time over the empty honeycombed flats. The first rider, Ira Fawley, twisted in his saddle and drank liquor from a leather canister; the second rider, Lloyd Logan, who was older and greying, looked down at his jug, but did not touch it. Ira hung the jug on the horn, satisfied, since in winter he habitually drank in contempt of the cold. His straight mane of yellow hair ruffled in the breeze, and his muskrat cap was strung

Reprinted by permission from *The Hudson Review*, Vol. X, No. 4 (Winter 1957–1958). Copyright 1958 by The Hudson Review, Inc.

over one square shoulder, decorative and mocking. He was a very powerful huge man with blue eyes that were austere and impersonal, an expression without malice or kindness. He always rode ahead, tense and erect, and he never rode at less than a canter. Twisting the reins savagely, he sent the tired gelding plunging down the little ravines and straining again up the sandy knolls. He looked back where Logan was following hard with his thin haughty face set in a grimace of fatigue, and he noticed that the sun was getting low. He leaned forward spurring the horse and listened to the silence regroup behind him on the slopes and bottoms. The silence did not bother him since he could crack it with an effort of his will. He lived a life of constant check and balance. The silence now was like silt from the dead sun through which he rode coldly, with dispassion.

As he rode he noticed how the sundown left the gulches ahead stained in shadows that lay in sleepy eddies of cold beneath the iridescent reaches of the broken jagged-edged flats. He was a keen observer, self-taught; his mind habitually worked at a level above his knowledge of words because he never quite forgot the faces, the mouths that said them. He had been thrown in with all kinds of men, and he had always listened, studied and remembered. He was at ease anywhere, at peace nowhere. All he had ever liked doing in life was riding alone through the sunlight or rain, unattached and unwatched. He was himself then, with no principles or interests beyond his own pride in being.

The horse staggered up another ridge beneath him, splaylegged, and he rode on through another wall of silence wrenching it aside with the rapine of his will. Logan's horse came crashing down beside him, and he turned with a wry glance at the man, then nodded toward the horizon.

"See it old man. Nothin' like Kaintucky. One mistake up there, and hit may be you'll come washin' down in the Spring on a headwater end over end like a log."

For a minute Logan only rode beside him, his thin eaglet's face tense and haggard, looking ahead to the surge of icy blue that lay beyond the dark outline of the hills and up, where the mountains rose supine and flawless in deep snow.

"I've had my fling," Logan said suddenly. He spoke with a

blatant heatless vehemence. "I'm through. I never intended followin' Clay thus far. Go ahead. Get him! . . . He stole your gear. There aint no faith left among mankind."

Ira reined up facing Logan: his eyes were lit by an amused quietness. Finally he bent, lifted the jug again and drank; his eyes motionless, he rewound it to the horn.

"More faith than aught of anything else," he said softly, as if Logan was not really there, fencing or pretending in the sunlight. "I'm goin' on. Not because I care about the money, nor him either. Lloyd, I think I just want to hit trail."

Logan looked away toward the mountains. Part of the craft and knowing had fled from his lean face. He looked round momentarily as if searching for comfort, and found only the abysses of shadows crouched round the sunny headlands.

"I'm headin' back before dark," he said warily. "A man of my years loses quickness." He rubbed his thighs. "A head aint any good when you've lost quickness."

Ira studied Logan's face, observant of the touch of fear there, mingled with guile, feeling the cold sting his own eyes. Then he laughed with slow joyless irony.

"What've you to fear?" he asked. "What's Clay got to lose either?"

Logan answered him by the chillness of his look, and he dismounted suddenly in the frosted turf by the knoll; then he unhooked his jug and twirled it up to his mouth. He drank casually but not deeply, wiped his trim mouth with the back of his hand and hung the jug back. His hands were steady, but a thin sweat glistened on his temples.

"How's a man to know?" he said—the bright, fierce affability. "Every man's got his aim. Clay figured he needed your money to make a new start. Now that's bad wisdom, call it what you will. Me, I aint never been further from here in twenty years than yonder meadows. I figure a man's got to hold what he has and be patient." He spat regretfully in the frost. "Look here, I got plenty now. For me. Leastways I aint dead yet. That's why I'm goin' back. It aint because it was your money he stole, nor because he's my cousin."

For a time Ira only sat the horse looking down at Lloyd Logan.

He saw the black silhouette of his own horse and of himself stretching over the former Indian trader, once the power of Cheyenne,
the leader over himself, Ira Fawley who had learned the power
and weakness of evil; now his pardner, a shrewdness in him where
the old crazy gleam had been. Times changed like shifting sands;
Ira's mocking mind played back and forth now between the man
before him and the man far up in the white cold, Clay the third
pardner—a quick bold schemer.

"I ought to've felled you both with my fists."

There was no sullenness in his expression, only his cold heedless eyes, his strong austere mouth. Logan bent his head and said
nothing. Ira watched a sand-devil whirl away into the blueing
distance; then whistling softly to himself he began to dismount.
His boots printed deep in the rime and sand, he stood half facing
Logan, quiet and poised, almost dreamy, towering over Logan as
he assembled and lighted the clay pipe. He did not remove his
eyes from Logan's face; he always lighted his pipe in the void of
the evening. From ten years of pillage, he had retained this thing
alone, this pipe that appealed to him.

Logan looked round him with lonesome quietness, and in the
blue of the dying day he began to tighten the saddle-girth. Ira
remained motionless, seeming to joy in the writhen snake-like
figures on the bowl of the pipe; all else was joyless. He was not now
thinking of Clay, but of Audrey Mitchell far behind him now in
Cheyenne village. Her eyes seemed to watch him now—not with
love or unlove, just shadowy and sheltering and without any
dimension. Then he turned his thoughts back to Logan, and there
was the feeling again. From the first, he had sensed Logan's and
Audrey's alikeness: back of the coldness of each of them lay a dust
of sentiment that he did not share—it made them mean in an
impulsive way, more lewd than he—and he had watched this
dust of pollen draw them together.

In the hollows it was purple, dark and pitted as Audrey's eyes
when hate filled them. He felt something bitterer than the dust—
a touch of bewilderment, and he laughed sardonically aloud.
Logan turned to look at him with a shrewd expression in which
there was also a mist of fear; he knelt and began to pry the dry
mesquite stalks, heaping them for fire. Ira watched an instant,

and drifted slowly over beside the crouched man. Then with the sharp toe of his boot, he prodded the heap of twigs asunder.

Logan's hands remained still, dangling at his boot-tips as the whites of his eyes turned slowly up. In all the purpling stillness there was no other movement.

"There's no need of fire," Ira said. "I'm goin' on. I want to be movin'."

Logan remained still a moment. Then he rose and seemed to scan again the emptiness around them. Eventually, the blithe smile touched his callous eyes.

"Clay made a bad mistake." He clucked his teeth. "No doubt of that. I'll just ride by Cheyenne and tell Audrey Mitchell about you . . . about Clay too. So there won't be no worryin' done."

Ira turned away, seeming to scent in Logan the yearning rise of seeded dust—toward something in her that for Logan was always spring. He did not care, knowing that Lloyd and Audrey would betray him; he felt himself merely alone, and after their bodies met, he would still be alone. He looked up; winds quick as little whippets played among the sage. His grey eyes became august, impersonal, as he put away the pipe.

"Go on and see Audrey," he said.

Abruptly, he turned to his horse, half-watching as Logan turned and began to mount. Behind Logan the gulches were gutted purple, but the white knolls would stay light until the sundown when every known object would swoon away. He felt this ability to lift his mind out of a scene in which he was caught, seeing it as if locating it forever, just as it escaped toward nothing at all.

Whirling, he vaulted the saddle with a single powerful leap while Logan sat his mount facing him. He noticed again Logan's ageless small body, the unsated little eyes.

Logan raised his palm in a gesture of parting, and his mouth shaped into some half-mocking regret.

"See you in a day or two, Ira. Hope you have a mite of luck up there. Remember though, you still got a share."

Ira looked at him in slow withdrawn contemplation. Then he laughed easily.

"It'll take more than you've got left to keep her tame," he said.

In the trance of stillness, Logan turned his face away, seeming to hesitate, then whirled the horse and plunged down the purple ravine.

For a while as he watched, Logan was only a moving figure down the precipitate dusk of the gulley, like a shadow he might have projected on the wall with his thumbs and wrists. There seemed nothing left of Logan but this shadow, just as, in his sudden memory, Audrey's body at night became like a nest of wet leaves, a soil in the inmost pitchblack of his mind where there was nothing else—only sometimes a sound like that of whirring wings—from a source beyond recollection.

Then horse and rider plunged upward again into light, real again, seeming to make some demand upon him—either sympathy enough to let him ride on, or hate enough to stop him, neither of which he possessed. His hand dropped away from the stock of his rifle. It was this demand that he had long since denied to Logan: between them there had never been a trust to betray nor any vow to break; just as there was nothing between Clay and himself but the one thing—some pretence of Clay's, an innocence crueller than hate.

He watched as the black horse and rider disappeared over the ledge of gloom, in a faint downbeat of hooves. Then he loosened the rifle in the sheath, his expression merely calm, austere, and he spun the gelding and rode on down the ravine.

It was a long hollow, and it led far away into the rutted semi-darkness. In the frosty sand he could still make out the faint hoof-prints of the horse ahead, though indistinct like bird-claws. Loneliness descended into the hollow around him, and to his mind Audrey already lay darkly secure and glutted, having fed on Logan beyond the dusty shades of her room. He thought of it without pleasure or pain. There seemed nothing for him to view, past or present, but what was there—the grey dunes, the coming night—and what was not there or anywhere near, the retreating figure of Clay. He did not mind the darkness: it was less harmful to his way of feeling than the skies of day; there was always the dearth, day or night, but he had learned to become graver, more brilliant than the people, the lives it took under.

He lighted the clay pipe, his expression calm with some appearance of gentleness or dreaminess, and as he rode he began thinking in the ironic glow that always followed what some men called mercy. To kill a man like Clay was a service to most men, but it was only another service or disservice to a man that he did not like. In the case of Logan whom he had long studied, killing would not be measurable: it was nothing. His mind felt quieter than usual, and he began to think of Clay. He planned to come on him by morning; no man could keep pace with himself for long. At midnight he would feed and water the horse in the hills, and by sunup he would be near the pass, in the narrow throat where Clay, tired and unsuspecting, would have rested and eaten. Trailing Clay, a man less predictable, more deadly than Logan, gave him a direction, somewhere to go; but it was only another road that led where he had already come, to the single dearth where he was, at least, no slave, no fool. Beneath the hardness of his sinews he was always aware of a pointlessness like night, and he felt himself becoming more interested now in this duel against silence and aloneness than in overtaking Clay before he reached the pass—there seemed nothing ahead or behind him. In a flush of irony he laughed aloud and flicked his spurs against the straining groin of the horse. He began to whistle a tune that had followed him somewhere, something sweet with mockery, like lightning on a hot summer sky.

> *Weep all ye little rains,*
> *Wail winds wail*

He rode on and on through the darkened hollow, half musing, half reflecting. Again he felt the past rise up in flashes; and the dark places, unknown, were still there: the one moment mainly that he could not place in time, when he stood alone, knowing that God was not there, that there was only dearth and dust in the skies, and that a man was better dead, and if he lived, self-success was all he could live for. But there was not even then any choice—he could not kill himself, because that would be to lose the unforgiveness.

He remembered feeling it all along, but he had not always known what it meant. Failure ran men's lives—it was their pain, their joy. As a boy he remembered watching from the shadows of wagons as the tall girls and drunken men danced and revelled round the bonfires, and he did not hate them, but felt only a mixed contempt and sorrow which made him unwilling to approach them. And he began to be alone. He could not understand failure—or rather he understood it too well. He saw it everywhere—the feverish wish for forgiveness on a young wife's face as she danced with her husband after going down on her back to a trader for a bolt of linen, men on their knees asking God to forgive them their failures; failure was all they knew. He understood that they, all of them, expected it of him too . . . until they were surprised and cowed by his rifle. Then it was as if he became a God in their eyes; they wanted kindness, pity at his hands who could have none for himself. He became ice: he knew he was cruel, but he was ice. There was no place where he belonged. But he did not care; pride and a sense of being always alone, even in the midst of people, were all that gave him peace. He had never hated anyone enought to hurt him—but he was in the world alone. He took Audrey away from her husband and others too he had taken away; his hands had built the ranch out of plunder and what men relinquished to him. He became quieter, more intelligent than they and stronger, as subtle as Logan. Men who were afraid of the silence and the empty spaces welcomed him, made room for him and crowded round him. But he wanted none of their attention—he was past needing it, almost past noticing it.

Ira woke as if from a forgotten revery to feel the brush of stunted trees against his thighs. Unwearied, though hungry, he looked up at the new moon that had just scaled the mountain peaks and revealed, for an instant, a hazy, wild, dreamy catamount of snow. He saw it then but as a trick of his mind, and his habitual expression, half melancholy, half amused, yet empty of feeling, did not change.

As he rode in deep concentration it was much later. The moon had risen over the white wastes of scrub-oak and he saw the snow— deep mysterious snow that led upward and outward in queer riddles of depth and height. Alertness spread in his mind. As he looked around, it was only another place that did not belong to him or match his needs, but he saw that he must think afresh to fathom it and keep the trail. The horse had eaten, but its trail-weary legs were unsteady, spindling; it would never be a good horse again. He began to ease its pace in order that it might not founder.

As he rode up the mountainside, he could see nothing but the many dimensionless white slopes on every hand. It was not until some time later that the horse bore him staggering against one huge white pinnacle which he had taken for shoulders of a bluff, and he discovered that it was a tree, its branches strung with snow-crystals and chains of ice. It came as a wry surprise to him, as if a cunning hand had thrown a guise among things. He felt the cold now, the air wore a new bleakness and was still: it did not break or swerve as silence would do—it was everywhere. The mountains in winter were not new to him, but there had been a change everywhere after a month of blizzards. In some way he felt drawn to it—as if it were what his own imagination had built, while at the same time he fore-knew the grave difficulty.

After a while in a gesture of contempt against the cold he bent over the lurching horse to find the whiskey canteen; he had felt it against his thigh a few moments earlier. But he found he could not locate it; there was only the spur of leather where it had always hung. The loss brought a small pulse of rage within him who usually felt no anger. He rode onward into the puzzling dark, think-ing of it, finally recalling what he should have known, that an hour or more ago he had dropped the empty jug into the trail. But for some time, he did not know what to make of the lapse of memory. It had not happened to him before; and he felt an influence in the night that he could not fathom. He began to try to think through it, but the nearest he could come was an idea similar to being lost; he was not lost, but somewhere a stage between where the familiar became harmful beyond recognition. He was bothered by two things that had passed quickly between him and the real, a shadow of forgetfulness and a shape of anger.

For a long time Ira rode upward into the dark cold with a certain new interest in it, the same content, into the small hours of what was somewhere the morning. He had reasoned that it would be three hours before the first streak of dawn and four before the sun arose. He saw that the path was deeper in snow now and wider, and it was very dark: he could not see the prints of Clay's stallion, only the white corpses of trees or boulders on the dimensionless slopes. His hands felt speared with cold; suddenly he rammed them into the wings of his jerkin. It was his habit to think always of his hands first, since they were himself; they made him somewhat different from the sum of things he did because the hands had never been tired—they could do more. He stared ahead into the crater of darkness. In the half jesting quietness of his mind there was no touch of anxiety; but he noticed that what had seemed new to him did not become old. It was a world of blizzards; it changed, altered, yet stayed the same. The white slopes threw off new upheavals of depth; the horse plunged by turns, thigh-deep in what seemed a rapid river of snow, then trod lightly through a dust of frost like fine and static hail. In the dispassion of his mind, he felt how the shifting and shuttling went on, and yet there was no place where change began or ended. He was no stranger to it, yet he felt already a small area of weariness and blankness in his mind where the image of the snow lay, though even this was something he had been awaiting.

Hours later he rode into the pass. He had ridden long as into a dream, but now day opened, light by light. First there was a winter glow which seemed to rise upward from the ice and frost as much as downward from the arisen sun, and then the single form of the snow, without object or source. Ira, viewing it, flexed his tireless body in the saddle while he fought the blue sea of cold. He had won through, beaten Clay to the pass. But as he looked at it, he felt some change in his relation to it—something he could do nothing about.

What had seemed in the darkness dimensionless was not: it was mass—a continuous white maze which was measureless, cold and serene with shining light. Beneath him there was the ice-flown river, now far extended over its habitual banks by the blockades below, the ice blueish along the banks below the falls where the river still flowed, stormed, around the blockades, sending up a volume of motionless sound between a roar and a sigh, and yet remaining mirrored beneath the ice. As he sat there, the daylight shone only on snow-fast pines and bushes, joined and flexed together in a stiff drifted membrane of snow. In the glare something held him as if entangled, caught, in the frozen flux, and his mind seemed suddenly small—there was nowhere an object in all that space where his gaze could settle and rest. Quickly, Ira recognized a terror: it stood off somewhere behind the spell of whiteness—it was something pure or something vicious, either one past thought. But as he felt it, he was prepared; he knew it would not turn him back—until he killed the one man he might ever want to kill, a lean, skilled betrayer, the man who was always free, innocent, for whom there was always a better place to go.

For a while he sat the shuddering horse motionless—it whinnied once in weariness and despair—and he began slowly to think how when Clay arrived he could see him approach in the frost-light before they came face to face. Looking down, he noticed that his hands were turning blue, and he struck them in a pain and a touch of grief that were new to him and rubbed them viciously on his leather jerkin to erase the feeling. Some second sense told him then that he would have to go up what seemed to be a cliffside above the falls in order to see into the distance.

He spurred the horse, and it launched upward beneath him in a last burst of speed. It gained the rock-cliff on slithery legs, and then, before any heed returned to him, started to sprawl headlong on the ice.

For a long minute, they were poised there; the horse beneath him sprawling back and forth in terror—long enough for him to think and look downward over the cliff and outward into space. He saw thirty feet below the ice-choked river, frozen hard in the middle in an ice-cage, with the blueish film along its sides where the ice was thin, diaphanous, and the deep water roiled. Then, as he flipped his powerful body free of danger, the horse's huge haunches struck him by chance, and he toppled over the falls.

When he sat up immediately on the ice-cage, he heard the river flowing on all sides and beneath him, and looking up with measured slowness he saw that the horse was gone from the cliffside. His back was wrenched and one arm stunned, and he rubbed them a moment while his concentration flowed back. He knew somehow that he had fallen into disaster.

Nothing had changed, and yet as he crouched on his knees, there was nothing the same. Everywhere around him, but now

apart from him, was the diaphragm of the snow-fast woods, broken
only somewhere by a green smear of myrtle or mistletoe, the snow
depending from each branch, each crevice in the stone in one
cohesive rage. He knew he was left alone on an island of ice. He
felt, at first, no anger or grief, only a kind of pain; with the passage
of all certainty, only a stab of awe. He sensed that he was trapped,
but he had been trapped before and had escaped through a working
on the minds of weaker men who were more eager to believe than
to know. But he knew now that he was alone. There was nobody
out there. What he had seen from the cliff was open country, and
far in the distance, on the plains, having turned back, was the figure
of Clay and his horse.

For a time he crouched there looking at the flowing water
beneath the thin blue scale of ice, swept clean of snow, on all sides
of the ice-cage. It half isolated him from the peaks and flutes of
snow, but it gave him this view of that forest of snow, as of a
separate world, sparse and shining, and cut off from him, as if
painted there. The morning dew was descending in frost particles
that bit his cheeks and fixed to his skin-cap and clothes. He struck
his wrists, but the frost-particles would not brush off—they clung
to him like iron flakes. He felt he had to think, but he knew that
thinking was vain. He was reluctant to face the river which he knew
was impassable, knew by the breadth and the rush of the water
under the thin ice, by the high, sheer cliffs rising over it.

He arose to his feet, his shoulder taxing him, and began to
search himself for equipment; he had his Bowie knife, a cartridge
belt but no gun, a piece of strong cord, and flints for lighting—but
there was nothing around him to kindle. He took the items from his
pocket and heaped them slowly with some great care or patience in
the glistening frost, delaying until the last moment any consideration
of fording the stream. He tramped hard and saw that the ice was
deep. After a long time, he realized that he could dig a shallow
trench in it, deep enough to get out of the wind, and his expression
became cool, impersonal with irony.

Then he turned almost angrily to look down at the river. His
slowed reason told him that in time the ice-cage would melt, but
that was months away. There was too much water, too much speed
in the water for the ice to freeze over so that he could walk across

it. He knew suddenly that his nearest chance lay in swimming the river.

Slowly, he looked at it. The river groped in identical forks of equal width about the ice-cage, while before him were the falls. On each side there were rock walls silvered over with snow, nearly too steep for climbing even if he managed to swim through the ice and gain the cliff. He tramped down to the edge of the thin ice. Kneeling he thrust his weight down until the ice trembled far out, cracked, and splintered into fragments like thin glass which thrust up sharp gleaming points before disappearing in the revealed torrent. He touched the water. How swift? His hand, touching it, was thrust aside. How deep? He did not have to guess—the water was clear: six feet or more down. Then he bent and ran his thumb along the sill of ice—it was not quite an inch thick, more or less in spots. His head would go beneath the ice-surface, but he would break through again as he swam amain. His head would break through, and the ice would quickly slit his throat—it would carve out his eyes and bite into his brain. And even if he reached the wall, there was no place to stand to fix the rope for ascent, with eyelids frozen closed and body hacked and broken.

He thought of it for a long time. He knew he did not fear the risk of death. But he feared something else: the slow disfigurement of his body, the minnows sucking at a random dismembered arm or hand. Yet even if he had not feared this, it was not his way to consider certain death.

He stood up, his senses shaken partly free of the single membrane of snow and frost across in the woodlands. After all his wandering, he had come to a place that held him, which was no place at all. Standing there, he felt no self-pity; life and death had long been too simple to him for that. Yet something inside him could not shun the lengthening shadow of time that faced him.

He stood a long time motionless—more time than he, at first, knew—until his mind suddenly grasped and held it all: the unspeakable. Then he knew that he would have to work fast against it.

Bending down, he picked up the knife, as if his first purpose—to dig a trench—were the only real one. He went quickly to his knees and drew with the cold blade a six-by-three box in the ice. Quite suddenly, as he began working, he felt himself sinking into a limitless personal revery, something that wanted not to know. Looking up, he saw only the towering cliffs, the unanswering steeples of snow. For an instant only, he had forgotten where he was. He dropped the knife and leaned hard for an instant on his palms in the chipped and powdered ice, until the palms were like fire and the little pains worked far up his wrists.

Time passed; there was no movement anywhere in the snow-fast woods or on the cage other than his own, yet much time had passed for him. He finished digging a narrow bed in the ice where his body could drop and the cold wind and mist could not strike him. He lay down in it to rest, his cold impersonal face looking up at the sky, no longer the sky of dearth, but a sky of ruse and cunning. As he lay there, the silence, the trap, the shape of death, were things he had to face without hope of conquest, but could not countenance without hate, and he had never hated what was real, only what was not. He felt his mind crawl, seeking escape. He had known it was too much. He lay still, clinging both to himself and the unchanging scene which seemed in some way also within him, though untouchable. Time left a gap. Then the cold fine-spun revery began. He saw John Stein lying dead on the floor the night of the silver robbery; and Audrey's husband, Bill Mack, a bull of a man, who had come for his wife, sitting with broken hands and broken face after the fight, weeping for shame and loss: he heard his own ironic half-sorrowing laughter and saw Audrey's flesh shining through her nightgown in the next room. They were the sad things, and to his half waking mind they were not real; shadows only, as people were, they grew deep in his mind and clustered without love, beneath memory. He remembered no love; he did not want it for himself since he had seen in it the elements of need and pity. Yet he remembered Audrey and her bitter laughter, because she was all that love was not. He felt his memory of these personal things become deeper, something between dread and assurance, shutting off somehow the deluge of snow.

The long day-dream stopped. He was cold and alone, the sky was greying with snow. Then something moved. A lone eagle flapped out of the fixation of snow and tramped skyward, drifting out of view. It was an arresting and painful sight which at first he did not wish to believe. Gone now—the solitary live thing—it signalized more perfectly his isolation. He was going to die. Unless the ice froze deeper in a few days, he would freeze or starve or drift into madness. He knew he had to have comfort and food. Now.

Ira pulled himself lurching out of the trough in the ice and tramped in converging circles until he felt warmer. Then he went down to the water where he had broken the ice and knelt. Looking down he could see a school of little fishes deep in the shadows of the rocks. He bent down and plunged hand and arm in to the shoulder, groping with numbed fingers in the rock crevices. The little fishes only sank beyond reach in the swift water and fanned their tails while their icy eyes scrutinized his fingers. He withdrew the hand slowly and looked down at it, a numbed blue thing with not much more feeling or use than a gourd. He struck the hand savagely, finding an object for rage, until the blood pounded red and the fingers were alive again. Looking down at the hand, his eyes were crisp with melancholy and hatred. As he remained motionless, watching the little fishes, they seemed to become more real to him than anything else, than himself, because he must have them to live —and yet they were something like a dream.

Time was measured only by the sun—past meridian and deep in what elsewhere would have been mid-afternoon. He had been sitting for a long time with his knife, the cord, and a piece of skin cut from the tail of his jerkin, patiently, carefully making a seine for the fishes. As he worked, he felt how he had salvaged pride again: he was himself again, and he felt he had something to pit against the silence, the membrane of snow, and the ice-cage—his strength, his memory, or something else, a newness in him born out of prolonged unsorrowing awareness. He had shrunk in the last five hours—he was smaller than he had known, less powerful against the throat-cutting ice, but he had more skill than it, more heart even than the fishes. As in the past he had pitted himself against men, divining weakness, now he had begun to measure himself against the smallest things, stones, a piece of cord, minnows, and a small seine.

He finished with the seine, and stood in the blue cloud shadows fastening it. He felt very hungry, now that hunger was past meaning. He fitted the seine over his thumb in a finger-stall, so that it resembled the loose fin of a fish or the web-foot of a fowl. Then he got up, hurried to the hole in the ice, and lay down on his belly. Fitting the seine, he thrust his arm down. He trapped five minnows. He raised the seine carefully and emptied the minnows on the ice beside him. Three were very small, not more than a mouthful, but two were large, three mouthfuls apiece. He needed at least fifteen fishes to keep his strength up. So he dipped again, spreading the seine and closing it in crab-like movements. In three dips he caught twenty fish as his skill increased. Then he dried the seine on the ice by rubbing it hard enough to shed the water. Without getting off his knees, he began to cut the heads from the fishes and to swallow them like raw eggs. He felt the last wriggle of one fish deep in his guts, and a well of comfort seemed to open its edges into which his mind, tired, unheeding, and thankless, sank. Looking up, he saw that the snow-packed clouds were ranged closer, greyer, and a slow hope of change dawned in his mind.

Then it was night, quite suddenly as if he had not waited, and the snow so long withheld was falling over him. Lying in the shallow scooped-out ice, he looked up at the night, sleepless with the cold that blew on the set reticence of his mouth. Tongues of cold worked up into his back or shoulder, and he had to turn from side to side. The sky was soft as black fur and the fluffy white snow dropped like ornate flowers out of it, smiting his face with touches like unwished kisses, until he would finally have to drag his sleeve up over his eyes and mouth. The cold was partly broken by the snow; it was a mild deceptive cold now: sometimes he half forgot how chill his hands were, especially the one hand, the fishing-hand, which had grown tender as a woman's. He lay imagining without belief that when the sky cleared a terrific cold would come; it would dry up the springs higher up in the mountains, and he would walk out freely over the ice. Day-dreaming, partly comforted, he watched the snow; but the pointless place within him glimmered, some part of his mind (he seemed to know) that had led him here—unlike Clay who had turned back—among mountains of ice. Loneliness did not enter him: he knew he did not want the company of men. What he knew he knew well: that there was no comfort in men. He remembered no man or woman who could look life in its face as he had done. Now, in his day-dream that was far from sleep, he began to remember: John Atherton who rode beside him on more than one raid, a boy of seventeen with grave girl's eyes, who worshipped him, who on the night after a bitter day was sent up as lookout and fell in with Ruby McHayes, the marshal's son, and agreed to lead McHayes and two others to where Ira slept, to receive in return the sum of one thousand dollars in gold and title to a small ranch McHayes owned. Something wakened Ira in time to see the three of them clustered off in the shadows, and he opened fire; the men ran off in panic, leaving John Atherton behind. He let him go—his hands became useless against him. But he was fascinated by what he had found, not the boy's love overcome, but the fear of himself that he had discovered in an instant of grief.

When his revery ended, the snow had already quit. Fitful as a dream it had not lasted long—not long enough to do anything any good or to alter the night. Down the clear skies came the slow mirror of stars, and he lay once again empty of hope, his hands bitten by the random snow-flakes, feeling the soft smudge of pain —chilblains—on one cheek beneath the harsh yellow growth of beard. He lay still in the habitual and hardened grace of his mind, waiting for nothing.

At dawn he awakened from a broken sleep. It was keenly cold and clear, like yesterday. For the first time a shadow of weariness crawled along the lines of his mouth, striking his eyes. Standing up, without awareness of motion, he saw that the snow lay now on the thin sheets of ice, but he saw the same moist spots where the roiling water bubbled through. Hungry again, with but five fishes to eat, he turned slowly and walked down to the hole in the ice. A very thin tier had formed over it. He cracked it with a touch of his toe. Across in the woods, as yesterday, the chain of snow and frost leagued tree and bush and twig in the soundless white flux, until as he stood there, he felt himself begin to sink at last into that attitude, that long chain without memory.

Then, abruptly, he saw a strange sight. Three deer, lovely as fauns, were tippling in the water near the falls overhead. How long they had been there without his seeing them he did not know. Their eyes upon him were brighter than oak-leaves, dense with beauty. Arrested, drawn slowly from out some void, he stared upward at them. As time passed, the deer that wore the ten-pointed antlers lifted its slender distant head skyward and led the herd back into the forest, while he stood rooted, viewing the procession. He felt nothing of mockery in them: they would perish as soon from the cold as himself. The ten-pointed stag waited, however, until the does had all passed on beyond the snow barriers. Finally, he tossed his helm against the white brake and disappeared.

Then fatigue, astonishment, and the wreckage of a brief hope touched him deeply. A mist of horror and want welled and froze in his eyes.

After a while, he was himself again—a dreaminess inside him where the hate and pride waited—a new even smaller self, kneeling with the seine at the hole in the ice, thrusting his arm into the ice-water. But he had not forgotten the deer—they would not leave his mind. As he worked without much success, watching the scrutiny of the minnows as they darted below, in and out of shadows, he would stop to pound his frozen hand back into sensitivity and munch at the five dead fishes. As the sun rose, the lonely eagle rose again from his rock-nest and tramped skyward and disappeared as before, leaving the air trackless, insane, perfect. As he worked, he felt desire rise and hurt him—oddly, because he had never founded a habit with women, it seemed that all he wanted in earth or sky was the shape of a woman near. Looking down at his hand passing through the water, he thought of woman not only as flesh and as food, but as the only escape. To die lying with a woman in his arms was all that he seemed to want. He felt a hate for the slimey chaste minnows, with a flesh not his own. There was something warmer and richer about a woman than even the female deer in the dawn. Not their bodies—he did not want to think of their bodies, sow-white, less lovely than the deer's. It was something else. He could not think what it was—in the past he had never noticed.

He chewed the minnows this time, bone and false flesh, eight of them slowly, so they would digest. Then he drank long from the chill water, and rubbing the numb hand went to sit alone on the ice. His hands were empty now, useless: they did not seem strong with potential. There was an enormous space between them; he felt as if the sky or the earth were thrust between them. He found himself clenching and unclenching them, but the sense of immensity remained. He knew quickly that he had to do something. So he began thinking how to build an ice-house in which to live. As he sat in the silence, his thoughts seemed to rush out to some sphere which was bereft either of ideas or objects. Finally he rose in a calm bitterer than fear and began to hunt for his knife in the snow.

As he labored, day passed—it was night, and slow keen dawn with no interval of snow this time and no sense of time now except for the rough-hewn blocks of ice flanking the narrow groin of the bed. He heard the water seethe and boil under the thin ice, and as he seined, he saw the deer on the cliffside—four of them with one buck, lissome and grave, lovelier than the dawn. They had come again, as if to remind him of time and of flesh. As they drank at leisure, they gazed at him with the fullness of their eyes. Then they filed back with the same eloquent calm, the roe leading, into the membrane of snow. He felt how they left in their wake a dust in his mind like an interrupted dream in which he saw rows of cankered flowers, white bones, dead leaves, the waste of things.

As he worked, he sometimes spoke aloud now, without caring, small urgent words addressed to the seine, the sun, the water, or the little fishes. He felt very hungry. But this time he caught no fishes: they scrutinized him but kept away in the shadows of the rocks, their sucking mouths mocking him as they fed among roots and lichen. His hand stone-cold, he had to stop. He noticed keenly that the hand felt different now, as if smeared with nitre. Yet in a way he could not think or worry about it: it only seemed to reveal the truth. He got up, sleep-walking, and going back fell face-down on the ice. He lay there, sprawled and motionless, his mouth pressed hot and hard on the ice. He had failed. He could not cry or pray: he merely seemed to give up with a terrible effort something about himself that was important—hope. Time passed. Then he rose and felt refreshed, and he began to work with narrow quiet effort on the escarpment of ice.

As he cut and hewed with the dulling knife, without any feeling of pride in the work, he began to think again. It was both thought and revery. He knew he had some need of objects to think with,

need of at least a scheme or a hope of one. But such things had
become madness to his mind. He had begun to think without these
things, with nothing but the blank backdrop of snow—but his mind
felt clumsy and slow: he had begun to think of certain ideas, not
known or recognized before, ideas that rose to take the place of
people, caused by people though there were no people in them, like
a plant risen from seed. The ideas made no sense to him: people
were full of deceit and cruelty, worse than himself, because he knew
his nature and was—had been—faithful to what he knew. But he
felt there was no use remembering that—it was past and he would
not live beyond a few days: he had to think and he had to think
through ideas and persons, and the ideas were never inside the
persons and the persons were never inside the ideas. This he had
always known, but he had not understood that the ideas could not
last beyond the memory, the people.

Last night late, half asleep, he began imagining to himself a
place where there were cool summery trees, a long lake shadowy
in the afternoons, and a house with a stone well. It meant nothing
to him—yet pleasure arose as he began to add things to the place,
using this and casting out that. It was strange how little he chose.
He discovered that one thing he wanted there besides the well was
a boat and a fishing-line: the boat had waxen oars and the fishing
line would not sever. He did not want a gun, oddly he did not want
a horse—in this place he did not want a woman. There were no
people there. It was a strange idea: it was terribly real to him, and
yet he knew it did not exist. In all his life he had never found any
place that was his, that suited him alone, like this.

Then his knife slipped and he cut his palm, slit it so that the
veins opened. He got up, lurched up drunkenly with the blood
trailing down, cursing in calm fury and despair. When he finally
got his hand into the ice-water it stopped bleeding instantly, and
when he took it out, it felt already healed. Surprised, yet somehow
willing to believe, as even the real, the evil nature of things, had
fluctuated, he went back to work, while the skies glowed again grey
with a with-held and nearly imaginary snow.

Then it was night again. In the groin of the ice now worn
smooth by the passage of his body, he lay in gaunt sleeplessness,

looking with hollow eyes from side to side at the chiseled masonry of ice that surrounded him. It was warmer now in the ice-bed— his hands and chilblained cheek would let him sleep if sleep came. But as he lay looking at what his hands and skill had done, seized out of the mouth of death, the masonry of ice seemed almost more grotesque than the ice-cage, the thin crust of ice over the rushing deep water, and the membrane of snow that nature had fashioned out of forests. He felt no joy in the work, and his mind heavy with sleeplessness and deep with yearning turned back into the daydream: the long lake, the sandy shoals, the boat, the lighted house, himself and silence. By night the night-owls came, flapping at his windows, by day the starlings scattering sound. Many kinds of insects browsed among the dragonflies on the surface of the lake: it was a place of much small-life. But among the shores was a herd of twenty deer. Sleeping or awake, he had begun to feel the necessity of this place. He remembered that even before evening he had lain down in the groin of ice and closed his eyes, thinking of it.

He fell into a deeper dream which was sleep, but the sound of a snow avalanche on the hills awakened him. He lay remembering the dream. Men and women of all kinds were searching for him everywhere, as they had once searched: they chased him out of a hotel (it seemed to be, but was not, Audrey's hotel, where he was least secure) and into the forests through tall trees until he came suddenly . . . where? Nowhere, nowhere at all. To that place in his mind. He lay deep in discouragement and shame because it seemed that he had been running from them all this time. Deep in fatigue, he realized finally that it was only a harrowing dream; but he felt he could not shake free of its power. He got up, standing in the vacant shell of the starless night, and dipped his face in the cold water to rid the dream. He wished he were dead. As he stumbled back, it seemed to him that a man— a dying man—who wanted only to dream had no business with even a few days of life. But he had no hope of dying.

Awakened by the dawn, he did not rise. He lay with the crimson hush over him without wishing to eat or work or see the fallow deer in the snow. Yesterday he had remarked the leanness of the deer, how their skeletons shone through the bronze coats: he felt he did not want to see them leaner or hungrier or not at all. He did not want to see the eagle tramp up the skies, forever free, or hear the chatter of the invisible horde of chipmunks. He believed he had already struggled longer than most men would have done. He wanted only silence.

But he felt he had some shadow of choice. His strong lean face was already hollowed; the yellow beard soiled by the entrails of fish lay like haircloth on the chilblains of his cheeks. He stood up over the ice-walls, feeling his sole solitary motion, and looked up at the falls: there were no deer, but he saw the familiar mud-stains in the snow. They would be pierced with the need for salt now; like himself they could exist but not live long. He thought how winter —the pure thing—was too strong for deer or men, until through habit or craft they learned how to conceal themselves from it. He was bemused by his own thoughts, the qualities in them, the lack of object. As he stood there thinking this way, he felt the utter truth: that for the deer, death and life, the impure design, did not fit what they were. They were braver than either: they laid their slender necks down, at last willingly, upon the gibbet of frost. With him it was the same, yet harder. He did not fit any idea, and he was always changing—what he thought or believed was not what he was. To fit death, part of him had to die first; then death could hold the rest, the nerve, the instinct. It would take prolonged nightmare to rid him of all the rest, before he could lay his head down. . . .

It was noon. There was a crescent of sun overhead. He looked up, surprised again, to find himself still alive at the end of some stage in time. He had finished the walls and eaten fifteen half-live fishes; he ate them slowly and lingered over them, half studying the stubborn life in them. But by this time, he had already made the discovery. The fishing-hand did not now resemble the other hand (the one he had cut), but was a strange hectic blue-red with a kind of grey fur on it around the wrist-bone. Looking down at it, he saw beneath the quicks of the nails little moons of grey matter. For a long time after he noticed it, he sat still on the ice— time leaped, and he could not tell where it went. He felt no surprise or dismay—for a while, no feeling at all.

Finally, he looked at the hand, judging its chance and rate of survival, seeing for the first time what dying would do. Then pity swarmed over him. He felt he would not give much for the chances of the hand beyond a day or two. He knew he would have to make for it a dry leather mitten, cutting it out of some warm part of his jerkin.

Then, without moving or thinking, he began timelessly to fashion the mitten. It was the hardest thing he had ever done because the hand was too stiff and clumsy to help its neighbor. As he worked, bent over, chill sweat broke on his face, and he noticed that there was a pulpiness there in his palm, plump without feeling, like a frost-melon. Suddenly his work slowed, and he noticed the enormous space between his hands: he felt himself teetering on some verge of immensity.

A few instants later, as he knelt there, he knew that he could not live with the hand: it was death joined to his life.

After the discovery, he felt free of the burden of hope or pride. He rose calmly and walked slowly around the ice-cage, without shrinking from the view of the snow-valanced woods beyond the strips of water, hearing without emotion the roar and hiss of the cataracts beneath the falls. The day felt like all the others, too real, and himself too visionary, too quiet and small. In the face of this fact, it seemed he could ask nothing, expect nothing. His lips parted, and he laughed at himself in single scorn; mocking himself, he stood at the brink, fondling with hatred the dying hand. He thought suddenly: should something happen and the ice freeze he would not know whether to walk across it or not. Would it be worth the effort to know? Was he worth the agony of dying? If there was a God, which he had never believed, a God of dearth and plenty, Who counted the little fishes he ate and those he vomited, He would have to believe a man worthy of the agony, which he was not, never could be. Ira remembered how the other, fair, hand had been healed, the left hand, the lesser one.

He was struck by a fear of his own bright thoughts; yet they seemed to leap inside him. He knew suddenly that he had always seen too much to accept any one man's faith, that he had felt lifelong sadness and rage that had fed the body and will, made either one strong to surfeit. And he asked himself, what else was there for them to feed—now or then or ahead of him? There was excitement, accomplishment, admiration, schemes to lay. There were all these things, and there was nothing. Nothing at all. Standing exhausted, looking down sightlessly at the mittened hand, he realized this viewpoint; but it was already useless to him, and it was somehow behind him like a dead skin. He looked down at the bloated hand and water came and stood in his eyes. Brokenly, he looked into the afternoon. In the spires of the trees snow glistered like tiny stars—clouds bearing snow trafficked overhead and dwindled to opal grey. A solitary crow sat on the windless air northward like an ibis. He turned to hunt the knife where in his panic he had left it.

Beyond the bizarre ice-wall he found the knife, blade buried. He clutched it, but he could not bring himself to use it. The casual cold and the misty sun seemed not to watch him, not expectant, and to act was not to find quittance from these. He mocked himself again, with bitter cruelty, knowing it was not enough. Even the crow had vanished, probably crop-full with gobbets from a deer's leaner, fresher heart, or possibly it had been only a lonesome rook. Cruelty that mounted to irony inside him was all he had left. He felt he would have liked to justify the hollowness of his heart with the bitter glee of a rape or a killing. Soul-rotten, hand stinking, he stood in the sweet snow, feeling himself for what he was, for what all men had engendered in his blood.

Whirling, he knelt in the snow beside the water. But he only crouched there very still. It did not seem worthwhile to do it, for himself or any man. He shuddered and felt a passion for death, a wish for it, steal over him.

Possibly an hour later, half mad in mind, he waded through the snow on his knees to the buried knife. He plucked it out, gripped the useless throbbing fingers between his knees, and reaped the hand at the wrist, with giant, patient toil and hacking, splitting blows. Then while consciousness remained and while foils of onrushing blackness stained the snow, he wound the loose flesh and cord over the stump of wrist and tied the slip-knots with his teeth. Even now, he did not know why he had done it. On his back in the ice before all brightness fled, he drew over the wound the mitten he had made.

An hour later, between savage pain and forgetfulness, he

dragged himself to the water, washed the clout of flesh and bone until the cold stopped the bleeding, re-tied the slip-knots, and wound over it the piece of his shirt. He finished with it, his mind slipping quickly backward into a hovering nightmare; as he got to his feet, stumbling toward the ice-bed, it leaped and seized his brain.

It was twelve hours later when his head cleared. But he had lain a long time struggling as the nightmare slowly withdrew out of the pits of his eyes. He sat up shocked, half aware of his motions, one hand already searching, to find himself lying by the hole in the water where another inch would have spelt drowning, looking up into another new dawn, in some way forgetful of the death that had for a while shared his mind. He sat erect, nearly dreaming, the crown of his head damp with the slush that had revived him. He felt how the fever had left him what seemed a soft nest of flesh without inwardness, and hunger and thirst had pierced deeper than desire. He recalled a madness, a stalking like a bear, monstrous around the lair of ice, before his senses were shrived. But he knew it was past now. The hand was all right—it was gone and the dry pain was harsh but such as might be endured. What was past seemed now deeply past—so that as he staggered up, he had lost part of what he had been. It was gone, transfigured, like the dead hand.

He simply stood looking narrowly into the sunrise. As his sight cleared, he saw that the deer had left their tracks and gone. But as he looked more carefully, he saw lying on the snow of the high clearing, yet very near him, a beautiful doe, her sides still seeming to quiver with departed life. It was at first too real to understand. Then it hurt him so that he went weak at the knees. Beautiful and full of impulse, she lay on the scaffold of snow, unknowable and without peers. Moments later he did not know the meaning. He could not tell if his ascription of beauty to the dead doe was born out of his mind as a need for food, or not. But there had been a perfection about his feeling that left him, whoever he had become, real.

Turning, he saw the dead lump of hand, pale green in the fresh fluff of snow like the claw of an otter, and veering slightly, he picked it up and dropped it down to the little fishes. Then he knelt again beside the water and drank from his other palm. Patiently, he bathed the wound, applying new cloth, all that remained of his shirt. Irony was gone in him, as he fitted the bloody mitten to his single hand and crouching again began searching the shadowy, porcelain rocks for the small fishes.

After the exertion and the nausea of chewing the minnows, he vomited and lay in the shell of ice, too weak to move. In his mind there was something like a bridge of dreams, necessary and real, flowing inward from what was not himself, then through himself to some stage beyond either. First, gusts of fever would return, lasting perhaps ten minutes at a time, in which the clarity of a wide suffering in which he only shared, as one among many, and older and richer than himself, was broken by the final nightmare that awaited him certainly, at last, no matter how he strove or what he became. But the common nightmares were not strong now, only palls and threats and empty husks of the part of him that had lost identity—the overweening part; and the new feeling he had which was like mourning, like tragedy, chased and released itself again out of the nightmares. In the place in his mind, there were new forms of things, a beautiful deer without a herd (all the herd had vanished, as if he had asked too much even in this), and a quality that overhung the shadowed lake like peace.

Finally, he slept.

In the afternoon he dragged himself to the water again and fished with all the strength he had left, caught five large minnows, chewed and ate them. They stayed in his stomach, the fever had passed, and strength budded slowly. Bending beside the water, he knew by these signs that he would live a day, possibly a week longer. Thinking began again, and now it had hardly any object by which to move. The thoughts settled in himself and there they lodged; they were short, new, and fresh.

Standing again, without hope, by the brim of water, he noticed the freshness, and how underneath it lay no melancholy or dread clustered beneath memory, and irony was something former, something dead. He stood a long while, aching and weary. He felt he had staked the hand against all the forces he knew, and had lost—or rather, he had surrendered it, given it up in order that he might know; both and yet neither. He noticed an odd completeness about the other hand now which had been absent in the two.

Freshness crowded his mind so that he turned toward the forests. He watched the newly arrived snowbirds flit aloft over the chains of hoar and frost, and revel at will near the fallen doe. His eyes became more grave, austere, as he pondered. If the snow came soon again in abundance, the body of the doe would escape the bills of the kites, and when Spring came, the grass would spring richer and more lush where she had lain, while his own body would be washed away in the thaws. He thought one would not know this country in the Spring, when the columbines set out their purple and yellow flags. These lovelinesses would hold his grief.

In the evening, heavy snow began. What had been moonlight was now a white cloud that covered his lonely body in the ice-trench. He lay wondering if the heavy cold would follow the snow and he would walk out alive, to last as long as he could with one hand. Then his mind turned to the secret place where there was, for him, Ira Fawley, forever a lake and a house, forever the single deer.

Fever fits returned as he lay awake thinking. Suppose he escaped? He could not think what he would do, walking out over the solid ice up into the woods, where he would go or why. Clay had returned in despair to the ranch, seeking mainly forgiveness from himself who afar off had killed some men and plundered. It was as if Clay—all of them—had outlasted his will, and so outlived his ability to forgive or not forgive. This was the penalty: the past, and the fury in it, were dead to him. He was a man who had missed many chances, and all that he might have felt or done, the honor he might have paid to one woman, lay, as if in one gesture to a fallen doe. If he lived, by what means would he live?—he felt deep in a forgetfulness like sleep. Yet he knew that all things—even people—were before him, and nothing behind. In some way he had not even known who or what he was, from that moment when, full of longing for death, he had in some sudden fit of self-denial, raised the knife. It was because he knew he had not done it for himself; since he, himself, wanted and craved nothing but death, and not to be alive like this, maimed, with the past dead. But he had felt driven to it by some unaccountable love for the living bone, whether of people or of animals, which had been selfless then, but was now all of him that remained. He could not close his eyes, despite the comfort of the snow.

It was crimson dawn again, still as if enchanted. He lay broad awake, feeling the new shrill cold bite through the heavy skin jerkin as he wound the stump of the wrist in the mitten again and grunted and shivered with the renewed pain. He had not eaten in twelve hours or more, and he was still a sick man, nearer to death than ever. He could feel the nightmare waiting—something shapeless—slinking across the dark edges of his mind where there would never be light. But he did not hurry. He stood up in the frost-littered air, noticing that the bright high fluting of the river was quiet, a murmur under the level reaches of snow. Where the hole in the ice had been there was only a dip and a faintly moist slough. He took up his knife and the piece of cord and walked to the high edge of the ice-cage. Then he stepped out weakly on the river. The ice swayed, crackled, but did not give.

Finally, without danger, he dragged his body slowly atop the cliff and sat, expended, a few steps from where the rifle had dropped: it lay outlined beneath the snow. But he did not reach to seize it. Standing there, he began to think of building a cabin, some kind of lean-to shelter beneath a tree. As he looked up, he saw a late deer come out of the woods, standing in the lee beside the dead deer where the water-hole had been, and scent the air. It did not fly from him, though it looked toward him. It was the roe, the king-deer; suddenly in his wake came four, then five females and a young buck. His eyes were austere as he looked at them. The deer beheld him there a few paces from his rifle. They had not come to drink. He knew they had come to stand where the bitter snow was shallow, and out of the blade of the wind. They had come into his hands, since they knew him well, and the scent of him had become alike wild. Yet not merely this. He felt it now, though he was not gifted with the words: the hope that had been the gulf, the shadow, was traced there—the nature that

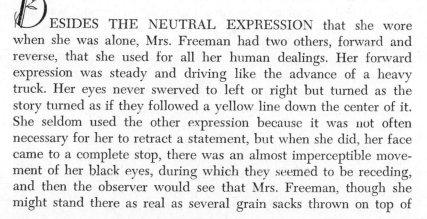

seemed looking in his direction, at last without fear, not at him, but on through him (at least through him) saw itself whole again, alive. As he stood there, it seemed only a passing feeling, but it came to him in deep need, a first sign of the man he had become— awakening him to that succession of things in which he had, at some cost to himself, witnessed for man in death's barrens, while out of the pitchblack of memory came a recognizable source of light.

FLANNERY O'CONNOR

Good Country People

ESIDES THE NEUTRAL EXPRESSION that she wore when she was alone, Mrs. Freeman had two others, forward and reverse, that she used for all her human dealings. Her forward expression was steady and driving like the advance of a heavy truck. Her eyes never swerved to left or right but turned as the story turned as if they followed a yellow line down the center of it. She seldom used the other expression because it was not often necessary for her to retract a statement, but when she did, her face came to a complete stop, there was an almost imperceptible movement of her black eyes, during which they seemed to be receding, and then the observer would see that Mrs. Freeman, though she might stand there as real as several grain sacks thrown on top of each other, was no longer there in spirit. As for getting anything across to her when this was the case, Mrs. Hopewell had given it up. She might talk her head off. Mrs. Freeman could never be brought to admit herself wrong on any point. She would stand there and if she could be brought to say anything, it was something like, "Well, I wouldn't of said it was and I wouldn't of said it wasn't," or letting her gaze range over the top kitchen shelf where there was an assortment of dusty bottles, she might remark, "I see you ain't ate many of them figs you put up last summer."

They carried on their most important business in the kitchen at breakfast. Every morning Mrs. Hopewell got up at seven o'clock and lit her gas heater and Joy's. Joy was her daughter, a large blonde girl who had an artificial leg. Mrs. Hopewell thought of her as a child though she was thirty-two years old and highly educated. Joy would get up while her mother was eating and lumber into the bathroom and slam the door, and before long, Mrs. Freeman would arrive at the back door. Joy would hear her mother call, "Come on in," and then they would talk for a while in low voices that were indistinguishable in the bathroom. By the time Joy came in, they had usually finished the weather report and were on one or the other of Mrs. Freeman's daughters, Glynese or Carramae. Joy called them Glycerin and Caramel. Glynese, a redhead, was eighteen and had many admirers; Carramae, a blonde, was only fifteen but already married and pregnant. She could not keep anything on her stomach. Every morning Mrs. Freeman told Mrs. Hopewell how many times she had vomited since the last report.

Mrs. Hopewell liked to tell people that Glynese and Carramae were two of the finest girls she knew and that Mrs. Freeman was a *lady* and that she was never ashamed to take her anywhere or introduce her to anybody they might meet. Then she would tell how she had happened to hire the Freemans in the first place and how they were a godsend to her and how she had had them four years. The reason for her keeping them so long was that they were not trash. They were good country people. She had telephoned the man whose name they had given as a reference and he had told her that Mr. Freeman was a good farmer but that his wife was the nosiest woman ever to walk the earth. "She's got to be into everything," the man said. "If she don't get there before the dust settles, you can bet she's dead, that's all. She'll want to know all your business. I can stand him real good," he had said, "but me nor my wife neither could have stood that woman one more minute on this place." That had put Mrs. Hopewell off for a few days.

She had hired them in the end because there were no other applicants but she had made up her mind beforehand exactly how she would handle the woman. Since she was the type who had to be into everything, then, Mrs. Hopewell had decided, she would not only let her be into everything, she would *see to it* that she was into everything—she would give her the responsibility of everything, she would put her in charge. Mrs. Hopewell had no bad qualities of her own but she was able to use other people's in such a constructive way that she never felt the lack. She had hired the Freemans and she had kept them four years.

Nothing is perfect. This was one of Mrs. Hopewell's favorite sayings. Another was: that is life! And still another, the most important, was: well, other people have their opinions too. She would make these statements, usually at the table, in a tone of gentle insistence as if no one held them but her, and the large hulking Joy, whose constant outrage had obliterated every expression from her face, would stare just a little to the side of her, her eyes icy blue, with the look of someone who had achieved blindness by an act of will and means to keep it.

When Mrs. Hopewell said to Mrs. Freeman that life was like that, Mrs. Freeman would say, "I always said so myself." Nothing had been arrived at by anyone that had not first been arrived at by her. She was quicker than Mr. Freeman. When Mrs. Hopewell said to her after they had been on the place a while. "You know, you're the wheel behind the wheel," and winked, Mrs. Freeman had said, "I know it. I've always been quick. It's some that are quicker than others."

"Everybody is different," Mrs. Hopewell said.

"Yes, most people is," Mrs. Freeman said.

"It takes all kinds to make the world."

"I always said it did myself."

The girl was used to this kind of dialogue for breakfast and more of it for dinner; sometimes they had it for supper too. When they had no guest they ate in the kitchen because that was easier.

Mrs. Freeman always managed to arrive at some point during the meal and to watch them finish it. She would stand in the doorway if it were summer but in the winter she would stand with one elbow on top of the refrigerator and look down on them, or she would stand by the gas heater, lifting the back of her skirt slightly. Occasionally she would stand against the wall and roll her head from side to side. At no time was she in any hurry to leave. All this was very trying on Mrs. Hopewell but she was a woman of great patience. She realized that nothing is perfect and that in the Freemans she had good country people and that if, in this day and age, you get good country people, you had better hang onto them.

She had had plenty of experience with trash. Before the Freemans she had averaged one tenant family a year. The wives of these farmers were not the kind you would want to be around you for very long. Mrs. Hopewell, who had divorced her husband long ago, needed someone to walk over the fields with her; and when Joy had to be impressed for these services, her remarks were usually so ugly and her face so glum that Mrs. Hopewell would say, "If you can't come pleasantly, I don't want you at all," to which the girl, standing square and rigid-shouldered with her neck thrust slightly forward, would reply, "If you want me, here I am—LIKE I AM."

Mrs. Hopewell excused this attitude because of the leg (which had been shot off in a hunting accident when Joy was ten). It was hard for Mrs. Hopewell to realize that her child was thirty-two now and that for more than twenty years she had had only one leg. She thought of her still as a child because it tore her heart to think instead of the poor stout girl in her thirties who had never danced a step or had any *normal* good times. Her name was really Joy but as soon as she was twenty-one and away from home, she had had it legally changed. Mrs. Hopewell was certain that she had thought and thought until she had hit upon the ugliest name in any language. Then she had gone and had the beautiful name, Joy, changed without telling her mother until after she had done it. Her legal name was Hulga.

When Mrs. Hopewell thought the name, Hulga, she thought of the broad blank hull of a battleship. She would not use it. She continued to call her Joy to which the girl responded but in a purely mechanical way.

Hulga had learned to tolerate Mrs. Freeman who saved her from taking walks with her mother. Even Glynese and Carramae were useful when they occupied attention that might otherwise have been directed at her. At first she had thought she could not stand Mrs. Freeman for she had found that it was not possible to be rude to her. Mrs. Freeman would take on strange resentments and for days together she would be sullen but the source of her displeasure was always obscure; a direct attack, a positive leer, blatant ugliness to her face—these never touched her. And without warning one day, she began calling her Hulga.

She did not call her that in front of Mrs. Hopewell who would have been incensed but when she and the girl happened to be out of the house together, she would say something and add the name Hulga to the end of it, and the big spectacled Joy-Hulga would scowl and redden as if her privacy had been intruded upon. She considered the name her personal affair. She had arrived at it first purely on the basis of its ugly sound and then the full genius of its fitness had struck her. She had a vision of the name working like the ugly sweating Vulcan who stayed in the furnace and to whom, presumably, the goddess had to come when called. She saw it as the name of her highest creative act. One of her major triumphs was that her mother had not been able to turn her dust into Joy, but the greater one was that she had been able to turn it herself into Hulga. However, Mrs. Freeman's relish for using the name only irritated her. It was as if Mrs. Freeman's beady steel-pointed eyes had penetrated far enough behind her face to reach some secret fact. Something about her seemed to fascinate Mrs. Freeman and then one day Hulga realized that it was the artificial leg. Mrs. Freeman had a special fondness for the details of secret infections, hidden deformities, assaults upon children. Of diseases, she preferred the lingering or incurable. Hulga had heard Mrs. Hopewell give her the details of the hunting accident, how the leg had been literally blasted off, how she had never lost consciousness. Mrs. Freeman could listen to it any time as if it had happened an hour ago.

When Hulga stumped into the kitchen in the morning (she could walk without making the awful noise but she made it—Mrs. Hopewell was certain—because it was ugly-sounding), she glanced

at them and did not speak. Mrs. Hopewell would be in her red
kimono with her hair tied around her head in rags. She would be
sitting at the table, finishing her breakfast and Mrs. Freeman would
be hanging by her elbow outward from the refrigerator, looking
down at the table. Hulga always put her eggs on the stove to boil
and then stood over them with her arms folded, and Mrs. Hopewell
would look at her—a kind of indirect gaze divided between her
and Mrs. Freeman—and would think that if she would only keep
herself up a little, she wouldn't be so bad looking. There was nothing wrong with her face that a pleasant expression wouldn't help.
Mrs. Hopewell said that people who looked on the bright side of
things would be beautiful even if they were not.

Whenever she looked at Joy this way, she could not help but
feel that it would have been better if the child had not taken the
Ph.D. It had certainly not brought her out any and now that she
had it, there was no more excuse for her to go to school again. Mrs.
Hopewell thought it was nice for girls to go to school to have a good
time but Joy had "gone through." Anyhow, she would not have
been strong enough to go again. The doctors had told Mrs. Hopewell that with the best of care, Joy might see forty-five. She had a
weak heart. Joy had made it plain that if it had not been for this
condition, she would be far from these red hills and good country
people. She would be in a university lecturing to people who knew
what she was talking about. And Mrs. Hopewell could very well
picture her there, looking like a scarecrow and lecturing to more of
the same. Here she went about all day in a six-year-old skirt and a
yellow sweat shirt with a faded cowboy on a horse embossed on it.
She thought this was funny; Mrs. Hopewell thought it was idiotic
and showed simply that she was still a child. She was brilliant but
she didn't have a grain of sense. It seemed to Mrs. Hopewell that
every year she grew less like other people and more like herself—
bloated, rude, and squint-eyed. And she said such strange things!
To her own mother she had said—without warning, without excuse,
standing up in the middle of a meal with her face purple and her
mouth half full—"Woman! do you ever look inside? Do you ever
look inside and see what you are *not?* God!" she had cried sinking
down again and staring at her plate, "Malebranche was right: we
are not our own light: We are not our own light!" Mrs. Hopewell

had no idea to this day what brought that on. She had only made
the remark, hoping Joy would take it in, that a smile never hurt
anyone.

The girl had taken the Ph.D. in philosophy and this left Mrs.
Hopewell at a complete loss. You could say, "My daughter is a
nurse," or "My daughter is a school teacher," or even, "My daughter
is a chemical engineer." You could not say, "My daughter is a
philosopher." That was something that had ended with the Greeks
and Romans. All day Joy sat on her neck in a deep chair, reading.
Sometimes she went for walks but she didn't like dogs or cats or
birds or flowers or nature or nice young men. She looked at nice
young men as if she could smell their stupidity.

One day Mrs. Hopewell had picked up one of the books the
girl had just put down and opening it at random, she read, "Science,
on the other hand, has to assert its soberness and seriousness afresh
and declare that it is concerned solely with what-is. Nothing—
how can it be for science anything but a horror and a phantasm?
If science is right, then one thing stands firm: science wishes to
know nothing of nothing. Such is after all the strictly scientific approach to Nothing. We know it by wishing to know nothing of
Nothing." These words had been underlined with a blue pencil
and they worked on Mrs. Hopewell like some evil incantation in
gibberish. She shut the book quickly and went out of the room as
if she were having a chill.

This morning when the girl came in, Mrs. Freeman was on
Carramae. "She thrown up four times after supper," she said, "and
was up twict in the night after three o'clock. Yesterday she didn't
do nothing but ramble in the bureau drawer. All she did. Stand
up there and see what she could run up on."

"She's got to eat," Mrs. Hopewell muttered, sipping her coffee,
while she watched Joy's back at the stove. She was wondering what
the child had said to the Bible salesman. She could not imagine
what kind of a conversation she could possibly have had with him.

He was a tall gaunt hatless youth who had called yesterday to
sell them a Bible. He had appeared at the door, carrying a large
black suitcase that weighted him so heavily on one side that he had
to brace himself against the door facing. He seemed on the point
of collapse but he said in a cheerful voice, "Good morning, Mrs.

Cedars!" and set the suitcase down on the mat. He was not a bad-looking young man though he had on a bright blue suit and yellow socks that were not pulled up far enough. He had prominent face bones and a streak of sticky-looking brown hair falling across his forehead.

"I'm Mrs. Hopewell," she said.

"Oh!" he said, pretending to look puzzled but with his eyes sparkling, "I saw it said 'The Cedars,' on the mailbox so I thought you was Mrs. Cedars!" and he burst out in a pleasant laugh. He picked up the satchel and under cover of a pant, he fell forward into her hall. It was rather as if the suitcase had moved first, jerking him after it. "Mrs. Hopewell!" he said and grabbed her hand. "I hope you are well!" and he laughed again and then all at once his face sobered completely. He paused and gave her a straight earnest look and said, "Lady, I've come to speak of serious things."

"Well, come in," she muttered, none too pleased because her dinner was almost ready. He came into the parlor and sat down on the edge of a straight chair and put the suitcase between his feet and glanced around the room as if he were sizing her up by it. Her silver gleamed on the two sideboards; she decided he had never been in a room as elegant as this.

"Mrs. Hopewell," he began, using her name in a way that sounded almost intimate, "I know you believe in Chrustian service."

"Well yes," she murmured.

"I know," he said and paused, looking very wise with his head cocked on one side, "that you're a good woman. Friends have told me."

Mrs. Hopewell never liked to be taken for a fool. "What are you selling?" she asked.

"Bibles," the young man said and his eyes raced around the room before he added, "I see you have no family Bible in your parlor, I see that is the one lack you got!"

Mrs. Hopewell could not say, "My daughter is an atheist and won't let me keep the Bible in the parlor." She said, stiffening slightly, "I keep my Bible by my bedside." This was not the truth. It was in the attic somewhere.

"Lady," he said, "the word of God ought to be in the parlor."

"Well, I think that's a matter of taste," she began. "I think . . ."

"Lady," he said, "for a Chrustian, the word of God ought to be in every room in the house besides in his heart. I know you're a Chrustian because I can see it in every line of your face."

She stood up and said, "Well, young man, I don't want to buy a Bible and I smell my dinner burning."

He didn't get up. He began to twist his hands and looking down at them, he said softly, "Well lady, I'll tell you the truth— not many people want to buy one nowadays and besides, I know I'm real simple. I don't know how to say a thing but to say it. I'm just a country boy." He glanced up into her unfriendly face. "People like you don't like to fool with country people like me!"

"Why!" she cried, "good country people are the salt of the earth! Besides, we all have different ways of doing, it takes all kinds to make the world go 'round. That's life!"

"You said a mouthful," he said.

"Why, I think there aren't enough good country people in the world!" she said, stirred. "I think that's what's wrong with it!"

His face had brightened. "I didn't inraduce myself," he said. "I'm Manley Pointer from out in the country around Willohobie, not even from a place, just from near a place."

"You wait a minute," she said. "I have to see about my dinner." She went out to the kitchen and found Joy standing near the door where she had been listening.

"Get rid of the salt of the earth," she said, "and let's eat."

Mrs. Hopewell gave her a pained look and turned the heat down under the vegetables. "*I* can't be rude to anybody," she murmured and went back into the parlor.

He had opened the suitcase and was sitting with a Bible on each knee.

"You might as well put those up," she told him. "I don't want one."

"I appreciate your honesty," he said. "You don't see any more real honest people unless you go way out in the country."

"I know," she said, "real genuine folks!" Through the crack in the door she heard a groan.

"I guess a lot of boys come telling you they're working their way through college," he said, "but I'm not going to tell you that. Somehow," he said, "I don't want to go to college. I want to devote my

life to Chrustian service. See," he said, lowering his voice, "I got this
heart condition. I may not live long. When you know it's something
wrong with you and you may not live long, well then, lady . . ."
He paused, with his mouth open, and stared at her.

He and Joy had the same condition! She knew that her eyes
were filling with tears but she collected herself quickly and murmured, "Won't you stay for dinner? We'd love to have you!" and
was sorry the instant she heard herself say it.

"Yes mam," he said in an abashed voice, "I would sher love to
do that!"

Joy had given him one look on being introduced to him and
then throughout the meal had not glanced at him again. He had
addressed several remarks to her, which she had pretended not to
hear. Mrs. Hopewell could not understand deliberate rudeness, although she lived with it, and she felt she had always to overflow
with hospitality to make up for Joy's lack of courtesy. She urged him
to talk about himself and he did. He said he was the seventh child
of twelve and that his father had been crushed under a tree when
he himself was eight year old. He had been crushed very badly, in
fact, almost cut in two and was practically not recognizable. His
mother had got along the best she could by hard working and she
had always seen that her children went to Sunday School and that
they read the Bible every evening. He was now nineteen year old
and he had been selling Bibles for four months. In that time he had
sold seventy-seven Bibles and had the promise of two more sales.
He wanted to become a missionary because he thought that was the
way you could do most for people. "He who losest his life shall find
it," he said simply and he was so sincere, so genuine and earnest
that Mrs. Hopewell would not for the world have smiled. He pre-
vented his peas from sliding onto the table by blocking them with a
piece of bread which he later cleaned his plate with. She could see
Joy observing sidewise how he handled his knife and fork and she
saw too that every few minutes, the boy would dart a keen ap-
praising glance at the girl as if he were trying to attract her
attention.

After dinner Joy cleared the dishes off the table and disappeared
and Mrs. Hopewell was left to talk with him. He told her again
about his childhood and his father's accident and about various

things that had happened to him. Every five minutes or so she would stifle a yawn. He sat for two hours until finally she told him she must go because she had an appointment in town. He packed his Bibles and thanked her and prepared to leave, but in the doorway he stopped and wrung her hand and said that not on any of his trips had he met a lady as nice as her and he asked if he could come again. She had said she would always be happy to see him.

Joy had been standing in the road, apparently looking at something in the distance, when he came down the steps toward her, bent to the side with his heavy valise. He stopped where she was standing and confronted her directly. Mrs. Hopewell could not hear what he said but she trembled to think what Joy would say to him. She could see that after a minute Joy said something and that then the boy began to speak again, making an excited gesture with his free hand. After a minute Joy said something else at which the boy began to speak once more. Then to her amazement, Mrs. Hopewell saw the two of them walk off together, toward the gate. Joy had walked all the way to the gate with him and Mrs. Hopewell could not imagine what they had said to each other, and she had not yet dared to ask.

Mrs. Freeman was insisting upon her attention. She had moved from the refrigerator to the heater so that Mrs. Hopewell had to turn and face her in order to seem to be listening. "Glynese gone out with Harvey Hill again last night," she said. "She had this sty."

"Hill," Mrs. Hopewell said absently, "is that the one who works in the garage?"

"Nome, he's the one that goes to chiropracter school," Mrs. Freeman said. "She had this sty. Been had it two days. So she says when he brought her in the other night he says, 'Lemme get rid of that sty for you,' and she says, 'How?' and he says, 'You just lay yourself down acrost the seat of that car and I'll show you.' So she done it and he popped her neck. Kept on a-popping it several times until she made him quit. This morning," Mrs. Freeman said, "she ain't got no sty. She ain't got no traces of a sty."

"I never heard of that before," Mrs. Hopewell said.

"He ast her to marry him before the Ordinary," Mrs. Freeman went on, "and she told him she wasn't going to be married in no *office*."

"Well, Glynese is a fine girl," Mrs. Hopewell said. "Glynese and Carramae are both fine girls."

"Carramae said when her and Lyman was married Lyman said it sure felt sacred to him. She said he said he wouldn't take five hundred dollars for being married by a preacher."

"How much would he take?" the girl asked from the stove.

"He said he wouldn't take five hundred dollars," Mrs. Freeman repeated.

"Well we all have work to do," Mrs. Hopewell said.

"Lyman said it just felt more sacred to him," Mrs. Freeman said. "The doctor wants Carramae to eat prunes. Says instead of medicine. Says them cramps is coming from pressure. You know where I think it is?"

"She'll be better in a few weeks," Mrs. Hopewell said.

"In the tube," Mrs. Freeman said. "Else she wouldn't be as sick as she is."

Hulga had cracked her two eggs into a saucer and was bringing them to the table along with a cup of coffee that she had filled too full. She sat down carefully and began to eat, meaning to keep Mrs. Freeman there by questions if for any reason she showed an inclination to leave. She could perceive her mother's eye on her. The first roundabout question would be about the Bible salesman and she did not wish to bring it on. "How did he pop her neck?" she asked.

Mrs. Freeman went into a description of how he had popped her neck. She said he owned a '55 Mercury but that Glynese said she would rather marry a man with only a '36 Plymouth who would be married by a preacher. The girl asked what if he had a '32 Plymouth and Mrs. Freeman said what Glynese had said was a '36 Plymouth.

Mrs. Hopewell said there were not many girls with Glynese's common sense. She said what she admired in those girls was their common sense. She said that reminded her that they had had a nice visitor yesterday, a young man selling Bibles. "Lord," she said, "he bored me to death but he was so sincere and genuine I couldn't be rude to him. He was just good country people, you know," she said, "—just the salt of the earth."

"I seen him walk up," Mrs. Freeman said, "and then later—I seen him walk off," and Hulga could feel the slight shift in her voice, the slight insinuation, that he had not walked off alone, had he? Her face remained expressionless but the color rose into her neck and she seemed to swallow it down with the next spoonful of egg. Mrs. Freeman was looking at her as if they had a secret together.

"Well, it takes all kinds of people to make the world go 'round," Mrs. Hopewell said. "It's very good we aren't all alike."

"Some people are more alike than others," Mrs. Freeman said.

Hulga got up and stumped, with about twice the noise that was necessary, into her room and locked the door. She was to meet the Bible salesman at ten o'clock at the gate.

She had thought about it half the night. She had started thinking of it as a great joke and then she had begun to see profound implications in it. She had lain in bed imagining dialogues for them that were insane on the surface but that reached below to depths that no Bible salesman would be aware of. Their conversation yesterday had been of this kind.

He had stopped in front of her and had simply stood there. His face was bony and sweaty and bright, with a little pointed nose in the center of it, and his look was different from what it had been at the dinner table. He was gazing at her with open curiosity, with fascination, like a child watching a new fantastic animal at the zoo, and he was breathing as if he had run a great distance to reach her. His gaze seemed somehow familiar but she could not think where she had been regarded with it before. For almost a minute he didn't say anything. Then on what seemed an insuck of breath, he whispered, "You ever ate a chicken that was two days old?"

The girl looked at him stonily. He might have just put this question up for consideration at the meeting of a philosophical association. "Yes," she presently replied as if she had considered it from all angles.

"It must have been mighty small!" he said triumphantly and shook all over with little nervous giggles, getting very red in the face, and subsiding finally into his gaze of complete admiration, while the girl's expression remained exactly the same.

"How old are you?" he asked softly.

She waited some time before she answered. Then in a flat voice she said, "Seventeen."

His smiles came in succession like waves breaking on the surface of a little lake. "I see you got a wooden leg," he said. "I think you're real brave. I think you're real sweet."

The girl stood blank and solid and silent.

"Walk to the gate with me," he said. "You're a brave sweet little thing and I liked you the minute I seen you walk in the door."

Hulga began to move forward.

"What's your name?" he asked, smiling down on the top of her head.

"Hulga," she said.

"Hulga," he murmured, "Hulga. Hulga. I never heard of anybody name Hulga before. You're shy, aren't you, Hulga?" he asked.

She nodded, watching his large red hand on the handle of the giant valise.

"I like girls that wear glasses," he said. "I think a lot. I'm not like these people that a serious thought don't ever enter their heads. It's because I may die."

"I may die too," she said suddenly and looked up at him. His eyes were very small and brown, glittering feverishly.

"Listen," he said, "don't you think some people was meant to meet on account of what all they got in common and all? Like they both think serious thoughts and all?" He shifted the valise to his other hand so that the hand nearest her was free. He caught hold of her elbow and shook it a little. "I don't work on Saturday," he said. "I like to walk in the woods and see what Mother Nature is wearing. O'er the hills and far away. Pic-nics and things. Couldn't we go on a pic-nic tomorrow? Say yes, Hulga," he said and gave her a dying look as if he felt his insides about to drop out of him. He had even seemed to sway slightly toward her.

During the night she had imagined that she seduced him. She imagined that the two of them walked on the place until they came to the storage barn beyond the two back fields and there, she imagined, that things came to such a pass that she very easily seduced him and that then, of course, she had to reckon with his remorse. True genius can get an idea across even to an inferior mind. She imagined that she took his remorse in hand and changed it into a deeper understanding of life. She took all his shame away and turned it into something useful.

She set off for the gate at exactly ten o'clock, escaping without drawing Mrs. Hopewell's attention. She didn't take anything to eat, forgetting that food is usually taken on a picnic. She wore a pair of slacks and a dirty white shirt, and as an afterthought, she had put some Vapex on the collar of it since she did not own any perfume. When she reached the gate no one was there.

She looked up and down the empty highway and had the furious feeling that she had been tricked, that he had only meant to make her walk to the gate after the idea of him. Then suddenly he stood up, very tall, from behind a bush on the opposite embankment. Smiling, he lifted his hat which was new and wide-brimmed. He had not worn it yesterday and she wondered if he had bought it for the occasion. It was toast-colored with a red and white band around it and was slightly too large for him. He stepped from behind the bush still carrying the black valise. He had on the same suit and the same yellow socks sucked down in his shoes from walking. He crossed the highway and said, "I knew you'd come!"

The girl wondered acidly how he had known this. She pointed to the valise and asked, "Why did you bring your Bibles?"

He took her elbow, smiling down on her as if he could not stop. "You can never tell when you'll need the word of God, Hulga," he said. She had a moment in which she doubted that this was actually happening and then they began to climb the embankment. They went down into the pasture toward the woods. The boy walked lightly by her side, bouncing on his toes. The valise did not seem to be heavy today; he even swung it. They crossed half the pasture without saying anything and then, putting his hand easily on the small of her neck, he asked softly, "Where does your wooden leg join on?"

She turned an ugly red and glared at him and for an instant the boy looked abashed. "I didn't mean you no harm," he said. "I only meant you're so brave and all. I guess God takes care of you."

"No," she said, looking forward and walking fast, "I don't even believe in God."

At this he stopped and whistled. "No!" he exclaimed as if he were too astonished to say anything else.

She walked on and in a second he was bouncing at her side, fanning with his hat. "That's very unusual for a girl," he remarked, watching her out of the corner of his eye. When they reached the edge of the wood, he put his hand on her back again and drew her against him without a word and kissed her heavily.

The kiss, which had more pressure than feeling behind it, produced that extra surge of adrenalin in the girl that enables one to carry a packed trunk out of a burning house, but in her, the power went at once to the brain. Even before he released her, her mind, clear and detached and ironic anyway, was regarding him from a great distance, with amusement but with pity. She had never been kissed before and she was pleased to discover that it was an unexceptional experience and all a matter of the mind's control. Some people might enjoy drain water if they were told it was vodka. When the boy, looking expectant but uncertain, pushed her gently away, she turned and walked on, saying nothing as if such business, for her, were common enough.

He came along panting at her side, trying to help her when he saw a root that she might trip over. He caught and held back the long swaying blades of thorn vine until she had passed beyond them. She led the way and he came breathing heavily behind her. Then they came out on a sunlit hillside, sloping softly into another one a little smaller. Beyond, they could see the rusted top of the old barn where the extra hay was stored.

The hill was sprinkled with small pink weeds. "Then you ain't saved?" he asked suddenly, stopping.

The girl smiled. It was the first time she had smiled at him at all. "In my economy," she said, "I'm saved and you are damned but I told you I didn't believe in God."

Nothing seemed to destroy the boy's look of admiration. He gazed at her now as if the fantastic animal at the zoo had put its paw through the bars and given him a loving poke. She thought he looked as if he wanted to kiss her again and she walked on before he had the chance.

"Ain't there somewheres we can sit down sometime?" he murmured, his voice softening toward the end of the sentence.

"In that barn," she said.

They made for it rapidly as if it might slide away like a train. It was a large two-story barn, cool and dark inside. The boy pointed up the ladder that led into the loft and said, "It's too bad we can't go up there."

"Why can't we?" she asked.

"Yer leg," he said reverently.

The girl gave him a contemptuous look and putting both hands on the ladder, she climbed it while he stood below, apparently awestruck. She pulled herself expertly through the opening and then looked down at him and said, "Well, come on if you're coming," and he began to climb the ladder, awkwardly bringing the suitcase with him.

"We won't need the Bible," she observed.

"You never can tell," he said, panting. After he had got into the loft, he was a few seconds catching his breath. She had sat down in a pile of straw. A wide sheath of sunlight, filled with dust particles, slanted over her. She lay back against a bale, her face turned away, looking out the front opening of the barn where hay was thrown from a wagon into the loft. The two pink-speckled hillsides lay back against a dark ridge of woods. The sky was cloudless and cold blue. The boy dropped down by her side and put one arm under her and the other over her and began methodically kissing her face, making little noises like a fish. He did not remove his hat but it was pushed far enough back not to interfere. When her glasses got in his way, he took them off of her and slipped them into his pocket.

The girl at first did not return any of the kisses but presently she began to and after she had put several on his cheek, she reached his lips and remained there, kissing him again and again as if she were trying to draw all the breath out of him. His breath was clear and sweet like a child's and the kisses were sticky like a child's. He mumbled about loving her and about knowing when he first seen her that he loved her, but the mumbling was like the sleepy fretting of a child being put to sleep by his mother. Her mind, throughout this, never stopped or lost itself for a second to her feelings. "You ain't said you loved me none," he whispered finally, pulling back from her. "You got to say that."

She looked away from him off into the hollow sky and then down at a black ridge and then down farther into what appeared to be two green swelling lakes. She didn't realize he had taken her glasses but this landscape could not seem exceptional to her for she seldom paid any close attention to her surroundings.

"You got to say it," he repeated. "You got to say you love me."

She was always careful how she committed herself. "In a sense," she began, "if you use the word loosely, you might say that. But it's not a word I use. I don't have illusions. I'm one of those people who see *through* to nothing."

The boy was frowning. "You got to say it. I said it and you got to say it," he said.

The girl looked at him almost tenderly. "You poor baby," she murmured. "It's just as well you don't understand," and she pulled him by the neck, face-down, against her. "We are all damned," she said, "but some of us have taken off our blindfolds and see that there's nothing to see. It's a kind of salvation."

The boy's astonished eyes looked blankly through the ends of her hair. "Okay," he almost whined, "but do you love me or don'tcher?"

"Yes," she said and added, "in a sense. But I must tell you something. There mustn't be anything dishonest between us." She lifted his head and looked him in the eye. "I am thirty years old," she said. "I have a number of degrees."

The boy's look was irritated but dogged. "I don't care," he said. "I don't care a thing about what all you done. I just want to know if you love me or don'tcher?" and he caught her to him and wildly planted her face with kisses until she said, "Yes, yes."

"Okay then," he said, letting her go. "Prove it."

She smiled, looking dreamily out on the shifty landscape. She had seduced him without even making up her mind to try. "How?" she asked, feeling that he should be delayed a little.

He leaned over and put his lips to the ear. "Show me where your wooden leg joins on," he whispered.

The girl uttered a sharp little cry and her face instantly drained of color. The obscenity of the suggestion was not what shocked her. As a child she had sometimes been subject to feelings of shame but education had removed the last traces of that as a good surgeon scrapes for cancer; she would no more have felt it over what he was asking than she would have believed in his Bible. But she was as sensitive about the artificial leg as a peacock about his tail. No one ever touched it but her. She took care of it as someone else would his soul, in private and almost with her own eyes turned away. "No," she said.

"I known it," he muttered, sitting up. "You're just playing me for a sucker."

"Oh no no!" she cried. "It joins on at the knee. Only at the knee. Why do you want to see it?"

The boy gave her a long penetrating look. "Because," he said, "it's what makes you different. You ain't like anybody else."

She sat staring at him. There was nothing about her face or her round freezing-blue eyes to indicate that this had moved her; but she felt as if her heart had stopped and left her mind to pump her blood. She decided that for the first time in her life she was face to face with real innocence. This boy, with an instinct that came from beyond wisdom, had touched the truth about her. When after a minute, she said in a hoarse high voice, "All right," it was like surrendering to him completely. It was like losing her own life and finding it again, miraculously, in his.

Very gently he began to roll the slack leg up. The artificial limb, in a white sock and brown flat shoe, was bound in a heavy material like canvas and ended in an ugly jointure where it was attached to the stump. The boy's face and his voice were entirely reverent as he uncovered it and said, "Now show me how to take it off and on."

She took it off for him and put it back on again and then he took it off himself, handling it as tenderly as if it were a real one. "See!" he said with a delighted child's face. "Now I can do it myself!"

"Put it back on," she said. She was thinking that she would run away with him and that every night he would take the leg off and every morning put it back on again. "Put it back on," she said.

"Not yet," he murmured, setting it on its foot out of her reach. "Leave it off for a while. You got me instead."

She gave a little cry of alarm but he pushed her down and began to kiss her again. Without the leg she felt entirely dependent on him. Her brain seemed to have stopped thinking altogether and to be about some other function that it was not very good at. Different expressions raced back and forth over her face. Every now and then the boy, his eyes like two steeel spikes, would glance behind him where the leg stood. Finally she pushed him off and said, "Put it back on me now."

"Wait," he said. He leaned the other way and pulled the valise toward him and opened it. It had a pale blue spotted lining and there were only two Bibles in it. He took one of these out and opened the cover of it. It was hollow and contained a pocket flask of whiskey, a pack of cards, and a small blue box with printing on it. He laid these out in front of her one at a time in an evenly-spaced row, like one presenting offerings at the shrine of a goddess. He put the blue box in her hand. THIS PRODUCT TO BE USED ONLY FOR THE PREVENTION OF DISEASE, she read, and dropped it. The boy was unscrewing the top of the flask. He stopped and pointed, with a smile, to the deck of cards. It was not an ordinary deck but one with an obscene picture on the back of each card. "Take a swig," he said, offering her the bottle first. He held it in front of her, but like one mesmerized, she did not move.

Her voice when she spoke had an almost pleading sound. "Aren't you," she murmured, "aren't you just good country people?"

The boy cocked his head. He looked as if he were just beginning to understand that she might be trying to insult him. "Yeah," he said, curling his lip slightly, "but it ain't held me back none. I'm as good as you any day in the week."

"Give me my leg," she said.

He pushed it farther away with his foot. "Come on now, let's begin to have us a good time," he said coaxingly. "We ain't got to know one another good yet."

"Give me my leg!" she screamed and tried to lunge for it but he pushed her down easily.

"What's the matter with you all of a sudden?" he asked, frowning as he screwed the top on the flask and put it quickly back inside the Bible. "You just a while ago said you didn't believe in nothing. I thought you was some girl!"

Her face was almost purple. "You're a Christian!" she hissed. "You're a fine Christian! You're just like them all—say one thing and do another. You're a perfect Christian, you're . . ."

The boy's mouth was set angrily. "I hope you don't think," he said in a lofty indignant tone, "that I believe in that crap! I may sell Bibles but I know which end is up and I wasn't born yesterday and I know where I'm going!"

"Give me my leg!" she screeched. He jumped up so quickly that

she barely saw him sweep the cards and the blue box back into the
Bible and throw the Bible into the valise. She saw him grab the leg
and then she saw it for an instant slanted forlornly across the inside
of the suitcase with a Bible at either side of its opposite ends. He
slammed the lid shut and snatched up the valise and swung it down
the hole and then stepped through himself.

When all of him had passed but his head, he turned and regarded her with a look that no longer had any admiration in it.
"I've gotten a lot of interesting things," he said. "One time I got a
woman's glass eye this way. And you needn't to think you'll catch
me because Pointer ain't really my name. I use a different name at
every house I call at and don't stay nowhere long. And I'll tell you
another thing, Hulga," he said, using the name as if he didn't think
much of it, "you ain't so smart. I been believing in nothing ever
since I was born!" and then the toast-colored hat disappeared down
the hole and the girl was left, sitting on the straw in the dusty sunlight. When she turned her churning face toward the opening, she
saw his blue figure struggling successfully over the green speckled
lake.

Mrs. Hopewell and Mrs. Freeman, who were in the back
pasture, digging up onions, saw him emerge a little later from the
woods and head across the meadow toward the highway. "Why,
that looks like that nice dull young man that tried to sell me a Bible
yesterday," Mrs. Hopewell said, squinting. "He must have been selling them to the Negroes back in there. He was so simple," she said,
"but I guess the world would be better off if we were all that
simple."

Mrs. Freeman's gaze drove forward and just touched him before
he disappeared under the hill. Then she returned her attention to
the evil-smelling onion shoot she was lifting from the ground. "Some
can't be that simple," she said. "I know I never could."

NELSON ALGREN

A Bottle of Milk
for Mother

I feel I am of them—
I belong to those convicts and prostitutes myself,
And henceforth I will not deny them—
For how can I deny myself?

WHITMAN

WO MONTHS AFTER THE Polish Warriors S.A.C. had had their heads shaved, Bruno Lefty Bicek got into his final difficulty with the Racine Street police. The arresting officers and a reporter from the *Dziennik Chicagoski* were grouped about the captain's desk when the boy was urged forward into the room by Sergeant Adamovitch, with two fingers wrapped about the boy's broad belt: a full-bodied boy wearing a worn and sleeveless blue work shirt grown too tight across the shoulders; and the shoulders themselves with a loose swing to them. His skull and face were shining from a recent scrubbing, so that the little bridgeless nose glistened between the protective points of the cheekbones. Behind the desk sat Kozak, eleven years on the force and brother to an alderman. The reporter stuck a cigarette behind one ear like a pencil.

"We spotted him followin' the drunk down Chicago—" Sergeant Comiskey began.

Captain Kozak interrupted. "Let the jackroller tell us how he done it hisself."

"I ain't no jackroller."

"What you doin' here, then?"

Bicek folded his naked arms.

"Answer me. If you ain't here for jackrollin' it must be for strong-arm robb'ry—'r you one of them Chicago Av'noo moll-buzzers?"

"I ain't that neither."

"C'mon, c'mon, I seen you in here before—what were you up to, followin' that poor old man?"

"I ain't been in here before."

Neither Sergeant Milano, Comiskey, nor old Adamovitch moved an inch; yet the boy felt the semicircle about him drawing closer. Out of the corner of his eye he watched the reporter undoing the top button of his mangy raccoon coat, as though the barren little query room were already growing too warm for him.

"What were you doin' on Chicago Av'noo in the first place when you live up around Division? Ain't your own ward big enough you have to come down here to get in trouble? What do you *think* you're here for?"

"Well, I was just walkin' down Chicago like I said, to get a bottle of milk for Mother, when the officers jumped me. I didn't even see 'em drive up, they wouldn't let me say a word, I got no idea what I'm here for. I was just doin' a errand for Mother 'n—"

"All right, son, you want us to book you as a pickup 'n hold you overnight, is that it?"

"Yes sir."

"What about this, then?"

Kozak flipped a spring-blade knife with a five-inch blade onto the police blotter; the boy resisted an impulse to lean forward and take it. His own double-edged double-jointed spring-blade cuts-all genuine Filipino twisty-handled all-American gut-ripper.

"Is it yours or ain't it?"

"Never seen it before, Captain."

Kozak pulled a billy out of his belt, spread the blade across the bend of the blotter before him, and with one blow clubbed the blade off two inches from the handle. The boy winced as though he himself had received the blow. Kozak threw the broken blade into a basket and the knife into a drawer.

"Know why I did that, son?"

"Yes sir."

"Tell me."

" 'Cause it's three inches to the heart."

"No. 'Cause it's against the law to carry more than three inches of knife. C'mon, Lefty, tell us about it. 'N it better be good."

The boy began slowly, secretly gratified that Kozak appeared to know he was the Warriors' first string left-hander: maybe he'd been out at that game against the Knothole Wonders the Sunday he'd finished his own game and then had relieved Dropkick Kodadek in the sixth in the second. Why hadn't anyone called him "Iron-Man Bicek" or "Fireball Bruno" for that one?

"Everythin' you say can be used against you," Kozak warned him earnestly. "Don't talk unless you want to." His lips formed each syllable precisely.

Then he added absently, as though talking to someone unseen, "We'll just hold you on an open charge till you do."

And his lips hadn't moved at all.

The boy licked his own lips, feeling a dryness coming into his throat and a tightening in his stomach. "We seen this boobatch with his collar turned inside out cash'n his check by Konstanty Stachula's Tonsorial Palace of Art on Division. So I followed him a way, that was all. Just break'n the old monotony was all. Just a notion, you might say, that come over me. I'm just a neighborhood kid, Captain."

He stopped as though he had finished the story. Kozak glanced over the boy's shoulder at the arresting officers and Lefty began again hurriedly.

"Ever' once in a while he'd pull a little single-shot of Scotch out of his pocket, stop a second t' toss it down, 'n toss the bottle at the car tracks. I picked up a bottle that didn't bust but there wasn't a spider left in 'er, the boobatch'd drunk her dry. 'N do you know, he had his pockets *full* of them little bottles? 'Stead of buyin' hisself a fifth in the first place. Can't understand a man who'll buy liquor that way. Right before the corner of Walton 'n Noble he popped into a hallway. That was Chiney-Eye-the-Princinct-Captain's hallway, so I popped right in after him. Me'n Chiney-Eye 'r just like that." The boy crossed two fingers of his left hand and asked innocently, "Has the alderman been in to straighten this out, Captain?"

"What time was all this, Lefty?"

"Well, some of the street lamps was lit awready 'n I didn't see nobody either way down Noble. It'd just started spitt'n a little snow 'n I couldn't see clear down Walton account of Wojciechowski's Tavern bein' in the way. He was a old guy, a dino you. He couldn't speak a word of English. But he started in cryin' about how every time he gets a little drunk the same old thing happens to him 'n he's gettin' fed up, he lost his last three checks in the very same hallway 'n it's gettin' so his family don't believe him no more . . ."

Lefty paused, realizing that his tongue was going faster than his brain. He unfolded his arms and shoved them down his pants pockets; the pants were turned up at the cuffs and the cuffs were frayed. He drew a colorless cap off his hip pocket and stood clutching it in his left hand.

"I didn't take him them other times, Captain," he anticipated Kozak.

"Who did?"

Silence.

"What's Benkowski doin' for a livin' these days, Lefty?"

"Just nutsin' around."

"What's Nowogrodski up to?"

"Goes wolfin' on roller skates by Riverview. The rink's open all year round."

"Does he have much luck?"

"Never turns up a hair. They go by too fast."

"What's that evil-eye up to?"

Silence.

"You know who I mean. Idzikowski."

"The Finger?"

"You know who I mean. Don't stall."

"He's hexin' fights, I heard."

"Seen Kodadek lately?"

"I guess. A week 'r two 'r a month ago."

"What was *he* up to?"

"Sir?"

"What was Kodadek doin' the last time you seen him?"

"You mean Dropkick? He was nutsin' around."

"Does he nuts around drunks in hallways?"

Somewhere in the room a small clock or wrist watch began ticking distinctly.

"Nutsin' around ain't jackrollin'."

"You mean Dropkick ain't a jackroller but you are."

The boy's blond lashes shuttered his eyes.

"All right, get ahead with your lyin' a little faster."

Kozak's head came down almost neckless onto his shoulders, and his face was molded like a flatiron, the temples narrow and the jaws rounded. Between the jaws and the open collar, against the graying hair of the chest, hung a tiny crucifix, slender and golden, a shade lighter than his tunic's golden buttons.

"I told him I wasn't gonna take his check, I just needed a little change, I'd pay it back someday. But maybe he didn't understand. He kept hollerin' how he lost his last check, please to let him keep this one. 'Why you drink'n it all up, then,' I put it to him, 'if you're that anxious to hold onto it?' He gimme a foxy grin then 'n pulls out four of them little bottles from four different pockets, 'n each one was a different kind of liquor. I could have one, he tells me in Polish, which do I want, 'n I slapped all four out of his hands. All four. I don't like to see no full-grown man drinkin' that way. A Polak hillbilly he was, 'n certain'y no citizen.

"Now let me have that change,' I asked him, 'n that wasn't so much t' ask. I don't go around just lookin' fer trouble, Captain. 'N my feet was slop-full of water 'n snow. I'm just a neighborhood fella. But he acted like I was gonna kill him 'r somethin'. I got one hand over his mouth 'n a half nelson behind him 'n talked polite-like in Polish in his ear, 'n he begun sweatin' 'n tryin' t' wrench away on me. 'Take it easy,' I asked him. 'Be reas'nable, we're both in this up to our necks now.' 'N he wasn't drunk no more then, 'n he was plenty t' hold onto. You wouldn't think a old boobatch like that'd have so much stren'th left in him, boozin' down Division night after night, year after year, like he didn't have no home to go to. He pulled my hand off his mouth 'n started hollerin', '*Mlody bandyta! Mlody bandyta!*' 'n I could feel him slippin'. He was just too strong fer a kid like me to hold—"

"Because you were reach'n for his wallet with the other hand?"

"Oh no. The reason I couldn't hold him was my right hand had the nelson 'n I'm not so strong there like in my left 'n even my left ain't what it was before I thrun it out pitchin' that double-header."

"So you kept the rod in your left hand?"

The boy hesitated. Then: "Yes sir." And felt a single drop of sweat slide down his side from under his armpit. Stop and slide again down to the belt.

"What did you get off him?"

"I tell you, I had my hands too full to get *anythin'*—that's just what I been tryin' to tell you. I didn't get so much as one of them little single-shots for all my trouble."

"How many slugs did you fire?"

"Just one, Captain. That was all there was in 'er. I didn't really fire, though. Just at his feet. T' scare him so's he wouldn't jump me. I fired in self-defense. I just wanted to get out of there." He glanced helplessly around at Comiskey and Adamovitch. "You do crazy things sometimes, fellas—well, that's all I was doin'."

The boy caught his tongue and stood mute. In the silence of the query room there was only the scraping of the reporter's pencil and the unseen wrist watch. "I'll ask Chiney-Eye if it's legal, a reporter takin' down a confession, that's my out," the boy thought desperately, and added aloud, before he could stop himself: " 'N beside I had to show him—"

"Show him what, son?"

Silence.

"Show him what, Left-hander?"

"That I wasn't just another greenhorn sprout like he thought."

"Did he say you were just a sprout?"

"No. But I c'd tell. Lot of people think I'm just a green kid. I show 'em. I guess I showed 'em now all right." He felt he should be apologizing for something and couldn't tell whether it was for strong-arming a man or for failing to strong-arm him.

"I'm just a neighborhood kid. I belonged to the Keep-Our-City-Clean Club at St. John Cant'us. I told him polite-like, like a Polish-American citizen, this was Chiney-Eye-a-Friend-of-Mine's hallway. 'No more after this one,' I told him. 'This is your last time gettin' rolled, old man. After this I'm pertectin' you, I'm seein' to it nobody touches you—but the people who live here don't like this sort of thing goin' on any more'n you 'r I do. There's gotta be a stop to it, old man—'n we all gotta live, don't we?' That's what I told him in Polish."

Kozak exchanged glances with the prim-faced reporter from the *Chicagoski,* who began cleaning his black tortoise-shell spectacles hurriedly yet delicately, with the fringed tip of his cravat. They depended from a black ribbon; he snapped them back onto his beak.

"You shot him in the groin, Lefty. He's dead."

The reporter leaned slightly forward, but perceived no special reaction and so relaxed. A pretty comfy old chair for a dirty old police station, he thought lifelessly. Kozak shaded his eyes with his gloved hand and looked down at his charge sheet. The night lamp on the desk was still lit, as though he had been working all night; as the morning grew lighter behind him lines came out below his eyes, black as though packed with soot, and a curious droop came to the St. Bernard mouth.

"You shot him through the groin—zip." Kozak's voice came, flat and unemphatic, reading from the charge sheet as though without understanding. "Five children. Stella, Mary, Grosha, Wanda, Vincent. Thirteen, ten, six, six, and one two months. Mother invalided since last birth, name of Rose. WPA fifty-five dollars. You told the truth about *that,* at least."

Lefty's voice came in a shout: "You know *what?* That bullet must of bounced, that's what!"

"Who was along?"

"I was singlin'. Lone-wolf stuff." His voice possessed the first faint touch of fear.

"You said, 'We seen the man.' Was he a big man? How big a man was he?"

"I'd judge two hunerd twenty pounds," Comiskey offered, "at least. Fifty pounds heavier 'n this boy, just about. 'N half a head taller."

"Who's 'we,' Left-hander?"

"Captain, I said, 'We seen.' Lots of people, fellas, seen him is all I meant, cashin' his check by Stachula's when the place was crowded. Konstanty cashes checks if he knows you. Say, I even know the project that old man was on, far as that goes, because my old lady wanted we should give up the store so's I c'd get on it. But it was just me done it, Captain."

The raccoon coat readjusted his glasses. He would say something under a by-line like "This correspondent has never seen a colder gray than that in the eye of the wanton killer who arrogantly styles himself the *lone wolf of Potomac Street*." He shifted uncomfortably, wanting to get farther from the wall radiator but disliking to rise and push the heavy chair.

"Where was that bald-headed pal of yours all this time?"

"Don't know the fella, Captain. Nobody got hair any more around the neighborhood, it seems. The whole damn Triangle went 'n got army haircuts by Stachula's."

"Just you 'n Benkowski, I mean. Don't be afraid, son—we're not tryin' to ring in anythin' you done afore this. Just this one you were out cowboyin' with Benkowski on; were you help'n him 'r was he help'n you? Did you 'r him have the rod?"

Lefty heard a Ford V-8 pull into the rear of the station, and a moment later the splash of the gas as the officers refueled. Behind him he could hear Milano's heavy breathing. He looked down at his shoes, carefully buttoned all the way up and tied with a double bowknot. He'd have to have new laces mighty soon or else start tying them with a single bow.

"That Benkowski's sort of a toothless monkey used to go on at the City Garden at around a hundred an' eighteen pounds, ain't he?"

"Don't know the fella well enough t' say."

"Just from seein' him fight once 'r twice is all. 'N he wore a mouthpiece, I couldn't tell about his teeth. Seems to me he came in about one thirty-three, if he's the same fella you're thinkin' of, Captain."

"I guess you fought at the City Garden once 'r twice yourself, ain't you?"

"Oh, once 'r twice."

"How'd you make out, Left'?"

"Won 'em both on K.O.s. Stopped both fights in the first. One was against that boogie from the Savoy. If he woulda got up I woulda killed him fer life. Fer Christ I would. I didn't know I could hit like I can."

"With Benkowski in your corner both times?"

"Oh no, sir."

"That's a bloodsuck'n lie. I seen him in your corner with my own eyes the time you won off Cooney from the C.Y.O. He's your manager, jackroller."

"I didn't say he wasn't."

"You said he wasn't secondin' you."

"He don't."

"Who does?"

"The Finger."

"You told me the Finger was your hex-man. Make up your mind."

"He does both, Captain. He handles the bucket 'n sponge 'n in between he fingers the guy I'm fightin', 'n if it's close he fingers the ref 'n judges. Finger, he never losed a fight. He waited for the boogie outside the dressing room 'n pointed him clear to the ring. He win that one for me awright." The boy spun the frayed greenish cap in his hand in a concentric circle about his index finger, remembering a time when the cap was new and had earlaps. The bright checks were all faded now, to the color of worn pavement, and the earlaps were tatters.

"What possessed your mob to get their heads shaved, Lefty?"

"I strong-armed him myself, I'm rugged as a bull." The boy began to swell his chest imperceptibly; when his lungs were quite full he shut his eyes, like swimming under water at the Oak Street beach, and let his breath out slowly, ounce by ounce.

"I didn't ask you that. I asked you what happened to your hair."

Lefty's capricious mind returned abruptly to the word "possessed" that Kozak had employed. That had a randy ring, sort of: "What possessed you boys?"

"I forgot what you just asked me."

"I asked you why you didn't realize it'd be easier for us to catch up with your mob when all of you had your heads shaved."

"I guess we figured there'd be so many guys with heads shaved it'd be harder to catch a finger than if we all had hair. But that was some accident all the same. A fella was gonna lend Ma a barber chair 'n go fifty-fifty with her shavin' all the Polaks on P'tom'c Street right back of the store, for relief tickets. So she started on me, just to show the fellas, but the hair made her sicker 'n ever 'n back of the store's the only place she got to lie down 'n I hadda finish the job myself.

"The fellas begun giv'n me a Christ-awful razzin' then, ever' day. God oh God, wherever I went around the Triangle, all the neighborhood fellas 'n little niducks 'n oldtime hoods by the Broken Knuckle, whenever they seen me they was pointin' 'n laughin' 'n sayin', 'Hi, Baldy Bicek!' So I went home 'n got the clippers 'n the first guy I seen was Bibleback Watrobinski, you wouldn't know him. I jumps him 'n pushes the clip right through the middle of his hair—he ain't had a haircut since the alderman got indicted you—'n then he took one look at what I done in the drugstore window 'n we both bust out laughin' 'n laughin', 'n fin'lly Bible says I better finish what I started. So he set down on the curb 'n I finished him. When I got all I could off that way I took him back to the store 'n heated water 'n shaved him close 'n Ma couldn't see the point at all.

"Me 'n Bible prowled around a couple days 'n here come Cat-foot Nowogrodski from Fry Street you, out of Stachula's with a spanty-new sideburner haircut 'n a green tie. I grabbed his arms 'n let Bible run it through the middle just like I done him. Then it was Catfoot's turn, 'n we caught Chester Chekhovka fer *him,* 'n fer Chester we got Cowboy Okulanis from by the Nort'western Viaduct you, 'n fer him we got Mustang, 'n fer Mustang we got John from the Joint, 'n fer John we got Snake Baranowski, n' we kep' right on goin' that way till we was doin' guys we never seen before even, Wallios 'n Greeks 'n a Flip from Clark Street he musta been, walkin' with a white girl we done it to. 'N fin'lly all the sprouts in the Tri-angle start comin' around with their heads shaved, they want to join up with the Baldheads A.C., they called it. They thought it was a club you.

"It got so a kid with his head shaved could beat up on a bigger kid because the big one'd be a-scared to fight back hard, he thought the Baldheads'd get him. So that's why we changed our name then, that's why we're not the Warriors any more, we're the Baldhead True American Social 'n Athletic Club.

"I played first for the Warriors when I wasn't on the mound," he added cautiously, "'n I'm enter' the Gold'n Gloves next year 'less I go to collitch instead. I went to St. John Cant'us all the way

through. Eight' grade, that is. If I keep on gainin' weight I'll be a
hunerd ninety-eight this time next year 'n be five-foot-ten—I'm a
fair-size light-heavy right this minute. That's what in England they
call a cruiser weight you."

He shuffled a step and made as though to unbutton his shirt to
show his proportions. But Adamovitch put one hand on his
shoulders and slapped the boy's hand down. He didn't like this kid.
This was a low-class Polak. He himself was a high-class Polak
because his name was Adamovitch and not Adamowski. This sort
of kid kept spoiling things for the high-class Polaks by always showing off instead of just being good citizens like the Irish. That was
why the Irish ran the City Hall and Police Department and the
Board of Education and the Post Office while the Polaks stayed on
relief and got drunk and never got anywhere and had everybody
down on them. All they could do like the Irish, old Adamovitch
reflected bitterly, was to fight under Irish names to get their ears
knocked off at the City Garden.

"That's why I want to get out of this jam," this one was saying
beside him. "So's it don't ruin my career in the rope' arena. I'm
goin' straight. This has sure been one good lesson fer me. Now I'll
go to a big-ten collitch 'n make good you."

Now, if the college-coat asked him, "What big-ten college?"
he'd answer something screwy like "The Boozological Stoodent-
Collitch." That ought to set Kozak back awhile, they might even
send him to a bug doc. He'd have to be careful—not *too* screwy.
Just screwy enough to get by without involving Benkowski.

He scuffed his shoes and there was no sound in the close little
room save his uneasy scuffling; square-toed boy's shoes, laced with a
button-hook. He wanted to look more closely at the reporter but
every time he caught the glint of the fellow's glasses he felt awed
and would have to drop his eyes; he'd never seen glasses on a string
like that before and would have given a great deal to wear them a
moment. He took to looking steadily out of the barred window
behind Kozak's head, where the January sun was glowing sullenly,
like a flame held steadily in a fog. Heard an empty truck clattering
east on Chicago, sounding like either a '38 Chevvie or a '37 Ford
dragging its safety chain against the car tracks; closed his eyes and

imagined sparks flashing from the tracks as the iron struck, bounced, and struck again. The bullet had bounced too. Wow.

"What do you think we ought to do with a man like you, Bicek?"

The boy heard the change from the familiar "Lefty" to "Bicek" with a pang; and the dryness began in his throat again.

"One to fourteen is all I can catch fer manslaughter." He appraised Kozak as coolly as he could.

"You like farm work the next fourteen years? Is that okay with you?"

"I said that's all I could get, at the most. This is a first offense 'n self-defense too. I'll plead the unwritten law."

"Who give you *that* idea?"

"Thought of it myself. Just now. You ain't got a chance to send me over the road 'n you know it."

"We can send you to St. Charles, Bicek. 'N transfer you when you come of age. Unless we can make it first-degree murder."

The boy ignored the latter possibility.

"Why, a few years on a farm'd true me up fine. I planned t' cut out cigarettes 'n whisky anyhow before I turn pro—a farm'd be just the place to do that."

"By the time you're released you'll be thirty-two, Bicek—too late to turn pro then, ain't it?"

"I wouldn't wait that long. Hungry Piontek-from-by-the-Warehouse you, he lammed twice from that St. Charles farm. 'N Hungry don't have all his marbles even. He ain't even a citizen."

"Then let's talk about somethin' you couldn't lam out of so fast 'n easy. Like the chair. Did you know that Bogatski from Noble Street, Bicek? The boy that burned last summer, I mean."

A plain-clothes man stuck his head in the door and called confidently: "That's the man, Captain. That's the man."

Bicek forced himself to grin good-naturedly. He was getting pretty good, these last couple days, at grinning under pressure. When a fellow got sore he couldn't think straight, he reflected anxiously. And so he yawned in Kozak's face with deliberateness, stretching himself as effortlessly as a cat.

"Captain, I ain't been in serious trouble like this before . . ." he acknowledged, and paused dramatically. He'd let them have it

straight from the shoulder now: "So I'm mighty glad to be so close
to the alderman. Even if he is indicted."

There. Now they know. He'd told them.

"You talkin' about my brother, Bicek?"

The boy nodded solemnly. Now they knew who they had hold
of at last.

The reporter took the cigarette off his ear and hung it on his
lower lip. And Adamovitch guffawed.

The boy jerked toward the officer: Adamovitch was laughing
openly at him. Then they were all laughing openly at him. He
heard their derision, and a red rain danced one moment before his
eyes; when the red rain was past, Kozak was sitting back easily,
regarding him with the expression of a man who has just been
swung at and missed and plans to use the provocation without
undue haste. The captain didn't look like the sort who'd swing back
wildly or hurriedly. He didn't look like the sort who missed. His
complacency for a moment was as unbearable to the boy as Adamovitch's guffaw had been. He heard his tongue going, trying to re-
gain his lost composure by provoking them all.

"Hey, Stingywhiskers!" He turned on the reporter. "Get your
Eversharp goin' there, write down I plugged the old rumpot, write
down Bicek carries a rod night 'n day 'n don't care where he points
it. You, I go around slappin' the crap out of whoever I feel like—"

But they all remained mild, calm, and unmoved: for a moment
he feared Adamovitch was going to pat him on the head and say
something fatherly in Polish.

"Take it easy, lad," Adamovitch suggested. "You're in the
query room. We're here to help you, boy. We want to see you
through this thing so's you can get back to pugging. You just ain't
letting us help you, son."

Kozak blew his nose as though that were an achievement in
itself, and spoke with the false friendliness of the insurance man
urging a fleeced customer toward the door.

"Want to tell us where you got that rod now, Lefty?"

"I don't want to tell you anything." His mind was setting hard
now, against them all. Against them all in here and all like them
outside. And the harder it set, the more things seemed to be all
right with Kozak: he dropped his eyes to his charge sheet now

and everything was all right with everybody. The reporter shoved his notebook into his pocket and buttoned the top button of his coat as though the questioning were over.

It was all too easy. They weren't going to ask him anything more, and he stood wanting them to. He stood wishing them to threaten, to shake their heads ominously, wheedle and cajole and promise him mercy if he'd just talk about the rod.

"I ain't mad, Captain. I don't blame you men either. It's your job, it's your bread 'n butter to talk tough to us neighborhood fellas—ever'body got to have a racket, 'n yours is talkin' tough." He directed this last at the captain, for Comiskey and Milano had left quietly. But Kozak was studying the charge sheet as though Bruno Lefty Bicek were no longer in the room. Nor anywhere at all.

"I'm still here," the boy said wryly, his lip twisting into a dry and bitter grin.

Kozak looked up, his big, wind-beaten, impassive face looking suddenly to the boy like an autographed pitcher's mitt he had once owned. His glance went past the boy and no light of recognition came into his eyes. Lefty Bicek felt a panic rising in him: a desperate fear that they weren't going to press him about the rod, about the old man, about his feelings. "Don't look at me like I ain't nowheres," he asked. And his voice was struck flat by fear.

Something else! The time he and Dropkick had broken into a slot machine! The time he and Casey had played the attention racket and made four dollars! Something! Anything else!

The reporter lit his cigarette.

"Your case is well disposed of," Kozak said, and his eyes dropped to the charge sheet forever.

"I'm born in this country. I'm educated here—"

But no one was listening to Bruno Lefty Bicek any more.

He watched the reporter leaving with regret—at least the guy could have offered him a drag—and stood waiting for someone to tell him to go somewhere now, shifting uneasily from one foot to the other. Then he started slowly, backward, toward the door: he'd make Kozak tell Adamovitch to grab him. Halfway to the door he turned his back on Kozak.

There was no voice behind him. Was this what "well disposed of" meant? He turned the knob and stepped confidently into the

corridor; at the end of the corridor he saw the door that opened
into the courtroom, and his heart began shaking his whole body
with the impulse to make a run for it. He glanced back and
Adamovitch was five yards behind, coming up catfooted like only
an old man who has been a citizen-dress man can come up catfooted, just far enough behind and just casual enough to make it
appear unimportant whether the boy made a run for it or not.

The Lone Wolf of Potomac Street waited miserably, in the long
unlovely corridor, for the sergeant to thrust two fingers through the
back of his belt. Didn't they realize that he might have Dropkick
and Catfoot and Benkowski with a sub-machine gun in a stream-
lined cream-colored roadster right down front, that he'd zigzag
through the courtroom onto the courtroom fire escape and—swish
—down off the courtroom roof three stories with the chopper still
under his arm and through the car's roof and into the driver's seat?
Like that George Raft did that time he was innocent at the Chopin,
and cops like Adamovitch had better start ducking when Lefty
Bicek began making a run for it. He felt the fingers thrust over-
familiarly between his shirt and his belt.

A cold draft came down the corridor when the door at the far
end opened; with the opening of the door came the smell of
disinfectant from the basement cells. Outside, far overhead, the bells
of St. John Cantius were beginning. The boy felt the winding steel
of the staircase to the basement beneath his feet and heard the
whining screech of a Chicago Avenue streetcar as it paused on
Ogden for the traffic lights and then screeched on again, as though
a cat were caught beneath its back wheels. Would it be snowing
out there still? he wondered, seeing the whitewashed basement
walls.

"Feel all right, son?" Adamovitch asked in his most fatherly
voice, closing the cell door while thinking to himself: "The kid
don't *feel* guilty is the whole trouble. You got to make them *feel*
guilty or they'll never go to church at all. A man who goes to church
without feeling guilty for *something* is wasting his time, I say."
Inside the cell he saw the boy pause and go down on his knees in
the cell's gray light. The boy's head turned slowly toward him, a
pious oval in the dimness. Old Adamovitch took off his hat.

"This place'll rot down 'n mold over before Lefty Bicek starts prayin', boobatch. Prays, squeals, 'r bawls. So run along 'n I'll see you in hell with yer back broke. I'm lookin' for my cap I dropped is all."

Adamovitch watched him crawling forward on all fours, groping for the pavement-colored cap; when he saw Bicek find it he put his own hat back on and left feeling vaguely dissatisfied.

He did not stay to see the boy, still on his knees, put his hands across his mouth and stare at the shadowed wall.

Shadows were there within shadows.

"I knew I'd never get to be twenty-one anyhow," Lefty told himself softly at last.

CYRUS COLTER

The Beach Umbrella

HE THIRTY-FIRST STREET beach lay dazzling under a sky so blue that Lake Michigan ran to the horizon like a sheet of sapphire silk, studded with little barbed white sequins for sails; and the heavy surface of the water lapped gently at the boulder "sea wall" which had been cut into, graded, and sanded to make the beach. Saturday afternoons were always frenzied: three black lifeguards, giants in sunglasses, preened in their towers and chaperoned the bathers—adults, teen-agers, and children—who were going through every physical gyration of which the human body is capable. Some dove, swam, some hollered, rode inner tubes, or merely stood waistdeep and pummeled the water; others—on the beach—sprinted, did handsprings and somersaults, sucked Eskimo pies, or just buried their children in the sand. Then there were the lollers—extended in their languor under a garish variety of beach umbrellas.

Elijah lolled too—on his stomach in the white sand, his chin cupped in his palm; but under no umbrella. He had none. By habit, though, he stared in awe at those who did, and sometimes meddled in their conversation: "It's gonna be gettin' *hot* pretty soon—if it ain't careful," he said to a Bantu-looking fellow and his girl sitting near by with an older woman. The temperature was then in the nineties. The fellow managed a negligent smile. "Yeah," he said, and persisted in listening to the women. Buoyant still, Elijah watched them. But soon his gaze wavered, and then moved on to other lollers of interest. Finally he got up, stretched, brushed sand from his swimming trunks, and scanned the beach for a new spot. He started walking.

He was not tall. And he appeared to walk on his toes—his walnut-colored legs were bowed and skinny and made him hobble like a jerky little spider. Next he plopped down near two men and two girls—they were hilarious about something—sitting beneath a big purple-and-white umbrella. The girls, chocolate brown and shapely, emitted squeals of laughter at the wisecracks of the men. Elijah was enchanted. All summer long the rambunctious gaiety of the beach had fastened on him a curious charm, a hex, that brought him gawking and twiddling to the lake each Saturday. The rest of the week, save Sunday, he worked. But Myrtle, his wife, detested the sport and stayed away. Randall, the boy, had been only twice and then without little Susan, who during the summer was her mother's own midget reflection. But Elijah came regularly, especially whenever Myrtle was being evil, which he felt now was almost always. She was getting worse, too—if that was possible. The Woman was money-*crazy*.

"You gotta sharp-lookin' umbrella there!" he cut in on the two laughing couples. They studied him—the abruptly silent way. Then the big-shouldered fellow smiled and lifted his eyes to their spangled roof. "Yeah? . . . Thanks," he said. Elijah carried on: "I see a lot of 'em out here this summer—much more'n last year."

The fellow meditated on this, but was noncommittal. The others went on gabbing, mostly with their hands. Elijah, squinting in the hot sun, watched them. He didn't see how they could be married; they cut the fool too much, acted like they'd itched to get together for weeks and just now made it. He pondered going back in the water, but he'd already had an hour of that. His eyes traveled the sweltering beach. Funny about his folks; they were every shape and color a God-made human could be. Here was a real sample of variety—pink white to jetty black. Could you any longer call that a *race* of people? It was a complicated complication—for some real educated guy to figure out. Then another thought slowly bore in on him: the beach umbrellas blooming across the sand attracted people—slews of friends, buddies; and gals, too. Wherever the loudest-racket tore the air, a big red, or green, or yellowish umbrella —bordered with white fringe maybe—flowered in the middle of it all and gave shade to the happy good-timers.

Take, for instance, that tropical-looking pea-green umbrella over there, with the Bikini-ed brown chicks under it, and the portable radio jumping. A real beach party! He got up, stole over, and eased down in the sand at the fringe of the jubilation—two big thermos jugs sat in the shade and everybody had a paper cup in hand as the explosions of buffoonery carried out to the water. Chief provoker of mirth was a bulging-eyed old gal in a white bathing suit who, encumbered by big flabby overripe thighs, cavorted and pranced in the sand. When, perspiring from the heat, she finally fagged out, she flopped down almost on top of him. So far, he had gone unnoticed. But now, as he craned in at closer range, she brought him up: "Whatta *you* want, Pops?" She grinned, but with a touch of hostility.

Pops! Where'd she get that stuff? He was only forty-one, not a day older than that boozy bag. But he smiled. "Nothin'," he said brightly, "but you sure got one goin' here." He turned and viewed the noise-makers.

"An' you wanta get in on it!" she wrangled.

"Oh, I was just lookin'—"

"—You was just lookin.' Yeah, you was just lookin' at them young chicks there!" She roared a laugh and pointed at the sexy-looking girls under the umbrella.

Elijah grinned weakly.

"Beat it!" she catcalled, and turned back to the party.

He sat like a rock—the hell with her. But soon he relented, and wandered down to the water's edge—remote now from all inhospitality—to sit in the sand and hug his raised knees. Far out, the sailboats were pinned to the horizon and, despite all the close-in fuss, the wide miles of lake lay impassive under a blazing calm; far south and east down the long-curving lake shore, miles in the distance, the smoky haze of the Whiting plant of the Youngstown Sheet and Tube Company hung ominously in an otherwise bright sky. And so it was that he turned back and viewed the beach again —and suddenly caught his craving. Weren't they something—the umbrellas! The flashy colors of them! And the swank! No wonder folks ganged round them. Yes . . . yes, he too must have one. The thought came slow and final, and scared him. For there stood Myrtle in his mind. She nagged him now night and day, and it was always money that got her started; there was never enough—for Susan's shoes, Randy's overcoat, for new kitchen linoleum, Venetian blinds, for a better car than the old Chevy. "I just don't understand you!" she had said only night before last. "Have you got any plans at all for your family? You got a family, you know. If you could only bear to pull yourself away from that deaf old tightwad out at that warehouse, and go get yourself a *real* job . . . But no! Not *you!*"

She was talking about old man Schroeder, who owned the warehouse where he worked. Yes, the pay could be better, but it still wasn't as bad as she made out. Myrtle could be such a fool sometimes. He had been with the old man nine years now; had started out as a freight handler, but worked up to doing inventories and a little paper work. True, the business had been going down recently, for the old man's sight and hearing were failing and his key people had left him. Now he depended on *him*, Elijah—who of late wore a necktie on the job, and made his inventory rounds with a ballpoint pen and clipboard. The old man was friendlier, too—almost "hat in hand" to him. He liked everything about the job now— except the pay. And that was only because of Myrtle. She just wanted so much; even talked of moving out of their rented apartment and buying out in the Chatham area. But one thing had to be said for her: she never griped about anything for herself; only for the family, the kids. Every payday he endorsed his check and handed it over to her, and got back in return only gasoline and cigarette money. And this could get pretty tiresome. About six weeks ago he'd gotten a ten-dollar-a-month raise out of the old man, but that had only made her madder than ever. He'd thought about looking for another job all right; but where would he go to get another white-collar job? There weren't many of them for him. *She* wouldn't care if he went back to the steel mills, back to pouring that white-hot ore out at Youngstown Sheet and Tube. It would be okay with *her*—so long as his pay check was fat. But that kind of work was no good, undignified; coming home on the bus you were always so tired you went to sleep in your seat, with your lunch pail in your lap.

Just then two wet boys, chasing each other across the sand, raced by him into the water. The cold spray on his skin made him jump, jolting him out of his thoughts. He turned and slowly scanned the beach again. The umbrellas were brighter, gayer, bolder than ever—each a hiving center of playful people. He stood up finally, took a long last look, and then started back to the spot where he had parked the Chevy.

The following Monday evening was hot and humid as Elijah sat at home in their plain living room and pretended to read the newspaper; the windows were up, but not the slightest breeze came through the screens to stir Myrtle's fluffy curtains. At the moment she and nine-year-old Susan were in the kitchen finishing the dinner dishes. For twenty minutes now he had sat waiting for the furtive chance to speak to Randall. Randall, at twelve, was a serious, industrious boy, and did deliveries and odd jobs for the neighborhood grocer. Soon he came through—intent, absorbed—on his way back to the grocery for another hour's work.

"Gotta go back, eh, Randy?" Elijah said.

"Yes, sir." He was tall for his age, and wore glasses. He paused with his hand on the doorknob.

Elijah hesitated. Better wait, he thought—wait till he comes back. But Myrtle might be around then. Better ask him now. But Randall had opened the door. "See you later, Dad," he said—and left.

Elijah, shaken, again raised the newspaper and tried to read. He should have called him back, he knew, but he had lost his nerve—because he couldn't tell how Randy would take it. Fifteen dollars was nothing though, really—Randy probably had fifty or sixty stashed away somewhere in his room. Then he thought of Myrtle, and waves of fright went over him—to be even thinking about a beach umbrella was bad enough; and to buy one, especially now, would be to her some kind of crime; but to borrow even a part of the money for it from Randy . . . well, Myrtle would go out of her mind. He had never lied to his family before. This would be the first time. And he had thought about it all day long. During the morning, at the warehouse, he had gotten out the two big mail-order catalogues, to look at the beach umbrellas; but the ones shown were all so small and dinky-looking he was contemptuous. So at noon he drove the Chevy out to a sporting-goods store on West Sixty-Third Street. There he found a gorgeous assortment of yard and beach umbrellas. And there he found his prize. A beauty, a big beauty, with wide red and white stripes, and a white fringe. But oh the price! Twenty-three dollars! And he with nine.

"What's the matter with you?" Myrtle had walked in the room. She was thin, and medium brown-skinned with a saddle of freckles across her nose, and looked harried in her sleeveless house dress with her hair unkempt.

Startled, he lowered the newspaper. "Nothing," he said.

"How can you read looking *over* the paper?"

"Was I?"

Not bothering to answer, she sank in a chair. "Susie," she called back into the kitchen, "bring my cigarettes in here, will you, baby?"

Soon Susan, chubby and solemn, with the mist of perspiration on her forehead, came in with the cigarettes. "Only three left, Mama," she said, peering into the pack.

"Okay," Myrtle sighed, taking the cigarettes. Susan started out. "Now, scour the sink good, honey—and then go take your bath. You'll feel cooler."

Before looking at him again, Myrtle lit a cigarette. "School starts in three weeks," she said, with a forlorn shake of her head. "Do you realize that?"

"Yeah? . . . Jesus, time flies." He could not look at her.

"Susie needs dresses, and a couple of pairs of *good* shoes—and she'll need a coat before it gets cold."

"Yeah, I know." He patted the arm of the chair.

"Randy—bless his heart—has already made enough to get most of *his* things. That boy's something; he's all business—I've never seen anything like it." She took a drag on her cigarette. "And old man Schroeder giving you a ten-dollar raise! What was you thinkin' about? What'd you *say* to him?"

He did not answer at first. Finally he said, "Ten dollars is ten dollars, Myrtle. *You* know business is slow."

"*I'll* say it is! And there won't be any business before long—and then where'll you be? I tell you over and over again, you better start looking for something *now!* I been preachin' it to you for a year."

He said nothing.

"Ford and International Harvester are hiring every man they can lay their hands on! And the mills out in Gary and Whiting are going full blast—you see the red sky every night. The men make *good* money."

"They earn every nickel of it, too," he said in gloom.

"But they *get* it! Bring it home! It spends! Does that mean anything to you? Do you know what some of them make? Well, ask Hawthorne—or ask Sonny Milton. Sonny's wife says his checks some weeks run as high as a hundred twenty, hundred thirty, dollars. One week! Take-home pay!"

"Yeah? . . . And Sonny told me he wished he had a job like mine."

Myrtle threw back her head with a bitter gasp. "Oh-h-h, God! Did you tell him what you made? Did you tell him that?"

Suddenly Susan came back into the muggy living room. She went straight to her mother and stood as if expecting an award. Myrtle absently patted her on the side of the head. "Now, go and run your bath water, honey," she said.

Elijah smiled at Susan. "Susie," he said, "d'you know your tummy is stickin' way out—you didn't eat too much, did you?" He laughed.

Susan turned and observed him; then looked at her mother. "No," she finally said.

"Go on, now, baby," Myrtle said. Susan left the room.

Myrtle resumed. "Well, there's no use going through all this again. It's plain as the nose on your face. You got a family—a good family, *I* think. The only question is, do you wanta get off your hind end and do somethin' for it. It's just that simple."

Elijah looked at her. "You can talk real crazy sometimes, Myrtle."

"I think it's that old man!" she cried, her freckles contorted. "He's got you answering the phone, and taking inventory—wearing a necktie and all that. You wearing a necktie and your son mopping in a grocery store, so he can buy his own clothes." She snatched up her cigarettes, and walked out of the room.

His eyes did not follow her, but remained off in space. Finally he got up and went into the kitchen. Over the stove the plaster was thinly cracked, and, in spots, the linoleum had worn through the pattern; but everything was immaculate. He opened the refrigerator, poured a glass of cold water, and sat down at the kitchen table. He felt strange and weak, and sat for a long time sipping the water.

Then after a while he heard Randall's key in the front door, sending tremors of dread through him. When Randall came into the kitchen, he seemed to him as tall as himself; his glasses were steamy from the humidity outside, and his hands were dirty.

"Hi, Dad," he said gravely without looking at him, and opened the refrigerator door.

Elijah chuckled. "Your mother'll get after you about going in there without washing your hands."

But Randall took out the water pitcher and closed the door.

Elijah watched him. Now was the time to ask him. His heart was hammering. Go on—now! But instead he heard his husky voice saying, "What'd they have you doing over at the grocery tonight?"

Randall was drinking the glass of water. When he finished, he said, "Refilling shelves."

"Pretty hot job tonight, eh?"

"It wasn't so bad." Randall was matter-of-fact as he set the empty glass over the sink, and paused before leaving.

"Well . . . you're doing fine, son. Fine. Your mother sure is proud of you . . ." Purpose had lodged in his throat.

The praise embarrassed Randall. "Okay, Dad," he said, and edged from the kitchen.

Elijah slumped back in his chair, near prostration. He tried to clear his mind of every particle of thought, but the images became only more jumbled, oppressive to the point of panic.

Then before long Myrtle came into the kitchen—ignoring him. But she seemed not so hostile now as coldly impassive, exhibiting a bravado he had not seen before. He got up and went back into the living room and turned on the television. As the TV-screen lawmen galloped before him, he sat oblivious, admitting the failure of his will. If only he could have gotten Randall to himself long enough—but everything had been so sudden, abrupt; he couldn't just ask him out of the clear blue. Besides, around him, Randall always seemed so busy, too busy to talk. He couldn't understand that; he had never mistreated the boy, never whipped him in his life; had shaken him a time or two, but that was long ago, when he was little.

He sat and watched the finish of the half-hour TV show. Myrtle was in the bedroom now. He slouched in his chair, lacking the resolve to get up and turn off the television.

Suddenly he was on his feet.

Leaving the television on, he went back to Randall's room in the rear. The door was open and Randall was asleep, lying on his back on the bed, perspiring, still dressed except for his shoes and glasses. He stood over the bed and looked at him. He was a good boy; his own son. But how strange—he thought for the first time—there was no resemblance between them. None whatsoever. Randy had a few of his mother's freckles on his thin brown face, but he could see none of himself in the boy. Then his musings were scattered by the return of his fear. He dreaded waking him. And he might be cross. If he didn't hurry, though, Myrtle or Susie might come strolling out any minute. His bones seemed rubbery from the strain. Finally he bent down and touched Randall's shoulder. The boy did not move a muscle, except to open his eyes. Elijah smiled at him. And he slowly sat up.

"Sorry, Randy—to wake you up like this."

"What's the matter?" Randall rubbed his eyes.

Elijah bent down again, but did not whisper. "Say, can you let me have fifteen bucks—till I get my check? . . . I need to get some things—and I'm a little short this time." He could hardly bring the words up.

Randall gave him a slow, queer look.

"I'll get my check a week from Friday," Elijah said, ". . . and I'll give it back to you then—sure."

Now instinctively Randall glanced toward the door, and Elijah knew Myrtle had crossed his thoughts. "You don't have to mention anything to your mother," he said with casual suddenness.

Randall got up slowly off the bed, and, in his socks, walked to the little table where he did his homework. He pulled the drawer out, fished far in the back a moment, and brought out a white business envelope secured by a rubber band. Holding the envelope close to his stomach, he took out first a ten-dollar bill, and then a five, and, sighing, handed them over.

"Thanks, old man," Elijah quivered, folding the money. "You'll get this back the day I get my check. . . . That's for sure."

"Okay," Randall finally said.

Elijah started out. Then he could see Myrtle on payday—her hand extended for his check. He hesitated, and looked at Randall, as if to speak. But he slipped the money in his trousers pocket and huried from the room.

The following Saturday at the beach did not begin bright and sunny. By noon it was hot, but the sky was overcast and angry, the air heavy. There was no certainty whatever of a crowd, raucous or otherwise, and this was Elijah's chief concern as, shortly before twelve o'clock, he drove up in the Chevy and parked in the bumpy, graveled stretch of high ground that looked down eastward over the lake and was used for a parking lot. He climbed out of the car, glancing at the lake and clouds, and prayed in his heart it would not rain—the water was murky and restless, and only a handful of bathers had showed. But it was early yet. He stood beside the car and watched a bulbous, brown-skinned woman, in bathing suit and enormous straw hat, lugging a lunch basket down toward the beach, followed by her brood of children. And a fellow in swimming trunks, apparently the father, took a towel and sandals from his new Buick and called petulantly to his family to "just wait a minute, please." In another car, two women sat waiting, as yet fully clothed and undecided about going swimming. While down at the water's edge there was the usual cluster of dripping boys who, brash and boisterous, swarmed to the beach every day in fair weather or foul.

Elijah took off his shirt, peeled his trousers from over his swimming trunks, and started collecting the paraphernalia from the back seat of the car: a frayed pink rug filched from the house, a towel, sunglasses, cigarettes, a thermos jug filled with cold lemonade he had made himself, and a dozen paper cups. All this he stacked on the front fender. Then he went around to the rear and opened the trunk. Ah, there it lay—encased in a long, slim package trussed with heavy twine, and barely fitting athwart the spare tire. He felt prickles of excitement as he took the knife from the tool bag, cut the twine, and pulled the wrapping paper away. Red and white stripes sprang at him. It was even more gorgeous than when it had first seduced him in the store. The white fringe gave it style; the wide red fillets were cardinal and stark, and the white stripes glared. Now he opened it over his head, for the full thrill of its colors, and looked around to see if anyone else agreed. Finally after a while he gathered up all his equipment and headed down for the beach, his short, nubby legs seeming more bowed than ever under the weight of their cargo.

When he reached the sand, a choice of location became a pressing matter. That was why he had come early. From past observation it was clear that the center of gaiety shifted from day to day; last Saturday it might have been nearer the water, this Saturday, well back; or up, or down, the beach a ways. He must pick the site with care, for he could not move about the way he did when he had no umbrella; it was too noticeable. He finally took a spot as near the center of the beach as he could estimate, and dropped his gear in the sand. He knelt down and spread the pink rug, then moved the thermos jug over onto it, and folded the towel and placed it with the paper cups, sunglasses, and cigarettes down beside the jug. Now he went to find a heavy stone or brick to drive down the spike for the hollow umbrella stem to fit over. So it was not until the umbrella was finally up that he again had time for anxiety about the weather. His whole morning's effort had been an act of faith, for, as yet, there was no sun, although now and then a few azure breaks appeared in the thinning cloud mass. But before very long this brighter texture of the sky began to grow and spread by slow degrees, and his hopes quickened. Finally he sat down under the umbrella, lit a cigarette, and waited.

It was not long before two small boys came by—on their way to the water. He grinned, and called to them, "Hey, fellas, been in yet?"—their bathing suits were dry.

They stopped, and observed him. Then one of them smiled, and shook his head.

Elijah laughed. "Well, whatta you waitin' for? Go on in there and get them suits wet!" Both boys gave him silent smiles. And they lingered. He thought this a good omen—it had been different the Saturday before.

Once or twice the sun burst through the weakening clouds. He forgot the boys now in watching the skies, and soon they moved on. His anxiety was not detectable from his lazy posture under the umbrella, with his dwarfish, gnarled legs extended and his bare heels on the little rug. But then soon the clouds began to fade in earnest, seeming not to move away laterally, but slowly to recede into a lucent haze, until at last the sun came through hot and bright. He squinted at the sky and felt delivered. They would come, the folks would come!—were coming now; the beach would soon be swarming. Two other umbrellas were up already, and the diving board thronged with wet, acrobatic boys. The lifeguards were in their towers now, and still another launched his yellow rowboat. And up on the Outer Drive, the cars, one by one, were turning into the parking lot. The sun was bringing them out all right; soon he'd be in the middle of a field day. He felt a low-key, welling excitement, for the water was blue, and far out the sails were starched and white.

Soon he saw the two little boys coming back. They were soaked. Their mother—a thin, brown girl in a yellow bathing suit—was with them now, and the boys were pointing to his umbrella. She seemed dignified for her youth, as she gave him a shy glance and then smiled at the boys.

"Ah, ha!" he cried to the boys. "You've been in *now* all right!" And then laughing to her, "I was kiddin' them awhile ago about their dry bathing suits."

She smiled at the boys again. "They like for me to be with them when they go in," she said.

"I got some lemonade here," he said abruptly, slapping the thermos jug. "Why don't you have some?" His voice was anxious. She hesitated.

He jumped up. "Come on, sit down." He smiled at her and stepped aside.

Still she hesitated. But her eager boys pressed close behind her. Finally she smiled and sat down under the umbrella.

"You fellas can sit down under there too—in the shade," he said to the boys, and pointed under the umbrella. The boys flopped down quickly in the shady sand. He started at once serving them cold lemonade in the paper cups.

"Whew! I thought it was goin' to rain there for a while," he said, making conversation after passing out the lemonade. He had squatted on the sand and lit another cigarette. "Then there wouldn't a been much goin' on. But it turned out fine after all— there'll be a mob here before long."

She sipped the lemonade, but said little. He felt she had sat down only because of the boys, for she merely smiled and gave short answers to his questons. He learned the boys' names, Melvin and James; their ages, seven and nine; and that they were still frightened by the water. But he wanted to ask *her* name, and inquire about her husband. But he could not capture the courage.

Now the sun was hot and the sand was hot. And an orange-and-white umbrella was going up right beside them—two fellows and a girl. When the fellow who had been kneeling to drive the umbrella spike in the sand stood up, he was stringbean tall, and black, with his glistening hair freshly processed. The girl was a lighter brown, and wore a lilac bathing suit, and, although her legs were thin, she was pleasant enough to look at. The second fellow was medium, really, in height, but short beside his tall, black friend. He was

yellow-skinned, and fast getting bald, although still in his early
thirties. Both men sported little shoestring mustaches.

Elijah watched them in silence as long as he could. "You picked
the right spot all right!" he laughed at last, putting on his sunglasses.

"How come, man?" The tall, black fellow grinned, showing his
mouthful of gold teeth.

"You see *every*body here!" happily rejoined Elijah. "They all
come here!"

"Man, I been coming here for years," the fellow reproved, and
sat down in his khaki swimming trunks to take off his shoes. Then
he stood up. "But right now, in the water I goes." He looked down
at the girl. "How 'bout you, Lois, baby?"

"No, Caesar," she smiled, "not yet; I'm gonna sit here awhile
and relax."

"Okay, then—you just sit right there and relax. And Little Joe"
—he turned and grinned to his shorter friend—"you sit there an'
relax right along with her. You all can talk with this gentleman
here"—he nodded at Elijah—"an' his nice wife." Then, pleased
with himself, he trotted off toward the water.

The young mother looked at Elijah, as if he should have hastened to correct him. But somehow he had not wanted to. Yet too,
Caesar's remark seemed to amuse her, for she soon smiled. Elijah
felt the pain of relief—he did not want her to go; he glanced at
her with a furtive laugh, and then they both laughed. The boys had
finished their lemonade now, and were digging in the sand. Lois
and Little Joe were busy talking.

Elijah was not quite sure what he should say to the mother. He
did not understand her, was afraid of boring her, was desperate
to keep her interested. As she sat looking out over the lake, he
watched her. She was not pretty; and she was too thin. But he
thought she had poise; he liked the way she treated her boys—
tender, but casual; how different from Myrtle's frantic herding.

Soon she turned to the boys. "Want to go back in the water?"
she laughed.

The boys looked at each other, and then at her. "Okay," James
said finally, in resignation.

"Here, have some more lemonade," Elijah cut in.

The boys, rescued for the moment, quickly extended their cups. He poured them more lemonade, as she looked on smiling.

Now he turned to Lois and Little Joe sitting under their orange-and-white umbrella. "How 'bout some good ole cold lemonade?" he asked with a mushy smile. "I got plenty of cups." He felt he must get something going.

Lois smiled back. "No, thanks," she said, fluttering her long eyelashes, "not right now."

He looked anxiously at Little Joe.

"*I'll* take a cup!" said Little Joe, and turned and laughed to Lois: "Hand me that bag there, will you?" He pointed to her beach bag in the sand. She passed it to him, and he reached in and pulled out a pint of gin. "We'll have some *real* lemonade," he vowed, with a daredevilish grin.

Lois squealed with pretended embarrassment. "Oh, *Joe!*"

Elijah's eyes were big now; he was thinking of the police. But he handed Little Joe a cup and poured the lemonade, to which Joe added gin. Then Joe, grinning, thrust the bottle at Elijah. "How 'bout yourself, chief?" he said.

Elijah, shaking his head, leaned forward and whispered, "You ain't supposed to drink on the beach, y'know."

"*This* ain't a drink, man—it's a taste!" said Little Joe, laughing and waving the bottle around toward the young mother. "How 'bout a little taste for your wife here?" he said to Elijah.

The mother laughed and threw up both hands. "No, not for me!"

Little Joe gave her a rakish grin. "What'sa matter? You '*fraid* of that guy?" He jerked his thumb toward Elijah. "You 'fraid of gettin' a whippin', eh?"

"No, not exactly," she laughed.

Elijah was so elated with her his relief burst up in hysterical laughter. His laugh became strident and hoarse and he could not stop. The boys gaped at him, and then at their mother. When finally he recovered, Little Joe asked him, "Whut's so funny 'bout *that?*" Then Little Joe grinned at the mother. "You beat *him* up sometimes, eh?"

This started Elijah's hysterics all over again. The mother looked concerned now, and embarrassed; her laugh was nervous and shadowed. Little Joe glanced at Lois, laughed, and shrugged his shoulders. When Elijah finally got control of himself again he looked spent and demoralized.

Lois now tried to divert attention by starting a conversation with the boys. But the mother showed signs of restlessness and seemed ready to go. At this moment Caesar returned. Glistening beads of water ran off his long, black body; and his hair was unprocessed now. He surveyed the group and then flashed a wide, gold-toothed grin. "One big, happy family, like I said." Then he spied the paper cup in Little Joe's hand. "Whut you got there, man?"

Little Joe looked down into his cup with a playful smirk. "Lemonade, lover boy, lemonade."

"Don't hand me that jive, Joey. You ain't never had any straight lemonade in your life."

This again brought uproarious laughter from Elijah. "I got the straight lemonade *here!*" He beat the thermos jug with his hand. "Come on—have some!" He reached for a paper cup.

"Why, sure," said poised Caesar. He held out the cup and received the lemonade. "Now, gimme that gin," he said to Little Joe. Joe handed over the gin, and Caesar poured three fingers into the lemonade and sat down in the sand with his legs crossed under him. Soon he turned to the two boys, as their mother watched him with amusement. "Say, ain't you boys goin' in any more? Why don't you tell your daddy there to take you in?" He nodded toward Elijah.

Little Melvin frowned at him. "My daddy's workin'," he said.

Caesar's eyebrows shot up. "Ooooh, la, la!" he crooned. "Hey, now!" And he turned and looked at the mother and then at Elijah, and gave a clownish little snigger.

Lois tittered before feigning exasperation at him. "There you go again," she said, "talkin' when you shoulda been listening."

Elijah laughed along with the rest. But he felt deflated. Then he glanced at the mother, who was laughing too. He could detect in her no sign of dismay. Why then had she gone along with the gag in the first place, he thought—if now she didn't hate to see it punctured?

"*Hold the phone!*" softly exclaimed Little Joe. "Whut is *this?*"

He was staring over his shoulder. Three women, young, brown, and worldly-looking, wandered toward them, carrying an assortment of beach paraphernalia and looking for a likely spot. They wore scant bathing suits, and were followed, but slowly, by an older woman with big, unsightly thighs. Elijah recognized her at once. She was the old gal who, the Saturday before, had chased him away from her beach party. She wore the same white bathing suit, and one of her girls carried the pea-green umbrella.

Caesar forgot his whereabouts ogling the girls. The older woman, observing this, paused to survey the situation. "How 'bout along in here?" she finally said to one of the girls. The girl carrying the thermos jug set it in the sand so close to Caesar it nearly touched him. He was rapturous. The girl with the umbrella had no chance to put it up, for Caesar and Little Joe instantly encumbered her with help. Another girl turned on a portable radio, and grinning, feverish Little Joe started snapping his fingers to the music's beat.

Within a half hour, a boisterous party was in progress. The little radio, perched on a hump of sand, blared out hot jazz, as the older woman—whose name turned out to be Hattie—passed around some cold, rum-spiked punch; and before long she went into her dancing-prancing act—to the riotous delight of all, especially Elijah. Hattie did not remember him from the Saturday past, and he was glad, for everything was so different today! As different as milk and ink. He knew no one realized it, but this was *his* party really—the wildest, craziest, funniest, and best he had ever seen or heard of. Nobody had been near the water—except Caesar, and the mother and boys much earlier. It appeared Lois was Caesar's girl friend, and she was hence more capable of reserve in face of the come-on antics of Opal, Billie, and Quanita—Hattie's girls. But Little Joe, to Caesar's tortured envy, was both free and aggressive. Even the young mother, who now volunteered her name to be Mrs. Green, got frolicsome, and twice jabbed Little Joe in the ribs.

Finally Caesar proposed they all go in the water. This met with instant, tipsy acclaim; and Little Joe, his yellow face contorted from laughing, jumped up, grabbed Billie's hand, and made off with her across the sand. But Hattie would not budge. Full of rum, and stubborn, she sat sprawled with her flaccid thighs spread in an obscene V, and her eyes half shut. Now she yelled at her departing girls: "You all watch out, now! Dont'cha go in too far. . . . Just wade! None o' you can swim a lick!"

Elijah now was beyond happiness. He felt a floating, manic glee. He sprang up and jerked Mrs. Green splashing into the water, followed by her somewhat less ecstatic boys. Caesar had to paddle about with Lois and leave Little Joe unassisted to caper with Billie, Opal, and Quanita. Billie was the prettiest of the three, and, despite Hattie's contrary statement, she could swim; and Little Joe, after taking her out in deeper water, waved back to Caesar in triumph. The sun was brazen now, and the beach and lake thronged with a variegated humanity. Elijah, a strong, but awkward, country-style swimmer, gave Mrs. Green a lesson in floating on her back, and, though she too could swim, he often felt obligated to place both his arms under her young body and buoy her up.

And sometimes he would purposely let her sink to her chin, whereupon she would feign a happy fright and utter faint simian screeches. Opal and Quanita sat in the shallows and kicked up their heels at Caesar, who, fully occupied with Lois, was a grinning, water-threshing study in frustration.

Thus the party went—on and on—till nearly four o'clock. Elijah had not known the world afforded such joy; his homely face was a wet festoon of beams and smiles. He went from girl to girl, insisting she learn to float on his outstretched arms. Once begrudging Caesar admonished him, "Man, you gonna *drown* one o' them pretty chicks." And Little Joe bestowed his highest accolade by calling him "lover boy," as Elijah nearly strangled from laughter.

At last, they looked up to see old Hattie as she reeled down to the water's edge, coming to fetch her girls. Both Caesar and Little Joe ran out of the water to meet her, seized her by the wrists, and, despite her struggles and curses, dragged her in. "Turn me loose! You big galoots!" she yelled and gasped as the water hit her. She was in knee-deep before she wriggled and fought herself free and lurched out of the water. Her breath reeked of rum. Little Joe ran and caught her again, but she lunged backwards, and free, with such force she sat down in the wet sand with a thud. She roared a laugh now, and spread her arms for help, as her girls came sprinting and splashing out of the water and tugged her to her feet. Her eyes narrowed to vengeful, grinning slits as she turned on Caesar and

Little Joe: "*I* know whut you two're up to!" She flashed a glance around toward her girls. "I been watchin' both o' you studs! Yeah, yeah, but your eyes may shine, an' your teeth may grit . . ." She went limp in a sneering, raucous laugh. Everybody laughed now—except Lois and Mrs. Green.

They had all come out of the water now, and soon the whole group returned to their three beach umbrellas. Hattie's girls immediately prepared to break camp. They took down their pea-green umbrella, folded some wet towels, and donned their beach sandals, as Hattie still bantered Caesar and Little Joe.

"Well, you sure had *yourself* a ball today," she said to Little Joe, who was sitting in the sand.

"Comin' back next Saturday?" asked grinning Little Joe.

"I jus' might at that," surmised Hattie. "We wuz here last Saturday."

"Good! Good!" Elijah broke in. "Let's *all* come back—next Saturday!" He searched every face.

"*I'll* be here," chimed Little Joe, grinning to Caesar. Captive Caesar glanced at Lois, and said nothing.

Lois and Mrs. Green were silent. Hattie, insulted, looked at them and started swelling up. "Never mind," she said pointedly to Elijah, "you jus' come on anyhow. You'll run into a slew o' folks lookin' for a good time. You don't need no *certain* people." But a little later, she and her girls all said friendly goodbyes and walked off across the sand.

The party now took a sudden downturn. All Elijah's efforts at resuscitation seemed unavailing. The westering sun was dipping toward the distant buildings of the city, and many of the bathers were leaving. Caesar and Little Joe had become bored; and Mrs. Green's boys, whining to go, kept a reproachful eye on their mother.

"Here, you boys, take some more lemonade," Elijah said quickly, reaching for the thermos jug. "Only got a little left—better get while gettin's good!" He laughed. The boys shook their heads.

On Lois he tried cajolery. Smiling, and pointing to her wet, but trim bathing suit, he asked, "What color would you say that is?"

"Lilac," said Lois, now standing.

"It sure is pretty! Prettiest on the beach!" he whispered.

Lois gave him a weak smile. Then she reached down for her beach bag, and looked at Caesar.

Caesar stood up. "Let's cut," he turned and said to Little Joe, and began taking down their orange-and-white umbrella.

Elijah was desolate. "Whatta you goin' for? It's gettin' cooler! Now's the time to *enjoy* the beach!"

"I've got to go home," Lois said.

Mrs. Green got up now; her boys had started off already. "Just a minute, Melvin," she called, frowning. Then, smiling, she turned and thanked Elijah.

He whirled around to them all. "Are we comin' back next Saturday? Come on—let's all come back! Wasn't it great! It was *great!* Don't you think? Whatta you say?" He looked now at Lois and Mrs. Green.

"We'll see," Lois said, smiling, "Maybe."

"Can *you* come?" He turned to Mrs. Green.

"I'm not sure," she said. "I'll try."

"Fine! Oh, that's fine!" He turned on Caesar and Little Joe. "I'll be lookin' for you guys, hear?"

"Okay, chief," grinned Little Joe. "An' put somethin' in that lemonade, will ya?"

Everybody laughed . . . and soon they were gone.

Elijah slowly crawled back under his umbrella, although the sun's heat was almost spent. He looked about him. There was only one umbrella on the spot now, his own; where before there had been three. Cigarette butts and paper cups lay strewn where Hattie's girls had sat, and the sandy imprint of Caesar's enormous street shoes marked his site. Mrs. Green had dropped a bobby pin. He too was caught up now by a sudden urge to go. It was hard to bear much longer—the lonesomeness. And most of the people were leaving anyway. He stirred and fidgeted in the sand, and finally started an inventory of his belongings. . . . Then his thoughts flew home, and he reconsidered. Funny—he hadn't thought of home all afternoon. Where had the time gone anyhow? . . . It seemed he'd just pulled up in the Chevy and unloaded his gear; now it was time to go home again. Then the image of solemn Randy suddenly formed in his mind, sending waves of guilt through him. He forgot where he was as the duties of his existence leapt on his back—

where would he ever get Randy's fifteen dollars? He felt squarely
confronted by a great blank void. It was an awful thing he had done
—all for a day at the beach . . . with some sporting girls. He thought
of his family and felt tiny—and him itching to come back next
Saturday! Maybe Myrtle was right about him after all. Lord, if she
knew what he had done. . . .

He sat there for a long time. Most of the people were gone now.
The lake was quiet save for a few boys still in the water. And the
sun, red like blood, had settled on the dark silhouettes of the
housetops across the city. He sat beneath the umbrella just as he
had at one o'clock . . . and the thought smote him. He was jolted.
Then dubious. But there it was—quivering, vital, swelling inside
his skull like an unwanted fetus. So this was it! He mutinied inside.
So he must sell it . . . his *umbrella*. Sell it for anything—only as
long as it was enough to pay back Randy. For fifteen dollars even,
if necessary. He was dogged; he couldn't do it; that wasn't the
answer anyway. But the thought clawed and clung to him, rebuking and coaxing him by turns, until it finally became conviction.
He must do it; it was the right thing to do; the only thing to do.
Maybe then the awful weight would lift, the dull commotion in
his stomach cease. He got up and started collecting his belongings;
placed the thermos jug, sunglasses, towel, cigarettes, and little rug
together in a neat pile, to be carried to the Chevy later. Then he
turned to face his umbrella. Its red and white stripes stood defiant
against the wide, churned-up sand. He stood for a moment moon-
ing at it. Then he carefully let it down and, carrying it in his right
hand, went off across the sand.

The sun now had gone down behind the vast city in a shower
of crimson-golden glints, and on the beach only a few stragglers
remained. For his first prospects, he approached two teen-age boys,
but suddenly realizing they had no money, he turned away and
went over to an old woman, squat and black, in street clothes—a
spectator—who stood gazing eastward out across the lake. She
held in her hand a little black book, with red-edged pages, which
looked like the New Testament. He smiled at her. "Wanna buy a
nice new beach umbrella?" He held out the collapsed umbrella
toward her.

She gave him a beatific smile, but shook her head. "No, son,"

she said, "that ain't what *I* want." And she turned to gaze out
on the lake again.

For a moment he still held the umbrella out, with a question
mark on his face. "Okay, then," he finally said, and went on.

Next he hurried down to the water's edge, where he saw a man
and two women preparing to leave. "Wanna buy a nice new beach
umbrella?" His voice sounded high-pitched, as he opened the umbrella over his head. "It's brand-new. I'll sell it for fifteen dollars—
it cost a lot more'n that."

The man was hostile, and glared. Finally he said, "Whatta you
take me for—a fool?"

Elijah looked bewildered, and made no answer. He observed
the man for a moment. Finally he let the umbrella down. As he
moved away, he heard the man say to the women, "It's hot—he
stole it somewhere."

Close by, another man sat alone in the sand. Elijah started
toward him. The man wore trousers, but was stripped to the waist,
and bent over intent on some task in his lap. When Elijah reached
him, he looked up from half a hatful of cigarette butts he was
breaking open for the tobacco he collected in a little paper bag.
He grinned at Elijah, who meant now to pass on.

"No, I ain't interested either, buddy," the man insisted as Elijah
passed him. "Not me. I jus' got *outa* jail las' week—an' ain't goin'
back for no umbrella." He laughed, as Elijah kept on.

Now he saw three women, still in their bathing suits, sitting
together near the diving board. They were the only people he had
not yet tried—except the one lifeguard left. As he approached them,
he saw that all three wore glasses and were sedate. Some school-
teachers maybe, he thought, or office workers. They were talking—
until they saw him coming; then they stopped. One of them was
plump, but a smooth dark brown, and sat with a towel around her
shoulders. Elijah addressed them through her: "Wanna buy a nice
beach umbrella?" And again he opened the umbrella over his head.

"Gee! It's beautiful," the plump woman said to the others. "But
where'd you get it?" she suddenly asked Elijah, polite mistrust entering her voice.

"I bought it—just this week."

The three women looked at each other. "Why do you want to sell it so soon, then?" a second woman said.

Elijah grinned. "I need the money."

"Well!" The plump woman was exasperated. "*No,* we don't want it." And they turned from him. He stood for a while, watching them; finally he let the umbrella down and moved on.

Only the lifeguard was left. He was a huge youngster, not over twenty, and brawny and black, as he bent over cleaning out his beached rowboat. Elijah approached him so suddenly he looked up startled.

"Would you be interested in this umbrella?" Elijah said, and proffered the umbrella. "It's brand-new—I just bought it Tuesday. I'll sell it cheap." There was urgency in his voice.

The lifeguard gave him a queer stare; and then peered off toward the Outer Drive, as if looking for help. "You're lucky as hell," he finally said. "The cops just now cruised by—up on the Drive. I'd have turned you in so quick it'd made your head swim. Now you get the hell outa here." He was menacing.

Elijah was angry. "Whatta you mean? I *bought* this umbrella—it's mine."

The lifeguard took a step toward him. "I said you better get the hell outa here! An' I mean it! *You thievin' bastard, you!*"

Elijah, frightened now, gave ground. He turned and walked away a few steps; and then slowed up, as if an adequate answer had hit him. He stood for a moment. But finally he walked on, the umbrella drooping in his hand.

He walked up the gravelly slope now toward the Chevy, forgetting his little pile of belongings left in the sand. When he reached the car, and opened the trunk, he remembered; and went back down and gathered them up. He returned, threw them in the trunk and, without dressing, went around and climbed under the steering wheel. He was scared, shaken; and before starting the motor sat looking out on the lake. It was seven o'clock; the sky was waning pale, the beach forsaken, leaving a sense of perfect stillness and approaching night; the only sound was a gentle lapping of the water against the sand—one moderate *hallo-o-o-o* would have carried across to Michigan. He looked down at the beach. Where were they all now—the funny, proud, laughing people? Eat-

ing their dinners, he supposed, in a variety of homes. And all the
beautiful umbrellas—where were they? Without their colors the
beach was so deserted. Ah, the beach . . . after pouring hot ore all
week out at Youngstown Sheet and Tube, he would probably be
too fagged out for the beach. But maybe he wouldn't—who knew?
It was great while it lasted . . . great. And his umbrella . . . he
didn't know what he'd do with that . . . he might never need it
again. He'd keep it, though—and see. Ha! . . . hadn't he sweat to
get it! . . . and they thought he had stolen it . . . stolen it . . . ah . . .
and maybe they were right. He sat for a few moments longer.
Finally he started the motor, and took the old Chevy out onto the
Drive in the pink-hued twilight. But down on the beach the sun
was still shining.

CARSON McCULLERS

The Sojourner

HE TWILIGHT BORDER between sleep and waking was
a Roman one this morning: splashing fountains and arched, narrow
streets, the golden lavish city of blossoms and age-soft stone. Sometimes in this semi-consciousness he sojourned again in Paris, or German war rubble, or a Swiss skiing and a snow hotel. Sometimes, also,
in a fallow Georgia field at hunting dawn. Rome it was this morning in the yearless region of dreams.

John Ferris awoke in a room in a New York hotel. He had the feeling that something unpleasant was awaiting him—what it was, he did not know. The feeling, submerged by matinal necessities, lingered even after he had dressed and gone downstairs. It was a cloudless autumn day and the pale sunlight sliced between the pastel skyscrapers. Ferris went into the next-door drugstore and sat at the end booth next to the window glass that overlooked the sidewalk. He ordered an American breakfast with scrambled eggs and sausage.

Ferris had come from Paris to his father's funeral which had taken place the week before in his home town in Georgia. The shock of death had made him aware of youth already passed. His hair was receding and the veins in his now naked temples were pulsing and prominent and his body was spare except for an incipient belly bulge. Ferris had loved his father and the bond between them had once been extraordinarily close—but the years had somehow unraveled this filial devotion; the death, expected for a long time, had left him with an unforseen dismay. He had stayed as long as possible to be near his mother and brothers at home. His plane for Paris was to leave the next morning.

Ferris pulled out his address book to verify a number. He turned the pages with growing attentiveness. Names and addresses from New York, the capitals of Europe, a few faint ones from his home state in the South. Faded, printed names, sprawled drunken ones. Betty Wills: a random love, married now. Charlie Williams: wounded in the Hürtgen Forest, unheard of since. Grand old Williams—did he live or die? Don Walker: a B.T.O. in television, getting rich. Henry Green: hit the skids after the war, in a sanitarium now, they say. Cozie Hall: he had heard that she was dead. Heedless, laughing Cozie—it was strange to think that she too, silly girl, could die. As Ferris closed the address book, he suffered a sense of hazard, transience, almost of fear.

It was then that his body jerked suddenly. He was staring out of the window when there, on the sidewalk, passing by, was his ex-wife. Elizabeth passed quite close to him, walking slowly. He could not understand the wild quiver of his heart, nor the following sense of recklessness and grace that lingered after she was gone.

Quickly Ferris paid his check and rushed out to the sidewalk.

Elizabeth stood on the corner waiting to cross Fifth Avenue. He hurried toward her meaning to speak, but the lights changed and she crossed the street before he reached her. Ferris followed. On the other side he could easily have overtaken her, but he found himself lagging unaccountably. Her fair hair was plainly rolled, and as he watched her Ferris recalled that once his father had remarked that Elizabeth had a 'beautiful carriage.' She turned at the next corner and Ferris followed, although by now his intention to overtake her had disappeared. Ferris questioned the bodily disturbance that the sight of Elizabeth aroused in him, the dampness of his hands, the hard heartstrokes.

It was eight years since Ferris had last seen his ex-wife. He knew that long ago she had married again. And there were children. During recent years he had seldom thought of her. But at first, after the divorce, the loss had almost destroyed him. Then after the anodyne of time, he had loved again, and then again. Jeannine, she was now. Certainly his love for his ex-wife was long since past. So why the unhinged body, the shaken mind? He knew only that his clouded heart was oddly dissonant with the sunny, candid autumn day. Ferris wheeled suddenly and, walking with long strides, almost running, hurried back to the hotel.

Ferris poured himself a drink, although it was not yet eleven o'clock. He sprawled out in an armchair like a man exhausted, nursing his glass of bourbon and water. He had a full day ahead of him as he was leaving by plane the next morning for Paris. He checked over his obligations: take luggage to Air France, lunch with his boss, buy shoes and an overcoat. And something—wasn't there something else? Ferris finished his drink and opened the telephone directory.

His decision to call his ex-wife was impulsive. The number was under Bailey, the husband's name, and he called before he had much time for self-debate. He and Elizabeth had exchanged cards at Christmastime, and Ferris had sent a carving set when he received the announcement of her wedding. There was no reason *not* to call. But as he waited, listening to the ring at the other end, misgiving fretted him.

Elizabeth answered; her familiar voice was a fresh shock to him. Twice he had to repeat his name, but when he was identified, she sounded glad. He explained he was only in town for that day. They had a theater engagement, she said—but she wondered if he would come by for an early dinner. Ferris said he would be delighted.

As he went from one engagement to another, he was still bothered at odd moments by the feeling that something necessary was forgotten. Ferris bathed and changed in the late afternoon, often thinking about Jeannine: he would be with her the following night. 'Jeannine,' he would say, 'I happened to run into my ex-wife when I was in New York. Had dinner with her. And her husband, of course. It was strange seeing her after all these years.'

Elizabeth lived in the East Fifties, and as Ferris taxied uptown he glimpsed at intersections the lingering sunset, but by the time he reached his destination it was already autumn dark. The place was a building with a marquee and a doorman, and the apartment was on the seventh floor.

'Come in, Mr. Ferris.'

Braced for Elizabeth or even the unimagined husband, Ferris was astonished by the freckled red-haired child; he had known of the children, but his mind had failed somehow to acknowledge them. Surprise made him step back awkwardly.

'This is our apartment,' the child said politely. 'Aren't you Mr. Ferris? I'm Billy. Come in.'

In the living room beyond the hall, the husband provided another surprise; he too had not been acknowledged emotionally. Bailey was a lumbering red-haired man with a deliberate manner. He rose and extended a welcoming hand.

'I'm Bill Bailey. Glad to see you. Elizabeth will be in, in a minute. She's finishing dressing.'

The last words struck a gliding series of vibrations, memories of the other years. Fair Elizabeth, rosy and naked before her bath. Half-dressed before the mirror of her dressing table, brushing her fine, chestnut hair. Sweet, casual intimacy, the soft-fleshed loveliness indisputably possessed. Ferris shrank from the unbidden memories and compelled himself to meet Bill Bailey's gaze.

'Billy, will you please bring that tray of drinks from the kitchen table?'

The child obeyed promptly, and when he was gone Ferris remarked conversationally, 'Fine boy you have there.'

'We think so.'

Flat silence until the child returned with a tray of glasses and a cocktail shaker of Martinis. With the priming drinks they pumped up conversation: Russia, they spoke of, and the New York rainmaking, and the apartment situation in Manhattan and Paris.

'Mr. Ferris is flying all the way across the ocean tomorrow,' Bailey said to the little boy who was perched on the arm of his chair, quiet and well behaved. 'I bet you would like to be a stowaway in his suitcase.'

Billy pushed back his limp bangs. 'I want to fly in an airplane and be a newspaperman like Mr. Ferris.' He added with sudden assurance, 'That's what I would like to do when I am big.'

Bailey said, 'I thought you wanted to be a doctor.'

'I do!' said Billy. 'I would like to be both. I want to be a atom-bomb scientist too.'

Elizabeth came in carrying in her arms a baby girl.

'Oh, John!' she said. She settled the baby in the father's lap. 'It's grand to see you. I'm awfully glad you could come.'

The little girl sat demurely on Bailey's knees. She wore a pale pink crepe de Chine frock, smocked around the yoke with rose, and a matching silk hair ribbon tying back her pale soft curls. Her skin was summer tanned and her brown eyes flecked with gold and laughing. When she reached up and fingered her father's horn-rimmed glasses, he took them off and let her look through them a moment. 'How's my old Candy?'

Elizabeth was very beautiful, more beautiful perhaps than he had ever realized. Her straight clean hair was shining. Her face was softer, glowing and serene. It was a madonna loveliness, dependent on the family ambiance.

'You've hardly changed at all,' Elizabeth said, 'but it has been a long time.'

'Eight years.' His hand touched his thinning hair self-consciously while further amenities were exchanged.

Ferris felt himself suddenly a spectator—an interloper among these Baileys. Why had he come? He suffered. His own life seemed so solitary, a fragile column supporting nothing amidst the wreckage of the years. He felt he could not bear much longer to stay in the family room.

He glanced at his watch. 'You're going to the theater?'

'It's a shame,' Elizabeth said, 'but we've had this engagement for more than a month. But surely, John, you'll be staying home one of these days before long. You're not going to be an expatriate, are you?"

'Expatriate,' Ferris repeated. 'I don't much like the word.'

'What's a better word?' she asked.

He thought for a moment. 'Sojourner might do.'

Ferris glanced again at his watch, and again Elizabeth apologized. 'If only we had known ahead of time—'

'I just had this day in town. I came home unexpectedly. You see, Papa died last week.'

'Papa Ferris is dead?'

'Yes, at Johns Hopkins. He had been sick there nearly a year. The funeral was down home in Georgia.'

'Oh, I'm so sorry, John. Papa Ferris was always one of my favorite people.'

The little boy moved from behind the chair so that he could look into his mother's face. He asked, 'Who is dead?'

Ferris was oblivious to apprehension; he was thinking of his father's death. He saw again the outstretched body on the quilted silk within the coffin. The corpse flesh was bizarrely rouged and the familiar hands lay massive and joined above a spread of funeral roses. The memory closed and Ferris awakened to Elizabeth's calm voice.

'Mr. Ferris's father, Billy. A really grand person. Somebody you didn't know.'

'But why did you call him *Papa* Ferris?'

Bailey and Elizabeth exchanged a trapped look. It was Bailey who answered the questioning child. 'A long time ago,' he said, 'your mother and Mr. Ferris were once married. Before you were born—a long time ago.'

'Mr. Ferris?'

The little boy stared at Ferris, amazed and unbelieving. And Ferris's eyes, as he returned the gaze, were somehow unbelieving too. Was it indeed true that at one time he had called this stranger,

Elizabeth, Little Butterduck during nights of love, that they had
lived together, shared perhaps a thousand days and nights and—
finally—endured in the misery of sudden solitude the fiber by fiber
(jealousy, alcohol and money quarrels) destruction of the fabric of
married love?

Bailey said to the children, 'It's somebody's suppertime. Come
on now.'

'But Daddy! Mama and Mr. Ferris—I—'

Billy's everlasting eyes—perplexed and with a glimmer of
hostility—reminded Ferris of the gaze of another child. It was the
young son of Jeannine—a boy of seven with a shadowed little face
and knobby knees whom Ferris avoided and usually forgot.

'Quick march!' Bailey gently turned Billy toward the door. 'Say
good night now, son.'

'Good night, Mr. Ferris.' He added resentfully, 'I thought I was
staying up for the cake.'

'You can come in afterward for the cake,' Elizabeth said. 'Run
along now with Daddy for your supper.'

Ferris and Elizabeth were alone. The weight of the situation
descended on those first moments of silence. Ferris asked permission
to pour himself another drink and Elizabeth set the cocktail shaker
on the table at his side. He looked at the grand piano and noticed
the music on the rack.

'Do you still play as beautifully as you used to?'

'I still enjoy it.'

'Please play, Elizabeth.'

Elizabeth arose immediately. Her readiness to perform when
asked had always been one of her amiabilities; she never hung
back, apologized. Now as she approached the piano there was the
added readiness of relief.

She began with a Bach prelude and fugue. The prelude was as
gaily iridescent as a prism in a morning room. The first voice of the
fugue, an announcement pure and solitary, was repeated inter-
mingling with a second voice, and again repeated within an elab-
orated frame, the multiple music, horizontal and serene, flowed with
unhurried majesty. The principal melody was woven with two other
voices, embellished with countless ingenuities—now dominant,
again submerged, it had the sublimity of a single thing that does

not fear surrender to the whole. Toward the end, the density of the material gathered for the last enriched insistence on the dominant first motif and with a chorded final statement the fugue ended. Ferris rested his head on the chair back and closed his eyes. In the following silence a clear, high voice came from the room down the hall.

'Daddy, how *could* Mama and Mr. Ferris—' A door was closed.

The piano began again—what was this music? Unplaced, familiar, the limpid melody had lain a long while dormant in his heart. Now it spoke to him of another time, another place—it was the music Elizabeth used to play. The delicate air summoned a wilderness of memory. Ferris was lost in the riot of past longings, conflicts, ambivalent desires. Strange that the music, catalyst for this tumultuous anarchy, was so serene and clear. The singing melody was broken off by the appearance of the maid.

'Miz Bailey, dinner is out on the table now.'

Even after Ferris was seated at the table between his host and hostess, the unfinished music still overcast his mood. He was a little drunk.

'*L'improvisation de la vie humaine,*' he said. 'There's nothing that makes you so aware of the improvisation of human existence as a song unfinished. Or an old address book.'

'Address book?' repeated Bailey. Then he stopped, noncommittal and polite.

'You're still the same old boy, Johnny,' Elizabeth said with a trace of the old tenderness.

It was a Southern dinner that evening, and the dishes were his old favorites. They had fried chicken and corn pudding and rich, glazed candied sweet potatoes. During the meal Elizabeth kept alive a conversation when the silences were overlong. And it came about that Ferris was led to speak of Jeannine.

'I first knew Jeannine last autumn—about this time of the year —in Italy. She's a singer and she had an engagement in Rome. I expect we will be married soon.'

The words seemed so true, inevitable, that Ferris did not at first acknowledge to himself the lie. He and Jeannine had never in that year spoken of marriage. And indeed, she was still married— to a White Russian money-changer in Paris from whom she had been separated for five years. But it was too late to correct the lie. Already Elizabeth was saying: 'This really makes me glad to know. Congratulations, Johnny.'

He tried to make amends with truth. 'The Roman autumn is so beautiful. Balmy and blossoming.' He added, 'Jeannine has a little boy of six. A curious trilingual little fellow. We go to the Tuileries sometimes.'

A lie again. He had taken the boy once to the gardens. The sallow foreign child in shorts that bared his spindly legs had sailed his boat in the concrete pond and ridden the pony. The child had wanted to go in to the puppet show. But there was not time, for Ferris had an engagement at the Scribe Hotel. He had promised they would go to the guignol another afternoon. Only once had he taken Valentin to the Tuileries.

There was a stir. The maid brought in a white-frosted cake with pink candles. The children entered in their night clothes. Ferris still did not understand.

'Happy birthday, John,' Elizabeth said. 'Blow out the candles.'

Ferris recognized his birthday date. The candles blew out lingeringly and there was the smell of burning wax. Ferris was thirty-eight years old. The veins in his temples darkened and pulsed visibly.

'It's time you started for the theater.'

Ferris thanked Elizabeth for the birthday dinner and said the appropriate good-byes. The whole family saw him to the door.

A high, thin moon shone above the jagged, dark skyscrapers. The streets were windy, cold. Ferris hurried to Third Avenue and hailed a cab. He gazed at the nocturnal city with the deliberate attentiveness of departure and perhaps farewell. He was alone. He longed for flighttime and the coming journey.

The next day he looked down on the city from the air, burnished in sunlight, toylike, precise. Then America was left behind and there was only the Atlantic and the distant European shore. The ocean was milky pale and placid beneath the clouds. Ferris dozed most of the day. Toward dark he was thinking of Elizabeth and the visit of the previous evening. He thought of Elizabeth among her family with longing, gentle envy and inexplicable regret. He sought the melody, the unfinished air, that had so moved him. The cadence, some unrelated tones, were all that remained; the melody itself evaded him. He had found instead the first voice of the fugue that Elizabeth had played—it came to him, inverted mockingly and in a minor key. Suspended above the ocean the anxieties of transience and solitude no longer troubled him and he thought of his father's death with equanimity. During the dinner hour the plane reached the shore of France.

At midnight Ferris was in a taxi crossing Paris. It was a clouded night and mist wreathed the lights of the Place de la Concorde. The midnight bistros gleamed on the wet pavements. As always after a transocean flight the change of continents was too sudden. New York at morning, this midnight Paris. Ferris glimpsed the disorder of his life: the succession of cities, of transitory loves; and time, the sinister glissando of the years, time always.

'*Vite! Vite!*' he called in terror. '*Dépêchez-vous.*'

Valentin opened the door to him. The little boy wore pajamas and an outgrown red robe. His grey eyes were shadowed and, as Ferris passed into the flat, they flickered momentarily.

'*J'attends Maman.*'

Jeannine was singing in a night club. She would not be home before another hour. Valentin returned to a drawing, squatting with his crayons over the paper on the floor. Ferris looked down at the drawing—it was a banjo player with notes and wavy lines inside a comic-strip balloon.

'We will go again to the Tuileries.'

The child looked up and Ferris drew him closer to his knees. The melody, the unfinished music that Elizabeth had played, came to him suddenly. Unsought, the load of memory jettisoned—this time bringing only recognition and sudden joy.

'Monsieur Jean,' the child said, 'did you see him?'

Confused, Ferris thought only of another child—the freckled, family-loved boy. 'See who, Valentin?'

'Your dead papa in Georgia.' The child added, 'Was he okay?'

Ferris spoke with rapid urgency: 'We will go often to the Tuileries. Ride the pony and we will go into the guignol. We will see the puppet show and never be in a hurry any more.'

'Monsieur Jean,' Valentin said. 'The guignol is now closed.'

Again, the terror, the acknowledgment of wasted years and

death. Valentin, responsive and confident, still nestled in his arms. His cheek touched the soft cheek and felt the brush of the delicate eyelashes. With inner desperation he pressed the child close—as though an emotion as protean as his love could dominate the pulse of time.

CARSON McCULLERS' *"The Sojourner"*

        At the surface level, there can be no question what "The Sojourner" is about. Unlike some of the other stories in this collection, it is written quite straightforwardly, in a clear, precise style. Its subject is exactly what is announced in the title.

The principal character, John Ferris, is literally a sojourner. His profession, as a foreign correspondent, is one that requires him to move from place to place, all over the world. Moreover, he is divorced; and, we shortly discover, a man of many casual love affairs; habitually unsettled. The main action of the story—the visit to his former wife and her present husband and children—presents him directly in the role of the hurried, awkwardly unexpected visitor. And by the time we see him back in Paris, his present, temporary "home," we have already learned enough about him to suspect that this too (his life with his mistress and her child) is probably *only* temporary—another "sojourn"—and to realize that he himself suspects it. Indeed, Ferris knows so much about himself, is represented as able so clearly to examine and define himself in his introspections, that there is hardly anything left for us (the readers) to do in this respect.

The question arises, then: where exactly is the element of the unexpected in the story, the sense of discovery and sudden insight, that is necessary for the effectiveness of any fiction? If we know so completely "how it is going to come out," in what way is it to interest us? In some other stories, even when there is no "suspense" in this sense, it is made up for by our feeling of superiority (with the author) to the characters. We detect, in a story like "A Diamond Guitar," a level of significance in the action that the participants cannot be supposed to understand. But in "The Sojourner" there is not even this satisfaction. Mrs. McCullers has chosen one of the most difficult of all character types to handle effec-

From COMMENTARIES ON FIVE MODERN AMERICAN SHORT STORIES, by John Edward Hardy, Verlag Moritz Diesterweg. Frankfurt/Main. Copyright 1962 by Moritz Diesterweg.

tively: a man neither very young nor very old, but merely adult, of at least average if not superior intelligence, acutely self-perceptive, and in a situation which, if it is a more than usually unhappy one, we still recognize as basically "normal." Divorce has become a commonplace of life in the modern world, nearly as much taken for granted and as normal as successful marriage. And, if Ferris is a member of a glamorous profession, and lives in places of glamorous name, New York and Paris, in glamorous circumstances, with a French mistress and so on— Mrs. McCullers has taken considerable pains in the story precisely to *de*glamourize it all, to show us that Ferris is a man completely disenchanted, living a life that has become for him the dreariest routine.

Yet, I think, the story is unquestionably interesting. But what we have to look for, in interpreting it, attempting to account for its effect, is not surprises, nor any grounds for feeling ourselves superior to the main character, setting an "esthetic distance" between him and ourselves —but, rather, just for the means by which Mrs. McCullers makes us *share* Ferris' experience. There is, if no radical change or reversal of the predictable order of events and insights, a subtle, gradual intensification of feeling that brings the narrative to a sure and final climax.

Ferris, we gather, has felt lonely before; he has also, it appears, felt many times that his life has been disorganized and to some extent wasted. This much, then, is nothing new for him. And the only "surprise," his chance glimpse of his former wife on the street, is something that simply *begins* the action. We somehow sense, moreover, that it is not going to lead to anything really spectacular—like an attempt to re-enter her life, or a decision even radically to alter the conditions of his own existence, to give up his job and not return to Paris, or whatever. As we might foresee from the time of our introduction to him, he goes on doing just what he has been doing before the encounter, picks up again the routine commitments of his existence. But he does it in a certain way, with a certain, new focus and intensity of feeling, or self-realization, that could not be from the beginning entirely predicted, and that gives the story its "point," its peculiar emotional impact.

This is expressed, principally, in his unaccustomed awareness of the children—Elizabeth's little son and daughter by her second marriage, and then his present mistress' child, Valentin. Ferris himself, we are left to suppose, has never fathered a child. He has until now avoided, as much as possible, contact with little Valentin; has apparently felt a trifle ashamed of him, indeed, on the one holiday they have taken together; and finds him, in general, a strange and rather disquieting child, is almost, in some obscure fashion, afraid of him. And, although he

knows that Elizabeth has the two children, he has managed to put the
fact out of his mind until the boy opens the door for him at the
Baileys' apartment, In short, not only has Ferris, as he secretly acknowl-
edges to himself, never really considered marriage to Jeannine—wanting
with this lie and the one about his good times with Valentin merely to
comfort himself (and Elizabeth and her husband) against the feeling of
his being so shut out from the joys of family life—but, if the fullness of
marriage is procreation, he has never been fully married to Elizabeth
either! He has, it is implied, always thought of life with a woman, in or
out of legal union, as simply a matter of the more or less satisfactory
intimacy of the *two* persons. (One of the minor ironies of the story, incidentally, is the way in which in his reminiscences of their life together,
seeing her in his mind's eye preparing for her bath and so on, Ferris
tends to glamourize Elizabeth—making her, in retrospect, more exciting
in the way of a "mistress" than Jeannine would appear to be.) What he
begins painfully to discover now, is the character of marriage as embodiment of the mystery of generation.

He realizes not only, more intensely than ever, that he is getting old,
but with a special terror that he has failed to reproduce himself. There
is a great deal of emphasis in the story on the theme of *time* and the
inevitability of its passage. This preoccupation of Ferris' is, in fact,
identical with his growing awareness of the children. He is terrified in
the realization (reinforced by the fact of his own father's death) that
he is nearing middle-age and has no children, through whom to continue his life. He has, in effect, all of his life tried to outrun time—
always flying (note the symbolic function of the airplane trip) from one
city and continent to another, and one woman to another, and pushing
out of his consciousness the fact that somewhere and sometime he must
stop. And his final realization now of the folly of his attitude toward
time is identical with a new insight into the meaning of love.

He has, it is apparent, always identified love simply with love of
woman—the sweetness of physical intimacy and possession. He realizes
now, for the first time inescapably, that women are also mothers; that
the possession of a woman leads, in the natural order of things, in time,
to children—also demanding love, and that perhaps of a kind finally
stronger and more perilous, more exacting, since it is beyond the satisfaction of desire, than the love of woman alone.

It is a fact of major significance that we never see Ferris' mistress,
Jeannine, and that in the final scene of the story he is alone with
Valentin. The effect is to put the woman (all women) entirely out of
the picture at last, leaving Ferris face-to-face with the essential question

whether he is capable of love without desire—capable not only of loving the child, beyond the woman, but a child who is not even his own, and one for whom he has always had, as we have noted, an instinctive aversion.

This, then, is the real theme of the story—the theme of love as defense against time and man's mortality. If it is still essentially the same theme that appeared on the surface at the beginning, it is rather more complex than we might have suspected at first glance. And we may ask ourselves now—looking back to my introductory remarks—whether we can have been so sure, after all, how the story was to "come out." Do we know, in fact, even at the end, how it comes out? It seems to me that Mrs. McCullers has left Ferris, finally, on the razor's edge. We may be tempted to see in the concluding phrase—"as though an emotion as protean as his love could dominate the pulse of time"—merely the pathos of his unacknowledged defeat. It is too late; "the guignol is closed." But is this the necessary implication? Is there not at least an even chance that his effort now will be successful, and this latest of the transmutations ("protean" changes) of his love the decisive one?

For something, in fact, *has* happened to Ferris in the course of the story. He was at the start the victim only of a vague disquietude of mind, urged on by an emotional whim to telephone Elizabeth. At the end, in the apartment in Paris with Valentin, his feelings run a violent range from terror to inexplicable joy and back again to desperation. And although the desperation is a fearful emotion, it is also one that shows him now, as he was not at the beginning, fully "alive"—to himself and his situation—not only understanding, but no longer trying to escape his understanding, accepting the facts: of his age, his exile, the irrecoverable loss of the beautiful wife and the healthy, happy children that might have been his. To the extent that the desperation embodies such acceptance, it might be interpreted as the first real hope for him, the first step toward a realistic determination to make the most of what he still does have—in Jeannine, and the sad, strange, unhealthy, but at least genuinely needful and responsive Valentin.   *J.E.H.*

ELLEN DOUGLAS

Jesse

HEN WE KNEW HIM, Jesse Daniels was already an old man. He had been draft age during the first World War, and had gone to France.

"I couldn't take my fiddle to the war with me," he told me, when we were talking about his travels one day, "but I took my Jew's harp and my sweet potato. I was already a good fiddler at that time, and a good drummer, too. Music come easy to me. I played with Louis Armstrong in New Orleans, 1915, 1916." He paused and looked at me as if to see if I was impressed.

"Louis Armstrong!" I said. "Did you really?"

He nodded. "Then I got drafted," he went on, "and when I come back to New Orleans after the war, all that old gang was busted up, kind of, some gone one way and some another. I played here and there—Vicksburg, Natchez, out to Texas, up to Chicago. I never liked Chicago and all them places much. Too cold. And no fishing to speak of. I'd play up there in the spring and summer some years and then come back here to Philippi in the winter. A man can make out in Philippi. Plant him a patch of greens, fish, get him up a little band. I always got two or three boys here willing to go in on a band with me, and we could make enough to live. Nowadays, though, it's even better. You get your unemployment every year a long time—some years I got it twenty or more weeks; and then when you get up my age you got your Social Security. So now I don't have to play nowhere if I don't want to. I had a job out to Minnesota two, three years before my Social

Security come in, playing concerts at a—a—you know what I'm talking about, Miss, one of them old peoples. . . ."

"An old people's home?" I asked.

"That's it," he said. "Nothing but old peoples. And they treat 'em so nice. They got the best of all kinds of food, and they got radios and TV's, everything. And they kept us on a long time just to play for 'em every night. They got beards."

"*What?*"

"Beards. Everyone of 'em, Miss. The men, I mean. Everyone of 'em got long beards. They don't let 'em cut 'em off. They some kind of special peoples. You know what I mean? They belongs to something or other special. Some kind of a house they calls it."

"Oh," I said. "Is it the House of David?"

"That's it, Miss. That's where they keeps they old folks. It was a good job—easy hours, steady work, good pay. But I'm glad to be home. I never did catch on to the fishing up there, and it seems to me the fishing down here gets better every year. I caught me around a hundred or more breams in Calloway's Blue Hole yesterday."

"Better not let the game warden hear about it," I said.

"No indeed, Miss. I sold half of 'em before I ever went home."

The first time I saw Jesse was the day I drove down to his house to interview him about teaching my son Ralph to play the guitar. We had heard of him from friends who had hired his little band to play at a party, and who knew that he gave guitar lessons. I had telephoned him to expect me, and following his directions had driven slowly along Pearl Street until I found his house. A neat, three-room shotgun house with a small vine-covered porch, it was one of only two recently painted buildings in the block; the others were weathered to a uniform soft gray.

Very few respectable Negroes live on Pearl Street, particularly if they have children. It's a noisy neighborhood, the red-light houses sandwiched in between night clubs like the *Casablanca* and the *Live and Let Live;* tumble-down fish markets, Chinese grocery stores, cafes and second-hand clothing and furniture stores crowded into a ten-block Negro slum. But it was an appropriate neighborhood for an old time jazz musician, and I thought nothing of Jesse's living there.

His house was a block from the *Casablanca,* a huge rickety old dance hall with an unsavory reputation, and two blocks from what was rumored to be an integrated house of prostitution. But it was a sturdy house, the small porch clean, the yard, unlike the cluttered yards of neighboring houses, broom-marked where it had been recently swept. An old washtub by the front steps was full of white petunias.

Jesse was waiting for me on the front porch when I arrived. As he stood up and came toward the car, my heart sank. I didn't think he could possibly teach anyone anything. He was a scarecrow of a man, a great, tall, loose bundle of sticks with a shambling walk. His long arms and legs seemed to have a will of their own, moving somehow in unexpected directions; his gestures were outlandish, extravagant, as if his arms and hands didn't know what he was talking about and always thought he was telling a wild story. He looked, too, as if he had deliberately dressed himself as ridiculously as possible. He had on an old, battered felt hat turned inside out, the upside-down brim tilted at a dashing angle, and a pair of jeans six inches too short. The black sticks of his legs showed above his shoes, so thin at the ankles I could have put my thumb and forefinger around them. I got out of the car and introduced myself to him, while he took off his hat and bowed and wagged his head self-consciously.

But when he began to tell me about himself and to discuss the lessons, he relaxed, and his face had a certain amount of sober dignity and self-possession that were reassuring. His eyes were small and alert, his high, sloping forehead merged into a shining bald dome fringed with stiff, short black hair, he had a long jaw, deeply lined from nostrils to chin, and a wide, kind mouth. He apologized for the way he was dressed, saying he had just come in from fishing, and we made sensible arrangements about hours and prices.

"I got to see if the boy's got talent before I know can I teach him," he said. "I come the first time free."

The arrangement we made was for me to pick him up every Monday and Thursday afternoon and bring him to my house, and then to take him home afterward. He charged a dollar and a half a lesson. When he came out to get into the car the following week, the day of the first lesson, he wore a sensible, dark suit, and a respectable if ancient hat.

Jesse lived almost two miles from our house, and I spent considerable time alone with him that year, driving back and forth. That was how we happened to have so much conversation. When we got to the house, he was all business, going straight with Ralph to his room, closing the door, and setting to work. They laboriously tuned their guitars, and played over and over again three or four boogies, of which Ralph does not even remember the names, and *The St. Louis Blues, Home on the Range,* and *The Red River Valley.* These songs apparently made up Jesse's whole repertoire—if he knew any others, he did not teach them to Ralph. Usually he did not sing the words to the songs, but hummed the tunes in his cracked old voice, interrupting himself now and then to call out the chord changes in the guitar accompaniment. Sometimes, in the course of a lesson, he would send Ralph out to borrow a cigarette from me; two or three times he came out himself, and in that case, at first, if I were having a drink or a can of beer, I would offer him one. But ordinarily, except for the faint sound of the guitars behind Ralph's closed door, I scarcely knew he was in the house.

Driving back and forth, Jesse and I talked a little about fishing or about Ralph's progress on the guitar, but mostly we talked about Jesse's life. Naturally, considering his age and profession, one of the first things I asked him was whether he had known Bud Scott, who was a famous old-time musician in our part of the country. I had heard him play when I was thirteen or fourteen, and had never forgotten it; he was coal black, enormously fat, and, when he sang, opened his huge mouth so that you could see all the cavernous red interior, and shouted out the words in a hoarse, raucous, gravelly voice that could be heard in the next county, even over the deafening, brassy tumult of his band. He died the year I heard him, but he had played for dances from St. Francisville to Greenville in my mother's day, and was one of our monuments, seeming until he died as indestructible as the Confederate soldier on his shaft in the courthouse yard. Jesse said, yes, he had known Bud well, in fact had played with him many times, and with his son, Bud, Jr., who after the old man died had what nowadays they call a "combo." I remembered that Bud, Jr. had played the night of the Natchez fire, and Jesse told me he was in the combo at that time. It was during one of his out-of-work periods, when he had come South to regroup, so to speak.

The Natchez fire was in late Spring 1939, and except for the 1927 flood, it was the worst thing that ever happened in our part of the country. I suppose it has been forgotten everywhere else; so many people have been killed since 1939. But it will be a long time before our Negroes forget it. The dance was in a ramshackle night club in Natchez, and all the colored young people in the county were there. The place was hung with Spanish moss, dry as tinder and flitted with some inflammable insecticide to get rid of the mosquitoes. Someone threw away a lighted match, or perhaps there was a spark of static electricity, no one ever knew exactly how it happened, but the place went off like a firecracker—simply exploded into flame. A few people near the front and back doors got out, but in the panic almost everyone was burned or suffocated or trampled to death—five hundred people. There was scarcely a Negro family in Natchez that didn't lose a child. Even in Philippi, a hundred miles away, we felt it. Everyone had connections with somebody who died in the Natchez fire.

Jesse told me that he just missed playing with Bud Scott, Jr., that night. At the time, he said, he had had a lady friend living in Ferriday, over the river from Natchez, and he was with her that day. She didn't want to go to the dance and persuaded Jesse to drive with her to Lake Providence instead, to visit her brother's family. He didn't even bother to get anyone in his place, he said. He didn't have that on his conscience. He just didn't show up. The next morning, getting up for breakfast, they heard about it on the radio. Bud Scott, Jr. and almost everyone in the band died in the fire.

Jesse told me he had been lucky like that all his life; even when he was living in Chicago during the twenties and thirties playing in what must have been mostly dives and speakeasies, he had stayed out of trouble.

"How did you manage?" I asked. "Weren't you scared of all those gangsters up there?"

"Yes, *ma'm,* I was scared. You *got* to be scared. And you got to keep your money in your bosom. I know plenty mens up there still sits with they back in a corner in the cafe—you know, where they can see the door and all, so nobody can sneak up on them. I had a friend up there wasn't scared, and he ended up in Lake Michigan with a concrete block to his feet. I warned him, too. I told him, 'You can get along fine up here if you keep your eyes and your mouth shut, and stay scared.' But he wanted to be a big man."

I asked Jesse once if he had ever heard the *Natchez Fire Blues* or the *Philippi Pearl Street Blues,* and he told me he knew them and knew the fellows who had written both of them. They are not good songs, only run-of-the-mill blues, or what we call *race music,* the kind that is played on the local radio stations (or used to be before rock and roll came in) every afternoon from one until five to advertise hair straighteners. Jesse laughed when I asked him about the *Pearl Street Blues,* and asked me if I had ever heard *Greenville Smokin', Leland Burnin' Down,* written by the same fellow. I said I had never even heard *of* it, and he shrugged and said, well, they didn't play it on the radio, and he reckoned there were white men in Leland, Greenville, too, who would think nothing of shooting any nigger they heard singing that song. I was curious, and two or three times afterward I tried to get him to play *Greenville Smokin', Leland Burnin' Down* for me on the guitar and sing it, but he never would. I even tried to get him to explain what he meant about the shooting part, and he seemed to try, but somehow he always got confused or got me confused. Once when I asked him about it, he said he didn't think the "bossman" would like it, and then I gave up. I realized that he did not want to assume anything, to take anything for granted. He was afraid of us.

I suppose people will wonder why it mattered to me, and sometimes I wonder myself; but I was troubled, and troubled people will grasp at any straw to vindicate themselves. It doesn't have to be anything that is important to anyone. I suppose, too, that my uneasiness is part of the reason we talked about the Natchez fire. I didn't want him to think I had dismissed it long ago, as so many white people have, as something that happened to a bunch of niggers.

He must have sensed what was going on in my mind, because one day just before we got out of the car in front of my house he said to me abruptly, for no reason that I could discover, "Miss, you such a good Christian, your daddy must be a preacher."

I'm not so foolish that I didn't know he was trying to flatter me, to say what he thought would please, but even if he had been sincere, what could I have said in reply? That the churches are crowded every Sunday with his bitterest enemies? That I might not be what he would call "a Christian" at all?

"No," I said, "he's not a preacher, but he's an elder."

"I knew it," Jesse said. "I knew he was bound to be saved."

One more thing I'll say about wanting to make Jesse Daniels my friend. I have a passion for talking over old times, for hearing from old people how it was at such and such a time in such and such a place; and particularly, if I can bring to bear anything out of my own recollections, can say, "That's right; of course; because I remember, or Gran told me something that fits right in with what you're saying." It gives me intense pleasure to hear my father tell how his father used to wad his old muzzle-loading shotgun with Spanish moss, aim it up into the holly tree in the front yard (Right there—that's the tree) and bring down enough robins to have robin pie for dinner. More than anything I want to hear *how it was*, to gather all the facts, and then to *understand*. For this reason it gave me a queer satisfaction to think of Jesse's driving to Lake Providence with his lady friend the day of the fire, sitting in the warm darkness on the little porch of her brother's house, laughing and drinking and slapping mosquitoes, going to bed and making love, and then getting up the next morning to hear the impersonal voice of the radio announcer describe the horror in which they had so nearly been consumed.

From the beginning my husband did not like Jesse. That is, he didn't dislike him, but he didn't take to him, and as time went on he had a number of things against him. In the first place, Jesse wasn't much of a musician, and Richard thought we were throwing our money away. He was right, too. Jesse came twice a week for more than a year, and I don't believe he taught Ralph a dozen chords. I'll never forget how embarrassed I was for Jesse one afternoon after the lesson when I persuaded him to sit down at the piano in the living room and play and sing for us. Richard had come home early, and I thought I would give him a chance to judge Jesse for himself. Jesse was delighted to play. He put his greasy hat on top of the piano and, drawing up the chair, sat down and banged away at the keys as loudly as if he were playing in a crowded night club, and shouted out the words. But his scarred and knotty old fingers faltered, struck wrong notes, and could not even keep the time. We sat stiff-faced and silent until he finished and then praised him as enthusiastically as we could.

He knew how terrible he had sounded. "I got to have a couple of drinks to get going," he said, "and then, too, folks dancing and hollering, that limbers me up. I can't do no good cold." He got up and bowed and scraped his foot to Richard with exaggerated servility. "I try it for you again one day soon, Bossman," he went on. "I work up a coupla pieces good."

Richard looked as astonished and horrified as if someone had slapped him. "Bossman," indeed! That was a little too much for him. And there was no reason, no excuse either of us could think of for servility. Richard had said nothing that could be interpreted as expecting or requiring it. Jesse just saw a white man and went into his act—like a firehorse at the clang of the alarm.

One reason he didn't see us more clearly and another reason for Richard's disapproval of him was that he was a heavy drinker. At least half the time he came to the house he was a little bit tight. He had to use so much of his energy and intelligence on trying to appear sober that he hadn't much left either for observing us or for teaching guitar. Even Ralph got to the place where he could tell whether Jesse had been drinking, and Ralph's experience with drinkers is negligible. After he told me a couple of times that Jesse hadn't made sense again that afternoon, I had to tell him not to come unless he was sober.

It didn't make much difference to him one way or the other. He made a good living. He taught guitar to half-a-dozen white children and piano to several Negro children. (It is hard to see how he kept his piano students, except that he was probably the only Negro piano teacher in Philippi.) He played almost every Friday and Saturday night at Negro dances and parties. He collected his Social Security, and his wife worked. He also "befriended" old people by helping them fill out forms for getting on the Social Security and the State old age pension, charging twenty-

five or fifty cents a person. He told me about this project one afternoon when I was driving him home—said he naturally felt sorry for
old folks who didn't have any education, and wanted to do his part
to help them. Of course, it is against the law to charge for such a
service. I happen to know that the agent at the local Welfare Department threatened several times to have him prosecuted. But
she never did anything about it. And Jesse continued to think of
himself as a very charitable man. Somehow the fact never penetrated that the social workers at the Welfare Department would
fill out the forms for nothing. Oh, he was an old scoundrel, all
right. To do him justice, though, I know that many of his "clients"
may have been afraid to ask the workers to fill out their forms, or
they may not have understood that they could, even if they had
been told so when they applied for their pensions. Besides, it is
commonly thought among the Negroes here that the Welfare Agent
has absolute power over the state's money and that she gives
pensions to those she likes and withholds them from those who
offend her; the caprices of the state legislature are always taken
for her personal caprices, and it may even be that in the interest
of prestige she fosters this misapprehension. Jesse's clients and
perhaps even Jesse undoubtedly thought that a neatly filled out
form would help win the agent's favor.

Before many months of our acquaintance with Jesse had
passed, I began to dread Ralph's guitar days. Sometimes it seemed
to me that he quite consciously tried to make me uncomfortable.
A chance remark, a nervous laugh, an exaggerated gesture, and
my afternoon was ruined. One day he told me how when he was
a teen-age boy working for a white family in Natchez he had had
to play horsey to the child in the house. "Man, that boy never got
tired playing horse," he said. "Not 'til he got up practically grown.
I can hear his maw now, when he was a boy big as Raff. 'Come on,
Jesse. Johnny wants to play horse,' and I'd have to ride him 'til my
knees shook. I'd ruther of picked a hundred pounds of cotton."
There was something in his voice and manner that made me want
to say, "But *I* had nothing to do with it."

"He does it deliberately," I told Richard that night. "He knows
how to make us squirm. And besides that, it's gotten so I can't
have a drink on Monday or Thursday afternoon until he's gone.

If he's sober, I don't want to start him drinking, and if he's drinking, I don't want to give him any more."

"You never should have offered him the first can of beer," Richard said. "After all, he's supposed to be working for you, not paying a call. You only gave it to him because he's a Negro."

"I was trying to be nice to him," I said.

Richard shrugged impatiently. "And get a little free credit for high principles," he said.

We talked half-heartedly that night of firing Jesse, but there was no one else in town to teach Ralph, and we were not spending enough money on the lessons to care much one way or the other. So we went on with them for almost a year and a half, until we found a white teacher, a high school senior who agreed to take Ralph on. Ralph learned more from that boy in a month than he had learned from Jesse in a year and a half.

About a month before we found the high school boy to teach Ralph, Jesse told me the story of his childhood. I was driving him home one hot Thursday afternoon in September, when the subject of where he had lived as a child drifted into the conversation. I don't know why we had never talked of his home before. I suppose I had been more interested in his adult life than in his childhood; and I had assumed, too, that he had been born either in or near Philippi, since it had been his headquarters for so long. But for some reason he mentioned Buchanan County that afternoon, and when I asked him if he had ever lived there, he said, yes, he had been born and raised in Buchanan County, ten miles from Pollock, the county seat.

"You live there any after you were grown?" I asked idly.

"No'm," he said. "I left."

"They say it's rough country over there in the hills," I said. "My father told me one time about a feud they had going when he was a boy, just like the Hatfields and McCoys, and they had to call out the National Guard to make them quit killing each other. Did you ever hear about that?"

"Yes, ma'm," he said. "I didn't live there at the time. I'd been gone from Buchanan County since I was thirteen. But I heard about it from some of my cousins down to Natchez. It didn't surprise me none. Them white folks been shooting each other for thirty years before they called out the Guard. I remember one night when I was a little bitty boy, they had a fight on the road going past the place where we lived. The white man owned the place and my step-daddy was out looking for a mare had got loose, and the white man got hit in the arm by a stray bullet."

"No wonder you left," I said. I was still trying to keep the conversation going.

Jesse did not answer and, when I glanced at him, he seemed to be deep in thought. His long arm, bent at the elbow, was half out the open window of the car. His shabby old hat was on his lap, and in his left hand he was absently rolling a dead cigarette back and forth. He never smoked in the car with me, and if he got into the car with a lighted cigarette, he always carefully put it out and either put it in his pocket or held it in his hand until he got out. He was perfectly sober that afternoon, dressed in his neat dark suit, his long face the picture of quiet dignity.

We drove on for a block, and stopped at the first of several traffic lights on the way to Jesse's house, before he spoke again. Then he repeated himself. "Born and raised in Buchanan County," he said. "Away out in the country from Pollock. I ain't been back there since I left. Thirteen years old when I left, and I been on my own ever since."

"That was pretty young to go on your own," I said.

"I had five brothers and three sisters, and I reckon they all dead but me."

"You must have been the baby, then," I said.

"No, ma'm. I had a baby sister," he said. "Died in my arms. So little I didn't know the difference."

I wasn't sure what he meant, although at first I thought he was saying that she was so small, so frail, he couldn't tell when the life went out of her. And I assumed that he was talking about sometime recently, that his sister had been an old woman when she died.

"What?" I said. I always hopefully asked him to repeat himself when our conversations got confusing, although sometimes the repetition only made them more confusing.

"I was ten years old at the time," he said. "And she was two. I was so little I didn't know she was dead."

"Oh, *Jesse*," I said. "Where was your mama?"

"My mama was dead," he said. "She been dead six months when the baby died. And so we had nobody but each other. I and her was the two youngest children, and the baby, she was a half to me. Like I told you, I had a step-daddy. *Gret,* big, black nigger, eyes like coals, *hot;* tall, big as a mountain he seemed like to me. I wasn't nothing but a skinny piece of nothing." He smiled and looked down at his thin arm. "I always been skinny," he said. "Food don't put no weight on me."

"But where was he?" I asked. "Who was taking care of you all?"

"*I* taken care of *her,*" Jesse said. He nodded his head, as if even now he could say that he was satisfied with the way he had cared for his little sister. "Ain't it hot?" he said.

We had turned now, down a dusty side street between rows of shotgun houses set on twenty-foot lots. I slowed down to let half-a-dozen little Negro boys who were playing ball in the street get out of our way. We raised a cloud of choking dust as we drove, even going so slowly, and it settled on dusty shrubs and porches, and in a gray film on the children's dark, sweat-streaked bodies.

"I loved that little baby," Jesse said. "She was the prettiest, littlest thing you ever seen. She was light like my mama. I takes my dark color from my daddy. She would follow me around and mind me good as if I was a man; and I had to be mama and daddy both to her, if I was but ten. I always loved children ever since, because she was took from me, I reckon, and I been sorry I had none of my own."

"But where was your step-daddy?" I said. "Weren't there any grown people around?"

"Well," he said, "us two lived together in a cabin on a place belonged to some white people over there in Buchanan County. My step-daddy was no good. Soon as my mama died he went off to work in the next county. Left us. And I was just as glad, I was so scared of him. He had a terrible hot rage on him. Most times I could run, but he would of kilt that baby sooner or later. He would come around maybe once in a month to see how we was getting along, and that was too soon to suit me. If I never saw him, it would of been too much. And like I told you, my other brothers and

sisters was all older than me, grown by the time my mama died—
twelve years old or more, and all but two out taking care of themselves. Them two left when she died. Oh, Lord, they was scattered
over the country. Some I don't ever remember seeing in my life.
And yet, my mama wasn't so old when she died. She had her first
when she was fifteen, so my uncle told me, once. I had this uncle,
see, my mama's brother, Will Hobson was his name, lived down the
road from us about five miles, and he used to come around regular
every week to see how we was doing. He would cut us a stack of
wood when we needed it. Yes, he was good to us. But he had
plenty children of his own, ten or twelve, and a mean wife. He
would of took us in, but she wouldn't have us." He hesitated and
then corrected himself. "I don't blame her. I did wrong to say she
was mean. She had more than she could feed already. And like I
say, he come around regular to see after us. The white people
where we stayed was good to us, too. They could just as easy have
took the house from us after my mama died and my step went off,
but they didn't. I used to go up to their house every so often and
they'd give me a sack of meal, and meat and molasses. I could
cook pretty good. They give us blankets, too, because my step, he
took all the covers when he went. And the white man come down
and turned a garden for me to plant greens and such that Spring,
but after all we didn't stay long enough to eat them. I fished, too.
I will say for myself, I could catch plenty fish even then."

He paused, and I said nothing, already so heartsick at the
story he was telling me that I wanted to hear no more of it. But
he went on after a minute.

"I didn't have no sense," he said. "I wasn't nothing but a kid."
He waved his arm at a cluster of children standing on a street
corner, quarrelling in loud voices. "No older than the biggest of
them. And so, I reckon the baby, she was sick two, three days,
probably, without me knowing it. She probably had a fever or something. Anyways, I remember she cried a lot, and I would put her in
the bed and get in with her to try and quiet her down. I got *so*
tired hearing her cry. And at night we would sleep together. One
Saturday night we was laying together in the bed, me holding her
and patting her. She'd been crying and crying most all day, until
I was so mad and tired I didn't think I could listen to her no more.
I was ready to go off and leave her. And all of a sudden she quit.

She just went to sleep. And I was glad. I was so tired I slept, too,
after she quit crying, all that night and most of the next morning.
When I finally got up, I tippied out in the kitchen to fix us some
breakfast without bothering her. But it was ready and still she
didn't wake. I ate and I didn't even go back in to her. Lord, I
needed a little peace. She slept and she slept. But I didn't think
nothing of it one way or the other. Least I can't remember I did.
I reckon I was still glad she was sleeping and not crying. So I let
her be all that day. And that evening, long about dusk-dark, my
uncle, the one lived down the road, come along and I was out in
the yard playing. I remember it all like it was yesterday. He was
a little bit of a man, not much taller than you, Miss. You wouldn't
thing he could of had all them children, much less taken care of
them. But he was *strong*. He could chop *wood*. I never seen a man
could handle a ax no better than him. And he could pick three
hundred pounds of cotton every day. I wished sometimes it would
of been so he could take me and my sister in that year. We wouldn't
of been no trouble to him, not if I could help it. Anyway, he come
along the road there by the house and stopped, and I was sitting
under a big old chinaberry tree in the front yard, just sitting,
playing some game or other to myself, I reckon, but I don't remember what.

"'How you all getting along, Jess?' he says.

"'Fine,' I say. 'We getting along just fine.'

"'You need me to cut you some wood this week?' he says.

"'No, sir,' I say. 'We got plenty, Uncle Will.'

"He squats down there in the dust by me under the chinaberry
tree, like he does 'most every week when he comes by, to talk
awhile.

"'What you been doing all day long, son? he says.

"'Just playing,' I say.

"'How your garden coming along?'

"'Greens is up. We ought to get a good mess by the end of the
week.'

"He looks all around the yard. 'Where the baby?' he says.

"'She in the house,' I say. 'She 'sleep.'

"'Taking a nap, huh?' he says.

"'Yes, sir, she been taking a nap all day.'

"'What you say, Boy?'

" 'She been 'sleep all day,' I say, 'and all last night, too. She ain't cried once.'

"Course by that, he knew something was wrong. 'Come on,' he says. 'We better go wake her up.'

"So we went in the house and she was laying up in the bed all under the covers as quiet, and I watched him, and he turned back the covers and felt her and she was cold. Dead." Jesse nodded his head. "I reckon she been dead all day," he said, "and all the night before, ever since she stopped crying. But I never knew it. We took and buried her that afternoon, my uncle and me."

I was so sick I couldn't say anything except, "Oh, *Jesse.*"

We had reached Jesse's neat little house on Pearl Street now, and I drew up to the curb and stopped. But he did not get out of the car. Instead he went on with his story matter-of-factly.

"My mama was third wife to my step," he said. "My own daddy died when I was no more than two or three. I can't remember him. Like I said, I was eighth child to him. And he was a settled man when my mama married him. She didn't marry again for a long time after he died. She went back and stayed with her own daddy until *he* died. And then she married my step. She was sorry afterwards; she left him two, three times, took me and what other kids was with her and tried to make it on her own, but she couldn't. You know, Miss, nobody going to give no lone woman with children no crop to make. How could she do it? And so she would have to go back to him."

He paused and looked at me as if waiting for my comment, but I could not speak. I gripped the steering wheel with both hands and stared at him, concentrating on keeping the tears from coming to my eyes. He went on quietly.

"She always done the best she could for us," he said. "Hard times or good, she seen we went to school. All but two of us, my uncle told me, finished the sixth grade. And me, of course, because she died when I was in the fifth. But I could already write a good hand. It come easy to me. And she could cook, too, and sew, better than most. It never seemed right to me how bad my step done her, and she a good woman. I heard when I was grown that he beat the first two wives he had to death. And my mama, you wouldn't know it from looking at a great, skinny old man like me, but she was a little bitty mite of a thing, like a bird, a little brown pecky bird. He killed her, too. Might not of struck the blow that did it, but he *killed* her. Wore her and beat her to death. I seen him more than once take her by the heels and throw her through the door."

"Oh, Jesse," I said. "Where were the police and the sheriff? Couldn't somebody do something about him?"

"Miss, nobody cared about things like that in them days," Jesse said.

"I don't see how a little boy could live through such times and not be crazy," I said.

"I run off from there when I was thirteen," he said. "For a while after my little sister died, I stayed with a old man down the road didn't have no children and needed somebody to help him around his place. Then that winter my step come back. Lost the crop he'd had in the next county and they wouldn't keep him on. He didn't have nobody to help him and couldn't make it on his own, so he come back and got me. He kept me two years and I had no place to turn. He beat me some, but I was getting a big boy. Not big enough to beat *him,* but big enough to outrun him if I got a start, and big enough to know I would be big enough to beat him soon. So one day when I was thirteen, he caught me. He like to kilt me before I got loose from him, whaling me with the buckle end of his belt. I tore my shirt half off and run out in the road by our house and stood there in the dirt crying and screaming like a baby. 'I'll kill you,' I screamed. 'I'll kill you. I'll kill you.' And he stood on the porch sweating and catching his breath, and laughed at me. But I would have. I left that day, and I never went looking for him, but if I'd ever of seen him again, I would of killed him. I still would. But he's dead now, bound to be."

Jesse put on his hat, opened the car door, and got out. He opened the back door and, reaching in, pulled out his battered guitar case. "Man, it's hot today," he said again. When he had closed the back door he bent down to the front window and took off his hat. "You see, Miss," he said, gesturing behind him toward the washtub by his front steps, "them petunias and merrygolds bloomed out, but my wife got chrysanthemums coming on now in the back. I'm going to bring you a bunch when they begin to bloom."

"That'll be nice," I said. "Thank you."

"Well," he said, "I'll be seeing you Monday. I thank you for the ride." He straightened up and put on his hat again. "May you and the cap'n have a pleasant week-end," he said.

Jesse only worked for us about a month after that day. He came to the next two lessons drunk, and Richard and I made up our minds that we had to find someone else to teach Ralph. We didn't tell Jesse why. I just said that I thought Ralph was too young, that he had learned as much as he could at his age and we thought he should drop the lessons until he was older. Jesse agreed.

"He ain't made much progress lately," he said. "He ain't got his mind on it."

I haven't seen the old man since, except at a distance. I heard that he had bought an old car, and then shortly afterwards that he had been arrested for drunk driving. He didn't call on us to bail him out.

But a strange thing happened recently. I woke up one night from a nightmare about Jesse. I couldn't remember anything about it except that it had been long and confused, with a great many people in it, and Jesse wandering in and out, a child no older than Ralph, but skinny instead of stocky as Ralph is, and having not a child's head on his shoulders but the long seamed face and high, domed forehead of his old age. I was choking with anxiety when I woke up, and two sentences kept repeating themselves over and over in my mind until to exorcise them and sleep again, I turned on the light and wrote them in the margin of a magazine on my night table. When I got up the next morning, I could not remember what I had written or why, in the night, it had seemed so important. I picked up the magazine and read, "There are those of us who are willing to say, 'I am guilty,' but who is to absolve us? And do we expect by our confession miraculously to relieve the suffering of the innocent?" I had written first, "Do we expect to *escape* the suffering of the innocent?" but I had scratched through *escape* and written, *relieve*. I read the sentences over several times, but they did not dispel the anxiety I still felt. I remembered then the reason I had written them. I had thought in the night that if I could remember those words, I would understand everything. But the words were only questions. It wouldn't have mattered if I had forgotten them.

ALBERT CAMUS

The Guest

----

*T*HE SCHOOLMASTER WAS WATCHING the two men climb toward him. One was on horseback, the other on foot. They had not yet tackled the abrupt rise leading to the schoolhouse built on the hillside. They were toiling onward, making slow progress in the snow, among the stones, on the vast expanse of the high, deserted plateau. From time to time the horse stumbled. Without hearing anything yet, he could see the breath issuing from the horse's nostrils. One of the men, at least, knew the region. They were following the trail although it had disappeared days ago under a layer of dirty white snow. The schoolmaster calculated that it would take them half an hour to get onto the hill. It was cold; he went back into the school to get a sweater.

He crossed the empty, frigid classroom. On the blackboard the four rivers of France, drawn with four different colored chalks, had been flowing toward their estuaries for the past three days. Snow had suddenly fallen in mid-October after eight months of drought without the transition of rain, and the twenty pupils, more or less, who lived in the villages scattered over the plateau had stopped coming. With fair weather they would return. Daru now heated only the single room that was his lodging, adjoining the classroom and giving also onto the plateau to the east. Like the class windows, his window looked to the south too. On that side the school was a few kilometers from the point where the plateau began to slope toward the south. In clear weather could be seen the purple mass of the mountain range where the gap opened onto the desert.

Somewhat warmed, Daru returned to the window from which he had first seen the two men. They were no longer visible. Hence they must have tackled the rise. The sky was not so dark, for the snow had stopped falling during the night. The morning had opened with a dirty light which had scarcely become brighter as the ceiling of clouds lifted. At two in the afternoon it seemed as if the day were merely beginning. But still this was better than those three days when the thick snow was falling amidst unbroken darkness with little gusts of wind that rattled the double door of the classroom. Then Daru had spent long hours in his room, leaving it only to go to the shed and feed the chickens or get some coal. Fortunately the delivery truck from Tadjid, the nearest village to the north, had brought his supplies two days before the blizzard. It would return in forty-eight hours.

Besides, he had enough to resist a siege, for the little room was cluttered with bags of wheat that the administration left as a stock to distribute to those of his pupils whose families had suffered from the drought. Actually they had all been victims because they were all poor. Every day Daru would distribute a ration to the children. They had missed it, he knew, during these bad days. Possibly one of the fathers or big brothers would come this afternoon and he could supply them with grain. It was just a matter of carrying them over to the next harvest. Now shiploads of wheat were arriving from France and the worst was over. But it would be hard to forget that poverty, that army of ragged ghosts wandering in the sunlight, the plateaus burned to a cinder month after month, the earth shriveled up little by little, literally scorched, every stone bursting into dust under one's foot. The sheep had died then by thousands and even a few men, here and there, sometimes without anyone's knowing.

In contrast with such poverty, he who lived almost like a monk in his remote schoolhouse, nonetheless satisfied with the little he had and with the rough life, had felt like a lord with his whitewashed walls, his narrow couch, his unpainted shelves, his well, and his weekly provision of water and food. And suddenly this snow, without warning, without the foretaste of rain. This is the way the region was, cruel to live in, even without men—who didn't help matters either. But Daru had been born here. Everywhere else, he felt exiled.

He stepped out onto the terrace in front of the schoolhouse. The two men were now halfway up the slope. He recognized the horseman as Balducci, the old gendarme he had known for a long time. Balducci was holding on the end of a rope an Arab who was walking behind him with hands bound and head lowered. The gendarme waved a greeting to which Daru did not reply, lost as he was in contemplation of the Arab dressed in a faded blue jellaba, his feet in sandals but covered with socks of heavy raw wool, his head surmounted by a narrow, short *chèche*. They were approaching. Balducci was holding back his horse in order not to hurt the Arab, and the group was advancing slowly.

Within earshot, Balducci shouted: "One hour to do the three kilometers from El Ameur!" Daru did not answer. Short and square in his thick sweater, he watched them climb. Not once had the Arab raised his head. "Hello," said Daru when they got up onto the terrace. "Come in and warm up." Balducci painfully got down from his horse without letting go the rope. From under his bristling mustache he smiled at the schoolmaster. His little dark eyes, deepset under a tanned forehead, and his mouth surrounded with wrinkles made him look attentive and studious. Daru took the bridle, led the horse to the shed, and came back to the two men, who were now waiting for him in the school. He led them into his room. "I am going to heat up the classroom," he said. "We'll be more comfortable there." When he entered the room again, Balducci was on the couch. He had undone the rope tying him to the Arab, who had squatted near the stove. His hands still bound, the *chèche* pushed back on his head, he was looking toward the window. At first Daru noticed only his huge lips, fat, smooth, almost Negroid; yet his nose was straight, his eyes were dark and full of fever. The *chèche* revealed an obstinate forehead and, under the weathered skin now rather discolored by the cold, the whole face had a restless and rebellious look that struck Daru when the Arab, turning his face toward him, looked him straight in the eyes. "Go into the other room," said the schoolmaster, "and I'll make you some mint tea." "Thanks," Balducci said. "What a chore! How I long for retirement." And addressing his prisoner in Arabic: "Come on, you." The Arab got up and, slowly, holding his bound wrists in front of him, went into the classroom.

With the tea, Daru brought a chair. But Balducci was already enthroned on the nearest pupil's desk and the Arab had squatted against the teacher's platform facing the stove, which stood between the desk and the window. When he held out the glass of tea to the prisoner, Daru hesitated at the sight of his bound hands. "He might perhaps be untied." "Sure," said Balducci. "That was for the trip." He started to get to his feet. But Daru, setting the glass on the floor, had knelt beside the Arab. Without saying anything, the Arab watched him with his feverish eyes. Once his hands were free, he rubbed his swollen wrists against each other, took the glass of tea, and sucked up the burning liquid in swift little sips.

"Good," said Daru. "And where are you headed?"

Balducci withdrew his mustache from the tea. "Here, son."

"Odd pupils! And you're spending the night?"

"No. I'm going back to El Ameur. And you will deliver this fellow to Tinguit. He is expected at police headquarters."

Balducci was looking at Daru with a friendly little smile.

"What's this story?" asked the schoolmaster. "Are you pulling my leg?"

"No, son. Those are the orders."

"The orders? I'm not . . ." Daru hesitated, not wanting to hurt the old Corsican. "I mean, that's not my job."

"What! What's the meaning of that? In wartime people do all kinds of jobs."

"Then I'll wait for the declaration of war!"

Balducci nodded.

"O.K. But the orders exist and they concern you too. Things are brewing, it appears. There is talk of a forthcoming revolt. We are mobilized, in a way."

Daru still had his obstinate look.

"Listen, son," Balducci said. "I like you and you must understand. There's only a dozen of us at El Ameur to patrol throughout the whole territory of a small department and I must get back in a hurry. I was told to hand this guy over to you and return without delay. He couldn't be kept there. His village was beginning to stir; they wanted to take him back. You must take him to Tinguit tomorrow before the day is over. Twenty kilometers shouldn't faze a husky fellow like you. After that, all will be over. You'll come back to your pupils and your comfortable life."

Behind the wall the horse could be heard snorting and pawing the earth. Daru was looking out the window. Decidedly, the weather was clearing and the light was increasing over the snowy plateau. When all the snow was melted, the sun would take over again and once more would burn the fields of stone. For days, still, the unchanging sky would shed its dry light on the solitary expanse where nothing had any connection with man.

"After all," he said, turning around toward Balducci, "what did he do?" And, before the gendarme had opened his mouth, he asked: "Does he speak French?"

"No, not a word. We had been looking for him for a month, but they were hiding him. He killed his cousin."

"Is he against us?"

"I don't think so. But you can never be sure."

"Why did he kill?"

"A family squabble, I think. One owed the other grain, it seems. It's not at all clear. In short, he killed his cousin with a billhook. You know, like a sheep, *kreezk!*"

Balducci made the gesture of drawing a blade across his throat and the Arab, his attention attracted, watched him with a sort of anxiety. Daru felt a sudden wrath against the man, against all men with their rotten spite, their tireless hates, their blood lust.

But the kettle was singing on the stove. He served Balducci more tea, hesitated, then served the Arab again, who, a second time, drank avidly. His raised arms made the jellaba fall open and the schoolmaster saw his thin, muscular chest.

"Thanks, kid," Balducci said. "And now, I'm off."

He got up and went toward the Arab, taking a small rope from his pocket.

"What are you doing?" Daru asked dryly.

Balducci, disconcerted, showed him the rope.

"Don't bother."

The old gendarme hesitated. "It's up to you. Of course, you are armed?"

"I have my shotgun."

"Where?"

"In the trunk."

"You ought to have it near your bed."

"Why? I have nothing to fear."

"You're crazy, son. If there's an uprising, no one is safe, we're all in the same boat."

"I'll defend myself. I'll have time to see them coming."

Balducci began to laugh, then suddenly the mustache covered the white teeth.

"You'll have time? O.K. That's just what I was saying. You have always been a little cracked. That's why I like you, my son was like that."

At the same time he took out his revolver and put it on the desk.

"Keep it; I don't need two weapons from here to El Ameur."

The revolver shone against the black paint of the table. When the gendarme turned toward him, the schoolmaster caught the smell of leather and horseflesh.

"Listen, Balducci," Daru said suddenly, "every bit of this disgusts me, and first of all your fellow here. But I won't hand him over. Fight, yes, if I have to. But not that."

The old gendarme stood in front of him and looked at him severely.

"You're being a fool," he said slowly. "I don't like it either. You don't get used to putting a rope on a man even after years of it, and you're even ashamed—yes, ashamed. But you can't let them have their way."

"I won't hand him over," Daru said again.

"It's an order, son, and I repeat it."

"That's right. Repeat to them what I've said to you: I won't hand him over."

Balducci made a visible effort to reflect. He looked at the Arab and at Daru. At last he decided.

"No, I won't tell them anything. If you want to drop us, go ahead; I'll not denounce you. I have an order to deliver the prisoner and I'm doing so. And now you'll just sign this paper for me."

"There's no need. I'll not deny that you left him with me."

"Don't be mean with me. I know you'll tell the truth. You're from hereabouts and you are a man. But you must sign, that's the rule."

Daru opened his drawer, took out a little square bottle of purple ink, the red wooden penholder with the "sergeant-major" pen he used for making models of penmanship, and signed. The gendarme carefully folded the paper and put it into his wallet. Then he moved toward the door.

"I'll see you off," Daru said.

"No," said Balducci. "There's no use being polite. You insulted me."

He looked at the Arab, motionless in the same spot, sniffed peevishly, and turned away toward the door. "Good-by, son," he said. The door shut behind him. Balducci appeared suddenly outside the window and then disappeared. His footsteps were muffled by the snow. The horse stirred on the other side of the wall and several chickens fluttered in fright. A moment later Balducci reappeared outside the window leading the horse by the bridle. He walked toward the little rise without turning around and disappeared from sight with the horse following him. A big stone could be heard bouncing down. Daru walked back toward the prisoner, who, without stirring, never took his eyes off him. "Wait," the schoolmaster said in Arabic and went toward the bedroom. As he was going through the door, he had a second thought, went to the desk, took the revolver, and stuck it in his pocket. Then, without looking back, he went into his room.

For some time he lay on his couch watching the sky gradually close over, listening to the silence. It was this silence that had seemed painful to him during the first days here, after the war. He had requested a post in the little town at the base of the foothills separating the upper plateaus from the desert. There, rocky walls, green and black to the north, pink and lavender to the south, marked the frontier of eternal summer. He had been named to a post farther north, on the plateau itself. In the beginning, the solitude and the silence had been hard for him on these wastelands peopled only by stones. Occasionally, furrows suggested cultivation, but they had been dug to uncover a certain kind of stone good for building. The only plowing here was to harvest rocks. Elsewhere a thin layer of soil accumulated in the hollows would

be scraped out to enrich paltry village gardens. This is the way it
was: bare rock covered three quarters of the region. Towns sprang
up, flourished, then disappeared; men came by, loved one another
or fought bitterly, then died. No one in this desert, neither he nor
his guest, mattered. And yet, outside this desert neither of them,
Daru knew, could have really lived.

When he got up, no noise came from the classroom. He was
amazed at the unmixed joy he derived from the mere thought that
the Arab might have fled and that he would be alone with no
decision to make. But the prisoner was there. He had merely
stretched out between the stove and the desk. With eyes open, he
was staring at the ceiling. In that position, his thick lips were
particularly noticeable, giving him a pouting look. "Come," said
Daru. The Arab got up and followed him. In the bedroom, the
schoolmaster pointed to a chair near the table under the window.
The Arab sat down without taking his eyes off Daru.

"Are you hungry?"

"Yes," the prisoner said.

Daru set the table for two. He took flour and oil, shaped a cake
in a frying-pan, and lighted the little stove that functioned on
bottled gas. While the cake was cooking, he went out to the shed to
get cheese, eggs, dates, and condensed milk. When the cake was
done he set it on the window sill to cool, heated some condensed
milk diluted with water, and beat up the eggs into an omelette. In
one of his motions he knocked against the revolver stuck in his right
pocket. He set the bowl down, went into the classroom, and put the
revolver in his desk drawer. When he came back to the room, night
was falling. He put on the light and served the Arab. "Eat," he said.
The Arab took a piece of the cake, lifted it eagerly to his mouth, and
stopped short.

"And you?" he asked.

"After you. I'll eat too."

The thick lips opened slightly. The Arab hesitated, then bit
into the cake determinedly.

The meal over, the Arab looked at the schoolmaster. "Are you
the judge?"

"No, I'm simply keeping you until tomorrow."

"Why do you eat with me?"

"I'm hungry."

The Arab fell silent. Daru got up and went out. He brought back a folding bed from the shed, set it up between the table and the stove, perpendicular to his own bed. From a large suitcase which, upright in a corner, served as a shelf for papers, he took two blankets and arranged them on the camp bed. Then he stopped, felt useless, and sat down on his bed. There was nothing more to do or to get ready. He had to look at this man. He looked at him, therefore, trying to imagine his face bursting with rage. He couldn't do so. He could see nothing but the dark yet shining eyes and the animal mouth.

"Why did you kill him?" he asked in a voice whose hostile tone surprised him.

The Arab looked away.

"He ran away. I ran after him."

He raised his eyes to Daru again and they were full of a sort of woeful interrogation. "Now what will they do to me?"

"Are you afraid?"

He stiffened, turning his eyes away.

"Are you sorry?"

The Arab stared at him openmouthed. Obviously he did not understand. Daru's annoyance was growing. At the same time he felt awkward and self-conscious with his big body wedged between the two beds.

"Lie down there," he said impatiently. "That's your bed."

The Arab didn't move. He called to Daru:

"Tell me!"

The schoolmaster looked at him.

"Is the gendarme coming back tomorrow?"

"I don't know."

"Are you coming with us?"

"I don't know. Why?"

The prisoner got up and stretched out on top of the blankets, his feet toward the window. The light from the electric bulb shone straight into his eyes and he closed them at once.

"Why?" Daru repeated, standing beside the bed.

The Arab opened his eyes under the blinding light and looked at him, trying not to blink.

"Come with us," he said.

In the middle of the night, Daru was still not asleep. He had gone to bed after undressing completely; he generally slept naked. But when he suddenly realized that he had nothing on, he hesitated. He felt vulnerable and the temptation came to him to put his clothes back on. Then he shrugged his shoulders; after all, he wasn't a child and, if need be, he could break his adversary in two. From his bed he could observe him, lying on his back, still motionless with his eyes closed under the harsh light. When Daru turned out the light, the darkness seemed to coagulate all of a sudden. Little by little, the night came back to life in the window where the starless sky was stirring gently. The schoolmaster soon made out the body lying at his feet. The Arab still did not move, but his eyes seemed open. A faint wind was prowling around the schoolhouse. Perhaps it would drive away the clouds and the sun would reappear.

During the night the wind increased. The hens fluttered a little and then were silent. The Arab turned over on his side with his back to Daru, who thought he heard him moan. Then he listened for his guest's breathing, become heavier and more regular. He listened to that breath so close to him and mused without being able to go to sleep. In this room where he had been sleeping alone for a year, this presence bothered him. But it bothered him also by imposing on him a sort of brotherhood he knew well but refused to accept in the present circumstances. Men who share the same rooms, soldiers or prisoners, develop a strange alliance as if, having cast off their armor with their clothing, they fraternized every evening, over and above their differences, in the ancient community of dream and fatigue. But Daru shook himself; he didn't like such musings, and it was essential to sleep.

A little later, however, when the Arab stirred slightly, the schoolmaster was still not asleep. When the prisoner made a second move, he stiffened, on the alert. The Arab was lifting himself slowly on his arms with almost the motion of a sleepwalker. Seated upright in bed, he waited motionless without turning his head toward Daru, as if he were listening attentively. Daru did not stir; it had just occurred to him that the revolver was still in the drawer of his desk. It was better to act at once. Yet he continued to observe the prisoner, who, with the same slithery motion, put his feet on the ground, waited again, then began to stand up slowly. Daru was about to call out to him when the Arab began to walk, in a quite natural but extraordinarily silent way. He was heading toward the door at the end of the room that opened into the shed. He lifted the latch with precaution and went out, pushing the door behind him but without shutting it. Daru had not stirred. "He is running away," he merely thought. "Good riddance!" Yet he listened attentively. The hens were not fluttering; the guest must be on the plateau. A faint sound of water reached him, and he didn't know what it was until the Arab again stood framed in the doorway, closed the door carefully, and came back to bed without a sound. Then Daru turned his back on him and fell asleep. Still later he seemed, from the depths of his sleep, to hear furtive steps around the schoolhouse. "I'm dreaming! I'm dreaming!" he repeated to himself. And he went on sleeping.

When he awoke, the sky was clear; the loose window let in a cold, pure air. The Arab was asleep, hunched up under the blankets now, his mouth open, utterly relaxed. But when Daru shook him, he started dreadfully, staring at Daru with wild eyes as if he had never seen him and such a frightened expression that the schoolmaster stepped back. "Don't be afraid. It's me. You must eat." The Arab nodded his head and said yes. Calm had returned to his face, but his expression was vacant and listless.

The coffee was ready. They drank it seated together on the folding bed as they munched their pieces of the cake. Then Daru led the Arab under the shed and showed him the faucet where he washed. He went back into the room, folded the blankets and the bed, made his own bed and put the room in order. Then he went through the classroom and out onto the terrace. The sun was already rising in the blue sky; a soft, bright light was bathing the deserted plateau. On the ridge the snow was melting in spots. The stones were about to reappear. Crouched on the edge of the plateau, the schoolmaster looked at the deserted expanse. He thought of Balducci. He had hurt him, for he had sent him off in a way as if he didn't want to be associated with him. He could still hear the gendarme's farewell and, without knowing why, he felt strangely empty and vulnerable. At that moment, from the other side of the schoolhouse, the prisoner coughed. Daru listened to him almost despite himself and then, furious, threw a pebble that whistled through the air before sinking into the snow. That man's stupid crime revolted him, but to hand him over was contrary to honor. Merely thinking of it made him smart with humiliation. And he cursed at one and the same time his own people who had sent him this Arab and the Arab too who had dared to kill and not managed to get away. Daru got up, walked in a circle on the terrace, waited motionless, and then went back into the schoolhouse.

The Arab, leaning over the cement floor of the shed, was washing his teeth with two fingers. Daru looked at him and said: "Come." He went back into the room ahead of the prisoner. He slipped a hunting-jacket on over his sweater and put on walking-shoes. Standing, he waited until the Arab had put on his *chèche* and sandals. They went into the classroom and the schoolmaster pointed to the exit, saying: "Go ahead." The fellow didn't budge. "I'm coming," said Daru. The Arab went out. Daru went back into the room and made a package of pieces of rusk, dates, and sugar. In the classroom, before going out, he hesitated a second in front of his desk, then crossed the threshold and locked the door. "That's the way," he said. He started toward the east, followed by the prisoner. But, a short distance from the schoolhouse, he thought he heard a slight sound behind them. He retraced his steps and examined the surroundings of the house; there was no one there. The Arab watched him without seeming to understand. "Come on," said Daru.

They walked for an hour and rested beside a sharp peak of limestone. The snow was melting faster and faster and the sun was drinking up the puddles at once, rapidly cleaning the plateau, which gradually dried and vibrated like the air itself. When they resumed walking, the ground rang under their feet. From time to time a bird rent the space in front of them with a joyful cry. Daru breathed in deeply the fresh morning light. He felt a sort of rapture before the vast familiar expanse, now almost entirely yellow under its dome of blue sky. They walked an hour more, descending toward the south. They reached a level height made up of crumbly rocks. From there on, the plateau sloped down, eastward, toward a low plain where there were a few spindly trees and, to the south, toward outcroppings of rock that gave the landscape a chaotic look.

Daru surveyed the two directions. There was nothing but the sky on the horizon. Not a man could be seen. He turned toward the

Arab, who was looking at him blankly. Daru held out the package to him. "Take it," he said. "There are dates, bread, and sugar. You can hold out for two days. Here are a thousand francs too." The Arab took the package and the money but kept his full hands at chest level as if he didn't know what to do with what was being given him. "Now look," the schoolmaster said as he pointed in the direction of the east, "there's the way to Tinguit. You have a two-hour walk. At Tinguit you'll find the administration and the police. They are expecting you." The Arab looked toward the east, still holding the package and the money against his chest. Daru took his elbow and turned him rather roughly toward the south. At the foot of the height on which they stood could be seen a faint path. "That's the trail across the plateau. In a day's walk from here you'll find pasturelands and the first nomads. They'll take you in and shelter you according to their law." The Arab had now turned toward Daru and a sort of panic was visible in his expression. "Listen," he said. Daru shook his head: "No, be quiet. Now I'm leaving you." He turned his back on him, took two long steps in the direction of the school, looked hesitantly at the motionless Arab, and started off again. For a few minutes he heard nothing but his own step resounding on the cold ground and did not turn his head. A moment later, however, he turned around. The Arab was still there on the edge of the hill, his arms hanging now, and he was looking at the schoolmaster. Daru felt something rise in his throat. But he swore with impatience, waved vaguely, and started off again. He had already gone some distance when he again stopped and looked. There was no longer anyone on the hill.

Daru hesitated. The sun was now rather high in the sky and was beginning to beat down on his head. The schoolmaster retraced his steps, at first somewhat uncertainly, then with decision. When he reached the little hill, he was bathed in sweat. He climbed it as fast as he could and stopped, out of breath, at the top. The rock-fields to the south stood out sharply against the blue sky, but on the plain to the east a steamy heat was already rising. And in that slight haze, Daru, with heavy heart, made out the Arab walking slowly on the road to prison.

A little later, standing before the window of the classroom, the schoolmaster was watching the clear light bathing the whole surface of the plateau, but he hardly saw it. Behind him on the blackboard, among the winding French rivers, sprawled the clumsily chalked-up words he had just read: "You handed over our brother. You will pay for this." Daru looked at the sky, the plateau, and, beyond, the invisible lands stretching all the way to the sea. In this vast landscape he had loved so much, he was alone.

STUDY QUESTIONS

"An Encounter"

1. What are the advantages and disadvantages of telling the story from the boy's point of view?
2. What is Joyce's purpose in disclosing the boy's fascination with Wild West stories? What bearing does this interest have on his encounter with the pervert?
3. Is the narrator duped by his own naïveté? Are there any indications of special perceptivity on his part?
4. How does Joyce use color symbolism in the story?
5. What kind of person is Father Butler? Do his remarks about *The Apache Chief* account for any traits in the boy's personality?
6. What does Mahoney's presence contribute to the story? Why has the speaker "always despised him a little"?

"The Two Faces"

1. The title underscores the story's theme of duplicity. In how many ways do you find this "Janus" metaphor relevant?
2. Precisely how does James' elaborate and highly refined style become an ironic comment on the action? What is the action?
3. What is James' purpose in keeping so much of the drama off stage?
4. All of this effect of hidden richness is achieved through technique, specifically the technique of point of view. Show how James manipulates the point of view.
5. Comment on the wit of the characters' names.
6. What purpose does the metaphor of sacrifice serve?
7. What is the relationship between the clothing symbolism and the theme of decorum?
   What does Miss Banker mean by her reply to Lord Gwyther's final question?

"The Battler"

1. Hemingway wrote a great deal of fiction about Americans in foreign countries. Here, the setting is American. But in what ways are the characters of this story, too, definable as "aliens"?
2. This story is distinctly of the type called the "initiation story," that is,

a story concerning a youth's introduction to the facts of adult experience. What does Nick learn that promotes his maturation?

There are a great many other stories of this type in the collection. Indeed, it would be all but impossible to compile an anthology of modern fiction without a number of stories on this theme. How do you account for the dominance of the theme, especially in the American stories?

3. Why is Bugs so polite to Nick? Is it only because he is a Negro and Nick a white man?

"The Christening"

1. In most stories there is a single character in whose actions, or reactions, we are centrally interested—about whom we can say that it is "his story." Who is that person in "The Christening"?
2. It is clear enough that the family is unhappy. There is a sense of an evil influence in the house, which has set them all against each other. But what is the source of the evil? Is it embodied primarily in any one person or is it altogether impersonal?

   The religious ceremonial of the christening is presumably intended in some way to relieve the "curse" upon the household, to invoke a blessing. If it would appear that this intention is not very well realized, who, or what, is responsible for the failure?
3. What is Lawrence's implicit attitude toward the religion? Does he despise it, admire it, or what? (Note especially, in this connection, the role of the minister and that of the father. How would you judge their sincerity? Which of the two is the dominant figure in the ceremonial?)
4. Is there any potential source of good in the life of the family? If so, what is it?
5. How important for the role of the father is his illness?
6. Why does Lawrence delay introduction of the brother until near the end?

"I Want To Know Why"

1. There are a great many references in the story to Negroes—all in one way or another complimentary. The boy even says at one point "I wish I was a nigger," although he feels that "it's a foolish thing to say." Negroes are, in his eyes, generally more trustworthy than white men, less affected and calculating, and in many ways more perceptive. In brief, Negroes represent to him many of the same values that he

associates with horses. What has this theme to do with that of his innocence and outrage?

2. Several times, the narrator interestingly (and unconsciously) ignores sexual distinctions in his remarks on beauty and love. The horse Sunstreak is a stallion; yet, "he is like a girl you think about sometimes but never see." Jerry Tillford, waiting for the horse to run, is compared to "a mother seeing her child do something brave or wonderful." The tall harlot, who is Jerry's choice at the bawdy house, is compared to "the gelding Middlestride, but not clean like him." These are only the most obvious examples. Again, what has this to do with the theme of innocence and evil?

3. The mature reader, of course, will not find Jerry Tillford's conduct quite so shocking and bewildering as it is to the boy. Is there anything in his behavior to suggest that the boy himself is not entirely innocent, that what he most fears is something within himself—that, in a sense, he already "knows why"?

4. In the literary tradition, the horse is as often a symbol of lust and violence, of "base nature," as of nobility and freedom, of the spiritual. For the narrator here, of course, only the latter associations are consciously in force. But what evidence might be adduced to show that Anderson—the author as distinguished from the narrator—is aware of the traditional ambiguity?

5. How does Anderson manage to communicate ironies of which the boy is wholly or partially unaware, while at the same time keeping to the juvenile idiom in the narration? Is the idiom entirely convincing and consistent?

"In the Penal Colony"

1. This story is clearly a fantasy. Yet, it is told in a straightforward, realistic style. What are the elements of this style? And why does Kafka choose to tell it this way, rather than to play up the sense of fantasy?

2. A great many "technical" details are given in the description of the machine. But it would be difficult if not impossible for a draftsman to make a clear drawing of the apparatus from this description. What is the purpose of this kind of deliberate obscurity?

3. Why does Kafka not give names to the characters of the story? (They are simply the explorer, the officer, the prisoner, the new commandant, etc.)

4. The story has been interpreted as an allegory. What are the character-

istics that seem to demand such an interpretation, and what do they signify?

Specifically, it has been argued that the officer and his machine, and the old commandant, represent the religion of the Old Testament, and the new commandant and his reforms, in opposition, the religion of the New Testament, or Christianity. Is there anything that seems inconsistent with such a reading?

Would it, perhaps, be more consistent to interpret the opposition of the old and the new orders in the colony as the opposition, rather, of two kinds of Christianity—medieval, let us say, and modern—or, as the opposition of orthodox Christianity and some kind of liberal humanitarianism?

If no one of these readings seems to offer entire consistency, if each fails to accommodate one or another element of the story, then what is the intent of its symbolism?

5. In certain respects, the story might seem to be an account of a dream. But there is no overt suggestion that this is so. Why does Kafka avoid making such a suggestion, and how, without it, does he achieve the dreamlike effect—despite the "realistic" character of the style which we have noted?

6. What is the significance of the explorer's actions at the end of the story? Does it appear that he has reached any clear-cut, final decision in the dispute between the officer and the new commandant? If so, what is his decision? If not, does this necessarily leave the reader unsatisfied with the conclusion?

7. There is a great deal of muted but irrepressible humor in the story. What is the function of the humor? Does it merely provide momentary "comic relief" from the horror, or is the one inseparable from the other?

Compare the story, in this respect, to those by Faulkner and Shirley Jackson. Which of the two is closer to Kafka?

"Railway Accident"

1. If the accident is "not really a first-class one," as the narrator admits, why does he tell about it? Are the events secondary to an unannounced intention? If so, is the tacit purpose fulfilled? How does Mann suggest what this purpose might be? Does he provide details which in any way undercut the speaker's purpose?

2. How does the scene on the relief train from Regensburg suggest a second meaning for the phrase, "not really a first-class" wreck?

3. What constitutes "adventure" for the speaker? Do the details of the journey, which arc "so clear in [his] memory," indicate a fascination with the unusual and catastrophic, like the derailment, or with the commonplace, like the man with the spats?
4. How would the speaker appear to his fellow passengers?
5. Does the narrator's being a writer have anything to do with his mock-superstitious confidence that he will escape another railway accident? (Note the conventional opening, his concern about the safety of his manuscripts, etc.)

"A Wagner Matinée"

1. Aunt Georgiana's renunciation of a musical career to go West is considered an irremediable mistake. Do her motives tend to make us more or less sympathetic with her in her error?
2. Does the nephew seem harsh and patronizing toward his aunt when she first arrives? Is his concern over her appearance a comment on the speaker himself? Why does he seem so fearful?
3. What brings about the change in the relationship from estrangement to recognition? How does Willa Cather emphasize the initial alienation and the growing affection? What is the basis for the final rapport between the speaker and Aunt Georgiana?
4. How would you characterize the speaker's response to music? Is Miss Cather's making pictorial associations with the musical themes justifiable or unjustifiable? In this connection, what significance has it that Wagner is the composer in question?

"The Jar"

1. This is a story with a great deal of "local color." How does the story communicate its essential humor to a reader who knows nothing of the country and its people?
2. Beyond the slapstick, what are the sources of comedy in the story? Are the characters primarily individuals, or representative, traditional types?
3. In what sense is Zi' Dima "the winner in the dispute"? Is our sense of justice satisfied by this outcome? What relevance has this question to question 2, concerning the source of comedy?
4. The jar might be referred to as a symbol. Is its symbolic value determined entirely by its status as a piece of property—the bone of contention between Don Lollo and Zi' Dima—or by what?
5. What is the role of Don Lollo's workmen in the story?

"Winter Dreams"

1. At the end of the story, what is the thing that Dexter has lost?
2. What has Dexter's business success to do with his success, or failure, in love?
3. One relevant meaning of "dream" here might be that of "idea" or "ideal"—the "image," of oneself, of other people, of life. If Dexter can be seen as a man who follows a dream, or dreams, of this kind, is it implied that financial success is merely the instrument of his purpose, or that it constitutes the ideal itself?
4. What social and psychological symbolism does Fitzgerald derive from golf—from the game, the golf course as meeting place and as landscape affected by changes of season, etc.?
   Need one have first-hand experience of the world of the country club, and of the "country-club mind," in order fully to appreciate this story?
5. What is the significance of the hero's name?
6. Besides that mentioned in question 3, what are other relevant meanings of the word "dreams" in the title? In what senses beyond that of mere reference to the season can the word "winter" be taken?
7. There are a number of physical improbabilities in the narrative, such as the details of Judy's appearance Dexter is supposed to observe when he meets her on the lake at night. Further, the writing is in many places marred by lush cliché; and even Dexter's final attitude might be regarded as rather painfully sentimental. How are these characteristics of the story related; and how, if at all, does it succeed in spite of them?

"A Rose for Emily"

1. Who are the "we" of the story? Why does Faulkner tell it this way, in the first person plural?
2. Three times Miss Emily refuses to accept the fact of death. What is the general significance of this refusal? Do the three instances differ in any essential ways?
3. According to a common interpretation of the story, Miss Emily is representative of "the South," and its social attitudes, and Homer Barron of "the North." But this rather obviously oversimplifies the pattern of dramatic oppositions in the story. How?
4. Does Faulkner deliberately play up the elements of horror in the story? How does his stylistic practice in this regard differ from that of Kafka, for example? Is the horror exploited "for its own sake"—that

is, solely for the purpose of exciting the reader's emotions—or has it some further thematic significance?

"My Oedipus Complex"

1. Although it aims also at other effects—of sentimental comedy—this story is in part a light satire. What are the satiric techniques, and what is being satirized?
2. This same life material might have been used for a very different kind of story—one of tragedy or high pathos. (Compare it to some of the other "boy" stories, or so-called initiation stories, in the volume.) How does O'Connor prevent our taking the attitude of ultimate seriousness which would defeat his comic intention with the story?

"When the Light Gets Green"

1. What is the significance of the title? Has "green" here anything of the same symbolic value that it has in Joyce's "An Encounter," or Welty's "A Curtain of Green"? Why is the grandfather's shaving mirror also "greenish"?
2. Especially in the light of the concluding paragraphs of the commentary, on the historical dimension of significance in the story, why does the story "end" with the death of Uncle Kirby in World War 1? What would this war, in distinction from the Civil War, represent to the narrator?
3. In the same connection, what is the importance of the fact that the narrator is apparently not an heir to the farm?
4. The commentary does not touch at all on the "landscape painting" in the story. But there is a great deal of it. What relationship to the development of theme has this attention to the outdoor setting?
5. What kind of poetry is it to which the grandfather is addicted? Is his taste related to the fact that "he never read poetry, he just said what he already knew"?

"Flight"

1. Many animals appear in the story, and there is a great deal of animal imagery—as in the frequent comparisons of Pepé to a snake, to a dog, etc. What has this to do with the theme of his becoming a man through his ordeal? If he is hunted down like an animal, is his own

and his mother's wish for him to achieve manhood simply defeated, or
is there another level of irony?

2. As he sets out on his errand to town, at the beginning of the story,
Pepé equips himself with a number of his father's things—signifying,
of course, his desire to play the man. He first loses the knife, which
is at once the proudest of his inheritances from his father and the
immediate instrument of his ruin, and then, during the flight, is di-
vested one by one of all the other articles. Do these losses make him
more, or less, a man?

3. In the scene at the house when Mama Torres is preparing Pepé for
his flight, there are repeated references to the changes in his face.
From a half-girlish one, it has become a man's face. Yet, when his
mother speaks of his being a man, and of his having a man's thing
to do, we are told that "he straightened his shoulders," and that "his
mouth changed until he looked very much like Mama." Does this
mean that his face has altered again, momentarily, so that he looks
like a woman? Or is it the opposite—a part of the new manliness?
Either way, there is an apparent inconsistency. Can the inconsistency
be justified?

4. It is more or less taken for granted, from the beginning of the flight,
that Pepé will not escape. Why does Steinbeck not leave this question
in doubt?

5. What is the significance of "the dark watching men"?

6. How important is religion in the story, and precisely in what way?

"Mr. Powers"

1. What is Miss Gordon's purpose in telling the story from the Cromlies'
point of view? They are "city people" and unfamiliar with back-
woods ways, but they do provide a dimension of understanding
when a country couple could not. Show how this understanding is
simultaneously an asset and a limitation.

2. How do Jack and Ellen Cromlie differ? Who is the more suspicious?
Who is more timid? And how are they alike?

3. Why does Ellen seem dissatisfied with her husband's explanation of
the basis on which Powers and his wife can continue to live together
after the accident? Comment on the ambivalence of attitude which
is reflected in her answer to Lucy's question at the end of the story:
"No," she said, "I don't want to speak to him."

4. What is Mrs. Foster's role in the story? Is her visit with Ellen Cromlie

over blackberry wine and ginger cookies merely an expression of rural neighborliness?

5. On several occasions, Ellen's eye is caught by certain configurations of light and shade. What is the telling quality of these images? What do they mean to Ellen?

6. Superficially a quiet and unobtrusive man, Mr. Powers has yet managed to make himself the main topic of conversation among the neighbors, to an extent that cannot be entirely accounted for simply by his notorious crime. He fascinates different people for different reasons, but perhaps we learn more about these other people, by the quality of their fascination, than we do about Powers. Does the reader have any definite and final impression of him which differs from those offered by the other characters? If so, how does Miss Gordon manage to communicate this impression? Finally, in what way does the problem of judgment relate to Ellen's preoccupation with light and memory?

"The Hint of an Explanation"

1. We are really given *two* series of hints in the story. One explains Father Martin's faith; the other explains the narrator's agnosticism. How does Greene place and contrast the two?

2. How important is time in the story? What is the relationship between the fictive present and Father Martin's flashback? (Perhaps it would be more accurate to refer to the story as having a "frame" structure— the account of the meeting on the train framing Father Martin's anecdote.) Are there any parallels in the details of the two narratives that underscore this temporal relationship?

3. Each of the travelers feels a certain rapport with the other. Father Martin says, "You are the first person—except for one—that I have thought of telling it to. . . ." The storyteller himself finds the anecdote "relevant" to his spiritual problem. How deep is this kinship?

4. What is Father Martin's concept of evil? How does Blacker embody evil?

5. In Blacker the "impossible paradox" of hating what you believe in is clear. Does this ambivalence apply also to the speaker? What form does the paradox take in the experience of Father Martin, both as a boy and as a man?

6. The three characters of the story might be taken to represent different aspects of the problem of free will. How would you define these aspects?

"A Crate for Kop"

1. Who is the central character of the story—Lasnow or Kop? Why?
2. It is apparent that Lasnow is disillusioned in the revolutionary cause in which he had once been a local leader. Why? Why does Kop want Lasnow to knock the cigarette holder out of his mouth, and why does Lasnow refuse?
3. What is the significance of the emphasis in the story on children, and children's toys and games?
4. Define the function of the boy (a person neither a child nor yet a man) who sells Lasnow the toothbrush, and who at the end is using the flattened sugar tongs to pick cigarette butts out of the grating at the railroad station.
5. What is the symbolic significance of the toothbrush? Of the sugar tongs? Of the railroad station?
6. There is a great deal of color imagery in the story—notably in Lasnow's thoughts about the candy sticks which he had once sold at Christmas, but less conspicuously in other places as well. What is its function?

"What You Hear from 'Em?"

1. Why does the "conspiracy" against her convince Aunt Munsie that Will and Thad are never coming back to Thornton to stay?
2. What is implied by the changes that Aunt Munsie undergoes after the conspiracy—her wearing a bandanna about her head, her "talking old-nigger foolishness," starting to reminisce about her childhood and her days as governess to Will and Thad, etc.?
   Is she more or less realistic in her outlook after having yielded to the new law and accepted the fact that Thad and Will will not return? Explain.
3. Would Taylor, as fictional historian of social change, be best described as a realist, a sentimentalist, or what?
   What is his attitude toward the status of Negroes in the different eras?
   The story also concerns the problem of male and female status in a changing society. How is this related to the racial question?
4. It is apparent that the white people of a town like Thornton have a tendency to "type" Negroes, that is, to avoid thinking of them as individuals. But Aunt Munsie has something of the same tendency with regard to white people; even Thad and Will she can distinguish only by their difference of girth, and they would seem to be im-

portant to her only as embodiments of her own sentiments and hopes. Does the reader, on this account, feel the less sympathetic with her in her final defeat? If not, why not?

"A Diamond Guitar"

1. We have observed that the prison is located in a Southern state. This regional setting, however, is hardly so important in this story as in Faulkner's "A Rose for Emily." Why not?
2. Mr. Schaeffer is a dollmaker; and his dolls are distinguished for their lifelike movements, with the wired limbs. In what way does this emphasize the pathos of his situation—his loneliness, his apparent lack of any family connections? Is not this hobby (and means of earning money) also ironically related to the fact that he is a condemned murderer? How?
3. Why does Capote give us only the vaguest information on what crimes the prisoners have committed? (Cf. my remarks in the commentary, that the men are not so much prisoners of the law and of bars and chains as prisoners of a dream.)
4. We have observed that Capote habitually writes about "outcasts" of society. In a sense, this is also true of Ernest Hemingway. But what is the essential difference between the two writers in their treatment of such people?
5. The final sentences of the story sum up Mr. Schaeffer's experience and illuminate the conflict once more. In what way?
6. "Feo" in Spanish means "ugly"; and a "Schaefer" in German is a "shepherd." What significance might these names have for the roles of the two characters?

"The Lottery"

1. In what ways is this story similar to Kafka's "In the Penal Colony"? In what respects essentially different?
2. Is there anything peculiarly American about the village and its customs?
3. What kind of ritual is it that the people are celebrating? What is the significance of the saying that Old Man Warner repeats: "Lottery in June, corn be heavy soon"? Of the references to the condition of the black box, to the change or disappearance over the years of certain portions of the ritual, to the rumor that in other communities the lottery has been abandoned, etc.?

"The Sergeant's Good Friend"

1. The title phrase, in reference to David, is clearly ironic. Is David himself aware of the irony at all levels?
2. Is there any evidence to indicate that the bus driver might be justified in his suspicion of the Sergeant's motives for cultivating David's friendship?

   What the General's widow says upon the discovery of the Sergeant's suicide, and her previous remark about her daughter's attitude toward him, might on the other hand tend to support Rant Thompson's first suspicion—that there was "something between" the Sergeant and Mrs. Williams.

   Why does the author leave these matters in doubt?
3. A partial answer to the preceding question might be that we are less interested in the character of the Sergeant himself than in David. But, what do we learn about David from his account of his friendship with the Sergeant? Specifically, David would seem to think that he has somehow betrayed the Sergeant—that the Sergeant had "looked at last into [his] real feelings," and that those feelings will not bear examination. Why? Is David's effort to expiate his guilt successful? Presumably, he is telling a lie when, on the way home from the funeral, he says that he had known the Sergeant's last name before. Why does he say this?
4. What relevance, to the story of his friendship with the Sergeant, has David's attitude toward the town and the countryside? His attitude toward his parents, and toward other neighbors? What is the significance of his reference to the street sign put up by Dr. Rogers, and to his father's remark that "if all that stuff about the Sergeant hadn't gotten in the newspapers, the sign wouldn't be there"?

"A Curtain of Green"

1. In her obsessive working of the "densely grown plot" behind her house, Mrs. Larkin would seem to be searching for something. What is she seeking, and what does she finally discover?
2. The commentary notes that in the crucial episode the story has moved into a realm of purely existential significance, beyond social considerations. How does Miss Welty manage to "transcend," so to speak, the very social elements—of sex, race, and class, Mrs. Larkin a white woman and a property owner, Jamey a Negro man and a day laborer—which she has deliberately introduced into the situation,

and which might have provided the occasion for violence in a more conventional kind of story about "the South"?

3. Comment on the importance of the references to birds in the story.

4. Clearly, the "curtain" or veil figure is central to the meaning of the story. In how many senses can the metaphor be applied to the events and character relationships?

5. Miss Welty's prose rhythms are intimately related to meaning. Show in detail how these alternating rhythms make convincing the otherwise illogical and abrupt changes in Mrs. Larkin's emotions.

"The Peaches"

1. This story is one of ten autobiographical anecdotes, or sketches, which Thomas collected under the general title *Portrait of the Artist as a Young Dog*. But the single story has its own unity and completeness. What is the principle of unity?

2. Does the story have more, or less, of the flavor of personal reminiscence—is it more or less "objective"—than, for example, Joyce's "An Encounter"? Why?

3. Does the author seek entirely to recapture the temper of the boy's mind? Or are we constantly aware that it is an adult who is telling the story, in recollection of his boyhood experience? On what characteristics of the narrative do you base your answer?

4. With reference to the title of Thomas' volume—what characteristics of the boy narrator's mind establish him as a type of the artist in opposition, say, to his friend Jack?

"The Enormous Radio"

1. How is the strange phenomenon of the radio's tuning in on life in the neighbors' apartments to be explained? Are Jim and Irene Westcott insane? Or has something either preternatural or of a technologically freakish character actually occurred? Or is the story to be read as a fantasy?

2. If a fantasy, is it also a satire? A satire on what?

3. It might seem to be in line with a basically satiric intent that Jim and Irene are presented from the first as so "average" in every way that they are almost without individual identity. Does this prevent our feeling very deeply sympathetic with them at the end of the story? Or, if in this final revelation of their presumably "true," hidden feelings about each other, we do respond to them for the first time as

whole persons—rather than mere statistical "types"—then how would one justify the previously impersonal, satiric treatment of them?

4. Does the story say something about the universal plight of modern, especially urban, man? In what ways is the radio an especially appropriate "medium," so to speak, for this purpose?

"The Forks"

1. To what extent does this story depend for its effect upon an assumption of certain conventional, popular notions about the life of priests?

2. Assuming that our sympathies are primarily engaged on the side of Father Eudex, in his conflict with Monsignor, what is the effect of his final decision to tear up the check, instead of signing it over to the strikers' relief fund? Is his integrity essentially compromised by this decision? If not, why not? If so, what is the author's intention in ending the story this way?

3. What has the visit of Mrs. Klein to do with Father Eudex's change of mind about the check?

4. Comment on the symbolic function of the automobile; of the meal which the two priests eat together.

5. The story might seem to imply that Christianity is an anachronism in the modern world—that the priesthood has no longer any real mission. So, at any rate, Father Eudex is tempted to feel. If this is not the author's implicit belief, what is?

    Or, is the final interest of the story psychological, with the question of the characters' faith having only circumstantial importance?

"The Wrath-Bearing Tree"

1. "The Wrath-Bearing Tree" is narrated from an omniscient point of view. Has this particular technique any bearing on the story's theme?

2. It might be said that nature in Marvin's story assumes the dimensions of a character. Given the definition of a character as an agent that both acts and is acted upon, would you agree with such a statement?

3. Upon what paradox does the whole significance of Ira's experience rest? In this connection, what is the particular significance of the maiming?

4. The herd of deer approach Ira in the final episode without fear. In what sense does he feel that their presence is a sign of "hope" for him?

5. In the story, what is "the wrath-bearing tree"?
6. How important is the frontier situation of the story, that is, its character of historical fiction? Would it be possible to modernize the story effectively?

"Good Country People"

1. Besides that of Joy-Hulga, what thematic significance have the names of the other characters in the story?
2. Comment on the relationship of horror and humor in the story. Compare Miss O'Connor's usage in this regard to that of Faulkner, or Kafka, or Shirley Jackson.
3. Is the theme of religious faith essentially, or only circumstantially, involved? What is the implicit attitude of the author toward religion?
4. In precisely what way is Hulga violated by the Bible salesman? What is the symbolic significance of the artificial leg in this connection? Of the glasses? (Note that, when he has first taken them and put them in his pocket, "she didn't realize he had taken her glasses. . . .") Why does Hulga want to think of the young man as a child?
5. What is the importance of the rural setting? How would you characterize Miss O'Connor's implicit attitude toward the virtues conventionally associated with life in the country? What has this to do with the theme of innocence and violation?
6. Does the grotesquery prevent the reader's feeling necessary sympathy with Hulga in her final predicament—i.e., has she (as well, perhaps, as all the other characters) been reduced to mere caricature? If not, why not?

"A Bottle of Milk for Mother"

1. Why does Algren use the epigraph from Whitman? Is its appropriateness in any way ironic?
2. Although the explanation that Lefty gives for his presence on the street—that he was going to buy "a bottle of milk for mother"—is patently a lie, it is significant that he attempts this *kind* of lie. How?
3. What is the significance of the fact that Lefty is still on his knees at the end of the story, and that Adamovitch does not stay to watch him then?
4. Bicek's cap is "pavement-colored." To what extent, and precisely in what ways, is he a product of big-city life?
5. The obvious, central theme of the story is that of the "quest for

identity"—a theme that, accompanying or involving that of the
"father search," it shares with a number of other stories in this collection. Compare Lefty's quest with those of some of the other heroes.

"The Beach Umbrella"

1. What is the symbolic significance of the umbrella itself? What is its
   connection with other things among Elijah's possessions, such as the
   ballpoint pen and clipboard he uses at the warehouse?
2. Why does Colter mention the haze from the Youngstown Sheet &
   Tube Company in the beginning of the story? Does this detail serve
   any other purpose than simply to create atmosphere?
3. The story begins with a description of the beach and ends with the
   sentence: "But down on the beach the sun was still shining." What is
   the importance of the emphatic "still"? What function does the beach
   as a place serve in the narrative?
4. The exact relationship between Elijah and his children is never fully
   stated. What would you surmise it to be, and how does Colter suggest
   its nature?
5. On one level "The Beach Umbrella" concerns a lonely man's search
   for companionship in a hostile world. There is also, however, an
   implicit indictment of society for failing to provide sufficient economic
   opportunity. Are these two themes interdependent? If so, in what
   ways do they support one another? If not, does their opposition
   create a flaw in the structure of the story?

"The Sojourner"

1. In many of these stories, the principal characters are distinctly admirable people, heroic in one way or another even when they have gross
   moral defects. We can hardly admire John Ferris, but we do sympathize with him. Why is it important to make this distinction—
   between sympathy and admiration—in dealing with fiction?
2. Although Ferris is, by virtue of years, an adult, yet the story is in an
   ironic sense an account of his "growing up." How does Mrs. McCullers play up this irony in the final scene with Valentin, and in the
   description of the child?
3. What is the effect of Elizabeth's little boy's saying that he wants to be
   a foreign correspondent, like Ferris, when he grows up? Is the
   remark, regardless of the boy's intention, entirely flattering to Ferris?
4. Why does Ferris not like the word "expatriate"? Is there anything
   distinctly American about him?

5. How are the musical references used to support the development of theme? What is the significance of the fugue, for Ferris, in opposition to that of the unfinished melody?

"Jesse"

1. What is the importance of the fact that Jesse doesn't any longer play very well, and is a poor teacher?
2. Why does the narrator's husband, Richard, so much resent being called "bossman" by Jesse?
3. Why won't Jesse sing the song "Greenville Smokin', Leland Burnin' Down"? (Greenville and Leland are two neighboring towns in the Mississippi Delta, plantation country.)
4. Why does Jesse's story of his childhood make it all but impossible for the white woman and her family to continue their friendship with him? What is the source of her guilt feelings?
5. After her dream, the narrator tells us that she wrote: "There are those of us who are willing to say, 'I am guilty,' but who is to absolve us? And do we expect by our confession miraculously to relieve the suffering of the innocent?" What is the relevance of this to the dream? Why does she change the word she had first written—"escape"—to "relieve"?
6. Why, in the dream, does the child Jesse have an old man's head?

"The Guest"

1. The title of the story most obviously refers to the Arab prisoner. What is the ironic significance of this name for him? Is there any sense in which the schoolteacher himself might be called a guest?
2. Why doesn't the teacher want to turn the prisoner over to the authorities? (Note that he does not feel any special, personal attraction to the man—indeed, that he seems rather to dislike him. Neither does he seem to be motivated by adherence to any very clearly defined, higher moral principle.)
3. Why does the prisoner choose to go on toward the town where he will be arrested when he is free to take the other road and escape?
4. In the light of the preceding questions, is there some ironic justification for the threatened revenge against the teacher by the Arab's friends? Explain.
5. What is the significance of the map on the blackboard? How is it appropriate that the warning to the teacher should be written there "among the winding French rivers"?

BIOGRAPHICAL NOTES

NELSON ALGREN

Mr. Algren was born in Detroit on March 28, 1909, studied journalism at the University of Illinois, and has spent most of his life, except for the war and the time he spent drifting around the Southwest, in or near Chicago. And the Chicago of newspaper headlines, police reports, and investigating committees—the tough West Side—is his theme and scene. He brings to life the broken, forgotten habitues of dives, junkies, boxers, immigrants, all of whom live in the shadow cast by the "El" which crisscrosses the Midwestern metropolis. There is a good deal of social protest in his fiction, but there is no sentimentality, no easy excuse for human behavior. His first novel, *Somebody in Boots* (1935), which decried the plight of "depression youth" was unsuccessful; but his later novel, *The Man with the Golden Arm* (1949), convincingly caught the West Side and sharply sketched many of its abandoned inhabitants. Its central character, Frankie Machine, is almost a legendary figure in American literature of the slum. The stories of *The Neon Wilderness* (1947) are no less powerful and, certainly, no less tales of dissent. He has also written a prose poem, *Chicago: City on the Make* (1951), which expresses that city's fear and fascination.

SHERWOOD ANDERSON

Anderson was born in Camden, Ohio, September 13, 1876. The son of a small-time saddle and harness dealer, he was rather haphazardly educated, and tried his hand at many odd jobs, soldiering, the writing of advertising copy, and management of a paint factory, before definitely undertaking a literary career. At this time, he was living in Chicago with his brother, the painter Karl Anderson, and had come under the influence of Theodore Dreiser, Carl Sandburg, and others, who encouraged him to continue his writing. His first considerable success was with the collection of stories *Winesburg, Ohio*, published in 1919. He continued writing from then until the end of his life, others among his better known books being *Poor White* (1920), *The Triumph of the Egg* (1921), *Dark Laughter* (1925), and *Death in the Woods* (1933). After 1925, he lived on a farm in Marion County, Virginia, where he edited two weekly newspapers. While on a South American cruise, he fell ill, and died March 8, 1941, at Cristobal, in the Canal Zone.

HEINRICH BÖLL

Böll was born in Cologne, Germany, on December 21, 1917, and since his return there in 1949 has continued to live in the city of his birth. His work is richly varied—satires, radio scripts, critical essays, stories, and novels. *Der Zug war pünktlich* (1949; translation, *The Train Was On Time*, 1956, by Richard Graves) was his first publication. This powerful novella recounts a soldier's five-day trip from his Rhineland home to a Galician town where he foresees his death. This stark account of human defeat was enthusiastically received by the disillusioned, postwar reading public in Germany. The popular enthusiasm waxed into critical acclaim with his subsequent works. In 1950 a collection of his short stories (actually composed before the novella) was published under the title *Wanderer, kommst du nach Spa* (translation, *Traveller, If You Came To Spa*, 1956, by Mervyn Savill). The twenty-five tales, most of which are plotless in the standard meaning of the term, deal with war and the postwar collapse in Germany. He has also published other short story collections, and a number of novels. In all his works, one large theme emerges: *Angst*, anxiety in its deepest, multiple meanings— the individual confronting the demands of war, society, religion, and himself. While Böll has come into his own in Germany and elsewhere in Europe, American knowledge and appreciation of his work lags behind.

ALBERT CAMUS

Camus was born on November 7, 1913, in Mondovi, Algeria, and is numbered among the most influential French writers of this century. Actually, his reputation—for his novels, essays, and plays—is worldwide, and as much as any author of his time he speaks not for a nation but for humanity. His first book is a collection of essays (1937); subsequently, he returned to his primary interest, the theatre. His famous novels appeared in 1946, *The Stranger*, in 1948, *The Plague*, and in 1956, *The Fall*. *Exile and the Kingdom*, a collection of short stories, appeared in 1958. Camus' overriding concern is the existential problem of the individual's isolation in a hostile world, and man's lonely struggle against the illogical forces of the universe. Man, as Camus sees him, must establish for himself the kingdom which God has failed to provide. Camus was the recipient of the Nobel Prize in Literature for 1957. He died January 4, 1960, in an automobile accident on a French highway.

TRUMAN CAPOTE

Mr. Capote was born on September 30, 1924, in New Orleans. He is an essayist, playwright, and novelist, as well as a short-story writer. In the main, his sympathies lie with the socially and psychically outcast, with children, with the congenitally incomplete and irresponsible of all kinds. His taste in locale favors the remote—Haiti, Africa, Russia, and the Gothic South. If there is much of the odd and hard about his work, there is also a tenderness which softens his preoccupation with the aberrant. His most important works are *Other Voices, Other Rooms* (1948), *The Grass Harp* (1951), and *Breakfast at Tiffany's* (1958).

WILLA CATHER

Born in Winchester, Virginia, December 7, 1876, Willa Cather moved with her family, while still a child, to Nebraska—where she was graduated from the University of Nebraska in 1895. Soon thereafter, she returned eastward, first to Pittsburgh as a newspaper writer and then a school teacher, and later to New York City, where she was an editor of *McClure's Magazine*. The rural-urban, Western-Eastern conflict of values is a recurrent theme in her fiction, and clearly reflects the pattern of her personal life, although her practical identity is usually elaborately masked—by such devices as the shifting of the action to another historical period, or the embodiment of her personality in a male character. Chiefly on the strength of such novels as *O Pioneers!*, *My Ántonia*, and *Death Comes for the Archbishop*, she is popularly, and vaguely, regarded as a champion of the frontier American virtues. But, as indicated in Richard Giannone's study of "A Wagner Matinée" (from *The Troll Garden*, a collection published in 1905), this is an oversimplification even of her earliest work. For a long time admired but little understood in the subtler intentions of her art, Miss Cather has only very recently begun to claim a proper critical appreciation. She was herself a discriminating critical theorist, as the essays in the posthumously published volume *Willa Cather on Writing* reveal. Although she traveled widely in Europe as well as in the United States, Miss Cather's one, tentative effort at the expatriate life, in France, was a failure. She spent her last years in New York City, where she died April 24, 1947.

JOHN CHEEVER

Mr. Cheever was born in 1912. At seventeen he was dismissed from preparatory school, but later he taught at Barnard College. In 1957 he wrote *The Wapshot Chronicle*, for which he won an award. Also, he has written several collections of short stories: *The Way Some People Live* (1943), *The Enormous Radio* (1953), *The Housebreaker of Shady Hill* (1958), *Some People, Places, and Things that Will Not Appear in My Next Novel* (1961). His stories appear frequently in *The New Yorker*.

CYRUS COLTER

In the anthology *Soon, One Morning: New Writing by American Negroes, 1940–1962*—from which "The Beach Umbrella" is taken—Mr. Colter is quoted as follows: "I live in Chicago and am a lawyer and state official. I have served for thirteen years now as a member of the Illinois Commerce Commission, concerned with the regulation of public utilities. I was born in Noblesville, Indiana, January 8, 1910, and began writing fiction only two years ago, as a weekend hobby. It's still a hobby—I have no illusions at fifty-two. I've had only four stories published, all in 'little' magazines. 'The Beach Umbrella' will be my fifth publication of fiction. My first story appeared about eighteen months ago in an Irish quarterly, *Threshold*, published in Belfast. Then followed stories in the Fall 1961 issue of *Epoch* (Cornell University), in the Winter 1961 issue of the *University of Kansas City Review*, and, the last one, in the Winter 1962 issue of *Epoch*." (This statement is dated April 29, 1962.) "The Beach Umbrella" has been prominently and favorably mentioned in reviews of *Soon, One Morning*. Although unnecessarily modest in his view of his writing, Mr. Colter would seem to be a man who knows what he is about. One would hope that he will continue to pursue his "hobby."

ELLEN DOUGLAS

Ellen Douglas is the pseudonym of a young Southern woman, married and the mother of several children, who was immediately and widely recognized as a fine new talent when her work first appeared in *The New Yorker* a few years ago. Her first novel, *A Family's Affairs*, which had been rather casually transmitted to the publisher through an insistent friend, won the Houghton Mifflin award for 1961. She talks, presiding calmly over her vigorous family the while, as quietly and beautifully as she writes. Her husband, a successful businessman, is also a poet and fiction writer, a musician, and a collector of musical instruments. "Miss Douglas" is so assuredly herself that she does not have to use her real name as author.

WILLIAM FAULKNER

Faulkner was born September 25, 1897, in New Albany, Mississippi, and lived most of his life in Oxford, seat of the University of Mississippi. He is generally recognized now as the greatest American novelist of the first half of the twentieth century. His education was irregular. He attended the University of Mississippi off and on for several years, but never graduated. During World War I, he joined the Canadian Air Force. Although most of his best work was published during the twenties and thirties—e.g., *Soldier's Pay* (1926), *The Sound and the Fury* (1929), *As I Lay Dying* (1930), *Sanctuary* (1931), *Light in August* (1932), *Absalom, Absalom!* (1936)—he received critical recognition in America only much later (the French were quicker to recognize his genius) and most of his earlier books were out of print until the mid-forties. The so-called Faulkner revival began with appreciations by Malcolm Cowley, in *The Portable Faulkner* (1946), and by Robert Penn Warren in an essay of the same year. Faulkner lived a quiet and deliberately obscure life, about which it is still difficult, on many crucial points, to distinguish between legend and objective fact. Although his critical reputation was by then well established, he received widespread public attention for the first time when he went to Stockholm in 1950 to receive the Nobel Prize for Literature. He published more than fifteen novels, two volumes of poetry, and several collections of short stories. His last novel, *The Reivers*, published in the year of his death, was a charmingly humorous study in the form of a childhood reminiscence, containing much of the intricately uproarious comedy for which he had been famous, but none of the horror and tragic violence which had accompanied the comedy in the works of his great period. He died July 6, 1962, and was buried in Oxford.

F. SCOTT FITZGERALD

Francis Scott Key Fitzgerald (a descendant of the author of the American national anthem) was born in St. Paul, Minnesota, September 24, 1896. He attended Princeton from 1913 to 1917, and served during World War I as a lieutenant in the army. Much to his regret, he was not sent to overseas duty. His first novel, *This Side of Paradise*, published in 1920, established him as a popular spokesman for the postwar "lost generation." With his wife, the former Zelda Sayre of Montgomery, Alabama, herself a writer, he lived for some years in France. The temporarily and rather frantically gay marriage was later marred by Zelda's mental illness, and Fitzgerald's own, slower and less decisive, emotional deterioration. The short story "Winter Dreams" is in some respects a preliminary study for his best-known and artistically most successful novel, *The Great Gatsby,* published in 1925. The later, more ambitious novel *Tender Is the Night,* with a European setting and themes and incidents which obscurely reflect aspects of his life with Zelda, was a long and uncertain time in the making, and when it appeared in 1934 was received with far less enthusiasm than the author had anticipated. A posthumously revised version, edited by Malcolm Cowley according to notes Fitzgerald had written before his death, was published in 1953. He was at work on a novel about the movie industry when he died. The fragment was subsequently published, in 1941, with the title *The Last Tycoon.* His short stories include those in *Flappers and Philosophers, Tales of the Jazz Age,* and *All the Sad Young Men.* A collection of essays and letters posthumously published (1945) under the title *The Crack-up* is especially interesting biographically. Fitzgerald died in Hollywood, December 21, 1940.

CAROLINE GORDON

Miss Gordon was born on Merry Font Farm, in Todd County, Kentucky, on October 6, 1895. She has taught fiction and creative writing at a number of universities, and at the moment she is a writer in residence at Purdue. Her yet expanding canon includes eight novels and numerous short stories, the most recent publication being a collection, *Old Red and Other Stories* (1963). In two of her books, *None Shall Look Back* (1937) and *Green Centuries* (1941), she returns to earlier times; and this move back into the historical past marks an aspect of her pervasive theme: a search for order and stability. This quest takes on a more spiritual character in other works. In *The Malefactors* (1956) the central character, a poet, loses his art; then, after a suffering search for a permanent value, he discovers God. Her other notable books are *The Women on the Porch* (1944) and *The Strange Children* (1951). Miss Gordon is also a literary critic.

GRAHAM GREENE

The son of a headmaster, Graham Greene was born in Berkhampstead, Hertfordshire, England, on October 2, 1904. He studied at Balliol College, Oxford, and, besides writing fiction, he has been a traveler, a film critic, and an editor. His productive career started with *The Man Within* in 1929. Some of his works he himself has called "entertainments," but the levity that the term suggests belies their underlying seriousness. *The*

Ministry of Fear (1943), for example, is a spy story but it also raises the problem of salvation. The spy-thriller conventions of mistaken identity and amnesia give way to portents of sanctity and selfhood. Besides "entertainments" he has also written books that earnestly and deliberately raise moral and theological issues. *England Made Me* (1935), *Brighton Rock* (1938), and *The Power and the Glory* (1940) examine the profound questions of man's relation to God and to society. He has given a moral estimate of the age, which mixes shocked acceptance of the human condition, as in *A Burnt Out Case* (1961), and a felt nostalgia for its irretrievable innocence.

ERNEST HEMINGWAY

A short-story writer, a novelist, and intermittently a war correspondent and big-game hunter, Hemingway was one of the most popular writers of his generation who could also make a continuing claim on the attention of serious critics. His short stories were collected in several different volumes. Probably his best novels are *The Sun Also Rises* and *A Farewell To Arms,* both antiheroic stories of Americans in Europe whose protagonists closely resemble each other and the author, and both written in the twenties. After the Spanish Civil War novel *For Whom the Bell Tolls,* at the end of the thirties, the quality of his work, and his critical reputation, generally declined. *Across the River and Into the Trees* (1950), for example, is largely self-imitative and spiritless. In some quarters, however, *The Old Man and the Sea* (1952), a short novel, was regarded as a redeeming achievement, and was cited in his election to the Nobel Prize in literature for 1954. He was born July 21, 1899, in Oak Park, Illinois. He served, during World War I, first as a volunteer ambulance driver and then as a soldier in the Italian army, and was seriously wounded. During the Spanish Civil War, and World War II, he was a correspondent. He died July 2, 1961, in Ketchum, Idaho, of a shotgun wound, believed to be self-inflicted.

SHIRLEY JACKSON

Miss Jackson was born in San Francisco in 1919. She has written several novels, *The Road Through the Wall* (1948), *Hangsaman* (1951), and *The Bird's Nest* (1954). But she is best known for her short stories, of which the best are contained in *The Lottery; or The Adventures of James Harris* (1949). Also, she has written a number of essays on the ironies of family life. She lives in Vermont, where her husband, the literary critic Stanley Edgar Hyman, teaches.

HENRY JAMES

Henry James, perhaps the most important American writer of fiction—certainly, the most influential—was born in New York City in 1843. He was privately educated, save for a brief stay at the Harvard Law School, and spent a large part of his life traveling in Europe. The affluence of his private life becomes an important ingredient in his fictive world where manners, society, art, and leisure present the dramatic occasions for the moral issues that occupy his attention. Very frequently, he juxtaposes whole cultures (particularly European and American) as a means of gauging the moral and esthetic sensibilities of their representatives. In the work of no other writer of fiction, with the possible exceptions of George Eliot and Jane Austen, is the art of conversation so highly developed and so dramatically purposive. His style matches the complexity and amplitude of his characters and themes. It is elaborate, elegant, intricate, and subtle. His earlier work is simpler, though by no means simple; and this phase of his career is best demonstrated in *Daisy Miller* (1879), *The American* (1877), and *The Portrait of a Lady* (1881). His more difficult, and more highly regarded, achievement came at the close of his long and productive life, and *The Wings of the Dove* (1902), *The Ambassadors* (1903), and *The Golden Bowl* (1904) amply testify to the beauty and mastery of James' final attainment. He became a British subject in 1915, and died in England in 1916.

JAMES JOYCE

Despite the comparatively small body of his work, James Joyce was one of the greatest writers of his age. Born in Dublin, February 2, 1882, and educated at the Jesuit schools of Clongowes Wood College and Belvedere College, and at University College, Dublin, he lived most of his mature life in self-imposed exile on the Continent, where he died January 13, 1941, at Zurich. Besides the volume of short stories, *Dubliners,* his works include the play *Exiles,* two small volumes of poems, *Chamber Music* and *Pomes Penyeach,* and three books usually referred to as novels. The first of these, *A Portrait of the Artist as a Young Man* (1920), is a novel in something of the traditional, formal sense of the term. *Ulysses* (1922) all but entirely escapes the usual limitations of novelistic form, and *Finnegans Wake* (1939) belongs to no previously known genre. Especially with *Finnegans Wake,* Joyce became one of the three or four writers in the history of European literature whose stylistic inventions amount to the creation of a new poetic language.

FRANZ KAFKA

Kafka was born in Prague, then a city of Austria-Hungary, July 3, 1883. The family was Jewish, prosperous, and moderately influential. Franz's entire life was overshadowed by a profound fear of his self-complacent and domineering father, whose approval he felt he could never win. He was educated in law at the German University of Prague, taking his doctorate there in 1906. For most of his tormented life thereafter, he held a civil service post by way of necessary pretense to existence in the ordinary world of affairs, but the realm of his real, inward experience was the episodic nightmare which is revealed in his books. The psychic disturbances generated in his relationship with his father, and later his awareness that he was hopelessly ill of tuberculosis, forced him to abandon the idea of marrying, in which he had seen his only prospect for happiness. After prolonged terror and physical suffering, he died in the Kierling sanatorium, near Vienna, on June 3, 1924. Very little of his work appeared during his lifetime. His friend, Max Brod, against Kafka's expressed will, published three incomplete novels after his death —*Der Prozess* (*The Trial*), *Das Schloss* (*The Castle*), and *Amerika* (*America*). The last is a disturbingly comic, imaginary adventure in a country which Kafka had never seen in actuality; but his America is at least as probable, even to Americans, as his Europe must be to Europeans. Other works available in English translation include *A Country Doctor* (short stories), *Parables, The Diaries of Franz Kafka,* edited by Max Brod, *The Penal Colony* (short stories), and *Dearest Father*.

D. H. LAWRENCE

David Herbert Lawrence was born September 11, 1885, at Eastwood, Nottinghamshire, England, the son of a coalminer. He was for a time a teacher in an elementary school, but after his literary reputation was established with the novel *The White Peacock* in 1911, he turned to a full-time career as a writer. He published several volumes of essays and travel sketches, besides plays, nine volumes of stories, eight volumes of poetry, and some fourteen novels. (He was also a painter of considerable talent.) His work, notably the novel *Lady Chatterley's Lover,* which appeared in several different versions, has been frequently involved in censorship proceedings. In the popular mind, he is principally identified as a champion of sexual freedom as the key to self-fulfillment; and his works have sometimes been criticized for excessive didacticism. But the critic F. R. Leavis, for example, has cogently defended the essential integrity of his artistic purposes. Lawrence spent lengthy sojourns at various times on the Continent and in America. In 1912, during a stay in

Bavaria, he became the lover of the German Baroness Frieda von Richthofen, and two years later married her in England. He died in France, near Nice, on March 2, 1930.

CARSON McCULLERS

Mrs. McCullers lives in the East now (where she has spent most of her time since arriving, at seventeen, to study at Columbia and the Juilliard School of Music); but she is a Southerner. She was born in Columbus, Georgia, in February 1917. The South has a strong bearing on her style and characters, as it does for most Southern writers, but the real "region" of her fiction is the human heart and its suburb, the mind. Her first novel, *The Heart Is a Lonely Hunter*, published in 1940, sympathetically, but not sentimentally, relates the torments of a deaf-mute's search for and loss of companionship. The promise which this first novel offered is most fully realized in a brief novel about a twelve-year-old girl, Frankie, whose entrance into maturity is hastened by her brother's wedding. Frankie's finding her place in these adult affairs powerfully conveys the sadness, the tenderness, and the difficulty of growing up. This novel, *The Member of the Wedding* (1946), when put into dramatic form for the New York stage in 1951, revealed Mrs. McCullers' gifts as a poetic dramatist. Her latest novel, *Clock Without Hands* (1961), intensifies the sadness so pervasive in her work into a hovering darkness—again, she marks the shadows cast on the human condition.

THOMAS MANN

Mann was one of the most eminent and influential writers of the first half of the twentieth century, his reputation having been firmly established on both sides of the Atlantic before he had reached his thirtieth birthday. He was born in Lübeck, Germany, one of the famous ports of the Hanseatic League, June 6, 1875—the descendant of a long line of prosperous, patrician merchants. His first novel, *Buddenbrooks*, a book in the tradition of the family saga, is in many respects clearly autobiographical. It traces the fortunes of the Buddenbrooks family through four generations, and presents a preliminary statement of nearly all the themes which were to dominate Mann's later fiction—including, for example, that of the northern and southern conflict of values in European culture, and that of the association of art with decadence. As in the story "Railway Accident," although seldom with this lightness of touch, the artist-protagonist in many of his fictions is a version of Mann himself, the writer inwardly torn between his sense of artistic mission and the instincts of his bourgeois heritage. Virtually all of Mann's important work is available in English translation. His *novellen,* elongated short stories, brought this form to near perfection. *Death in Venice, Tonio Kröger, Disorder and Early Sorrow,* and *Mario and the Magician* would offer an interestingly varied sampling. *The Magic Mountain* remains his best-known novel, although its comparatively realistic treatment of a modern situation makes it hardly less formidable an undertaking for the reader than the legendary-historical narrative of the *Joseph and His Brothers* tetralogy. As an essayist, as well as incidentally in his fiction, Mann was an erudite and penetrating critic of literature, the visual arts and music, and politics. An inveterate enemy of the Nazi movement, Mann left Germany in 1933, four years after he had received the Nobel Prize in literature, and in 1944 became a citizen of the United States. In 1953 he returned to Europe, residing in Switzerland until his death on August 12, 1955, at Zurich.

JOHN MARVIN

Mr. Marvin was born in 1924 on a farm in northeast Colorado in the dustbowl. He holds degrees from the University of Denver and attended The Johns Hopkins University for a time. His published short stories have appeared in *The Hudson Review* and his critical pieces in *Faulkner Studies,* of which he is also a coeditor. Presently, he is working on a novel along with his duties as a teacher of creative writing.

FLANNERY O'CONNOR

Miss O'Connor was born in Savannah, Georgia, in 1925. She studied in the South and then went to The State University of Iowa. She first published a novel, *Wise Blood,* in 1952; but it was her collection of short stories of 1955 that aroused a great deal of interest in her work. In the ten pieces of that volume there is a vision of humanity which sees the final importance of man's everyday actions and problems. An accident recalls divine grace; a fatuity, man's spiritual vulnerability; a madness, the uncorrected vision of evil. The characters have a side-show appeal and a fearful unpredictability; but, as Miss O'Connor reveals them, they also have human warmth. Her latest novel, *The Violent Bear It Away,* appeared in 1960. She lives in Milledgeville, Georgia, where she raises peafowl and, according to the latest dispatch, keeps "Tommy Traveler," a pony.

FRANK O'CONNOR

Born in Cork, Ireland, 1903, O'Connor attended the Christian Brothers school in Cork, but did not enter a university. He was for a time one of the directors of the famous Abbey Theater in Dublin. But the drama is a secondary interest for him, and his some twenty collections of short stories contain his finest work. William Butler Yeats once compared his contribution to Irish literature with that of Chekhov to Russian. His stories have enjoyed a special success in America, and he was married in 1953 to an American woman, Harriet Rich, of Annapolis, Maryland.

LUIGI PIRANDELLO

Pirandello was born in Girgenti, Sicily, June 28, 1867. He studied the classics at Girgenti, Palermo, and Rome, and took a doctorate in philological studies at the University of Bonn, Germany. From 1897 to 1921 he was a professor of Italian literature in Rome, a post that he was forced to take on account of the ruin of his father's mines by a flood. The latter years of his married life were vexed by financial anxieties, which might have been responsible in part for the pessimism of the plays he began to write shortly before his wife's death. The best known of his plays is *Six Characters in Search of an Author* (1921). Besides forty plays, his works include some three hundred stories, several collections of poetry, critical essays, and seven novels. He was awarded the Nobel Prize for Literature in 1934. Afterward, he divided most of his income among his three children, and spent the rest of his life in obscure travels from one country to another, as if acting out the themes of loss of identity and the search for freedom which had informed much of his writing. He died in Rome, December 10, 1936.

J. F. POWERS

James Farl Powers was born on July 8, 1917, in Jacksonville, Illinois. Like many beginning writers, he was first introduced to the reading public by a "little" magazine—in this instance, *Accent*. In 1947 (he first published a story in 1943) the best of his early efforts were collected in *Prince of Darkness, and Other Stories*, the book for which he is still best known. After *Accent* it was *The New Yorker* that published his work, and in that magazine one is likely to find Mr. Powers' fiction as he develops it. His skill as an observer is best demonstrated in subtly shaded portraits of the clergy, whose private lives and conscience are caught with penetrating insight and sympathetic irony. His second collection of short fiction, *Presence of Grace* (1956), brings together his two major preoccupations—Roman Catholicism and the American Midwest. He recently published his first novel, *Morte D'Urban* (1962), concerning a priest's struggle with the world.

JOHN STEINBECK

Steinbeck was born February 27, 1902, in Salinas, California. He graduated from the Salinas High School, and spent four years at Stanford University as a special student. Before achieving success as a novelist, he worked as a bricklayer, caretaker, chemist's assistant, and migratory fruitpicker. Having matured during the depression years, Steinbeck wrote powerfully, if often sentimentally, of the common and laboring man. His typical successes in this vein are *In Dubious Battle* (1936), *Of Mice and Men* (1937), *The Long Valley* (1938), and his masterwork *The Grapes of Wrath* (1939). Since the thirties, he has published *Sea of Cortez* (1941), a work of nonfiction which is his most comprehensive philosophical statement, *Cannery Row* (1945) and *Sweet Thursday* (1954), which return to California folk materials, and, among others, *The Winter of Our Discontent* (1961), a comic indictment of declining American values. In 1962, he received the Nobel Prize for Literature.

PETER TAYLOR

Born in Trenton, Tennessee, in 1917, Mr. Taylor spent his early life in Nashville, Memphis, and St. Louis. He started to write and publish before his graduation from Kenyon College (1940), and since that time has written one novel, *A Woman of Means* (1950), and three volumes of short stories, *A Long Fourth and Other Stories* (1948), *The Widows of Thornton* (1954), *Happy Families Are All Alike* (1959). The major concern, to which all his work returns in various ways, is the disintegration of the family as a meaningful unit. This domestic decline is dramatized—and universalized—through the life of the middle-class South. Most characteristically, his angle of vision is from the city, the vantage point from which he contrasts the stability of the past as represented in its agrarian tradition with the disorder of the present. There is a sadness about this historic change, a sadness enhanced by a "haunting tenderness." There is no violence, only quiet detachment and gentle humor. His newest book is *Miss Leonora When Last Seen and Fifteen Other Stories*.

DYLAN THOMAS

Thomas was born in Swansea, Wales, on October 27, 1914. For a year he was a newspaper reporter and then tried his hand at a number of odd jobs, but above all he was a poet. He first appeared in print when he was sixteen or seventeen, and at nineteen he published his first volume. His principal collections include *18 Poems* (1934), *The Map of Love*

(1939), *New Poems* (1942), and *In Country Sleep, and Other Poems* (1952). Predominantly, Dylan Thomas is concerned with the psychic division between what man thinks to be true and what is true. From the countless other artists who address themselves to this split, he is distinguished by a tone of impatient exuberance, an engaging gift of gab, his complete Welshness (in both setting and language), his metaphorical extravagance, and, of course, his wit. By and large, there are three general subjects in his work: childhood, the body, and religion. Through all his themes there runs an innocence; but one finds nowhere an immaturity. His prose works exhibit the same temper of mind and the same preoccupations, and are frequently to be distinguished only by technical characteristics from the poetry proper. *Portrait of the Artist as a Young Dog* appeared in 1940. Other titles are *Under Milk Wood* (1954), *Quite Early One Morning* (1954), and *Adventures in the Skin Trade* (1955). His charming sketch, *A Child's Christmas in Wales*, appeared in 1959—like several of the others, a posthumous publication. Thomas was world-renowned as a reader, or performer, of his poetry—and, between platform appearances, as a party guest. While on such a reading tour of this country in 1953, he died in New York City, on November 9.

ROBERT PENN WARREN

Born April 24, 1905, in Todd County, Kentucky, the section that provides the background for his novel *Night Rider*, Warren is one of the leading poets, critics, and editors of his generation, and a playwright as well as a short-story writer and novelist. He has won two Pulitzer Prizes, one for his best-selling and perhaps artistically most successful novel *All the King's Men* (1946), and the other for *Promises* (1957), a volume of poems. The dominant themes of his fiction and poetry, his connection with the so-called Fugitive Group at Vanderbilt during the twenties, his teaching experience at Louisiana State University and his coeditorship of *The Southern Review,* have stamped Warren as primarily a Southern writer. But for many years he has lived principally in the eastern United States, and in Europe. He has taught at many different American universities, and is now a member of the Yale faculty. His more important novels, besides *All the King's Men,* are *Night Rider* (1938) and *World Enough and Time* (1950). He is coauthor and coeditor of several textbooks and anthologies, with Cleanth Brooks and others—one of these being *Understanding Poetry,* which is sometimes largely credited with having caused a revolution in the teaching of poetry in American colleges. His volumes of poems include *Eleven Poems on the Same Theme* (1942),

Selected Poems 1923–1943 (1944), *Promises* (1957), and *You, Emperors, and Others* (1960). A volume of selected essays appeared in 1958.

EUDORA WELTY

This gifted lady was born on April 13, 1909, educated at Mississippi State College, the University of Wisconsin, and Columbia, and now lives in the city of her birth, Jackson, Mississippi. She, too, began her career in a "little" magazine (*Manuscript,* in 1936); but it did not take long for her fiction to attract a wider public. Critics immediately recognized her first collection of stories, *A Curtain of Green* (1941) as distinguished both in technical mastery and dramatic forcefulness. Her first novel, *Delta Wedding* (1946), firmly established her reputation, and it also presented critics with the central difficulty of her fiction. The structural simplicity, the stylistic precision, and deft characterization, as finished and effective as they are, do not satisfactorily account for her achievement. There is a hidden richness about her work just as there is a veiled other side in her fictive world. Fantasy, the unconscious, even humor, strongly convey their counterparts—a stark reality, a calculation, a tragedy. Or she can work in the reverse and provide the apparent and let it suggest the ineffable. Again, within the personally imposed boundaries of her "region," Miss Welty probes as deeply as any writer. Her achievement is best found in, besides *A Curtain of Green* and *Delta Wedding, The Wide Net* (1943), *The Ponder Heart* (1954), and *The Bride of the Innesfallen* (1955).

ELLINGTON WHITE

Ellington White is the author of far too few stories, which have appeared in *The Sewanee Review, The Kenyon Review,* and other literary journals. He is married to the poet Jean Farley, and lives with her and their children on a farm in his native Virginia, where both husband and wife manage exasperatingly if charmingly to distract themselves from their writing—he with fishing, and she with an improbable collection of pets. However, White has profitably combined his talents as prose stylist and fisherman in articles for *Sports Illustrated.* He studied at Johns Hopkins, and is now a teacher of literature and creative writing at the college in Farmville.